THE OZARK TRILOGY

The World of Ozark

K. Jollie '81

SCALE
0   4000 mi.

Wilderness Areas

THE OZARK TRILOGY

Twelve Fair Kingdoms

The Grand Jubilee

And Then There'll Be Fireworks

Suzette Haden Elgin

University of Arkansas Press

Fayetteville

2000

LIBRARY OF CONGRESS CATALOGING-IN-PUBLICATION DATA

Elgin, Suzette Haden.
     The Ozark trilogy / Suzette Haden Elgin.
          p.   cm.
     Contents: Twelve fair kingdoms—The grand jubilee—And then there'll
be fireworks.
     ISBN 1-55728-592-6 (alk. paper)
     1. Fantasy fiction, American. I. Title.
PS3555.L42 O9 2000
813'.54—dc21   99-051760

CONTENTS

Twelve
Fair Kingdoms

Brightwater

I should have known that something was very wrong when the Mules started flying erratically. I was misled a bit, I suppose, because there were no actual *crashes,* just upset stomachs. The ordinary person on the street blamed it on turbulence; and considering what they understood of the way the system worked, that was as reasonable a conclusion as any other. However, I had full access to classified material, and I knew perfectly well that it was magic, not aerodynamics, that kept the Mules flying. And magic at the level of skill necessary to fly a bulky creature like a Mule was not likely to suffer any because of a little disturbance in the air. You take a look at a Mule sometime; it surely isn't built for *flight.*

Even someone who's gone no farther in magic than Common Sense Level knows that the harmony of the universe is a mighty frail and delicately balanced equilibrium, and that you can't go tampering with any part of it without affecting everything else. A *child* knows that. So that when whatever-it-was started, with its first symptoms being Mules that made their riders throw up, I should of known that something sturdy was tugging hard at the Universal Web.

I was busy, let's grant me that. I was occupied with the upcoming Grand Jubilee of the Confederation of Continents. Any meeting that it doesn't happen but once every five hundred years—you tend to pay it considerable attention. One of our freighters had had engine trouble off the coast of Oklahomah, and that was interfering with our supply deliveries. I was trying to run a sizable Castle with a staff that bordered, that spring, on the mediocre, and trying to find fit replacements before the big to-do. And there were three Grannys taken to their beds in my kingdom, afflicted with what they claimed was epizootics and what I knew was congenital cantankerousness, and that was disrupting the regular conduct of everyday affairs more than was convenient.

So . . . faced with a lot of little crises and one on the way to being a big one, what did I do?

Well, I went to some meetings. I went to half a dozen. I fussed at the Castle staff, and I managed to get me in an Economist who showed some promise of being able to make the rest of them shape up. I hired a new Fiddler, and I bought a whole team of speckledy Mules that I'd had my eye on for a while. I visited the "ailing" Grannys, with a box of hard candy for each, and paid them elaborate compliments that they saw right through but enjoyed just the same. And I went to church.

I was in church the morning that Terrence Merryweather McDaniels the 6th, firstborn son of Vine of Motley and Halliday Joseph McDaniels the 14th, was kidnapped, right in broad daylight . . . when the man came through the churchdoor on a scruffy rented Mule, right in the middle of a Solemn Service—right in the middle, mind you, of a *prayer!*—and rode that Mule straight down the aisle. He snatched Terrence Merryweather in his sleeping basket from between his parents, and he flew right up over the Reverend's head and out through the only stained glass window he could count on to iris—Mule, basket, blankets, baby, and all, before any of us could do more than gape. February the 21st, that was; I was there, and it was that humiliating, I'm not likely to forget it. The McDaniels were guests of Castle Brightwater, and under our protection, and for sure should of been safe in our *church*. And now here was their baby kidnapped!

Although it *is* possible that kidnapping may not be precisely the word in this particular instance. You have a kidnapping, generally there's somebody missing, and a ransom note, and whatnot. In this case, the Reverend shouted an AAAAmen! and we all rushed out the churchdoor; and there, hanging from the highest of the three cedar trees in the churchyard in a life-support bubble, was Terrence Merryweather McDaniels the 6th, sucking on his toe to show how undisturbed *he* was by it all. And the Rent-a-Mule chewing on the crossclover against the church wall, under the overhang. There was no sign of its rider, who could make a claim to speed if to nothing else.

We could see the baby just fine, though we couldn't hear him. And we knew he was safe in the bubble, and all his needs attended to indefinitely. But he might as well of been in the Wilderness Lands of Tinaseeh for all the good that did us—we didn't dare touch him.

Oh, we had Magicians there skilled enough to put an end to that bubble and float the baby down to his daddy's arms without ruffling one bright red hair on his little head. If we hadn't had them, we could of gotten them in a hurry. It wasn't that; it was a matter of diagnosis.

We had no way, you see, of knowing just what kind of magic was on the forcefield holding that bubble up in the tree and keeping it active. Might of been no problem at all, just a bit of Granny Magic. *Ought* to of been, if the man doing it couldn't afford but a Rent-a-Mule. And then it might of been that the mangy thing was meant to make us think that, and it might of been that if we so much as *jiggled* that baby we'd blow the whole churchyard—AND the baby—across the county line. We're not much for taking chances with babies, I'm proud to say, and we weren't about to be hasty. The way to do it was to find the Magician that'd set the Spell, or whatever it was, and make it clear that we intended to *know,* come hell or high water, and keep on making it clear till we got told. Until then, that baby would just have to stay in the cedar tree with the squirrels and the chitterbirds and the yellowjays.

Vine of Motley carried on a good deal, doing her family no credit at all, but she was only thirteen and it her first baby, and allowances were made. Besides, I wasn't all that proud of my own self and my own family at that moment.

Five suspicious continental delegations I had coming to Castle Brightwater in less than three months, to celebrate the Grand Jubilee of a confederation they didn't trust much more now than they had two hundred years ago. Every one of them suspecting a plot behind every door and under every bedstead and seeing Spells in the coffee cups and underneath their saddles and, for all I knew, in their armpits. And I was proposing that they'd all be safe here—when I couldn't keep one little innocent pointy-headed baby safe in my own church on a Solemn Day?

It strained the limits of the imagination somewhat more than somewhat, and there was no way of keeping it quiet. They'd be having picnics under the tree where that baby hung in his pretty bubble and beaming the festivities out on the comsets before suppertime, or my name wasn't Responsible of Brightwater.

In the excitement we left the Solemn Service unfinished, and it took three Spells and a Charm to clear that up later on, not to mention the poor Reverend going through the service again to an empty church reeking mightily of garlic and asafetida. But the clear imperative right then was a family meeting; and we moved in as orderly a fashion as was possible (given the behavior of Vine of Motley) back to the Castle, where I turned all the out-family over to the staff to feed and cosset and called everyone else at once to the Meetingroom.

The table in the Meetingroom was dusty, and I distinctly saw a spiderweb in a far window, giving me yet another clue to the competency of my staff and strongly tempting me to waste a Housekeeping Spell or two —which would of been *most* unbecoming, but I never could abide dirt, even loose dirt—and I waved everybody to their chairs. *Which* they took after brushing more dust with great ostentation off the chair seats, drat them all for their eagerness to dot every "i" and cross every "t" when it was my competence in question, and I called the roll.

My mother was there, Thorn of Guthrie, forty-four years old and not looking more than thirty of those, which wasn't even decent; I do not approve of my mother. I said "Thorn of Guthrie" and she said "Here" and we left it at that. My uncles, Donald Patrick Brightwater the 133rd—time we dropped that name awhile, we'd wear it out—and Jubal Brooks Brightwater the 31st. Jubal's wife, Emmalyn of Clark, poor puny thing, she was there; and Donald's wife, Patience of Clark, Emmalyn's sister. And my grandmother, Ruth of Motley, not yet a Granny, since Jonathan Cardwell Brightwater the 12th showed no signs of leaving this world for all he was 109 years old . . . and it was said that he still troubled Ruth of Motley in the nights and scandalized the servingmaids in the chamber next to theirs. And I could believe it. We could of used him that day, since his head was as clear as his body was said to be hearty, but he was off somewhere trying to trade a set of Charms he'd worked out for a single Spell he'd been wanting to get hold of at least the last five years . . . and the lady that Spell belonged to not *about* to pass it on to him, if he spent five more.

As it was, that meant only seven of us in Meeting, not nearly enough for proper discussion or voting, and you would of thought that on a Solemn Day, and with guests in the Castle, there'd of been more of us in our proper places. I was put out about the whole thing, and my mother did not scruple to point that out.

"Mighty nervy of you, Responsible," she said, in that voice of hers, "being cross with everybody else for what is plainly your own fault." I could of said Yes-Mother, since she despises that, but I had more pressing matters to think of than annoying my mother. She'd never make a Granny;

she was too quick with that tongue and not able to put it under rein when the circumstances called for it, and at her age she had no excuse. She'd be a flippant wench at eighty-five, still stuck in her magic at Common Sense Level, like a child. Lucky she was that she was beautiful, since men have no more sense than to be distracted by such things, and Thorn *was* that. She had the Guthrie hair, masses of it, exactly the color of bittersweet chocolate and so alive it clung to your fingers (and to everything else, so that you spent half your life picking Guthrie hair off of any surface you cared to examine, but we'll let that pass). And she had the Guthrie bones . . . a face shaped like a heart, and great green eyes in it over cheekbones high arched like the curve of a bird's wing flying, and the long throat that melted into perfect shoulders. . . . And oh, those breasts of hers! Three children she'd suckled till they walked, and those breasts looked as maiden as mine. She was well named, was Thorn of Guthrie, and many of us had felt the sharp point of her since she stepped under the doorbeam of Castle Brightwater thirty-one years ago. I have always suspected that those Guthrie bones made her womb an uncomfortable place to lie, giving her a way to poke at you even before you first breathed the air of the world, but that's a speculation I've kept to myself. I hope.

"Well, now that we're thoroughly disgraced in front of the whole world," sighed my grandmother, "what do we propose to do about it?"

"This is *not* the first manifestation of something cockeyed," said Jubal Brooks. "You *know* that, Responsible."

"There was the milk," my grandmother agreed. "Four Mundy's in a row now it's been sour straight from the goat. I assume you don't find *that* normal, granddaughter."

"And there was the thing with the mirrors," said Emmalyn. "It *frightened* me, my mirror shattering in my hand like that."

I expect it did frighten her, too; everything else did. I was hoping she wouldn't notice the spiderweb. She was a sorry excuse for a woman; on the other hand, we couldn't of gotten Patience of Clark without taking the sister, too, and all in all it had been a bargain worth making.

Patience was sitting with her left little finger tapping her bottom lip, a gesture she made when she was waiting for a hole to come by in the conversation, and I turned to her and made the hole.

"Patience, you wanted to say something?"

"I was thinking of the streetsigns," she said.

"The streetsigns?"

"Echo in here," said my mother, always useful.

"I'm sorry, Patience," I said. "I hadn't heard that there was anything happening with streetsigns."

"All over the city," said my uncle Donald Patrick. "Don't you pay any attention to anything?"

"Well? What's been happening to them? Floating in the air? Whirling around? Exploding? What?"

Patience laughed softly, and the sun shone in through the windows and made the spattering of freckles over the bridge of her nose look like sprinkled brown sugar. I was very fond of Patience of Clark.

"They read backwards," she said. "The sign that should say 'River Street' . . . it says 'Teerts Revir.'" She spelled it out for me to make that clear, though the tongue does not bend too badly to "Teerts Revir."

"Well, *that,*" I said, "is downright silly."

"It's all silly," said Patience, "and that is why I was laughing. It's all ridiculous."

Emmalyn, whose freckles just ran together and looked like she hadn't bothered to wash, allowed as how she might very well have been cut when her mirror shattered, and that was not silly.

I looked at them all, and I waited. My uncles, pulling at their short black beards the way men always do in meetings. My mother, trying to keep her mind—such as it was—on the discussion. My grandmother, just biding her time till she could get back to her embroidery. And the sisters—Emmalyn watching Patience, and Patience watching some inner source of we-know-not-what that had served us very well in many a crisis.

Not a one of them mentioned the Mules, though I gave them two full minutes. And that meant one of three things: they had not noticed the phenomenon, or they did not realize that it was of any importance, or they had some reason for behaving as if one of the first two were the case. I wondered, but I didn't have time for finding out in any round-about fashion.

"I agree," I said at once the two minutes were up, "it's all silly. Even the mirrors. Not a soul was harmed by any one of the mirrors that broke—including you, Emmalyn. Anybody can smell soured milk quick enough not to drink it, and the other six days of the week it's been fine. And as for the streetsigns, which I'm embarrassed I didn't know about them but there it is—I didn't—that's silliest of all."

"Just mischief," said Jubal, putting on the period. "Until today."

My mother flared her perfect nostrils, like a high-bred Mule but a lot more attractive. "What makes you think, Jubal Brooks," she demanded, "that today's kidnapping—which is a matter of major importance—is connected in any way with all these baby tricks of milk and mirrors?"

"*And* streetsigns," said Emmalyn of Clark. Naturally.

"Jubal's quite right," I said, before Thorn of Guthrie could turn on Emmalyn. "And I call for Council."

There was a silence that told me I'd reached them, and Emmalyn looked thoroughly put out. Council meant there'd be no jokes, and no family bickering, and no pause in deliberation for coffee or cakes or ale or anything else till a conclusion was come to and a course agreed upon.

"Do you think that's really called for, Responsible?" asked my grandmother. She was doing a large panel at that time, mourningdoves in a field of violets, as I recall. Not that she'd ever seen a mourningdove. "As Jubal said, it's only been mischief so far, and pretty piddling mischief at that. And there's no evidence *I* see of a connection between what happened in church today and all that other foolishness."

"Responsible sees a connection," said Patience, "or she would not have called Council. And the calling is her privilege by rule; I suggest we get on with it."

I told them about the Mules then, and both the uncles left off their beard-pulling and gave me their attention. Tampering with goats was one thing, tampering with Mules was quite another. Not that they knew what it meant in terms of magic, of course—that would not of been suitable, since neither had ever shown the slightest talent for the profession, and I suppose they took flying Mules for granted as they did flying birds. But they had the male fondness for Mules, and they had anyone's dislike for the idea of suddenly falling out of the air like a stone, which is where they could see it might well lead.

"It has to do, I believe," said Patience slowly, "with the Jubilee. That's coming up fast now, and anybody with the idea of putting it in bad odor would have to get at it fairly soon and move with some dispatch. I do believe that's what this is all about."

She was right, but they'd listen better if she was doing the talking, so I left it to her.

"Go on," I said. "Please."

"I'm telling you nothing you don't know already," she said. "The

Confederation of Continents is not popular, nor likely to be, especially with the Kingdoms of Purdy, Guthrie, and Farson. And Tinaseeh is in worse state. The Travellers hate *any* kind of government; they are still so busy just hacking back the Wilderness that they don't feel they can spare time for anything else, and they for sure don't want the Jubilee. A Jubilee would give a kind of *endorsement* to the Confederation, and they are dead set against that. And then there're all the wishy-washy ones waiting around to see which way the wind blows."

"'A thing celebrated is a thing vindicated,'" quoted Ruth of Motley. "They all know that as well as anybody."

"The idea," Patience went on, "would be to make it appear that there's so much trouble on the continent of Marktwain . . . so much trouble in the Kingdom of Brightwater specifically . . . that it would not really be safe for the other Families to send their delegations to the Jubilee."

My conscience jabbed me, for she was right; and it had been niggling at the back of my mind for some time, though I'd managed to ignore it up to now by worrying about dust on the banisters and coffee deliveries for Mizzurah.

Donald Patrick scooted his chair back and stared at me, and then scooted it up again, and said damnation to boot, and my grandmother went "Ttch," with the tip of her tongue.

"Five years of work it's cost us," he said, glaring around the table. "Five years to convince them even to let us *schedule* the Jubilee! Surely all that work can't be set aside by some spoiled milk and a few smashed mirrors!"

"*Precisely*," I said, flat as pondwater. "And that is just the point. You see, youall, how it will look? First, parlor tricks. Then, a kind of tinkering —nothing serious, just tinkering—with the Mules. And then, to show that what goes four steps can go twelve, the baby-snatching. Again, you notice, without any *harm* done."

"Aw," said Jubal, "it's just showing off. A display of power. Like throwing a dead goat into your well."

"That it is," I said. "'See what we can do?' it says. . . . 'And think what we *might* do, if we cared to.' *That's* the message being spread here. Think the Wommacks will fly here from the coast knowing their Mules may drop out from under them any moment, to come to the support of our so-called Confederation?"

"Disfederation," murmured Patience of Clark. "A more accurate term at this point."

"Patience," I said, "you hurt me."

"Howsomever and nevertheless," she said, "it's true. And anything but a sure hand now will wreck it all."

We sat there silent, though Emmalyn fidgeted some, because it wasn't anything to be serene about. Marktwain, Oklahomah, and probably Mizzurah, agreed on the need for the Confederation of Continents; and their Kingdoms were willing to back it as best they could. But the whole bulk of Arkansaw lay between Marktwain and Mizzurah, and the Ocean of Storms between all of us and either Kintucky or Tinaseeh; and the three loyal continents all put together were not the size of Tinaseeh. Since the day the Twelve Families first landed on this planet in 2021, since the moment foot was set on this land and it was named Ozark in the hope it would prove a homeworld to our people, those of us who preferred not to remain trapped forever in the twenty-first century had been in the minority.

The Twelve Families had seen, on Old Earth, what the centralization of a government could mean. They had seen war and waste and wickedness beyond description, though the descriptions handed down to us were enough to this day to keep children in Granny Schools awake in the long nights of winter, shivering more with nightmare than with the cold. Twelve Kingdoms, we had. And at least four of them ready to leap up every time a dirty puddle appeared on a street corner and shout that this was but the first sign, the first step, toward the wallowing in degradation that came when individuals allowed theirselves to be *swallowed up* (they always said "swallowed up," playing on the hatred every Ozarker had for being closed in on *any* side, much less *all* of them) by a central government. . . . And several more were in honesty uncommitted, ready to move either way.

I ran them by in my mind, one by one. Castle Purdy, Castle Guthrie, Castle Farson, Castle Traveller—dead set against the Confederation and anxious to grab any opportunity to tear the poor frail thing apart and go to isolation for everything but trade and marriage. Castles Smith, Airy, Clark, and McDaniels, and Castles Lewis and Motley of Mizzurah, all with us—but perhaps only Castle Airy really ready, or able, to put any *strength* behind us. It was hard to know. When the Confederation met at Castle

Brightwater, one month now in every four—to the bitter complaints of
Purdy, Guthrie, Farson, and Traveller about the expense and the waste
and the frivolousness of it all—those six voted very carefully indeed. That
is, when we could manage to bring anything to a vote. Only Castles Airy
and Lewis had ever made a move that went three points past neutrality,
and that rarely. As for Castle Wommack, who knew where they stood?
One delegate they sent to the meetings, grudgingly, against the other
Castles' delegations of four each and full staff; and the Wommack delegate
came without so much as a secretary or Attendant, and spent most of his
time abstaining. We were seven to five for the Confederation—maybe.
Maybe we were but two against ten, with six of the ten playing lip service but ready to bolt at the first sign of anything that smelled like real
conflict.

My mother made a rare concession: she addressed me by term of
kinship.

"Daughter," she said, making me raise my eyebrows at the unexpected mode of address, "what do you think we ought to do?"

"Ask Jubal," said foolish Emmalyn, and I suppose Patience kicked
her, under the table. Patience always sat next to Emmalyn for that specific purpose. Ask Jubal, indeed.

"*Think* now before you speak," said Ruth of Motley. "It won't do
to answer this carelessly and get caught out, Responsible. You give it careful thought." She had finally forgotten about her embroidery and joined
us, and I was glad of it.

"I think," I said slowly, "that things are not so far out of hand that
they cannot be stopped. Vine of Motley is crying herself into hiccups up
in the guestchambers at this very moment, and no doubt feels herself
mighty abused, but that baby is safer where he is than in her arms. Signs
and mirrors and milk make no national catastrophe, and Mules that
behave like they'd been drinking bad whiskey are not yet a disaster. The
point is to stop it *now,* before it goes one step further. The next step might
not be mischief."

"What is called for," said my grandmother, nodding her head, "is a
show of competence; that would serve the purpose. Something that
would demonstrate that the Brightwaters are capable of keeping the delegations, and all their kin, and all their staffs, safe here for the Jubilee."

"I sometimes wonder if it's worth it," sighed Donald Patrick. "I sometimes think it might be best to let them go on and dissolve the Confederation and all *be* boones if that's their determined mind! The energy we put into all this, the *time,* the *money.* . . . Do you know what Brightwater spent in food and drink alone at the last quarterly meeting?"

"Donald Patrick Brightwater," said Ruth of Motley in a voice like the back of a hand, "you sound like a Purdy."

"I beg your pardon, Mother," said my uncle. "I hadn't any intention of doing so."

Strictly speaking, it was not fair for him to be rebuked. As the ordinary citizen was ignorant of what kept the Mules flying in the absence even of *wings,* so was Donald Patrick ignorant of the peril every Ozarker faced if we could not establish once and for all a central government that could respond, and respond with speed, in an emergency. The decision to maintain that ignorance had been made deliberately, and for excellent reasons, hundreds of years ago, when first the menace of the Out-Cabal had been discovered by our Magicians. And that decision would stand, for so long as it was possible, and for so long as disputations in political science, and intercontinental philosophy, and planetary ecology, and the formidable theory of magic, could be substituted for a truth it had been sworn our people would never have to learn.

"First," I said quickly, "there's finding out where this attack is coming from. That's the easy part."

My mother crossed her long white hands over her breasts to indicate her shock and informed us that *first* we had to get that baby down out of that tree.

"Mother, dear Mother," I said, "you know that's not so—that baby is all right. Unlike the rest of us, that baby is protected from every known danger this planet can muster up. Not so much as a bacterium can get through that bubble to harm Terrence Merryweather McDaniels, and he will be tended more carefully there than a king's son."

It was only a figure of speech; there were no kings in our kingdoms and never had been, and therefore no king's sons. When First Granny had stood on Ozark for the first time, her feet to solid ground after all those weary years on The Ship, she had looked around her, drawn a long breath, and said, "Well, the Kingdom's come at last, praise be!" and we'd had "kingdoms" ever since for that reason alone. But it had the necessary effect. Thorn of Guthrie made a pretense of thinking it over, but she knew I was right, and she nodded her lovely head and agreed with me that the baby probably represented the least of our problems. Except insofar as it stood for an insult to our Family and our faith, of course (and it was at that point that I realized the Solemn Service had been left unfinished).

"I say call in the Magicians of Rank, then," said Jubal Brooks, "and have them to find out which one of our eleven loving groups of kindred has set itself to bring the Confederation down about our heads. *Literally* about our heads."

"No," I told him, hoping he was right that it was only one. "No, Jubal Brooks, that's all wrong. It would maybe be *fastest,* depending on the strength and number of the Magicians ranged against ours, but it's all wrong as to *form.*"

"I don't see it," he said.

"A symbol," said Ruth of Motley, spelling it all out for him, "is best answered by a symbol. Not by a . . . meat cleaver."

"And what symbol do we propose to offer up for this motley collection—no offense meant, Mother—of shenanigans? Cross our hearts and spit in the ocean under a full moon?"

"A Quest, I expect, Jubal," I said, straight out. I had been thinking while they were talking, and level for level, that seemed right to me. And the women nodded all around the table.

"In this day and age?" sputtered Donald Patrick, and threw up his hands. "Do you realize the antiquated set of hidebound conditions that go with mounting up a *Quest?* Responsible, you can't be serious about this!"

"Well, it *is* fitting," said his mother, saving me the trouble. "As Responsible and Patience have pointed out, the entire campaign against us to this time has been a single symbol, what would be referred to in classical terms as a Challenge. OUR MAGIC IS BETTER THAN YOUR MAGIC, you see. No harm has been done, where obviously it *could* have been, had they been so minded. Very well, then—for an old-fashioned Challenge we shall offer an old-fashioned Quest. It is appropriate; it has the right ring to it."

"Foof," said Donald Patrick. "It's absurd."

"Indeed it is," I agreed, "and that's the whole point."

"We might should ignore the whole thing," he said. "For all we know."

"We do, and there will be no Grand Jubilee of the Confederation of Continents of Ozark, Donald Patrick Brightwater—and yes, I *do* know, down to the penny, what all this has been costing us. Nor will we have another *meeting* of the Confederation, I daresay, for a very long time. Whoever is doing this, they would be *delighted* to have us ignore it all, and everybody snickering behind their hands at us for cowards and weaklings . . . and it is in the hope that we will be fools enough to do that that they've kept every move to pestering only and not gone forward to injury. If they can bring us down for two cents, why spend two dollers?" I was completely out of breath.

"They have overplayed their hand," said Patience, "with this matter of the McDaniels baby."

"I believe so," I said. "It was a mistake of judgment. They should of kidnapped one of Jubal's Mules instead."

"And hung it in a cedar tree? In a life-support bubble?" Her brown eyes dancing, Patience of Clark was clearly trying not to imagine Jubal's favorite Mule being cleaned and fed and curried up in the cedar tree; and losing the battle.

"It would of been safer," I said. "*I* might of been busy enough not to take it for anything more than a prank; and *they* would of had still more time to make nuisances of themselves—and undercut the confidence in our security staff—before the Jubilee."

"Responsible, that's but eleven weeks away!" Patience broke in, the laughter in her eyes fading. "That's mighty little time."

"All the more reason to talk less and do more," I said. "Here's what I propose."

I would take our best Mule, from Brightwater's champion line, called Sterling and deserving of her name. I would make a brief and obvious fuss around the city in the way of putting together suitable outfitting for a journey of a special kind. I would let the word of the Quest be "leaked" to the comset networks. And then, I would do each Castle in turn, staying only just long enough at each to make the point that had to be made. Responsible of Brightwater, touring the Castles on a Quest after the source of magic put to mischief and to wickedness—just the thing. *Just* the thing!

"Even Tinaseeh?" asked Jubal dubiously.

"Even Tinaseeh. Certainly."

"It's a nine-day flight by Mule from here to Tinaseeh," he said. "At least. And you do a Quest, you do it by foot or by Mule, Responsible, no getting out of *that*. Nine days, just that one leg of the trip."

"As the crow flies," I acknowledged. Not that it would of taken *me* nine days, but there was no reason to let Jubal Brooks know more than he needed to know. "I will not head straight for Tinaseeh across the Oceans of Remembrances and of Storms, dear Uncle. I am touring the Twelve Kingdoms on solemn Quest, please remember. First I will go to Castle McDaniels. Then a short flight to Arkansaw, a mere hop across the channel to Mizzurah, on over to Kintucky, and then—and *only* then —to Tinaseeh. Then Oklahomah, quick around *it,* and back home."

"But, my dear *niece,*" he said—Jubal Brooks was stubborn, grant him that—"though it's but one day from Kintucky's southernmost *coast* to the coast of Tinaseeh, that one day will set you down not at Castle Traveller but on the edge of the largest Wilderness Lands on Ozark. Larger than the entire land area of this continent, for example; I strongly doubt you'll do the trip over *that* in less than three days, and you'd *still* have two days ahead of you before you reached the Castle gates!"

My grandmother stepped in then; the man was getting above himself, but tact, of course, was necessary. Men are a great deal of trouble, I must say.

"Jubal Brooks," she said, firmly but courteously, "Responsible was properly named. I suggest we do her the courtesy of trusting her in this."

"Distances," he began—the man was ranting!—"are distances. Name or no name—"

We might of wasted a lot more time on that kind of thing, if there hadn't been a knock on the door just as he was hitting his stride. For all that we were in Council, we could spare time to answer the door, and we did. Nobody was there, of course, leading Emmalyn to look puzzled and Patience to look innocent, but it served its purpose.

I dismissed Council with thanks, letting Jubal run down naturally as we all filed out, paid a visit to the guestchambers only to be told that the baby's parents had gone with full ceremonial tent to camp in the bed of needles beneath their son and heir, taking along the infant daughter of a servingmaid to see to the problem of Vine of Motley's milk—a practical solution, if a bit hard on the servingmaid—and then I ran for the stables.

So far as I was concerned, we were late already.

McDaniels

2

So close to home, I didn't dare take chances; and so I let my Mule fool about and waste hours in the air on the first stage of my journey, to Castle McDaniels. I wore an elaborate gown of emerald green; under it I had on flared trousers of a deeper green, tucked into trim high boots of scarlet leather, with silver bells about the bootcuffs and silver spurs all cunningly worked. And I had over *that* a tight-laced corselet of black velvet embroidered in gold and silver, and it was all topped with a hooded traveling cloak of six layers black velvet quilted together with silver thread in a pattern of wild roses and star-in-the-sky-vine and friendly ivy. My scarlet gloves matched my boots and my riding crop matched my spurs, and around my throat on a golden chain was a talisman almost not fit for the sight of decent people, except that decent people could be counted on not to know what it meant and anybody that knew what it meant would sure not mention it. All in all it was a purely disgusting sight. When I flew I preferred honest denims, and over them a cloak of brown wool. And spurs and riding crop to fly a Mule were about as sensible as four wheels and a clutch to sail a ship—but none of that was relevant.

I was a *symbol,* and a symbol carrying out a symbol. I was, by the Twelve Corners, a Meta-Symbol, and I intended to look the part if it choked me. They, whoever they might turn out to be, would have leisure to compare the style in which Castle Brightwater did these things with their scroungy brigand on a mangy rented Mule. I would see to that, and I intended to rub it in and then add salt, if I got the chance.

I brought Sterling down smartly at the entrance to Castle McDaniels without raising so much as a puff of dust, and I called out to the guard-maid at the broad door to let us in.

"Well met, Responsible of Brightwater!" she hollered at me; and I mused, as I had mused many and many a time before, on the burden it gave the tongue to greet either myself or my sister Troublesome (not that many greeted *her!*). A regular welter of syllables, and I hoped the Granny that did it got a pain in her jaw joints. When I was a child, the others made me pay for the inconvenience, ringing changes on it all the day long. Obstreperous of Laketumor, they liked to call me. Preposterous of Bogwater. Philharmonic of Underwear. And numerous variations in the same vein. On the rare occasions when my sister and I shared the same space, they liked to call us "Nettlesome and Cuddlesome."

We have a saying, an ancient one: "Don't get mad; get even." It stayed my hand when I was young enough to mind such nonsense, and now I would not stoop the distance necessary to get even. But it still rankles at times. As when a skinny guardmaid bellows out at me before all the world, "Well met, Responsible of Brightwater!"

"Well met yourself," I said, "and why not good morrow while we're at it?"

"Beg your pardon?" She had a slack jaw, too, and it dropped, doing nothing to improve the general effect.

"As should you," I said crossly. "The year is 3012, and 'well met' went out with the chastity belt and the spindle."

"I have a spindle," she said to me, all sauce, but she must not of cared for the expression on my face; she left it at that.

"What's your name, guardmaid?" I asked her, while I waited for the idea to reach her brain that someone should be notified of my arrival.

"Demarest, I'm called. Demarest of Wommack."

Demarest . . . it was a name that had no associations for me, and she was far from home.

"Would you tell the McDaniels I'm here, Demarest of Wommack?" I asked her, giving up. No doubt the McDaniels, like myself, were having trouble finding Castle staff that could even begin to meet the minimum needs of their jobs. It made me sorry, at times, that robots were forbidden to us. True, they were the first step toward a population that just lay around and got fat and then died of bone laziness; I understood and approved the prohibition. But they would of been so useful for some things. Pacing off the boundaries of a kingdom, for instance, which had to be done on foot, every *inch* of it . . . and letting people into Castles.

She looked at me out of the corner of blue eyes under straightcut coppery bangs, and she tugged at the bellpull hanging at her right hand, and in due course the Castle Housekeeper appeared and opened the front doors to me. She did not, I'm happy to say, tell me I was well met; but she called stablemaids to take away the Mule and unload my saddlebags, and she showed me into a small waiting room where a fire burned bright against the February chill. And she saw to it that someone brought me a glass of wine and a mug of hearty soup.

I settled my complicated skirts and maddening trousers, and drank my soup and wine, and soon enough the arched door opened and in came Anne of Brightwater, my kinswoman and a McDaniels by marriage, to greet me.

"Law!" she said from the doorway, looking me up and down. She was blessed with a plain name and plain speech both, and I envied her the first at least.

"Look like a spectacle, don't I?" I acknowledged.

"My, yes," said Anne.

"I'm supposed to," I said. "You should see my underwear."

She agreed to forego that experience, and came and sat down and stared at me, shaking her head and biting her lower lip so as not to laugh.

"Well, Anne?"

"Oh, I'm sure you've good reasons," she said, "and I have sense enough not to want to know what they are. But I'll wager not a single Granny saw you leave in that getup, or more than your boots and your gloves would be rosy red."

I chuckled; I expected she was right.

"Welcome, Responsible of Brightwater," said Anne then, "and how long are we to have the misery of your company?"

Plainer and plainer speech.

"Can you put me up for twenty-four hours, sweet cousin?"

"In the style you're decked out for?"

"If you mean must there be dancing in the streets, Anne, no, I'll spare you that."

"What, then? You didn't just 'drop in' on your way to buy a spool of thread somewhere."

Anne pulled her chair near the fire, folded her arms across her chest, fixed her attention on me, and waited.

"I, Responsible of Brightwater," I recited, "am touring the Twelve Castles of Ozark, Castle by Castle, in preparation for the Grand Jubilee of the Confederation. Which is—as you'll remember—to be convened at Castle Brightwater on the eighth day of this May. And I begin here, dear cousin, to do you honor."

"And because Castle McDaniels is closest."

"And," I capped it, "because a person has to begin somewhere. There is one advantage; if I start with you, then it follows that you're first done with me."

"Ah, yes," she sighed, "there is that."

She leaned back in her chair and sighed again, and I tried to keep my spurs from making holes in her upholstery.

"What's required?" she asked me.

"One party," I said. "A very small one. In honor of my tour, you know. In honor of my Quest."

"In honor of the Pickles."

"The Pickles? Anne!"

On Earth, we are told in the Teaching Stories, there was a food called pickles, made out of some other food called cucumbers. On *this* world, Pickles are small flat squishy round green things, and they bite. They certainly are not good to eat, even in brine, and we grant them a capital letter to keep the kids mindful not to step on them barefoot.

"Well," said Anne of Brightwater, "it's just as sensible."

"It would be just as well," I said, "not to mention the Pickles in your invitations."

"Responsible, dear Cousin Responsible, I *despise* parties! I *always* have despised them, and you know it. Why don't you be too tired, instead?"

The fire crackled in the fireplace, and a nasty wind howled round the Castle walls, and I knit my brows and glared at her until she sighed one more time and went away to give the necessary orders. My mention as she stepped into the hall that she'd best expect a comset film crew did nothing for her expression, but she went on; and I got myself out of my spurs and hung them over a corner of her mantel.

There could be no treason here—and that *was* what all this foolishness in fact amounted to, of course, plain treason—not in Castle McDaniels. The Brightwaters and the McDaniels had been closer than the sea and its shore ever since First Landing, and if there was anyone in this Castle who was not kin to me by birth or by marriage, or tied to me by favors given and received, it was some ninny such as stood guardmaid. Nevertheless, a Quest was a Quest, and it had to be done according to the rules. I had had a boring flight, tooling along through the air and waving to passing birds; and I would have a boring supper with Anne's boring husband, and then we would all have a boring party and be boringly exhausted in the morning. And then before lunch I would be able to take my leave for Castle Purdy.

At which point a thought struck me, and I pulled my map from my pocket and unfolded it. Upper right-hand corner of the pliofilm, the small continent Marktwain, with the Outward Deeps off its coasts to the east. To the south of Marktwain, Oklahomah, a tad bigger. To the west, and dwarfing both, the continent of Arkansaw, with little Mizzurah almost up against its western coast and sheltered some from the Ocean of Storms by its overhang to the north. Then across the Ocean of Storms, in the northwest corner of my map, was Kintucky, big as Oklahomah but with only the Wommacks to manage the whole of it. And last of all, filling the southwest corner, the huge bulk of Tinaseeh, the only one of our continents to have an inland sea, and its Wilderness Lands alone as big as either Kintucky or Oklahomah. And the empty Ocean of Remembrances, filling all the southeast corner.

True, the most obvious route, and the one I had described to the arguesome Jubal, was straight over to Arkansaw. But Arkansaw was shared by Castles Purdy and Guthrie and Farson. And those were three of the most likely to have something to hide from me and require an investment of my time.

An alternative that might save me time in the *long* run would be to fly straight on south to Castle Clark on Oklahomah, and make a quick circuit of Castles Smith and Airy, both of which—along with Clark—were loyal to the Confederation. I could maybe do the entire continent in eight, nine days, counting one to a Castle for the required ceremonial stopover, before I moved on to Arkansaw and more reasonable sources of trouble.

The McDaniels children found me poring over my map and gathered round to look over my shoulder, all nine of them. The room shrank around me; not a one of them that was not a typical McDaniels, big and stocky and broad-shouldered (and if female, broad-hipped as well). It got very crowded in that room.

"This is a nice map you've got," said one of the younger of the herd, a boy called Nicholas Fairtower McDaniels the somethingth—I could not remember the what-th there for a minute. The 55th? No; the 56th. I was embarrassed; if there is one thing expected of us it is knowing people's *names,* and this boy was a second cousin of mine.

"What are you looking for, Responsible? It's a nice map, like Nicholas says, but there's a lot on it."

"She's looking for the kidnapper—"said the very littlest, and instantly clapped both hands over his mouth. "I forgot," he said around his fingers.

Either Anne or their father then had threatened them with dire events if they mentioned that baby; still, it *was* a McDaniels baby, and it was not surprising that they'd be interested. Manners were hard to get the hang of.

"I am trying to decide," I said, ruffling the boy's hair to show I didn't intend to take notice of his lapse, "which is the best way to go when I leave in the morning. Like you say, there's a lot of choices."

The children hadn't any hesitation at all—zip due west to Arkansaw, as any fool could see. Except for one of them. Her name was Silverweb, and she was fifteen years old and not yet married; perhaps it was her intention to become a Granny without the bother of waiting around to become a widow. She was a handsome strapping young woman, with a pleasant face; she bound her hair back in an intricate figure-eight of yellow braids that I could never of managed, and she carried herself with dignity. I made a mental note to compliment Anne on this daughter—her only daughter —who seemed to me to show promise.

She laid a well-tanned finger that showed she wasn't afraid of a little sun to my map, and traced a different route. Castle Clark, on Oklahomah's northeast corner. Castle Airy, at the southern tip . . . Oklahomah came very near being a triangle. Then to Castle Smith, in the northwest corner. My choice exactly.

"Do it that way," she said. "Then over to Arkansaw, only an easy morning's ride. And you're at Castle Guthrie."

"Faugh, Silverweb," said one of her brothers, "she can't do that at all. You heard Mother—Cousin Responsible is touring all twelve Castles on solemn Quest. The way to do it is go straight on to Arkansaw, then Mizzurah, then Kintucky, then Tinaseeh, then *end up* in Oklahomah, and back to Marktwain."

"If she ever gets out of Tinaseeh," said another. "Horrible old place,

Tinaseeh is, and full of things that would as soon eat you alive as look at you."

"Not as horrible as your room!"

I moved out of the way so as not to get my costume spoiled, grateful that the map was indestructible, and let them shove and carry on for a bit to get it out of their systems. Silverweb, calm among the turmoil, held fast that it would be just as sensible, and twice as pleasant, and break no rules that *she'd* ever heard of, if I went the other way round.

"But then she's got all that open ocean between Tinaseeh and Oklahomah to fly! Look at it, would you? A person could fly over that and never be heard of again—it must be . . . three days across? Five? Six?"

"It's got to be done at one end or the other," scoffed his sister. "Better to do it when the worst is over and she can take her time. She'll be plain worn out, by then."

"What makes you think so, Silverweb?" the boy taunted, for all he had to stand on his tiptoes to look her in the eye. "She's Responsible of Brightwater, Silverweb, she's not a *tourist!*"

Silverweb's chin went up and the blue eyes almost closed. She took one step forward and the boy fell back two. Second of nine she was; it couldn't be easy. And the other eight all male . . . it was enough to constitute a substantial burden.

Silverweb. I added it up in my head—she was a *seven*. Withdrawal from the world . . . that went with not marrying . . . secrets and mystery . . . that fit the hooded eyes and the intricate figure of her braids. From what I could see, this one was properly named, and living up to it.

As of course she would be. There were no incompetent Grannys on Marktwain to cause trouble with an Improper Naming, as had been known to happen elsewhere from time to time.

I let them squabble, Silverweb winning easily, and relaxed as best I could given the way I was dressed, enjoying the sight of them all if not the sound. I had my route chosen now—as Silverweb had had the wit to lay it out, and it was not designed solely in terms of distances and points of the compass. I would do quickly the friendly territory of Oklahomah; and in that way I'd have a bit extra where it was less than friendly.

The party was pleasant, more a dance than a party, and a credit to Anne. She'd invited people enough to fill the Castle's smaller ballroom,

and had managed to muster a respectable crowd, considering the short
notice and a thunderstorm that had already been scheduled and could not
of been postponed without distorting the weather for the next three
weeks. Anne and I stood in a corner back of the bandstand where the
Caller was hollering out the dances, both of us in slight danger from a
flying fiddle bow but willing to risk it for the sake of the semi-privacy. I
despised parties as much as Anne did, probably more, and I couldn't dance
even the simplest dances, much less the complex things they were weaving on the tiles that night in honor of my visit.

> "Star in the shallows, flash and swim,
> Lady to her gentleman and parry to him!"

"Wherever do they *learn* to do all that?" I marveled.

> "Circle has a border to it, touch it and run,
> Muffins in the oven till their middles are done!"

"You should of been taught," said Anne. "They had no right to leave
you ignorant just because you might of enjoyed yourself."

"There wasn't time," I said, which was the plain truth. Plus, I was
awkward, always had been.

> "Braid a double rosebud, smother it in snow,
> Swing your partner, and dosey-do!"

> "Step on a Pickle in the dark of night,
> Grab your cross lady, and allemande right!"

"It's not fair," she insisted. "I hear your brother's the best dancer
in three counties, and turning all the girls to cream and butter. And I'll
wager they saw to it that your sister learned every dance that was worth
knowing."

I snorted. "Nobody ever 'saw to it' that Troublesome did anything,
Anne of Brightwater. What she wanted to do, she did. What she cared to
know about, she learned. Anything else was just so much kiss-your-elbow."

> "Sashay down the center, rim around the wall,
> Single-bind, double-bind, and promenade all!"

I couldn't even understand these calls . . . dosey-do and promenade-the-hall went by often enough to let me know it was dancing, but the intricacies of it were beyond me. I couldn't decide whether I minded that, either, though on general principles I was not supposed to fall behind on anything that mattered to any sizable proportion of Ozarkers, "sizable" being defined as more than three. It looked to be hot work, and I fanned my face with my blank program in sympathy.

"Young people!" I said, ducking the bow. "They do amaze me."

Anne gave me a sharp look, and I looked her right back and waited. Whatever she had to say, she'd say it; she'd said enough about my blue-and-silver party dress, which was even more preposterous in the way of gewgaws and lollydaddles than the one I'd arrived in. And my high-heeled silver slippers with the pointed toes.

"My daughter, Silverweb," she said to me, and I noticed that she was talking with her teeth clenched, and spitting out the syllables like she couldn't spare them, "Silverweb, my dear cousin, is a 'young people.'"

"And a fine one," I agreed. "That's a likely young woman, and I plan to keep my eye on her in future. I wager she'll go a considerable distance in this world."

"*Silverweb*," Anne said again, "is *fifteen years old*. And you, Responsible of Brightwater, you remarking on the habits of these 'young people' like a blasted Granny, have had precisely fourteen birthdays, and the fourteenth not more than six weeks ago!"

It wasn't often I stood rebuked lately, not since we'd finally managed to pack my sister off where she couldn't do any harm to speak of or leave me holding the bag if she was bound and *determined* to live up to *her* name. But this was one of the times, and I had it coming. Not that we are given to considering only the calendar years on Ozark, we know many other things more worth considering. But my speech had not been genteel. It was the sort of thing my mother would of said, and I wished, not for the first time, that I had the skill of blushing. That, like the ability not to fall over my own big feet, had been left out of my equipment. And the more ashamed of myself I was, the more I looked like I didn't care at all—I knew that. I only wished I knew what to *do* about it.

Anne of Brightwater was not as tall as I was, and she had a usual habit of gathering herself in that made her seem even smaller, but she was making me feel mighty puny now, there mid the music and the boom of thunder. A trick like a cat does, puffing herself up to be more impressive.

"It is *hard* for Silverweb," said my kinswoman, spitting sparks now along with the syllables, "seeing you come here, dressed like a young queen and treated like one, off on a Quest before all the world and it taken *seriously*—oh, they are, don't you worry, they are taking it very seriously! While she stands aside and must hear herself called 'one of the McDaniels children.' Had you thought of that?"

I had not thought of it, obvious though it surely should have been. I looked at the tall grave girl who was a year my senior, moving easily through the squares in a simple dress of gray silk sprigged with pale green rosebuds, and her only ornament a shawl of dark gray wool in a Love-in-the-Mist knotting, with a pearl fringe . . . and perhaps the single wild rose in her yellow hair. I remembered the way I had sat that afternoon, "watching the children," with a pretty fair estimate of the expression that must of been on my face at the time, and I felt a fool. Had I called her "one of the children" in her hearing? Surely not . . . but supper had been boring, as expected, and I'd not paid a great deal of mind to curbing my tongue.

"The mother lion defends her young," I said lamely, and the nearest Fiddler got me back of the ear, making me jump.

"And a stitch in time saves nine!"

I winced and stared at the floor, and Anne drew her skirts around her with a swish like ribbon tearing and went off and left me standing there all alone as she headed for the ballroom door, managing to tangle herself up with two couples in a reel before she sailed out into the corridor and slammed the door behind her.

She would be back later to apologize. After all, I had not *chosen* to be Responsible of Brightwater. It was none of my doing. A Granny had chosen that role for me and I filled it as best I could, and no doubt there were good reasons. Some of them I knew, and some I could guess, though there seemed a kind of fuzz between them and my clear awareness; others I would learn in time, and some I would be told. When I was buried they would be written on a sheet of paper narrow as my thumb, in the symbols of Formalisms & Transformations, and tucked between my breasts and buried with me. Somewhere, if she still lived, there was someone who knew every one of those reasons at this very moment, and no doubt the knowledge lay heavy on *her* shoulders; I hoped they were broad.

I was *behaving* like a fourteen-year-old, I realized, and I smoothed my ruffled feathers and set my quarrel with Anne aside, along with the futile lamenting about my lack of elegances. Spilt milk, all of it, and I'd spill gallons more before I saw my own Castle gates again. The only important question I needed to concern myself with was: could there be mischief here, if not treason, despite the fact that the McDaniels were close to the Brightwaters as our skins?

I listened, then, with more than my ears—my ears were too full of fiddle and guitar and dulcimer to be useful in any case—and only silence came back to me. Here I might be annoying, and I might be read up and down, but here I was loved, and here the Confederation was seen as a worthy goal to be worked toward. I found no small thing that I could worry about, and I worried easy; nor would I be spending this night casting Spells to troll for echoes that I might of missed hearing through the music.

Thunder boomed again, less intimidating than Anne, and I poured myself another glass of punch and retreated further into the protection of the tall white baskets of flowers and ferns that surrounded the bandstand. And seeing as how the McDaniels set as fine a party table as was to be found anywhere, I had another plate of food. I would be off in the morning early, I decided, and skip the breakfast. That way I wouldn't have to face Silverweb of McDaniels again and risk putting my foot deeper yet in the muck than I had already, from being self-conscious over slighting her so today.

My pockets were deep and my skirts full enough to hide plenty of lumps. I made sure I had both a midnight snack and a breakfast squirreled away before Anne came back to tuck her arm through mine and tell me what a crosspatch she'd been over nothing.

"It wasn't 'nothing,'" I said resolutely, "and I had every word you said coming to me, Anne. But I want you to know it wasn't *meant* to be the way it looked, and I wish you'd tell Silverweb that once I'm gone. And I thank you for bringing my manners to my attention here and now, close to home; it would not be so easy if you were the lady of Castle Traveller."

"Just use your head," she said, and tears were in her eyes, because she saw I was truly sorry. Anne of Brightwater had a quick temper, but a heart that melted at blood heat, nearly. "And watch your tongue."

"I'm trying," I said. "I'll get the hang of it."

I had for sure *better* get the hang of it, and that with some speed.

"You'll tell Silverweb?" I asked her. "Promise?"

"I'll tell her. And she will understand. Silverweb is a deep one."

Clark

3

The next day I was able to be a little more sensible. Leaving, I still wore my spectacular traveling outfit, but the minute I was well over the water and out of sight of the fishing boats I brought Sterling to a full stop in midair and changed into something that didn't make what was already misery doubly so.

Balancing on Muleback for that kind of thing takes practice, and properly fastened straps and backups, but I was more than up to it—I'd had lots of practice. Mostly it requires pretending you are flat on the ground, while at the same time not exactly forgetting that it's a good ways down.

I took the Ocean of Remembrances at a leisurely pace; it was a three-day flight from Castle McDaniels to the first landfall on Oklahomah, and since I'd done Castle to coast in about fourteen minutes flat I had time to make up over the ocean.

I cut the Mule back to half her regulation speed, and I balanced a very small dulcimer—all I'd been able to fit in my saddlebags, but not all that bad—over her broad neck, and I sang my way dry through a steady wind and plenty of rain by way of a Weather Transformation that it was fully illegal for me to know. Sterling disliked the dulcimer, and she probably disliked my voice even more; it was a good deal like her own. Just as I was never called upon to dance at parties, I was never called upon to sing (anywhere), and I reveled in my opportunity, here at a height where there was nobody to clap hands over their ears and beg me to leave off tormenting them. I do *know* a lot of ballads, not to mention every hymn in the hymnal, and I enjoyed myself tremendously.

There is some inconvenience, of course, to making any lengthy ocean voyage by Mule, our oceans being almost completely empty of islands or reefs. A person could get through one day without *too* much hassle, provided you neither ate nor drank the day before nor during the flight itself. But once you went beyond that single day the inevitable happened, and considerable gymnastics were required of both rider and Mule. (This was not the least of the reasons why Ozarkers for the most part went by boat from continent to continent, and it made it unlikely that I would meet any other citizen on Muleback as I went along, which was all to the good in the interests of modesty.) Only for the sake of a symbol would anything so unhandy be undertaken by a reasonable person, and few had that sort of symbol to deal with.

I had ample time to think about the distances and times of flight that would be expected of me, when my throat and my fingers got tired. Brightwater to McDaniels, one very long day, and then three more to Oklahomah. Three days roughly for each leg of the triangle from Castle Clark to Castle Smith, Castle Smith to Castle Airy, and back again almost to Clark for the best take-off across the channel to Arkansaw—*that* a day's flight only, and a short day. Three days' travel for Castles Farson and Guthrie, a day's flight to Mizzurah; two days there and two to Castle Purdy. Four days across the Ocean of Storms to Kintucky, provided the ocean didn't do too much living up to its name and force me to put in an extra day for the benefit of the population. Ten days from Kintucky to Tinaseeh. Then the longest leg over water . . . the McDaniels children had not been too far off in their estimate of the flight time from Tinaseeh's southeast tip back to Oklahomah; it was a good five days, even with fair weather and a tailwind. And then four days home. Fifteen days, even cutting it very close, I'd be expected to spend flying over water. And far more than that for the land distances, with stops at the same intervals expected of anyone else.

Since I was all alone I indulged myself, and turned the air blue to match the stripe between Sterling's ears, which were still laid back in protest against my concert. I could of done the whole *trip,* the actual flying time, in about an hour total, just the amount of realtime involved in take-offs and landings, and there was no time to spare with the Jubilee coming in May, and February almost over. But whereas a Magician of Rank could have done it that way and nobody would of done more than maybe fuss mildly about people that felt obliged to show off, having a *woman* do such a thing would cause about the same amount of commotion as a good-sized groundquake. And the damage would not be repairable by stone and timber. I could shave an hour here and half an

hour there and get away with it, but not much more, not without causing more trouble than I could conveniently put an end to. The word
would be well out by now, and people in the towns and farms—and on
the water along the coasts, too—would be expecting to look up and see
me fly by all in emerald and black and gold and silver and scarlet, at *reasonable* points of time. Aeronautically reasonable.

I could think of no cover story that would get me out of any of that
time, except that (the Twelve Corners be praised) I would be able to do
most of my make-up time in the Wildernesses instead of over the oceans.
The likelihood of anybody observing me in mid-ocean once I got away
from the coasts was too small to be worth considering; I would do a decorous few miles in sight of land, SNAP to a suitably remote spot in the nearest Wilderness, and camp there to wait out the time it "should" of taken
me to fly that far. Enough was enough. Muleflight was fine for formal
occasions, for short-time travel, and for racing and hunting, but it was
one of the most boring ways ever devised for going long distances.
Sterling, like any other Mule with a sense of self-respect, refused to go
through the completely superfluous leg movements in the air that travel
over ground or in the water would of required . . . it was a lot like sitting on a log (a small log) floating through the air, and if it hadn't been
for the wind blowing past you it would of been easy to believe that you
weren't moving at all. Over the water even the wind wasn't all that much
diversion. It wasn't tiring, and twelve full hours of it was no great strain
on either Mule or rider, but, *law,* it was boring. I intended to keep it to
a minimum.

The coast of Oklahomah is peaceful land. Pale golden sand sloping
gently down to the water on one side and gently up into low green hills
on the other, and the weather always easy there. There were boats out,
farther from the land than I had really expected them to be, and I made
my arm tired waving at their passengers before I began my descent. *And
managed to drop my poor dulcimer into the Ocean of Remembrances in
the process.* New motto: never try to balance a dulcimer across a Mule's
neck, keep from falling off the Mule, and wave to a boat captain below
you at the same time.

Sterling and I settled down toward the land, and I saw that my expectations were correct; the word had gone out. Although Castle Clark was
no more than three miles up from the shore, where it had a view that

melted both heart and mind as it faced out toward the sea, there was a delegation of some sort waiting to meet me. I wouldn't have to hammer on the gates of Castle Clark as I had had to do at Castle McDaniels; we were going in in a small, and I hoped a tasteful, procession.

The Clarks' Castle staff wore dark brown livery, trimmed at cuff and hem with yellow and white. Four of the staff were there on Muleback (all, by their insignia, Senior Attendants), the Clark crest embroidered on their right shoulders. I had always liked that crest; two stalks of wheat, crossed, yellow on a field of brown, and a single white star above the wheat—nothing more. It pleasured the eye and was a credit to the Granny that'd devised it when the Castle was built.

"Good morning, miss," they said, which was a great relief, and I good-morninged them back again. And then they told me that dinner was waiting for us at the Castle, which pleasured me even more. I hope to outgrow my appetite one of these years, but I was hungry again.

"And a message from Castle Smith waiting, miss," said one.

"What sort of message, Attendant?"

"Don't know, miss. I was told to greet you, ask you to dinner, and say the message was waiting. That's all."

We turned the Mules, and they followed me, four abreast and a mannerly four Mule-lengths behind, across the sand and up the hill ahead of us. The Mules had no objection to the hard-packed beach, but floundered once we were above the tideline; I was pleased to see that none of the animals following me took the all too common Mulish tactic of stopping dead and refusing to move, sinking deeper all the while into the sand. They were well trained, and they struggled through the powdery stuff without hesitation, though I'd no doubt they'd of said a good deal if they'd had the chance. Not one brayed, a sure sign of good management in the stables, and once we reached the road their hoofs tapped smartly along the white pavement. Very orderly, and I liked order. I was in a good mood, and prepared to be in a better one, as we went through the gates and dismounted in the courtyard, and I was led straight on to a long balcony on the second floor that looked out over the hills to the sea.

There sat the Clarks. Nathan Terfelix Clark the 17th, with a beard like a white bush trimming up his burly chest, and not a hair on his head, in compensation. His wife, Amanda of Farson, the one with the chins. Their three daughters, Una, Zoë, and Sharon, and the husbands of the two eldest at their sides. Let me see . . . it was Una that had scandalized her parents by marrying a Traveller, and gone on to scandalize the Families nearby by loving him far beyond what was either decent or expected, and that would be him, Gabriel Laddercane Traveller the 34th, in the suit of black. The Travellers were unwilling to give up *any* of their ancient trappings, and they dressed still as they had the day they stepped off The Ship in 2021. Zoë's husband was a kinsman, Joseph Frederick Brightwater the 11th, and looked pleased to see me. And an assortment of babies, all of them beautiful. I've never seen an ugly baby—but then I've never seen a genuinely *new* one, either—I'm told that might dent my convictions.

And there sat Granny Golightly.

She gave me the shivers, and it pleased me not to have her where I had to see her oftener. She stood not quite five feet tall, she weighed about as much as a Mule colt, and she was an Airy by birth, which had been an astonishing long time ago. If my reckoning was right, Granny Golightly had passed her one hundred and twenty-ninth birthday recently; next to her I was a flyspeck on the windowpane of time. I intended to go lightly near her, for sweet prudence' sake, and as befit her name.

"Hello there, Responsible of Brightwater," they said to me, and waved me to an empty chair in the sunshine. Dinner was chowder—I counted eleven kinds of fish!—and dark ale, and cornbread properly prepared and so hot the butter disappeared when it touched it, and a fine pair of salads, one fruit and one vegetables. And a berry cobbler that I knew nobody at Castle Brightwater could of brought off, including my own self.

Finishing that cobbler, and thinking back on the rest of the meal, I understood fully how the Clarks acquired their bulk, and I forgave Amanda her chins. What I did not understand was the trim waists of the daughters, especially Una, who accounted for five of the children. Perhaps since they had grown up eating this way they had developed a natural immunity. Or perhaps this was a company meal and they usually ate like the rest of us at noon; I had, after all, been expected here.

"Responsible of Brightwater," said Nathan Terfelix, "there's a message here for you from Castle Smith. Man arrived with it this morning almost before we had the gates unlocked, and what he was in such a hurry for I have no idea. *Or* interest. Knew you couldn't get here before noontime."

"Took off as fast as he arrived, too," Amanda added. "He wouldn't even stop for a cup of coffee."

She raised her head and nodded at a young Attendant standing near the door, and he brought me an envelope and laid it in my hand without a word. He looked to be about eleven, and if I was any judge his livery collar itched him; this must be his first year in service.

"Amanda," I said as he backed away, "the young man's collar is badly fit. Someone should see to it."

Granny Golightly cackled, which was trite.

"Not going to miss a trick, are you, Responsible of Brightwater?" she demanded. "Going to see that our *livery* fits the servants right, are you? You plan to inspect the stables while you're here, and run your little white fingers up and down the banisters?"

"I beg your pardon, Granny Golightly," I said. "I did not mean to criticize."

"Lie to me, young missy, and you'll rue it," she snapped. "Criticism you gave, and criticism we got, and I'll see to the tadling's collar myself, this afternoon. *And* to the careless seamstress that made it too tight in the first place, whoever *she* may be! All we need is sloppy staff giving Responsible of Brightwater bits to add to her long list!"

This was ordinary behavior for a Granny, and I paid it no mind; it had been years since I'd made the mistake of getting into a wrangle with a Granny bent on public performance. She went on like that for quite some time, under her breath, while I turned the envelope from Castle Smith over in my hands, and the young husbands disappeared one at a time on mumbled errands.

Creamy white paper, thick as linen, and an envelope that ought to of held something of importance—which it had to hold, if it could not of been sent by comset in the ordinary way but had to be carried here by human hand. Seven inches square if it was one, and the Smith crest stamped on it both front and back, *and* an official seal! And inside it, all alone in the middle of a sheet of matched paper like lonely raisins in a pudding, the following words:

> We regret that Castle Smith will be unable to entertain you
> at this time, due to a family crisis. Any questions you might
> have can be asked there at Castle Clark, and well answered.
>
> > In cordial haste,
> > Dorothy of Smith

The eldest daughter of the Castle, Dorothy of Smith . . . carrying out a minor social duty? Or what? Dorothy was a pincher; I remembered her as a child at playparties and picnics, always quick with her wicked little fingers, and running before you could get a fair chance to pinch her back. She would be fourteen now, just about three months older than I was. And since she'd bid me ask questions, I asked one.

"Begging your pardon, Granny Golightly," I said, and the Granny stopped her nattering and looked up from her cobbler. "Amanda, do you or Nathan either of you know of any 'crisis' at Castle Smith?"

Amanda looked blank, and Nathan frowned, and Granny Golightly forgot her pose long enough to give me a sharp look between bites.

"Crisis," said Nathan.

"What kind of crisis?" asked Amanda.

I waved the note. "Doesn't say," I said. "Just disinvites me."

"Now that won't do, young lady," Granny Golightly jumped in, "for you invited your *own* self on this particular traipse-about! There was *no call* sent out from the Twelve Castles, demanding the drop-in of Responsible of Brightwater at her earliest convenience, not as *I* know of—and I would know."

"Gently, Granny," said Zoë of Clark, and leaned over to pick up a baby. For ballast perhaps. "Gently!"

"Flumdiddle," said the Granny.

"I withdraw the accusation," I said, "and you are quite right—I had no invitation. Not here, either, but you've seen fit to be hospitable and I thank you for it. I will remember it."

"On your list!" said Granny. "See there?"

"And," I added, "I will remember the way the Smiths set their hands to the same plow—what to do with Responsible of Brightwater, all inconvenient and uninvited. *Unless*—unless there truly is trouble at Castle Smith to back this up."

Silence, all around the table. Mules braying in the stables, and seabirds crying out as they whirled above us, but no words, nor did I really expect many. Ozarkers do not talk behind one another's backs, excepting always the Grannys, who do it only as part of their ritual and are careful that it leans to harmless nonsense.

"Anybody sick there?" I asked finally.

"Might could be," said Zoë. "It's that time of the year. We have a few people here down with fevers . . . nothing serious, but fevers all the same."

"I was thinking more on the order of a plague," I said flatly.

More silence.

"All right," I said, "is there marrying trouble there? Or birthing trouble? Or naming trouble?"

"If there is," said Granny Golightly, "Granny Gableframe is there and she'll see to it."

"Responsible," said Amanda of Farson, "you're touring the Castles, as I understand it, because you intend to find out who hung the McDaniels baby in your cedar tree—"

"Flumdiddle!" said Granny Golightly again. Emphatically.

"Trite, Granny Golightly," I said between my teeth, and she wrinkled her nose at me.

"I say flumdiddle because no other word that's accurate sits well in my mouth," she had back at me. "If all you wanted to know was who did that foolish baby trick, you have Magicians of Rank as could find that out for you without you setting out on a Quest! Amanda, you can't see any farther than the end of your nose."

"Gently, Granny," said Zoë again, and her sisters each reached for a baby, too. They appeared to use the little ones like a kind of armor in this Castle; any sign of tension and everybody grabbed a baby. I wasn't sure what it signified, but it was distinctive.

"What were you going to say, Amanda?" I asked, keeping my voice as courteous as I could and hoping for a chance at this Granny another day.

"I meant to say that the Smiths are easily offended. That's well known."

"If they think you suspect *them* of doing that sorry piece of business— and with you coming uninvited they'll for sure think you *do* suspect them, since you've never done such a thing before—you'll put their backs up," said Nathan Terfelix. "They're stiff-necked and over proud. They won't bear being spied upon."

"Do *you* see my visit as being spied upon?" I asked, taken aback, and then regretted it; Golightly was on me quick as a tick.

"Most certainly!" she said, little wrinkled cheeks red as wild daisies. "*Most* certainly! And why not, seeing as that is what it is?"

"Oh, my," I sighed, "this won't do."

"Now, my dear, that's just Granny's way of talking," said Amanda. "You mustn't mind it."

Telling me, was she, about the Grannys and their way of talking? Even Sharon looked embarrassed, and the silent Una made a little noise in the back of her throat and stared down into her coffee cup.

"Your Granny," I said quietly, "is doing what she's good at. Stirring up trouble. Sowing dissent."

The old lady's brows went up, and I thought she was going to rub her hands together with glee at finally getting to me. But she waited, to see if I'd go on.

"I see no reason why youall can't know why I'm here," I told them. "Nor why the tour of the Castles. For sure, I could of found out without leaving my own bedroom—with the help of a Magician of Rank, of course—"

"What are you up to with a Magician of Rank in your bedroom?" Granny interrupted, scoring one point.

"—who kidnapped the McDaniels baby," I went right on. "That's not in question. The point is that somebody, or some one of the Families, is doing one piece of fool mischief after another to try to make people back out of the Jubilee. Especially people that've been against it all along and are just looking for an excuse to stay away. Finding out *who's* doing the mischief is not really the point—though it serves as Quest Goal, naturally, and I'll do it as I go along. The point is to show that Castle Brightwater is not to be put down by mischief, magical or otherwise."

"A symbol," said Amanda.

"A Quest for a Challenge," said Golightly, who knew her business. "Quite right."

"But nobody *here* is against the Jubilee!" said Zoë, looking both outraged and puzzled.

"Of course not," I agreed, "but do *think, Zoë* of Clark!"

She jogged the baby a bit, and then she nodded.

"You couldn't go only to the Castles you suspect," she said. "That would tip your hand."

"Green *roosters,* the girl's stupid!" shrilled Granny Golightly, and Zoë winced. I thought I might have to take this Granny in hand; and then I reminded myself sternly that the internal affairs of Castle Clark were none of my business, as long as they remained allies of Brightwater.

"And why am I stupid, Granny?" demanded Zoë, and good for *her!*

"She means," I said gently, "that the problem is not tipping my hand—the Families that I suspect know who they are already. Traveller, Purdy, Guthrie, and—I'm sorry, Amanda—Farson. The reason for all this folderol is that a Quest must be done in a certain fashion, or it is *not* a symbol. A Quest is *one* thing, done under rigid constraints, one step at a time—"

"And plenty of adventures as you go along!" said Granny. "That's *required!*"

"One step at a time," I went on, working uphill, "flying our finest Mule, wearing my finest gown . . . and so on. Done any other way, it's not a Quest at all, it's just the daughter of Brightwater gallivanting around the planet uninvited and unexplained. That would be something quite different, Zoë. Brightwater doing this as a Quest, and doing it to the letter of the rule—that says we mean business, and no mistake about it."

The early shadows were beginning to stripe the balcony, and the wind was coming up cold. The older children began shooing the younger ones inside, and the Clark daughters passed along the babies in their laps to the staff to be carried in. High time, too, to *my* mind.

"I see," Zoë said, rubbing her arms and drawing a shawl around her shoulders from the back of her chair. "Yes, that's clear."

Nathan Terfelix pulled at his beard—which I would have enjoyed pulling myself—and poured one half-cup of coffee all around to finish off the pot.

"What do *you* think, Responsible of Brightwater?" he asked; and there was no banter in his voice. "I take no insult on the part of my wife—the Farsons have never shown signs of love for the Confederation, and your logic can't be faulted. Nor is she responsible for her family's doings on the other side of Arkansaw, if doings there be. But what do you think of the chances for this Jubilee?"

"Fair to middling," I said. "Provided I do this right."

"I don't see it," said Sharon of Clark. "The Jubilee is a celebration, a giant party. It's a lot of trouble for Castle Brightwater, but if they're willing, why should anybody else care?"

I looked at Granny Golightly and waited for a remark about the girl's stupidity, but apparently she didn't think twelve was old enough yet to demand the attentions of her tongue. She glared at me, but she held her peace.

"The Travellers," I told the child, "the Purdys, the Guthries, the

Farsons . . . all of them want the Confederation set back to meeting one day a year like it once did, pure play-acting with no muscle to it. And each Castle absolutely to its own self the rest of the time. Every meeting, Sharon of Clark, the Travellers move to go back to that one day a year, the Farsons second that, it goes to a vote, and it goes down seven to five or eight to four, depending. *Every* meeting . . . that's the first thing happens after the Opening Prayer. The Jubilee, now, may look like a giant party, but it means a kind of *formalizing* of the Confederation that's never been done yet. Those Families would like to see it fail, like to see the other Families do as Castle Smith has done here—send letters around politely regretting that due to some 'crisis' they could not after all attend the Jubilee. You see that?"

Sharon of Clark drew her brows together and sighed. "Well, it makes no sense atall," she said crossly. "Don't they know anything? Don't they know that if it wasn't for the Confederation we'd have *anarchism?*"

"Anarchy, child," said her father. "The word's *anarchy.*"

"Well, *that,* then! Don't they even care?"

She was positively abristle with outrage, and I gave the Granny credit for that; Sharon of Clark had been properly taught. I doubt she knew anarchy from a fishkettle, but she'd learned it for a word to shudder at, and that was all that was likely to be required of her.

"Perhaps they don't care, Sharon," I said carefully. "And then perhaps they only don't understand. If we knew the truth of it, might could be we'd be able to change their minds on the subject."

Amanda of Farson said nothing, there being little she *could* say, and I paid her the courtesy of not questioning her on her own sympathies, while her child nodded solemnly. Amanda had been a Clark by marriage now over forty years; it was not likely that she still held to her Family's prejudices. Even if she did, certainly she would not be involved in sabotage coming from that quarter. A woman *actively* disloyal to her husband's house would go back to her own, as a matter of honor; she would not live as his wife and work against him.

"Speak openly, Responsible of Brightwater," said Granny Golightly then, "and look in my eyes when you speak. Do you suspect treason here?"

I looked her eye to beady eye, and I spoke flat out. "For sure and for certain, Granny Golightly, I do *not.* Nor, till I had this scrap of paper from

Castle Smith, did I suspect it on all of Oklahomah. It was my idea that I'd stop quickly at each of the three Castles here, where I knew the loyalty to the Confederation wasn't in question, and so doing gain maybe a little extra time to spend in other places."

"She speaks the truth," said the Granny, showing an amount of overconfidence that didn't specially surprise me. "And *I* will speak the truth, returning her the favor, and then we can all get inside out of this blasted wind and get *comfortable*."

She leaned forward and tapped her skinny fingers together as she steepled them, peering at me over the steeple. "There's no trouble at Castle Smith," she said, "but not your treason, either. No one at Smith's doing *magic* as shouldn't be doing it, or for evil ends."

"I wonder," I said.

"I'm *telling* you," she snapped, "and I know of what I speak. You can cease wondering. I am the Granny of this Castle, and the senior Granny of the five that share the housekeeping of Oklahomah among us, and I *tell* you, Uppity—*fourteen,* aren't you! what an age for wisdom!—I tell you there's no need to set your stubborn foot in Castle Smith. It's as Nathan Terfelix says; they're stiffnecked and you've insulted them, and they haven't the sense to see what you're doing, any more than Sharon there did, or the babies."

"Not going would save me time," I hazarded.

"Don't go, then," she said, and stood up with more creakings and poppings than an old attic floor in cold weather. "Who's there to suspect? Granny Gableframe, her that was a Brightwater by birth, and a McDaniels by marriage forty-seven years? Can you see her allowing such goings-on? And there's whatsisname . . . Delldon Mallard Smith the 2nd, and twice is enough if you ask me, no more gumption to him than a nursing baby for all he thinks himself a power in the land. And his three brothers, each of them as much a bully as he is, but scared of him, more fools them . . . and all their poor burdened wives, doing their best to clean up after their worthless menfolk. . ."

"Granny Golightly," I said quickly, "I think I follow you."

"*That* one," she said, shaking her finger under my nose and not a bit slowed down, "that Delldon Mallard, now, he is just *stupid* enough to set himself up proud and claim he should have been made an exception of, though he knows very well you skip a station on a Quest and you risk the whole thing. He was a stupid little boy, he was a stupid young man, and he's growing stupider with every passing year. I can just *see* him thinking himself fit to be an *exception* and sitting around his supper table bragging that he's shown Brightwater a thing or two! But he's a poor, pitiful, pathetic, puny fool. He couldn't sour milk any way but spitting in it."

Whew! She was outspoken. Too outspoken. There were still staff near us, and what their family allegiance might be was unknown to me. And children, who are not always good at guarding their tongues.

"Want *me* to hush," she said, her mouth twitching, "you pass the Smiths by. Or I'll say the rest, to convince you—and I know a passel more, young woman."

I was sure she did, and it was clear that she was prepared to lay it all before us, and the devil take the consequences.

"Granny Golightly," I said, "I'll make a bargain with you, if you'll hush now."

"State it!"

"You spread the word for me," I said, "with a suitable story . . . some *good* reason why I did not go to Castle Smith. You know the conditions on a Quest—mere refusal of admittance to a location is no excuse. I need a plague, or a dragon, or a bomb, or whatever you like, I leave it to you. But something that will be sufficient to make by-passing that Castle *not* a spoiling of my Quest! Something clearly and wholly beyond my control, you understand me?"

"I do," she said. "And I'll see to it."

"Your word on it? And nobody else harmed, mind!"

"My word, given already," she said impatiently, "and done as it should be. I'll spread the story and it will be ample, and no edges lopping over. My promise on it, Responsible of Brightwater!"

I stood up then, too, and it was like a congregation following the choir; they all followed the Granny and me and stood along with us, and the servingmaids moved in to clear away the tablestuff.

"Then I'll stay the night here, if you'll have me for supper, too," I said, "and then go on sometime tomorrow to Castle Airy. The matter of Castle Smith I'll leave to Granny Golightly, with my thanks."

"Make it good, Granny," said Una—the first time she'd spoken all that time except to chide or cosset a child.

"Never you mind," said the old woman. "I've been a Granny a very long time now, I know my doings."

Maybe.

Since she would cover my tracks for me, it made no difference if the guilty one *was* at Castle Smith; as had been plainly stated, I had not even needed to leave home to find out who that was. But the Smiths now . . . I'd seen Delldon Mallard Smith at meetings, and for sure had always found him a pompous bore, with an "uh . . . uh . . . uh . . ." for every other word out of his mouth. But I didn't know there was dry rot in his brain, which was how the Granny made it sound, and it was of course a credit to the Smith women that I didn't. If the men at the Castle were as foolish as Granny Golightly had said them to be, plain out and aloud in front of one and all, then there might be one or more of them fool enough to be mixed up in this somewhere, or to prove a weak link at an inconvenient moment.

It didn't matter, I decided. I felt quite confident about Granny Golightly's powers of invention. By the time I landed Sterling at Castle Airy some truly wondrous tale would have spread from one end of Ozark to the other to explain why I had not favored Castle Smith with a visit, and that was all that was of any present importance. The rest of it could wait till a later time.

I followed them into the Castle, looking forward to my room and a rest and a proper bathroom, and as a show of solidarity I scooped up a random baby from a low bench in the hall under a round window.

When in Clark . . .

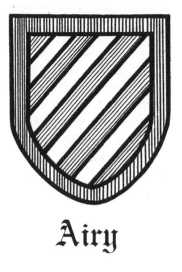

4

Airy

Castle Clark did very well by me; a small formal supper for twenty-four interesting couples, and the young man provided for me able to discuss several other subjects besides Mules and the weather, and then a truly impressive breakfast on the Castle balcony with what appeared to be half the county invited, and both a Taleteller and a Ballad Singer laid on. I left happy; dulcimerless, but mighty well fed, and my traveling costume fresh from the attentions of Granny Golightly herself—who I'd wager had not bothered to wash or press it but confined her "work" to a Housekeeping Spell—and I went over the next step in my head as Sterling and I headed out.

Castle Airy sat at the southernmost tip of Oklahomah; like Castle Clark it overlooked the sea, but there was a great difference between the tender hills of Kingdom Clark's seacoast and the hulking sheer cliffs that Castle Airy sat on. Their lands *had* no beaches; you pulled a boat up into the sucking caves that pitted the lower borders of the looming seacliffs at your own peril. Between the borders of Clark and the lands paced off by Daniel Cantrell Airy the 9th and his five sons in 2127 lay a broad expanse of Wilderness. Technically speaking it, it was at least a three-day flight from Castle to Castle, and considering the time involved it was going to be a piece of luck for me that I could by-pass the visit to Castle Smith after all.

I had no intention *what*soever of spending three full days—much less four—in the air. According to the maps there was an isolated stretch of thick forest roughly mid-Wilderness; once I got beyond the area where people were likely to be around, I intended to SNAP straight to that spot and spend two of my days in a pleasant contemplation of the Wilderness, some long naps that I was badly in need of, and catching up an account book I had dutifully brought with me having to do with trade in supplies for magic and a good two months out of date. I could then fly in on the third day and join the Airys for supper, with all as it ought to of been.

Nor need I stay at Castle Airy long; they were loyal there. They were as romantic . . . quaint, to put it frankly . . . in their loyalty to the Confederation as the Travellers were in their resistance to it. Held a Confederation Day every blessed year on December 12, with speeches and bands and bunting and whatnot, the only one of the Kingdoms to have such an innovation. Stamped the Confederation Seal all over everything, and flew its flag beside the flags of Airy and Ozark at the Castle gate. Any day now I expected them to begin opening souvenir stands or publishing a Confederation *Gazette*.

Why they were like that, it was hard to say; if we knew why any Family developed as it did rather than in some other fashion, *that* would be knowledge. I'd put that a sight higher than any of the scientific discoveries that had earned their originators a Bestowing of land in the past ten years. Or past one hundred, for that matter.

I jumped suddenly as a squawker flew by me, drawing a bray of disgust from Sterling and scaring the squawker into a plunge that I thought for a minute might prove fatal to the ugly thing. It was a male, its blue-and-white-speckled comb rigid with terror and its raucous call twice the volume a female could muster. And I supposed it had lost its eggs, along with its way, or forgotten the difference between up and down, assuming it ever had known it. It surely had no business being two hundred feet up in the air interfering with me and my Mule.

"Never mind the fool thing, Sterling," I said, and soothed her with a sturdy smack to the shoulder. "It's gone now, and if it doesn't kill itself it's headed back to the farm where it belongs."

The Mule snorted, reminding me of Granny Golightly, who I was well pleased to have behind me this fine morning, and I smacked her once more for good measure. What makes a Mule think a whack on the shoulder is a caress is a mystery, but it appears to be the way of it. Or perhaps they are sickened by lovepats, and look on the thumping as some kind of comradely, *Mule*-worthy activity. Mules are the only creatures on Ozark that are capable of telepathic communication with a Magician, but refuse to have anything to do with the process; their position appears to be that we should mind our own business and leave them to mind theirs, and they maintain that *most* effectively. You try mindspeech on a

Mule—say to let it know there's a storm ahead and you'd appreciate it taking cover in a hurry—you'll get yourself a headache that'll last you three days. There are, among the Teaching Stories, two or three that have to do with young Magicians looking on this situation as a challenge and trying to *force* a Mule to mindspeech; they're gory, as Teaching Stories go. Myself, I leave the mind of the Mule strictly alone.

I stopped thinking about Mules and thought about landing, which was going to be possible fairly soon. I hadn't seen any sign of habitation now for a considerable time, and on Oklahomah there was mighty little to block your view once you got ten feet above the trees. I took one more look at the map to be sure I had my coordinates straight, waited twenty more minutes for good measure, and SNAPPED, to Sterling's great relief. The less of this formal travel the better, so far as she was concerned, and she didn't need to use her psibilities to make that plain. Her braying didn't become exactly *musical*—that would be overstating the case a tad—but it took on a definite tone of musical *intention*.

The land below us as the air rippled and cleared was so tangled that I pulled back up to give it another good look; I had no desire to land in a bramble thicket or some such. There was nothing down there but forest, big old trees with their branches all twined and knotted in one among the other and their roots humping out of the ground, and I was hard put to it to see a break where we could set down. It would be dark down there, for sure, and not a likely place to run into anybody, give it that. Then I saw the glint of water to my right, a middle-sized creek by the look of it from where I was, and I turned that way. We could head down above the water and make a landing slow to the bank, unless it was thickets all the way to the edge.

I had to try twice before we found a break in the undergrowth—no wonder nor Clarks, nor Smiths, nor Airys had cared to claim any of this stretch. It'd have to have diamonds under it to make it worth fooling with. I finally located a little bend in the creek where it eased back into a kind of tumble of boulders, several of them big enough for a Mule to stand on with a foot or two of space to spare, and I brought Sterling down. Seeing as how I didn't want to slide into the water and ruin my clothes totally, I brought her to a full stop in the air first and then we stepped sedately onto the nearest flat place. She was good, but she couldn't land naturally with *no* room for a run-in.

And then I looked around me, and I was satisfied. There could of been forty people in those woods within ten feet and not one of us would of known the others existed, it was that tangled. Dark! My, but it was dark. We'd come down out of clear skies and a brisk wind and scudding little puffs of cloud, all bright and sparkling; down here it was pure gloom. *Very* satisfactory.

I had a microviewer with me, and six trashy novels on fiche that I couldn't of gotten away with taking time to read at home. I could feel my resolve to work on the account book fading away at the very look of this place; it was designed by its Creator for a good read if ever I saw a place that was, and the serious stuff could wait. I would settle in here in this back-of-nowhere and indulge myself while the chance lay there begging to be taken.

I pulled the smaller saddlebag off the Mule's back and set it down, careful *it* wouldn't slide, and set myself down beside it. The first step, even before I led Sterling down to drink (provided she waited for me to do that, which was not anything to lay bets on), was to change my clothes. I was just pulling off one of the last of my complicated garments when I got into trouble I hadn't anticipated.

Whatever it was that had slapped me into that cold water had been big, and because I'd had my head covered up in swathes of lace and velvet I hadn't seen or heard or smelled it coming. I hoped I'd given the dratted clothes a hard enough pitch to keep them dry, but not hard enough to throw them into a bramblebush . . . or I'd be spending my planned period of self-indulgence manifesting a new set just like them, out here in the middle of nowhere, by magic, with nothing but my emergency kit and whatever happened to grow handy for makings.

On the rough principle that what had knocked me into the water was not a water creature itself, since it had been on the bank at the time, I dove for the bottom of the creek. It was murk down there, naturally, no nice clear ocean all pretty with water like a gemstone, but it seemed to be clean water, and flowing, and there were no deepwater weeds in my way to get caught in. And about the time I was congratulating myself on that, I discovered that I'd made a major mistake.

I'd never seen one before, but I recognized the shape of it well enough when I got my eyes open, even through the dark of the water and the stuff I'd stirred up going in. Only one thing on this planet goes with six legs and is the size of the shadow that twisted just ahead of me (I hope), and I was in sizable trouble. The cavecat can climb anything, and it can swim, and it lives to kill; four of the legs are for running, and the other two for slashing and clawing, and the clawing involves eight three-inch razors to every paw. Not to mention its *teeth,* of which it has more than it needs by a goodly number.

There are not supposed to *be* giant cavecats on Oklahomah. Kintucky, maybe, just maybe, though I'd never heard of one showing up there the past thirty years. But the way of things was supposed to be that cavecats had been wiped out everywhere except in the Tinaseeh Wilderness— where I was convinced the Travellers not only didn't try to get rid of them but *encouraged* them, just to keep everybody off. Nevertheless, this was *not* Tinaseeh, nor yet Kintucky, this was placid, long-settled Oklahomah, with its Wilderness not much more than a pocket hanky as Wildernesses go, and that *was* a giant cavecat in the water ahead of me. Right smack dab ahead of me. And I could see how, in this backwood tangle, the Family hunts might of missed a specimen or two.

I didn't know how well they swam, but I knew if it got to me it would drown me, even if it had to surface and just hold me under with its middle legs while it had all the air it wanted or needed. And I needed air badly, myself. The bottom was right there, and praise the Twelve Corners, it was rocky—I gave myself a hard shove off the cobbly rocks and shot toward the light, with the cat right behind me, and I scrambled out onto the bank and hollered for Sterling.

Mules. If she'd been there, where I'd left her not two minutes before, I might have been able to SNAP out of that particular hard place before the cat made it out of the water. She wasn't there, though, nor anywhere in sight. Gone looking for something edible, probably.

"Sterling, you damn Mule, you, damn your ears and your tail and your bony rump besides!" I shouted, and then I made the very close acquaintance of hundreds of pounds of soaking wet cavecat.

It pulled me in with one front paw and held me to its chest, which stank the way you'd expect wet cat to stink and then some, and started off across the rocks on the bank. Almost dainty, the way it picked its footing, and in no hurry atall. Like any cat, it intended to play with me awhile before it made its kill, and no doubt I was an unusual play-pretty for the nasty thing. If there'd been any people around here in a long, long time

we would have *known* there were still cavecats on Oklahomah . . . and I
made a note, as it carried me, that when I got back—*if* I got back—word
had to be sent to the three Castles to clear them out.

It's amazing how much time a person has to think in a situation like
that. Time stretches itself out in front of you, and everything goes to the
slowest of all motions, and we went positively stately over those boulders and under arches of trees and through an assortment of bramble
thickets. I was bleeding badly, and I was pretty cross, but I didn't intend
to let either interfere with me staying alive. I relaxed, and let just enough
blood fall to keep the cavecat's nostrils contented, and sort of cuddled
back into its smelly wet embrace. And waited.

The problem was the selection of a suitable countermeasure.
Common Sense magic would only get me killed—would of had me dead
before this, considering the blood I ought to of been losing. The cavecat obviously did not know how frail the hides of humans were, nor that
they could die from the loss of their body fluids before it had a chance
to have its fun. Common Sense magic was not enough, nor Granny
Magic. The question was, would Hifalutin Magic do it, or did I have to
move clear on up to Formalisms & Transformations? (*And* make up your
mind quick, Responsible, things may *seem* slow, but this animal is covering the ground at a smart pace and its cave cannot be much farther away!)
I needed to be ready the instant it set me down and stretched out to bat
me around between its front paws and watch my interesting attempts to
get out of its reach—that *instant.*

I decided I was not expendable, and whatever firepower I had I'd best
use it at its most potent. There was nobody around to see and wonder at
a woman using that level of magic, and if there had been I would not have
been in any mood to care. Formalisms & Transformations it would be,
and all out—now which one? I was a mite short on equipment.

The cave smelled worse than the cavecat, which I wouldn't of
thought possible in advance. Not that it was fouled—no cat does that,
whatever its size—but it had lived there a long time, and it was a tom,
and it had marked out all the limits of its territory with great care. It
slouched in under a hole in the ground that I doubted I would of spotted as the entrance to anything, and it was suddenly darker than the inside
of your head. Not a ray, not a *mote,* of light was there in that cave . . . I
had the feeling it was small; no echoes, no water dripping. Just a hole in

the ground, perhaps, and not a *real* cave such as we had flushed these creatures out of long ago on Marktwain. Real enough to die in, however, had I intended to die. Which I didn't.

It stretched out, long and lazy and reeking, and laid me down between its paws. And it stretched *them* out, hairy bladed bars on either side of me like a small cage of swords, and it gave me a gentle preliminary swipe with the right one, and batted me back the other way with the left one, to see me roll and hear me whimper.

The Thirty-third Formalism was suitable, and I used it fast, doing it rather well if I do say so myself. Lacking gailherb, I used a strip of flesh from the inside of my upper arm to guarantee Coreference; lacking any elixir, I used my own blood to mark out the Structural Description and the desired Structural Change. Make do, my Granny Hazelbide always said; and I made do. It smarted. On the other hand, I would of been embarrassed, dying in a place like this at the whim of a creature with five hundred pounds of brawn and maybe four, five ounces of brain. It would not have been fitting.

When the cavecat lay purring quietly, content with the fat white pig it now thought was what it had caught originally (assuming it thought at all), and which I had Substituted for my own skinny white form, I gathered my battered self together and crawled on my stomach back out into what passed in these parts for daylight. I found myself regretting very much that there was no way to do a single Formalism—let alone a Transformation —while being clutched to a cavecat's bosom. Like a Mule landing, I had needed a *little* space, and I'd gotten mighty beat up before it became available. I was going to have a good night's work ahead of me cleaning up all this mess, and maybe longer. I looked like something blown through a door with rusty nails in it, and most assuredly my appearance was not anything that would impress the Airys if they could see me now. Or before tomorrow morning, I rather expected.

"Botheration," I said, and hollered for Sterling one more time. She turned up at once, naturally, now that I didn't need her to save my life, and looked at me with the most Mulish distaste.

"Don't like my smell, do you?" I muttered. I didn't blame her; I didn't like it either. "Let's get back to the water," I said, "and I'll do something about it."

I didn't know the coordinates, or even the general direction, and I

was too tired and too weak to SNAP even if I had known them. So I just
followed her tail. I could count on her to take me back to where we'd
landed, since she wouldn't be enjoying all these brambles and brush any
more than I was. I wanted water, and the medicines in my emergency
kit, and the denims I'd been about to put on when this adventure—

I stopped short, right there. I stopped, battered as I was, and the
elaborateness with which I blistered the air all around me impressed even
Sterling; her ears went flat back against her head.

"And plenty of adventures as you go along! That's *required!*" she'd
said, had dear old Granny Golightly, and I'd ignored her and gone right
on talking without so much as an acknowledgment that I'd heard her
mention the matter. Nor had I thought of it since. If I hadn't been so
young I'd of thought I was getting old.

This *changed* things.

Sterling brayed at me, and I hushed her.

"Wait a minute now," I said. "Let me think."

There were but two possible readings. One, this had been an accident, no more, and my simplest course was to heal my wounds and settle
and furbish myself to appear at Castle Airy as if I'd had no hair disturbed
on my head since I flew out from Castle Clark. *Two*—this was Granny
Golightly's doing—and she had an amazing confidence in my abilities if
it was, or an outright dislike for me—and I should somehow or other
contrive to have myself rescued by somebody else . . . or whatever. Clear
things up just enough to stand it, maybe, throw myself over the Mule's
back at the proper time, and straggle into Castle Airy a victim just short
of death.

Foof. I didn't know what to do. From Granny Golightly's perspective I'd been getting off easy; two Castles stopped at already, and not one
adventure to show for my trouble yet—hardly the way that things were
supposed to be laid out. Under the terms of the Constraints set on a
Quest, its success was directly proportional to the number and the sever-
ity of the adventures encountered along the way, and Golightly might
well have felt she had a duty to support me more than I might of cared
to be supported. And if Granny's story explaining my by-passing Castle
Smith was a cavecat mauling, and I showed up unmarked and spoiled
it—there'd be trouble. But how was I to know?

*Un*til Sterling and I made it out onto the bank of the creek again, me fretting all the way and her whuffling, and there, in the absolute middle of nowhere, naked and alone out on a bare gray boulder, sat a pale blue squawker egg. No nest, no squawker, no coop. No farmer. Just the egg. Granny Golightly was mean, but she wasn't careless; the question was neatly settled, and a few more points to her. I wondered just how far that one's range extended?

Well, it was dramatic, I'll say that for it. There I was at the gates of Airy before the eyes of their greeting party, clinging to Sterling's mane with one poor little gloved hand, my gorgeous velvets sodden with blood and my hair hanging loose below my waist in a tangle of brambles and weeds and dirt. I chose a spot that looked reasonably soft, pulled up the Mule weakly, moaned about a twenty-two-caliber moan, and slid off gracefully onto the ground at their feet in a bedraggled heap. If I'd been watching, I'm sure my heart would of ached for me.

They carried me into the Castle at full speed, shouting for the Grannys (the Twelve Corners help this poor Family, they had *three* of the five Grannys of Oklahomah under their roof!), and I allowed a faint "a cavecat . . . a huge one . . . back there . . ." to escape my lips before I surrendered consciousness completely. (Under no circumstances did I intend to undergo the ministrations of three Grannys in any other condition *but* unconsciousness.)

I woke in a high bed in a high room, surrounded by burgundy curtains and hangings and draperies and quilts. The Travellers were addicted to black; with the Airys it was burgundy. And crimson for relief of the eye. There was a plaster on my chest, and another on my right thigh; a bowl of bitter herbs smoked on the wooden chest at the foot of my bed, and the taste in my mouth told me I'd been potioned as well.

I ran my tongue around my teeth, and sighed. Bitter-root and wild adderweed and sawgrass. And wine, of course. Dark red burgundy wine. And something I couldn't identify and didn't know that I wanted to. Either none of the Grannys here held with modern notions, or the dominant one didn't. Phew.

"She's awake, Mother," a voice said softly, and I let my eyelids flutter wide and said the obligatory opening lines.

"Where am I? What—what happened to me?"

"You're in Castle Airy, child," said a voice—not the same one—"and you're lucky you're alive. We would of taken our oaths there were no cavecats left on this continent, but you managed to find one, coming through the Wilderness. Whatever possessed you to *land* in the Wilderness, Responsible of Brightwater? Oklahomah's got open land in every direction if you needed to stop for a while . . . why the Wilderness?"

I had expected that one, and I was ready for it. "My Mule got taken sick all of a sudden," I said. "I hadn't any choice."

Time then for some more obligatories.

I struggled to a sitting position, against the hands of the three Grannys who rushed forward in their burgundy shawls to hold me back, and demanded news on the condition of my beloved steed.

"The creature is just fine, child," said the strongest one, pushing me back into the pillows with no quarter given. "Not a mark on her, the cat was only interested in you. And I'll thank you not to flop around like a fish on a hook and undo all the work we've done repairing the *effects* of its interest!"

I sighed, but I knew my manners. I said a lengthy piece about my gratitude and my appreciation, and swallowed another potion which differed from the earlier one only in being even nastier, and at last I found myself alone with only the three Grannys and the lady of the Castle and my obligations settled for the time being.

The lady was a widow, her husband killed in a boating accident years ago, which was the only reason the Castle had three Grannys. It was in fact a Castle almost entirely of women; every stray aunt or girlcousin on Oklahomah with poor prospects and not enough gumption to go out as a servant came here to shelter under the broad wings of Grannys Forthright, Flyswift, and Heatherknit. And over them all, the beautiful woman who sat at my side now, smiling down at me, Charity of Guthrie. A three she was, and she lived up to the number; in everything that Charity of Guthrie did, she succeeded, with a kind of careless ease, as if there was nothing to it at all. Her hair fell in two dark brown braids, shot with white, over her shoulders, and her sixty-odd years sat lightly on her as the braids. The Guthrie women wore remarkably well.

"Sweet Responsible," she said to me, "we are so happy you're here . . . and so sorry that your visit has to be like this! We had a dance planned in your honor tonight, and a hunt breakfast tomorrow morning, and a thing or two more besides; but obviously you must stay right here in this bed, and no commotions. I've already sent the word out that you'll be seeing nobody but us, and that only from where you lie. Poor child!"

The poor child was all worn out, and could see that even with an excessive pride in the skill of her Grannys this woman was not likely to believe her recovered from the attack of that cavecat overnight. Loss of blood. Loss of skin. Shock. Blow on the head. Being dragged along. Whatnot.

Since there was no help for it, I gave up and closed my eyes. I was going to see to it, one of these days, that Granny Golightly paid dearly for this delay, not to mention all the arithmetic she'd put me through working this out so that all parts of it came out right *aerodynamically*. Aerodynamicadamnably. Not to mention in addition the potions, which were beyond anything in my personal experience to date.

I slid down into sleep like a snake down a well, surrendering. Tomorrow would be soon enough to try to convince them that someone as young and strong as I was could not be kept down by a cavecat, or even by three Grannys . . .

5

Guthrie

The women at Castle Airy were anything but docile, and I was no match for them. Under ordinary circumstances I might of had at least a fighting chance, but I was not operating under ordinary circumstances; I was being the badly mauled victim of a cavecat attack, and I lost almost two precious days to that role. I would dearly of loved to make up the lost time on the crossing from Oklahomah to Arkansaw, but it would not do. The sea below me was not an open expanse with a rare bird and a rare rocktip to break it; it was the narrow shipping channel between the two continents, and about as deserted as your average small-town street. All up the Oklahomah coast and all the way across the channel I flew, at the regulation sixty-mile-an-hour airspeed for a Mule of Sterling's quality. It was proper, it was sedate, and it was maddening; it was a number well chosen, being five times a multiple of twelve, and the members of the Twelve Families found it reassuring and appropriate, but it was *not* convenient.

Below me there were at all times not only the ponderous supply freighters, but a crowd of fishing boats, tourboats, private recreation vehicles, and government vessels from a dozen different agencies. Near Arkansaw's southernmost coast I even saw a small golden ship with three sails of silver, a craft permitted only to a Magician of Rank.

It didn't surprise me, it warmed my heart, for all it made me have to dawdle through the air. We Ozarkers, from the beginning of our history, even before we left Earth, had always had a kind of lust for getting places by water. If an Ozark child could not afford a boat, that child would set anything afloat that it was strong enough to launch—an old log was a particular favorite, and half a dozen planks nailed together into an unreliable raft marked the traditional first step up from log-piloting.

What *was* in some way surprising was that we had bothered with the Mules; it hadn't been a simple process. When the Twelve Families landed they found the Mules living wild on Marktwain in abundance, but much complicated breeding and fine-tuning had been required before they were brought to a size where a grown man would be willing to straddle one on solid ground, much less *fly* one. And the twelve-passenger tinlizzies we built in the central factory on the edge of Marktwain's desert were more than adequate for getting people over land distances as needed, as well as solving the problem of what to do with the most plentiful natural substance produced by our goats and pigs.

But the memories of Earth, Old Earth, were still strong, and we were a loyal, home-loving people. We hadn't been such fools as to take with us on The Ship the mules of Earth, seeing as how using that limited space for a sterile animal would of been stupid; but every Ozarker had always fancied the elegance of a team of well-trained mules . . . and the Mules *were* a good deal like them. Especially in the ears, which mattered, and in the brains, which mattered even more.

We had brought with us cattle and goats and pigs and chickens and a few high-class hounds, but of all that carefully chosen lot only the pigs and goats had survived. Most of the other animals had died during the trip, and the few that made it to landing or were born on Ozark soon sickened, for no reason that anyone could understand, since we humans breathed the air of Ozark and ate its food and drank its water with no ill effects. And then to find the Mules! For all that they stood only four feet tall and had tails that dragged the ground, they looked like something of home, and we had set to breeding them for size, and we braided and looped their tails. And "discovered" that they could fly sixty miles an hour. In the one most essential way of all they differed from their Earth counterparts—they were not sterile.

The people on the boats below me waved, and I waved back, as I wound my way carefully above them, doing my best not to fly directly over any vessel. Sterling was well trained, but there were limits to her tolerance for the niceties, and I wanted no unsavory accidents to spoil the image I was trying so hard to establish.

It was well into afternoon when I began to head down toward the docks that crowded Arkansaw's southeastern coastline, and there was a chill in the air that made me appreciate my layers of clothing. The docks

were crowded, almost jammed with people, some carrying on their ordinary daily business, and some no doubt there to gawk at me, and I decided
that a landing would only mean another delay that I could not afford. I
chose the largest group of people I could see that appeared to have no
obvious reason for being on the docks, and dipped low over them, gripping Sterling hard to impress her with the importance of good behavior.
My intention was to fly low enough—but not too low—exchange cheerful greetings in passing as I flew by, and then get on with it. It was a simple
enough maneuver, something that could be brought off by a middling
quality Rent-a-Mule with a seven-year-old child on its back. I didn't
want the people down there to think me uppity and standoffish, nor did
I want to waste time, so I chose my moment and sailed gracefully down
the air toward the waiting Arkansawyers—

    And crashed.
    Three Castles I'd visited now, without the slightest hint of that dis-
turbance of flight that had made me suspicious in the first place. And
now—not over a Wilderness where nothing could suffer but my stomach, not over a stretch of open ocean with the occasional freighter, but
twenty feet up from a dockful of sight-seeing women and children—my
Mule suddenly wobbled in the air like a squawker chick and smashed
into the side of a storage shed on the edge of the dock. The last thought
I had as *I* flew, quite independently, off her back, was that at least we
hadn't hurt anybody, though from the screams you'd of thought them all
seriously damaged. And then my head and a roof beam made sudden contact, and I stopped thinking about anything atall.

    When I woke up, I knew where I was. No mistake about it. The
Guthrie crest was carved into the foot of the bed I lay on, it hung on the
wall of the room beyond the bed, little ones dangled from the curving
brackets that held the lamps, and it was set in every one of the tiles that
bordered the three big windows. Furthermore, the woman sitting bolt
upright in a hard wooden chair at my right hand, where turning my head
to look at her would put me nose-to-shoulder with an embroidered
Guthrie crest, not to mention more clouds of Guthrie hair, was no
Granny. It was my maternal grandmother, Myrrh of Guthrie, and I was
assuredly under her roof and in her Castle.

They had taken off my boots and spurs, but my clothing showed no sign whatsoever of a trip through the air into the side of a dock shed, nor did my body. I wasn't likely to forget the thwack I'd hit that shed with, but I hadn't so much as a headache, nor a scratch on my lily white hand. Being as this was somewhat unlikely, I looked around for the Magician of Rank that had to be at the bottom of it.

"Greetings, Responsible of Brightwater," he said, and I was filled with a sudden new respect for those who found my mother's physical configurations distracting. He had chocolate curls, and the flawless Guthrie skin and green eyes, and the curve of his lips made me think improper thoughts I hadn't known lurked in me. He was tall, and broad of shoulder, slim of waist and hip . . . and then there was the usual garb of his profession to be put in some kind of perspective. A Magician of Rank wears a pair of tight-fitting trousers over bare feet and sandals, and a square-cut tunic with full sleeves caught tight at the wrists, and a high-collared cape that flows in a sweep from his throat to one inch of the floor, thrown back in elegant folds over one shoulder to leave an arm free for ritual gestures. There'd never been a man that getup wasn't becoming to, and the fact that it was all in the Guthrie tricolor—deep blue, gold, and forest green—was certainly no disadvantage.

I shut my eyes hastily, as a measure of simple prudence; and he immediately checked my pulse, combining this medicinal gesture with a thoroughly nonmedical tracking of one strong finger along the most sensitive nerves of my wrist and inner arm. It was my intention not to shiver, but I lacked the necessary experience; and I was glad I could not see the satisfied curl of those lips as he got precisely the response that he was after.

"Responsible of Brightwater, open your eyes," he said, in a voice of all silk and deep water, "and swoon me no fabricated swoons. You had a nasty knock on your head, you broke a collarbone and three ribs, and you were bruised, scratched, abraded, and generally grubby from head to foot—but you, *and* I might add, your fancy Mule, are in certified perfect condition at this moment. Every smallest part of you, I give you my word. That was the point of calling me, my girl, instead of a Granny."

"Confident, aren't you?" I said as coldly as possible, repossessing myself of my arm, and Myrrh of Guthrie remarked as how I reminded her very much of my sister, Troublesome.

"Neither one of you ever had any manners *what*soever," she said, "and my daughter deserves every bit of trouble the two of you have given her . . . bringing you up half wild and about one-third baked."

I took the bait, it being a good deal safer to look at her than at him, and I opened my eyes as ordered.

"Hello, Grandmother," I said. "How nice to see you."

"*On the con*trary!" she said. "Nothing nice about it. It's a disaster, and I'm pretty sure you know that. The young man on your left, the one you're avoiding because you can't resist him—and don't concern yourself about it, *nobody* can, and very useful he is, too—is your own kin, Michael Stepforth Guthrie the 11th. You be decent enough to greet him, instead of wasting it on me, and I'll guarantee you safe conduct past his wicked eyes and sorrier ways."

There was only one way to handle this kind of scene; some others might of been more enjoyable, but they wouldn't have been suitable. I sat up in the Guthrie bed, propped on my pillows, put a hand on each of my hips right through the bedclothes, gritted my teeth against the inevitable effect, and I looked Michael Stepforth Guthrie up and down . . . slowly . . . and then down and up, and then I looked him over once more in both directions.

"Twelve roses," I said, "twelve sugarpies, and twelve turtles! You are for *sure* the comeliest man ever my eyes have had the pleasure to behold, Mr. Guthrie. Your buttocks, just for starters, are superb . . . and the line of your thigh! Law, cousin, you make my mouth water, on my word . . . turn around once, would you, and let me see the swing of your cape!"

Not a sound behind me from Myrrh of Guthrie; and I didn't glance at her, though I would of loved to see her face. Michael Stepforth's eyes lost their mocking laughter and became the iced green I was more accustomed to see in Guthrie eyes. I faced the ice, smiling, and there was a sudden soft snapping sound in the nervous silence. One rib, low on my right side.

"Petty," I said, and found the pain a useful distraction, since not breathing was out of the question. "Cousin, that was *petty.*"

The next two ribs sounded just like an elderly uncle I'd once visited that had a habit of cracking his knuckles, and breathing became even more unhandy.

"See where bad manners will get you?" observed Myrrh of Guthrie.

"And as for *buttocks*—at fourteen a woman does not mention them, though I must agree with your estimate of Michael's. Who will now leave us alone, thank you kindly."

I didn't watch him sweep out of the room. His mischief had immunized me temporarily against his charm; you don't feel the pangs of desire through the pangs of broken ribs.

"Uncomfortable, are you?" said my grandmother, but she had the decency to move to the end of the bed where I wouldn't have to move around much to look at her while we talked.

"I wouldn't have him on my staff," I said crossly, hugging my ribs.

"He's an *excellent* Magician of Rank," she said. "Such quality doesn't grow on every bush, and I've need of him."

"And if he takes to breaking *your* ribs, Grandmother?"

She chuckled. "The man has principles," she said. "Infants and old ladies . . . and anyone he considers *genuinely* stupid, I believe . . . are safe from his tantrums. And do *not* ask me which of the three categories I have my immunity under, or I'll call him back."

I sniffed, and gasped at the result; the breaks would be neat, and simple, but they were a three-pronged fire in my side. And what can't be cured for the moment must be endured for the moment.

"Grandmother," I said, "while we're on the subject of manners, would you care to explain why my visit has to be called a 'disaster'? That strikes me as mighty sorry hospitality. Castle Guthrie wealthy as sin from the shipping revenues, *and* the peachapple orchards, *and* your share of the mines in the Wilderness. You telling me you can't afford to put up one girlchild for twenty-four hours?"

"It's the twenty-four hours that we can't afford," she said, and she sounded like she meant it. "This is not one of your la-di-da city Castles, we're *busy* here. Right now we're so busy—I want you gone within the hour, young lady. With your ribs set right, of course."

"Not possible," I said firmly.

"Responsible," she said, "you exasperate me!"

"Myrrh of Guthrie," I said back, "you bewilder *me*. Here I lie, your own daughter's daughter, three ribs broken by your own Magician of Rank, not to mention whoever or whatever was responsible for that encounter my Mule and I had with the architecture that graces your docks—"

"That was not the work of Michael Stepforth Guthrie!"

"And how do you know *that?*"

Her lips narrowed, and she turned a single golden ring round and round on her left hand. Her wedding ring, plain except for the ever-present crest.

"I am not entirely ignorant," she said, which I knew to be true, "and though he's skilled he's like any other young man, a regular pane of glass. I know what he was doing at the time of your undignified arrival."

"If he's as skilled as you say, he's equally skilled at pretending to a transparency that's convenient for his purposes. Who trained him?"

"His father. And a Magician whose name you'll know . . . Crimson of Airy."

Crimson of Airy . . . now there was a name. It was a concoction absolutely typical of Castle Airy, and in dreadful taste, but she had lived up to it. She was a *one,* and she had everything that went with being a one, and of the five women to become Magicians on Ozark in the thousand years since First Landing, only Crimson of Airy had made any mark. If it hadn't been forbidden, she'd have been a Magician of Rank herself, no question; and I knew her reputation. That of the father of Michael Stepforth Guthrie I didn't know, but my never hearing of him—plus the fact that he'd allowed a woman to meddle in his son's education for the profession—told me all I needed to know.

Myrrh of Guthrie leaned toward me and I burrowed into my pillows hastily, for it looked to me as if she was going to grab my shoulders and shake me, broken ribs and all. But she caught herself.

"I know what you're thinking," she said. "You're thinking that it's our Michael Stepforth that's been souring your milk and kidnapping babies and making your Mules giddy, purely because he'd be able. I'll grant you he's that good, I won't deny it—but he's been far too busy here to be involved."

"Too busy for such piddly stuff as souring milk? And sending some trash into a church after one little baby, with the Spell already set?" It's not that easy to scoff with three broken ribs, but I scoffed. "Dear Grandmother," I said, "with every word you speak you undo three others. Either the man's a bumbler and an egotistical fraud—which I'll not accept, not if Crimson of Airy taught him his tricks, and very lucky we are that *she's* dead at last!—or he is more than clever enough to tend to whatever brews here at Castle Guthrie and carry on all that other mischief with one of his long clever fingers, just on the side! And the *latter*, Myrrh of Guthrie, the *latter* is the truth of it!"

"You say that only because you don't *know* what's brewing here!" she hissed at me. "It's been weeks, if not months, since he's had more than snatches of sleep . . . the Farsons are at our backs and at our throats, the Purdys are determined to ruin us all and have ignorance and black luck enough to do it, and you come here, *now,* at a time like this!"

"Grandmother!" I lay back, easy, and realized that I was a rattled young woman and that the pain was fast getting to me. "Grandmother, *what* are you talking about? I agree that the Purdys make bad neighbors; very well. Granted. They seem forever determined to win whatever foolishness awards are going round. But the only ruin the Purdys will bring is ruin to themselves, and the Farsons have their own Kingdom to run."

"You're ignorant," she said flatly. "Plain ignorant!"

It was possible, I was beginning to realize, that I was. I had more than a strong suspicion that I had been *deliberately* ignorant . . . and I would of given a large sum for the intelligence reports that lay in my desk back at Brightwater. I had read them, I would never have *not* read them, but had I perhaps been reading them with a selecting eye for what I preferred to find there, and ignoring patterns that would have required some effort?

My grandmother stood up suddenly, hurting me as she jarred the bed and well aware that she hurt me.

"I want you up," she said, "since you won't leave. Up and able-bodied. If you insist on meddling in our affairs because Brightwater can't manage its own, then I intend you to hear just what it is you're meddling *in!* You lie there, and I'll send Michael Stepforth—oh, hush your mouth, he'll do what needs doing on orders from me, and no nonsense out of him!—and an Attendant will be here in one hour to bring you down to the Hall. Where we'll tell you what you've gone and blundered into!"

"I know my way, Grandmother," I reminded her mildly. "I've been here before."

"An Attendant will come for you," she said again. "I'll hear no more of our lack of hospitality out of you, or from anyone else. And a Reception and Dance in your honor this evening, missy, as befits a Castle rolling in its wealth!"

My grandmother was furious, that was quite clear without her slamming the door behind her and making all the crests hanging about rattle on their hooks. I hadn't expected warmth here, but this exceeded my expectations; I was amazed. And where was her husband, her own sixth cousin with the utterly prosaic name and the utterly prosaic manner? The most boring of all the Guthries? Ordinarily he would at least have been mentioned, if not present for our little altercation . . . where was James John Guthrie the 17th in the midst of my welcome?

"A man's name is chosen for euphony," I said aloud, "and James John Guthrie is not euphonious. It sounds like three rocks landing on a pavement, and the third one bouncing."

Whereupon something replied, after a fashion. Considering what I had said, "Shame, shame, shame, you wicked chiiiiiiild!" did not really follow.

I topped it.

"Three times six is eighteen," I told the thing, and then there were eighteen of them, and I was glad I hadn't decided to say nine times nine.

"Really!"

"Shame, shame, shame, you wicked chiiiiiiiiiiiild!" they all said in chorus. Eighteen giant seagulls, four feet tall and a wingspread to match, standing round my bed flopping those wings and ordering me in perfect harmony to be ashamed of my wickedness.

If they'd been real I'd have turned all eighteen into fleas and deposited them neatly in the high collar of Michael Stepforth's cape, perhaps, but I was far too miserable to waste my time working Transformations on fakes. I closed my eyes instead and let the pseudobirds do their chant while I tried hard not to breathe, and after ten, eleven repetitions their creator finally appeared in my doorway—not bothering to knock—and came striding in, walking through one of his birds to reach my side.

"Look up, please," he said crisply.

"Why? To view your little flock? No, thank you. I don't care for squawkers."

"Seagulls."

"They look like squawkers to me," I said. "Might could be your Spells are faulty."

(I *wished!* I tried to imagine a faulty Spell worked up by Crimson of Airy, and found the thought ridiculous.)

"You look up here or I'll put all the gulls in bed with you," he said placidly. "And you wouldn't like that; they're awfully dirty."

It was a pain as bad as the pain in my ribs to have to put up with his sass; on the other hand, I wasn't about to give in to the temptation to do magic beyond my permitted level under this one's nose. Much as some old-fashioned staple along the lines of turning him into a reptile would have done me good, much as I longed for the tiny satisfaction of maybe just snapping one of his perfect fingerbones, I was not that foolish. Even if I could have managed something like that with all my supplies packed away in a wardrobe and three of my ribs broken, there was no sense to giving him any further smallest advantage. I lay still, and I looked up.

Hmmmmm. Structural Description . . . Structural Change . . . Coreferential Indexes. All properly formal and not a fingertip out of place. The double-barred arrow appeared in the air, glowing gold, quivering slightly, and the pain faded away as the arrow did. Perhaps ninety seconds total time. I was impressed. It always takes longer to undo things than to do them, and more formal operations are required. He was as good as my grandmother said he was. I grinned at him.

"Ask me no fool questions," he said grimly, "and don't offer me any more of your uncalled-for and unappreciated assessments of my person. Just thank me, please, and show you have *some* breeding."

"Thank you kindly, Magician of Rank Michael Stepforth Guthrie the 11th," I said promptly. "You are certainly handy at your work, and I intend to mention it everywhere I go." And I batted my lashes at him, and crossed my hands over my breasts.

"Your Attendant will be along soon," he said, looking clear over my head and out the window, "and you are now in perfect condition. And leave off your spurs, you'll mark up the stairs. We're waiting for you—patiently—down in the small Hall."

"And your bill? For services rendered, Michael Stepforth?"

"Courtesy of the house," he said. "No charge." He raised both his hands in the mock-magic gesture of the stage magician, fanning his fingers open and shut and open again. And then he turned on his heel and swept out of the room, the cape swirling about him. And the gulls made a soft little noise and disappeared.

I thanked the Attendant and walked into the Hall, where I had spent a number of reasonably pleasant Hallow Evens and Midsummer Days over the years. There had been children then, and costumes and candy, and cakes and beer and an atmosphere of frolic. There was none of that today.

They sat in high-backed chairs about a table at the far end of the room, filling a windowed corner through which I could see the sun going down. Myrrh of Guthrie. The previously absent James John, looking rumpled. Michael Stepforth Guthrie. Two unmarried sons in their late teens, whose names I did not remember. And one Granny, whose name I *did* know. Whatever else I might neglect, I did not neglect the Grannys; I had a file on every one of them, and I knew it by heart, and they didn't gather an Ozark weed that I didn't know it. This one was a harmless old soul, name of Granny Stillmeadow, that specialized in liniments and party Charms, and I chose the chair next to hers and let her pat my knee.

Supper appeared the minute I took my place, and by the time I'd been introduced to the two boys it had been served and we were well into it. And if Myrrh of Guthrie was serious about the Reception and Dance scheduled for that same evening there was surely no time to fool about. I didn't recognize the beast that I was eating, but I recognized it for a beast, and I knew both the vegetables. And I was sure they wouldn't poison me in front of the servants, so I fell to. And I listened.

Castle Farson, it appeared, had been sending bands of traders across the Wilderness to the Guthrie docks, and offering higher bids for supplies than those authorized to the Guthrie personnel. The Guthries were willing to allow that that might have been due to an unfortunate incident in which a charge set by a Guthrie mining crew had caved in a gem mine on the very edge of Kingdom Farson. However, it seemed that although the mine was in Wilderness Lands and therefore technically common property, the Farsons felt that the Guthries were demanding more than their share of the profits from the mine, which meant their miners might just conceivably have been harassing the Guthrie miners who *set* the charge. (What the Purdys had been doing through all this, and whether they'd been getting any of *their* legitimate share of the profits, was not mentioned.) But it did come up that a Purdy had managed to get himself killed—according to both the Guthries and the Farsons, it was deliberate, which I found it hard to believe, even for the Purdys—in a spectacularly disgusting way. (Granny Stillmeadow was of the opinion that only a Magician of Rank could of arranged it, considering the curious shape the body had assumed before it was found.) And this getting killed had happened in the Farson Castle Hall, while the Guthries were there protesting the latest iniquity perpetrated by the Farsons, and a Farson Granny had cried "Privilege!" and they'd had to call a three-Kingdom hearing, which by law had to be held on common ground in the Wilderness, and was still going on, and that was costing an arm and a leg and another arm. And a Purdy spy had hacked her ridiculous way through the Wilderness to tell the Guthries that the Farsons were stealing them all blind by working another gem mine on the Purdy's southern border, tunneling from its Wilderness entrance clear under the Guthrie lands—which was something the Guthries already knew—*but,* since the poor thing had ruined herself for life scrabbling around on foot through the underbrush and whatnot and getting lost over and over to bring information that she had *thought* would prove the Purdy loyalty to the Guthries, and since she claimed to have been assaulted by a farmer in a ditch along the way (which the farmer denied, but the Granny was of the opinion he was at least bending the truth, if not breaking it), it made it a debt of honor for Castle Guthrie to avenge when the fool woman fell into a well and drowned herself—

That did it. That *did* it! To think that *these* were three of the Kingdoms staunchly claiming that they should be left to manage their own affairs! It beat all, and some left over!

"Wait!" I shouted. "Just *stop!*"

They all put down their silverware and stared at me, and the Granny clucked her tongue.

"You interrupted, child," she said. "Ill-bred of you. *Ill*-bred!"

I whistled long and low, and pushed my plate away from me.

"What *was* that?" I asked. "The roast, I mean."

"Stibble," said James John Guthrie, whose absence was now well explained. He would be very busy indeed with all *this* going on.

"Stibble?"

"Something like a pig and something like an Old Earth rabbit."

"I don't believe it."

"Nevertheless. Granny there named it for us."

"How big?"

He made a measure in the air. Two feet, roughly, and about so high.

"Did you like it?" he asked.

"Yes, I did," I said. "I just wanted a name for it."

"It's new," said James John. "Our Ecologist developed it . . . oh, about a year and a half ago. A little bit of this, a little bit of that."

"And made no mention of it?"

He raised his eyebrows and speared another bite of stibble roast.

"You folks going hungry on Brightwater?" he asked me innocently. "Famine on Marktwain, is there? Starving populations on Oklahomah?"

He knew very well that the law said we all shared. If the Guthrie Ecologist had found a reliable new foodsource, the announcement—and all details—was supposed to go out to all the Twelve Castles, share and share alike. But I let it pass.

"There is no way," I said, "that I can remember all of this hoohah about you Guthries and Farsons and Purdys."

"Poor things," said Granny Stillmeadow. "The Purdys, I mean."

"And no reason why you should remember," said Myrrh of Guthrie like a scythe falling. "I don't recall asking you for help. I don't recall sending any dispatches demanding rescue, and we can handle it ourselves, thank you very much. If *you'll* just stay home."

"The *wickedness* of those Farsons," bellowed James John Guthrie, "and the *ineptitude,* I might say the stupidity, of those Purdys, defies belief, and brings a decent man to—"

"Talk too much," pronounced Granny Stillmeadow. "Shut your face, James John Guthrie, the young woman's been told it's not her concern."

Well! So she could granny when it was needful after all! I patted *her* knee.

"Granny Stillmeadow," he said doggedly, "you have not heard what those people did today. I am here to tell you—"

Granny Stillmeadow, and Myrrh of Guthrie, and I myself fixed him with chilly stares, and Michael Stepforth cleared his throat ominously, and both the sons looked down at their plates, and the man gave it up, his voice trailing off while the servingmaids came forward and took away all evidence of the stibble roast, and the two vegetables, and the bread and butter and gravy and salt and coffee.

"No dessert," said Myrrh of Guthrie, "because of the Reception and the Dance."

One of the young women looked up at that and offered that there was a bread pudding ready in the Castle kitchen if her lady wanted it, and no trouble atall, but Myrrh waved her away.

"You do *see*," she said to me, "why I told you we hadn't time right now to play games with you?"

No, as a matter of actual fact, I did not see. I'd never heard such a tangle of nonsensical tales in all my life, and I couldn't imagine how any group of supposedly competent grown-up people had allowed things to reach such a pass. However, I now had a certain feeling of conviction about one thing—whatever was going on here on Arkansaw, it was keeping the Guthries so busy they had little time to even think about the Jubilee, much less plot against it. That didn't mean I didn't have my guard up, not with that canny Magician of Rank sitting there to remind me. The Guthries could of put all this together as one gigantic distraction, in the hope that I'd feel obliged to stay on and try to settle it, for instance; that would of been perfectly plausible. I didn't *think* so. It all had the ring of truth, however ridiculous; but I wasn't putting it entirely out of my mind. But I was reassured a good deal by the number of lies I'd been told in the space of one brief hour . . . well, call them distortions, lies may be too strong a word . . . and the lack of craft behind them. The Farsons were feuding with the Guthries; and the Guthries were feuding with the Farsons; and the Purdys were caught in the middle trying to play both sides. That much was obvious. The rest of it I wouldn't give two cents for.

It might be I'd have to do some serious digging before I left Arkansaw, and for sure I'd have to keep a wary eye and ear from here on out on Michael Stepforth Guthrie, but I needn't waste time at Castle Guthrie. Reception. Dance. A little breakfast. And on to Farson.

It wasn't going to be a pleasant night, of course; the Magician of Rank would see to that, hoping to provoke me to some indiscretion he could use later on, and wanting his own back for my shaming him before the Missus of the Castle that afternoon. I could count on lizards in my bed, and sheets that *felt* like bread pudding, and bangs and thumps and clanks, and mysterious flames dancing in the corners, and probably—no, for *sure*—the whole room rocking and swaying all night like a small boat in a high wind. I might sleep through some of it, and then I might not. Depending on how ingenious he was. And how spiteful.

I looked at him, and he looked back at me slow and steady, that beautiful mouth curling and the lashes half-lowered over the sea-green eyes. I felt my own traitor lips part, and I firmed them tight, and I saw the devil dance behind those lashes.

I was learning; my sympathy for my mother's victims increased.

Farson

6

"Responsible of Brightwater," said the Attendant, in that dead voice that seemed to have been droning on for hours and hours. I gripped my glass, leaned on the table, and shook this latest hand; it belonged, said the Attendant, to one Marycharlotte of Wommack, wife of Jordan Sanderleigh Farson the 23rd. I didn't even bother to add up the letters and see what number "marycharlotte" came to, which was some index of my exhaustion; she could be any number she chose, including the horrible four, she could be a one like Crimson of Airy and a threat to my life and the Kingdom of Brightwater . . . I no longer cared.

I stood in the line with the Attendant at my side, and the people filed past and were introduced by couples, or one at a time, and I had begun to suspect that they were recirculating that line; it trailed out the Hall door and dissolved into a milling crowd of faces and names I'd long since lost all track of. If a single face had come around twice, or three times for that matter, I doubt I'd have been able to spot it—by now they all looked just alike to me.

I was very nearly out on my feet, and the wine the Castle staff kept pouring into my glass was no great help. White wine I might have replaced with water and gotten away with, but not red; nothing else liquid on Ozark is that color, except blood, and a glass of blood in my hand would of made a mighty poor impression.

Michael Stepforth Guthrie had had some innovations to offer on magical harassment in the guestchamber that had outdistanced even my broadest expectations, and before long I'd settled down to taking notes on his efforts, since it was clear I wasn't going to get any sleep. I'd been grateful for my virginity before it was all over, since that had limited his

legal span of effects some, but nonethe*less*—when I'd given up all hope
at dawn and staggered out of my bed I'd been in sorry shape. And then
there'd been the requisite eighteen hours of flight to Castle Farson, which
I'd had to do every one of its minutes in plainstyle—no SNAPPING. So far
as I'd been able to tell, the whole continent of Arkansaw was innocent
of empty areas, even in the Wilderness Lands; Sterling and I had looked
down on a constant scurry of activity beneath us the whole time, and had
been promptly greeted by Arkansawyers of one kind or another each time
we landed for a brief rest stop.

And the Farsons themselves were terrifyingly efficient. Met me at the
door, fed me and wined me, saw me to a room to change my bib and
my tucker, saw me back down to the Hall for this party, which was clearly
intended to fill all the remainder of this evening, and *no* discussion. Not
a word. "Welcome, Responsible of Brightwater, pleasant to see you."
"Beg your pardon, Responsible, but you've caught us at a right busy time,
we'll just have to make do." "Step this way, please, miss." "Notice the
view from that window, child, it's much admired." "Fine evening, isn't
it?" And on and on.

I could tell from the clustered packs of guests around the Hall and
the scraps of their talk that floated my way that it was much the same stuff
the Guthries had been talking. Perfidy, wickedness, and ineptitude; the
ghastly Guthries and the pitiful Purdys. But no one brought any of it to
my ears—we remarked on my costume, and how pretty it was; and on
my Mule, and how handsome *she* was; and on the weather, and how fine
it was; and the party, and how pleasant *that* was. No more.

I'd made a few early stabs at talking of the Jubilee, and had learned
immediately that the Farsons were either far more subtle than the
Guthries, or else under some sort of orders regarding the topics of their
converse. "You'll be at the Jubilee in May, no doubt?" (That was me, all
charm.) "May is a *fine* month, we always enjoy May!" (That was whoever, moving on down the line toward the punchbowl, smiling.) I got
flustered, and then I got mad, and then I got grim; and as the evening
went on I reached a cold plateau of determination that floated on my second wind and a very good head for wine. I stopped asking, which got
me no information, but at least deprived them of the satisfaction of ignoring my questions.

More hands. Something something of Smith, wife of something

something the 46th. Accompanied by himself, the something somethingth. My teeth ached from smiling, my behind ached from riding, and my spirit ached from boredom, and it went on and on.

"There," said the Attendant. A variation.

"There?"

"That's the last of them, Miss Responsible."

"You're sure?"

"I am," he said. "That's all, and I can't say I'm sorry."

I looked, and it did appear that there were no more people lined up to my right with their hands all ready to be shaken by the guest of honor, Responsible of Brightwater. And a good thing, too; the Farson Ballroom was huge, but it was straining at the seams. I'd have said there were four hundred people there; surely I had not shaken *four hundred hands?*

I set down my glass on the table, careful not to snap its stem for spite, and gathered up my elaborate blue-and-silver skirts.

"Give my compliments to your Missus and my host," I told him, "and tell them I'll be down to breakfast in the morning. Early."

He raised his eyebrows, but it was not his place to question my behavior, and I surely didn't give a thirteen what he thought of it. If he thought I was going to fight my way through this roomful of sweating phony smilers to find the Farsons, if he thought I was going to *thank* them for their bold as brass campaign to wear me right down to a nub, he could think twice more. Manners be damned, I was going to my bed.

I showed him my back and went out the closest door, into the corridor that led to the stairs toward my room. But I was being watched; another Attendant appeared at my side the instant I reached the door, carrying a bowl of fruit, a tray of bread and butter, and a tall decanter of that accursed Farson wine.

"This way, miss," he said, and he led on politely, looking back now and then as we wound up stairs and down corridors, down stairs and through tunnels, round turrets with more stairs and across echoing rooms lined with the family portraits of generations of Farsons, until we came at last to a door I had seen before and knew full well could have been reached by a direct route taking maybe six minutes flat.

"Your room, miss," he said, opening the door to let me pass.

"Thank you for the grand tour, Attendant," I said through my teeth, and he bobbed his head a fraction.

"No trouble atall, miss. No trouble atall; I had to come this way anyhow."

And then he set the food and drink down on a table and left me, blessedly, alone.

I was so angry that I was shaking, and so tired that I was long past being sleepy. The second was a point in my favor, as I had work to do, but the first wouldn't serve. You can't do magic, at whatever level, when you're in a state of blind rage. (Well, you can, but you risk some effects you aren't counting on and that may not exactly fit into your plans.)

I threw myself out flat on the narrow elegant guest bed, kicking off only my shoes, and whistled twenty-four verses of "Again, Amazing Grace." No way to tell which was which, since I was only whistling; but I kept count by picking one berry from the fruit bowl for every verse I finished, and setting them out on my lap in sixes till I had four sets. By that time I was a tad hyperventilated, but I was no longer furious; I had in fact reached a stage of grudging admiration.

After all, the Farsons had given me nothing tangible to complain of. I'd been properly met, a full complement of Attendants in red and gold and silver livery at my beck and call. I'd been dined and wined to a fare-thee-well. I'd had a servant at my elbow every instant, and often half a dozen. I'd been guest of honor at the biggest party I ever remembered seeing, and formally introduced to who knew how many scores of distinguished citizens of Kingdom Farson, and all their kith and kin. And now here I lay in state in one of their best guestchambers, and it had been *my* choice that I'd not stayed below in the Ballroom to receive whatever honor had been next on their list for me.

Thinking about it, staring up at the vaulted ceiling high above my head, I chuckled; it had been done slick as satin, and I had not one piece of information to show for all those hours—nor one legitimate complaint. Well done, well done for sure.

I got up then and went into the bathroom, where I was pleased to see that the facilities were not marred by any nostalgic antiquation, and made myself ready for the night.

Three baths, first. One with hot water, and one with cold, and one with the proper crushed herbs from my pack. Then my fine white gown of softest lawn, sewn by my own hands; I pulled it nine times through a golden finger ring, and examined it carefully—not a wrinkle, it was ready to put on. My feet bare, and a black velvet ribbon round my neck; my hair in a single braid, and I thought that would do. I had nothing really fancy planned for this night, just a kind of easy casting about for wickedness, if wickedness was to be found here. I didn't expect any; for all their sophistication in handling one lone inquisitive female, this Family was just as taken up with the continental feud as the Guthries had been. I was just checking.

I set wards, Ozark garlic and well-preserved Old Earth lilac, at every door and window, laying the wreaths so anyone passing would be certain I slept no matter what went on. I didn't bother warding against Magicians, just ordinary folk and a possible inquisitive Granny; if the Farsons cared to send a Magician, or better yet a Magician of Rank, to check on me, I wanted *that* person to come right on in. I'd be saved hours of Spells and Charms that way, and I had nothing in mind for the night that was forbidden to a woman.

I set two Spells, Granny Magic both of them, and the leaves in the bottom of my little teacup formed unexciting figures both times. I didn't need the bird to tell *me* there was travel in my future, not with all of Kintucky and Tinaseeh still ahead of me; and I didn't need the fine hat that formed high on the right side near the rim to let me know diplomacy was indicated.

And then I moved up a tiny notch, with the idea of making assurance doubly sure, and ran a few Syllables.

I said:

ALE.

BALSAM.

CHERRYSTONE.

DEVIL IN DUNG.

EMBLEM IN AN EGG.

FOGFALL IN THE FOREST.

EGGSHELL IN AN EEL.

DUNG ON DEWDROPS.

COBBLESTONE.

BOWER.

ALE.

Now that's a simple bit, you'll agree. Your average Granny might not be quite so free with dung, but I saw no flaw in it all; and I cast my gold chain on the bed where I was kneeling at my work, fully expecting to see it fall in yet one more reassuring shape, after which I would call it a night and get some well-deserved sleep.

Then I took a look at what I'd got, and backed off to give it room, and backed off some more, and remembered Granny Golightly. What *was* that old woman's range, anyway? Her and her plenty of adventures required . . .

It loved me, that was clear. It licked my face, and it licked the velvet ribbon round my neck, and it slobbered down both the front and the back of my gown with pure affectionate delight, and rolled over on the Farsons' good counterpane to have its stomach scratched, and even flat on its back it kept on licking every part of me it could reach.

This the wards would never hold for, especially if it began to hum to me, which was likely if it got any happier. I scrambled off the bed, with it after me anxiously, licking and snuffling and falling over things at my heels, and I doubled the garlic and hung a ring of it on the doorknob. For good measure I took my shammybag of white sand and laid out a pentacle at the door, with the door itself serving as one of the five sides. Only then did I pause, doing it in the middle of the pentacle just to be extra safe, whereupon it knocked me over and devoted its tiny mind and heart and its enormous tongue to licking me *absolutely clean.*

It was called a Yallerhound, though it was nearer brown than yellow, and only by the most strained courtesy a hound. Like the giant cave-cats, it had six legs; like the Mules, its tail dragged the ground; unlike the Mules, so did its ears and its body hair. It was seven feet long, not counting the tail, and about five feet high, and its aim in life was to love people and keep them *clean.* It had a purple tongue the size of a hand towel, from the eager attentions of which I was already soaking wet from head to foot. And it now had decided that my hair wasn't clean enough, and would probably drown me before it was satisfied about *that.*

I couldn't help myself, this was too much, and made twice as awful because it would of won me no sympathy from anybody—some part of me, somewhere inside, could still see that it was funny. But most of me was at the end of all its ropes. I lay down in the middle of the pentacle, making sure no part of me lopped over any borders, curled up in a ball to protect as much of me as possible from the damned Yallerhound, and I bawled and cried and carried on till I was limp. The poor stupid creature cried with me, keening high and thin.

When I woke up it was a quarter after two, and I was ashamed of myself. Women, after all, are expected to *cope*. There I lay, decked out all ladylike and delicate for magic, as was proper; and there *it* lay, curled round me and humming a tune in that thin little voice that went so badly with its size and made it obvious that the creature was mostly hair. And both of us soggy in a puddle of Yallerhound lick—and the sticky tears of two species. It was enough to rouse the last word I remembered being spanked for using—it was enough to make a person say "puke." Ugh.

I felt better for the sleep, however, and whatever I felt was all the Yallerhound cared about, especially if what I felt was something positive. Now that I'd had my conniption fit, I had to *think*.

To begin with, there was the source of this animal. No Granny on Ozark (and so far as I know we have all the Grannys there are) could teleport anything as big as either a giant cavecat *or* a Yallerhound. I knew Granny Golightly had had her signature on that cavecat back on Oklahomah, but it might of been she'd only had to encourage one that was already there. But I'd bet my velvet neckband it was on this Yallerhound as well, and that was a different matter altogether. Yallerhounds don't just happen to turn up in bedrooms, popping out of empty air, and that had to mean she'd had some help. From a Magician of Rank, who, other than me, would be the only individual with enough skill and strength to bring this off. And I had a pretty good idea I knew *which* Magician of Rank.

Not Michael Stepforth Guthrie; I thought he'd had fun enough for a while. The one I had in mind was called Lincoln Parradyne Smith the 39th, resident of that same Castle Smith that had so coolly disinvited me to visit, Magician of Rank to the continent of Oklahomah, and surely handy to good Granny Golightly.

He'd have been delighted to help her; I rather expected that almost any one of the Magicians of Rank on this planet would of been. I'd been twelve years old the first time a sign from the Out-Cabal had obliged me to convene a Colloquium of the Magicians of Rank (and what a difference two years makes . . . I hadn't even noticed the attractions of Michael

Stepforth Guthrie). And I'd been warned to be prepared for their hostil-
ity, but it hadn't been warning enough. It was like sitting too close to a
wall of fire to be shut in a room with them; I flamed inside with the waves
of hatred beating against me from that crew of arcane males, and I'd been
sick for days afterward.

A strange sickness. I lay in my bed, so weak I could not lift my head
from my pillow even to drink, and perpetually thirsty, and the skin of my
body cold as mountain river water while I burned and burned within. I
had not known that so much pain could be.

"They consumed your energies, child," our Granny Hazelbide had
said, sitting beside me and holding my icy hands in her warm ones, and
every now and then letting a spoonful of water trickle one drop at a time
down my throat. "Sucked 'em right up like a pack of babies at the teat;
and they'll do it every time."

I'd asked her with my eyes, because I couldn't talk—how long? And
she'd shaken her head.

"This first time, sweet Responsible, sweet child? No way of telling,
just no way atall. What you're doing, lying there on a cross of ice and
fire mingled . . . oh yes, child, I know! I've never been through what
you're bearing, praise the Twelve Corners, but I do *know!* . . . what you're
doing there is renewing yourself. It may take days and it may take weeks
and there's not a blessed thing anyone can do to help you. But there's
one good thing—each time it will be shorter. As you get older, and
stronger, and more experienced at this yourself . . . why, you'll get to
where you don't *mind* them any more than a pack of babes!"

A spasm had racked me, all my muscles flickering under my skin, and
she'd sat there calm as a boulder, it not being one of the times when she
felt expected to cluck and fuss and dither. She'd sat there eleven days, and
when it was over she told me I'd done well.

"A short time, for your first time," Granny had said. "That speaks
well for the future, child."

They hated me, one and all, did the Magicians of Rank—though they
no more understood why than the Yallerhound would have. Nor why
they should have felt compelled to come at my call, me no more than a
little pigtailed girl; nor why they couldn't get up and go home, but had
to sit and listen to my pronouncements, as if I had a rank and they had
none; nor why their voices left them if they tried to speak upon the sub-

ject, ever. It was a mystery, and one that they weren't privy to, and there weren't supposed to be any mysteries they weren't privy to. They were, after all, the Magicians of *Rank*.

So, if one of them could do me a little hurt . . . just a small hurt, you understand, just a plaster for their aching egos . . . I was in fact surprised that they'd chanced the cavecat, it might have *really* hurt me; and I could be sure I'd been watched every minute in the crystal that Lincoln Parradyne Smith kept in his magic-chest. He must of been very confident he could reach me in time if I couldn't manage by myself, or he never would of risked it. The Yallerhound, on the other hand, was just funny. It couldn't hurt me even if it wanted to, which it didn't, short of falling on me by accident off a Castle roof, or something of the kind.

"The Yallerhound," I said aloud, which delighted it and set it humming up and down a nineteen-tone scale that was awful beyond all imagining, "is a harmless creature. However, it weighs almost one hundred pounds and a bit, and it eats more than a half-grown Mule, and it will never, never stop licking you."

We would of made a pretty sight, Sterling and me and my saddlebags, and the Yallerhound riding behind me licking my neck and my hair as we flew by. Not to mention the fact that, given the magic I was supposed to be able to perform, we would of *had* to drop like a stone. A Mule couldn't carry that much weight, even if it was precious cargo instead of stupid beast. I had to make up my mind what to do with the thing.

I could simply leave it here, a "gift" to the Castle, and claim I had no idea where it had come from—which was, in a sense, true. They'd never forgive me, and they'd probably shut it up in the stables to die of heartbreak and the conviction that it had done something wrong—but I could do that.

I could claim that *their* Magicians had sicced the silly thing on me, and gain a few points that way, since they wouldn't be able to prove that they hadn't. But the results for the innocent Yallerhound would be the same, if I left it behind.

I could buy another Mule to carry it and take it with me—thus guaranteeing that I'd look like a fool and be greeted like one at every Castle left on my itinerary.

Or I could try to do something with more flair to it, and maybe some justice. Like send it back to its Granny, O! True, I shouldn't be able to do that. True, she'd know that I had. But she couldn't tell on me without telling what *she'd* done, and what she'd done was a pure disgrace. *Therefore!*

"My pretty Yallerhound," I said, frantically ducking the purple tongue and encountering it all the same, "do you know what I think? I think you should go right back to where you came from! Poor Granny Golightly has got no Yallerhound to love her, and I'll bet she's dirty as seven little boys dividing up syrup in August. She undoubtedly, indu-*bita*bly needs a Yallerhound to look after her, don't you think?"

Its eyes got wide and its tongue paused long enough for me to wipe my face off once. It had just enough brain to know I was talking about it, as well as to it. I tapped it on its nose, gently, and I scratched it on its hairy stomach, gently, and I set to work.

Crystals were not my style, but I didn't need one. I had no trouble finding my lady Golightly in my mirror. She slept curled like a scrawny baby in a high bed on the third floor of Castle Clark, under a thick red comforter stuffed with squawker feathers, and a smile of innocent bliss upon her face.

I dumped the Yallerhound right on top of the smile.

Motley

7

I sat in the library at Castle Motley, drinking coffee so strong you could of stood a spoon up in it easy, still weak-kneed from the recent shenanigans but pleased that I'd arrived here without any unbecoming incidents. Sterling had flown across the narrow channel to Mizzurah with nary a wobble, no more creatures of any size or description had joined me as I flew, and if there was an adventure headed at me for this station on the Quest it had yet to arrive. And I was willing to wait.

We were even having a *pleasant* conversation—something I'd been missing for quite a while now. Me and my host, Halbreth Nicholas Smith the 12th, and the lady of his Castle, Diamond of Motley. Just the three of us. There was a small informal supper planned for the evening, I'd been told, and a hunt breakfast the next morning, but no great to-do's. That suited me; I had another slice of fresh hot bread with blazonberry jam, braced myself against the coffee, and relaxed.

Diamond of Motley was a placid woman, gone stout and not the least bothered by it, with her red hair wound around her head in a coronet of thick braids that was about as becoming as measles but otherwise perfectly suitable. She had eleven children and an unshakable serenity; just looking at her rested me. Hearing her say that she and hers were looking forward to the Jubilee *delighted* me.

"Diamond of Motley," I said, "that does me good! It's a great occasion for Ozark, and it *should* be looked forward to. I've not heard much talk along that line since I left Brightwater."

"You've been where now, Responsible?" her husband asked me.

"McDaniels, Clark, Airy, Guthrie, and Farson."

"A shame you had to miss Castle Smith," said Diamond. "Who'd of thought there was still a cavecat left on Oklahomah?"

"*I* wouldn't," I told her. "But I learned."

"Well, Smith's gain is our loss," said Halbreth Nicholas, gallant as you please, "you're here the sooner. Think you missed anything in particular there?"

I looked at him, not sure what he meant, and he was tamping down his pipe and staring into it like he was looking for omens.

"According to a rumor as came this way," he said carefully, still eyeing the tobacco, "Smith wasn't expecting you anyhow . . . it's going round that there was a note sent asking you not to come."

Ah, the close-mouthed Smiths; this would be their doing. Gabble, gabble, gabble, all the time.

"As it happened, that's true," I said. "They sent me a letter."

"Signed by?"

"Dorothy of Smith—the oldest."

Halbreth Nicholas lit his pipe and took a long draught. He was a Smith himself, and head of this Castle only because there'd been no Motley sons in the last generation. If my memory served me right, he'd be the second cousin of the blusterer that filled the same role at Castle Smith.

"She say why?" he asked me.

"They claimed a family crisis."

"Hmmph." He blew a fine smoke ring, and he watched it rise, and he said no more. Which was only to be expected. I wanted to say something comforting about everybody having relatives they'd as soon they didn't have to own up to, but that kind of thing was the proper remark for a Granny, not a Castle daughter, and I held my peace.

Diamond of Motley was not so inhibited—after all, it wasn't *her* relatives. She asked me straight out, leaning over to pour me more coffee and push the jam dish closer to my plate:

"Does it make you suspicious of them, child?"

"You know what's been going on at Castle Brightwater," I said.

"Been on all the comsets. Soured milk, smashed mirrors, kidnapped babies, and such truck. Everybody's heard all about it by now."

"Well," I said, "it's one of those which comes first the squawker or the egg things, to my mind. If Castle Smith is guilty of all this mischief, then telling me not to stop by their door makes them look guiltier. On the other hand, if you're guilty, doing something like that tips your hand so plain and easy that you can't imagine anyone with half a brain doing it; that makes them look as innocent as the babe kidnapped. On the *other* hand, if you were guilty and wanted to look innocent, doing something so outrageous as that would be a canny move. It goes round and round."

"So it does," she said, "and what's your own opinion?"

The question put me in a very awkward position. There sat her husband, him a Smith by birth and close kin to those at Castle Smith this minute, and she asked me such a thing? She was a typical six, and properly named, and her husband stepped into the breach and saved me neatly.

"Shame on you, darlin'," he told her, "putting the young woman on the spot like that. How can she say right in front of me and under my own roof that she suspects my close kin of treason against the Confederation? At least let her finish with her food before you throw her into a bog like that!"

"Oh," she said, "you know, I didn't think?"

"I'm sure you didn't," he observed, and he touched her cheek gently. It was clear he doted on her, and that was nice. "But you must try, now and again."

Then he surprised me.

"Would you like to know what *I* think?" he asked abruptly.

"Indeed I would. If you're willing to say."

"I am," he said. "Delldon Mallard the 2nd, for all he's my cousin, and his three brothers with him, never have had sense enough to pound sand in a rat hole. They're ornery enough to do the kind of foolishness that's been coming down, that's a point against them; and they're silly enough not to see that they're surrounded on all sides by Families loyal to the Confederation, and would be well advised to run with the pack at least until the Jubilee gives us all a chance to see how the land lies. *But,* and nevertheless, I don't think they could of carried it off this long without making some fool mistake that would of given them away—that's a point for them. And furthermore, Granny Gableframe's at Castle Smith, and I don't believe she'd put up with it for a minute, nor do I believe they could put it past her. Now *that,* my dear, is what *I* think."

"And so thought the Clarks," I said, nodding my head. "*Including* Granny Golightly."

"Wicked old lady, that one!" put in Diamond of Motley. "Downright wicked!"

"Grannys aren't wicked, Diamond," said her husband firmly. "They're just contrary, and it's expected of them. She's a tad worse than some of the others, might could be . . . but she has an image to live up to."

"And," I concluded, "so think I. I don't believe Castle Smith is in this."

"And the others?" They asked me together, right in chorus.

"The McDaniels and the Clarks, not a chance of it," I said. "As for the Airys, you know how they are, I don't know where they get it from. The Guthries and the Farsons, from what I can tell and the tales they're spinning, are bent on carving up one another and the poor Purdys along with them. If they've thought of the Confederation in the last two months, I'll be surprised, and the Jubilee? If they don't want to go, they just won't. And everything you said of the Smiths applies to the Purdys . . . if they were playing these tricks they'd of betrayed themselves early, early on."

"And us, my dear?"

I smiled at him, and had some more coffee. "I just got here," I said. "Suppose you tell me how you feel about these things."

"It won't take long."

"All the better."

"Mizzurah is a mighty small continent, and it's right off the port bow, if you'll allow the figure, of Arkansaw and all that feuding and carrying on. We've got the Wommacks and the Travellers on our flanks, and a hell of a lot of ocean—beg your pardon, ladies—all around, and nobody but Castle Lewis to rely on should all of the others decide to move in on us. Guthries, Farsons, Purdys, Wommacks, and Travellers, that is. They have us cut off completely from Marktwain and Oklahomah."

"Which means?"

"Which means we're in an interesting position, if you like interesting, but a chancy one. You'll find the Lewises as strong for the Confederation as the Airys, though a mite less drivelly about it, and they'd stand firm in any crisis; but they're even smaller than we are, they couldn't hold out a week. And we couldn't defend them. Therefore, I tell you quite frankly, Responsible of Brightwater, that Castle Motley stands for the Confederation of Continents, and does so openly—but you can't count on us for anything dramatic."

He was right, if unromantic. Mizzurah was the smallest of the six continents, and it sat all alone in the middle of the oceans with its three great neighbors hemming it on all sides. Castle Motley was in no position to make rash promises.

"But you'll be at the Jubilee?" I asked him, hoping.

"We'll be there," he assured me. "You heard my wife; her and the children, they're looking forward to it, and a lot of our staff. It's a rare chance when we can get away and see something besides our own Castle yard. We plan to leave very shortly, as a matter of fact, because we're going by water everywhere we can—no Mules for *my* household, thank you, except flat on the solid ground, and no more of 'em then than's absolutely required. But we can't offer you anything else but our presence, and no daring political moves—you might as well know that."

I wondered if he knew anything that I didn't, and couldn't see what I'd lose by asking.

"Halbreth Nicholas, do you expect some daring moves from somebody else?"

He knocked out his pipe and set it down, and then he counted out his propositions with the side of one palm on the flat of the others.

"First," he said, "there's already those trying to scuttle the Jubilee outright. Correct?"

"Correct."

"I think you'll be able to stop that . . . this Quest of yours is an exaggeration, but it's caught people's fancy, and I believe they'll come to see what happens next, if for no other reason. Dragons and a tourney in the courtyard at Castle Brightwater, maybe?"

I grinned at him.

"Second," he went on, "assuming, as I do think we can assume, that there *will* be a Jubilee, even if one or two of the Families boycott it—and frankly, I doubt that strongly; like I said before, every one of them is curious, and if anything's going to happen they don't want to miss it—*if* the Jubilee does come off as scheduled, I look for a formal move to dissolve the Confederation."

"Happens every time we meet," I said. "That would be no surprise."

"*Not* exactly," said Halbreth Nicholas, "not exactly. Nobody's proposed that seriously within anybody's memory. No, what always happens is the move to cut it back to one day a year, and then that's voted down . . . by how much depending on how the Wommacks are wobbling that month."

"My dear," said Diamond of Motley, "I'm afraid I really don't see much difference. In effect, that is."

"Oh, there's a difference," he said, "yes, there is. True, that ritual meeting would make the Confederation an empty pretense, a regular little bug of a planetary government and not worth spitting at. But so long as it met even that long, they'd only have one meeting's worth of satisfaction. Brightwater'd move to return to meeting four times a year, Castle Lewis'd second, and the vote would go as usual—seven to five or eight to four. *Dissolving* the thing, meaning no meetings *atall,* would be quite a different thing altogether."

I felt a chill between my shoulders . . . not that I hadn't had the same idea cross my mind, but if it came this easy to him there might be many others sharing it.

"You think they could do it, Halbreth Nicholas?"

"I think they'll for damned sure try."

"But do you think they can bring it off? The vote has always gone against them, even on the meeting cutback . . ."

"But weak votes, young woman, weak votes," he said solemnly. "You can't count on the Wommacks, them and their curse. It may well be you can't count on the Smiths, considering this latest development. If all our neighbors pulled out, I'm not prepared to say you could count on the Motleys or the Lewises, either."

"Halbreth Nicholas Smith!" said Diamond of Motley, so shocked her spoon rattled in her cup.

"My dear," he said, "we must face facts. Castle Motley is not self-sufficient, nor Castle Lewis either. If Arkansaw, Kintucky, and Tinaseeh decided to blockade us so that no supplies could be shipped in from Oklahomah or Marktwain, just where do you think we'd be? We can grow vegetables and fruit here, and raise a goat or two, but that's about it. No sugar, no salt, no coffee, no tea, no metals, no supplies for the Grannys or the Magicians, no manufactured goods to speak of. And where do you think our power comes from, Diamond of Motley? It comes from the Farsons and the Guthries, who can equally well cut it off. No law says they have to sell to us."

"Our windmills," she said. "Our solar collectors—and our *tides.*"

I tried to imagine the population of Mizzurah managing with its windmills and its solar technology and its tides, with all the huge hulking bulk of three continents cutting off both wind and water on three sides, and it raining or cloudy three quarters of the year or more, and I admired Halbreth Nicholas for not smiling. She was a good woman, was Diamond, but she hadn't much grasp of logistics.

"No," he said, but he said it respectfully, "I'm afraid they wouldn't suffice, Diamond. The Lewises, now, they are just pig-headed enough that they might go the rest of us one better!"

"Withdraw from the withdrawal, you mean."

"Exactly. And live on greens and goatmeat, and burn . . . oh, candles, for all I know. They might. But not us, Responsible, and I want that understood. I've many families here depending on me and they're not expecting to go back to Old Earth standards and the year 2000. And I don't intend to ask it of them."

"You'd vote for dissolving, then."

"If it was clear that that was the way it was going—yes. Regardless of how the Lewises might decide. It's not my druthers, young woman, but it's the facts of life. We are dependent on Arkansaw, Kintucky, and Tinaseeh, and there's no way to change that short of moving the continent of Mizzurah to a new location just off *your* coast. Are your Magicians of Rank up to a project like that?"

Moving Mules was one thing; moving continents was quite another; I didn't try to answer.

"Law, but you've made a gloomy day of it, Mr. Motley!" said his wife. "I hope you're proud of yourself!"

I was quite sure he wasn't; in fact, I was quite sure he was ashamed. He would of liked to hear himself saying that if the vote came to end the Confederation his delegates would be right there at the front telling the rotters to do their damndest and to hell with them. Begging the pardon of any ladies present, of course. That went with the image he'd of *liked* to have of himself. But he was a practical man, and an honest one, and he knew he'd do what went with that. Diamond of Motley was right; he'd made it a gloomy day.

I went off to my room to rest for a while before supper, and found a servingmaid waiting there, pretending—not very skillfully—to still be unpacking my saddlebags and clearing up. She looked eleven, but had the frail look of a Purdy to her, too, which meant she was probably my own

age or a bit more, and her hair was falling down from the twist she'd put
it in and hanging down around her face. My fingers itched to set it right—
I can't abide a sloppy woman—but I didn't know her and I couldn't take
liberties.

"Hello, young woman," I said, friendly as I could manage in my
dreary mood, "are you having a problem with some of those things? What
is it, a fastening you can't get loose?"

"No, miss," she said, "I'm managing." And dropped my hand mirror on the floor, smashing it to smithereens. No magic, just plain fumble-
fingers.

"Oh, Miss Responsible, I'm sorry!" she said, and bit one finger. She'd
be chewing on her hair next. "I'll get you another one, miss, there's a
hundred of 'em down in the corner of the linen room! What do you
fancy, something plain? Or a special color? The Missus has a weakness
for a nice pale blue, and flowers on the back . . ."

Her hands were trembling, and her voice was a squeak, and I stared
at her long and hard while she dithered about the variety of mirrors the
Motleys had to offer for as long as I could stand it, and then I told her to
sit down.

"Miss?"

"*Do* sit down," I said, too cross to be gentle, "and tell me what is the
matter with you. And your name."

"My name? Is there something the matter with my name?"

She had to be a Purdy; her eyes were wild like a squawker got by
the neck.

"I did not mean to imply that there was anything wrong with your
name, young woman," I said, "I just asked you what it might *be*."

"Oh!" she said. "Well, I hoped . . . I mean, only the Wommacks
have women as aren't properly named, and—"

"That's not true," I interrupted, wondering if she'd had any education atall. "I daresay there's no Family on Ozark that hasn't had a girl or
two Improperly Named over the years; the Grannys aren't infallible. The
Wommacks just did it more spectacularly than anybody else ever has and
got famous for it, that's all."

As they surely had. It hadn't been a matter of naming a Caroline that
should have been an Elizabeth; they'd named a girlbaby Responsible of
Wommack, and it had been a mistake. That's a sure way to get famous.

One more time, I thought, and asked her: "Will you tell me your name, then, and what the trouble is?" And if she wouldn't I fully intended to put her over my knee for her sass.

"Yes, miss," she said. "Ivy of Wommack's my name."

A two. She was properly named. And I was right glad I had not let it slip that I'd taken her for a Purdy.

"And your problem?"

She stared down at the bed she was sitting on and gripped the counterpane with both hands, silly thing, as if it wouldn't of slid right off with her if she'd done any sliding herself.

"Oh, Miss Responsible," she said in a tiny, tiny voice, "I have all the bad luck I ever need, I have more than *anybody'd* ever need, and I don't need any more, and I'm afraid—oh, law, miss, they say there's been a Skerry appeared!"

Well. That did take me aback a bit, and I sat down myself.

"Who told you so, Ivy of Wommack?" I demanded.

"Everybody!"

"Nonsense. You haven't talked to everybody."

"Everybody I've talked to, then," she said stubbornly. "They're all talking about it, and they're all worried."

"And what are they saying? Besides just, 'There's been a Skerry appeared.'"

"There's an old well, down in the garden behind the Castle church, miss—the water's no good any more, but oh, it's pretty, with vines growing all over it and the old bucket hanging there, so it's been left. And they say that last night—there were full moons last night, miss—they say there was a Skerry sitting on the edge-rim of that old well. Just sitting there."

"At midnight, I suppose."

"Oh yes . . . just at midnight, and under the full moons. Oh, Miss Responsible, I'm glad I didn't see it!"

She hadn't much gumption, or much taste. I would dearly have loved to see it, if it was true. A Skerry stands eight feet tall on the average, sometimes even taller, and there's never been one that wasn't willow slender. They have skin the color of well-cared-for copper, their hair is silver and falls without wave or curl to below their waists, male or female. And their eyes are the color of the purest, deepest turquoise. The idea of the full moons shining down on all that, not to mention an old well covered with wild ivy and night-blooming vines . . . ah, that would of been something to see and to marvel on.

Except there were a few things wrong with the whole picture.

"*Who* told you they saw the Skerry?" I insisted. "Who?"

And I added, "And don't you tell me 'everybody,' either."

"Everyone in the Castle is talking about it," she said. Drat the girl!

"Not the Master nor the Missus," I said. "I've been with them these past two hours, and I've heard not one word about a Skerry."

"Everybody on the *staff,* I meant, miss. It was one of the Senior Attendants . . . he'll go far, they say he knows more Spells and Charms than the Granny, and he's a comely, comely man . . . he was down there by the well last night with a friend of mine"—she looked at me out of the corner of her eye to see if I was going to make any moral pronouncements about that, but I ignored her, and she went on—"and they *saw* it, sitting there in the full moonlight, all splendid with the light fair blinding on its long silver hair, they said."

"And then they told everybody."

"Well, wouldn't you?" she asked me, and I had to admit that I might have. You didn't see a Skerry every night, much less under full moons at midnight in a Castle garden.

"But you notice they didn't tell the Family," I said. "That's mighty odd, seems to me. Seems to me that would of been the *first* thing to do."

The girl rubbed her nose and stared down at the floor, scuffing one shoe back and forth. Not only sloppy, but wasteful, too.

"The Housekeeper told us not to," she said sullenly. "She carried on about it till we were all sick of listening—what she'd do if we bothered the Master and the Missus with it . . . *bothered* them, that's how *she* put it!"

"Well?" I asked her. "Do you have any inkling in your head why she might of taken it that way?"

She sniffled. "I don't know," she said. "I just know I'm scared. And it's *not fair*—I already had my share of bad luck."

"Ivy of Wommack," I said patiently, "have you given this tale any thought atall? Other than to fret yourself about it, I mean?"

"What way should I be thinking about it?"

"Well, for starters, where do the Skerrys live?"

"In the desert on Marktwain," she said promptly.

"Quite right. In the desert on Marktwain. The only patch of desert on this planet, girl, and *left* desert only out of courtesy to the Skerrys. They *were* here first, you know, and it was desert then."

"Yes, miss."

"And since that's true, and Skerrys can't live outside the desert, why in the name of the Twelve Gates and the Twelve Corners would one turn up on Mizzurah, many and many a long mile from its desert, and of *all* unlikely places, sitting on a *well* brim? Skerrys *hate* water, can't *abide* water, that's why they live in the desert!"

Her mouth took a pout, which was no surprise.

"Really," she said, "I'm sure I'm no expert on Skerrys, and it wouldn't be proper if I was, and as to how it got here, my friend says it would have to be by magic, and she got that from the Senior Attendant, and he's on his way up in the world—he's no fool!"

"Tell me again," I said. "Exactly. What did they say?"

"Kyle Fairweather McDaniels the 17th, that's the Senior, and my friend—never mind her name, because she wasn't supposed to be out of her bed at midnight, much less with Kyle Fairweather—they say that they were down by the well and they saw the Skerry as plain as I see you."

"Walked right up and touched it, did they? Said howdeedo?"

"Miss!"

"Then how did they know it was a Skerry?"

"Well, miss, what *else* is eight feet tall and has copper skin, and silver hair as hangs down to its knees? I ask you!"

"It was sitting on the well, Ivy of Wommack, not standing. You said so yourself. How could they see that it was eight feet tall? And as for the copper skin, a bit of Hallow Even paint will do that—I've done it myself, and I'll wager you have, too—and a silver wig's easily come by."

"They were *sure*."

"Were they?"

"They *were*."

"They were out where they should not of been, doing what they should not of done—"

"I didn't say that."

"Well, I say it, missy," I snapped at her, "and I say it plain, and between their guilty consciences and the moonlight, it was easy for anybody atall to play a trick on them. And more shame to them for scaring the rest of you with such nonsense . . . what trashy doings!"

"You don't believe it, then, miss?"

"Certainly not. Nor should you, nor anybody else."

She sat there beside me, quieter now, though she'd switched from wrinkling up the counterpane to wringing those skinny little hands that looked like you could snap them the way Michael Stepforth Guthrie'd snapped my ribs. Only with no need for magic, nor much strength, either.

"Feel better now, Ivy of Wommack?" I asked her finally, and I hoped she did, because I wanted a rest and a read before my supper. I was willing to finish unpacking for myself, if I could just get rid of this skittish creature.

"You know what's said, miss," she hazarded. I *wished* she would stop wringing her hands before she wore them out.

"What?" Though I knew quite well.

"That if a Skerry's seen," she breathed, and I could hear in her voice the echo of a Granny busy laying out the lines, "that there has to be a whole day of celebration in its honor. A whole day of no work and all celebration . . . or it's bad luck for all the people that know of it. And I've worked this livelong day, and so has all the staff!"

"That, I suppose, is why your 'friends' spread the news around," I said. "Sharing out the bad luck."

"Maybe," she said. "Might could be that's why."

"Covering their bets," I said tartly. "If they didn't really see a Skerry, no harm done. If they did, the bad luck that comes from not following the rules gets spread out thin over the whole staff, instead of just falling on the two of them. You think that over, Ivy of Wommack."

She sighed, and allowed as how I might be right, but she didn't know, and I occupied myself with sending her on her way. She'd forgotten all about finishing my unpacking, fortunately, and it took me three minutes to do what she'd left and fix what she'd messed up, and then I stretched out on the bed bone-naked under the covers and took up my most trashy novel.

There was a certain very small, you might say tiny, bit of risk here. For a Skerry to show up on Mizzurah, at midnight, or at any other time, might fit right into some Magician of Rank's idea of an adventure for this particular stage of my Quest. And if so, I was asking for powerful trouble —maybe not right now, maybe not for a long time, but *someday* it would come—if I didn't speak up and demand the day of festival to honor its appearance.

Furthermore, if a Magician of Rank *had* teleported a Skerry out of its desert and onto the edge of the Motleys' well, the Skerrys were not going to be pleased about that. Not at *all* pleased. They'd asked precious little of us, when The Ship landed; just to be let alone. And whizzing one around the planet in the middle of the night was distinctly not leaving it alone as promised.

I tried to remember when a Skerry had last been seen, putting my microviewer down for a minute . . . not in my lifetime, I didn't think. In my mother's, perhaps; it was dim in my memory. But *that* Skerry had come walking out of the desert on Marktwain of its own free will, and had walked right down the street of a town on the desert's edge in broad daylight. It had been an honor, and I believe Thorn of Guthrie said there'd been festival for two whole days. . . .

No. I made up my mind. It had to be a trick, played on the Senior Attendant and his foolish lady friend, and no more. For my benefit, perhaps, meant to distract me and delay me if I believed it, but only a trick all the same. No Skerry would cross all the water between Marktwain and Mizzurah and sit on a well in the middle of the night for two young Castle staff to gawk at. And no Magician of Rank would dare tamper with a real Skerry in that way.

I was not going to take any such obvious bait, and that was all there was to that.

I went back to my book.

8

Lewis

I left for Castle Lewis after the hunt breakfast, not staying for the hunt itself on the grounds that I had to hurry, and since that was obviously true no one made more than the objections politeness demanded. Mizzurah was so small, and so heavily populated, that anything but ordinary Muleflight was out of the question, and I flew through a blustery spring day, sedate and proper, and reached Castle Lewis only just before the sun began to go down behind the low hills. Sterling was bored, and so was I, and we did nothing fancy; just came down slow and easy over the broad lawn that spread round the Castle, and waited for developments. The wind was brisk enough that the Mule was shivering, and I got down and took an extra blanket from my pack and began rubbing her down.

Castle Lewis was small against the darkening sky, small and tidy, with a central gate and two towers to each side, and a tower at each of its corners. No frills, no fancy battlements and balconies, just a plain small sturdy Castle, and I liked the look of it.

The front gates opened as the sun slipped out of sight completely, and three men came running out with solar lanterns—economy here, I noted, and I approved. They'd been well exposed and threw a fine bright light across the grass, as they should do. One of the men put a shawl around me, very respectfully; one took over the task of rubbing Sterling down, making protesting sounds because I'd started the process myself; and the other stood stiff as a pole, waiting for something.

"Where *is* that woman?" demanded one of them, and called over his shoulder: "Tambrey! Tambrey of Motley! What's keeping you, woman? Responsible of Brightwater at your gate half-frozen, and dropping with hunger and entirely tuckered out, and what are you doing in there, counting your fingers to see if you've lost one? Will you get *out here?*"

"I'm not that tired, Attendant," I said sharply, "and not that cold, and not that hungry. I'll last the night."

"That doesn't excuse her, miss," he said firmly. "She knows her duty, and she's expected to do it." And he turned his head again and shouted "Tambrey!" and then made a remarkably expressive noise of disgust.

"It's all right," I said, "never mind the woman. One of you to take my Mule to the stables, and two to see me to my host and hostess—I can surely make do with that?"

But they wouldn't have it that way, and we stood there in the wind while a soft rain began to fall in the deepening darkness, and I knew that I was up against it. The famous Lewis propriety, than which only the Travellers' could be said to be more extreme. I could stand there and drown, for all they cared, I'd not enter their Castle attended by other than a female, and I envied my Mule. At least she was going to be warm and fed and dry, any minute now.

When Tambrey did appear, which to give her credit was not many minutes later, she didn't come from the gates but out of the cedars that bordered the Castle lawn. She was a pretty thing, too, and I couldn't see her being a servingmaid long; her hair was hidden by the hood of her cloak, but her face was perfection, and I was willing to place my bets on the rest of her.

The men grumbled at her, but she paid them no mind at all, and from the way they dropped their complaining I was reasonably certain they were used to that, too.

"Welcome to Castle Lewis, Responsible of Brightwater," she said, "and let's get you in out of this damp this minute and a mug of hot cider in your hand!"

Oh yes. I had forgotten. I'd get nothing stronger than cider from the Lewises unless it came from a Granny's own hand and was vouched for as being the difference between my total collapse and my blooming health. And not hard cider, either; it would be the pure juice of the Ozark peachapple, mulled with spices, and hot as blazes, and innocent enough for the baby that still hung safe outside the Brightwater church. The Lewises kept to the old ways with a vengeance.

We went through the gates into a small square courtyard, planted with low flowers in neat square beds, and raked paths between them, and on to where the Castle door shone wide and welcoming. In the door stood two I'd heard a great deal of, but knew hardly at all: Salem Sheridan Lewis the 43rd, and his wife, Rozasharn of McDaniels.

"Here she is," said Tambrey, handing me through the door like a package, so that the Lewises both had to step back a pace to avoid me running them down, "Responsible of Brightwater, safe and sound! Miss, Salem Sheridan Lewis the 43rd; and the Missus of this Castle, Rozasharn of McDaniels."

"Thank you kindly, Tambrey," said the woman Rozasharn, and the beauty of her voice caught my ear. I hoped she would sing for us, later, if the quality of her speech was any sign of her ability.

Salem Sheridan was another matter. His wife gathered me into her arms as if we'd known each other all our lives; but he snapped his fingers and ran everybody through their drill. Had my Mule been seen to and stabled? Good. And had my bags been brought in and taken up to my room? Good. And was the mulled cider ready in the east parlor? Good. And would Tambrey see to my unpacking? Good—and I was to have extra blankets, mind, it was going to be cold. And would supper be on the table in *precisely* one hour? Good! And it was all "Yes, sir!" coming the other way. It said something for Tambrey of Motley's ingenuity that she'd been able to find her way past this one and into the cedars—there'd be no sloppy staff here.

I had time only to wash a bit, tidy my hair, and change from my traveling costume into something less elaborate, before suppertime, the cider still burning my throat. I was traveling light, as was necessary; there was the splendid traveling outfit, the blue-and-silver party dress, the gown of lawn for magic, some underclothes and a nightgown, a sturdy black shawl, and one plainer dress that I'd not yet had an opportunity to wear. And that was all.

I held up the last dress and looked it over dubiously; it had alternating narrow stripes of the Brightwater green and scarlet, with a neck cut low in front and rimmed in back by a high ruff of ivory lace that would require me to put my hair up. It had long sleeves caught at the wrists with lace-trimmed wide cuffs as well, and the stripes themselves were shot with silver-and-gold threads.

I'd seen nothing like it here; only modest high-necked round-collared gowns without ornament even to their cut. The Lewis crest was a green cedar tree on an azure field, with a narrow border of cedar-trunks russet round, and except for a button or two that bore that device I'd seen only the plain and the spare. Even Rozasharn, presumably dressed for company, had been wearing a dress of a heather blue with a skirt scarcely full enough to swing with her hips as she walked, and plain little round white buttons down its high front.

True, I was a guest. And true, the conditions on a Quest demanded a certain amount of spectacle, and I had to abide by them. But I could see nothing in the garments that Tambrey had hung for me that would not of looked foolish at the Lewis supper table.

Well, there was my nightgown . . . it was moss green flannel and had the proper cut and simplicity, and I couldn't see that the Lewises would recognize it for what it was if I could keep my own face straight. I belted it with a narrow braid of gold cord, since it had no proper waist, and added a single silver pendant—a small flower meant, I believe, to represent a violet, but innocuous enough for any occasion—on a narrow green velvet ribbon. Then I used a matching ribbon to tie my hair back simply at the nape of my neck and looked at the effect in the long glass mirror in my guestchamber.

My grandmother would of been scandalized, my *mother* would of fainted, but I was of the opinion that I could get away with it. I only had to remember not to let a servingmaid see me in it tomorrow morning when she brought up my pot of tea. That would have meant the word going out that I'd either been too lazy to change into my nightgown and had slept in my dress, or that I'd been so addled I'd worn my nightgown to supper, neither of which would do.

Kingdom Lewis had just one product for sale—cedar, cut from the progeny of the three seedlings the family had somehow managed to nurse through the whole trip to this planet, and which now they alone seemed to have the skill to grow. Under any other touch the trees turned brown and died, like grass not watered, but the Lewises had the green thumb, one and all of them, and the rows of cedars grew stately in every spare field of the small Kingdom and all along its narrow roads. Even in the great Hall inside Castle Lewis, a giant cedar grew out of earth left open for its roots in the time of building, dropping its needles everywhere for the staff to sweep up but smelling like heaven, and every windowsill had a small seedling growing in a low bowl.

Nor had they stinted themselves in the use of the timber. The Castle gleamed with it, and the table at which I sat down to supper was a single massive slab of russet cut from the heart of an ancient monster of a tree and rubbed till it glowed like coals burned low in a hearth. They had had sense enough not to cover it up with some frippery cloth, either, and had set chairs round it of the same glowing wood.

Me in my nightgown, I drew one up and sat down, spreading my napkin in my lap, and I said, "This table is beautiful, Rozasharn of McDaniels. I've never seen anything to match it." Nor had I.

"My husband's great-great-grandfather made it with his own hands," she answered, "and I do its polishing with mine."

"It *was* a single plank?"

"That it was; they waited a very long time for a cedar to grow the proper size for this, and while they waited the Lewises ate off plain boards laid across trestles. Then the one tree made this table and all the chairs . . . and no polish or oil has ever been set to it except by a Missus of this Castle, all these years."

"I've seen a few housethings made from cedar," I said. "Chests, usually." And I stroked the satiny wood. "But nothing like this."

"Magic-chests!" breathed a child at my right hand, and I turned my head to see him better. He was young, and his chair not tall enough to bring him much above the edge of the tabletop, but not young enough to be willing to submit to the indignity of sitting on a stack of pillows; he made do by craning his neck.

"My son, Salem Sheridan Lewis the 44th, called Boy Salem," said his father from the head of the table, and he introduced the other five children that had joined us for the meal. And the Granny, the youngest on Ozark and one of the sternest—fifty-nine-year-old Granny Twinsorrel. I bid them all a good evening, and helped myself to the soup.

Salem was a patient child; when the introductions had gone all the way around and the grownups were eating, he said it again, but this time he was asking.

"Magic-chests?" he asked me. "All of cedar?"

"Usually," I told him. "Because it keeps everything so safe."

His dark blue eyes shone, and I found him a handsome child despite the lack of three front teeth and the presence of a crazy-quilt assortment of scrapes and scabs and scratches. I expect he had fallen out of one or more of the cedar trees recently.

"What's in a magic-chest, Responsible of Brightwater?" he asked me then, and he held very still, waiting for me to answer. Which meant he'd asked it before, and it had done him no good. It would do him no good this time, either.

"Herbs and simples and gewgaws," I said casually. "And garlic."

"In a *cedar chest?*" The child was shocked, and I chuckled.

As it happened, the Magicians *did* keep their garlic in their magic-chests, but they saw to it that the smell of the stuff was on hold while it was in there.

"That's right," I said. "Garlic."

"When I am a Magician of Rank," said the boy with utter solemnity, like a Reverend pronouncing a benediction, "I won't do that. Or I'll make a Spell to take the smell off so it doesn't spoil the wood."

Smart little dickens, that one. I could tell by the twitch at the corner of his stern father's lips that this was a favorite child—the name told me that in any case—and that his promise was noticed. But the Master of the Castle spoke to him in no uncertain terms.

"When *you* are a Magician of Rank!" he said. "Many a long, long year of study lies between you and that day, Boy Salem, if it ever comes— *which* I doubt. And many a difficult examination. You had best get your mind off garlic and concentrate on learning the Teaching Story you were set this week—you didn't have it right yet last night, as I recall."

"Or," added a sister who looked to be about thirteen, with the same pansy blue eyes but considerably less scuffed up and battered as to the rest of her, "you'll end up like your cousin Silverweb."

"I'd not be such a ninny as *that*," scoffed the boy, "not ever! You know that, Charlotte."

"Silverweb of McDaniels?" I set my soup spoon down and used my napkin hastily. "Has something happened to her?"

"Nothing serious, Responsible," said Rozasharn of McDaniels, "and nothing that can't be mended. She's been left too long unmarried, and this is where that sort of thing leads to."

"I hadn't heard," I said. "What's happened?"

"Well," said Rozasharn, "as I understand it Silverweb decided you needed somebody to be guardmaid—or companion, who knows? to be company at any rate—on your Quest. And that young one packed a pair of saddlebags, stole a Mule from the McDaniels stables, and started off after you."

"She didn't get far," observed her husband, handing the meat platter down the table. "Her daddy caught up with her before noon the following day and took her straight back to Castle McDaniels."

"For a licking," said the one they called Boy Salem.

"Not for a licking," corrected Granny Twinsorrel. "Boy Salem, you'll never make a Magician if you don't learn to turn on your brain before you begin rattling off at the mouth. Young women of fifteen don't get lickings, it wouldn't be proper."

The boy snorted, and wrinkled up his nose.

"Not fair," he said. "Not fair atall."

"What *did* they do to her?" I asked reluctantly, not really sure I wanted to know. I had high hopes for Silverweb, and I bore a certain guilt for having ranked her when I was at Castle McDaniels.

"Packed her off to Castle Airy in disgrace," said Salem Sheridan. "And to the tender care of all three of the Grannys there. Seven weeks and a day, she's to be servingmaid to those Grannys. I do expect that will have some effect on her."

Poor wretched Silverweb . . . I knew what that would mean. She'd hem miles and miles of burgundy draperies, and then be made to take the hems out and do them over till her fingers bled. She'd boil vats of herbs half as tall as she was, stirring them for hours at a time with a wooden staff. And she'd pick nutmeats—they'd have her doing that with *bushels* of nuts, staining her fingers black where they weren't bleeding. And scrubbing the Castle corridor floors with gritty sand. And worse.

"Oh, what *ever* made her take such a notion?" I asked, cross in spite of feeling sorry for her.

"Like I said," said Rozasharn, "she's been left too long unmarried. Silverweb's going on sixteen, and that's far too old. It's a wonder she's not done worse."

"And she *may* have," put in one of the older children. "Our daddy says Silverweb of McDaniels could very well of dressed like a man and kidnapped that baby out of your church, Responsible of Brightwater! He says she's plenty big enough and strong enough—and bold enough, too."

"I was there," I protested, "and I can't believe that, not atall! I'm *sure* it was a man . . . and I'm sure it wasn't Silverweb of McDaniels. She's a fine young woman, I give you my word on that; she's just maybe a bit strong-minded."

"She ought to have a husband and two babies to occupy her energy by now," said Salem Sheridan, "and I fault her parents for that. Though I agree she's got to be punished for running off, and for taking the Mule without permission, and the rest of it. That's fitting, and expected."

"She'll live through it," said Granny Twinsorrel. "And maybe she'll learn a thing or two about pride."

"Now, Granny—" Rozasharn began, but the woman cut her off sharp.

"Pride is all that's keeping that one spinster," said Granny Twinsorrel, "simple pride. Her father's offered her three marriages, each one fully suitable, each of the men with land and a homeplace and a good future ahead of him. And Miss Yellow-Haired High-and-Mighty wouldn't accept any one of the three. Two fine men from Kingdom Guthrie, and one of our *own*—and none of them good enough for her. Pride, that is, and it'll lead her to no good end."

"They say," said Rozasharn, "that she has ambitions. And if that's true, she'll make no marriage, Granny Twinsorrel."

She *has ambitions.* In front of the children, that would mean that Silverweb intended to become a Granny the hard way, and go virgin to her grave; and there was no reason for a woman to do that unless she had her eyes out for a chance to become a Magician as well as a Granny. Which was "having ambitions."

I frowned into my soup, but went back to eating it. Silverweb was none of my business, and no reason for her to come between me and my supper.

The rock that whistled past my ear went into the bowl of mashed sweet potatoes, which weren't enough to slow it down any, and on beyond to hit the far wall with a resounding smack. Whoever had thrown it had put considerable muscle behind it, and I couldn't say it made my stomach calm. But not a one of the Lewises moved, or paused in their eating, or turned a hair, so far as I could tell. An Attendant stepped forward from the door and picked up the rock, and went off with it somewhere, while the Lewises went right on with their meal.

"Rozasharn of McDaniels," I said, my voice more a quiver than I'd intended it to be, "how many more of those are we likely to be favored with this evening?"

"Half a dozen, maybe," she said. "Maybe a few more, maybe a few less."

"Well, don't you *mind* having rocks thrown at you like that?"

"Gracious, child," said Granny Twinsorrel, "those rocks aren't being thrown at us. It's a bit of fuss in *your* honor—started about the time you crossed the border of Kingdom Lewis, I calculate, which is why we were a mite disorganized when you arrived, and will stop when you move on. We don't plan to pay the fool thing any attention, it will only make it worse."

"Nobody's been either hurt or bothered," said Rozasharn soothingly. "You'll notice there's not even dust in the potato dish."

"We can put up with it," said Boy Salem, backing her up. "Besides, I like to see what it does."

What it did next may have amused Boy Salem, but it didn't amuse me in the slightest. Nobody wants a live lizard in her soup, and since Rozasharn of McDaniels was so calm about all this I strongly wished it had been in her bowl instead of mine.

"Tch," said Granny Twinsorrel. "Now that was rude."

"Can I fish it out?" asked Boy Salem. "Is it real? Can I get it out for you?" He was fairly hopping up and down in his chair.

It was real enough, about four inches long, and a bright poisonous green. It put back its narrow head and hissed at me, and I fancied it was a little warmer there among the potatoes and the jebroots than it cared to be.

"Never mind, Boy Salem," I said disgustedly. "I'd best do it myself, I believe."

Granny Twinsorrel's voice came sharp and sudden. "Don't you put silver to it, young woman!" she told me. "It's not the creature's fault. Use your fingers."

I knew that much, but I didn't sass the Granny; I reached into my soup with two careful fingertips, caught the little animal by the tip of its tail, and lifted it out into the air still spitting.

"Can I have it?" demanded Boy Salem. The child was outrageous, and his brothers and sisters stared at him in amazement. Eben Nathaniel

Lewis the 17th, twelve years old and already with a rigid look to him like his father, turned that look on Boy Salem in a way that would of frozen the child stiff if it'd had any power behind it.

"A Spelled creature like that, Boy Salem?" said Eben Nathaniel. "Your head's addled!"

The Granny stepped over to my chair and took the lizard from me, which was a good deal more appropriate than letting Boy Salem have it for a pet, and a servingmaid slipped the bowl of soup away and replaced it with a fresh one, and handed me a new spoon.

Whereupon a small frog, same shade of green, croaked up at me from among the vegetables. And I set the silverware down again.

If this was the beginning of an adventure, I didn't fancy it; there were quite a few nasty and downright dangerous things that would fit into a soup bowl.

"Keep changing the bowls," ordered Granny Twinsorrel, without a tremble to her voice, and we sat there while the process went on.

Bowl three, a much larger frog, darker green.

Bowl four, a skinny watersnake, banded in green and scarlet and gold, and about as long as my forearm.

Bowl five had a squawker in it, which was at least a change from the reptiles.

"Granny?"

"Hush, Rozasharn," said the woman; she was made of ice and steel, that one was, and she hadn't yet even bothered to behave like a Granny . . . certainly she'd yet to speak like one.

"You, young woman," she said, "just keep changing the bowls; and you, Responsible, you keep taking the creatures out. We'll see how this goes."

She stood at my left hand and I passed her whatever I got with each bowl. I must say the children were fascinated, especially when, after the tenth move, the bowl itself suddenly grew larger.

The Granny made a small soft noise—not alarm, but it showed she'd taken notice—and Salem Sheridan Lewis set down his own spoon and spoke up.

"I don't like that," he said. "I don't like that atall."

I didn't like it either, and I didn't know that I was going to like what came next in my alleged soup. There were several possibilities . . . it could

go from harmless creatures to poisonous ones, and I moved back from
the table enough to dodge if a snake that killed was to appear coiled up
before me next. It could go to *nasty* creatures, along the line of the
squawker, but dirtier—say, a carrion bird. Or it could go to *things,* and
that left a wide latitude of choices.

"Responsible of Brightwater," said Salem Sheridan, "put your spoon
in that bowl—this has gone too far."

But Granny Twinsorrel raised her hand, her index finger up like a
needle, and shook her head firmly.

"No, Salem Sheridan," she said, "we'll see it out awhile yet."

"Responsible of Brightwater is our *guest!*" Rozasharn of McDaniels
protested.

"As were Halliday Joseph McDaniels the 14th and his wife and son,
at Castle Brightwater not too many days past," said the Granny.

"I *am* sorry about that," I said, keeping my eye on the soup bowl as
I talked, "but I was truly not expecting mischief right in the middle of a
Solemn Service. And I am sorry that yourall's supper is being spoiled on
my account, I assure you."

"This is more fun than supper," said Boy Salem.

"This is more fun than a *picnic,*" said Charlotte, and there was general
agreement among the young ones. And I had to admit that from their point
of view it *was* all very entertaining; no doubt they'd be pleased to have me
back any time, even if it meant they all went hungry while I was there.

The entity responsible for all this fooled us, next go-round. It was
neither a coiled poison-snake, nor a carrion bird, nor yet a loathsome
mess of stuff mixed and coiled—another possibility—that gazed up at me.
It made the children clap their hands, all but Eben Nathaniel, who was
old enough to know better. And I felt Granny Twinsorrel's hand come
down hard and grip my shoulder.

"Is it real, *too?*" breathed one of the little girls, before Boy Salem
could put in his two cents' worth.

"Certainly not," said their big brother Eben Nathaniel with contempt. "There's no such thing."

And the boy had it right. There was no such thing as a unicorn, not
on Old Earth, not on Ozark, and what sat before me was only an illusion. But it was beautifully formed. About eleven inches high, not counting the gleaming single horn all fluted and spiraled, as pure white as new

snow, with its flawless tiny hoofs delicately poised in the soup broth and its beautiful eyes perfectly serene, soup or no soup. It even had about its neck a tiny bridle of gold, with a rosette of silver.

"*That* now," said Granny Twinsorrel, "you'll not touch! That's torn it. Just put your silver spoon in the bowl, Responsible of Brightwater."

The children were crying out that that would kill it, and Rozasharn of McDaniels was reassuring them that you can't kill what doesn't exist, and Salem Sheridan looked grimmer than a lot of large rocks I'd seen in my time.

Like a soapbubble, the instant my silver spoon touched the soup, the creature disappeared with an almost soundless pop. I sat there thinking, while Boy Salem—who had mightily wanted to keep the little unicorn, and I didn't blame him, I would of liked to have it my own self—was comforted. The Granny picked up the offending bowl and handed it to the servingmaid, who looked scared to death but managed to ask, "Shall I try again, then?"

"One minute," said the Granny. "Just keep your places and hold on. I intend to have my supper this night, and have it in *peace*."

She plunged her hand deep into her skirt pocket—which showed me she'd either been prepared for at least some of this or always went prepared, just in case—and pulled out wards enough to seal off a good-sized mansion. The noses of the children quivered some at the reek of the garlic, and I didn't blame them. I was sorry I dared not take off the smell . . . but we'd had scandal enough, I judged, for one evening. Garlic that didn't smell and worked nonetheless would have been an offense to decency, and we'd just have to put up with the current odiferous situation for the sake of the little ones.

When every door and window was properly warded the Granny went back to her chair and sat down.

"*Now,*" she said, "let us begin again, before we all starve and none of the food left's fit to eat. Let the soup be served, and give Responsible of Brightwater a different bowl again, and put fresh hot broth in everybody else's."

"The Granny's put out," said the servingmaid in my ear, as if I couldn't of seen that for myself, and she set down a fresh bowl of soup at my place. Where it stayed soup, though I took my first bite gingerly. I had no interest in something like a mouthful of live worms and straight pins.

"Responsible of Brightwater," said Salem Sheridan Lewis then, all of us sedately eating our soup, "because I approve of the Confederation of Continents, and because I despise mischief—not to mention treason—I approve of this Quest of yours. Our Granny has explained clear enough the manner in which it must be done and the reasoning behind it—and as I say, I approve. But I'll be right pleased when you are safely home again and we Families can go back to a normal way of life. Unlike Boy Salem there, I don't care for this sort of thing . . . it stinks of evil as well as the garlic."

Another apology seemed in order, and I made it, but he waved it aside.

"You're doing what's necessary," he said, "and from what we've heard—and seen!—it hasn't been pleasant for you so far. No need for you to be sorry for doing your plain duty."

Rozasharn of McDaniels paused between two bites and looked at Granny Twinsorrel.

"Granny," she asked, "is Responsible in any danger? Any real danger, I mean, not just folderols like this exhibition at my table?"

"Don't ask, Rozasharn," said Granny, "you'll only rattle cages. Just eat your supper."

"There's berry pie," somebody said, and I was glad to hear it. It would take more than a few creepy-crawlies in broth to spoil my pleasure in berry pie.

"What I *won't* do," Salem Sheridan Lewis went on, as if nothing had been said in between, "is have any celebration of all this. It does not strike me as seemly in any way, and I won't have it."

"But, my dear—" Rozasharn began, or tried to begin; he went right on without so much as pausing.

"I know the conditions," he said. "I know there must be some mark of your visit, and I'll not interfere with the course of things by denying you that. But it will *not* be a playparty, or a festivity, or a hunt—nothing that implies I enjoy or condone such devilment as we've just watched. Tomorrow morning, after an ordinary breakfast—properly warded, if you please, Granny Twinsorrel, and no frogs in the gravy for my breakfast biscuits, thank you!—after a *perfectly ordinary breakfast,* we will have a parade. A *solemn,* I might say a *dignified,* parade. Three times round the Castle, three times round the town, with Responsible riding between me and Rozasharn. That satisfactory, Responsible of Brightwater?"

"Quite satisfactory," I said. "But I'd like to put in a word."

"Go right to it."

"I understand your feeling about what happened just now, but I'm not at all sure that it's got anything to do with wickedness."

What I meant was that I was a lot more convinced that I could lay all this to Granny Golightly and her Magician of Rank hotting up my Quest for me than to the traitor behind the misuse of magic on Brightwater. But Salem Sheridan Lewis was not interested in my opinions.

"Magic," he said, looking at me like a bug on a pin beneath his gaze, "is for *certain* purposes. Crops. Healing. Weather. Dire peril. Naming. It is *not* for the usage we saw it given at this table, and I'll have in the Reverend and the Granny both as soon as you're gone to clean out the last trace of it. I have no trouble atall recognizing sin when I see it, young woman."

I held my tongue.

"Now," he went on, "this parade. We'll begin at seven sharp, and anybody not there on the mark will be left behind. Is that clear? Not to mention what will *happen* to any such person when we get back—I want our support set out unmistakable for all to see, and be done with it."

"You stand for the Confederation, then?" I asked, while the berry pie was being handed round. It might not of been necessary, but I liked my knots well tied, and this was a man of strong opinions.

"Responsible of Brightwater," said the Master of Castle Lewis, in a voice like the thud of an iron bell-clapper, "if every last turn-tail Kingdom on this *planet* votes against us, Castle Lewis stands for the Confederation. We'll be at the Jubilee, never you fear, and our votes where they belong."

"Hurrah!" shouted Boy Salem. Unfortunately. An Attendant scooped him out of his chair like a sea creature out of its shell, and off he went— reasonably quietly—under the young man's sturdy arm. There was apparently a standard procedure in these cases.

I rested easy that night at Castle Lewis. Granny Twinsorrel warded my room double, and my nose had grown dulled to the garlic by the time I finally found myself in one of the high hard narrow beds the Lewises considered regulation. Not even a dream to disturb me. But the sun that came flooding through my windows in the morning woke me early enough; and when Tambrey of Motley knocked at my door with my wake-up tea she found me already in my traveling dress, sitting sedately in a cedar rocker waiting for her, and only my bare feet to show I'd not been up long.

I drank the tea slowly, enjoying the peacefulness of the morning, and the well-run propriety—a tad constraining, but well-run—of this Castle, and gave over my thinking to how I'd doll Sterling up for this parade. It had to be elegant, and it needed to be memorable, but I must not *over*do it or I'd offend my host. It was a neat little problem, and the kind of thing I liked to ponder over, a good way to begin a morning.

I settled finally on something a bit beyond what Salem Sheridan Lewis would of liked, and a bit less than what *Sterling* would have—she was vain, even for a Mule. Rosettes in her ears in the Brightwater colors, and streamers braided in her tail—which I could triple-loop, for good measure—and me in my splendiferous traveling garb.

We went three times round the Castle, and three times round the town, as specified, the people lining the streets in Sundy best and cheering us on our way, holding up the babies to gawk at the glitter going by. Salem Sheridan even unbent so far as to put a single Attendant at the head of the parade with a silver horn, and allowed him to blow one long note at every third corner.

But I did not get to hear Rozasharn of McDaniels sing even one ballad, not even one *hymn,* though I asked politely enough as we returned from our three times round. That would have been too much like frivolity to suit either Rozasharn's husband, or Granny Twinsorrel, or, for that matter, Eben Nathaniel Lewis the 17th.

"She sings in church," said Salem Sheridan, "and does a very good job of it. And that's sufficient."

It was days like this that I could see the advantages of the single state most clearly.

Purdy

9

The party the Purdys gave for me went very well—I threw in a little something here and there of my own, to make sure it would. The pies that would of gotten salt in place of sugaring didn't after all—that got noticed in time. And the beer that had gone flat because somebody left it sitting out overnight acquired some new bubbles in a way that wasn't strictly natural. And when Donovan Elihu Purdy the 40th got his boot toe under a rough spot in the rug and was headed for a broken hip sure as an egg's got no right angles, he managed to land—without doing her any harm, and in fact she looked as if she rather enjoyed it—in the lap of a woman of fine substantial size. Instead of flat out on the floor.

What I was doing was known as meddling, and it was not looked on with any special favor. One of the first things a girl learned in Granny School, right there at the beginning with keeping your legs crossed and how not to scorch milk, was "Mind your own business and leave other people *be*." I hadn't forgotten.

Howsomever, I was fed up to here by that time with listening to every clattering tongue on Ozark meanmouthing the Purdys. My tolerance had been first reached and then exceeded. I had even realized, a lot more belatedly than did me any credit, that I was guilty of the same thing myself. Taking that silly Ivy of Wommack for a Purdy, for instance, for *no other reason* than that she was silly and looked like she didn't eat right. There was a name for it all, and not a very nice name either—*Prejudice*, that was its ugly name.

And I'd had time to muse some on the essential *meanness* of human beings. Isolated as they were, the Twelve Families had had no people of black skin among them, nor any of brown or yellow, either. Probably there was a smidgen of Cherokee blood someplace, from the long-ago days, but it had hundreds of years since disappeared in the inundation of Scotch, Welsh, and Irish genes that the Ozarkers carried. Only the brown eyes here and there had survived our outrageous *white*ness. And so, lacking anybody colored differently than ourselves to make our scapegoat, we'd picked the Purdys out for the role.

And of course they *filled* it, once elected, which encouraged everybody to go on with it. Naturally they did. Nothing is more sure to make you spill the tray you're carrying than knowing for certain and certain that everybody's just watching you and waiting for you to do that. Waiting so they can look at each other, and all of them be thinking, even if they scruple to say it: "Purdys! Really, they beat all!"

As I say, I'd gotten a bellyful of that, and it was on my list of things to be tackled when I got some leisure again. High time we took some Purdy daughters in hand and taught them what a self-fulfilling prophecy *was,* and how to go about canceling one.

We had a fine party, therefore. The food was good, including those pies, and the drink was good, and the bouquet presented to me with a nice rhyme on the Castle bandstand by three little girls of just the sort I had in mind was fresh and beautiful. The one sprig of blisterweed I saw behind a red daisy I threw over the bandstand railing without anybody seeing me, and I had my leather gloves on at the time. No harm done, and an easy job later getting the poisonous oil off the glove.

The Purdys were plainly worried about how much the Farsons and the Guthries had seen fit to tell me of their recent doings, and I saw no harm in that. I dropped hints; and one by one they took me aside to confess some piece of foolishness and tell me how much they regretted it. Which is good for the soul, the stomach, and the disposition.

By the time it was all over, and me tucked up in my bed—an *ample* bed, for a welcome change, that a person could stretch out in it without falling off on the floor—the Purdys were fairly glowing. They'd done themselves proud, and done me honor, and nothing had Gone Wrong. And you could see what a new and delightsome feeling that was for them.

I lay there and reviewed it in my mind as I fell asleep, and I was well satisfied. It was a start, and I'd carry it further when I got home. As for treason . . . not the Purdys. They were doing well to just get through the ordinary day, without introducing any magical complications.

And then the Gentle came to me in the night, and woke me with full formality. I was not expecting that.

"Responsible of Brightwater," it said at my bedside, "you who bear the keys and keystones, daughter of all the Grannys and mother of all the Magicians and all the Magicians of Rank—awaken and speak with me!"

I can't say I was addressed like *that* often. It brought me bolt upright instantly, clutching the bedclothes. There'd been a Responsible of Brightwater hundreds of years ago who'd perhaps been called all those things, and may have deserved them, for all I knew, but it was a new experience for me, and my teeth needed brushing, and I had not the first faintest notion what I was supposed to say. This constituted a kind of diplomatic exchange between two humanoid races, and for sure required all the formality there was going, but how exactly did you be formal in your nightgown and all mussed and grubby from sleep, and taken wholly and entirely by surprise?

I'm ashamed to say that I settled for, "Dear goodness, just a minute, please!" and added, "I shall return at once," for good measure, hoping that at least sounded hifalutin, and bolted for the dressingroom that went with my guestchamber in Castle Purdy. There wasn't time to change the night-dress, but I did add my shawl and tend to my hair and teeth and face, and I was back in my bed propped up on the pillows for audience before the Gentle could of counted to twenty-four. *Nervous,* but I was there.

This was a real Gentle, no baby trick like the Skerry on the well curb; and it was waiting for me patiently, standing there beside my bed in silence, till I should collect myself and respond in some sensible fashion. I saw that it was a female—*she,* then, was waiting for me patiently. I searched my memory for the old phrases, and prayed they'd be the right ones.

"I am happy to see you, dear friend of the Twelve Families," I began, "more happy than I can say." Was that right? I hoped so. "And may I know how you are called?"

She told me, and I found I could say it competently enough. Her name was T'an K'ib; not too difficult for an Ozarker tongue. It was for the sake of our rare speech with the Gentles that we had added the glottal stop to our Naming alphabet all those many years ago; for all the sounds of their language except that one the alphabet of Old Earth served well enough. (Not that the Gentles were interested in their name-totals, despising all magic and anything to do with magic as they did. But it delighted First Granny to put a twenty-seventh letter in the alphabet. Three nines, nine threes—*much* improved over the twenty-six we'd always had to make do with previously.)

"Greetings, T'an K'ib," I said slowly, "and I beg your pardon if my words don't come easily . . . your people visit us rarely, and we have little chance for converse. You honor me; I thank you for coming and welcome you in the name of Castle Brightwater."

It was an honor, and no mistake. The Gentles were a people so ancient we could scarcely bring the numbers to mind; their history was said to be a matter of formal *record* for more than thirty thousand years. By their reckoning we Ozarkers had only just popped up on this planet like mushrooms in a badly drained yard, and we merited about the same degree of attention. They considered us a backward and primitive race—and were probably right, from their perspective—and they saw us only when absolute necessity demanded. I had never seen a Gentle before, nor my mother either; I believe that Charity of Guthrie's mother claimed to have.

T'an K'ib wore only a hooded cloak, and wore that out of deference to Ozarker morals, I assumed. A being that is covered head to foot with soft white fur has little need for clothing. She was not quite three feet tall, if my guess was right (and I was good at judging such things), and I knew she was female because she had no beard or neckruff. Her eyes, the pupils vertical like a cat's, were thick-lashed and the color of wood violets, the deepest purple I had ever seen in a living creature.

We understood the Gentles, after a fashion; they were physically quite reasonable for the planet. The Skerrys, that were the only other intelligent species native to Ozark—unless you counted the Mules, and perhaps you'd better—we didn't understand at all. Not how their skeletons supported their height; not how their metabolisms functioned; not anything about them. No one had ever found or seen or (praise the Twelve Corners) stolen a Skerry bone, but whatever its substance was it had to be something different from what held us Ozarkers upright in our skins. The Gentles, on the other hand, could be looked upon as roughly equivalent to furred Little People without wings; and we'd been well acquainted with several Little Peoples before we ever left Old Earth. The Gentles did not alarm us; *we* alarmed *them*.

"And I greet you in the name of all the Gentles," she said to me. "We are troubled, Responsible of Brightwater, sorely troubled. I come to you on behalf of all my people to ask that you put an end to that trouble."

I wondered what sort of power she thought I had, to word her request like that, and doubted she would of known what to make of me peeling pans of potatoes at Brightwater because the Granny needed all the servingmaids to gather herbs, and had set *me* to make certain of that day's mashed potatoes. We had myths aplenty of the Gentles, and tales among the Teaching Stories; it looked as though they might also have myths of us. The idea that I figured in those myths, and maybe prominently, made me uneasy.

"I will do whatever I can do," I said.

"You can do whatever is necessary," she said at once. "And whatever is *dyst'al*."

Dyst'al. One of the few words of the Gentle speech that we understood, and fortunate for us that they had not had the same trouble learning our Panglish. *Dyst'al* meant something like "unforbidden and permitted and not beyond the bounds," and something like "good for all the people," and something like "characteristic of the actions of a reasonable and wholesome person having power," and something like "well mannered." She was telling me, clear enough, what she expected. Whether I could fulfill those expectations remained to be seen.

There was only a sliver of moonlight; she stood in the feeble ray that fell through the near window. I would have liked some light myself, because it was hard enough to judge the voice of a non-Terran even when you could see the features of the face clearly. I had learned that early, watching the threedy films again and again. But the Gentle preferred the dark, would not care for the exposure, and would be greatly offended if I were to set a glow about her; I would have to strain my ears and hope for the best.

"Be comfortable, friend T'an K'ib," I said, "and tell me what it is you want of me. Will you sit here near me, so that I may hear you more easily?"

She went to the foot of my bed and stepped handily up to sit on its turned rail, using the blanket chest placed there as a kind of step to climb on. She settled her cloak around her and let the hood fall back, and by the feeble moonlight I saw that her ears had been pierced five times—in each there hung five separate tiny crystals. *Five* crystals; this was no mere messenger, and I bowed my head slightly to acknowledge her rank.

"May I begin?" she asked.

"Please do."

"We are the Gentles," she said, "or so you call us; we are the
Ltlancanithf'al. We have been on this planet for fifty thousand years. In
our caves the inscriptions name our ancestors for more than thirty thousand of those years . . . we go far, far back into time. My people, daughter of Brightwater, were here *long* before yours."

"That is certainly true," I said carefully.

"Our claims are prior."

"That, too," I said. "Of course."

"And when your people came here, and your vessel fell into the
Outward Deeps, and only by the grace of the Goddess did any one of
you escape to set foot on our land, your people made *treaties,* Responsible
of Brightwater. Solemn treaties. We ask that they be honored."

Oh, dear. Never mind the slight conflict in the myths of the Landing,
this was no time to compare tales and quibble over the identity of res-
cuers. The question was, what did she mean—they asked that the treaties
be honored? That any Ozarker would have violated the treaties was
beyond conception, I would have staked my life on that. We *do not* break
our word.

"My friend T'an K'ib," I asked, "do you come here to tell me that
my people have violated their sworn oaths? A Gentle does not lie—but
I find that hard to believe."

And if I was wrong, and they had? I thought of blustering Delldon
Mallard Smith, the ugly man of the ugly name . . . and I thought of the
easy malicious ways of Michael Stepforth Guthrie, and I cast around in
my mind for other possibilities. No Granny would of tampered, but the
men were another matter. And if they had—what was I to do? I felt four
years old on the outside and four hundred years old on the inside, and I
hoped my brain was not as cold as the rest of me. I longed for a pentacle,
and my own Granny Hazelbide, and the safe walls of my own Castle
around me. And here I was, of all unhandy places, at Castle *Purdy.*

"Responsible of Brightwater," she said, "I would not tell you that
we are certain; I would not go so far. It may be that there has as yet been
no violation. It is to forestall such a thing that I am come to you this
night."

"Tell me, then," I said. "I will listen until you have told me everything that disturbs you; and I will not interrupt."

And she began to talk, in the faintly foreign archaic Panglish the First

Granny had taught her people, and that I had learned from many boring hours listening to the microtapes while I begged to be let go out and play instead. I blessed every one of those hours now, seeing as I understood her with ease, and I supposed she'd spent fully as many hours herself listening to the Teachers of her people, who passed down the knowledge of Panglish without benefit of tapes or any other thing but their wondrous memories and their supple throats.

There was trouble, she told me. Much trouble on Arkansaw, where the Guthries and the Farsons were even more openly feuding than had been admitted to me, by her account. Where the Purdys were frantic, trying desperately to play both sides of the feud, but faced with an eventual choice made under great pressure. There were, she told me, strange comings and goings in the nights.

"There was a meeting in what you choose to call the Wilderness Lands of Arkansaw," she said, "not three nights ago. The men there were not all of Arkansaw, some had come very far . . . some wore the crests of Kintucky and Tinaseeh, the Families known as Wommack and Traveller. It went on all the night long—our children had no sleep—and then, as *thieves* comport themselves, all stole away at first light. A Gentle does not spy, I remind you; thus, I cannot tell you what they spoke of. What we heard we heard only because a loud voice in the night carries far in an ill-mannered throat . . . but they were not telling each other pleasant tales to while away the hours. That much was clear."

She stopped for a moment, and I waited, and then she went on.

"It was sworn, Responsible of Brightwater, sworn and sealed—the Gentles were to be left alone. And none of your magic was to touch our people, for all of time. Nor were we ever to be part of your . . . feuding. If you have forgotten, I am here to remind you—so read the treaties."

I let my breath out, slowly, wondering where in me the knowledge was that I supposedly could put to use in circumstances such as these. I felt no revelations bubbling within me, no sealed-off memories with their locks dropping away.

"Has a hand been raised against you?" I asked T'an K'ib. "Any hand? Any weapon?"

"Not as of this night."

"Has any sharp word been spoken? Any threat made? Has any Ozarker actually breached the privacy of your homes, T'an K'ib?"

"Not as of this night."

"None?"

"You must understand," she said, no edge to her voice, but firm, "that what *you* consider a hand raised, or a sharp word, or privacy breached, may not be the same as what a Gentle would so judge. There are many, many thousands of us in the caves of the Wilderness Lands of Ozark, daughter of Brightwater, and we live in peace, and our lives are not tainted by sorcery. We have made adjustments unasked, when the mines of your people cut well beyond the limits given them, and we have not begrudged those adjustments, though no law held us to them."

I could imagine, thinking of the Farsons and Guthries and Purdys, always wanting to cut just a little deeper into a vein, probably shaking the Gentles in their sleep and filling their homes with gemdust, or worse. And I was ashamed.

"When I return to Castle Brightwater," I said, my voice harsh in my throat, "I will see that that is put right. *That* I can do. There will be no more encroachments on your territory, and where such has taken place, your 'adjustments' will be readjusted. My word on it, and my apologies."

She made an easy gesture with her head, as if to show how little this mattered; I, the Ozarker, felt bigger and greedier, as I was no doubt meant to feel.

"If it can be done, so be it," she said, "if not—what is past is past. But if the three Families of the continent of Arkansaw go to open war among themselves, and if the Families of Kintucky and Tinaseeh join them, blood will flow in the Wildernesses and it may well be *our* blood. That we cannot allow, daughter of Brightwater. *That* would be in violation of *all* treaties."

"War, T'an K'ib? Your people fear *war?*"

I suppose I sounded foolish; she sounded indulgent.

"It is not an exotic word," she said. "Think of guns and lasers and bombs and gases and missiles. All very small and simple Panglish words, and well known to you."

"Dear friend, dear T'an K'ib," I protested, "Ozarkers do not go to war—it was the violence of one human hand raised against another, much of it part of war and much of it without any explanation but madness, that drove us here in The Ship one thousand years ago. As a Gentle does not lie, T'an K'ib—an Ozarker does not *war!*"

"You yourself," she pointed out, "have let pass the word 'feud' without protest. Our Teachers are quite clear on the meaning of that word, and it is violent."

"Ah, T'an K'ib," I said, almost weak with relief, "it is not what it appears to be atall. This is a misunderstanding."

"Explain, please."

"You know of the Confederation of Continents of Ozark?"

"Your government," she said flatly.

"As much government as we have," I said, "and hard won. We are at a tricky *political* crossroads, we of the Confederation. And the Families you name, the ones that have so disgracefully disturbed the harmony of your homes, they are not plotting violence. They are plotting against the Confederation . . . they are plotting the casting of *votes,* not the launching of missiles! Nothing more, T'an K'ib; nothing less. There is not even a question of dominance among them."

"That makes no sense," she said. "I beg your pardon if I speak sharply, but it makes no sense."

"If," I said, "one thinks carefully of the Ozarkers—and no reason, the Twelve Corners granted, why your people should ever do anything of the kind—it does make sense. And no offense taken. First, no Ozarker lifts a hand against another, not since we left Earth; the only exception would be the occasional child, that must be taught it can't hit its playmate because there's a toy they both want at the same time, and the occasional drunken fool, that is promptly seen to and differs little from the child. I'd hazard that even among *your* people the young and the foolish must learn."

"Granted," she said.

"But what the dissenting Families want is not that one should be superior to the rest, but that all should be equal, and *no* dominance. What they want, T'an K'ib, is isolation."

"It is an absurdity."

"No doubt," I said reluctantly, my loyalty giving me a bit of trouble around the edges. "Nevertheless—it is so."

"There must be community," she said, "and this is a small planet. What you describe is anarchy."

I was reminded, a moment only, of Sharon of Clark . . . but there was a difference. This was no child who faced me, prattling memorized cant from Granny School. This was a diplomat, high in the ranks of a people whose sophistication surpassed ours as Granny Gableframe's surpassed a babe's. She knew quite well what anarchy was, and she knew what went with it. No doubt her people had seen its effects a time or two in their long history. No doubt it meant, to her and to them, rape and pillage and murder, barbarian hordes pouring through the cavehomes and tearing out the ancient tunnels as they went. She had no reason to believe an Ozarker ungoverned would behave any differently.

"They want to go back to being boones," I said, wishing sadly that there was some way to make her understand us—us aliens.

"It is not a concept that I know," said T'an K'ib. "The Teachers do not mention it."

"Nor is it a concept that will burden you unduly," I told her. "A very long time ago—by Earth reckoning—on the planet from which my people came, there was a man whose name was Daniel Boone. If he had a middle name, we have no record of it—I'm sorry. And it is written that whenever the time came that Daniel Boone could see the smoke of a neighbor's chimney from his own homeplace, those neighbors were too near, and he moved on."

The Gentles lived in chambers carved beneath the earth, and it was said that they observed a stringent privacy of manner. But they lived crowded close as twin babes in a womb, and their families were not small. I doubted she would see much sense to the story of Daniel Boone.

She was silent and small, sitting there thinking over what I had said, and possessed of a kind of presence that much larger creatures might have envied. I wished that we could have been friends. I wished that I could have visited *her*—but the Gentles saw to it that none but a very small Ozarker child could enter the doors they set up. I would never know, unless I looked in a way that the treaties forbid me, what it was like inside the caves of the Gentles. And, I reminded myself sternly, it was none of my business to know.

"Responsible of Brightwater?" she asked, finally.

"Yes, dear friend?"

"It may be that what you say is true, though it does not seem reasonable."

"To the best of my knowledge, it is true, however it sounds. And I believe my knowledge on *this* matter is reliable."

"I see . . . I *think* I see."

I thought she would leave me then, but she sat quietly, not even a shape any longer since the moonlight had waned. Evidently whatever this was, it was not over.

"Friend T'an K'ib," I hazarded, "do you want something else of me? You have only to ask."

"Your guarantee."

"Of no war? Consider it given. Of an end to mining beneath your bedchambers and your streets? Of course, I guarantee it; that it ever happened was due only to carelessness, not to malice. When I speak to the Families guilty of that, they will be deeply ashamed."

"No," she said. She shook her head, and I heard the crystals in her ears sound, softly. Little bells in the darkness. "That is not all."

"What, then?"

"*Whatever* it is that your people are about," she said, "however it may be, whether this desire to be a boone that you describe to me, or a feud, or a greater evil . . . Your guarantee, daughter of Brightwater, that we Gentles will take *no part* in any of it! No part, however small! Not even by accident . . . as you say, by carelessness."

Well, I never liked lying. I liked lying to a Gentle even less than I liked ordinary lying; since they did not lie, they were as vulnerable to it as they would have been to the kick of a boot. More so; the kick they could at least have seen coming. However, there are times when a person does what she must. I gave her her guarantee, all solemn and sealed and packaged in phrases that made me feel silly even to use them, and she went away as unheralded as she had come, leaving me to toss fretfully through the rest of that night. My conscience was raw in me.

What I hadn't dared tell her was that there was only one way that I could make my guarantees real. What her myths said I had in the way of power I did not know; her people had royalty, and perhaps the ancient rights that went with that. I had none.

I could do what she asked of me, yes. But only in one way. Only by setting wards of the strongest (and from her point of view, the foulest and most barbaric) magic known to me, around every cave and every burrow and every smallest scrap of Wilderness her people inhabited. It was a flagrant violation of the treaties she had mentioned with every other breath; it was also the only way that what had to be done *could* be done. And at that it would have to wait till I was back at Castle Brightwater and had all my laboratories and my Magicians at my disposal—and I had not told her that, either. I supposed she would tell her people there was to be no delay.

I knew perfectly well that she would rather have died, and all her kin with her, than be protected by the magic they so abhorred—by "sorceries." For sure, it would *not* be judged *dyst'al*. And I did not intend to be the person that shattered illusions that had lasted tens of thousands of years, or the person that ended up with the lives of such a people and their blood on her hands. It might be there was some other way out, something I should have thought of, but it did not come to my mind, and I was colder than I had ever been in my life; and I gathered what little of my wits I had left about me, and I lied.

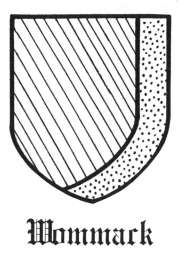

Wommack

10

Castle Wommack sat high at the northwest corner of Kintucky, in a landscape of tangled trees and thick ground cover, steep hills and ragged cliffs and crags; only Tinaseeh was wilder, and not by much. The Castle was bigger than it needed to be, rambling along the edge of a bluff above a ravine at the bottom of which there surely flowed a river, though I couldn't see it from the air. I would of guessed it to be at least twice the size of Castle Brightwater, and larger than any castle on Arkansaw, the Farsons' included. And I could understand why, though I might privately question the use of so much time and energy for a single structure. The natural stone it was built of was abundant—if they hadn't used it to build the Castle they'd of had to cart the stuff away and fill up ravines with it, after all. Every time I flew low to get a look at the land I saw stretches where boulders big as squawker coops were strewn around like so much carelessly flung salt, leaving the vegetation to grow over and around and in between the jutting stones as best it could . . . and I was not looking at the Wilderness Lands, mind you. This was the "cleared" area of Kintucky.

Furthermore, even the size it was, Castle Wommack was dwarfed by the country round it, and looked like a doll's castle more than a proper human dwelling. No doubt they drew some comfort from its size through the long winters when the winds howled down those ravines and ripped up huge trees by the roots, to pile them in heaps against the bald faces of the bluffs. I could see the point to it.

It was four days' hard flying at regulation speed from Castle Purdy to Castle Wommack, and except for a brief stretch over the Ocean of Storms between the two continents I had not done any distance by SNAP-PING. I was running out of anything to read, for one thing. And then this country was new to me, the Twelve Corners only knew when I might get back this way again, and I felt it behooved me to see all I could and note it well.

Once I left the coast of Arkansaw and was beyond the shipping lanes, all the way over that vast country up almost to the edge of the town built around Castle Wommack, I saw nary a soul. There were farms—clearly very large farms, and why not?—spread out over the surface of the land. And every now and again I would see the telltale white line of a fence built of that same stone, running along the edge of a cleared field, or catch sight maybe of light glancing off solar collectors on a roof. But not until I actually neared Booneville, the capital (and only) city of Kintucky, not till I saw the Castle ahead of me, did I begin to see people. Kintucky had only been settled in 2339, just ten years before Tinaseeh, and the latest figures I had for the whole kingdom showed under seven thousand citizens living here. More than a third of those lived in or near Booneville itself.

They met me properly at the Castle, and made me welcome; Jacob Donahue Wommack the 23rd, a widower these past two years, and his five sons and seven daughters, and numerous wives and husbands. There was a band playing as I brought Sterling down on the roadway winding up to the Castle gates, and people lining both sides throwing flowers and waving bright banners. Seven Attendants in green and silver Wommack livery followed me up the ramp and through the gates. And where I could catch glimpses of the streets and buildings of the town I saw that they'd hung garlands everywhere there was something to hang a garland *on*. Booneville was decked out for full festival in my honor, and I was surprised; I supposed it must come of the loneliness out here, and so few occasions for any kind of partying. Considering the hasty excuses for celebrations thrown together along my way so far, it made me smile; I tried, without any success, to imagine my cousin Anne at Castle McDaniels going to all this trouble for me, or the stern Lewises even *countenancing* such a fuss.

The inner court of Castle Wommack, inside the gates, was the size of a respectable playing field; you could have raced Mules there without much inconvenience. And they had it set up for a fair, with long tables of food and drink, and strolling singers and dancers, and a whole play being put on on a stage that fit neatly into a far corner, and crowds of young people milling in their Sundy best. They led Sterling away to their stables and then turned their energies to entertaining me, with a dogged determination that was at first highly flattering. And then, after a while, it began to make me uneasy.

I was sitting on a low bench with Jacob Donahue and three of his daughters, watching twelve couples move through an elaborate circle dance done to the tune of dulcimer, guitar, and fiddle, finishing my fourth mug of excellent dark ale and much too full from the food they'd been plying me with, when I finally realized that things were genuinely *odd*. True—they were celebrating my visit as no other Castle had even considered celebrating it, so far as I could tell. True—the sounds in the inner court, and those that floated in over the walls from the town, were all laughter and song and merrymaking and pleasure. But there was something strange . . . and then, all at once, I knew what it was.

The broad front of Castle Wommack, five stories high of pearly white stone, forming a great muleshoe shape around that court, had windows everywhere. I took time to count those on the first story alone, and there were forty of them; multiply that by five and you got roughly two hundred windows facing on this court, give or take a dozen for variations.

And every last blessed one of them was not only empty of the people I would of expected to see looking down on the fair and taking part from above us; it was closed tight as a tick, and shuttered.

I clapped politely for the circle dance as it drew to its close, and clapped again for the musicians, and took time to smile at a small boy that had decided he was a juggler and was doing three pieces of fruit considerable harm right under my nose. And then I stood up, brushed off my skirts, and said: "I'll be going in now, ladies; Jacob Donahue Wommack."

A daughter named Gilead, freckled and slender and twenty-odd, stood up with me. "It's much pleasanter out here," she said, "and I can recommend the cake they're setting out down beside the stage; it's extra good lightcake, and you haven't had any of it yet, I don't believe."

"The reason it's pleasanter out here," I said, measuring my words to make them fall with proper force, "is because whoever is in *there*"—I pointed to the front of the Castle proper—"is suffocating."

"Daddy," said Gilead of Wommack, "I believe she's noticed."

"That I have," I snapped.

"My dear young woman," Jacob Donahue began, but I cut him off short.

"I'll be going in now," I said. "If you care to come with me, you're welcome; if you prefer to stay out here while your faces crack, pretending to be having fun, that's your privilege. Youall do just as you like—but *I* am going inside and see what's back of your shutters."

I looked at them again, row on row of heavy wooden eyes all shut tight and black against the stone, and I shuddered. A good job they'd done of keeping me distracted, that I'd sat out here for near two hours and not seen that!

"We'll go with you, Responsible," said Gilead, and the other two stood to join us. "But most of these people *are* having fun, and I'm pleased that they are. It's a hard life here, and not much in the way of party times—don't let's spoil it for them."

The false cheer dropped off Jacob Donahue like a scarf off a sloped shoulder as he stood up, slowly, and I could see that he was in fact wholly miserable.

"Like Gilead says," he told me, "we'll come along . . . but I'd be grateful if we do it without drawing any attention. I've no more mind to spoil the others' day than my daughters have. You, girls, you see to it that Responsible is sort of tucked away among the rest of you, and don't act as if we were in any hurry to get anywhere."

We *strolled,* therefore, over to the Castle and in through its front door. My feet were itching to run, as much from annoyance at my own thick head as anything else, but I did as Jacob Donahue bid, and—eventually—we were inside.

Inside, and the door closed behind us, and the silence of an empty church. Not one laugh, not one note of music, came through those shutters, which was no doubt the intention. The fair might as well of been back on Marktwain; it did not exist inside this Castle.

"Well, well, well," I said, "this is a pretty pass! What's happening here at Castle Wommack to account for this?"

From the top of a stairway ahead of me a woman's voice called down, and I peered up in the dimness to see if I knew the face that went with it, but it was a stranger. She wore plain enough dress to suit even the Lewises, her hair was pulled back and tucked into a kerchief, and she carried a basin of steaming liquid in her hands.

"We've sickness here, young miss of Brightwater," she said in a bitter voice. "*That's* what's 'happening' here! Mr. Wommack, there's another three taken with it just since you went out this morning, and I'm truly scared at the way Granny Goodweather looks. . . . I don't know what to do for her, and the Magician says he doesn't either—what next, I ask you, Mr. Wommack? I'm at the end of my wits!"

"Your Granny is sick?" I asked. I was astonished. A Granny was human, of course, but it was their job to *tend* the sick, not lie among them. It was obligatory for a Granny to suffer from "rheumatism," that went with the territory, but I couldn't remember any Granny ever being *really* sick for more than an hour or two, or dying any other way than peacefully in her bed at an age well beyond one hundred years.

"Both of them, miss," said the woman on the stairs. "Granny Goodweather was taken first two days ago; and then yesterday Granny Copperdell as well . . . and they'd both been poorly, I'd remarked on that."

I turned on the Wommacks behind me to demand of them exactly what they'd been *doing* about this—sick Grannys, indeed!—but one look was enough to close my mouth. They were Wommacks, that was all that was wrong with them; they'd of done nothing, or as near to nothing as couldn't be noticed.

The Purdys, now, were forever in some sort of mess, and usually by their own stupidity. But they did put some effort into their actions. (They would in fact have been better off if they'd learned to put in less; usually they got themselves so entangled and benastied that it took more effort to extricate them than it would of just keeping them out of it all from the beginning.)

With the Wommacks, it was different. They were capable people, and intelligent, and sensible. About most things, that is. So long as whatever obstacle faced the Wommacks couldn't be laid at the door of the famous Wommack bad *luck,* they just turned to and took care of things. Bad luck, though, the Wommack curse, the long burden of paying and paying for the Granny that had laid out the Improper Name . . . anything that seemed due to that, they just gave up on, on the principle that it was no use trying in such a situation. This, I gathered, was one of those situations.

I tucked up my skirts then and ran up the stairs toward the woman that still stood there, the water in her basin getting colder by the passing minute, if it was water, and paid the family behind me no more mind.

"You're Castle staff?" I asked the laggard nurse, and she nodded.

"Your name, please."

"Violet," she said. "Violet of Smith."

"Very well, Violet of Smith—take me this instant to the sickroom, and let me see how bad things are in this place!"

"Which sickroom, miss?" she asked me. "We've nothing but sickrooms on this whole second floor."

"How *many* are down?" I demanded, but she only shrugged.

"I've lost count, miss . . . might could be thirty, might could be twice that."

"And both your Grannys."

"And both our Grannys."

"Well, take me to Granny Copperdell, then," I said, "and set down that basin—whatever it is, it's no use to anybody now."

She turned without a word, but I had to take the useless basin from her hands myself, and I followed where she led me. I could smell the sickness now, and I wanted those windows open at the front of the Castle, and fresh air in here as fast as it could decently be accomplished.

"Are many people sick in the town?" I asked her, wishing she'd hurry.

"Oh no, miss," she said. "Not in the town. Only in the Castle."

Hmmmph. That would be fuel for the dratted Wommack curse, of course.

She knocked twice at a doorway, and then opened it and stood aside to let me pass, saying, "That's Granny Copperdell there in the bed, miss, and I hope you can do something for her, for I surely can't. And I'm too busy to stay with you, so you'll excuse me, please." And she was gone.

"Well, Granny Copperdell!" I said, making it a cautious challenge. "So this is how you run things!"

Hers was the only bed in the room, and she was tiny in it; three featherbeds under her, I was willing to wager, and half a dozen pillows propping her up in them.

"Land, who is it bothering me *now?*" came from the depths of the bedclothes, and I saw an encouraging flurry. "Can't leave an old woman to die in peace, can you? Come near me and torment me again with one of your so-called Magicians and you'll find *out* if I'm sick, I warn you, and me that's *sick and tired* of *warning* youall! Magicians! Phaugh—what's a Magician know about healing? No more use than—Well, who *be* you?"

It did my heart good. She might be sick, but she surely was not dying. She was behaving absolutely as a Granny ought to behave, and that meant I'd get useful information here at least.

"It's only me, Granny Copperdell, Responsible of Brightwater," I said. "And sorry to see you so poorly. May I come sit by you there?"

"Come ahead," she ranted, "come right ahead! Why ask? If it's not one sort of meanness, it'll be another . . . why can't you stay home where you belong 'stead of meddling in our affairs, and tormenting an old woman as is about to draw her last breath?"

I tried the bed, but it was impossible; you sank into the featherbeds and disappeared from sight unless you weighed no more than a Granny, and that did not apply to me.

"You get a chair and get yourself off my bed!" she ordered me, whacking at me with a handkerchief like I was a gerdafly; and I did so gladly, pulling the chair up close beside her head.

"Now, Granny Copperdell," I said firmly, "there's no need for you to keep on with your carry-on. It doesn't impress me, and I'll be no use here if I don't hear some sense and hear it quick."

"Likely," she said. "Likely!"

"Granny, you know I'm right," I said, "you a Brightwater by birth; and every Castle on this planet knows quite well why I'm traveling round it. You're in a wild place here for sure, but this high up the reception on your comsets is certain to be perfect. *You* know why I'm here!"

"Took you long enough," she muttered.

"No comset on my Mule, Granny," I said. "I've been four days, and all of them *long* days, flying here, and I've landed only to make my camp and sleep; I've had no news. If I'd known there was trouble here I'd not of stopped for anything."

She sighed then, and settled back, and I plumped up her pillows for her.

"Speak up, Granny Copperdell," I said. "For I've had not one sensible word out of anybody else in this house—what am I up against?"

"Three days ago, it began," she said. "You'd already of left Castle Purdy, I reckon."

"Started sudden?"

"A child's sitting on a windowsill, playing with a pretty and eating a biscuit, happy and fit as a bird," she told me. "And then in two breaths that child is burning alive with fever, and racked head to foot with misery, and writhing like a birthing woman, fit to break your heart. I've never seen anything, not anything, so quick."

I touched her forehead, though she pulled away from my hand; it was blazing hot.

"What kind of sickness is it?" I asked her.

"Well, I wish I *knew* that!" she said, fretting, and turned her head side to side on the pillows. "Think I'd be lying here like an old fool if I knew that? If I knew even the name, it might could be I'd know what to tell the idiot females in this Castle to do . . . what's its name, that's half the battle won any time."

"And the Magician doesn't know either."

I said that under my breath, thinking out loud, and regretted it immediately. A Magician could set bones, and take out sick and useless organs such as an appendix, and deal with cancers. If it had been any of those, the Magician would already have taken care of the matter. And there was no Magician of Rank on Kintucky.

"I'm sorry, Granny Copperdell," I said, before she could start on me. "I wasn't thinking straight; just forget I said it. But you help me . . . tell me the symptoms of this stuff. Even the little things that you don't really think matter."

"High fever," she said, reciting it like a lesson. "Racking pain in every joint and bone and muscle. That's likely the worst of it, that pain. All the lymph glands swollen and tender, especially in the armpits. A bloody flux, and pain high on the right of the belly. Rash around the ankles and the hands, and a flaming red patch over both cheeks. Sores in the mouth, sores in the privates. . . . Hurts to breathe, hurts to swallow, hurts to hear any noise much over a whisper—that's why the windows are shuttered, child."

"What have you tried for it?"

"Everything a Granny knows, and some made up new," she said. "And none of it any use." She was in no danger, but she was exhuasted, and I was wearying her more. "I'm not a good patient for you to be observing," she said accurately, "I'm hardly touched with it yet, and tough as I am I doubt it'll get much worse. You go look at the others and you'll see what it's like."

"Can I get you anything, Granny, before I do that?"

"You can get *on* with it, and leave off pestering me!"

I plumped the pillows up again, and checked to see that the water was easy to her reach, and I went on out and closed the door behind me. She'd keep a long while yet.

Ah, but the others; they were another matter altogether. I counted fifty-one, and they were truly sick. Even Granny Goodweather. She didn't so much as ask me my name when I leaned over her, and that frightened me.

They lay in their beds and they twisted, slowly—I can think of no other way to describe it. As if they hung from intolerable bonds. One arm would stretch, the fingers spread like claws, pushing, pushing till I thought the fingerjoints would crack, and then the other arm, pushing against some unseen wall. And then the legs, one at a time, stretching till the soles of the bent feet lay flat against the mattress. And no more would the foot reach its terrible extension than it began to move back upon itself . . . and then the arms would start. It was like a horrible, endless, solemn, tortured, dance of death; and it was very clear that it hurt them like raw flames. There were women from the town trying to tend them, but I could see that they weren't accomplishing much. Changing the bedlinens and bathing flesh, bringing them water to drink and soothing the little ones . . . that seemed to be it.

As for treason, the thought was indecent. The Wommacks were so grimly convinced their whole household was cursed that they considered the most absolute neutrality no more than their duty toward their fellows. Even when they were without other troubles to distract them, no Wommack took sides, for fear their bad luck would rub off on the side they'd chosen. With things as they were here right now, I could put all else out of my mind and consider only this sickness.

As it happened, I did know what it was. But I wasn't that surprised the Grannys hadn't recognized it, especially since they'd come down with it almost immediately themselves. They'd not really had time to think before their own fever set in, and it was not a common disease.

I went down the stairs and found the Wommacks still gathered there silently, waiting for me, and I had a strong suspicion looking at them that most—including the Master of this Castle—would be in their beds themselves before the day was out. Considering the number sick upstairs, they'd made a brave showing, and I credited them for that; but not a one that wasn't white around the mouth, and the red tinge coming up on their cheeks, hectic, and a line of beads of moisture at the edge of the coppery hair to betray them further. All that time out in the sun with me had surely done them no good, and I'd of bet the party food they'd put down lay heavy in their stomachs this minute like Kintucky stone.

"I know what it is," I said to them, not bothering to dawdle and back and fill.

"But neither of the Grannys had any idea, nor the Magician either!" objected a thin boy by the name of Thomas Lincoln Wommack the 9th.

"Well, I *do*," I said, "whoever does or doesn't, and the Grannys would of known, too, if they hadn't been taken themselves before they could run it down. What you have upstairs, by my count, is fifty-one cases of something called Anderson's Disease. Or, if you prefer less formality, some call it deathdance fever—which does describe it. And looking at youall, I see a few more cases to add to the count—you'd better every one of you get to your beds."

"And those upstairs?" asked Gilead.

"You need capable people up there, taking care of your sick," I said. "Not townswomen wandering around wondering where to fling water next. It's no trifle, this disease, people can *die* of it! Why haven't you sent for help?"

They looked at me, and I looked back, and I said a broad word, not caring particularly if I did shock their sensibilities. They hadn't sent for help because, being the Wommacks, they figured it would be no use anyway. Bad luck was bad luck, and those as were marked for death would die, and a lot of similarly superstitious nonsense. And I was very grateful that none of them knew something I wasn't going to take time to think about right now, which was that Anderson's Disease was *not* contagious. If they'd known that, and it running through their castle like wildfire, I daresay they'd of just given up and died on me on the spot; I had no plans of telling them.

"Shame on you!" I said. It was uppity of me, and not kind, especially toward Jacob Donahue, who was a good fifty years my senior. But I was thoroughly disgusted. The idea of half a hundred people stretched on the rack for the last three days while helpless hands were wrung and mournful moans were made about the Wommack curse . . . it turned my stomach. Eventually I would have to face the problem of just who among the Magicians of Rank was behind this monstrous cruelty, but not now. Now what mattered was putting an end to that cruelty, and without delay.

"You need a Magician of Rank here," I said, "and you need him at once. There's two good ones on Arkansaw—"

"We'll have nobody from Arkansaw," said Jacob Donahue Wommack.

"I beg your pardon?"

"I say, we'll have nobody, Magician of Rank or anybody else, from Arkansaw. Not in this Castle."

"In the name of the Twelve Gates and the Twelve *Corners,* Jacob Donahue Wommack, why *ever not?*" I shouted at him. "Have you seen those people upstairs?"

"I've seen them. I live here."

"Then—"

"They're feuding on Arkansaw," he said doggedly, "and have been these past six months. No talking them out of it, either—we've had good men trying. And we want no part of it."

"At a time like *this,* you—"

I was so furious it's likely just as well that Gilead cut me off.

"Responsible of Brightwater," she said, "since distance makes no difference to a Magician of Rank, then it also makes no difference where he comes from. Do think of that."

True enough. Since a Magician of Rank was not only allowed, but *expected* to take his Mule by SNAPS instead of trundling along at sixty miles an hour, and since there was, strictly speaking, no time taken up by that process except leaving and landing, she was quite right.

"What will you accept, then?" I asked them, trying to sound a tad less arrogant.

"Anywhere but Arkansaw," said the Master of Wommack. "Anywhere atall."

"From Castle Motley, then," I said. "I don't know the man well, I've only seen him once or twice, but they say he's highly skilled. To go on with, he's a Lewis by birth, and that means he cuts *no* corners—everything done strictly by rule, and strictly by the book. And we'll have Diamond of Motley send a Granny along as well, to give him a hand."

"You think it's worth a try?" asked Gilead.

"I do." Worth a try . . . I had no stomach left for arguing with these people. If and when I ever got back home, and the Jubilee over and done with, and could put my mind to something new in the way of planning, I would tackle the problem of superstition gotten out of hand in far corners. We for sure wanted the people accepting the system of magic by which this planet functioned; to lose that would be roughly comparable to losing photosynthesis, or gravity, or two and two coming up five. But this was 3012, not 1400 of Old Earth. Some balancing needed doing, clearly, or this crew would be throwing entrails and dunking for witches.

Somewhere in the back of my mind a kind of icy voice spoke up to point out that the list of things to be seen to in some vaporous unspecified "later" was getting longer and longer; and I told it to shut up. Now was not the moment for either accounting or reform.

"Jacob Donahue," I said, "will you show me where your comset room is, so that I can send for help? Or do you plan to stand there like that till everybody upstairs is dead in their beds?"

That brought him out of it, as I had expected it would.

"I'm not helpless, young woman," he said, "nor yet crippled. I'll send the message myself." And he spun on his heel—staggering only a little at the turn with his fever—and left us, with his children staring at me accusingly. I'd made their daddy unhappy, and they didn't care for that.

There was a low bench against the wall beside the Castle door at the foot of the stairs; I went on down and sat there, leaning my head gratefully back against the chilly stone. I was trembling all over. And young Thomas Lincoln came over to stand in front of me.

"Will the Magician of Rank be able to fix everybody?" he wanted to know.

"Well," I said wearily, "those as aren't too far gone, yes—he'll be able to fix them about as fast as you can say 'Magician of Rank.' He won't be able to help anyone that's really near to death—that's interfering with the laws of things, Thomas Lincoln. I'm sorry, but that's the straight of it."

"We should of sent for him sooner," said the boy.

"That you should."

"Wommacks don't care to be beholden," he told me stiffly.

"Then Wommacks must live with the consequences of their doings," I said right back.

"Responsible of Brightwater, don't be hard on the boy," one of the daughters pleaded, but I wasn't interested. If they'd called for a Magician of Rank the instant their Grannys had said they didn't know what sickness they were dealing with, *nobody* would have been in any danger. Not one person. Now . . . a lot of time had passed, and a lot of suffering endured. Now, they'd be losing some of their own, to their own stupidity.

The time had come for another judicious lie, and I mustered up the strength to provide it.

"It will spread to the town unless it's seen to," I said, "and on beyond—it's stuff that spreads like wildfire. Only two things have kept that from happening before this, you hear me there? One is the size of this place, with you able to keep everybody in a room of their own; that's helped. But primarily, my good Wommacks, what's kept your illness inside this Castle is nothing but *good luck*. Plain old miraculous twelvesquare common garden variety *good luck*. Now you think on that."

A drop in the bucket, but mine own drop.

"And if your father should happen to forget, because he's got the stuff himself and I'd judge his fever's headed for this roof, the name of it is Anderson's Disease, and the access code for the computers is somewhere in the 441's. If—"

And there sat a Magician of Rank, in full regalia, with Granny Scrabble of Castle Motley seated before him on his Mule, right in the front hall on the clean-scrubbed flagstone floor.

"Mercy!" I said, and decided to stay where I was. They could get down off that animal's back, and call for an Attendant to take it away, all by themselves. I was duly impressed.

"Shawn Merryweather Lewis the 7th," said the man, "and Granny Scrabble. Both of Castle Motley, at your service."

"It's all upstairs," I told him, "and there's enough of it to last you. Fifty-odd sick of Anderson's Disease. And two of them Grannys—you might see to those two first, so they can help."

I watched them up the stairs with a feeling of relief as wide as the Castle front; it was a pure pleasure to put some of this in other hands and know they were capable. I could tell by the set of his shoulders, and the way he wasted not one second—not to mention the fact that the Granny had not opened her mouth either to fuss or to oppose him—that Shawn Merryweather Lewis the 7th could handle all of this without any further attention from me.

"Responsible of Brightwater," Gilead's voice came softly, then, "let me see you to your room. We're not completely without breeding here, though it may look some like it at this moment."

"No," I said, "you've shown breeding and to spare, Gilead of Wommack. I give you my word—*no*where on Ozark, in no Kingdom of the Twelve Families, have I been treated with the ceremony I was treated with here. And I can't really say as I expect Castle Traveller to top you. It just wasn't the best way to handle things . . . us down here celebrating while your people were in that pitiful state upstairs."

"We weren't thinking clearly . . . or maybe we don't know *how* to think clearly," she said in a voice both dull and bitter.

"Gilead," I said, "it's not lack of breeding you've shown this day, but lack of proportion. Lack of *balance,* Gilead. And I lay it to just one place— you are sick yourself; of course you can't think clearly. Now I'll take you up on the offer of the room, because I'm worn out, and I intend to sleep the rest of the day, unless I'm needed. But you'll take me nowhere—I want every one of you to your *own* beds, and that right smartly—and I'll see to myself. Just give me instructions. So many flights of stairs, so many halls, so many doors—I'll find it, you just number them off."

Gilead of Wommack stood there, rubbing the end of her nose with one finger and frowning, all of them looking like they'd drop around her, and me doing my best to be patient. And then she said, "I know!" and put her arm around Thomas Lincoln. "Thomas Lincoln? You go holler at your uncle to see Miss Responsible to her room! Move, now!"

His uncle. I thought a bit; who would that be? I kept good enough reckoning of the Families near Marktwain, and could give you the names of all direct lines on Ozark, but I hadn't every aunt, uncle, and cousin at the tip of my tongue.

And I had forgotten this one. I had forgotten all about him, or I would have run like a baby that's pulled a Mule's tail by mistake. I'd heard about him, more than enough to warn me off and make me careful, espe- cially since my experience with Michael Stepforth Guthrie'd provided me with some new data on my current state of vulnerability to manly charms . . . but I had purely forgotten all about him.

When he stood before me, I looked into his eyes, and him smiling, and *knowing;* and I saw that I could fall forever into those eyes, and drown for all of time, and still not get to the bottom of what lay behind them. I was not ready for that yet, not by any number of long shots.

Traveller

11

I had been warned about him, most certainly—I'd been properly raised —but I had only been five years and one month old. Me and fourteen other little girls, all at Granny School together. All listening to the Teaching Stories and getting them by heart, like any other little girls.

And my own beloved Granny Hazelbide, holding me tight between her bony knees, and pinching my chin between her first finger and her thumb until it hurt, so I couldn't look away.

"Pay heed, now," she had said, scaring me as well as the others sitting in a circle on the floor of the schoolroom watching. "This has come to Responsible of Brightwater, as it happens, but it might of been any of you, *any one* of you! Might could be it still will . . . you pay heed."

He had been there in my five-year-old palm, which was already hard from climbing trees and weeding with an Oldtime Hoe, and already quick with every kind of needle (some of them not very nice). And in the leaves at the bottom of seven cups of tea, made seven times on seven consecutive days. And in the swing of the golden ring on its long chain. They'd tried again and again to read a fartime that hadn't him in it, but all in vain; he was always there.

It was called a Timecorner.

"I can't see round it," said Granny Hazelbide. "Nor can any Magician, or even Magician of Rank. Can't anybody see round it, for it's purely and wholly sealed off from *this* time."

You see I had not exactly forgotten it. More accurately, I had just shut it away in that corner of my head where things that didn't bear thinking about were stored. But I couldn't recall it coming to my mind the past five years at least, which was doing a pretty good job of keeping it

at the bottom of the heap. I had no trouble getting to it, when the time
came. It had these parts:

FIRST:

For a Destroyer shall come out of the West; and he will know
you, and you will know him, and we cannot see how that
knowledge passes between you, but it is not of the body.

SECOND:

And if you stand against him, there will be great Trouble.
And if you cannot stand against him, there will be great
Trouble. But the two Troubles will be of different kinds. And
we cannot see what either Trouble is, nor which course you
should or will take, but only that both will be terrible and
perhaps more than you can bear.

THIRD:

And if you fail, Responsible of Brightwater, the penalty for
your failure falls on the Twelve Families; and if you stand, it
is the Twelve Families that you spare.

FOURTH:

And no matter what happens, it will be a long, hard time.

Well, you talk of your curses! I recall suggesting to Granny Hazelbide
that the whole thing would be more suitable for my sister, Troublesome,
and no doubt that was true. And I remember being told that things were
far more often *un*suitable, and for sure *that* was true. And then I had put
it away, and I believe I had expected it to be something I had to face
along around the age of forty-nine or so. That would of seemed like giving me at least a running start.

Since it was thirty years and more before I had planned for it, and
since I was certainly not ready either to stand *or* fall, and since I was in
the middle of a Quest at the time, not to mention a Grand Jubilee dangling just ahead of me, I chose the most prudent course I saw before me.
This was no time for theatrics. This was no time for flinging myself in
the teeth of the winds to see what was at the very bottom of that teacup.
I was *busy!*

I knew him all right, and he knew me, and when I fled him like a
squawker hen flees a carrion bird he was laughing fit to kill. I did not
spend the night at Castle Wommack, nor so much as go to the room

where they'd put my belongings. My weariness melted away like snow
in the sun, a servingmaid brought me my packed bags right there where
I sat on that bench against the wall, tapping my foot, and a stablemaid
brought round my Mule; and I flung the saddlebags over Sterling's back
and took off from the middle of the fair still going on in the Castle court,
while *he* stood on the steps with his hands on his hips, laughing. What
Gilead of Wommack or any of the others thought, I had no idea, and I
didn't wait to see.

It was ten days' travel, regulation speed, from Castle Wommack to
Castle Traveller, most of it over Wilderness that had never even been
walked through, from the far northwest tip of Kintucky to the far southern coast of Tinaseeh. And if there was one person any ten flown miles
I'd be mighty surprised, which meant that I didn't have to be careful.
There'd be nobody around to appreciate it, and in my state just then that
was a blessing.

I SNAPPED straight from the edge of Kintucky's farming country to the
exact center of the Tinaseeh Wilderness—a five-day journey in right on
seven seconds—and headed Sterling down toward the treetops I saw below
me. I camped in a cave that would have satisfied a human-size Gentle, and
rested the full five days. I needed the rest. Then I waited two more days
for good measure, putting them to sensible use gathering herbs growing all
around my camp; and I SNAPPED to the coast of Tinaseeh's Midland Sea. I
flew in to Castle Traveller in the ordinary way, right on time.

By then I'd acquired a certain new respect for the Family Traveller,
and a feeling that their name was a fitting one and well earned. Tinaseeh
made Kintucky look like a kitchen garden.

"There it is, Sterling," I said as we came in. "Castle Traveller, just
as described." First, an outer keep of upright Tinaseeh ironwood logs,
standing side by side with their wicked points an exact twelve feet tall—
not an inch deviation allowed anywhere. Then two inner keeps, made
exactly the same way, one within the other. At the heart of the third
keep, the Castle itself, not much bigger than Castle Lewis. And there was
no town, though it had the name of one and one was planned—Roebuck.
The buildings of "Roebuck" hugged in orderly rows to the walls of the
Castle keeps. There'd been no time yet on Tinaseeh for such a thing as
a separate town.

According to the computers, there were exactly eleven hundred and
thirteen people on this continent, and all but a half-dozen were Travellers,

Farsons, Guthries, and a stray Wommack or two. And every structure here was built of Tinaseeh ironwood, which would not burn, and could only be cut with a lasersaw, and which could—with sufficient patience— be tooled by laser to an edge that a person could shave with. I had seen friendlier-looking places.

I was met at the gates of the outer keep by an Attendant, who sent me under escort to the gate of the next keep beyond, where they passed me on to a third to take me up to the Castle gates, and not a word said the whole time beyond regulations.

"Greetings, Responsible of Brightwater; follow me."

I followed.

I had not expected parties here, or parades, or fairs. I knew better. A formal dinner—for twelve—I had expected. And I was prepared for one Solemn Service after another; that would strike the Travellers as entertainment enough. Ordinary Solemn Service on Tinaseeh began on Sundy at 7:00 of the morning and lasted past noon, to be followed by another session after a two-hour break for dinner. I had anticipated that a *company* Solemn Service might well provide me with preaching enough to fortify me against all the evil I'd have to contend with for the next year or two. I'd expected a *substantial* edification of my soul.

But I was not prepared for what actually did take place, which was that ten minutes after I'd freshened up—with an Attendant standing in my door waiting with an eloquent back to me, seeing that I didn't tarry over it—I was taken without further ado to a formal Family Council. Hospitable, it wasn't, and I felt a sudden steadying in my stomach. This— which was glorified sass, by the look of it—was more in my line of experience than what I'd just been through at Wommack. If it turned out sufficiently extravagant it would even give me something I needed badly . . . something to keep my unruly mind in order yet a while.

The Meetingroom had walls of varnished ironwood, and it held a group of people that appeared to be put together of the same unappealing substance, seated in straight chairs around a long narrow table. They reminded me of the side-by-side upright logs that fenced their keeps, and my traveling costume stood out in the grim and the gloom like a carnival garb.

"Young woman," said the man at the head of the table, "I am Jeremiah Thomas Traveller the 26th; be seated."

I sat, and he named them off. His wife, Suzannah of Farson. His three oldest sons: Jeremiah Thomas the 27th, Nahum Micah the 4th, and Stephen Phillip the 30th . . . why he wasn't Obadiah Jonas I couldn't imagine; perhaps Suzannah had pleaded for some relief. His three oldest daughters still at home—Rosemary, Chastity, and Miranda, every one of them a six. His brother, Valen Marion Traveller the 9th. And his own mother, now a Granny in this Castle, Granny Leeward. Not another wife, not a husband, not a child; just the in-Family.

"And I," I said, "am Responsible of Brightwater. As you are aware."

"We are that," said Suzannah of Farson. "It could hardly be missed." Her reference was to my outfit, which was in marked contrast to her own dress of dark gray belted with black. I smiled at her, sweet as cinnamon sugar, and waited the move.

"We have called this Council in your honor," she said, "and would like to begin. But you've had a long journey—are you hungry? Or thirsty? We can have coffee brought, and some food, if you need it."

"Thank you," I said, "I had breakfast before I left."

"Considerate of you," said Suzannah. "We have little time to waste here on Tinaseeh. It's a hard land, and not meant for the shiftless."

"Proceed, then," I told her. "You've no need to coddle *me*, I assure you; I'm perfectly comfortable. And I've been in Council a time or two before. I expect you'll find me able to tolerate yours."

"Are you trying to be insolent, missy?" said the Granny, her mouth tight. "Or does it just come natural to you?"

I considered the question, and I looked her up and down, and no looking away from her pale blue eyes, either; and I decided that her question was serious, not just grannying, and deserved a serious answer.

"It's a cold welcome you've offered me, Granny Leeward," I said, "and not the way an Ozarker's brought up to treat a guest. As it comes natural to youall to be unpleasant, it comes natural to me to be unpleasant in return. I'm told I'm good at it."

"Guests," said Granny Leeward, "are *invited*. You were not."

"True enough," I said. "And you're not the first to point it out to me."

"There are those," she said, "as would of taken instruction the first time they heard it—and not needed a second statement of the obvious."

"There are those," I said, "as let every little thing put them off their duty. I am *not* one of those."

Silence. And then the Granny, who appeared to have been designated spokesperson for this collection of alleged living beings, began in earnest.

"I call for Full Council," she said.

"Seconded." And the ayes went round.

"Explain your purpose here, Responsible of Brightwater," she continued. "And speak up plain. It's a long table."

"There's been magic used for mischief on Marktwain," I said easily. "You know all about that. And a baby kidnapped from out of a Solemn Service, which is not decent. And in Full Council it was decided that it might be a good idea to spell out the particulars to the Twelve Families, as well as find the maker of the mischief. And it was agreed that I was best equipped to do that—and here, therefore, I am."

"You're a girl of fourteen!" she declared.

"You're a woman of eighty-six. Neither number is significant."

"And what fits a girl of fourteen—it *is* of significance, missy, for it means you've neither wisdom nor instruction nor experience—what fits a girl of fourteen to go gallivanting around the planet on a Mule, dressed like a *whore,* pestering decent folk and creating trouble everywhere she goes?"

Well, she was a Granny of eighty-six, and I was a girl of fourteen, as had just been stated. I took the bait she'd laid for me as easy as if I'd never heard the word before.

Granny Leeward had been holding a black cloth fan, using it to tap the table with to emphasize the ends of her phrases. By the time she got to "everywhere she goes" she was holding as pretty a nosegay of black mushrooms as you'd care to see anywhere. And they had me.

Her hand didn't even quiver, though I knew the mushrooms stung her—I'd made sure of that, while I was digging myself a hole to fall in—and she laid them out before her on the table and folded her arms.

"There's your answer," she said. "Just as I told you."

Jeremiah Thomas Traveller the 26th looked at his timepiece and nodded with satisfaction.

"Well done, Granny Leeward," he said. "Three minutes flat."

"Mighty sensitive to words, aren't you, child," said their dear old Granny, "for someone who sets herself *so* high she presumes to teach the Twelve Families their manners?"

Law, how it galled! I'd of given years off my life to have back the last five minutes, and sense enough to do them over right. But that's not how the world works, as I could hear myself telling other people, and there was nothing I could do but be silent and see where this would lead me.

The Master of the Castle told me.

"Personally," he said, "I was inclined to think Granny Leeward was exaggerating some when she told us her estimate of your abilities. I have daughters of my own, and they do sometimes play about with Spells and the like, when they get to be your age—it's a stage, and they grow out of it. But you seem to have got somewhat beyond that, Responsible of Brightwater."

"I sincerely beg your pardon," I said sadly. "I'm afraid I lost my temper—and I'd ask you to lay *that* to my age, too, if you would. It won't happen again."

"How could it happen at all?"

I didn't answer, but he wasn't about to drop it.

"How does it happen at *all*," he insisted, "that a girl of fourteen, whatever special place she may have in the frame of things, is able to set a Spell like that one you just set, and her against a skilled Granny?"

I saw Granny Leeward's lips twitch at that; she knew very well no Spell nor Charm would have turned her fan into those mushrooms. That had required a Substitution Transformation, and an illegal one, and it had been incredibly stupid of me. A simple Spell would of been more than enough . . . I could of just heated up the fan a little bit, and had my temper fit that way. But the Granny wouldn't betray me to a male; she lowered her eyes, and she kept her silence.

"I've studied a good deal," I said carefully, "and I've had good teachers. Nonetheless, it wasn't nice of me. As I said, I regret I did it, and I apologize, most respectfully."

"Well, Granny Leeward told us you knew a few tricks," said her son, "and that she figured it wouldn't take her five minutes to prove she was right—and it took her three. I don't mind telling you, young woman, I don't approve of it atall. I'm sorry my family had to see it happen."

"And so is Responsible of Brightwater," said the Granny, twisting the knife. "Pride," she added, "goes along before a fall."

"I'm afraid 'sorry' won't cut it," said Jeremiah Thomas. "No; I'm afraid it will take more than just *sorry* to make me easy with something like you under my roof."

Here it came again; I didn't bother to ask.

"I'll have your sworn word," he said. "And I'll have it now."

"Sworn to what?"

"That you'll use no magic—not *any* level, Responsible of Brightwater, not even Common Sense—so long as you are, as you yourself point out, the guest of this Castle and this Family, and under my roof. Since it's clear you've no sense of what's decent, you'll make do on mother wit alone."

"Are you that afraid of a few tricks?" I taunted him. "From a girl of fourteen?"

"Indeed I am," he said, "*indeed* I am! This is a respectable household, and the people within it not accustomed to scandal. We follow the old ways here, and we have a wholesome respect for the power of such as you, no matter how you come packaged. If you came into my house with a loaded gun, you'd have to give it up while you stayed here, as would you a flask of poison, or a laser, or any other such truck. And I'm a lot more afraid of magic unbridled than I am of any of those."

He turned away from me then and spoke to the son that bore his name.

"I hope you see," he said gravely, "and I hope you will spread the word among our people, that this is what can be expected when the old ways are *not* observed. I'll count on you to go over it with considerable care when you speak to our households next—might could be that will tame a few of those not thinking in the proper *way* of the Jubilee this young woman's been sent around to sponsor."

"As a matter of fact, sir," the answer came, "it seems to me it might be an excellent idea to discuss this whole thing *at* the Jubilee. It would perhaps be instructive for the other Families to hear about."

My gown was drenched with my own cold salt sweat, and my hair clung to my neck like wet weeds. I'd found my guilty, no doubt about that; it could hardly have been clearer if they'd had it branded on their foreheads. The venom from around that table, where almost no one had spoken one word, or more than stared at me, was as real as my two hands before me, and it battered at me in waves. I admired the cool control of this Granny—most would have been setting wards.

It was a tidy trap, grant them all that. If I accused them of using magic to wreck the Jubilee, or of turning it against Castle Brightwater, as I surely could have, there were ten grown men and women in this room prepared to swear that they'd seen me carry out an illegal act of magic right before their eyes, under their own roof, and against one of their own. And they would be telling the truth. If I'd been against the Confederation my own self, I could hardly have done it graver harm, and for sure I'd of been better off listening to my uncles, staying home, and ignoring the whole thing.

And if I gave them the oath they asked for—as I would have to do, no question about it, and their Granny there to see that I left no corners dangling—there'd be no passing this night in undoing by magic the folly I'd wreaked. I'd lie in my bed and I'd pray, and I would maybe cry some; but I'd do no magic. Not even to look ahead and see just how much chance there was of *any* solution to the problem.

"Well, let's have your promise," said Jeremiah Thomas. "Our Granny assures us that your wickedness doesn't extend to violating your own word, and she's proved she knows your measure. No magic, Responsible of Brightwater, for so long as you are within the continental borders of Tinaseeh. *None.*"

He was very sure of himself; we'd gone from "under my roof" to the whole continent at remarkable speed. But then, he was in a position where he could *afford* to be sure of himself.

"I promise," I said. "Certainly."

"Put your hands on the table so we can see—"

"Oh, Jeremiah Thomas," said Granny Leeward pettishly, "that's not needful! What do you think she's going to do, cross her fingers? This one does not play games."

"That I do not," I agreed.

"Nor do we," said the Granny. "Bear that in mind."

"It does not seem to me," said Jeremiah Thomas slowly, "that just saying she promises is enough, in this case. Have another look at those mushrooms there, making the table nasty with their rot, will you, Granny Leeward? She might—"

"She gave her word," said the Granny. "That's all that's required."

"Let her give it in full, then," said her stubborn offspring. "And I'll be satisfied."

I knew the sort of thing that would appeal to him, and having no choice *what*soever, I gave it to him.

"For so long as I am within the continental borders of Tinaseeh," I intoned, "I will do no magic, of any sort or kind, at any level, for any reason whatever, no matter what may come to pass—not even to safeguard this house or those within it, not even to safeguard myself. My word on it, given in full." There.

I saw the Granny's eyebrows go up at the phrase about safeguarding their house, but she didn't say a word. I knew then that there must be at least a couple of Magicians of Rank in this Castle at this moment—I knew of three that very well could be—and if there were one or two I *didn't* know about besides, it wouldn't be past believing. She was far too calm, knowing what she knew, not to have quite a backup behind her own legal skills.

"Well?" I asked him. "Will that do it?"

"If Granny Leeward approves."

"Oh, it's enough," said that one, "and a bit more."

"In that case," he said, "we can get on with the business of this Council."

I had thought tricking me into my present position of total helplessness *was* the business of his Council; but it was apparently no more than item one on the agenda.

"My sons have a few questions to ask of you, young woman," he said. "We'll need a bit more of your time."

They wanted to know a lot of things. What arrangements I had made for seeing to it that the Families would be safe at Brightwater during the Jubilee—from "malicious magic," to use their term, and their using it struck me as astonishing gall considering that they were its source. It amounted to saying, "If we come in with fifty vials of deadly poison to spread around, what have you got on hand that will be able to stop us?" They wanted to know details of the *schedule* for the Jubilee; if, presumably, I had ways to keep it going, then how much time would have to be "wasted" on frivolity before we could get down to the real purpose of the meeting? What the real purpose of the meeting *was*. Why I felt such an outlay of time and trouble and money was justified, when there were Wildernesses to be cleared and roads to be laid and wells to be dug and windmills and solar collectors to be built and crops to be planted and fish to be caught, and game to be hunted, and other *serious work* that went understaffed and underfunded and would grow more so while we fooled away time at Brightwater. What did I assume would be accomplished by this "gaudy display" that couldn't have been taken care of at an ordinary meeting of the Confederation of Continents? How many were being invited from each Family, and how many had accepted? Where would they all be staying, and who'd see to their comfort? Did I give my guarantee that it would be not only safe for children, but an *edifying* experience—and if not, how did I propose to justify leaving them all behind? Would all the Magicians of Rank be present at the Jubilee, and all the Magicians, and for that matter, all the Grannys? And if so, why—who needed them there and for what? And if not, why not, and what would they be doing behind our backs instead?

It went on and on, and it was thorougher than could be excused by any motive except wearing me out and humiliating me, and rubbing my nose some more in my sudden position of servility to their will. I had no trouble with any of the questions; they set them in turn, each son asking three, and then politely yielding to his brother. Every word I said was information already available to them in the proceedings and proclamations of the Confederation over at least the last three years, and there'd not been a single Confederation meeting where one of those sons—and sometimes the father as well—had not sat as delegate. My throat got raw, and my back got tired, and they went on and on, learning nothing they didn't already know.

"That's enough," said Suzannah of Farson at last, long after I'd decided they intended to keep it up all night.

"Granny?" said Jeremiah Thomas.

"Been enough a long while," said Granny Leeward, "and you've made your point. I've heard nothing that made my ears stand up, and you'll not wear *that* one out just prattling at her—your sons are showing off, and they begin to irritate me some. You forget your own position on moderation, Jeremiah Thomas?"

He flushed, and the sons looked whiter and grimmer than ever, but he didn't cross her. He just pointed at the mushrooms, now, I'm happy to say, a really stinking mess of putrid black on their tabletop, and said, "What about those?"

"I'll see to them," said the Granny. "Never you mind."

"You wouldn't dare touch them," I said coldly.

"You think not, missy?"

"I *know* not!" As I did. I'd have handled them with a great deal of care my own self.

"I'll have them seen to, then," she told her son. "Comes to the same thing."

Jeremiah Thomas Traveller stood up, then, and adjourned the Council, took his lady on his arm and led us all out of there, and sent me on to my room with another of his silent Attendants.

I was right about the Magicians of Rank. When I woke that night and felt the heat of my skin, I cursed myself bitterly for not taking precautions sooner, before I'd had my hands tied by my own oaths. I could take the search for the source of the epidemic at Castle Wommack off my long list of postponed duties—I'd found it. And anybody that could bring themselves to lay innocent women and children low with Anderson's Disease, just for display, was unlikely to scruple at providing someone like me with the same unpleasant experience. And knowing that, I'd surely ought to of taken some steps to prevent it; like a lot of other things, it hadn't entered my mind.

I sent word to Granny Leeward by way of the guardmaid outside my door, and the Granny sent back a full crew. Four of them, all in Traveller black, though two of them had no right to wear it. They stood around my bed and smiled down on me, hands behind their backs.

"Twenty-four hours from now, Responsible of Brightwater," said one, "you'll be fit as a fiddle."

I felt the terrible need to twist and writhe, and my breath burned in my chest as I drew it, but I'd encountered pain before that matched this and surpassed it, and I'd had some practice in dealing with the stuff. I'd not give them the satisfaction of seeing one of my smallest toes move while they watched; and I lay still as a pond while the spasms moved over my muscles like live snakes, and I smiled back.

"I didn't know you were all still in training," I said, forcing the words through a throat that threatened to shut tight on me. "A competent Magician of Rank could stop this in twenty-four seconds."

They went right on smiling, and allowed as how Granny Leeward had said that it would do my soul good to have the deathdance fever for twenty-four hours.

"The Granny gives you orders, does she? You don't mind that?"

I was looking for a weak spot, but they knew what I was up to, of course, and they ignored me. A smugger quartet of elegant males I'd never laid eyes on, and they reminded me of my mushrooms—before the rot set in, of course. There I lay, forbidden to so much as wish on a star till I left Tinaseeh; and there they stood, able to add a notch or two to their accounts with Responsible of Brightwater, in perfect safety. It would have been too much not to expect them to enjoy it.

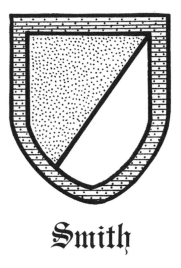

Smith

Now it's true that when I proposed a Quest as the way to demonstrate Brightwater's status, symbol returned in kind for symbol given, I was completely serious about the idea. I don't want that misunderstood. No Ozarker takes any formal construct of magic—and a Quest is one of the most rigorous of those—lightly. Like I said, you go tampering and tinkering with an equilibrium as delicate as the system of magic, you're going to cause radical distortions in places you never even considered would be touched. I was *absolutely* serious in my choice. And the choice I made had had solid motivations back of it.

Those that wanted to undermine the Confederation could have gone about *their* task in the most mundane way, you see. They could of simply boycotted meetings, straight out and without concern for who joined them at it. They could of started banging heads in the straightforward physical sense, though the public outrage at that would of backfired on them by the third blow landed—still, they could have. More reasonably, they could of used economic strategies of one kind or another, though for those on the wilder continents where self-sufficiency was a long way off yet that might of carried heavy penalties for their populations. But they had not chosen any of those measures, nor yet anything like them. They had made their decision to go at it on the level of magic—and the principle of fighting fire with fire is sufficiently venerable to make the idea of going back at them the same way look perfectly sound. Fighting magic with science has never been handy.

But let's grant it now and be done with it, the Quest was not all I had available to *me,* by a long shot. True, they'd flung a gauntlet and made a planetary display of a very special kind; not so much what they actually did—as had been made plain at that first Brightwater Council—but their clear notice as to what they thought they *could* do if they took the notion. We couldn't of just let that pass, not and kept our place among the Families as the informal—but only actual—seat of central government for Ozark. It was a dare they'd made, and a contemptuous dare at that, right up to the baby-snatching; and I'd figured that last move was made not so much because they weren't sure how far they should go, but because I kept dawdling around and not responding, and time was awasting. They'd meant to shake me loose from my dawdling, and hanging the baby up in the cedar tree did accomplish that.

But looking back . . . looking back and feeling a lot more than the six, seven weeks older I actually was when I at last left Castle Traveller behind me, I could see that I had gone butting my head where it was not necessarily called for. Now that it was all over but the dirty work I began with, and the dirty work I'd piled up along the way, I could see all the other alternatives I had censored right out of my head at the time.

I could have assembled the Magicians, from all three levels, by a full call-up at Brightwater, and made some kind of spectacular display of my competence there; and then sent them all back home to think about that awhile. I could of delegated the whole process to the Magicians of Rank from Marktwain, Oklahomah, and Mizzurah, and let *them* demonstrate our magical strength to the others, with whatever judicious behind-the-scenes string-pulling that might of required on my part. I could, for the Twelve Corners' sakes, just of used the comset for a display of our abilities, planet-wide. Or I could of seen to it that one highborn baby in every Kingdom popped into a tree during a Solemn Service at the same identical instant—my Magicians of Rank could have managed that easily, and it would of put the rest on adequate notice that they'd best pull back.

I hadn't considered, hadn't even brought up, any of those things.

It was clear to me, as I headed away from Tinaseeh with my ego as bruised as my body, that what I had really wanted had in far too many ways been just what the Grannys were claiming it was as I made my rounds. I had, I guess, wanted to show off, and to do it personally and get full credit; and I had been champing at the bit for an excuse to get away from Brightwater and all the dull routine of my duties there, not to mention the preparations for the Jubilee that others had had to carry on with while I took my vacation. The speed with which I'd gotten underway was the speed of guilt—I had just grabbed at the Quest concept, all loaded with tradition and symbolic significance like it was, for an excuse.

If there'd been any of the Marktwain Grannys present at that meeting in February, they might well have found a way to stop me; I wished mightily now that someone had. But neither my mother nor my grandmother had had a chance against my willfulness, and it was not the way of Patience of Clark to step in and take action unasked.

No, I'd had a dandy idea for getting away from it all for a while, and had gone about it pigheaded as you please, and how it was all to be managed now or at the Jubilee, I surely did not know.

"Sterling," I said, looking down on the Ocean of Remembrances just before we SNAPPED over all that boring endless water, "I've been a blamed fool. And I only hope I've learned enough from it to pay me back."

She brayed at me twice, and slid sideways in a truly spectacular wobble that set me grabbing the straps and fighting for control of my stomach. They were still at it . . . and I smacked her hard on the shoulder, and held fast, and swallowed bile, and got out of there.

I had a better understanding now of the lay of things, Castle to Castle, there was that. I had a picture of sorts, thanks to the Gentle, of the trouble brewing on Arkansaw and where that might yet lead. I'd had a first look at my own personal nemesis, foretold these nine years, and had gotten away from *him* intact but for my pride, this time. And every one of the Families, excepting the Smiths, had had a chance to deal with me directly on its own turf. I suppose that would do for a short list.

I was also tired, and ten pounds thinner, and had been mauled about pretty extensively, and had maybe ignored a Skerry sighting because I hadn't wanted to bother with it. I had allowed myself to be trapped by a passel of Travellers, like a child, and had no way of knowing what action they might take against me at the Jubilee with the new knowledge they had, and their determination to make good use of it. And my original task, the Goal of my Quest—bringing home the *exact* name of the traitor or traitors—that still had to be done.

I've mentioned pride before; I have it in abundance. It was one thing to admit to myself that Granny Golightly had had the right of it and I'd just taken off because I wanted to gallivant. It was one thing to admit that my fancy triumphant symbolic Quest had been more a series of accidents and misfires than anything else, when it hadn't been plain boring. Lying to your own self is a sure way to go to hell in a handbasket, and the time had come to 'fess up. But that was to my *own* self. I was not about to go back to Castle Brightwater, march into the halls and say—to Jubal and Emmalyn's great satisfaction, and my mother's—"Well, youall were right. It was a silly thing to do in the first place, and I'm worse off than I was before I left. Begging your pardon." Oh no! Bruised ego, bruised spirit, bruised body, all the blacks-and-blues of me notwithstanding, I would arrive home with an appearance of having won this one, come what may. Come what *may*.

And that was why I was now coming in over Castle Airy, instead of heading for home. Airy was a Castle of women, used to cosseting women and always willing to cosset one more, and I intended to take full advantage of that. I was going to let Charity of Guthrie and her daughters and nieces and cousins, and her three resident Grannys, feed me up and make over me and listen to my troubles and spoil me generally until I had accomplished what I'd set out to accomplish and could go on home in a state of sufficient dignity to at least fool Emmalyn of Clark and Thorn of Guthrie.

It was possible, if you were traveling by Mule, to fly into Castle Airy through a great arch cut in its front wall over the sea for that express purpose. I slowed Sterling and we moved in through the opening and down onto the easy-arced ramp at its base, me with a wary hand on the Mule's bridle against another of those wobbles, and straight into the sidecourt of the Castle where the stables were.

A stableman came forward to see to the Mule and greet me, and I slid gratefully down from Sterling's back onto the flagstones of the court, and stood there a minute to brace myself.

"You weren't expected, Miss Responsible," said the stableman, "and you arrived a bit sudden. I sent a servingmaid as soon as I saw you coming in over the water, to tell the ladies; somebody should be here directly to take you to the Missus."

"Thank you," I said. "I appreciate your courtesy."

"You look tired, miss," he said, and I admitted that I was tired—but not how tired.

"It's been a long trip," I told him. "A lot of flying and a lot of company behavior, which is worse. A day or two'll right me. You take my Mule on, if you will, and see to her; I'll wait right here."

He gave me a long considering look, and stood his ground.

"Believe I'll wait until somebody comes for you," he said. "I don't care that much for the look of your eyes, nor your peakedy face, and Charity of Guthrie'd put me back to peeling roots in the kitchen if I went on off and you fainted or some such trick. Your Mule'll keep awhile."

I didn't argue with him—he meant well—and we stood there in silence, me not being up to polite conversation and him not seeming to mind, until a young woman came hurrying toward us from a side corridor, with Charity of Guthrie herself right behind her.

Charity took one look at me, wrapped her arms round me, and rocked me like a baby.

"Poor child," she said, "you're worn clear out. You're the color of spoiled goat-cheese and not much more appealing-looking. What in the world have you been *doing* to yourself?"

"I should of sent you a message I was coming," I said, all muffled against the burgundy front of her dress. (And I would have, too, if I hadn't known I could shave a bit off my traveling time by not letting people know precisely when I was taking off and landing.)

"Never you mind that," she said, "I'm glad you came, and no warning needed. It'll be a cold day in a mighty hot place when this Castle can't put up one scrawny girlchild on short notice. You're welcome here any time." And she hugged me close again, bless her, and bless her some more. I can't remember when I've needed hugging worse.

She sent the man off with Sterling into the usual racket the Mules made greeting one another, told the servingmaid that had come with her to take my things up to the guestchamber I'd had before, and led me straight up to her own sitting room where she settled me in a rocker, with a quilt over my feet and a mug of strong hot coffee in my hand.

The Grannys came drifting in, then, one by one, and the daughters, and we soon had a roomful. And the Grannys lost no time.

"Well, youngun, how'd it go?" said Granny Heatherknit; she was senior here, at one hundred and eleven. "Your famous Quest, I mean . . . did you do enough damage to satisfy your craving?"

Charity of Guthrie's lips tightened, but I looked at her hard over my coffee and she made no move to call them off. We both knew this had to be gotten through sooner or later, and it might as well be sooner.

"Went well enough," I said judiciously. "Well enough—considering."

"Considering?"

"Considering that not a one of you helped me in any way *whatso*-ever," I said. Bedamned if I'd count that squawker egg out in the Wilderness; Granny Golightly had owed me that one.

"Not a one of who?" said Forthright. "Not a one of *what?*"

"Not a one of you Grannys," I retorted. "Near thirty of you there are here on this planet—"

"Twenty-nine, child, twenty-nine!" said Granny Heatherknit.

"Nearly thirty," I insisted, "and you did not one thing to help me the whole time I was gone."

"*For* which," said Granny Flyswift, jabbing the air in front of her with her knitting needles, "*for* which there are three good and sufficient reasons! *One*—this was your own tomfool idea, and none of ours, and none of our advice asked before you set out on it, hot out of here like a Mule with a burr under its tail! *Two*—you know the conditions on a Quest . . . adventures aplenty required and supposed to be unpleasant, or it doesn't count—and Granny Golightly herself reminded you of that in case it'd slipped your mind! And *three*—the best way for any child to learn that a flame'll burn him is to let him stick his finger in it; that makes for remembrance."

"Yes, ma'am, Granny Flyswift," I said. I had it all coming.

"Now what did you learn that's useful to anybody but your stubborn self, missy?" demanded Granny Heatherknit again.

Charity's daughter Caroline-Ann, sitting on a windowseat with her skirts drawn up and her legs tucked under, asked if that couldn't wait till I'd had some supper. She was twelve years old, and a lot like her mother.

"*No*-sir," said Granny Heatherknit. "She's still able to sing for that supper, and I'm right interested in her tune."

"Well," I said, "I learned that a girl of sixteen as can put her hair up in a figure-eight and knows all the modern dances should not be called a child or treated like one."

The Grannys peered at each other and snickered; and I wondered what foul task they had poor Silverweb of McDaniels doing that very minute.

"And, I learned that a giant cavecat stinks, in more ways than one. I learned that broken ribs are as inconvenient the second time as the first, and that where everybody's trying to keep the corks in their homebrew nobody has much time for the export trade."

"So far, so accurate," said Granny Heatherknit. "Go on."

"I learned that being licked to death is nasty."

"No argument with that."

"I learned that just about anything propped up in the moonlight and painted the right color is sufficient to turn a guilty head. I learned that one continent can hold two very small birds, and only one of them have gumption enough to fly. I learned that just because a Granny isn't using the old formspeech doesn't mean her garlic won't work."

"She's only fifty-nine," snorted Granny Flyswift. "Give her time, she'll outgrow her notions."

"She did very well," I told the old woman. "Very well indeed."

And I went on. "I learned that a Family truly *set* on a curse can bring one down on them. And, last of all, I learned that a person can't knit with both hands tied together."

"Think not?" said Flyswift.

"Well, *I* surely couldn't."

Granny Heatherknit scrunched up her eyebrows over her glasses— which she didn't need and doubtful she ever would—and I could see her counting.

"You left out Castle Purdy," she said. "What happened there?"

"There's what I will tell," I answered, "and there's what I won't." (And about the Gentle coming to see me—I wouldn't.)

"Hmmmph," said Granny Heatherknit. "That might be the most important piece of all."

"None of it," said Caroline-Ann of Airy sadly, "meant anything to *me*. As usual."

To my surprise, Granny Heatherknit turned to her and spoke almost gently; that girl must have a way with her.

"Caroline-Ann," said the Granny, "if you keep in mind that what Responsible of Brightwater's doing is trying to see how much she can *not* tell—despite being asked most politely—you'll understand why you found her remarks on the murky side. She's riddling, can't you hear that?"

"It didn't rhyme," said Caroline-Ann. "I never recognize riddles when they don't rhyme."

"Well, take the list she gave you and rhyme it, then," said Granny
Heatherknit. "Set it to a tune for us, Caroline-Ann . . . good exercise for
you, and we'll have something new for tale-telling makings."

"Granny Heatherknit, that would be *hard!*" objected Caroline-Ann,
and that seemed to me accurate. "You don't mean I have to?"

"Think you should," said the Granny, and the other two nodded
their agreement.

"Pheew!" said one of the huddle of girls on the floor below the sill
where Caroline-Ann was. "Glad it's you and not me, Caroline-Ann!"

"Easy rhymes," said Granny Flyswift calmly. "Cat. Rib. Bird. Knit.
Suchlike. You can manage that, Caroline-Ann; we give you three days,
and then we'll hear it."

"Oh, *blast!*"

Caroline-Ann sat up straight and dropped her legs over the sill, careful not to kick anybody. "Naturally I had to open my mouth with three
Grannys in the room! *Botheration!*"

I felt sorry for her, but I needn't have; it took her only half an hour
to do the task set, and we had the song from her right after supper that
night. It went like this:

CAROLINE-ANN'S SONG

A girl of sixteen as can put up her hair
in a figure-eight knot, and can do it alone,
and can dance through the figure-eights smartly as well—
that girl is no child, but a woman full grown!
  That's what I learned, said the daughter of Brightwater,
  That's what I learned.

The smell of a cavecat is ranker than bile,
and a cavecat's attentions are close to its chest,
and a cavecat that moves a mysterious mile
has a second rank odor that's risky at best!
  That's what I learned, said the daughter of Brightwater,
  That's what I learned.

A rib as is broken will ravage your breath,
and the second time round it will ravage your pride,

and it's cold comfort knowing while choking to death
that none of the damage shows on the outside!
    That's what I learned, said the daughter of Brightwater,
    That's what I learned.

A cellar of homebrew with corks to be set
and a hot spell ahead as makes setting them hard
keeps a family home from the market and road,
keeps a family corked to its Hall and its yard!
    That's what I learned, said the daughter of Brightwater,
    That's what I learned.

A Yallerhound's neither a hound nor a dog,
it's a bag full of water with a topcoat of hair;
it will drown you in slobber for the sake of pure love,
let the Yallerhound owner think well and beware!
    That's what I learned, said the daughter of Brightwater,
    That's what I learned.

A chair in the moonlight all painted with gold
is easily taken for royalty's throne,
and a conscience that's guilty can easily see
a scepter and crown in a rock and a bone!
    That's what I learned, said the daughter of Brightwater,
    That's what I learned.

Two little pretty birds sharing one nest,
hidden away in the littlest tree;
one has a leash on and sorrows to know it,
and envies the other that dares to fly free!
    That's what I learned, said the daughter of Brightwater,
    That's what I learned.

A Granny should cackle and gabble and nag,
and twist her tongue round to the formspeech and motions,
but garlic still wards if she knows her craft right,
and as she adds years she'll no doubt drop her notions!
    That's what I learned, said the daughter of Brightwater,
    That's what I learned.

A Family as goes through its days set on gloom,
talking of curses and harping of fate,
eyes to the past and determined to suffer,
will get what it asks for served up on its plate!
> That's what I learned, said the daughter of Brightwater,
> That's what I learned.

A person whose hands are tied tight at her back,
a person who's bound like a goat to a spit,
a person in such a predicament can't
neither gather nor sow, neither broider nor knit!
> That's what I learned, said the daughter of Brightwater,
> That's what I learned.

And there was a nice pre-verse to it, too, for times when there might be those singing back and forth:

What did you learn as you flew out so fine,
splendid on Muleback, dressed like a queen?
What did you learn, daughter of Brightwater?
Tell us the wonderful things that you've seen!

I could see how, throwing that in every time a verse came round, you could use up a good part of an evening with that song. And I was especially impressed with Caroline-Ann's solution to the fact that there's no way anybody can sing my awkward name. It was a fine song, every syllable and note in its proper place, and it added a certain respectability to my Quest, which was why the Grannys had demanded it, of course. I expected to hear a good deal in future of this daughter of Airy.

I passed two blissful days being mothered by Charity, and teased by her Grannys, and generally catching my breath, and by the end of the third day I felt able to face my role in this world once again. I was grateful to Castle Airy for that, because I had arrived in a sorry condition. And I kept humming Caroline-Ann's song.

And then on the third night, I set about catching myself a serpent. Or serpents, as the case might be.

I waited until all the Castle was sound asleep, and then I took my three baths: one hot, one cold, and one of herbs. I pulled my lawn gown through the small gold ring and saw that it passed without wrinkle or raveling to show for the trip, and I slipped it over my head. I put my black velvet ribbon around my neck, and braided my hair. I set wards and double-wards, which took some time; the guestchamber I was in had three doors and eight windows, and there had to be a pentacle at every one of them, and a double one at the corridor door where the Grannys might pass in their night-prowls.

It was past midnight before I was finally able to climb up into the center of my bed, set a pentacle round *me* with white sand from my shammybag, and take what was needful out of my pouch.

A bowl of clearest crystal, exactly the size of my closed fist, crystal so clear you had to look twice to see it was there. A vial of water from the desert spring on Marktwain that was holy to Skerrys, Gentles, *and* Ozarkers, and exactly twelve drops of that water poured into the bottom of the tiny bowl. My shammybags—one full of sand, one of fresh herbs, one of dried herbs, one of talismans. My gold chain, and my gold ring. Everything else I needed was inside my head.

I laid them all out around me within easy reach, and I crossed my legs and sat up straight, and realized that in no way was I tired any longer. Youth does have its compensations.

Now—we should see what we should see!

The needed Formalism was an Insertion Transformation; I wanted a name where I had a null term now, and I wanted more than just "Traveller" to fill that null.

I set down the Structural Index in a double row of herbs, and the Structural Change I laid right underneath it. I set the bowl of desert water in the space of the null term, and I made the doublebarred arrow with my hands above the water.

"Let there be," I said over the whole, "a name, sub-N; and let there be a filling of the null term, sub-T; and let there be no alteration of the underlying structure, sub-S!"

The whole of it looked correct, but I checked it over one more time, for rigor—

—and then I closed it off with the symbol ⊕.

I watched the water closely while it dimmed and clouded and bubbled, and finally cleared again. And then I jumped like a child stuck with a pin!

I'd expected a Traveller, naturally (and maybe half a dozen more of them, one for every time I repeated the Transformation, since I could change only one term at a time); and I had *for sure* expected to see a man! Despite the mention that Silverweb of McDaniels was husky enough, if properly clothed, to pass for a man and fly a Rent-a-Mule through a church, I'd been convinced no female was behind any of this.

But the face that looked up at me from the water, no bigger than my thumbnail but clear in every smallest detail, and certainly clear in its utter terror, belonged to none of the Travellers and to no man. . . . It was Una of Clark.

Una, the silent domestic daughter of Clark, the doting mother of five with the amazingly slim waist . . . whose *husband* was a Traveller. Whose husband wore the Traveller black despite all his years in his father-in-law's cheerful Castle.

I never, never would have suspected her. Never! She had seemed to me the dullest woman I'd come across on this planet, up to and including the gawkiest and rawest servingmaid just decided to try her luck in a Castle and still not sure where the doors were. And she had fooled me. Fooled me pure and simple!

"Una of Clark!" I said over the water, a couple of times. "Una of *Clark?*" Had it been Sterling looking out at me, I could not of been more astonished.

Then I tensed—fooling me that well, she might have other skills equally foolsome. If the water began to boil in that crystal bowl again, or cloud over, I wanted to be ready to set a new Transformation on it before she got away from me. But the minutes passed, with only the sound of my heart beating loud in the room, and there was no change—only the tiny, so tiny, shivering figure in the water; and very gradually I had all of her, not just her face.

You can't speak, of course, when you're trapped in blessed spring-water by a Transformation, nor can you move. I appeared to have her at my mercy, and I had the rest of the night to decide what to do about that. Which was not so much time; the clock had just struck two.

I was not precisely *free* in this; I could go just so far and no farther. Murder's murder, whether you do it with a hatchet or a Transformation, and it's not allowed. It would have tidied things up, and I will admit it even crossed my mind, though that shocks me, because I was so put out; but it could not be done. A Deletion Transformation to remove Una of Clark from the matrix of this universe was certainly *possible,* but it would violate the primary constraint on all magic: it is not *allowed, ever,* to change the Meaning of things. To do that is the use of magic for evil, and the moral penalties for evil by hatchet are a good deal less severe. They, at least, are administered by people. I'd come within a hair's breadth of violating that constraint when I tampered with Granny Leeward's fan, and a very good thing I'd watched the shaping of that nosegay when I lost the rest of my mind; if she'd cared to, she still could of fanned herself with the mushrooms.

Since my choices were pretty rigorously constrained, it didn't take me long to select among them. At twenty minutes of three I had finished a bounded Movement Transformation, and I faced Una of Clark, dry now in the night wind and back to her standard size, on a narrow rock ledge at the foot of the cliffs where Castle Airy stood. The waves crashed over the rock where we were, and I motioned her to move back into the small cave I'd noted as I flew in that day.

"Don't you come near me!" she screamed at me, and threw up her hands before her face to shield it. "Don't you *dare!*"

"If you drown here, Una of Clark," I shouted back at her, the wind taking my words and making clattering skeletons out of them, "if you fall into that sea that boils not ten inches from the tip of your dainty white foot, it will be your *own* fault! And I'll not be mourning you, you'll have saved me a great deal of trouble! Get back away from the edge, as I tell you now, and into that cave—move! Get!"

"I'm afraid, I'm afraid," she whimpered, hunkering down into the wind. "Oh, I don't dare move. . . . I'm so afraid!" Drat the woman; I did not really want her to drown, and it looked as though she might. The stone under our feet was like glass, polished by the constant wind and water, and the wind gusting high, and some of the waves were striking us to our knees and more.

"Well, you *ought* to be afraid," I countered, "you surely ought! That ocean is as near bottomless as makes no difference, woman, and you're going into it sure if you don't pull back!"

I saw her sway as the spray was flung against her . . . and fool that she was, she *did* move—closer to the rim of the ledge.

Law, I had no time for foolishness; I traced the double-barred arrow in the air and Moved her myself, safe into the narrow shelter cut by the water, and I followed her in just inches ahead of a wave that would have had us both sure, not a second to spare.

It was dark in there, and I set a glow around her and around me, so that we could see one another. The roar of the waves was under us and all around us, too, it was everywhere, and with each one the whole mountain seemed to shudder under our feet; but we were safe enough there until the tide rose.

"Witch . . ." she hissed at me . . . a serpent she was, right enough . . . her teeth chattering, back pressed to the cave wall and her bare feet curled to the curve of the hollowed rock. And she said it once again, a good deal bolder. "Witch!"

"Nonsense," I said. "I'm nothing of the kind."

"Oh," she said, "you're not a *witch?* Reckon you didn't snatch me out of my bed and trap me first in some . . . some *noplace* . . . where I saw nothing, heard nothing, felt nothing, but your wicked face over me as big as all the sky, and your eyes boring down on me, each of them big as a Castle gate . . . and then you brought me here, you SNAPPED me here! Think I don't know that's the only way you could drag a decent woman halfway round a continent through the night from her husband's side?"

"Oh, stop it," I said, and sat down on the bare rock in pure disgust. I had been prepared to feel some challenge here, maybe some respect for my opponent, but I was just *plain* disgusted. She was the one responsible for what had been happening to the milk and the mirrors and the street-signs, all right—the springwater does not lie, nor do the Transformations fail. But the interference with the flight of the *Mules?* Just as I'd been too slow to see that when I should of seen it right off, I'd misunderstood it completely when I finally got to it, and gone to an awful lot of unnecessary trouble as a result of my blindness.

"Here I thought the reason that everything was just *barely* over the bounds of half-done was cleverness," I said crossly, wishing I dared smack her face and knowing the thought was shameful. "Here I thought that just making the Mules wobble a tad instead of making them crash was a way of showing your *finesse,* and a way of hinting at what dread things you might do if you chose to! You realize that? And all along, all this miserable long time, Una of Clark, it was just that you aren't very *good* at what you do! All along, with your piddling little tricks, you've been doing the *very best you could,* haven't you? Why, we had the whole damned thing clean backwards! *Damn!"*

"Well, it worked, didn't it?" she spat at me, and she had me there.

And then she hid her face against her shoulder and screamed into the darkness, over and over that same foolish word—"Witch! Witch! Witch!" —until I was nearly distracted. I suppose that was what Gabriel Laddercane Traveller the 34th had used against her, all through the nights of their marriage, lying beside her in their bed, whispering while he stroked her thighs and that slim waist, convincing her to tackle magic far beyond what she was trained in or fit for or had any legal right to even think of. If he'd truly convinced her that she was doing battle against witchcraft when she raised her weak hand against me . . . it did not excuse her, but I could see how he might have used that as a lever. Especially with her far gone in the sickness of Romantic Love; it would of served his needs well, and paid him for his long exile from his father's house, and explained why he'd put up with it over these long years instead of taking her away. The threads that ran to this night were sticky ones, and they clung.

"Well, now, what am I going to do with you?" I asked her, and myself, out loud. "What am I going to do *about* you, Una of Clark?"

I'd lost all taste for harming her, she was only pathetic; but she couldn't be allowed to go on with her mischief, bungling as it was, all the same. Nor could she be allowed to go back and talk about *any* of this, and I was by no means sure she had brains enough to see that.

"Una?" I said sharply. "Una of Clark? You look at me!"

"No! You'll turn me into something horrible if I do!"

Turn her into something horrible? What did she think she'd done to *herself?*

"Look at me, you foolish, *silly* woman!"

She lifted her head then, and her eyes were like two huge flat fish in her white face. Most unappealing.

"Una, what did you think you were trying to do?" I asked her. "Maybe if you tell me that I'll be able to see my way."

To my astonishment, she raised her hands beside her face, spread her fingers wide as they would stretch, and recited straight at me—

ASS.

BEDPOLE.

CHAMBERPOT.

DEAD OF THE NIGHT.

EGG-ROTTEN BIRD DUNG.

FISTFULS OF MEALY WORMS.

NIGHT OF THE DEAD.

POTCHAMBER.

POLEBED.

ASS.

I was flabbergasted. As nasty a Charm as I'd heard anywhere, and bold as brass about it, terrified as she was. But no elegance. *No* style! And put together all cockeyed to boot. I'd seen six-year-old girls do a sight better than that, and without anything nasty in it to help them along, either.

I said:

AIR.

BALSAM.

CINNAMON.

DENY ME NAUGHT.

EVERMORE WEEPING.

FOLLOW ME EVERYWHERE.

EVERMORE SLEEPING.

DOUBLE MY WORTH.

CINDERMAN.

BELLTONGUE.

AIR.

"And," I added, "if you'd like to go on to twelve syllables and back, in twelve sets of rhymed pairs, I'm ready. But do hurry, Una of Clark, because I intend to be in *my* bed before breakfast."

By that time, when she began to sob hopelessly, choking and sputtering, I wasn't surprised. I wondered what her life was going to be like, from this night on; she wasn't built for a burden like this, and her husband had chosen a poor instrument to break to his evil.

"See where foolish love will lead you?" I said to her sorrowfully. "See where it will lead you, woman? Into *folly,* into *shame,* into *disgrace.* . . . Why didn't you tell him to do his *own dirt?* What would your father and mother say of you, Una of Clark, if they only knew what you have done?"

She only blubbered harder, and I was sick of watching her.

"I'll tell you what I'm going to do," I said, "and I suggest you listen to me more carefully than you've been listening to your Reverend these last few years. For I'm not playing with you, and I warn you—I'm no Granny, to just put toads in your bed and rashes under your armpits and keep your cakes from rising. You do understand that?"

"What *are* you, really?" she hissed at me. "What *are* you?"

"Nor am I a witch," I went right on, ignoring that, "for if I were, you would have been at the bottom of that ocean long before this, and you know it very well. If I were a witch, Una of Clark, I'd set a Substitution Transformation. And another woman that looked just like you and talked just like you and walked just like you and moaned in the loving arms of Gabriel Laddercane Traveller *just like you* would go home from here—but she would not *be* you. You would be feeding the fishes and she would be only a Substitute, and nobody would ever know."

"Go ahead, then—you can do it, why *don't* you, and leave off torturing me?"

"Because I'm *not* a witch, I'm a law-abiding well-brought-up woman, that you've caused a lot more trouble than there's any excusing you for, that's why!"

"Then what are you going to do?" she whispered. "Make me ugly? Make me crippled? Oh dear saints, Responsible of Brightwater, what is it going to be?"

"Your mind is a cesspool," I said, staring at her. "A cesspool. Make you ugly and cripple you indeed!"

"Tell me!"

"What I am going to do is set a Binding Spell on you," I said. "That and nothing more. Seven years, Una of Clark, you'll say no word about this night or about what you know of me, or about what you've done. And seven years, you'll do no magic you haven't earned the rank for. You not even a Granny or any chance of ever being one. . . . I'll bind you seven years; and then you're free to do your worst."

She went limp against the rock; I was glad there wasn't any place for her to fall to.

"The reason I'm stopping there," I went on as I made my preparations, "is because I am *not* a witch! And because I have no desire to go beyond what's decent. You're a woman—and you're a Clark by birth. I am willing to wager that in seven years you'll achieve enough wisdom, that when the Spell is at its end you'll guard your own mouth out of shame and simple decency. I'm willing to take a chance on that."

And if I was wrong, I could bind her then again, of course; I'd be on the watch.

She just huddled there and bawled, every other word some stuff about what was she going to tell Gabriel Laddercane, more shame to her, and I got on with my work.

It took me only a little while, and then I Moved her carefully back to Castle Clark, to the bed where—might could be—her husband had not yet even missed her. If he had, that was her problem, and it was up to her to figure out some way to get out of it. I'd done all I was willing to do, and more than she deserved, out of regard for her Family, and pity for her folly, and out of the kind of distaste that comes from dealing with an enemy that's really no match for your skills. There's a game called shooting ducks in a barrel—I don't play it. Never have.

And before the servingmaid tapped on my door with my pot of morning tea, everything was put away. Every sign of the wards and the pentacles swept clear, not a speck of sand from my shammybags on the Airy floor. And I lay there in my plain nightgown with the covers tucked up around my chin, and a smile on my face that suited my pose, like I'd not lifted a finger all that weary night.

Now I could go home.

13

I don't mind saying that it went well, though it's bragging, for it's no more than the plain truth. My leavetaking may have had an unseemly abruptness due to my hightailing out of there before my common sense (or somebody else's) could stop me, but my homecoming went off as slick as I could possibly have desired it. And the rough edges I well knew were there didn't so much as show their shadows on the surface that was available for examination to others.

I timed it so as to fly in to Castle Brightwater right at the end of breakfast on a sunny April morning. And the last ten miles I rode Sterling along the winding roads of the Kingdom, between the hedges of butter-yellow forsythia newly in bloom, and the fields of fruit trees covered with blossoms thick as snowflakes. Every blade of grass and every new leaf and bud was that perfect green that comes only in April, and that was what the Brightwater green was meant to stand for (and never quite matched). And although the people didn't cheer me—we didn't hold with such display on Marktwain, and hadn't for hundreds of years—I knew they were glad to see me coming back. I knew by the smiles on their faces and the fact that they were out in the fields working in their Sundy best, and this not Sundy. I kept my own face straight and pretended not to notice . . . in fact, I worked at *really* not noticing, seeing as how if I arrived at Castle Brightwater puffed up with anything that a sharp eye could spot as pride the family would be on me like carrion birds on a new-dead squawker, and I'd come out of it blistered.

Nobody came out to meet me, which was reasonable enough. I wasn't company here, I *lived* here, and I had to whistle for a stablemaid to come take Sterling off my hands. Then I stopped and indulged myself, just for a minute, since nobody seemed to be looking. I never would of imagined I could be so glad just to be home.

Ours was the first Castle built, and the Castle proper is not one of the shelters the Twelve Families set up when The Ship landed and they were new to this planet. The one the Brightwaters built was made of logs

that can't match Tinaseeh ironwood even half-way for durability, but
have kept well enough under cover; and it sits within the front courtyard
of the Castle as a constant reminder—lest we should ever forget—of our
humble beginnings here. It had seven bedrooms round a common room;
and forty-four Brightwaters—men, women, and children, and one fine
hound that had quickly died—slept and ate and passed their very limited
leisure time under that wooden roof.

When I was at home I hardly saw the loghouse, I was so accustomed
to it, but it was new to my eyes this morning, and I let them linger on
it, glad it was still there for the children of all the Twelve Families to visit
and play at living in.

And then I turned my eyes to the Castle itself, and it pleasured me,
too. It was perfectly square, and a modest but satisfactory two stories high.
It had twelve towers; one at each corner, one at the center of each wall,
one on either side of the front doors, and two extra in the front wall for
fancy. The Brightwater flag flew from every one of the tower roofs, and
I noticed that someone had polished the brass weathervane (an Old Earth
rooster that was one of the few material things granted space in The Ship
that could only be called a luxury), and that it turned briskly in the wind
at the top of the tower spire where it had been fastened more than nine
hundred years ago. I smiled; they'd claim that was done for spring cleaning, but I knew better—we were a good week away from spring cleaning time. It was done to welcome me home.

I knocked at the Castle doors, and they slid apart without a sound to
let me in; someone had oiled them, too, for there'd been a grating scrape
to them when I rode out in February. The Castle Housekeeper stood
there casually watching three servingmaids polish the same banister over
and over again, and she looked up as I stepped under the doorbeam and
pretended to be surprised.

"Well, if it's not Miss Responsible," she said. "Good morning to you,
miss!"

"Good morning to you, Sally of Lewis," I said, and I greeted each
of the servingmaids by name as well, including the one whose apron had
a grease spot, for which there was no excuse in my front Hall. "I'm
home," I said.

"We see you are," said Sally of Lewis. "And we're glad—it's been a
long time."

It had been that; nearly eight weeks, and at that I'd made a bit better time than I'd deserved.

"The Family's still having breakfast, miss," said Sally of Lewis. "They're just finishing the coffee and there's still hot cornbread on the table. The cooks happened to make extra this morning."

It was amazing. I found that not only was I anxious for some Brightwater cornbread and butter, I was even anxious to see my mother. I believed I was even anxious to see Emmalyn of Clark, and I couldn't remember that idea ever passing through my mind before. I had clearly been away too long and was going weak in the head.

I went down the corridors to the room at the back of the Castle where we liked to have breakfast and supper both. It looked out on a wide field that was a riot of wildflowers in the spring and a riot of scarlet and golden leaves in the fall, and through which there flowed a quite respectable creek that you could catch glimpses of from the windows. That creek had been First Granny's only condition for choice of the Brightwater land. "I don't care what else it has or hasn't," she'd declared. "Volcanoes, canyons, banana trees, swamps, anything you fancy—but it has got to have a creek or I won't build even an *out*building on it. Keep that in mind!"

"Well, Responsible," they all said as I went in the door. And various other equally original greetings. Granny Hazelbide settled for "Decided to come back, did you?" and a full-scale Granny glare.

"Sit down, Responsible," said Patience of Clark, "and help yourself to the cornbread. Unless you want to change first, of course."

I looked down at myself, at the black velvet corselet and the silver-and-gold embroidery and the scarlet leather gloves, and all the rest of it. "No," I said, "I'll have my breakfast first. And then I plan to take all this off, and burn it."

"*You'll* do no such thing!" said Granny Hazelbide, dropping her silverware with a clatter onto her plate. "Waste not, want not, young woman—you think money grows on trees? You'll take that truck off and give it in to the staff for cleaning and storing away proper; and then next time you take a notion to play the fool you'll already have your fool outfit to hand. But spare us your spurs, please—they clank, and furthermore, they'll scratch the floorboards. And take off your gloves; they'll be all over Mule."

Emmalyn of Clark told me what a pretty outfit it was, and how much she admired it, and how she had thought of that as I left but hadn't had a chance to express her admiration, and I thanked her politely.

"I think, personally," said Thorn of Guthrie, "that it is a tad Too Much."

"A *tad!*" exclaimed Granny Hazelbide. "Why, she looks like a circus, or a—"

I interrupted with considerable haste, remembering how I'd reacted the last time I'd heard the word I was reasonably sure she was just about to use.

"Dear Granny Hazelbide," I said, sitting down and reaching for the hot cornbread and the butter, "you weren't here to advise me when I left, you see, you were ailing. I left in something of a hurry, and I did the best I could."

"Hmmmph," said Granny, "your 'best' is pretty puny, Responsible. And I am scandalized that either your mother *or* your grandmother let you leave this Castle looking like a—"

Well, there was clearly no hope for it.

"Granny Leeward of Castle Traveller said I looked like a whore," I said blandly. If the word had to be used I might as well do it myself and spare my sensibilities as best I could.

"Shows what *she* knows," muttered Granny Hazelbide instantly, just as if she hadn't had the exact same word on the tip of her fibbing tongue. "Had *her* way, you'd have gone on Quest in a black nightgown and a bonnet, I reckon."

"I expect I would," I said. "I expect."

The same crew was there that had been at the meeting in February; except that Jonathan Cardwell Brightwater the 11th sat beside Ruth of Motley, and the Granny was present. My mother looked a vision, as always, in a gown the exact color of the forsythia bushes; and she brought up the subject at hand without preliminary, as always.

"Well," she said, "did you find out who we owe for our sour milk? And all the rest of it? And did you find out who put that baby up in the cedar tree? I am of the opinion, myself, that the McDaniels are growing somewhat more than just tired of camping under that tree and watching their baby through a life-support bubble, and I rather imagine that if you could see your way clear to do something about that they'd be properly grateful. Not that I'd want to hurry your breakfast, of course."

Prick, prick, prick . . . that was Thorn of Guthrie. Prick you here and when you jumped, stick you somewhere else.

"Mother," I said, "I learned everything I went to find out, and a good deal more I never suspected, and we can take care of the baby matter in just a minute. I do intend to finish my breakfast."

"Well?" she demanded. "Who was it?"

"Can't tell," I said, shaking my head with what was intended to look like sincere regret. "I *am* sorry about that."

"You can't tell?" Jubal Brooks and Donald Patrick did that in chorus, both outraged, and my grandparents looked at each other significantly and said nothing.

"Told you she wouldn't," said Granny Hazelbide smugly. "She's ornery; always was, always will be. You'll get nothing out of her."

"Not true, Granny," I answered, "you'll get a good deal out of me. I will be calling Full Council later . . . after supper, Mother, you needn't think about it now . . . to tell you about a lot of things that need discussing badly."

"Your 'adventures,' I suppose," said my grandmother Ruth.

"They were not of my choosing, Grandmother," I reminded her, "they went with the choice of *measure* to be taken, all duly voted on by you and everybody there at the time. I'll take my fair share of blame, but I warn you I'll not take what's not *coming* to me . . . and I learned a lot that will need tending to before the Jubilee."

Patience of Clark looked at me like I'd said a broad word.

"Responsible," she said, "do not say that to me. Do not even *suggest* that. We're going under for the third time already in 'what has to be done before the Jubilee' . . . don't you make it worse." And I knew then whose shoulders had taken on the load for me in that part of the field while I'd been gone.

However, Patience meant food to prepare and rooms to clean and suchlike, and training new staff. I was thinking of a promise made to a Gentle in a Purdy guestchamber, and settling the question of whether we should—or could—try for a delayed celebration of the claimed appearance of a Skerry, just in case. And there was the matter of the feuding on Arkansaw to be laid out for them, and just how the rest of the Families might fit in to that, and how that would tend to complicate both the security arrangements and the seating ones.

I would not be taking up with them the matter of what I'd done at

Castle Traveller, nor what might be done in advance of the Jubilee to
forestall their putting my blunder to use; that I'd have to deal with myself,
in private, and I had a feeling in my heart that I knew the answer already.
Nothing to be done but wait, and deal with it when it came, I'd wager,
though I'd search the timelines as far as my wit and skill would take me,
on the off chance. But that would not be on the Council agenda.

Nor would the name of Una of Clark. Much good seven years of
silence was going to do us if I didn't observe it myself.

"I found out who was back of all the mischief," I said calmly, "and
that we had the thing hindside to, and I put a stop to it. There'll be no
more wobbly Mules, I promise you. But for the sake of the Families
involved, there'll be no passing on of names, either, from my lips or any
others."

"Families involved . . ." That was Jubal Brooks. "Then there were
more than one."

"In a manner of speaking, Jubal Brooks," I said.

In a manner of speaking. The Travellers for sure—I'd not been
wrong in thinking them guilty; without the strokings and whisperings of
Gabriel Laddercane Traveller the 34th there'd of been no shenanigans
from Una of Clark. She'd of bounced her babies on her knee, and doted
on her husband, and died a good woman. And no way of knowing who'd
put Gabriel up to that, nor how many long years it might well have been
planned. And the Clarks for sure, by reason of Una's direct hand. But
only those two, I thought, only those two. I'd not repeated the Insertion
Transformation that night at Castle Airy, to see if any other faces would
turn up in my bowl of springwater. I'd been rushed, and I'd been disgusted, and there'd not been either the time or the proper mood. And
to make certain sure, I'd be doing that now I was home. I didn't expect,
however, to trap anyone else. If there'd been any other name to babble,
Una of Clark would of let it fall, in sheer terror.

"You're mean not to tell, Responsible," said Thorn of Guthrie. "But
then you were always mean."

I smiled at my plate, and listened to Granny Hazelbide put her in her
place, which she did more than adequately. My mother could not abide
being left out of anything, even when it was for her own good and clearly
for the general welfare. Granny dressed her both up and down, and she
subsided. And when that was over, we all walked down to the churchyard.

Vine of Motley and Halliday Joseph McDaniels the 14th *did* cheer as they saw us coming, and I could see their point. Eight weeks camped under that tree must have been wearisome, even in the sort of luxury accommodations they'd provided for themselves. And I could well believe that Vine of Motley's arms itched to hold her own baby, instead of the servingmaid's she'd nursed these past two months. In her place I'd of been impatient, too, and I was glad I hadn't waited to change my clothes after all.

"Hurry up," I told the Magician of Rank that had joined us in some haste at the Castle back doors. He was called Veritas Truebreed Motley the 4th, a name some found overly fancy—which accounted for its only coming round four times in all these years—but there was no quarrel with his skill. Once I'd assured him that whatever held that baby couldn't be anything much more complicated or dangerous than Granny Magic, and clumsily done at that, he didn't waste either time or energy. At fifty-three going on fifty-four he was a sure and experienced man with his Formalisms & Transformations, and he made no fuss whatever over bringing Terrence Merryweather McDaniels the 6th down to his parents. He didn't even bother with herbs; he just scuffed a few cedar needles into suitable patterns, flicked his fingers with the supple ease of long practice, and the baby floated right down to his daddy, gurgling and cooing and obviously without so much as a heat rash to mar his perfection.

"Oh, Halliday Joseph McDaniels, *do* give him to me!" cried Vine of Motley. "Please let me have him!"

"Certainly, darlin'," said Halliday Joseph, grinning so I feared he'd crack his face. And he passed the child over to Vine of Motley and took the servingmaid's baby in exchange.

She popped up instantly and relieved him of *that* burden, and I made a mental note that she was to be rewarded handsomely for her part in all of this. Discreetly, but handsomely. Her name was Flag of Airy, for the Ozark iris that looked quite a lot like the pictures we had from Earth; and she was, as I recalled, just on fifteen, and wife of an Attendant that was a Clark by birth. I thought that a small Bestowing of an acre or two of farmland would not be out of place, and I'd have it seen to. Two months was a long time to watch your own child suckled at another woman's breasts, and to know that your first task when you had it back— *if* you had it back, because she would not of been human if she hadn't worried that something might go wrong—would be weaning that babe to a cup. No, a couple of acres to put a small house on would not strain Brightwater, though the land we still had to give away was almost gone— this was a time that justified parting with it, even beyond the Family proper. And Flag of Airy would be pleased to be the lady of a house instead of a servant in Castle Brightwater. It wouldn't make it up to her completely for what she'd sacrificed, I didn't suppose; having no baby myself I was a poor judge. But it seemed to me it ought to lessen the ache a little.

Happy! We were for sure happy that day. The McDaniels insisted on packing up and heading for home at once (they didn't say "before something else happens" but no doubt they were thinking it), and nobody there that wouldn't of done the same in their place, though we protested politely. But the rest of us were in no mood for any kind of labor. The air was golden, the cedar sighed over us, and the churchyard was a credit to its Maker with white and yellow and purple violets, and young daisies, and all the spring flowers of Earth that had, praise be, taken to the soil of Ozark without so much as a dapple to their leaves to show strain. There'd be plenty of work to do later, after supper; it would be a long Council, and we'd all come out of it sobered, even with me keeping back the worst of it.

For the moment, though, we weren't worrying about that or any-thing else. I set aside my corselet and cape, my boots and gloves— *carefully*, under the sharp eyes of Granny Hazelbide—and rolled up my puffed and beornamented sleeves to feel the warm sun on my arms. We sent for a picnic from the Castle. And we lay all through that day under the cedars (I had to send the Lewises a note thanking them, I thought, while I was tying up loose ends . . . I had not known how much I loved those three cedars they'd nurtured in our churchyard until I lay there lazy under them and saw them with fresh eyes); and we talked of minor things. The children ran wild and wore themselves into stupors before it was time to head home for supper, playing circle games and tag and hide-and-seek and Little Sally Waters all over the churchyard, and wading in the creek while their mothers scolded halfheartedly and turned a blind eye and deaf ear most of the time.

I managed to tie down tight again in that corner of my mind reserved for the awful my encounter with the young uncle at Castle Wommack.

That I would look at when the Jubilee was over, unless, the Skies help us all, he *came* to the Jubilee. Stuff that away, Responsible, I told myself hastily; sufficient unto the day is the evil thereof, and if it happened I'd have to deal with it then. I wasn't going to let it spoil my homecoming day, not that nor any of the rest of it. Not this one day.

"Glad to see you appreciate your homeplace, missy," said my Granny, giving me a wicked dig in the ribs to be sure I was paying attention. "Grass wasn't quite as green as you thought it'd be elsewhere, eh?"

"Don't torment me, Granny Hazelbide," I pleaded with her. "I'm so comfortable . . . and so glad to be here! Leave me in peace."

"Leave you in *peace?*"

"Please, Granny Hazelbide. Pretty please."

"Think you deserve peace, young lady?" she demanded.

"No, Granny, I doubt I deserve it atall," I said frankly. "I just *asked* for it—I didn't say I had it coming to me."

She chuckled. And patted my knee.

"All right, then," she said. "Long as you're staying honest with your poor old Granny."

She didn't believe I was honest for a minute, nor did I, but it appeared she was willing to call temporary truce. I closed my eyes, so full of my undeserved bliss that I couldn't hold any more, and took a nap. *That* at least, considering the way I'd been having to spend my nights, I had earned.

END OF BOOK ONE

The Grand Jubilee

PART ONE

1

"Oh, Great Gates," said Jewel of Wommack. "I'll never manage it."

Her brother looked down at her and grinned.

"Afraid you'll fall in the water, are you?" he teased. "Tell you what, dear heart, I'll carry you down the landing ramp."

"You touch me, Lewis Motley Wommack," she said between her teeth, "and I'll scream you a scream they'll hear all the way to Castle Brightwater."

He leaned one elbow on the gunwale, set his chin in his hand, and looked at her sideways, considering. She had a scream that was deservedly famous, did Jewel, and the potential scene had a certain appeal for him. There they'd be, pulling up to the mooring, the great ship easy in the calm water of the harbor, and all the passengers crowding politely onto the ramp three abreast. And there'd be all the elegant citizens waiting on the landing in their Sundy best—*Jubilee* best!—standing under the ancient trees that shaded them and watching the delegations and their households disembark. And there *he'd* be, carrying his screaming squalling sister through all the decorous lines of pleasant people . . .

"Don't you think it," she said firmly. "Don't you even *think* it! You'll rue it, I swear you will."

"Will you set a Spell on me, little sister?" he asked, mock-terrified before her prowess, and then he gathered her against him and held her close to his side. It was a good deal like holding a sapling whipping in the wind, if you'll allow a sapling the skill to curse without ceasing; but she was no more trouble to him than the buttons on his cloak. He could have held half a dozen more like her, all screaming and spitting, and not begun to exert himself.

Jewel was fighting him only for the principle of the thing, having learned in the course of her twelve and a half years that it was a useless activity for any other purpose. She had seen her brother lift a full-grown man over his head and throw him into a tree, and he hadn't even been angry at the time, just slightly fussed. And then she had an idea.

The wicked point of the broochpin that she'd had at her throat took him right in the armpit, where there was little clothing and less muscle. The group behind them stepped back hastily at his roar of pain, and Jewel braced herself to be flung over the side. It would spoil her gown and her cloak and her fine new shoes, and she would lose her hat and her travel-bag in the process. It would mean being hauled in dripping wet before the grave watching eyes of Silverweb of McDaniels, that she could see standing among those waiting on the Landing, and somebody near enough her age that she'd half hoped to have her for a friend. But it would be worth it all. She'd happily have swum ten miles before all the Grannys of Ozark assembled, in a full set of winter clothes and wrapped in a quilt to top it off, if it would of gained her one point against Lewis Motley Wommack the 33rd. For all that she worshipped the ground he walked on and the air he breathed.

"Well?"

"Well what, Jewel of Wommack?"

"Well, aren't you going to pitch me overboard?" She braced herself again, and then felt her cheeks flood crimson as he patted her on the bottom like a Mule colt, right in front of all those people.

"No, Little Wickedness, I'm not going to do any such thing," he said. "Smile pretty now, there comes the land—and I expect you to walk that ramp like a highborn lady, which you are, and if you *do* fall in and shame us all I'll put you over my knee right there under those trees soon as you're fished out. Provided I don't let you drown, that is."

The men had tied the lines, and the First Officer secured the gleaming ironwood steps that would allow the passengers to walk up to where the ramp met the gunwales instead of scrambling over on a rope ladder like the crew was used to doing. There were a few cheers from the younger children, hastily hushed by their elders, and Jewel heard the resounding smack of a sturdy hand against someone's backside. That, she thought, would be a Purdy female, and a Purdy child; neither Wommack nor Traveller would of laid hand to one of their offspring in public—or needed to.

"Why?" she demanded softly, still clutched to her brother's side—and then she realized that in the noise of the landing, everyone talking quietly but everyone talking at once, she didn't have to be quiet, and she shouted it at him. *"Why?"*

"Why what?"

She wiggled violently, and he set her aside with a courtly smile, not scrupling to tickle her ribs as he did so.

"Why aren't you going to throw me overboard?"

"One, it would give you far too much satisfaction," he said promptly. "Two, I've already told you—a dozen times, if I've told you once—I intend to be careful of the Wommack reputation at this Jubilee. I'm tired to death of being only one cut above the Purdys—they're stupid and we're cursed, that's a fine bedamned arrangement! And I'll not risk a scandal before ever we set foot to Brightwater land, Jewel of Wommack. Not if you run a sword through my armpit instead of a pin."

She would of liked to say she was sorry, but she didn't dare. If there was one thing that made her brother furiouser than somebody doing something outrageous, it was that somebody saying they were sorry, afterwards. She stood shaking in her finery and trying to get her breath back, and she held her tongue.

"All right now," he said, and gave her a gentle push toward the steps. "Here we are, and this is the famous Brightwater Landing, and I'm right behind you. No simpering, no giggling, no lollygagging, sister mine. Move!"

She moved. The press of people behind her would have moved her in any case. Up the nine shining steps; and then, with a hand from the First Mate to steady her against the gentle rocking of the ship, across the narrow space and her foot on the landing ramp that stretched out into the harbor. And down the ramp between the rows of flags brilliant in the May breeze, in front of all those staring people—not that they stared openly, but she knew they watched her, all the same. She turned an ankle once, but no one would of guessed; Lewis Motley was at her elbow and he steadied her instantly.

"It's *miles* long, this ramp!" she fretted. "Suppose that's to give the Brightwaters ample time to look everybody over as they land!"

"No," he told her, "it's so the ramp will reach out into the harbor far enough to let people land from an oceangoing ship with a deep draft. You have a mind, Jewel, and known to be spectacular; use it. Nobody's looking at you."

"They are!" she insisted.

She knew they were, in her bones. She was not quite sure when it had begun; one day she was a child, fresh out of Granny School and not caring if the whole world looked at her nor even thinking they might care to. And the next she knew herself the center of everyone's attention, at all times. For the women at Castle Wommack to tell her that this came of being twelve and would disappear with turning thirteen, approximately, was no help to her. Thirteen might as well of been ten years away as four months, for every day stretched out long and lanky before her full of ordeals. They had told her who knew how many times. Her nose was *not* too pointed; her freckles were *not* ugly; the copper-colored hair that fought its way instantly out of any attempt she made at bringing it to order was not untidy; her breasts and hips were not too big; her legs were not too long. It didn't help any. Her days were a misery and she endured them, that being a woman's place in this world; but she defied anyone to expect her to enjoy them.

"Jewel, sister Jewel," he said as they stepped off the ramp onto the stones of the Landing—sure enough, each one was a good four feet square, and blinding white, just as she'd been told!—"I am counting on you."

She would have clung to him in despair and hidden her face against his chest; but he knew that, of course, and he was gone in an instant. He disappeared into the clusters of talking people like thread into a needle's eye, and was out of her sight.

"Jewel." The voice at her elbow was like a blessing pronounced twice; she turned joyfully to greet it. There stood Gilead of Wommack, Jewel's niece despite her seventeen years; and Jacob Donahue Wommack the 23rd, Gilead's father and the Master of Castle Wommack; and there stood Grannys Copperdell and Goodweather, both bristling with impatience to get on with it, whatever it might be; and all the rest of her homefolks.

"Oh, I am so glad to see you!" she declared, doing her best to disappear into the middle of the group, and she meant it most fervently. Whatever it was that her beloved brother was "counting on" her for, she intended to postpone it as long as possible.

"Lewis Motley's upset her," said Gilead to the others. "I knew he would."

"She's no business letting him," snapped Granny Copperdell.

"Granny," objected Jacob Donahue, "the child's only twelve!"

"When I was twelve I had a babe at my breast," said the old lady, "and it would of been a cold day in a warm place before any nineteen-year-old lout such as that one would of upset *me*."

Jewel had no doubt that was true. Indomitable twelve-year-olds such as that make good Grannys, and Granny Copperdell was one of the finest.

"If I had a babe at *my* breast," said Jewel staunchly, "I'd have it hind-end to, and youall know it."

"Jewel of Wommack!" Gilead was shocked, and the Dozens only knew what the Attendant and the servingmaid bringing up the rear with the smaller children thought. But both Grannys cackled with appreciation, and Jewel saw that as a good sign and took up her position between them. She could think of few safer places to be than flanked on either side by a Granny in a good mood.

A Brightwater Attendant, splendid in his livery of emerald green piped with narrow silver braid, the crest on his shoulder looking to be embroidered only yesterday, stepped forward then to greet them, making his proper salutations with a flourish.

"If you'll follow me," he said pleasantly, "I'll take you to your lodgings at the Castle and see you settled in."

Lewis Motley, popping up as unexpectedly as he'd disappeared, spoke from the back of the cluster of Wommacks.

"All of us?" he asked.

"Beg your pardon, sir?"

"I said, all of us? That is, is there *room* for all of us?"

"At Castle Brightwater?" The Attendant was clearly flabbergasted.

Lewis Motley Wommack shrugged politely, and made it obvious that he was being too well bred to mention the four hundred some odd rooms at Castle Wommack, or its vast acres of land.

"Ignore him," said Jacob Donahue immediately, "and accept my apologies. He has no manners whatsoever and never did have. And keep an eye on him while he's under your roof, because he can't be trusted. I've done my best with him, poor orphan that he is, but it's been a hopeless and a thankless task. He grows wickeder with every passing year."

Lewis Motley chuckled, and Jewel wondered grimly how he'd of been behaving if he *hadn't* been concerned for the Wommack reputation; and the Attendant, confused but doggedly set on his duties, explained that although Castle Brightwater was nothing like the size of Castle Wommack, it could surely manage to put up the delegations of the other eleven Families of Ozark without strain. Gilead moved forward smoothly to soothe the poor man with a steady flow of distracting questions, and Granny Goodweather leaned back and pinched the unruly younger brother's cheek—a Granny's privilege, however much it might hurt, and however much the red wheal it left might mar the effect of the young man's splendid beard.

They were handed into five of a long line of gleaming carriages, each with the Brightwater crest on its door and harnessed to a matched team of four Mules, and Jewel began to enjoy herself in spite of everything. It was one thing to watch the doings at Castle Brightwater on the comset while she sat at home at Castle Wommack, and it was quite another to actually be here. The carriages were a fine touch, and she could tell she wasn't the only one to think so. Lizzies would of taken them up to the Castle far more quickly, twelve at a time, but a lizzy had none of the elegance of a four-Mule carriage. They were speckledy Mules, a soft gray flecked all over with a darker shade of the same; their harness was gray leather with silver fittings; and their tails had been done in an intricate five-strand braid, not just looped up and fastened in the usual way. And their hoofs! Jewel had never seen Mules with their hoofs, that were naturally a kind of nothing clayey color, stained a jetty black. It was purely splendid, and polite of the Mules to allow it done.

And then there were the crests; a crest on the door of a lizzy would of been like a lace collar on a goat. It was well carried out, and a few points for the Family Brightwater.

Somewhere down the line the remark came—"Waste, waste, and never an end to it!"—and nobody had to look back to identify the source. That would be someone from the Traveller delegation, going through the obligatory rituals in his thrifty suit of coarse black cloth and his plain black coat. The Travellers considered *anything* either pleasant or attractive to be a "waste."

"*They* are going to be a nuisance," said Gilead, and her father nodded.

"Fiddle," said Granny Copperdell, "they just make for balance. Everybody else says 'how nice' and the Travellers come in all together with 'what a waste' and it evens it all out. Keeps us from getting carried away with delight and debauchery. Right useful of them, if you want my opinion on the matter."

"The eeeeequilibrium of the yuuuuuuuniverse is a fraaaaaail and—"

"Lewis Motley Wommack!" The Granny's voice whipped through the air in the open carriage, and Jewel tried not to wince. "You mock the Reverend, and on a Sundy at that, and I'll see you pay dearly for it!"

Jewel listened to the laughter in his voice, tucked under the charming apology that came properly and without a second's hold-back, and wished she could stick him with her broochpin again. There was nothing in all the known universe that her brother feared, and nothing so far as she knew that had ever bested him—excepting perhaps Responsible of Brightwater, who'd run away from him and left him laughing till the tears poured down into his beard on the steps of Castle Wommack, and she hadn't the least idea what all *that* had been about . . . but his own brash fearnaught ways were no reason to risk bringing down the wrath of the Powers That Be on the heads of all the rest of the household.

At her side, Granny Copperdell touched her wrist. "You'll be having your hands full, child," she said. And Granny Goodweather on the other side, though she didn't leave off looking round her at the fields and farms of Brightwater, so much a park by comparison with the rough-hacked land at home on Kintucky, nodded a sturdy agreement.

"*My* hands full? Why? Of what?" Jewel's heart sank—here it came. Holiday or no holiday, Jubilee or no Jubilee, there'd be something; there always was. Botheration!

"Keeping Lewis Motley Wommack the Thirty-third in order, child," said the Granny solemnly. "Not a job *I'd* fancy."

Jewel was absolutely silent. Not a word entered her mind that she dared give voice to. But the Grannys went on, and spared her the trouble of trying to frame the questions without the broad words.

"You keep in mind, now," said Granny Copperdell, "you are the only woman in your brother's line. Your parents both dead since you were only babies, no other sisters, and him not married—that makes you responsible for his doings. You may well find out that you'd abeen better off with a half *dozen* babies, time this is over."

"It'll grow you up some," said Granny Goodweather calmly, and patted Jewel's knee. "And high time. You're near on marrying age, we can't have you shirking your duties and hiding in grannyskirts forever."

"It's not fair!" Jewel announced, her outrage sufficient at last to let her speak. "And I don't fancy it either!"

"Fair!" scoffed Granny Copperdell. "I ever tell you this world was fair, Jewel of Wommack?"

"No," she said, speaking sullen into her own collar. "No, I can't say as you ever did."

"Well, then," said both the Grannys together. And then the carriage pulled up at the gates of the Castle and everyone was suddenly moving about, gathering up what they'd laid down for the ride, and there was no more time for discussion.

Inside the Castle, Responsible of Brightwater sat at the desk in her bedroom, going over for the tenth time the welcoming speech that she would be giving to open the meeting tomorrow morning, including the elaborate agenda she was counting on to give her time to see how the wind blew. There must be no smallest niche of time left over tomorrow in the scheduled activities to allow the anti-Confederationists to begin their moves. She could count on their obsession with manners to keep them from tampering with that agenda on Opening Day; and good use she'd best make of it, seeing as she could count on nothing for the other four days. The only possibility she could safely exclude was murder— there hadn't been a murder on the continent of Marktwain in the entire one thousand years of its history—but that left a mighty long list of other kinds of disorder and disarray.

"Keep 'em busy!" she said out loud, and made herself jump.

She was nervous, that was for sure. Her mother had remarked on it. Her uncles and her uncles' wives and all the children, and even the Housekeeper, had remarked on it. Until Granny Hazelbide had told them all to leave her be, in no uncertain terms.

"She has enough to think of now," the Granny'd said, shaming them all—and they deserved it—"without you forever tormenting her. The Confederation of Continents might go down for good and all this week, after five hundred years of nursing it along, and she has *that* to think of. And if it doesn't fall, the Twelve Gates only knows what shape it'll be in after the Travellers get through chopping away at it. If she wasn't nervous I'd be calling in the Magician of Rank to see to her *head,* and I'll thank youall to *hush!*"

Responsible grinned, remembering. It was rare that a Granny, or anybody else, came to her defense. It had been a pleasant experience, and one she wouldn't mind repeating a time or two.

"You really worried, Responsible?" her grandfather had asked, sounding sorry for his teasing.

"Some," she'd said.

"They're not such fools as to think that without the Confederation things'd be even half proper—they'll just make the usual noises, and then back down like they always do. No need for you to fret."

She surely did hope he was right . . . And he ought to be. He ought to be!

On the wall before her hung a battered map of Ozark, the six continents set out in their oceans, and a pin stuck firmly at the site of each Castle. Black pins for those Families she knew to be dead set against the Confederation and ready to bring it down, come what may—Travellers, Guthries, and Farsons. And the Purdys thrown in, seeing as they'd not have the courage to stand against the other three. Red pins for those she knew to be loyal—Castle Airy, Castle Clark, Castle McDaniels, Castle Motley, Castle Lewis, and her own Brightwater. Green pins for those as might move either way, depending on what happened over the next few days—the Smiths, and the Wommacks. Six months ago the pin that marked Castle Smith had been a red one, but no longer. Their behavior had grown more and more odd, and the Attendant set to watch had told her half an hour ago that every one of the other Families was arrived and safely settled in the Castle, but no sign of the Smiths and no word from them. That did nothing to reassure her.

It looked, providing you were ignorant, as if things were fairly safe for the Confederation. Six for, only four against, and two undecided: sway those two and it could be eight to four and an easy sweep; lose them and it would be six to six, a standoff. But that would be your impression *only* if you were ignorant, and Responsible of Brightwater was not. Castles Lewis and Motley could be as loyal as they liked, there was little they could do to help. Two tiny kingdoms sharing one continent not much more than an oversized island, the total not much bigger than Brightwater Kingdom alone. The great bulk of Arkansaw loomed to their east, all of Kintucky to their west, and Tinaseeh—largest of the six continents and held by the Travellers—to their south. If the Confederation did not stand, the Lewises and the Motleys would be hard put to it to do more than make speeches. They could not survive without the help of their neighbors.

And yet, she could not bring herself to believe that there was really any danger beyond that of the anti-Confederationists wasting this precious week in stalling and wrangling so that none of the necessary work could get done. They had a lot to say about independence, but she was inclined to agree with her grandfather; they must have sense enough to know the terrible price of isolation.

Responsible sighed, and stamped her foot in frustration. She had cast Spells half the night, she'd done Formalisms & Transformations till her hands ached, and she'd gotten only one answer. An answer she could of gotten with Granny Magic alone, reading leaves in a teacup. *Trouble* ahead, she kept getting—as if she didn't know that! Something was wrong with her data, or something had been wrong with her methods, she had no least idea which; and there was no one she could ask for their opinion, seeing as how everything she was doing was illegal or worse. It fretted her, having no idea what *kind* of trouble.

There was a knock at her door, and she called "Come in!" expecting an Attendant telling her it was time for the banquet in the Castle Great Hall, but it was her own Granny Hazelbide.

"Granny!" she said, laying the thick sheets of paper down on the desk and resigning herself to the fact that there'd be no more reviewing of that speech. The Granny would of come to fuss at her about something, or perhaps a dozen somethings, then there would be the Banquet and the Dance, and then she must sleep or she'd not be fit to *give* the speech. She was so tired now that the words on the paper blurred when she looked at them.

"Responsible," said the Granny back at her.

"What can I do for you?"

"Do for me, indeed!"

"Well, then, what can you do for *me?*" asked Responsible patiently. "What is it, Granny Hazelbide? Has the Housekeeper run off? Is the food spoiled? Do we expect a hurricane off schedule?"

"Mercy, you're the cheery one," said Granny Hazelbide.

"If something weren't fretting you, you wouldn't be here, Granny, and we both know that. And if something's fretting you, then for me to be cheery would be foolishness. What's gone wrong?"

The Granny sat herself down in a rocker where Responsible would have to turn her chair around to look at her, and folded both arms across her narrow chest.

"For one thing," she said, cross as a patch, "the Castle's full of every kind of devilment ever invented."

"Granted," said Responsible. "And?"

"For another, it's so crowded you can't find a place to sit nor a place to stand, nor much air to breathe—and the Smiths aren't even here yet. And if I know *them,* they'll bring every piddling relation they can scrape from under a rock, and three dozen Attendants, and a servingmaid to every chick and child—a delegation of one hundred even, I'll wager you my smallest thimble and my oldest shammybag!"

"More nearly fifty, Granny," said Responsible. "You exaggerate."

"Still too many, *I* say!"

"Granted," said Responsible. "But it's their way, and none of our business to object to it."

"I-dislike-it-all," said Granny Hazelbide, each word separate and alone as it left her mouth, like a solemn pronouncement; and Responsible couldn't help but laugh.

"Granny," she chided, "you've known these last twelve months and more that this was coming. And you've known how it would be. We've gone over it and over it, and my mother has not held back *her* comments at any time. I don't know how it is her voice hasn't worn grooves in the floors by this time, complaining. There's been ample time to mope and moan and carry on over it, and we'd all come to an agreement that it was worth the trouble. Why are you bothering me about it now?"

"I have a funny feeling," muttered Granny Hazelbide, rocking slowly and staring at the floor.

"A funny feeling."

"That's what I said."

"What does your funny feeling tell you?"

"That there's trouble coming."

Responsible shrugged.

"And what were you expecting?" she asked patiently. This conversation was wearisome, and a waste of time as well, unless the Granny knew something that might be useful. If she did, she was going to make Responsible work for it.

"Know who's in the room next to yours?" asked the Granny suddenly.

"For sure," said Responsible, surprised at the question. "Anne of Brightwater, and her boring husband, Stewart Crain McDaniels the Sixth. And if I know Anne, and I do, they'll have the youngest tadling they brought along sleeping in their bed with them for safekeeping."

"Wrong," said the Granny.

"I arranged it myself."

"So you did, but it's been changed, and your uncles both approved it and remarked as how nobody should bother checking with you since you were so busy, bad cess to 'em both."

Responsible reached both arms above her head and stretched. Law, but she was tired! And asked the Granny, as politely as her strained tolerance would allow, to tell her what she'd come to tell.

"Who've they given me for nearest neighbor, dear Granny Hazelbide?" she pleaded. "Leave off teasing, now, and tell me."

"Don't sass me, missy!"

"Granny, tell me!" said Responsible. "Or I'll go back to work on my speech. Notice that it's on *paper?* None of your pliofilm sheets for this ceremony—I'd put it on a set of stone tablets if I could carry them."

"Granny Leeward," said the old woman abruptly, and left it at that.

Responsible took a deep breath before she tried answering, and folded her hands in her lap where they wouldn't betray her. And then she said, casual as she could make it: "They've put Granny Leeward in the room beside mine?"

"That they have. It seems she wasn't comfortable where she was, and it seems the air is better on the side of the Castle nearest you, and it seems she can't abide the view where the rest of the Traveller delegation has their rooms because it reminds her of a tragic experience she had as a child, and it seems the beds in none of the other rooms will suit her back, which she declared to be frail, though the woman has pure steel for a backbone. But she faced me down and butter wouldn't of melted in her mouth—and the upshot is that you're one side of the wall and she's on the other."

Responsible thought about that for a while, and the Granny rocked. And then she asked, "And what do you think it means?"

"Trouble." Granny Hazelbide's mouth was a little puckered line.

Responsible's mind, despite the control she tried for, took her back to the long table at Castle Traveller, and the black fan in Granny Leeward's hands, and then the jetty mushrooms, where the fan had been, rotting on the table.

"Responsible of Brightwater," demanded Granny Hazelbide sternly, "why are you shivering?"

"You said 'trouble' your own self, ma'am. And I respect your opinion."

"There's more to it than just mischief," said the Granny. "Like I said, I have a funny feeling."

"Think she'll strangle me in my bed?" ventured Responsible, her voice careful and light. It wouldn't do to have the Grannys feuding.

"I'll wager she could, without leaving her own."

"Ah, but she wouldn't! She's a Traveller born, Granny Hazelbide, and she'd be drawn and quartered naked before she'd use illegal magic."

"I'll grant you that much, but you mark my words—"

"Mark mine," put in Responsible. It wasn't polite to interrupt a Granny, but when Granny Hazelbide said to mark her words you were in for a good hour's worth to mark, and she just simply didn't have the strength.

"Mark mine," she said, "the woman's done it to torment me, purely because she delights in tormenting me. Nothing more. And I don't intend to let her have the satisfaction of thinking she's achieved her purpose."

"It's possible," said the Granny. "I suppose it's possible."

"And you, I'll thank you to help me rather than hinder me in this. All I need is that woman thinking she has *you* upset; it won't do, Granny! I need you serene, not all in a fidget."

Get in a staring match with a Granny, you can wear your eyes out, and Responsible's eyes already burned from no sleep and the hours poring over papers. But she held firm, and it was the old lady who gave way first.

2

Every Ozark child was familiar with the building called Confederation Hall, whether they lived five miles away or clear on the far side of the Ocean of Storms. Little girls in Granny School, and the boys under the instruction of their Tutors, became familiar with it whether they would or no, and at a very early age. They drew it on sheets of pliofilm and took the pictures home to be fastened up on the housewalls; they made lopsided models of it from Oklahomah's thick blue clay and gave them to their fathers for desk ornaments. The girls embroidered it on heavy canvas, with name and date beneath; the boys built it of scrap wood and carved their names with the points of their first good knives.

It was red brick, two stories high plus a tiny attic said to be haunted by a half dozen dead Grannys, with tall narrow arched windows framed in stone, and stone steps leading up to a central door. And the whole sitting square in the middle of a broad green lawn with a walk all around. A spanking-white bandstand stood in the left front corner of the lawn as you faced the Hall door, and the other corner had a statuary group lasered out of Tinaseeh ironwood. There on the pedestal block was First Granny, wading ashore with her skirts pulled up just high enough to show her shoetops; and there was Captain Aaron Dunn McDaniels, standing on the shore and reaching a hand to her; and there stood a miscellaneous child beside him looking very brave. The inscription across the base read: FIRST LANDING—MAY 8, 2021.

Confederation Hall was authentic Old Earth Primitive, right down to the solar collectors on its roof. And the children knew why. "Not *every* thing on Earth was bad," the Grannys and the Tutors told them. "When the Confederation of Continents was established in twenty-five twelve, meeting then just one week in the entire year, Confederation Hall was built as it was to *remind* us of that. It represents some of the good things."

Ordinarily it was a building empty enough to have an echo in its corridors. Even during the one month in four when the Confederation met, the delegations and their staffs weren't large enough to dent its emptiness, running as they did to two or three men and a single staff member. And the other eight months there was nobody at all there but an Attendant to show visitors around, one official to keep up the records and the archives, and a few servingmaids to see to the cleaning. The Travellers disapproved of that; if they'd had their way it would of been closed up tight except during meeting months. But the Traveller children were taught to make the embroidered pictures and the wooden models just like everybody else's.

Today it was a long way from empty. Responsible of Brightwater, standing at the speaker's podium in the Independence Room, ran her eyes over the crowd of delegates with satisfaction. Not one Family had boycotted the Jubilee, leaving the assembly without its full complement of votes; the message had come in that morning before breakfast, the Smiths were delayed but they would be there. Not every seat was filled—though every seat in the balcony was—and there were empty rows at the back. But it was a satisfying turnout, and when the Smiths did arrive they'd take up a goodly number of those empty spaces.

Twenty-eight of Ozark's twenty-nine Grannys, lacking only Granny Gableframe of Castle Smith, filled the first row of the balcony, a sight Responsible had never seen before and wasn't sure she could handle with a straight face. They looked like twenty-eight matched dolls up there, each with her hair knotted up high on top of her head as required, each with the same thin sharp nose and tight-puckered mouth, every last one of them in the same crackly gown and triangular shawl and high-topped shoes, and round eyeglasses perched halfway down their noses whether they needed them or not. Not to mention the twenty-eight sets of flying knitting needles. Responsible looked away from them hastily, feeling unseemly laughter tugging at her mouthcorners, and concentrated on the Travellers instead. That was dampening enough to end all hazard of either laughter or smile. And talk of waste! The Traveller delegation, by her rapid count, numbered twenty-four ebony-coated men. Quite a contrast with the grudging tokens they sent to regular meetings, and each and every one of them entitled to speak to any question raised, *plus* offer a rebuttal. They had men enough there to tie up the floor for hours at a time.

At her side, in the big square-cut chair reserved for the leader of the meetings, sat her uncle Donald Patrick Brightwater the 133rd, fidgeting.

Since her father had been dead these seven years, it was Donald Patrick that would take over on behalf of Brightwater once she finished the welcoming speech. And he was itching to get at it, too, she could tell. It was made particularly clear when he grabbed her elbow and hissed at her under his breath to get started.

Responsible didn't intend to be hurried. There were still people moving into the balcony doors to stand and try to get a glimpse of the proceedings below, and the delegates hadn't yet left off rustling documents and muttering to one another. She'd not begin to speak till she had silence in the room, and she was not through looking her audience over. She'd had a bad moment when she saw who was included in the Wommack delegation, though she ought to of known Lewis Motley Wommack wouldn't let himself be left behind. A Grand Jubilee would come along only once every five hundred years; you miss your chance at one, you weren't likely to get a second try. She would have to deal with the problem he presented as it *was* presented.

"Responsible!" said her uncle, too cross now to be discreet. "*Will* you get on with it? At this rate it'll be noon and time for dinner before we get past your performance!"

He had been opposed to her making the speech at all.

"It's not appropriate," he'd complained, three Family meetings in a row, while his wife sat and lived up to her name and waited for him to exhaust himself. Patience of Clark wasted no words on her husband unless she was convinced he couldn't be relied on to talk himself into silence unassisted.

Donald Patrick had had arguments he considered potent. In the first place, he'd pointed out, women were not allowed in the business sessions of the regular Confederation meetings; therefore, a woman ought not to be allowed in this one. In the second place, if the excuse for having a woman present on the Hall floor was her social function as hostess of this to-do—*which* he could grudgingly see might be reasonable—then that welcoming speech should not be made by Responsible, it should be made by her mother, as Missus of this Castle. Thorn of Guthrie had raised her brows at that and allowed the ivory perfection of her face to be marred by a frown that was as downright ugly as any expression Responsible had ever seen her use, and had declared as how she'd have nothing to do with it; and no argument of Donald Patrick's would sway her.

"*Why* won't you do it?" he'd demanded, smacking his fist in the palm of his hand. "I will feel like a plain fool sitting there listening to a fourteen-year-old girl—"

"Going on fifteen," put in Granny Hazelbide.

"—a fourteen-year-old girl giving the welcoming speech on behalf of this Castle and this Kingdom. And so will every member of the Brightwater delegation. And so would *you*, Thorn of Guthrie, *and* you, Responsible, if you had any decency at all, or any respect for your father's memory, rest his soul!"

Thorn of Guthrie had looked at him and sighed, and then she turned to Responsible and said, "Well, Responsible, will you abide by my order and let your uncle do the honors?"

Responsible had said no, and Thorn of Guthrie had said "You see?" and Donald Patrick Brightwater had stomped out of the room in a black mood that had lasted well past suppertime.

Responsible had made an effort at calming him, in the few chinks of time available to her, promising that as soon as the speech was over she'd move to the balcony and mind her manners for the rest of the week. And Patience of Clark had put as much of her skill into soothing him as she'd considered reasonable.

But he sat beside her as unresigned and as infuriated as he'd been from the beginning. When Responsible began to speak, the silence having grown tangible enough to suit her, she felt almost obliged to be ready to leap aside at any moment and prevent him from snatching the sheets of paper out of her hands. He had his eyes fixed on the brilliant bunting that circled the room at the level of the balcony and ran across its front rail, with the crests of the Twelve Families hung in strict alphabetical rotation at each looped-up swath, and an expression of propriety slapped onto his face like a mask. But like all men, when sitting rankled him his thigh muscles kept tensing, and he would inch forward in the chair, and then recollect the situation and jerk suddenly bolt upright again. And then start it all over, tugging at his beard and then crossing his arms over his chest and then tugging at the beard again. He put Responsible in mind of a five-year-old too far from the bathroom, and she hoped his manners would last him till she finished.

She knew the words of the speech by heart, every one of them the perfect word. All about the solemnness of this occasion. Commemorating that great day five hundred years ago when after much struggle the Twelve Families had set aside their fears of anything remotely resembling a central government and allowed the Confederation of Continents to be formed. Commemorating the slow but steady progress as they moved from meeting one week in the year, a token foot in the waters, toward the present one month in four. A couple dozen sentences about the wickedness and corruption of Old Earth that had driven them away and into space, and the mirroring sentences that congratulated the Confederation for letting none of those varieties of wickedness arise here on Ozark. She rang the changes and pushed the buttons, and she could of done it all in her sleep, so far as the words went.

But the manner of *saying* those words—the modulation of her voice and the phrasing, the set of her features and the positions of her body—that was a very different matter. That demanded considerable fine-tuning, a constant eye on the men she faced, an adjustment for a frown here, a careful pacing of a phrase for a wandering expression there; it took her mind off both her uncle *and* Lewis Motley Wommack the 33rd.

If it hadn't been for that, she'd of been delighted to let Donald Patrick read the *words;* and if it hadn't been for that, and the fact that her mother knew full well she hadn't the skill to control this roomful of males, Thorn of Guthrie would of insisted on her right to read them and backed Donald Patrick in every objection he raised. Thorn had no reluctance for the limelight.

A thousand years had gone by here on Ozark, and who knew how many billions before that on Earth; and still men spoke solemnly of the power of logic, the force of facts and figures, and remained convinced that you persuaded others and won their allegiance by the words you said. It would of been funny if it hadn't been such pathetic ignorance, and there were times when Responsible wondered whether the males of other inhabited worlds suffered from the same ancient illusion.

It would for *sure* have been helpful if she could of known whether the members of the Out-Cabal shared the same faith in the power of the surface structure of language. In fact, it would of helped to know whether those three beings were males of their species, just for starters.

She put that thought out of her head instantly; it was distraction, and a sure certain way to lose her audience and run into objections to her plans for this day.

In the balcony the Grannys noted appreciatively the skill with which Responsible wooed her unruly crowd, and Granny Hazelbide felt she was justified in her pride at having brought the girl up. She stood up there, bold as brass before the restless males, and she played them as easily as a person that lived by fishing would play a little stippleperch in a creek. It looked easy when she did it, and Responsible looked cool and easy herself in her elegant gown of dark green with a pale green piping round its hem and collar. But Granny Hazelbide had held the girl's head all the night before while she'd first vomited everything she'd eaten and drunk at the Banquet and the Dance—which wasn't much—and then retched miserably on an empty stomach and cursed the weakness of her body. Not more than an hour's sleep all told had she had, Granny Hazelbide was certain of it, but none of that showed now. Not a tremble of her hands, brown hands that showed the hard work they did, against the creamy paper. Not a slightest hesitation of that voice, though her throat must of been raw. Smooth as satin, bold as brass, cool as springwater, that was her girl.

It wasn't working on the Brightwater men, naturally; they were used to Responsible and took her about as seriously as they did the serving-maids. And the Travellers were fighting it, staring up at the ceiling to break the hold of it upon them. Granny Hazelbide sincerely hoped they'd hear from their women later about their ill-bred behavior. But it was working on everybody else, they were just this side of trance, and the final paragraph would finish them off. Not a one had protested as Responsible read off the list of events that would fill Opening Day, and the comset screen on the front wall behind her spelled out the lengthy agenda in small bright lights.

There was to be a Memorial Address by the Reverend Terrence Patrick Lewis the 5th, head of the church of this Kingdom. There was a Commemoration Ceremony. There were three separate Awards Ceremonies for service to the Confederation, and at each of those there'd be awards speeches and acceptance speeches and folderols. There was a noon banquet, with two guest speakers. There was a reading of the Articles of the Confederation, with a commentary to follow from the senior Magician of Rank pointing out the satisfying parallels between the structure of the Articles and the notations of Formalisms & Transformations. When Responsible got through, there were not five unscheduled minutes available from the end of her welcoming speech to the Closing Prayer that would—so the lights recorded—be pronounced at six o'clock precisely that afternoon, just in time for supper. And Granny Hazelbide could tell by the backs of their necks and the set of their shoulders that the Traveller

men were silently lamenting the loss of time before they could get on with
what they'd be seeing as the real business of this Jubilee, and that the
restraint was unsettling their stomachs. She wished she could of hoped
they'd empty those stomachs as Responsible had hers, but it wasn't likely.
No doubt the Travellers had to answer *some* calls of nature, but the idea
that one of them might be so human as to vomit went beyond the bounds
of imagination. That would, after all, be *waste*.

She felt the eyes of Granny Leeward on her then, her that was a
Traveller born and bred, as Responsible had reminded her, and she didn't
like it. The woman was uncanny, and she held some trump card—that
much had been clear from the way Responsible went white when her
name was mentioned, as well as from the arrogance of her behavior. She'd
all but shoved the other Grannys aside taking the central place in the balcony row this morning, and she hadn't scrupled to do it without so much
as a beg-your-pardon, either. Some trump card. Something that Granny
Hazelbide had no clue to, but that came near unsettling *her* stomach.

Wickedness in a Granny was unthinkable; they were human like any
other human, and they could make mistakes, but in everything moral
they were above reproach. And it therefore made no sense that she should
suspect Leeward of evil intent . . . but something there nagged at her.

Responsible had matters well in hand and needed no attention. She
had turned the meeting over to her pettish uncle with casual ease and
gone out into the hall to climb the stairs to the balcony. The men were
still half stupored from the word patterns flowing over and around them,
a situation Donald Patrick would no doubt put an end to in short order.
He couldn't talk for beans, never had been able to. But it was his meeting now, and Granny Hazelbide could afford to give her mind over fully
to the problem of Granny Leeward, where logic *did* apply.

No Granny could do deliberate evil, that was a given. It would turn
inward and destroy her if she tried. She would sicken, and the evil would
show plain in her eyes and in her flesh. Not Granny Leeward; the woman
was rail-thin and had a nose like a fishhook, but she had the radiant bloom
of health. It followed then, followed as the night the day (and praise be
that had never failed yet), that Granny Leeward planned no wicked act
toward Responsible of Brightwater or anybody else. She *could* not.

And yet, wherever Granny Leeward moved, the other Grannys
pulled away from her, drew back their stiff skirts. The woman that sat at
her right hand now, Granny Golightly of Castle Clark, was not over-

fastidious. She was famous for her mischief, and for a certain cavalier disregard of the consequences of that mischief. Still she was edged to the right in her seat in a way that crowded her next neighbor and could not be comfortable, but preserved her from any chance of touching Leeward —it kept a full two inches of space between them. That provided the second given: it was not just herself, Granny Hazelbide of Brightwater Castle, as looked at Leeward and saw darkness puddling round her skirthems; it was all the Grannys.

And that provided the third. Twenty-seven Grannys could not be wrong. She might be overly suspicious herself, because she had raised Responsible of Brightwater and knew the Travellers had set themselves to bring down the Confederation the girl was sworn to maintain. One or two others might have a hidden soft spot for Responsible, those as had known her well years ago, a child visiting the Castles of near kin. But every *one* of them, even those that scarcely knew the daughter of Brightwater, was pulling back from Granny Leeward like she was a source of polluted water. That many Grannys, all turning against one of their own—that had never happened before. Not ever. Generations ago, when the poor soul at Castle Wommack had nearly brought the whole system crashing down around their heads by giving a Wommack girlbaby an Improper Name, and the Twelve Gates knew there was cause and aplenty for resentment, no Granny had turned on the foolish one. And Granny Leeward had done nothing yet this day but sit there and watch the proceedings, knitting sedately on an unidentifiable strip of dark-gray work—probably underwear for the young girls of Traveller, scratchy to subdue the natural passions the Travellers feared inflamed them all—knitting and watching. And breathing. She'd done nothing more.

Granny Hazelbide saw Responsible come in at the side door and motioned to her to come take her seat; she'd had enough and then some, and she meant to head for home. It was all very well leaving matters to Responsible and mouthing platitudes about lying in beds once they were made, but she loved that child. She had a few tea leaves to brew, and a few Charms and Spells to try, and furthermore she intended to set strong wards in Responsible's bedroom, where she slept not twenty feet away from Granny Leeward's bed. And might could be she'd take a nap; she wasn't as young as she had been.

Responsible accepted the seat gratefully, however much it might annoy her uncle to look up and see her there among the Grannys instead of in the back row as he would consider fitting for her age and station. She was worn completely out; if there was a reserve of energy left in her someplace, she didn't know its location and hoped she wouldn't find herself obliged to seek it.

Here she could keep an eye on her uncle, and an eye on the delegations, and her presence would make it plain to Granny Leeward that she wasn't afraid of her. She *was* afraid of Lewis Motley Wommack the 33rd, but she was safe from him up here, and she intended to surround herself with respectable females of all ages and degrees until she was back in her room with her door barred against all untoward possibilities that might involve him.

There'd been a good deal of sympathy for the sister, young Jewel of Wommack, when the Attendants had brought the gossip back from the Landing. Two Grannys telling that child she had to keep her brother in order, more shame to them, and if they thought it was good for Jewel's character she hoped they both came down with pimples on their nosepoints. It wasn't fair to the girl, especially since she would surely believe them, and torture herself through the whole Jubilee—instead of enjoying herself as she ought to of been allowed to do—following that wicked young man around and worrying about how to see that he did no harm.

Personally, Responsible had no intention *what*soever of turning her safety from Wommack over to his sister. Jewel was beautiful, and it was said that she was astonishingly learned, and she had the awkward elegance that meant the beauty would be the lasting kind. But Responsible had looked her full in the eyes at last night's Dance, going down a Reel, and what she'd seen had been the clear innocent eyes of a child. A wise child, but a child all the same. Responsible of Brightwater was prepared to love the girl—she was irresistible—but she would take care of herself her *self*.

And she'd speak to the two Grannys. They'd no right to spoil the girl's entire holiday with their rearing practices—the Gates only knew when she'd get another one, stuck there on Kintucky. Let them bring her up properly when they had her home again at Castle Wommack; that struck Responsible as quite soon enough.

3

She could not move, not even to shake one skinny finger at him; she couldn't talk except when it pleased him to permit her that privilege, which was rarely. But short of actually putting her into pseudocoma, there was no way that Lincoln Parradyne Smith the 39th could dull the red rage that glowed in the eyes of Granny Gableframe, and he didn't consider the coma justified by the situation. In fact, he found himself admiring the amount of hate the old lady managed to express without word or motion. There was an ancient saying—"If looks could kill . . ."—and it surely applied here. He'd seen some looks in his time, but this one was spectacular, even for a Granny.

"You might just as well stop glaring at me like that, my dear Granny Gableframe," he'd told her. From the very beginning. "I'm not impressed," he'd said, "not in any way, not to any degree. You may glare at me all day and all night—all you are going to get from it is a headache." It hadn't discouraged her any.

Lincoln Parradyne didn't mind, though he didn't look forward to the moment when he would have to turn her loose and put up with her tongue-lashing.

"How long can you keep her like that?"

Lincoln Parradyne glanced at the man that stood beside him, wondering if he could be serious, and sure enough he appeared to be, and so he shrugged his shoulders and raised his eyebrows and said, "Till she dies, if I like."

"Well, I don't want her dying," objected Delldon Mallard Smith the 2nd, "whether you like or not!" And all three of his brothers, standing round the Granny's bed, indicated that they strongly agreed with that sentiment.

The Magician of Rank asked himself, from time to time, which one of the four Smith brothers was the stupidest. Delldon Mallard the 2nd was the biggest; Whitney Crawford the 14th was the handsomest; Leroy Fortnight the 23rd was the fattest; and it appeared that the most cowardly of the set was Hazeltine Everett the 11th. But for stupidity, it was hard to choose among them, and the fact that they were his blood kin was a heavy burden to him.

"You hear me, now?" demanded Delldon Mallard. "I want no misunderstanding. That's our Granny and we love her, and if it just happens that she can't quite be brought to go along with what's needful without a certain amount of pressure being applied, all right; but she's just an old lady and she's frail, and I don't want—"

Lincoln Parradyne was completely out of patience. The man would ramble on for half an hour if he wasn't stopped, and all of it nonsense.

"I don't want to hear what you don't want," he said tiredly. "I have no *interest* in what you don't want! Your requirements were quite clearly specified, Delldon Mallard—you wanted Granny Gableframe in a state where she could not interfere with your plans, and I've provided you that. If she were one of the servingmaids, I could also have seen to it that her condition wasn't marred by . . . irritation. But this is a *Granny,* cousin, not a dithering girlchild."

Leroy Fortnight snorted from the foot of the bed, where he was alternately kicking the bedpost with his boot and punching it with his fist.

"What's the matter?" he asked, snickering. "Isn't your magic good enough to keep her down? One little old scrawny woman?"

"I don't believe I'd talk to Lincoln Parradyne like that," hazarded one of the others. "Not unless you fancy him laying you out the same way as the Granny. You think you'd like that, Leroy Fortnight?"

Delldon Mallard cleared his throat. "That," he said firmly, "would . . . uh . . . be illegal. *Illegal.*"

"Do you suppose," marveled the Magician of Rank, staring at the big man with true astonishment, "that what I've done to Granny Gableframe *isn't* illegal?"

"Well . . ."

"Well? *Well?*"

"I don't really think so," said Delldon Mallard. He was the oldest, and Master of this Castle; he felt a sense of responsibility and wanted his position made unambiguous. "I don't really think that legality enters in here, you know. I . . . uh . . . gave the matter a good deal of thought before I asked the Magician of Rank to do this. And I'm satisfied in my own mind that what this represents is a kind of . . . uh . . . contest. That is, if the

Magician of Rank was to perform a Transformation like this and paralyze just *any* old lady, say, just any old lady at all, why, that would . . . uh . . . be a different kind of thing. *That* would be illegal, I'd be obliged to agree. But not with the Granny here . . . She, uh, has her own magic, and as I said—"

"Sit down!" said the Magician of Rank. "Delldon Mallard Smith the Second—shut *up* and sit *down*."

"Now I don't see that there's any call for you to speak to me like that," began Delldon Mallard. And then he saw Lincoln Parradyne set one hand on the bedstead and stretch out the other toward him, and he sat down instantly and closed his mouth.

"I believe," said Lincoln Parradyne through clenched teeth, "that I had better explain this to you gentlemen just one more time before we leave for Castle Brightwater. You do not appear to me to have it straight in your minds. Not at all."

"Now, Linc—"

"Be still!" thundered the Magician of Rank. "You listen to what I say, you listen with both ears for once! Do I have your attention?"

The silence indicated that he did, and he went on.

"It is true that the Granny has magic of her own, surely; you'd be in sorry shape if she didn't. Your girls would be born and given names at hazard, the way it was done on Old Earth, if the Granny weren't at hand to choose a Proper Name. Your crops would fail and your goats would go dry. There would be rot and mildew and dirt and vermin inside the Castle, and there'd be blight and ignorance and dirt and vermin outside it. There'd be nobody to heal your sick—I give you my word neither the Magicians *nor* the Magicians of Rank have time these days to see to your sniffles and your bellyaches. But as for there being a contest between us, between myself and Granny Gableframe . . . think of a contest between twelve grown men and one four-year-old boy, and you'll have something to compare! The odds are about the same."

"Well," said Delldon Mallard, tugging at his bottom lip, "I think we'd need an interpretation on that. I wouldn't want anybody saying as how I wasn't fair. It might could be that you know a few tricks the Grannys don't, Lincoln, I'm willing to grant you that. But I do believe your ego has a tendency to run away with you." He chuckled softly, all tolerance and indulgence, and his brothers echoed him; and the Granny lying helpless under the counterpane closed her eyes as if she could bear no more.

Lincoln Parradyne stared at the man, oldest of the Smith boys, Master of Castle Smith, and wondered whether he could control himself. I keep your Mules flying, he thought. Without my help a Mule could no more fly than it could knit. I see to your weather, so that no rain falls except where it's needed, and I control the snow and the wind and all things that have to do with the heat and the cold, with wet and with dry . . . Because of the Magicians of Rank you have never known a blizzard or a drought or an earthquake. Or a disease that lasts more than a week, and even those we could shorten to minutes if we didn't feel that the week was good for your coddled little characters. We see to—

He stopped, suddenly, in the middle of his silent recital, feeling foolish. There was some question as to just who it was he was trying to convince, since nobody could hear him. And if anyone could have, he'd of been guilty of spreading knowledge allowed only to the other Magicians of Rank and that accursed girl at Brightwater.

"No point in arguing with him," said the handsome brother. "No point atall. Delldon sets his mind to a thing, there's no changing it. And his mind is for sure set on this."

"You're quite right," said Lincoln Parradyne grimly. "If Delldon Mallard has his mind set to do something he knows is wrong, there's no hope of swaying him from whatever excuse he comes up with to justify that wrongdoing."

"You think we're doing something wrong?" Leroy Fortnight turned on his oldest brother. "Think he's right? If he's right, I'm here to tell you, I'm not going to go through with this, Delldon Mallard."

Lincoln Parradyne walked out of the room and left them listening attentively to their brother's endless explanation of why what might be wrong at some other time, if somebody else were doing it, in some other situation, was *perfectly* justified at this time, in this situation, with the brothers Smith doing it. He had no doubt that Delldon Mallard would be able to convince them; their consciences were no more tender than their manners, and they were accustomed to giving in to Delldon's arguments. They had spent their *lives* giving in to Delldon's arguments. He himself had no stomach for listening to it again, however, and he felt a certain twinge of his own conscience at the thought that the Granny had no choice but to endure it in silence.

If she had known what a mire of ignorance and ineptitude she would spend her time dealing with, would she have chosen this Castle as her residence, he wondered? Though someone had to, and Gableframe was a good deal tougher and better fit to manage it than most. For himself, if it were not that to leave would have meant abandoning his own kin . . .

Outside the door, he nearly fell over a cluster of the Smith women, all hovering there wringing their hands—always excepting Dorothy, who was convinced that her father's plan was a brilliant stroke. She smiled at Lincoln Parradyne, and then curtsied slowly, a deep court curtsy ending in a wobble that turned her face a dusky red.

"Better practice that some more," he said. As if he didn't know how many hours she had spent practicing it, standing in front of the tall mirror in her bedroom. The flush on her cheeks deepened, and he thought for a moment that she would cry. She cried easily, fat tears always right at the surface and trembling in her eyes. It was a curious characteristic in a female like Dorothy, who was just plain *mean,* right down to the core; no doubt she'd outgrow it.

"How is Granny Gableframe?" asked one of the women, her voice tight as a banjo string in dry weather. "How does she feel?"

"She feels thoroughly miserable right now," said the Magician of Rank, "as would you, if you were in a similar condition."

"But she's all right."

Lincoln Parradyne sighed. They were so determined, these Smiths, to have all their cake, frosted and frilled on the shelf, while they savored it to the last bite.

"She is not 'all right,'" he said crossly. "Of course not. There are perhaps a dozen different ways to cause a person to suffer from motor paralysis, some of them more unpleasant than others, but none of them could be said to be precisely desirable. However, she's in no danger, if that's what you mean."

"It must be terrible—not being able to move anything but her eyes . . ."

"No," he said, making his way through them and answering her over his shoulder as he headed down the corridor. "On the contrary, it's very restful. Good for the Granny to have a little holiday from tearing round the Castle tongue-lashing and nagging and fretting, in my opinion. Her major problem is that she refuses to relax and enjoy it."

Her major problem, if he'd been able to explain it to them, was of course that she knew what he'd done and why, and was in a flaming rage because her own magic skills weren't adequate to reverse such a simple process.

He could feel them staring after him, and he kept his back to them till he reached a corner he could turn. The Smith women, all but Dorothy, disapproved of what was going on, which showed considerable good sense on their part. Too bad they hadn't exerted that good sense in marrying elsewhere, and left the four brothers to bachelor splendor and an end of the marred line.

They would be easier to manage once the whole group had left the Castle and was headed for the Jubilee—they'd take no chances of embarrassing their men in front of other people, whatever their personal opinions might be. He'd even considered letting the Granny go along, and manipulating her through the remaining days of the Jubilee; there were Formalisms & Transformations that would have made it possible for him to do that, and her absence was sure to create suspicion. But although her behavior would of passed well enough with the ordinary citizen, he was by no means sure that his control would not have been spotted by the other Grannys—or by Responsible of Brightwater. He had decided, finally, not to risk it, and to accept the consequences of the alternatives open to him.

In the corridor a Senior Attendant stopped him, to report that everything was ready for the Smith delegation's journey to the Jubilee.

"You're sure of that, now?" he asked the Attendant sharply. "If anything has been forgotten, it won't be amusing—for us *or* for you."

"Twenty-seven trunks they loaded on the ship," said the Attendant, stolid as always. You didn't get to be a Senior Attendant in this Castle unless you learned to hide your emotions. "Checked the count myself to make certain sure of it. And I was most particular that the one you marked with the *x*, it got put on board early this morning, and well at the back. The lizzies are out front to take you all down to the dock, and in perfect order—I had the airjets seen to not ten minutes ago, and the batteries as well, in case the cloud cover doesn't lift. Nary a thing on your list, sir, that I *haven't* seen to."

"Good man," said Lincoln Parradyne. "I appreciate good service, and I remember it."

"That's known," said the man. "And the drape of your cloak needs attention, if you don't mind my saying so."

The Magician of Rank glanced at his shoulder and murmured agreement: what was supposed to be seven neat folds in an orderly cascade was more like the casual pleating of a little girl's skirt, and that would tell him something about allowing himself to be provoked by his cousins into flailing his arms around and shaking his fists at the ceiling. He adjusted the cape's arrangement with swift fingers, and refastened the silver bar that drew the falls together and held them back out of the way of his right arm.

"There," he said, "will that do it?"

"That's proper, sir," said the Attendant.

"Then will you go along and pass the message to the rest of our group? Tell them to meet me by the front gate and look sharp about it—it'll be late in the Second Day before we reach the Jubilee, even if we have fair winds all the way." Which he'd see that they did; it was going to be crucial for them to arrive at *exactly* the right moment in the proceedings.

"I'll do that," said the man. "But I do think it's a shame Granny Gableframe went on ahead of the rest of you. It would of pleasured her a good deal to ride in the lizzy and give you all what-for the whole way to Brightwater on the ship. Granny Gableframe's partial to water and to company, that's also known."

"The Granny would of been uncomfortable on this trip," said Lincoln Parradyne casually. "At her age and with her rheumatism?" He clucked his tongue. "It was much better for her to have me fly her in on the Mule, and avoid all that commotion."

The Attendant had known the Granny a long time. He gave him a look that couldn't exactly be described as disrespectful, but let Lincoln Parradyne know what the man's opinion was of his estimate of the old lady's constitution; and the Magician of Rank snapped at him to get a move on, before things could become more complicated than they were already. It was a fine kettle when the staff of a Castle had more brains than the Family they were hired to serve, and he sincerely hoped the situation wasn't widespread. When he got back he'd review the whole bunch, and any that showed signs—like this man—of being sharper than they needed to be to carry out their duties would have to be replaced.

And then he sighed, and went quickly to his rooms to fill in the final character of a Transformation he'd had ready and waiting for completion these last three days. He wasn't eager to do it, but it was necessary. The Granny was going to have his hide in small scraps for the work that had deprived her of movement and of speech, that could be counted on already. What she would do about this last task of his, the one that would provide the Castle temporarily with a new cat—of origin unknown, but much too beautiful not to be spoiled and watched over—he didn't even care to contemplate. If things went as he hoped, she might forgive him; on her deathbed, maybe, she might forgive him. If the Smith brothers, or one of their nervous women, made some mistake that put a kink in the plan—which was likely—she would never forgive him.

And *then* Delldon Mallard Smith the 2nd would have a chance to see his "contest"! Years of it. Years of the Granny doing her Charms and Spells, setting them against him with her little mouth puckered tight as her heart must be in her chest; and years of him, Lincoln Parradyne Smith the 39th, canceling out each and every one of them. The chance of the Granny getting one past him was too small to be worth considering, but the amount of *time* he was going to have to spend in the feud would pile up into a respectable amount of misery over the years. Grannys lived to a formidable old age, and he'd never known one to mellow.

It would have made things so much simpler if they could of brought her around to see things their way and cooperate with them—if not to help them, at least not to interfere. But she had told them flat out what she thought of Delldon Mallard's great plan.

"Flumdiddle!" she'd said. "Goatwallow! Cowflop!" And a half-hour string of more of the same, with a persistent refrain on how they'd all taken leave of what pitiful supply of sense they'd been born with, and the litany of ancient oaths for coda and elaboration.

Lincoln Parradyne didn't agree with the Granny. Every means of foreseeing he had at his disposal had been clear: the road would be a tad bumpy for what they had in mind, and its duration would depend on the skill of those carrying it out—but they *would* bring it off. That was enough for him; the potential once it was done was everything he had ever wanted and had thought hopelessly out of his reach. Well worth the risk, and the problems could be faced as they came along. He was only anxious to begin.

4

Opening Day dragged on, and Responsible dragged on through it, up in the balcony. The breeze through the windows of the Independence Room was heavy with the smell of early summer flowers, and the soft hum of the red Ozark bees on whose ministrations those flowers depended, and the combination was an effective sedative. Nothing that was going on inside did anything to lessen its effectiveness, either. She supposed she must have heard worse speeches and more boring ones, somewhere, sometime, but she could not during that interminable day think of an example. If the overdose of tedium didn't take any of the starch out of the Traveller delegation, it could only be due to their bizarre practice of spending all of every Sundy listening to a single extended sermon, *with* elaborate developments and codas and commentaries and extrapolations, and emendations on the extrapolations, and scattering slightly truncated versions of the same throughout the rest of the week. They were calloused to this kind of thing, both ears and rears, and could of endured a lot more of it, she supposed. Everyone else, however, including their allies the Farsons and the Guthries, was exhausted long before the Closing Prayer. The way some of the delegates had slumped down in their seats by midafternoon had all twenty-seven Grannys still present—and for sure still straight as spikes in *their* seats—clicking their tongues fit to drown out their knitting needles.

Responsible was satisfied with the effect. She much doubted that the population had stayed glued to the comsets to watch the proceedings of *this* day, and she figured to of lost the majority of them well before noon. She doubted even more that they'd tune in their sets to more of the same tomorrow, and that suited her purposes. If there was going to be a battle on the floor of the Independence Room, the fewer Ozarkers that knew about it and had time to get excited about it, the better. And she had seen to it that there were plenty of other ways to spend your time than sit at the comsets, or even in the balcony, while the days of the Grand Jubilee went passing by.

There were four different plays—one religious, one historical, one comedy, one adventure—going on in Capital City at all times, and enough different ones in their repertoires to be sure there'd be no repetition. Three dance troupes were on duty, two indoors and the other moving around the city, and ordered to make themselves available anywhere they were asked. Four sports exhibitions, including one laid on especially for the tadlings. Checkers tournaments everywhere she had a leftover corner. Two speech competitions, tours through the caves for the romantic of mind and tours through the farms for the practical. Mule races for the daring, and all-day nonstop sermons for the conservative. Down at the Landing there was an inexhaustible picnic, where you could sit and eat in comfort, passing your time in gossip and watching the ships come and go in the harbor. Outside the city borders the largest fair ever put on anywhere would be going on all five days, with every kind of game and exhibit and performance, every variety of food and drink, rides all the way from the sedatest of merry-go-rounds to a thing called Circle-Of-Screams that was guaranteed to make you get off and sit down for half an hour to review your sins. She had something for everybody, something for every time, and comcrews everywhere to beam out the doings to those that couldn't come to Brightwater. The doldrums on the channel given over to the Confederation Hall assembly were not going to be able to compete for attention.

There'd been plenty of opposition to the scope of the celebration, even from her grandfather, Jonathan Cardwell Brightwater the 12th, who didn't as a rule care what *anybody* spent, so long as they extended him the same privilege.

"Are you *sure* all that's needful, Responsible?"

She'd heard that till the time came when she suggested they get a sign made and save their throats. And she'd ignored it. Yes, it was needful, and furthermore it was the one and the only Jubilee she expected ever to be involved in; she'd not have it said that Brightwater stinted, or offered its guests anything less than the very best there was to offer.

"Pride, missy!" the Granny had said, shaking her finger. "Just *pure* pride! And where do you reckon it'll lead you, one of these days?"

She took a deep breath, remembering, and then, finally, the Reverend said "Amen!" and it was over, and the delegations began to file out of the Hall. The band in the bandstand at the corner of the lawn struck up a rousing march at the sight of the first man stiff and blinking at the light and the air, and that did get them moving a bit more briskly. The Grannys and Responsible brought up the rear, everybody else having left the balcony hours before, and she made certain that the Grannys surrounded her on all sides. Invisibility was her goal, and she achieved it clear to the gates of Castle Brightwater and across the courtyard to the open front doors, where the Grannys scattered and forced her to hurry for cover. A narrow cramped corridor that ran the length of the Castle and was meant to give the staff a speedy way in or out of any of the rooms had served both her and her sister Troublesome well when they were children; it served her admirably now.

Nevertheless, when she finally reached her room on the third floor, she found that all her painstaking precautions had been a waste. She could of come straight up the front way and saved herself fifteen minutes of walking time, and had a herald before her crying, "Make way for Responsible of Brightwater!"—it wouldn't of made any difference.

Lewis Motley Wommack the 33rd was waiting for her, sitting on the floor with his knees drawn up and his arms clasped around them, leaning back comfortably with his head against the wall beside her bedroom door.

"Oh, law," she said, "wherever did you come from?"

"Afternoon, Responsible of Brightwater. Same place you did—that repository of hot wind and tiny minds we choose to call Confederation Hall."

She ignored that, and said, "Good afternoon, Lewis Motley Wommack, and you'll miss your supper if you don't hurry. The delegates are intended for the first serving in the Great Hall . . . you want to end up eating with the children?"

He cocked his head and raised his eyebrows at her, and looked her up and down, and she took one step backward before she caught herself.

"You ran away from me once," he said solemnly.

"So I did."

"You plan to repeat that?"

"If I do, you'll no doubt notice," she snapped.

He smiled and leaned his head back again and closed his eyes; it was clear he'd no intention of moving from her door. She could, of course, have had him removed—or removed him herself, if the commotion either would cause had seemed justified. It would of been an interesting problem of manners if it had not concerned her quite so personally.

It is called a Timecorner, Granny Hazelbide had said, holding her tight between knees so bony they hurt her even then, in front of all the other five-year-olds, *and we cannot see around it.* Could she run away from a Timecorner twice?

And then there was the question of what, precisely, *he* knew. He had glanced at her when she sat exhausted on a bench in his Castle hall, and for sure, just as the Prophecy had said, he had known her and she had known him, in some way that she could not account for. But had some Tutor told him, years ago, that the day would come when there'd be hard times for the entire population of Ozark on account of his behavior with Responsible of Brightwater, and hers with him? No matter what she did, said the Prophecy, there'd be hard times—but nowhere did it say there was a way of escaping. It might could be that he sat there now, insolent by her door as if he'd been near kin, because he too had been told that what lay before them was not to be avoided, and he wanted to get it over with and put it behind him. And it might could be he knew nothing at all, that no gossip from those little girls had found its way to Castle Wommack over those eight years, and that he sat there for reasons he understood not at all.

"Lewis Motley Wommack," she said, watching him closely, "why are you here on my doorsill?"

"To see Responsible of Brightwater," he answered, perfectly easy. "I've come for audience."

"Audiences," she said carefully, "are held with queens and kings. We've no such nonsense here, young Wommack."

He opened his eyes then and looked at her, and Responsible turned her own eyes swiftly away and stared at the floorboards of the corridor, that were polished and gleaming for the Jubilee till she could see a dim reflection of herself staring back at her. She was in no hurry to look at him directly; one look into those eyes of his and the world had swung away from beneath her, once before. In the seconds it had lasted she had fallen endlessly, before she had managed to break free and run.

"You are a kind of royalty," he said, and she could feel his smile like sunlight on her flesh. "I don't know what kind, nor does anybody else— but I mean to find out."

"You talk rubbish," she said.

"And you tell lies—and we're even. Look at me, Responsible of Brightwater, her that travels round the Castles on Solemn Quest, with boots of scarlet leather and whip and spurs of silver . . . her that can command a Magician of Rank as easily as I command an Attendant—oh, yes, my fine young lady, we *do* hear these things, and the servingmaids *will* talk, for all you caution them . . . *Look* at me!"

Because she had the feeling that escape, if escape there might be, or perhaps the mercy of delay, lay specifically in *not* looking, she shook her head like a stubborn child ordered to recite, and stared unrelenting at the floor. And that was her undoing. You can't keep a wary eye on a serpent unless you watch him, and his hands were gripping her shoulders before she knew he'd moved.

"I tell you," he said in a voice that held the promise of endless patience, "look at me! Am I so ugly as all that? So terrible I'll turn your face to stone?"

She struggled in his hands and turned her head away, and with no trouble at all he used one of those hands to hold her fast and the other to tilt her face up. She could feel the warmth radiating from him where he stood, not half an inch between her body and his, and she put all her strength into pulling away from him, with her eyes tight shut.

"Responsible of Brightwater," he scoffed, "I expect you were not Properly Named. Poor little girlbaby, your Granny clabbered the thing. Timorous of Brightwater, that's more like it. Cowardice of Brightwater, might could be. My little sister has more courage than you."

That bothered her not at all. She'd been hearing nonsense intended to provoke her to foolishness all her life, and except for that single mistake with Granny Leeward, none of it had succeeded in a very long time. What she'd heard from all around her lately made his taunting no more than prattle. But his physical strength was a different matter. There was no legal way she could break loose from his grip, short of screaming for help like a terrified child—and nothing would of brought her to such a shameful pass.

There was no help for it. And once her mind was settled to that, she wasted no more time. She opened her eyes and looked at him.

No one would have called him handsome, but he was wondrously beautiful. His head was thick with curls of coppery Wommack hair, copper with lights and fire in it, and she knew from the look of his wrists

and throat that naked he would gleam in the light with that copper everywhere. He had the beauty gnarled trees and rough cliff faces have, with
no elegance to him anywhere—except for his eyes. They were blue, like
any Wommack eyes, but a blue so dark that it put her in mind of the violets that grew deep in Brightwater's forests in the last days of March and
were so useful for simple Spells. The eyes had *great* elegance, and an utter
authority, and they were as dangerous as she had remembered; she looked
full into them, mustering her courage, and once again the floor dropped
from beneath her feet and she was helpless.

"Come into my room," she said to him, in a voice she had no mas-
tery of and hardly recognized, suspended in endless blue. It was, she
decided, like being trapped in glass—blue stained glass. She had a sudden
image of herself in a pointed church window, marked off all around with
a leading of black, and perhaps a Mule beside her and a squawker above
her head, and cleared her throat quickly. Laughter would not be appropriate, however much it might tempt her.

"You're not afraid for your reputation?"

"I have no reputation," she told him. And that was so. Everything
had been said of her, and much of it was true. "Are you afraid for yours?
Or have you forgotten how doors work?"

He rubbed at his nose with the hand that wasn't occupied in holding her, but he made no move to touch her door.

"It's warded," he said.

Responsible gathered together enough of her attention to sniff the
air, and to set aside the smell of him that flooded her senses, and was
amazed that she'd not noticed the garlic sooner. Granny Hazelbide had
been by here, and would no doubt have hung garlic wreaths round
Responsible's neck if she'd dared.

"My doors," she told him, "are always warded, one way or another,
and always will be. Make up your mind, Lewis Motley Wommack—you
have waited all this time here at my door, and played a foolish child's
game of Look Into My Eyes with me, and now I am going *through* that
door. Do you follow me or not?" And she added, "Mind, I'm not running from you. You're free to keep me company."

Once they were inside he sat in the rocker by her window that
Granny Hazelbide had chosen the night before, and she took another and
pulled it over facing him.

"Well," she asked, "you suffer any ill effects from the wards?"

He looked himself over, and he took his time about it, and then he allowed that there seemed to be no change.

"I haven't been turned into any kind of varmint, there's that," he said. "Nor struck dead, nor my wits scrambled. There's that."

"Did you expect such stuff?" she marveled. "Wards are to keep evil *out*, not create it! What kind of Tutor did you have, there at Castle Wommack, that he didn't teach you even that?"   .

"You are highly valued, daughter of Brightwater," he answered, "though it's not considered polite to mention it. Very highly valued indeed. I've heard that song"—he sang the chorus in a pleasant enough voice that would one day be deep—

> "What did you learn as you flew out so fine,"
> splendid on Muleback, dressed like a queen?
> What did you learn, daughter of Brightwater?
> Tell us the wonderful things that you've seen!"

"All the way to Kintucky," she said, wondering, "all that way, you've heard Caroline-Ann of Airy's song?"

He ducked his head, mock-humble. "Even in the Kintucky outback," he said, "we have comsets. I know all the verses—shall I prove that?"

"Mercy, don't! I'd feel a fool for sure, sitting in my own room and hearing you sing a song about me."

"Well, then," he said, "because you are so highly valued, I'd thought it might be harder to find myself alone with you. I was prepared for . . . oh, at least a Granny in a fury, to bar my way."

"And so she would, if she knew you were here," said Responsible.

"And what will she do when she finds me here?"

Responsible shook her head in amazement. "Young Wommack," she said, "you are downright ignorant, not to mention insulting. Even here, 'in the Brightwater outback,' we know to knock on doors. Even Grannys don't enter rooms without leave—why should she find you here? I don't intend to give her leave."

He stood up at that, drew closed the curtains at all three of her windows, and went and stretched himself full length on her bed. She liked the look of him against her white counterpane, and she told him so.

He didn't pause to acknowledge the compliment.

"You learned many things, touring the Castles, having adventures," he said. "Now come learn something useful."

She was still thinking she would do no such thing when she lay down beside him. Her counterpane was turned down, and her clothes and his lay in a jumble on her rug, and the thought still lingered. Only when she noted that she had been right, that the copper hair covered him in all but two or three specific places, did she abandon that idea and concede that she was indeed about to learn something.

"I am *not* ready for this," she announced.

And there are times when the land is not ready for the rain, but it falls all the same.

He ran his fingertips over her thighs, and set his lips to her nipples, and he was not overly careful how much of his weight she had to bear.

"I dislike that," she said clearly.

"This, too?"

"I dislike that even more."

"You lie," he said.

She surely did. Everything his body had promised, shirted and trousered and cloaked, it delivered in abundance. Her loins arched toward his touch and she knew most clearly the meaning of longing. She was all out of patience, the aching of her body for him was unbearable, and if she had known any manner of hurrying him she would not have scrupled to use it. Unfortunately, she was operating this time from a position of total ignorance, and she could only grit her teeth till she shuddered, and wait.

"You're an anxious creature," he said finally, and he lifted her onto the gold of his belly and set her gently where she might ease her own need. It was not what she had expected at all, and certainly not what her experience in the stables and goatbarns had led her to expect, and she moaned in desperate frustration.

"It's impossible," she said. "It can't be *done* this way!"

"Lady, lady," he answered her, "I promised to teach you something useful. For sure it *can* be done this way, if you will only—there!"

Nothing she had heard or read or imagined had prepared her for what it was like to have the full thrust of his maleness within her, and she forgot everything in her determination to draw from him every last measure of the ecstasy offered.

"You see?" he said roughly.

She did, most certainly she did, and when he would have held her away from him she cried out fiercely and slapped at him, frantic in her determination to achieve something—her body knew what it was, though her mind did not—and he laughed and let her have her way for a while.

Until she hovered just on the edge of that achievement. And then, ignoring her teeth and her hands, he held her still in torment against him.

"Oh, dear heaven, dear heaven," she moaned, "let me *loose!*"

"Shhhhh . . . hush . . ."

"No! I can't bear it, I can't bear it another second . . ."

She fell against him, broken in despair, sobbing and past all pride, and he made a soft noise of satisfaction, gripped her in those sure hands, and held her while the shudders racked her, more and more swift, and her breath tore at her throat, and then he said:

"Now, Responsible of Brightwater. Now I shall show you the most useful thing of all."

And he grasped her hips and moved her, and suddenly she knew that she would die of joy, and he muffled her screams against his shoulders and let her take of him everything that she wanted. It took a very long time, and not once did he make a sound.

She had heard women speak, married women and women of experience, of what happened *after* the act of love. Some men, it seemed, would talk to you. Others would fall asleep. Some would demand food; among the Traveller males, she had heard it said, there were those that would drop to their knees and give thanks for the blessings just received.

This man, however, was doing none of those things. He had raised himself on one elbow and was staring at her as if he had never seen anything like her before anywhere. Responsible had no illusions about her beauty, she had Thorn of Guthrie to compare herself with every day of her life; it could not be that which put such an expression on his face. And she was reasonably sure that the look he bore was not the usual afterlove expression.

"What," he demanded harshly, "was *that?* What the Twelve Bleeding Gates *happened?*"

Responsible reminded him that she had been the virgin here, not him, which made that a foolish question. "There are a number of words to choose from," she added, "always depending on your degree of delicacy. Pick the one you like the best."

"That's not what I meant." And then, "You didn't notice anything unusual?"

Responsible made an exasperated noise and climbed over him abruptly, heading for her bath. The bed was a sea-marsh, and she was not much better.

"Young man," she said over her shoulder, "I have never lain with a man before you. If there was something unusual, I wouldn't know it. What do I have to compare with you?"

He followed her into the bathroom and joined her in the hot water, still frowning, and the frown lasted until they both were clean and once again clothed, and sitting in the two rockers as sedately as if nothing but conversation had ever passed between them.

"I must have imagined it," he stated.

"No. I am convinced that it truly did happen. I was there, Lewis Motley."

"Responsible of Brightwater, do you remember what you said to me, just at the last?"

It hardly seemed proper, but then nothing they'd done in the past hour had been proper. She thought for a moment, and then answered him to the best of her recollection.

"I said . . . 'My lovely one, it is so wonderful to be inside you.'"

He cleared his throat, and directed her to think about that.

"Doesn't it seem to you," he asked, "that the anatomy is just a tad scrambled?"

She thought about it, and saw what he meant.

"Isn't it always like that?" she asked. "After all, it's mighty close contact."

"Not that close," he said. "No. It is not always like that. In fact, it is not ever like that."

She set her lips, and found that she was no longer afraid of his eyes.

"It *was* like that," she declared. "I was there, and so were you, and for certain sure it was precisely like that. And if you didn't want it to be like that, you should have provided a lecture as you went along."

He was going to be a very stubborn man, she thought, immovable as a mountain; a natural force like a tide or a storm, against which you could break into a thousand pieces, and he would never notice. And she thought, somewhat more than a little belatedly, of the Timecorner Prophecy. There was a lot in there about what would happen if she "stood before him." She doubted that what she'd done could be so described.

"Law," she whispered, more to herself than to him, "I wonder what will happen now?"

He swore, and stood up to stand with his back to her, staring out of her window, holding back one curtain with his hand.

In honest bewilderment she asked him, "Why are you angry?"

"I'm not angry," he said, but he didn't turn around, and she knew that now *he* lied.

"Lewis Motley Wommack," she said, "go eat with the children. They'll be serving them now."

He left her without another word, and she sat there rocking until the last light was gone from her room and she rocked in full darkness. She wasn't sorry for what she had done; nothing that pleasant could be a thing to regret. And her fear of him was gone for good and all. But the consequences of what she had done, now there was something to ponder on. For one thing, she was vulnerable to a number of unpleasant things that her virginity had protected her from until now. The Magicians of Rank would not need to be half so constrained in their constant wearing away at her, now that she lacked her maidenhead, and the first to take a look at her tomorrow would know that. As would the Grannys, one and all. But the Prophecy had been most specific: whatever it was that she would loose upon this world, she and Jewel of Wommack's brother, the harm would not come from knowledge shared by their bodies. That was laid out unmistakably.

She knew his body well now, and intended to know it a great deal better; and with his skill he no doubt knew everything there was to know about hers. But if it was not that, not that knowledge that held the danger, what *was* it then? They had not talked as much as you did over the ordinary cup of coffee.

"Botheration," said Responsible, and decided she didn't want any supper.

She would take off her sheets, for they reeked of salt, and sleep that night on her counterpane. Let Granny Leeward lie on the other side of the wall and wonder why the daughter of this Castle had not appeared for supper; the daughter of this Castle would be sound asleep and not caring.

Tomorrow would be burden enough, when she had to face them all and see in their eyes—even Leeward's—that they knew of the change in her. Tomorrow there'd be no eternal agenda of ceremonies and prayers to hold back the plans of the delegations set to bring down the Confederation, the fools! Tomorrow she would sit in the balcony and watch, alert for the slightest move, the least word, the beginning of crisis, the turn that would mean it was time to call on the loyal delegations and find a way to put the necessary words in their mouths.

Tonight, she would sleep.

5

Responsible was sitting over the last cup of the pot of tea the servingmaid had brought her when the knock came at her door. She set the cup down, made sure her nightgown was decently arranged, and called, "Who's there?"

"Granny Leeward here, Responsible of Brightwater. Granny Leeward of Castle Traveller. May I come in?"

"You sound nothing *what*soever like a Granny," said Responsible deliberately. "I do believe you're a fraud and a sham, whoever you may be."

There was a silence, time enough for her to have another sip of her tea. It was her favorite cup, emerald-green china with a rim of silver, and sturdy enough to drink from half awake without worrying that she'd crush it, the last unbroken one of a set used for company meals when she was still in Granny School. She despised the cups her mother and grandmother chose to start their days with, delicate white porcelain with the Brightwater Crest on the side, big enough to hold maybe three good swallows, and so frail they felt like eggshells in your hand. She could face those later in the day if need be, but not before breakfast, and at no time did she admire them.

"Responsible of Brightwater, you bar your door to me, you'll rue it! A fine day it'll be when a wench of fourteen keeps me standing in a hall saying howdydo to the bare boards, and I'll thank you to keep that in mind, missy!"

"Ah," said Responsible, "now I hear you use formspeech, I recognize you for a Granny after all! Please to come in, Granny Leeward."

The old woman was dressed and ready for the day, all in her customary black, and her pale-blue eyes so cold in her bony face that they put Responsible in mind of two small dead fishes, side by side.

"Have a rocker," she told her, "and make yourself comfortable. Have you had your tea this morning or shall I send for you some?"

"I've been through with my tea this past hour," said Granny

Leeward, chill and snappish, "and waiting till I heard the sound of your cup on your saucer so I'd not wake you. You keep mighty highclass hours, to my way of thinking."

"Proceedings don't begin at Confederation Hall till nine," said Responsible, "and it's a while yet till it strikes seven. Ample time for what I have before me today."

"You've mighty little before you, this day and some days to come." The Granny sat down in a rocker, carefully settling her heavy skirts around her, and folded her hands in her lap. "That's what I've come to tell you about—and mind, I'll have no sass from you."

Responsible had some more tea and waited the move, and after the silence had stretched a ways Granny Leeward continued.

"You'll recall, I expect, that I was present—and quite a number of the other members of our delegation with me—when you put on your disgraceful performance at Castle Traveller a while back."

"I do recollect that, yes."

"And you do agree that it was—disgraceful."

"I messed up your fan a tad," said Responsible coldly, "but I did you no harm. And I believe Castle Traveller's budget will run to a fan or two."

"Sin," said Granny Leeward, like a stone falling. "It was *sin,* what you did."

"No," said Responsible. "It was illegal. The two things are not the same."

"Only a Magician of Rank has the authority to do what you did that day," said the Granny, chopping off every word, "and *that's* the illegal part. The sinful part is a woman even knowing what you obviously know, and having no more decency than to use that knowledge, and in full daylight before a dozen respectable people on top of *that*. And it was an ugly trick, missy, a purely *ugly* trick!"

"If there was sin—which I don't admit to—it was in losing my temper and falling into the trap you and your kin set for me. I'd say that was more stupidity than wickedness."

Granny Leeward gave her a narrow look, and as Responsible had expected, there came a sudden look of understanding in her eyes. She'd be seeing that look a lot oftener than she cared to today.

"I see you've added a *new* wickedness to your inventory," said the old woman. "You're a *bold* hussy, I'll grant you that."

Responsible sighed, and set her tray on the night table by her bed.

"Granny Leeward," she said, "you've come to chastise me for my foolishness at Castle Traveller—call it sin if you please, I'll not waste my breath arguing theology with you before breakfast. Well and good; I'm not proud of it. There you sat, leading me on and fanning yourself with that black fan; and all I had to do was heat up its handle a tad to advise you I intended to be treated with respect. There was no call for me to turn that fan into a handful of mushrooms—"

"Black and *rotting* mushrooms, with the smell of death on 'em!" interrupted Leeward, and Responsible nodded.

"Quite right," she said. "The black was appropriate, seeing as how you Travellers find it the only fit color for human use, but there was *no* call to make them rot in your hand. You caught me with a child's trick, and I'm well and thoroughly ashamed that I took that bait. But it seems to me you made me pay for that already, Granny Leeward. How greedy for revenge *are* you?"

The old woman snorted, and her face was stiff with contempt.

"I wouldn't want any misunderstanding between you and me," she said, leaning back in the rocker and steepling her fingers. "Not any misunderstanding whatsoever. Might could be I should clarify this for you."

"I'd be grateful," said Responsible.

Granny Leeward counted the points off one at a time. "What you did to *me*," she said, "practicing an illegal act of magic, and a foul one, on my person—that goes unpunished still. You lay for a day with deathdance fever, that the Magicians call Anderson's Disease, as payment for carrying out your ugliness before the Family—that's paid. Your offense to me still stands, and I'll call that in when I choose; I don't choose just yet, Responsible of Brightwater, not just yet. And that's not why I'm here."

"You're not clarifying *much*, Granny Leeward, but your narrowness of spirit. Perhaps you could try a little harder?"

"There are six delegates from Castle Traveller as will sit in the Independence Room this day, and as saw what you did," hissed Granny Leeward, "and they're ready and willing to denounce you before the entire convention of delegates, the audience in the balcony, and those watching on their comsets. That make it clearer?"

"Mighty gallant, your men," said Responsible. "It must make you proud."

"A female such as you, missy, ought not to have the gall to ask for gallantry. Well on the way to being a witch, and clear the other side of being a fornicator, and you talk about gallantry? That's for decent women, not for your kind."

"You're plain-spoken," said Responsible. "That's useful in a Granny."

"Didn't I say I'd take no sass from you? Your memory gone with your maidenhead?"

"A compliment is not sass," said Responsible, with as much sass as she was able to muster. "I judge Grannys as I judge Mules, and you rank high. Now speak your piece."

Those pale-blue eyes . . . she had not been surprised to see them like dead fish, but spitting blue fire was surprising. It would have been pleasant to think that the old woman might be tricked in return, brought to a sufficient pitch of fury to lead her into some indiscretion of her own, leaving the two of them in a more balanced position; but it wouldn't happen. To begin with, they were alone, and if the Granny was being humiliated there was no one to see or know it but herself. And to go on with, Responsible was certain the woman knew nothing beyond Granny Magic, all of which was legal for her to use.

Granny Leeward leaned forward, stabbing the air with her pointing finger, and she laid it out for Responsible so there could be no confusion in any least particular.

"Either you stay clear away from Confederation Hall," the Granny said, "where you cannot interfere in what's none of your business and never has been, or my son will stand before the entire assembly this morning and denounce you—leaving out *no* details, keep that in mind!—and the rest of those as saw you will back him up. Now I reckon that is clear as springwater, but if it's not I'll be glad to embroider it for you some."

Responsible sank back against her pillows and whistled long and low and silent. Now she'd heard it, it was obvious, but she hadn't expected it. Which was an interesting measure of her strategic skills.

"Botheration," she said aloud, and thought a word that she'd never heard spoken, though it was claimed to exist.

"Keep your botherations to yourself," said the Granny, "and the Travellers won't add to them. We've other doings to concern us, and telling that sorry tale about you would only use up another day on top of the one you wasted for us yesterday. But if you insist on coming into the Hall, spite of what I've said to you, we *will* waste that time, I promise you, and I'll not scruple to stand in the balcony and add my voice to the testimonies."

"I believe you have me," said Responsible, taking another drink of tea. "All things considered."

"That we do," said Granny Leeward. "That we surely do, and if ever a female deserved it, you qualify."

"Blackmail doesn't burden your conscience, Granny?" Responsible asked.

Granny Leeward sat straight and pale. "We walk a narrow line at Castle Traveller," she said. "We keep the old ways, and there's none of the rest of you as does. We know, the Gates be praised, the difference between a sin and its name. That's a difference not to be despised, nor yet forgotten."

"Explain me that, Granny Leeward—and its application in this matter of you and me. I don't see it."

"I'll explain you nothing! You need moral instruction, you've a Granny here, and a Reverend as well, though he's a poor thing. This universe has one primary law—as ye sow, so shall ye reap—and *we* abide by that. I come here as no instrument of blackmail, Responsible of Brightwater; I come as an instrument of justice!"

"I wonder," mused Responsible, and the Granny drew herself up in the rocker, bridling all over with outrage. Responsible had heard about people bridling, and read the phrase, but this was the first time she'd ever seen it.

"On Old Earth," she said casually, "there were those so convinced of their purity, so sure they were instruments of justice, that they put others to the rack and the fire out of concern for their immortal souls. Now I suggest to you that you might want to keep that in mind your *self*, Granny Leeward. There's ugly, and then there's ugly."

Granny Leeward stood up like she'd sat on a straight pin, shaking all over with a rage she wouldn't stoop to express, and Responsible made a mental note—this was one who did not handle well any criticism that struck at her morality. It might be useful to know that one day. And while she had it going, she drove it home.

"And it doesn't burden your conscience that you Grannys are charged to *help* me, not hinder me?" she demanded. "I find *that* curious."

The Granny's face closed, shut, and if the rage was still there she mastered it. She gave no sign that she'd heard Responsible's last question.

"I'll leave it to you to furnish your excuses for your absence," she said, looking right through the girl. "You lie easy enough, it should cause you no special trouble. Just you stay away from the Hall. And I'll have your word on it."

"You have it," said Responsible wearily. They were tiresome, these Travellers, with their never-ending insistence on guarantees. "And now you *do* have it, I'll thank you to leave. I have work to do, and I'd best get at it."

Granny Leeward headed for the door, but she stopped there long enough to shake her finger some more and say a few sentences on the subject of pride going before a fall, and peace coming to them as deserved it and misery to those as didn't, and just deserts. Responsible rode this out in silence—she had no intention of easing any wounds she might have inflicted on this one—and the time finally came when the woman had either exhausted her supply of moral justifications or tired her own tongue, and she went out the door, leaving a vast silence behind her.

Responsible lay there and whistled her way through three choruses of "Once Again, Amazing Grace," as a calming measure, and gave her situation some careful thought.

Under her bottom pillow, for example, there was a cylinder no bigger than a needle, and in it a list written on pliofilm and headed "Things To Do When I Get Home." Weeks it had been there, shoved out of sight till she could find time to tackle it, and there'd been nights when she'd had the feeling it burned her head right through the feathers and heavy pillowslips. Might could be she'd make her way through some of the items on that list after all, while she was staying away from the Hall.

And then, might could be she'd take advantage of the opportunity to just *lie* here? She was that tired.

She reached under her pillow, knowing the foolishness of the lying-about idea, and took out the cylinder, unscrewed the top, and pulled from it the sheet of pliofilm. It had been so long curled it wouldn't lie flat, of course, and she hadn't any inclination to take it over to her desk where she could spread it on the leather surface to cling properly; she made do with gripping its edges and ignoring the way it wound itself round her fingers.

Eight items she had written there, she noted with disgust. Eight tasks. And when she'd set out on the Quest in February there'd been only the first. Somehow, riding back into Brightwater in April, there'd been the idea in her head that she could get them all out of the way before the Jubilee. Like many another fool idea she'd had lately.

First of all, there was the task she'd set out with: to go over the Castle's secret account books, those that couldn't be trusted to the Economist and required her personal attention.

Next came the matter of determining whether there really had been a Skerry seen at Castle Motley; and if there had been—which she doubted even more strongly now than she had when the servingmaid had blurted out the tale to her—declaring a day of celebration separate and special for the event as custom demanded. It'd be a tad late, but better a tardy observance than none at all. Provided she found any evidence that the servingmaid's story had had a scrap of truth to it.

Third was the promise she had made in the night to the Gentle, highborn T'an K'ib. She had given her word: the Gentles would be involved in *none* of the Ozarkers' doings, as already specified by the treaties signed centuries ago. Furthermore, Responsible intended to see that every inch of the Gentles' territory taken from them by the careless mining operations of the Arkansaw Families was restored, and restored in either its original condition or with improvements to the ancient race's own specifications. T'an K'ib had not insisted on that, treating it as a minor matter, but Responsible saw it differently. The Arkansawyers knew quite well where the boundaries of their lands joined those of the Gentles, and the temptations of a few tons of ore or a vein of choice gemstones were no excuse for violating those boundaries.

Fourth, she had to see to the matter of the growing prejudice against the Purdys. Prejudice was one of the things that had driven the Twelve Families from Old Earth in the first place. They'd all been white, sure enough, but they'd heard more than they cared to tolerate about "ignorant hillbillies" and "white trash" and they'd seen the black and brown and yellow peoples of Earth suffer at the hands of ignorant and vicious people their own color. And now, somehow without anybody's remarking on it as it grew, the Purdys had become the "white trash" of this planet. When anybody did a stupid thing, the first remark you heard was "A body'd think you were a Purdy born and raised!" Nasty, that's what it was, and she would *not* have it; it shamed her that she had not noticed it sooner.

You didn't put an end to prejudice by proclamations, though; it grew slow, and it died slower. What was required was for the next few groups of Purdy girlchildren to spend their Granny School time spread all round this planet, clear away from the constant expectation of the grown-up Purdys that they would *always* fail in whatever they did. A few dozen confident, self-assured Purdy females to go home and do missionary duty —that's what was called for.

And then, for number five on her list, she had written down "Wommack superstition clear out of hand." As it was, and no doubt about it. A Wommack cut his finger, it was because of the Wommack Curse. A Wommack spoiled a roast because she had her mind elsewhere, the Curse again. Every mistake, every natural mishap that the universe laid on a Wommack—be it ever so like the mishaps and mistakes that were laid on every other soul on Ozark—lay it to the Wommack Curse. That had to be seen to, and quickly; there had to be a sufficient run of good luck for the Wommacks to put some chinks in their curse consciousness. And thinking of Lewis Motley Wommack, she smiled to herself; she might find it possible to get in a few licks on *that* job with no strain to herself at all.

Sixth was the trivial task of making certain that nobody but pitiful Una of Clark, lost in her worship of her husband beyond all limits of decency, had been back of the mischief that had plagued Brightwater early in the year. Milk that came spoiled from the goats, mirrors that shattered, Mules that flew like squawkers drunk on fallen fruit fermented in the sun—and the one kidnapped baby, with no harm done to him. Responsible had no doubt this one was trivial, for Una of Clark had been too broken with terror the night she'd confronted her with her crimes not to have cried out the names of anyone that'd helped her—always excepting the husband. Una of Clark would have died unhesitatingly, plunged off the seacliff and into the waters boiling below her, before she spoke any word that might mean the smallest peril for Gabriel Laddercane Traveller the 34th.

Responsible tried, briefly, imagining herself obsessed in that way with Lewis Motley Wommack, convinced the sun rose when he came in the door and set when he went back out it, trembling at his least frown and melting away when he smiled on her. She ran it round her head for a minute or two, checking, but it made no sense to her any way she viewed it. Praise be for small favors.

Next to last on the pliofilm was the Bestowing of two acres of land on Flag of Airy and her husband, in recognition of their service to Castle Brightwater; and seeing that, the guilt did bite at her. Most of the things on the list she could truly say there'd been no time for; they required careful planning and ample time. But not this, this was an hour's easy work. She had plain and simply forgotten about it.

And finally . . . "See to the feuds on Arkansaw," she'd written with the stylus.

See to them!

Responsible rolled over onto her stomach and struck the pile of pillows with her fist. See to them, indeed. How was she to "see to" the incredible antics of three Families, bent on feuding, set on feuding, bound and *determined* on feuding? Guthries, Farsons, and Purdys, bad cess to them all, and the poor Gentles right in the middle of it! Just what she'd been thinking when she'd scribed there so casually "See to the feuds" she could *not* imagine. Must have been after she crashed into the side of that dockshed and addled her head.

It was a long list, and she figured that to carry it through she needed maybe a staff of fifty Magicians, and fifty more miscellaneous, and for all she knew an army wouldn't be a bad idea, whatever an army might be like. She could begin with the Castle accounts, and throw in the Bestowing in a hurry, but the rest of it?

She knew an assortment of words she was forbidden to use, and she ran through them as she'd run through the list, all the while she was rolling up the pliofilm and stuffing it back in its case to bury once more underneath the pillows. And she'd only gotten to the tenth of her prohibited pronouncements when there came the thundering at her door that she'd been expecting with half an ear for some time now.

"Come on in, Granny Hazelbide, before you destroy my door for good and all," she hollered, resigned to what could not be avoided and wouldn't improve by being put off. "Come on in here and tell me all about my sins!"

The Granny fairly flew through the door, and banged it to behind her. She had on a crackling crisp dress of shiny dark blue, caught at the neck with a brooch handed down in her family all the way from First Landing, if she was to be believed. Her feet were shod in high-heeled pointy-toed black pumps with a shine that hurt your eyes, and so narrow Responsible knew they hurt her. Granny Hazelbide prided herself on the neatness of her foot. And on her head was a black straw hat to match the pumps, and a black veil ready to be pulled down over her face in the latest style, with a cluster of dark-blue violets with velvet petals and velvet leaves and velvet stems wound round wire to top off the headgear. She was a regular fashion plate, was Granny Hazelbide, and she was in a fury.

"Whatever are you doing lying there in that bed like the Queen of the Shebas?" she demanded, advancing on Responsible like a skinny tornado. "You make me late for the Opening Ceremonies, girl, and I'll take a switch to your bare tailbone, for all you're near fifteen and fancy yourself full grown! I'll give you two minutes—two minutes, do you hear?—to make yourself fit to be seen and go out this door with me! Laws and Dozens, Responsible, we're late this minute!"

"Granny, Granny," soothed Responsible, "you'll have a heart attack if you go on like that, and I'll have to call in a Magician to set you right, and for sure I want no Magician hanging round my bed on a beautiful morning like this! I suggest you *calm* yourself a tad."

The old lady's lips drew tight, and her brows met over her nose, and she leaned over Responsible's bed like she was ready to whack her with her pocketbook.

"Calm myself!" she said. "When you lie there and face me down, cool as you please, and it half past eight in the morning? Have you taken sick, missy, or leave of your senses—which one?"

"Neither one, Granny Hazelbide," said Responsible. "Neither one. I've just run into a sort of a snag."

Granny Hazelbide leaned over farther, and tipped the girl's chin up to look into her face, turning it this way and that till it made her neck ache. And then she let her fall back, suddenly, and Responsible was grateful it was pillows she'd had to fall on. Even so, the resulting thump shook her some.

"You call that a snag, do you," said the old woman disgustedly. "A snag! What'd you go and catch yourself on it for, if you saw it as such a hindrance, eh, Responsible?"

"Granny, darlin'—"

"'Granny, darlin'!' You mark my words, Responsible of Brightwater, there'll be a few words from your Granny darlin' about this, once she's leisure enough to speak them. But losing your maidenhead, though it's a disgrace to us all and a piece of foolishness the likes of which doesn't come by *often,* it's no excuse for you to lie in bed and miss the Second Day at Confederation Hall. Now get yourself out of there and into your clothes, and let's us *go,* Responsible! Snag, huh! *Who,* pray tell, was it got past my wards on this room?"

"I'm not about to tell you, Granny," said Responsible. "Not *about* to, so you needn't push it. Nor, I'm sorry to say, is that the snag I had in mind."

"What you have in mind doesn't bear repeating before decent folk such as myself, I'll wager!"

"How you *do go* on!" said Responsible admiringly. "You'll outgranny all the other Grannys yet, and think how proud I'll be then! Seeing as how I had the raising of you.

"However," she added quickly, before the Granny could catch her breath and start on her again, "if you plan to hear the Opening Prayer you'd best go on, and I'll explain later. It's not a short explanation."

Granny Hazelbide stared at her, and set her arms akimbo.

"Responsible," she said, "is there really an explanation? Worth my being late for?"

"You'd have to tell me that after you heard it," said Responsible. "Depends on how much you fancy the Opening Ceremonies, I'd say."

Granny Hazelbide pulled up a chair and sat down in it without a word, as Responsible had known she would; and she listened—her mouth puckering tighter and tighter with every passing minute—while she heard a carefully edited version of the mistake made at Castle Traveller and this morning's visit from Granny Leeward. And then she spoke her mind, and Responsible was glad she'd only made it a tale of giving all the staff at Castle Traveller toothaches. She'd been afraid that might be somewhat too mild to convince, since many an Ozark woman not a Granny and with no hope of ever being one picked up a scrap or two of Granny Magic, though few would dare use what they knew. Granny Hazelbide didn't find the transgression a light one; that became clear in a hurry.

"Stupid!" she said fiercely. "That's the only word for you, missy. Just purely *stupid!* How could you let yourself be wrenched round to such a state—and the Travellers, of *all* Families to find yourself beholden to! So Granny Leeward called you a whore—does calling make it so? Prior to this morning, that is! I reckon she used the word again when she was in here, and this time with good reason!"

"No," said Responsible, "as a matter of fact the word she used this time was 'fornicator.'"

"And how'd you respond to *that*? You put warts on all the Mules in the stables? Rashes on all the servingmaids and Attendants? Sink all the boats at the Landing? What kind of conniption fit did you throw over 'fornicator'?"

"Well," said Responsible, "I don't mind 'fornicator' especially. It lacks the little extra bit; it makes no claim that I *sell* my favors, you'll note. I was able to restrain myself."

"And now there you are, barred from the Hall."

"So I am."

"Shame on you, girl!"

"Want me to call her bluff and go, Granny?"

"Great Gates, no! There's no bluff to that woman. If she said she'd make a scandal of you before the whole world and its brother-in-law that's exactly and precisely what she would do. You stay away, just as she bid you, and be glad she's not made it worse."

"Well, then, Granny, what I need from you is not more tongue-lashing. What I need is for you to go on along and be my eyes and my ears. I can watch on the comset, for sure, but it'll give me only such scraps of what's going on as the comcrews find interesting. Whoever's speaking, and a shot of the balcony now and again, and no more. I won't be seeing who passes notes to who else, or who walks out in a huff, or who falls asleep that you might of expected to pay close attention, or who gets together in huddles in the rows. I need you to watch for me, and listen close, and send word if you see *anything* that appears to you to be out of line."

"And what'll you do if I do see mischief? I'll see plenty afore this week's over, you know. What do you plan to do about any of it, missy?"

"That depends on what it is," said Responsible patiently. "Might could be there'll be nothing I can do; might could be I can be useful. But unless I have you to report to me, we'll never know which."

"And what will you be doing in between my reports, besides lolling in your bed and sniffing the posies?"

Responsible thought of her hateful list of "to do" tasks.

"I'll find a way to pass my time," she said with assurance.

"Rolling in his arms, no doubt!"

"Granny Hazelbide," said Responsible, mock-serious, "you have an evil mind."

The Granny clicked her tongue against her teeth till Responsible wondered the tip didn't bleed.

"Shiftless *and* shameless!" she ranted, shaking her finger at the girl smiling up from her pillows. "What would your *mother* say?"

"That she couldn't believe any man would of wanted me," said Responsible promptly. "You know that. Especially when there's such competition as Silverweb of McDaniels around, all unspoken for and never been kissed. Now do please go on to the Hall, dear heart? Please? It'll be time soon for the Travellers to begin their move, and I'd be pleasured to know how they open the game. You can come back tonight and lecture me on my morals till you drop in your tracks if that appeals to you; so far as I know, nobody ever talked a maidenhead back into its place, but I'll listen respectfully if you fancy trying. But not now, Granny Hazelbide, not *now!*"

The Granny went out of the door, proclaiming woe and thunderations all the way down the hall, and Responsible locked her hands behind her head and stared up at the ceiling until she could hear her nattering no longer. And then she stared a good half hour longer, thinking. She might have put her list away, but she could still see it plain as plain in her mind's eye.

"This very day," she told the ceiling at last, "this very *morning*— what's left of it—I'll see to the Bestowing of Flag of Airy's two acres."

And then what? the ceiling gave her back.

"And then," she said, carrying it on, "I believe I'm going to need some help. I do believe that I'd better send for my sister."

That silenced the ceiling. What it would bring on in the way of response from other sources, once it was known that Troublesome of Brightwater might be coming down from her mountaintop and into the city, would not be silence. Responsible chuckled, thinking about it.

And realized that, come to think of it, she *missed* her sister. Mean as she was, outrageous as she was, impossible as she was sure to be, she missed her. And she'd had no idea.

6

The Bestowing was drawn up in black ink on snow-white paper, marked with the Brightwater Crest and sealed with the Brightwater Seal, before noon of that day. Responsible had looked over the Kingdom's maps, displayed for her on the comset screen, with great care; and she had chosen two acres plus a bit of riverbank left over, a nice piece of land only eleven miles out from Capital City, tucked into an arm of the river between two big farms and overlooked this long time because it was so small.

"Too small to be any use," said her grandmother Ruth of Motley when Responsible carried it downstairs to the small sittingroom.

"Too *large,* to my mind!" her mother had objected. "We've almost no land left to give, Responsible; if somebody actually did a deed worthy of gratitude, Castle Brightwater would be hard put to it to find any acres to Bestow. I don't approve, myself; I don't approve at all."

"Responsible didn't expect you to," said Ruth of Motley comfortably. "It'd spoil your image. *I* approve, and I'll speak for both my husband and my sons: none of them would grudge the young woman her two piddling little acres."

"I don't see," said Responsible's mother stubbornly, "what Flag of Airy has done to merit a Bestowing. The last one we gave—and it's been eleven years ago, mind, before Responsible ever saw daylight!—was twelve acres to the young man that tried to save the lives of Jewel of Wommack's family. You remember that, Ruth?"

"I'm not senile," answered Ruth of Motley, giving Thorn of Guthrie a look as she bit through a strand of embroidery floss that spoke of a preference for setting her teeth elsewhere.

"Grandmother, you'll ruin your teeth," said Responsible automatically. She'd been saying that ever since she could remember, and she'd learned it from hearing everyone else say it. But Ruth of Motley never paid it any mind, and her teeth gleamed bright as they ever had. Then she realized what Thorn of Guthrie had said, and she looked at her mother and tried for a casual face.

"I didn't know that happened here," she said. "Thought it was on Kintucky."

"*No*-sir," said Thorn of Guthrie. "The Wommacks were here at Brightwater on a visit, the old man and that young wife of his—she was no more than a child, and he had no business marrying her, if you ask me, not that anybody ever has—and Jacob Donahue Wommack's wife, and the two children. Praise the Gates, they left the tadlings home . . . But the others went down in the river, there where that root tangle is just past the bend, right out there beyond the Castle grounds. And they all died, trapped in the roots and sunken logs, with the boat turned over on top of them. And," she wound it up, "it was the young man as near drowned him*self* trying to save them that had the last Bestowing of land from this Kingdom. They were perfect fools, you know—going out on the river, and it in flood, and not knowing what kind of mess there was trapped in that tangle, but they wouldn't hear no; nothing would do but they should have a day on the river—and they paid in full."

"That was a sorry day," Ruth of Motley added. "Everybody carrying on about the Wommack Curse, like it wouldn't of happened if anybody else had been in that fool boat. I remember it well."

"And *that* young man did something worth notice, Responsible. He must of gone down a dozen times trying to free the Wommacks, and at the last they had to hold him back to keep him from having another go at it when he was so exhausted he'd never in the world have come up again himself."

"Mother," said Responsible reasonably, "do think. If, as you put it, somebody did something that *really* called for a gift from Brightwater, those two little acres wouldn't serve anyway. But they'll please Flag of Airy and her husband, both of them fine young people. There's room enough for him to raise a house, and her to put in a garden that'll feed the two of them and a few tadlings as the years go by. Don't be selfish, Mother—it's not becoming."

"Wait till the men are home," said Thorn of Guthrie, "and we'll see what they say. Not to mention Patience of Clark."

"I'm not likely to make any Bestowing without the whole Family's approving," protested Responsible. "What do you take me for?"

"Responsible," said Ruth of Motley mildly, "don't tempt your mother."

"Yes, ma'am."

"The document's well drawn, and you were wise to do it and have it out of the way. Put it in the desk over there, and then after supper tonight we'll call a short Meeting and send the vote around. But there'll be no trouble."

"I *still* say—" Thorn of Guthrie began, but her mother-in-law cut her off. Enough was enough.

"Thorn of Guthrie," she said, "for two long *months* Flag of Airy saw her own babe suckled at the breasts of Vine of Motley, so her milk would not dry up before we Brightwaters got Vine's own child back to her arms. And in that two months she bore a heavy load. Responsible is quite right."

"Fiddle!" said Thorn of Guthrie. "I've suckled two daughters myself, one of them there before you, and I'd have welcomed anyone that cared to take the task from me. I don't see it."

Ruth of Motley rolled her eyes toward the ceiling, and then bent over her embroidery in silence. She was doing a panel of ferns and flowers that required a good deal of attention, and she intended to waste no more effort on her sharp-tongued companion.

There they sat, the two of them: Ruth of Motley with her needle-work, one piece after another till the Castle was smothered in the stuff, and Thorn of Guthrie with yet another of the endless series of diaries she'd been scribbling away at for thirty years. They were almost alone in the Castle. It wasn't large, as Castles went; but today, with nearly every-one gone to the fair or the Hall or some one of the other entertainments, it seemed a vast echoing cavern.

The question Responsible had been dreading came just as she thought she was going to make it out the door without either of them thinking of it.

"Responsible!"

"Mother, I'm just on my way to put this Bestowing document back in my desk for safekeeping."

"Your grandmother said to leave it here, and you heard her; and besides, I want to ask you something."

Thorn of Guthrie sounded determined; Responsible turned back with a sigh, went to put the Bestowing document in the sittingroom desk, and then stood waiting.

"How come you aren't down at Confederation Hall your*self* this morning, along with the Grannys?" her mother asked her, and Ruth of Motley looked up from her work for the answer.

"Don't plan on going," said Responsible, short and sharp.

"You don't plan on going?"

"Echo in here," said Ruth of Motley, as was her habit.

"Whatever do you mean, you don't plan on going? All the fuss you've made, all the dust you've raised over this week of nonsense—and you stand there and tell me you don't plan to go?"

Responsible stuck to her guns.

"That's right, Thorn of Guthrie."

"Well, that beats all!"

Her rescue came from an unexpected source. Ruth of Motley had turned back to her work, but she spoke attentively enough.

"I think that's wise of you, Responsible," she said. "I think that's *very* wise. Not a thing you can do to change what's going to happen in that Hall, and for you to sit there and watch it going on and torturing yourself over it would be pure foolishness. You're better off keeping busy here till it's all over and we know how far they've gone. Not to mention the fact that there's plenty of neglected work right here for you to turn your hand to while everybody else is off gawking at the delegations and going to carnivals."

That satisfied her mother, and Responsible blessed Ruth of Motley for her solid common sense. Here she'd been fully prepared to face them all down and just plain refuse to *say* why she was staying away from the proceedings, same way she'd refused ever to say who she'd learned had kidnapped the McDaniels baby, and to bear the fuss that went with the refusing. Just because no amount of thinking had brought a plausible reason to her mind. And now Ruth of Motley had taken the load right off her back, all unexpected and unasked. And while Thorn of Guthrie was still occupied in counting off all the things she wanted Responsible to see to while she was staying home and not tormenting herself, she slipped away, much relieved. It was time she turned on the comset in her room and had a look at what was happening; by now they'd have finished with the Opening Prayer, and whatever leftover trivia there'd been from the day before—and unless she was far wrong in her thinking, Jeremiah Thomas Traveller would of been recognized by the Chair and would be holding forth.

She wasn't wrong, either. She sat in her favorite rocker, the blue one with a back high enough to rest her head against, and paid the figure on the wall the compliment of *her* attention. Like many another thing in Castle Brightwater, the comset could have done with some repair. That had been sacrificed to the budget for the Jubilee, and every so often the projections ceased to be threedys and became flat as paper cutouts. But the sound was reliable, and that was the main thing; she knew well enough what they looked like.

Jeremiah Thomas had just begun, and the speech promised to take some time, for he was not only Master of his Castle, he was a Reverend, ordained before he passed his sixteenth birthday, and he knew how to spin out the sentences.

She had tuned him in just as he was finishing off his thanks to the Brightwaters for the "splendid program" of Opening Day—the hypocrite! —and allowing as how it had been a historic occasion fitly and abundantly observed. But now it was time for them to turn from ritual observance to the serious business of this meeting—and he proceeded to explain just what that meant to him.

"Mister Chairman"—he rolled it out—"Senior and Junior Delegates and Aides, gentle ladies that honor us by gracing the balcony of this grand and glorious Hall . . . and all the citizens of the six continents who join us this day through the miracle of technology . . . I stand before you now with a heavy heart. A *heavy* heart!"

Responsible hoped it was heavy. She hoped it was a stone of Tinaseeh marble in his sly vicious breast, and well supplied with sharp little points.

"Why, you ask, is my heart heavy?"

I don't ask any such thing.

"Because, my dear friends, my dear colleagues, I have no choice open to me today but to speak the truth. Oh, not that I am not reluctant to be the first to do so—for many among you know what that truth is, and did I wait long enough you might well speak it for me! Not that the truth does not stick in my *throat* . . . no! I *am* reluctant! I *do* find it hard to force the words to come forth, as come forth they surely must! But I tell you all, my conscience will not let me rest until I have said what *must be said*." He let his voice fall to a hush. "All night last night I knelt on the bare boards of my chamber floor—"

There wasn't a guestchamber in Castle Brightwater with bare boards to its floor, nor a servant's room either, but Responsible could see that it wouldn't of sounded nearly so dramatic for him to talk of kneeling for hours on soft rugs.

"—and I *wrestled* with my conscience! *Must* I, I asked myself . . . *must* I, I asked the Holy One Almighty . . . must I, Jeremiah Thomas Traveller the Twenty-sixth, be the one to speak this truth?"

He paused to let that settle over the heads of his listeners, and then he answered his own question.

"And the answer came back to me—it came back YES! And it came back YES! again!"

Just like him, thought Responsible, pleased to see him go flat and black on her wall, barely a flicker, to drag the Holy One into this and spread the blame.

"Oh, my friends," he said, "oh, my colleagues—"

Careful! You'll be saying dearly beloved next!

"—I shuddered then. I shuddered . . . for the truth I must pronounce, the truth my conscience *compels* me to pronounce—that truth is not a joyous truth! That truth is not a merry truth! That truth is not a truth cast in a spirit of gaiety . . . unless, unless . . . but let me come back to that! For now, let me only tell you that the truth is sometimes a sad and solemn burden, and that this is such a time—but I *will* speak it, nonetheless; and I do not fear to do so."

He went on then, to remind them one and all of the reasons that had brought the Twelve Families from Old Earth to Ozark one thousand years ago. He talked of the air of Earth, that could not be breathed; of the water of Earth, that no one dared drink till it had been made so foul by chemicals that it burned the throat and offended the nose; of the soil of Earth, so poisoned that the food it grew was unfit for human beings to eat, that had taken in pollution till it could give back nothing else. He talked of the pollution of human*kind* as well, every hand set against every other; of the dank misery of the slums where the world's poor had scrabbled from dole to dole. He spoke of the shame of the so-called holy men who threw out in their daily garbage the finest foodstuffs chemistry could produce, while billions lay swollen-bellied in the dust, dying of starvation. He talked of the politicians, that lived like great ticks upon the bodies of the citizens they had sworn to serve, bleeding them of their substance and fattening upon it till the bureaucracies were swollen to monstrous size. He spent a number of superb sentences upon the doctors, become so callous and so arrogant and so divorced from the people that they could heal nothing but their bank balances; and a few more upon the lawyers, who had lusted after the suffering of others and profited by it; and still more for those that had dared to call themselves teachers, while they spent their useless lives spreading ignorance and demanding ever more money for the pitiful job they did . . .

On and on and on . . .

Would he *never* stop? Responsible tried to imagine any gathering of women where such a monologue would of been tolerated past the five minutes it took to see where it was heading, and failed. No female would of sat still for the wasted time. Not a word that he said, looming there in his antiquated black suit, flickering with the straining of the comset— which was certainly poorly—standing there with a *tie* round his scrawny neck as a symbol of his bondage to the ancient nonsense he spoke against— not a word they hadn't all heard a hundred dozen times. Not a turn of phrase they didn't hear every three Sundys or so at Solemn Service . . . and he had no skill of control. He had the preacher's skill. He could put one word after another without ever a stumble or a pause; but they sat for his mellifluous bombast out of politeness, not because they enjoyed it— and because they were men, and had no better sense.

Granny Hazelbide had said it as well as ever she'd heard anybody say it, long ago at Granny School. "Men," she'd said, "are of but two kinds. Splendid—and pitiful. The splendid ones are rare, and if you chance on one, you'll know it. What I tell you now has to do with the *rest* of 'em —as my Granny told me, and her Granny told her before that, and so back as far as time will take you." They'd all leaned forward, because her voice told them something important was coming, and she'd gone on. "If," she said, "a man does something properly, that's an accident. That's the first thing. As for the sorry messes they make in the ordinary way of things, that's to be expected, and not to be held against them—they can't help it. That's the second thing. And the third thing—and this is to be *well-remembered*—is that no man must ever know the first two things."

Granny struck her cane on the floor, three times hard, to underline that. "When a man spills something, it's your place to catch it before it touches, snatch it before it falls, and be sure certain he thinks he caught it himself. Men—all but those rare splendid ones—they're frail creatures; they can't bear much."

"And a woman?" one of the little girls had asked timidly. "How about a woman?"

The Granny had gripped her cane till her knuckles gleamed like pearls. "There is *nothing*," she said in a terrible voice like ice grinding together, "more despicable than a woman who cannot *Cope!*"

Thump!

"You remember that now!" she told them. "You keep that *firmly* in mind!"

"It's not fair!" It had run all around the circle, where they were sitting on the floor with their legs tucked neatly under them. "It's not fair atall!" And she'd turned on them, brandishing the cane over their heads—Responsible remembered how that cane had seemed ready to crash down upon her head, and how she'd trembled—and she'd said, "*Fair!* This is the real world, and it is as it is. Let me never hear any more from you about *fair!*"

She jumped, then, no longer a five-year-old at Granny School, once again a woman near grown watching a foolish man and listening to his useless words. The word that had made her jump, thundering out of the wall, had been "Jubilee!" She had missed, in her reverie, the part where he'd compared all those tribulations of Old Earth with the tribulations he now claimed to see building on Ozark, and had laid them at the feet of the Confederation of Continents.

It didn't matter, she'd heard it from him before, along with the part about the money wasted by the Confederation that should be staying in the treasuries of the individual Kingdoms where it belonged, where it had been honestly earned and should be honestly disbursed. She knew where he was in the speech—it was time now to make the motion to dissolve the Confederation—and what was he yelling Jubilee about? She leaned toward the wall, not wanting to miss this.

"A Jubilee!" he was saying, voice like butter melting, voice like syrup on cakes, voice like rosy velvet against the cheek, "A Jubilee is a time of rejoicing and coming together in celebration. And I wouldn't have you think I begrudge you your Jubilee—you have *earned* your Jubilee. I do not propose to take it from you. What I propose . . . what I propose is that we make this a new Jubilee, a true Jubilee, a Jubilee in honor of the celebration that will then go on for all the days that remain of this week! A celebration not of serfdom, not of slavery, but of independence! A celebration of our decision to stand upon our own feet at long, long last, sovereign states governing themselves as befits *men* . . . no more cowering under the skirts of Brightwater! Let us, my dear friends, oh my dear friends, let us celebrate not the Jubilee of the Confederation—but the *Jubilee of Independence!*"

The whooping and the cheering and the shouts of "I so move!" and "Second the motion!" came through loud and clear, and Responsible had to admit, much as she despised to do it, that that had been a clever touch. Grim old Jeremiah Thomas, he'd managed to get rid of the role of ghost at the feast, managed to paint himself benevolent and warm of heart and in *favor* of people enjoying themselves—and at the same time, the motion to dissolve the Confederation permanently had been passed and set up for debate, just as he'd wanted it to be.

She reached up and switched off the comset, no longer interested. It would be the standard procedure now, and it would take all of the following day at least. Every Senior Delegate would be allowed to speak to the question, first of all. Then every Junior Delegate, should any of them want to add something—and most were sure to, they had so few opportunities to be heard. And after that, there'd be the round of rebuttals, when anybody that wished to raise objections to the speeches could put that in. And the final summing up by the Chair . . . all of that, before the motion could be put to a vote. It would be tedious.

She could count on some of them. The McDaniels, the Clarks, and the Airys, for sure; she could count on them to point out and underline what it was going to be like for the frontier continents with no comsets and no supply freighters, hacking out their existences with a few thousand people that hadn't been here to vote for any such condition. She could count on the Travellers to scoff at that and allow as how people weren't such puny creatures as some thought they were, and how a hard life here meant a fair life Hereafter, and how misery was what built *men*—she could be sure of that. There'd be the Purdys, saying nothing . . . and the Smiths helping them . . . but doing it at great length, trying to play both sides against the middle they could only just barely glimpse. The Lewises and the Motleys, they'd help specify as far as they dared what sovereign statehood was going to be *like,* once the rhetoric was done with and the hard-

scrabble was before you . . . And the others? No way to know, and nothing much to do but wait. It seemed to her the chances were good, in *spite*
of the rhetoric, and she was sick to death of watching the delegates caper
about, and weary to death of hearing them talk, and she turned them off
as she would have pinched a bug between her fingers.

And because of that, she missed the entrance of the Smith Delegation,
filing sixteen strong into the back rows of the room, just in time to add
their "Ayes!" to the vote for the Traveller motion. And she didn't hear,
until after Granny Hazelbide came to her room just before supper, of the
stir it had caused when people had seen that Granny Gableframe wasn't
with them.

7

Jewel of Wommack was out of her bed at the first sound from Lewis Motley's guestchamber and into her nightrobe; by the time he closed his door—so softly—behind him and turned around, she was standing outside her own door with her arms folded over her chest and her foot tapping on the cool stone floor.

"Hush!" he said at the top of his lungs; and then he roared at her: "You mean to wake up the whole Castle? Don't you have any consideration at *all* for other people? You think you're the only person in this Castle that—"

Jewel backed hastily into her room, dragging her laughing brother after her by a death grip on his left earlobe. Scandalized, she pushed the door to with her free hand, praying that nobody had heard his carrying on.

"Lewis Motley Wommack!" she said, stamping her foot at him—a wasted effort on the thick rug with its pattern of intertwined roses and ivy, but the only gesture short of biting him that she could think of in her fury. "You are a worthless, wicked man, and a disgrace to our Family, and you will drive me clean to *distraction* if you do not cease your dreadful ways! Haven't you got any shame at *all?*"

"No," he said, "I don't suppose I have."

She glared at him, back to the door and determined he'd not go through it without going through her as well, determined she'd not cry no matter what he said or did, and silently cursing the mother who'd left her with this burdensome animal to torment her all her life long. He'd never marry, not him, she knew it; he could not bear the idea that there was anybody that had a claim on him, anybody he had to answer to for any smallest thing. She'd be a creaking old woman of ninety-nine and she'd *still* be accountable for his behavior.

"I wish I was dead," she announced bitterly. And then she changed her mind. "No, I wish *you* were, and then I'd have some peace!"

Lewis Motley Wommack the 33rd, all in black like a Traveller male, and a hood to cover the copper hair that might catch the glint of a stray

light and give him away, lifted his little sister into the air and shook her
gently at arm's length, well beyond the reach of her nimble fingers.

"Nasty, nasty child," he said, "wishing your one and only brother
laid out in his cold narrow grave, and him only nineteen! Whatever
would people say if they could hear you now?"

"That you'd driven me *mad,* that's what they'd say! And they'd be
right!"

"*What* do you care about Responsible of Brightwater?" asked Lewis
Motley in his most reasonable voice. "What has she ever done for you
that you should have such tender scruples about her?"

"My scruples," hissed Jewel of Wommack, "my scruples are for any
living creature that strikes your fancy! *Any* creature—always excepting
your Mule, of course. You take right good care of your Mule."

He swung her down into his arms, gave her a hug that took all her
breath away, set her back on the bed she'd come tearing out of, and
allowed that he did see to the comfort of his Mule.

"A Mule," he said, "is worth a man's respect. Won't do fool things
no matter who tries to make it; keeps itself to itself and has no patience
for human nonsense; works hard for its keep and asks no quarter of anybody or any thing; and'd take your hand off as soon as look at you if you
don't play fair. Mules, my dear, are *entitled.*"

"And women? They don't do for you and make over you and plain
lie down and beg for the privilege of dying for you, Lewis Motley
Wommack? They're not worth the consideration you give a Mule, just
because they won't bite your hand off?"

"The day I find a woman that's as admirable as a Mule," he declared,
"I promise to treat her well. *You,* for example; you show signs of developing into something as valuable as a Mule. Provided you get over spying
on every move I make."

"Lewis Motley," she said, shivering all over with simple fury, "how
many women now have you notched off to your count? How many girls
are there in Kintucky that get up from their beds in the morning crying
and go back to them at night with the tears not dry on their faces, because
of you? How many now have you taken on, molded to your liking—
law, you turn every *one* of them into the same pitiful slavish creature,
over and over again—and then dropped the way you'd drop a playpretty?
How *many,* dear brother?"

"You've been keeping my count for me," he chuckled. "I don't bother."

And he added, "Responsible of Brightwater's a different matter. I think you can leave her off your list."

"I should think *so!* I should just purely and completely think so . . . And the idea that you are off to bedevil her again . . . Lewis Motley, you break my heart, you truly do."

"Think I *can* bedevil her, do you? I appreciate the compliment."

The tears flooded Jewel's eyes, in spite of her resolve, and she hated her voice for the way it betrayed her, quavering and quaking like a little girl's.

"Why do you spy on her?" she managed to choke past the lump in her throat.

"Why do you spy on *me?*" he countered. "The Grannys ordered you to, I suppose."

Jewel bit her lip and glared at him, though he'd gone all blurry through her tears. As if she'd answer that!

"Little sister," he said then, "you might just as well resign yourself and sleep the sweet sleep that's due you, because there is no way in this world you can change a single thing that's bothering you. Hear me, Jewel? No way atall. No way you can change me into a staunch and upright stick of a Lewis—or another version of my righteous brother Jacob. I have only four more days and nights in Brightwater, and if I'm to discover Miss Responsible's secrets I have no time to waste. The days are useless, since I have to spend them in that Hall listening to the idiot pontification of the pack of fools we've chosen to call Continental Delegates . . . And if you interfere with my use of the nights . . . Jewel, love, I can't let you do that."

"Whatever secrets Responsible of Brightwater has," said the girl wearily, knowing it was no use and never would be, "they're none of your business."

"I intend to *make* them my business," he told her. "I intend to find out why it is that a skimpy little female, not yet fifteen and homely to boot, is bowed to and scraped to like she is. I intend to find out what there is about her that is so special it sets her apart even for the Grannys— and I intend to find out why the Magicians of Rank speak of her the way they do."

"Which is what way?"

"Like a pestilence," said her brother. "Like a plague. Like an evil that goes far and beyond all other evils. That scrawny little piece! I intend to know why."

"*Why* must you know that?" she shouted at him, no longer caring who heard; might could be if somebody heard they'd come along and object and he'd be ashamed to go prowling the halls in the middle of the night. "Even supposing it's true—and I don't see it, Lewis Motley, I don't see it at all, I think it's all your imagination and Responsible has just had the sorry luck to be born to a do-nothing mother and a scandalous sister and a pack of worthless men that leave everything to her to do, and have since she was old enough to talk—and the only difference between her and a couple dozen other girls I know is that the family as makes a slave of her happens to own the oldest Castle on Ozark instead of a poorscratch farm! But just suppose you're right—why must you find out about it? What business is it of yours, that makes it your place to go prowling the Castle where we're guests when decent people are in their beds, poking and prying—what gives you the right, Lewis Motley?"

"Ah, Jewel," he laughed, "you can't expect me to let a mystery like this go by me! I may never get another chance at it—I may well never get off Kintucky again, and Kintucky's got not a single mystery to call its own. A *secret,* Jewel of Wommack, exists for but one reason—to be found out. And I'm off now to worry at this one."

The heavy door closed behind him, but she wasn't fooled; she knew him far too well. She let the minutes pass, let him stick his head back in and bid her a mocking goodnight with his apologies for forgetting, before she really let herself weep. He hadn't caught her that way for over two years now, and she was proud of the record.

She looked up at the ceiling and found no answers written there, and announced to the Holy One that she had by the Twelve Gates and the Twelve Corners done her best, for all that she'd failed as usual, and then she lay down and cried herself to an exhausted sleep.

Lewis Motley was grateful to his sister in the long run; though he wouldn't ever have admitted it to her, he found her a good deal superior to any Mule—or any female—he'd ever encountered, and he enjoyed her company even when she was at her most frantic. Jewel of Wommack was never dull, and there was no putting her down by any fair means; give her another year or two and she'd be a match for anybody, himself included. She had a way of finding the strands of an argument, laying out each one casual as if it were nothing at all—with all its sub-propositions attached—and then tying the whole thing off, while everybody else was still muddling around in search of their opening remark. He admired that, if it did sometimes cause him inconvenience; and this time, with her futile protest, she had saved him a half hour's boring wait at least. As it was, he'd no more than reached the narrow corridor running the length of the Castle, the one Responsible thought she used so discreetly, and found himself a narrow niche to hide in, when she came along. The timing couldn't of been better.

She was wearing a long traveling cloak for which there could be no excuse in the warm May night if she'd nothing to hide, and she fairly flew along the corridor and out the door at the back of the Castle, with him right behind her. They crossed the Castle yard and took the path down to the stables, a parade of two; and he saw in the last fading light of Ozark's three moons that she had a gathering basket over her arm. At one o'clock in the morning, whatever did she need with a gathering basket? He could feel himself warming to his task.

Not a Mule brayed as they came up to the stables, and that wasn't natural. The Mules should of been raising the devil of a fuss. If not about her—he was willing to admit that it was just possible the Brightwater Mules had seen to it that all the others stabled there these nights knew who she was and that she had every right to be there, seeing as the fact they wouldn't mindspeak a human didn't mean they wouldn't mindspeak one another—then about him. Any Mule worth the price its tail would fetch for a loomwarp would be braying to warn her he was behind her in the night, and the Mules in these stables were the very finest of their breeds. Something was all wrong, delightfully and fascinatingly wrong, in the Kingdom of Brightwater.

He waited by the stable corner, back pressed to the wall and only that smallest part of his face absolutely necessary to see her come out not hidden; and in three minutes flat there she was, without the awkward basket, mounted on a Mule with two sets of saddlebags over its back. He had barely time to throw himself bareback on one of the Mules that Brightwater had made available for its guests before hers had taken to the air and gone over the Castle wall into the darkness.

He followed her at a safe distance down a street where the flowering trees arched thick and met over the roadway, making it a tunnel of heavy scent—how the citizens of Brightwater stood it he couldn't imagine, it was so sweet it turned his stomach. She was a tiny figure ahead of him, the street curving away down a hill and out of his sight, but her Mule had a white blaze to each ear, and he marked her by that. He'd have no trouble keeping up with her, and no chance of losing her, especially with the mysterious silence that had somehow been imposed on every living thing that could ordinarily have been expected to sound an alarm.

And then she was gone.

One moment she was there, the two little white spots in the darkness clear as two candles ahead of him, and the next there was no sign of her anywhere. Only the darkness and the absolute silence and the perfumed night air, and him alone like a fool and with no idea how to get back to the Castle. He'd been far too interested in where she was going to pay any attention to the route they'd followed.

But he'd learned something that would be worth the wandering around hunting he'd have to do to retrace his path. He went a bit farther, and he got down from the Mule and walked a few nooks and crannies to make certain sure, but he hadn't really had any doubts. A Mule, a high-class and expensive and well-trained Mule, had a top speed of sixty miles an hour. But there was a way the Magicians of Rank had, called SNAP-PING, that took those Mules from point to point as near instantly as made no difference. *Only* the Magicians of Rank could do that. The Grannys couldn't. The plain Magicians couldn't. Just the nine Magicians of Rank, and no other living creature.

Except Responsible of Brightwater. That she had SNAPPED somewhere, and would get herself back the same way, he had not the least doubt. Lying in her bed, feeling not just their bodies mingling but somehow their minds as well, so that he was her and felt her deep within him, and she was no longer a maiden on her way to being a woman but was *him,* taking her own maidenhead, he had known there was more to her than just the knot of political intrigue he'd suspected. And for the sake of knowing what it was he'd fought back the gorge that rose in him at the sensation of being female, at having the privacy of *his* body invaded—let alone the privacy of his mind! He felt cold sweat on his forehead, remembering; it had been like having something you would never put

your hand to, something you'd carry out of an old barn wiggling at the
end of a rake and at arm's length, with your head turned aside, and having it moving in your head, somewhere back of your eyes . . . Lewis
Motley shuddered, for all the warmth of the night air.

Oh, he was not surprised that she could SNAP a Mule. He would not
of been that surprised if he'd seen her SNAP without the Mule beneath
her; and the word "witch" came to him all unbidden. It would be a good
question to ask the Grannys: what happens to a man that takes the virginity of a witch?

He turned his own Mule and took it back through Capital City,
watching for the towers above the trees till he found the Castle, flew over
the high stone wall and down to the stable door, and put the Mule away
in its stall with a ration of grain for its trouble. Then he found himself a
place to sit against the stable wall, hidden behind a rack of hanging bridles
and gear, and settled in to wait for Responsible's return. And still, not a
Mule brayed.

It was almost three when she came back, and he had fallen asleep in
spite of himself. Bad enough trying to stay awake all day while the men
in the Hall droned on and on with their everlasting nonsense; to make a
nightwatch of it as well, two nights in a row now, was beginning to tell
on him. Jewel would of been pleased to know that, no doubt. What woke
him was the sound Responsible made transferring something—a number
of somethings, and it frustrated him mightily that he couldn't see what
they were—from the Mule's saddlebags into the gathering basket.

The Mule was lathered, and she set the basket aside, hung the saddlebags on a hook in a corner of the stall, and began to rub it down . . . He
could hear the rough hiss of the stable blanket against its hair. He sat bolt
upright against the wall, doing his best not to breathe, and was pondering what to do next when she spoke up.

"Lewis Motley," she said briskly, right along with the rubdown,
"you'd be a good deal more comfortable in your bed than you are against
that wall. We pride ourselves here at Brightwater on making our guests
comfortable . . . but then we've never had to allow for them sneaking up
and down the halls and through the stableyards and roaming all around
the town half the night. Might could be our arrangements'll need to be
changed. Tea, maybe, served for the guest with a sudden urge to go riding after midnight. And a sofa in the stable instead of that hard floor."

The idea that she'd known he was here all along, let him follow her down the garden path, and expected him to be waiting—the humiliation of it left him without a word to say.

"Well?" she said. "No answer, Lewis Motley? You Wommacks have curious manners, if I do say so myself, and I surely do. Only person I've ever known with more gall than you is my sister Troublesome, and she has her reasons. You have your reasons, young man?"

He cleared his throat, took a deep breath, and launched into an ordinarily reliable account of the manner in which he ached for her fair white body and was willing to spend any number of waking nights on hard floors for an opportunity to clasp it to him once again. It wasn't his very best version, but it was the one that came quickest to his otherwise vacant mind, and she listened to it all the way through politely enough.

"Do tell," she said, at the end of it, and he wasn't all that surprised. It had had its uses with any number of young females, the ones Jewel expected him to worry about their crying and puling through their days and their nights. But it was not all that likely to prove effective with the daughter of Brightwater—he'd heard the welcoming speech she gave the delegations, and noted the easy way she lulled them.

"Shall I try a different one?" he asked her. "I have an assortment."

"Never mind," she said. "Considering you spent most of last night sitting out in my hall and got nothing for your trouble, and then most of this one in the company of our Mules, I'll settle for the piece you just recited. Now I suggest we go to bed, or you'll be late back to your room and the whole Castle will be scandalized."

He followed her warily, feeling no more lust for her than he'd felt for the borrowed Mule. It had been far too easy, and he'd gotten off much too lightly; he might have been led round the barn, but he wasn't so addled he didn't realize *that*. Not to mention that she must know he'd seen her disappearing act, seeing as how she knew everything else he'd done this past forty-eight hours or so. And he tread the halls softly, knowing they had barely an hour before the Castle staff roused to start this day. To say nothing of the Grannys, that felt anybody abed after five in the morning wasn't worth spitting over, and tended to set even that hour back once they passed the century mark. Might could be that with the press of time and the number of curious circumstances he'd not be called upon to muster up even a pretense of that absent lust; which would be just as well.

But he needn't have worried. Responsible of Brightwater had him naked in her arms with a speed that made him wonder if she was still using witchcraft, and in ten frantic minutes it was all over, tangle of bodies, tangle of minds, and all. He lay there drenched with sweat beside her, trying to get his breath, and complimented her on her efficiency.

"I'd of preferred a more leisurely course to things," she said, "*if* I'd had my druthers, but there are times when every second must be made to count. This was one of those times."

"Well, I thank you for your hospitality," he said lamely; he hoped he had strength enough to get back down the corridors and up the stairs to his room. Maybe he could claim he'd broken a leg and buy himself a few hours' sleep—for a few hours' sleep, at that moment, he would have been more than willing to break a leg.

"Tired, Lewis Motley Wommack?" she asked him.

"Oh, no," he said. "I can hardly wait to get to the Independence Room and sit through today's round of speeches on the cursed *Confederation*."

"Law, how you lie!"

"Right enough. And I wish you'd tell me, before I rush off to my important affairs of the day, how you *do* that."

"Do what? Lie? It's you as does the lying."

"Tell me how you run around inside my head like you do, Responsible of Brightwater . . . Tell me that, and stop your throwing dust in my eyes."

Responsible raised herself on one elbow and stared at him, and he thought what a shame it was she wasn't beautiful, plain witches not really fitting his concept of the thing, and she said with an absolute seriousness that inclined him to believe she spoke the truth: "If I could keep from it I wouldn't do it, since I'm well aware you dislike it."

"You can't keep from it? That's a dubious claim."

"I don't go where I'm not wanted," she declared. "Not deliberately. Might could be that as I get more practice at this, I'll learn to control my head somewhat better. I get . . . carried away, you see. It's a distracting sort of activity."

She did indeed get carried away, and he prudently made no comment on that. She was a lusty woman, and he pitied any man handed the task of keeping her satisfied for the next fifty years.

Just the thought of it and the sweat turned icy on his body, making her go "Tsk!" beside him.

"I'd warm you up, my friend," she said gently, "but there's not time. Nor time for you to shower, I'm sorry to say. Unless you want every Granny in this Castle to see you sashaying down the halls, you'd best get yourself under way and save the tidyup for your own rooms."

"Tell me one thing," he said.

"If you don't ask," she cautioned, "I won't be obliged to refuse you."

"Where did you go?" he continued, determined to gain as much as he could. "Near on three hours you were gone, Responsible of Brightwater —where were you?"

She was silent, except for the laughing; and he sighed and dragged himself out of her bed before he could fall asleep in it. He wasn't going to find out by asking, she'd made that clear; and the idea of turning her into the sort of maudlin mess he was accustomed to producing, where she'd do or say anything just to keep him from leaving her side—that was ridiculous. He was young, but he wasn't stupid.

"I intend to find out, you know," he told her, pulling his clothes on any old how. "I do intend to find out."

"Intend all you please," she mocked him—mocked him, damn her! "I'll not spoil your fun by telling you."

"And how do you know I won't get up today in front of the Grannys and the whole world assembled, and tell them that you disappear in the night on a Mule, and have the power to lay silence on the creatures, and make something indescribable of the act of love?"

She was calm as a pond. "I know that," she answered, "because first of all that would put an end to your fun, for sure and for certain—you'd never find anything out that way. And secondly, because for all the wickedness you so pride *your*self on, young Wommack, you have a code of honor of your own—and it doesn't include tattling. You'd never stoop to that."

"Might could be I'd see it as my duty as a citizen to speak up," he said, struggling with his hood. "If there's anything I can't abide, you know, it's failing in my duty as a citizen."

"Like Jeremiah Thomas Traveller?" she teased. "Burdened with the truth and heavy of heart, but oh, law, you asked the Holy One Almighty if you should tattle and the answer came back YES! and it came back again YES!"

He closed her door behind him as loudly as he dared, leaving her still chuckling on her drenched narrow bed among the pillows, and limped desperately toward his rooms and a scalding shower. He was by no means confident he'd live through this day, nor certain he cared to; and the Gates help anybody that crossed him till he'd had a chance at some sleep.

When Jewel of Wommack stuck her head out her door at him as he passed it he said only, "Don't chance it!" and she popped it right back in again without another word.

8

Responsible sat at her desk, the private account books before her, and worked, doggedly. It was work that had needed doing before she had left the Castle in February; it was work that needed doing now; and it would make an excellent device for forcing the hours of this day to go by.

At nine o'clock sharp she'd tuned her comset for automatic printout, and she would not miss one word spoken. The speeches and their rebuttals, the Chair's summary and the results of the voting—assuming they got to the voting today, which was not all that likely—would be transcribed silently onto pliofilm and deposited in the comset slot where her copy of the day's news still lay unread. She had waked up that morning, an hour after Lewis Motley Wommack left her bed, to the sound of a late spring rain drumming on the roof and against the north windows, and usually that would of been her idea of an ideal setting to curl up in her bed with the news-sheet and her pot of tea. But she'd had no stomach for the "news" this morning. None of what had happened at Confederation Hall would be news to her—except the things that mattered most but would not be printed on the pliofilm. And anything new that had happened beyond the narrow focus of her present interest, anything that was of importance and might deserve her attention, she did not want to know about right now. She had no attention left to give such things, and would do a slapdash cattywampus job of tending to them—far better to have them wait till this meeting was over and she knew where matters stood.

She was tired, from tension and from lack of sleep; the shower she'd had before her tea had not driven away the gritty feeling under her eyelids nor the ache in her muscles. Nevertheless, she sat at her desk and she studied the columns of figures, forcing them not to blur by squinting fiercely until she added a headache to her other problems and was tempted—just *slightly* tempted—to squander a Spell or two on her self.

"Pay attention, Responsible," she told herself sternly, "and don't be such a frail little flower." A good hard pinch would wake her up fairly effectively, and save the energy she might well need for real magic before this week was over. She applied the pinch, swore softly, and looked again at the columns of numbers.

There was, for example, the one hundred thirteen dollers entered under the ambiguous heading "Herbs Needed." Herbs needed by whom? For what? And how could anybody spend one hundred thirteen dollers on herbs at one time? The Grannys gathered their own herbs, as did she and the Magicians; only the Magicians of Rank were considered so busy that their herbs must be provided for them by others.

She laid down her stylus, cross at the ambiguous entry, cross that she hadn't demanded details when it had come through on the private budget line in the first place, and went to the comset. She punched in the computer locations for the budget category, seven numbers in sequence, and the infowindow lit up for readout on such matters as the cost of goatfeed and Mule blankets in the month of April 3012, which was not yet quite what she wanted. The restricted access code numbers switched the computer's search to the areas that interested her.

She typed in the date of the entry, the words, and then, AMPLIFY.

GAILHERB	EIGHTY DOLLERS EVEN
BENISONWEED	THIRTY–THREE DOLLERS EVEN
SOURCE	MARKTWAIN WILDERNESS,
	NORTHEAST EDGE,
	2119.4 BY 941.0 APPROX
GOAL	CASTLE AIRY
BENEFICIARY	CHARITY OF GUTHRIE

The readout winked off, flashed once more as a concession to her human frailties, and winked off, leaving the word WAITING behind.

Responsible thought about it.

IS REPEAT DESIRED? The computer was short on patience.

She ignored it, and thought some more. Then she typed in: DISPLAY ALL OTHER DETAILS RE ENTRY.

ALL DETAILS DISPLAYED. WAITING.

"Wait, then," said Responsible, and turned it off. She was satisfied. Charity of Guthrie, widowed Mistress of Castle Airy, took in every damaged creature that Ozark produced. Any citizen involved in some shabby Family altercation that would not bear the light of day or of the courts;

any girl suffering the nine-month effects of careless love; any young person unable to face the long haul up through the world from servingmaid or apprentice or hired man to heading an independent household; any weak or shamed or injured or frightened person, anyone simply in need of refuge, could be sure of a warm welcome at Castle Airy. And three Grannys lived under that roof, to help Charity live up to her name. If she'd felt she needed one hundred and thirteen dollars worth of gailherb and benisonweed, so be it.

Responsible checked the item off and went on to the next one. And then her stylus slowed as she wondered . . . had any of the Twelve Kingdoms planned ahead, against the possibility that the Confederation would fall and they would no longer be able to depend upon Brightwater for such things as herbs? It was very simple for them now; whatever their Castles required, they punched in their order on their comsets and it arrived by supply freighter. And in an emergency, there'd be Veritas Truebreed Motley the 4th, Brightwater's own Magician of Rank, SNAPPING in on his Mule with the supplies in his saddlebags almost before the person asking had stopped entering the order. The Castles had been taking that for granted for hundreds of years now, like the weather; might some of them have thought about preparing for a new kind of winter?

Sure enough. The computers told her, as they'd have told her sooner if she'd had sense enough to ask. In the last six months there'd been a steady series of orders in from Castle Traveller. Herbs, they'd ordered, both healing and magic. Magic supplies in abundance. Bags of the holy sands from Marktwain's desert, and flagons of the sacred water from its desert spring. Lengths of fine cloth needed for the ceremonies of the Magicians and the Magicians of Rank. Gold cloth for the sails permitted only to the small silver ships of the Magicians of Rank. Unguents and potions; musical instruments and bolts of velvet; silver horseshoes and silver daggers. And coarse salt, in huge amounts.

The list was too long to represent genuine need, and she ought to of seen it; but they'd been clever about it. A little here, a little there, and all of it scrambled to look like the ordinary orders of a busy Castle . . . Only when the computers had it neatly sorted and totaled could you see what they were up to. They'd been stockpiling, had the Travellers, hoarding all those items they might find themselves hard put to locate for a while if they didn't have Brightwater to call upon.

The hypocrisy of it made Responsible's mouth twitch. Independence! Oh, yes. Stand on your own feet, be boones, be true *men;* no more hiding behind the skirts of Brightwater. But first, be very sure you've bled Brightwater of all the necessities for that independence.

Castles Guthrie and Farson, on the other hand, that ought to have been doing the same thing, had put in nothing more than a few routine orders. They were so obsessed with the details of the fool wrangling going on on Arkansaw that they'd had no time to spare for the obvious. Responsible had no illusions that they would of refrained from hoarding on any kind of moral grounds.

She typed in rapid instructions; there would be no more deliveries of supplies to Tinaseeh, nothing else to Castle Traveller, that did not have her personal approval. She'd not have a legitimate need neglected, but neither would she allow Castle Traveller to strengthen their hands any further at Brightwater's expense.

Noon passed, and still she worked, and the soft hiss as each filled sheet of pliofilm landed in the OUT slot on the comset never stopped; they were working right on through dinner, then, at the Hall. She kept grimly to her figures and her bits of data, refusing the temptation to take a look now and then at the words that might be on those sheets. There were only a few alternatives, and as her magic had truly told her, every one of them carried trouble with it. Should the Confederation stand, there would be trouble: the anti-Confederationists' resentment would be greatly increased by their defeat, and by their public humiliation at the Jubilee. The plotting, the niggling attempts to undermine the assembly, the constant dragging of feet when action was needed, would go right on as they had all these years, disrupting the equilibrium of Ozark. Should the Confederation fall, there would be trouble: twelve sovereign states to establish themselves, to construct alliances and formal relationships one with another—a way of life entirely new and untried. And then there was the possibility about which she could make no reliable prediction: the most militant of the anti-Confederationists—say, the Travellers, the Farsons, and the Guthries— they might simply *secede.* That was also possible, if things did not go their way, and if the problem of saving face seemed to them heavier than the consequences of secession.

At which point she realized that her method of concentrating on her work and refusing to think about these things was to run them round and round her mind, thinking all the time, "I absolutely refuse to think about what will happen if . . ."

"Dozens!" she said out loud, and then, "Bloody oozing Dozens!" If there was a worse oath than that one, she didn't know it; if there was any justice, she'd be struck dead here where she sat, and then she wouldn't have to worry about any of it any longer. "As I sow, so shall I *reap?*" she demanded of the universe in general. "How about You doing a little reaping, now I've done so benastied much sowing?"

The small message bell on her comset rang then, a poor substitute for the bolt of lightning she was lusting after; there was a message for her. No doubt the Farsons wanted their rooms changed; they always did, whenever they came to visit, as a matter of principle.

She laid down her work, doing it little harm, since she'd been paying no real attention to what she was doing for the past half hour at least, and pushed the MESSAGE stud.

"Twelve Corners and Twelve Gates!" the thing squawked at her; she didn't even recognize the voice. But the voice was prepared for that, which meant it had to be somebody accustomed to the vagaries of Brightwater's low-budget communications equipment. "It's Granny Hazelbide," it went on. "You turn your comset on, missy, this minute—the Smiths have just demanded to be heard out of turn because, by their lights, they've already missed *several* turns—as if that was anybody's fault but their own, but your uncle's fallen for it—and from what I see before me, unless you look quick you're going to miss something like you never imagined in all your borned days! And so am I if I tarry *here* any longer!"

TERMINATE, said the computer.

Responsible frowned; she had no desire to miss out on anything that had brought the Granny to that pitch of excitement, but the suggestion that anything the Smiths might say or do would be worth her time was one of the more dubious ideas she'd heard lately. A Granny tumbled over the balcony edge from leaning too close, a Junior Delegate gone berserk and racing up and down the center aisle—something like that might be interesting, but the Smiths? The Smiths were dullness raised to its utmost potential.

Nevertheless, if Granny Hazelbide thought there was something happening, it was likely there was, and Responsible hit the proper switches. And there stood Delldon Mallard Smith the 2nd, risen to give *his* speech on the subject of the motion to permanently dissolve the Confederation of Continents. And his brothers, all four of them, and all four eldest sons, standing in the row alongside him—to give him moral support, no doubt.

She scowled at his image—the man'd never said a word worth hearing in all the years of his life, if what people said of him was to be credited, and her own limited experience with him led her to believe that it was— and listened for a clue to what had had the Granny all in an uproar.

"—that I . . . uh . . . understand from the very depths of my *manhood*, the utmost recesses . . . uh . . . of my soul, the plea that my distinguished colleague from Tinaseeh has made to all of us and its . . . uh . . . its significance. It strikes a chord that resonates in *this* breast!" And he pounded on the breast in question to demonstrate the awesome sincerity of his feelings; Responsible snickered. "But we Smiths," he went on, "we Smiths were not taken by surprise at Castle Traveller's move, nor do we . . . uh . . . take it lightly . . . uh . . . lightly. Knowing, knowing I say, that it was sure to come at this Jubilee—my friends, it was long over*due!*—we turned our finest minds to what it must mean . . . for all of us. Not only for Castle Smith, but for every Castle on this planet. And what came to us, like a . . . uh . . . *revelation!* . . . was that since First Landing our people have been ignoring something of great importance. *Great* importance!" He paused dramatically, a great bulk in a swath of cloaks that must have been torment in the heat, and clasped his hands before him, leaning toward his audience.

"Think!" he said. "What *was* it that First Granny herself said, as she waded out of the waters of the Outward Deeps and set foot on this gentle land, one . . . uh . . . one thousand years ago? Every schoolchild knows the answer to that question! She said—she *said:* 'Glory be! The Kingdom's come at last!' The *Kingdom!* I tell you, my friends, my colleagues, gentle ladies, citizens all over this beautiful and bounteous . . . uh . . . planet— we have missed the significance of what First Granny said for *one thousand long years!* For that, that was a *Naming!*"

Responsible was glued to the set now, not because what he said was so fascinating but because for the life of her she could not see where it was going to lead. What *could* he be trying to get at?

"Now," he said, clearly warming to his subject, "what *is* a Kingdom? Is it a piece of land? Is it a building? Is it a set of . . . uh . . . coordinates? That may well sound like a simpleminded question to . . . uh . . . some of you—but I ask you, I ask you to give it some serious thought. When one of our Grannys names a girlbaby Rose, we ask ourselves—what does that *mean?* We add up the values of those letters, and we look carefully and with respect at their . . . uh . . . total, and we ask ourselves—what is their *significance?* And we don't call that simpleminded, for we know that Naming is serious . . . that the very . . . uh, the fabric of our lives depends upon Proper Naming! And when First Granny called this a Kingdom, what, we must ask ourselves—one thousand sorry years late!—what did she *mean?*"

As any fool knew, Responsible thought, tapping her fingernail impatiently against her front teeth, she meant that we'd finally reached a homeplace and that she was fervently grateful to be off The Ship and out of the water and once more have her feet on solid ground. So?

"I'm not going to *tell* you what she meant," Delldon Mallard said, his voice heavy with layers and layers of dramatic emphasis—he must have practiced, thought Responsible—"I'm going to *show* you!"

For a moment she lost sight of him, as the comcrews swung their cameras round the room and up toward the balcony to give their viewers a glimpse of what was happening. On the floor of the Hall, where Delldon Mallard stood with his four brothers in their places and the four eldest sons each at their father's elbow, an Attendant rose at every one of them's right hand, and waited at rigid attention. And up in the balcony, the Smith women were standing, each with a servingmaid at *her* right hand! Marygold of Purdy, wife of Delldon Mallard and Missus of their Castle; the wives of each of the three brothers, lined up beside Marygold in the back row; and Dorothy of Smith, eldest daughter of the Castle. All over the Hall, the Smiths and their staff were standing—to do what?

The cameras swung dizzyingly back again—the comcrews must have been flustered by the turn of events—and focused on the Master of Castle Smith. His face was the very picture of a man with grave thoughts on his mind, though Responsible doubted he'd ever had a truly grave thought, and he jerked his chin imperiously toward the Attendant that flanked him.

Responsible watched it; but she didn't believe it. Even seeing it with her own eyes, she thought that last night's labors, last night's revels, and this day's tedium had driven the last of her senses to distraction. It could not be that she was really seeing the Attendant lift away—with a flourish—

the heavy cloak that covered his Master, to reveal beneath it yet another cloak; this one of purple velvet, sweeping from the high ruff at his throat all the way to the floor and trimmed all the way round its edges and its sleeves with a foot-wide border of snowy fur. Nor could she really be seeing the magnificent velvet outfit, all tucks and smocking and studding, beneath that purple cloak, or the—yes, dear heaven, it was a scepter—suddenly in his hand!

"You are seeing it," she told herself sternly. "*Behold* . . ."

From a carven box the Attendant took something else, and he placed it with laborious pomp upon his Master's brow. A crown, beyond all question a crown. It shone under the lights the room required in the gloom of the rainy day, a heavy golden crown with a puffed insert of velvet and fur to match the cloak . . .

She began to believe it, and she sank right down on the floor to watch the spectacle as it was repeated all over the room at the Hall, flickering there on the screen. His brothers weren't quite so splendid as Delldon Mallard, their heads were decked with coronets and they held no scepters; the sons, miniatures of the brothers except for an extra gewgaw or two on the costume of Delldon's boy, looked miserable with both the heat and the attention. And up in the balcony, while every Granny clutched her knitting to her breast in shock, the servingmaids removed the outer cloaks of the Smith women and completed the final touches to *their* gaudy array.

"I give you," bellowed Delldon Mallard Smith, "my brothers—the Dukes of Smith!" He swung his arm wide in a gesture of presentation, and the Attendant next to him ducked hastily, but not quite hastily enough. "I give you my son, the Crown Prince Jedroth Langford Smith the Ninth! My nephews, who will be Dukes one day, and now bear proudly the title of Baronet! I give you my wife and my consort, Queen Marygold of Purdy, Queen of my Kingdom!" And on and on down the list, ending with the Crown Princess, Her Gentle Highness Dorothy of Smith.

Dorothy, that had always been a pincher. Marygold of Purdy, that had never sent in an order totaled correctly in her life, even when it was for just one item. The Royal Family.

Delldon Mallard Smith wasn't through, of course; that would of been too much to expect. "That," he went on, giving the back of the seat ahead of him three solid thumps with his scepter and making everybody sitting there jump, "*that* is what a Kingdom is! It has a King! A Queen! All those things that properly . . . uh . . . belong to a Kingdom, it has those things! And when every Family of Ozark has fulfilled its responsibility to First Granny, when every Kingdom has its King and its Queen, *then* at long last we shall see an end to the tribulations that we have suffered these last ten centuries . . . For it was not the Confederation of Continents that brought our troubles upon us—begging your pardon, Delegate Traveller, but that is . . . uh . . . a misinterpretation. It was the failure, the failure to establish twelve *proper* Kingdoms as First Granny intended us to do!"

An Ozarker hesitated to shoot at a sitting duck; but there was one careful question, put by a delegate with his eyes fixed on the ceiling above him and not on the man he addressed. He wondered, just wondered, why First Granny had never seen fit to *mention* this dreadful mistake.

It didn't bother the King of Castle Smith. The whole thing having come to him in a dream, it all being a *revelation,* as he reminded them he had already stated, he knew the answer to that.

"Just plain stubborn," he said flatly. "She wouldn't stoop, not First Granny! If we were such plain fools we couldn't see it, why, we could . . . uh . . . just suffer the consequences. And we *have*—and we've deserved them every last one. It tears at the heart to think of it, First Granny sitting through all those long years waiting, waiting for . . . uh . . . somebody to see the light, and going to her grave with her wishes still denied her . . . It makes a man . . . it brings a man close to tears." And he wiped ostentatiously at the corner of one eye with a bit of his white fur cuff.

Responsible would have given half her repertoire of Formalisms & Transformations at that moment for a chance to see the faces of the Grannys up in the balcony, listening to a pitiful fool make out the first of their number to have had less sense than *he* had.

There was more, but she was past hearing it. She had thought, she truly had thought that she had considered every possible alternative. But she had been sorely mistaken, for this had never crossed her mind. Not only had it not come in a dream, like a revelation, it had not even drifted through a nightmare! Why, even on Old Earth, even before the Twelve Families left it in disgust, there had been no more Kings and Queens that she knew of. Maybe somewhere in the backwaters of that dying world there'd been a relic monarchy or two, but for the true nations of Earth the days of royalty had been the days of fantasy and fairy tale—and that was one thousand years ago.

What would they do now, she wondered, not sure she really cared anymore; she couldn't decide which word was more fitting—"tragic" or "hilarious"—and her head felt entirely scrambled. This explained a number of things, all in a swoop. Why Granny Gableframe wasn't here; no Granny would have countenanced such a charade. Why the Smiths had come late—to call even more attention to their foolish selves and their ridiculous plan, and to avoid the consequences of coming so unhandily late in the alphabet. Why the Smiths had so rudely shut their Castle doors to Responsible when it had been their turn to show her hospitality on her Quest—they'd been afraid that she would see something that would give their scheme away and lose them the advantage of surprise.

Surprise they had, and no question about it. The loudest silence Responsible had ever heard lay over the Independence Room; she fancied she could hear that silence spreading out all the way to the Castle. And Delldon Mallard Smith, fool that he was, was not such a fool as to lose that advantage. While he faced no more than a pack of stunned and dumbfounded males, with the females above him helpless to interfere, he called out, "Mr. Chairman, I move we put the motion to a vote *now!* With no further delay!" "Second!" bellowed the Dukes of Smith in chorus. And the Chair, her own uncle, in his own state of shock, quavered, "All in favor say aye," and the ayes came out of mouths that no more knew what they were saying than if they'd been babes in the cradle—and the act was done.

And in the Smith row, where she'd not seen him before, Responsible saw the beaming face of Lincoln Parradyne Smith the 39th, Magician of Rank of Castle Smith. He was pleased, ah, he was *delighted;* he'd be dancing in the aisle any minute now. What had he done to Granny Gableframe, she thought, to keep her away, and keep her from warning Responsible that this monstrous thing was in the planning? If he'd harmed the old woman, Responsible would see that he paid . . . but he no doubt knew that. If there'd been any hazard he'd not of been grinning the way he was.

It was over. Over!

Not done properly, of course. Few of the delegates had had their opportunity to speak, and no rebuttals had been offered. Any one of the neglected men could of cried "Point of order!" and demanded that the procedures be observed, that had been their right; but they had not. The Travellers had no doubt been holding their breaths for fear someone *would* come to his senses enough to halt what Delldon Mallard had set in motion. And the Brightwaters, like everyone else, had been vacant-minded with amazement, and miserable with embarrassment, and had let the opportunity pass by and the ayes fall from their mouths as if they didn't matter . . .

"*Men!*" shouted Responsible then, outraged to the point of physical sickness, and she kicked the ailing comset with all her strength. "Bad cess to every last *one* of them!"

She was not alone in her opinion.

Down the center aisle of the Independence Room strode a figure that ought to show Delldon Mallard Smith and his Dukes and Princes what majesty was. She stood almost six feet tall; she was slender as a blade of grass, but there was no hint of frailty to her; a black braid was wound round her head in a coronet that was natural in its magnificence and needed no gold to set it off. And her beauty! In the long periods of time that passed between her rare opportunities to see her sister, Responsible tended to forget the almost awesome beauty that Troublesome of Brightwater carried so casually. She wore a riding costume of plain brown leather, faded and worn, and the heels of her riding boots rang against the polished marble floor, and there was no ornament on her anywhere. She needed none, and Responsible hoped the Smith women were aware of the contrast, them in their gleaming crowns, and their necks and hands hung with baubles like something up for sale on the cheap!

Troublesome needed nothing to carry her voice, either. She gave the Chair—Donald Patrick Brightwater the 133rd, him of the popular name—one glance of contempt that should have withered him into fragments right then and there, and turned to face the remnants of Ozark's government. And while she shouted at them, her voice echoing back from the walls, Responsible wept and clapped and cheered, and so did the Grannys, one and all.

"Now you've done it, you cursed fools!" shouted Troublesome of Brightwater. "Now you've gone and done it! I've seen foolishness in my day, I thought I'd seen all the kinds of foolishness there were, but you have topped it all! The year three thousand and twelve, this is; a time when we could if we so chose travel from star to star across our skies; a time when the marvels of magic have taken from the backs of our people the burdens that other ages thought the natural lot of humankind forever-more. A time of wonder—if we chose that it should be . . . But you, you Smiths! You *Smiths!* You choose to throw us back into the darkest of Dark Ages; shall we have the pox, too, to make our Kingdoms more authentic? Eh, *Your Majesty?*"

She waited, and when nobody challenged her, she went on.

"And I'm a fool, too," she said, "to stand here wasting my voice on youall. My fellow fools, I should be saying. My dear, fellow fools . . . You've done it, you're a Confederation no longer; you've thrown away five hundred years of striving toward a respectable system of government, thrown it away for a mass of confusion and a pile of chaos, thrown it away for a cheap parlor trick that left you all gawking at the funny man and his funny hat and his funny scepter . . . I speak for Brightwater—no, dear Uncle, you stood and let this pass without a word, don't you interfere with me now, and don't you *presume* to speak for us!—I, Troublesome of Brightwater, *I* speak for this Castle and this Kingdom, and I tell you to get out of this room and out of this Hall and out of my sight! You sicken me, you disgrace this ancient building . . . Goats have more sense than you, I'll let them in here; Brightwater will stable its Mules in here, they have an intelligence that merits it. But you! Fools! In the name of the Twelve Bleeding Suffering Gates, begone from here before I take a whip to your pitiful *backs* . . . and don't you think, don't you think for one breath, that I wouldn't! You deserve whatever happens to you now . . . and Brightwater will weep no tears for you!"

Her voice ran them from the room as surely as if it had been a whip, and in the magnificence of her rage she was as sure a scourge as an earth-quake or a flood would have been, and even the Magicians of Rank went scurrying out of the Hall with all the speed they could manage.

As for the Royal Family . . . they were a tad encumbered in their heavy velvets, and no doubt suffering greatly from the heat in them. And Responsible cackled like a squawker in its coop to see two of the Baronets —Baronets! they could at least have gotten the titles right!—chasing down the aisles after the little golden circlets that had fallen from their unac-customed heads.

9

Granny Hazelbide came straight to Responsible's room to tell her about what she'd missed.

"Law, you'd of been proud of your sister!" she said, rocking fast. "You saw her order that pack of cowards and ninnies out of the Hall; you should of seen 'em scurry, like something was yapping at their tail-feathers, and all the 'royal' Smiths tripping over their purple trains!" The Granny smacked her knee and chortled deep in her throat. "And then your sister went all around that Hall, child, and she locked every window in every room, all three stories of them, and she locked the back door and the side doors, and then she threw the bolts and slammed the front door as well. Left the place tight as a cast iron egg, she did. And then she marched out to get her Mule—know where she'd hitched it?"

"To the statue on the lawn, I expect," said Responsible.

"Quite right, *quite* right, and tied up to First Granny's left ankle! She untied that Mule and rode it right down the street and out of town with never so much as a look back at anybody, but there was no trouble atall reading what she was thinking purely from the look of her back! Not to mention the Mule's, but we'll leave that lie. I never thought to see such a sight as I saw today, never in all my life—and I'm sorry you weren't there. Your delegates were damned fools, which comes as no surprise; but your feisty sister! Law, Responsible, she was a privilege to behold and an honor to observe!"

"I didn't even get to say hello to her," said Responsible slowly. "And I wanted to, Granny—I realized, the other day, I've been missing her."

Granny Hazelbide stretched out her hand and tucked in a strand of the girl's hair that had come loose from the ribbon binding it back. "She came when you sent for her, child," she said gently. "There's nobody else alive she'd do that for."

"I suppose I'll have to make do with that."

"I reckon you will—and appreciate it."

"Granny?"

"Yes, child?"

"Tell me how that happened."

"Tell you where one end of a wedding ring starts and the other ends, you mean? It's that kind of question."

Responsible ignored her, and kept worrying at it.

"How," she demanded, "after all the planning, and all the discussing, and all the saying what we'd do if this happened and how we'd do if that happened, and all the rest of it . . . *how could such a fool thing happen?"*

"You've put your finger on it," said Granny Hazelbide. "We had all our preparations made, like you said, for many a different comealong; but we never thought to prepare against a *fool* thing! And that is how they got us. You can use all the logic you like, seeing what this cause will do for this consequence . . . but nobody's so wise they can plan for fools. There's no logic *to* a fool, Responsible, just no logic atall—remember that."

Responsible swallowed hard, and nodded, not that it would do her much good to remember it.

"What's happening now, Granny Hazelbide?" she asked. "I don't have the heart to go see for myself."

"Just about what you'd expect to be happening," said the Granny. "As fast as they can pack up, the Families are riding out of here, flying out of here, sailing out of here. They can't look each other in the eye, and for *sure* they can't look at the Brightwaters! They're stuffing their faces in the diningrooms, making their hastiest excuses to your mother, and then heading for their homes like the sorry shamed creatures they rightly ought to consider theirselves."

She fanned herself briskly; she'd come as close to a run on her way here as a woman of ninety could get, and she was feeling the warmth.

"It'd of been a mighty different thing if it'd been done *right*," she went on. "Say the Confederation *had* fallen, in spite of the speeches and the rebuttals, there'd still have been the other three days of the Jubilee. Jeremiah Thomas Traveller would of organized it all so each of the Twelve Kingdoms could of met in smaller rooms of the Hall, and he'd of had trade treaties going, and plans drawn up for Parliaments or some such all around, and brand-new Ambassadors flying back and forth from room to room, feeling important . . . It wouldn't of been what we wanted—but it would still of been a Jubilee, and done with dignity! This was a Mule of a different breed, Responsible. None of 'em quite realizes yet what's been done, none of 'em wants to admit they behaved like tadlings deciding who's to be It—they just want to be gone, with their tails between their legs. Purple velvet tails, in the case of the Smiths."

"Well," said Responsible bitterly, "the Economist should be happy. This will save Castle Brightwater three days' rations for near on two hundred people, and a respectable number of Mules."

"It's a sorry mess, child, and a scandalous waste."

"Not just for us, Granny—think of the Lewises. They've got no money to spend on frills like trips to Brightwater, but they sent twenty-four, and every last one of them in Sundy best . . . I know how long they had to save to do that."

"There was no way we could of known," Granny Hazelbide insisted.

"There should of been!"

"And there should be only bliss and glory, but there isn't. How many nights did you spend casting Spells, trying to see your way through this, Responsible? Not even the Magicians of Rank could say how it would come out. All any of you got for your efforts was 'There'll be trouble'! *I* remember."

She stood up then, and brushed her skirts down, looking grim. "And I'm sorry to have to tell you that there's a piece of trouble left over," she muttered.

"Ah, Granny! A piece of trouble—we haven't even seen the beginning of the troubles yet!"

"This is something . . . more ordinary."

"What? What's happened?"

"Well, now, it seems as there's a Bridgewraith."

"Oh, Granny Hazelbide!" Responsible knew she must look despair doubled and pleated, but it was too much. "Not now!"

"Now," sighed the Granny. "You recollect that little bit of a bridge on Pewter Street, the one they call Humpback, though it has about as much of a hump as I do—that's where she is."

"You know who it is?"

"For sure I do. It's Mynna of McDaniels. But there being strangers in town, and young people as weren't here when Mynna died—she's been taken home twice already. They say her mother's in a sorry state, Responsible; Mynna's been dead it must be twenty years this October. Two of the Airy Grannys are down in the diningroom this minute telling

those as are left eating not to pay Mynna any mind no matter how she
cries and begs; but it won't be easy. Mynna was a pretty little thing, and
she's standing on the bridge crying fit to kill, wearing the blue dress she
had on the day she tripped and fell off that bridge into the water. Hit her
head on a rock, Mynna did, and drowned in water not even six foot deep,
and her a good strong swimmer for a girl of ten. I remember it like it was
yesterday."

"I'd better—"

Granny Hazelbide stopped her, pushing her back into her chair with
one firm hand.

"You'd 'better' nothing—you stay right here," she said. "I'll be going
along to Humpback Bridge myself, soon as it's dark, and I'll take Mynna
of McDaniels' hand and lead her back to the graveyard where she belongs.
That's Granny business, and not suitable for you to concern yourself
with it."

"She won't *stay* in the graveyard, Granny—they never do."

"Then I'll go down and lead her back every night for so long as it
takes to convince her, and two or three times a night if it's needful. And
some of the other Grannys'll spell me. A month or two, she'll settle back
down."

Responsible rubbed at her eyes with both hands; the sandy feeling
was a torment, and tonight, somehow, she'd have to get some sleep. But
she said, "I don't mind going down there, Granny."

"Nor do I," said the old woman, "nor do I. And I'm not worn out
with all this the way you are. At ninety a body doesn't need much sleep."

"I thank you—and I do mean it."

"I know you do, child. And I'll have a little something sent up to
you to *see* that you sleep this night. Mind you drink it all down, you're
falling over in your tracks."

Responsible nodded, and leaned her head back in the chair, weary
to her bones and beyond.

At the door, the Granny stopped suddenly and stood with one hand
on the knob.

"One more thing, Responsible," she said, "and I reckon you'd best
hear it from me. I'd be averse to your hearing it from Granny Leeward,
for example, and if I know that one she'll be at you with it before supper—
or your mother will, one. It'll be no surprise to you."

"What is it, Granny?" Responsible wondered if there ever would be an end to this day.

"They're saying that the Bridgewraith's come out because Troublesome was here in the town."

Responsible closed her eyes and smiled.

"They would say that," she said. "What else have they got to blame things on? Couldn't be their own fault, after all."

"Like I said," the Granny answered. "I didn't think you'd be surprised. And now I'll be going."

The door closed behind Granny Hazelbide, and Responsible sat and rocked and thought and rocked and thought some more. She sent a tentative thought out, feeling for Lewis Motley Wommack, and found him already on board a ship pulling away from the Brightwater Landing, and skittish under her mindtouch as a wild Mule colt. Taking note of that, she let it drop; he had a right to his privacy.

It wasn't as if he hadn't made it amply clear to her how he felt about mindspeech and mindtouch—exactly the same way the Mules felt about it, so far as she could tell, though he'd not done to her yet what the Mules did when a Magician was fool enough to try to take advantage of their telepathic abilities. The headache she had was from having the world fall in on her; she couldn't lay it on the shoulders of Lewis Motley.

PART TWO

10

At Castle Smith, Lincoln Parradyne Smith the 39th was not at all surprised to find something sitting on the Castle's front steps waiting for him. It was a beautiful cat, grant him that, but he didn't care much for the look of it at that moment. Its back was arched like a snare, the claws on all six paws were out and at the ready, its long silver hair stood out all over it like the quills of the fabled Porkypine; and it hissed and spat at him in a remarkably eloquent manner.

The Magician of Rank had been expecting his reception; in the trunk marked with an *x* there'd been packed not only the thirteen crowns, the king's scepter, and the rest of the royal paraphernalia, but also a sack of heavy leather with a drawstring round the top. He whipped that out of a deep pocket inside his cloak, dropped it over the cat—that had been too occupied cussing him out in her limited vocabulary to be wary—and pulled the string tight. Then he tucked the bag under his arm, much like carrying a bag full of snakes but perfectly safe, and headed up to his rooms at the fastest pace consistent with the dignity of his position.

Inside his rooms he lost no time; he went straight to the heavy magic-chest, hewn of the precious cedar that only the Lewises could coax to grow, and pulled out what was needful, laying the squalling sack inside it where he could slam down the lid if the animal thought of anything he hadn't anticipated. He drew a pentacle of adequate size on his floor, pouring out the coarse salt that made its borders well over an inch wide for safety; and at each of its five corners he laid two silver daggers set down in a cross. He stepped back and looked at it, and decided that though it wasn't elegant it would serve, and then in one swift motion he loosed the puckerstring to the sack, threw the thing into the middle of the pentacle and leaped back well out of harm's way.

"You *are* angry, you dear old thing," he murmured at the cat, that's fur had now taken to giving off sparks all on its own, "and I can't say I blame you. Hold on a minute, and I'll give you a chance to tell me what a vast number of unspeakable things I am."

He had a sudden temptation, almost overpowering, to run the Granny through a set of changes on the way to her proper shape—say a mourning dove, first; and then maybe a ponderous turtle; and then maybe a nanny goat; and so on. But he fought it off. She was going to be trouble enough as it was.

He set up his Structural Index and his Structural Change with great care—it wouldn't do to alter so much as the sprigged flowers she'd had in the pattern of her dress goods—and he raised his hands to trace the double-barred arrow in the air. It was a simple Substitution Transformation, and it didn't take long; one quiet crackle from the golden arrow, and there stood Granny Gableframe good as new and twice as fractious.

The pentacle had been more than sufficient to hold the cat, furious as it had been; the Granny was something else. She hitched up her skirts to avoid the salt, kicked aside a set of the crossed silver daggers with one pointy-toed shoe, stepped contemptuously right out of the magic shape and right up to *him,* and jabbed her finger into his chest. He felt the blood come, even through his tunic, and sighed; it was one of his favorite tunics.

"Now, Granny—" he began, but she cut him off in midsyllable.

"*You,*" she said, "are so far beneath contempt that you're not worth wasting spit on. If you were sitting on the edge of a piece of paper, you'd be able to swing your legs, you're that *small!* You are a worthless, sorry, vile excuse for a Magician of Rank, and if I'd the power I'd strip you of that rank, for you don't deserve it any more than your *bed* does. Oh, I can't do it, I know that well, but I can wish, and I'm a powerful wisher, Lincoln Parradyne, just a *powerful* wisher! And it might could be the just One as runs this universe'll see fit to do what I can't—I can pray for that, *with*out ceasing! And when you've laid me in my grave at last and think you're shut of me, Lincoln Parradyne Smith the Traitor, you watch, you watch close—you'll see my face in every mirror and it'll be telling you what filth, what slime, what blasphemy you are . . . You'll see my face in every cup you lift to your lips, you'll hear my voice at your ear all the day long and all the night long and it'll be cursing your immortal soul, *with*out ceasing! Vile serpent, vermin out from under a swamplog, you and your false lying tongue, you'll find me in your pocket when you reach in for a shammybag, you'll find me in your shoe when you stick your stinking foot into it, you'll find me in your buttonholes when you . . ."

It went on and on, earning his considerable admiration before it was over, and he didn't doubt a single word of it; and all the time that fingernail in his chest, poke, poke, poke, and he took it in silence. He had every bit of it coming to him.

"Never before," she said finally, her voice gone to a gravelly rasp but not one bit weary, "never before in the one thousand years we've watched this world turn under the three moons, *never* has a Magician of Rank raised a hand—by magic or in ordinary human mischief—against a Granny! You are the very first to have that sorry distinction, Lincoln Parradyne Smith, and whatsoever it may have gained you now it will bring you more evil in payment than you ever knew existed! The universe, false Magician, *is not mocked!*"

"Granny Gableframe," he hazarded then, since she appeared to have at least paused for a breath, "do please notice that I've done you no harm—none. I know the staff of this Castle, they'll have fed you on breast of fowl and thick cream all the time we've been gone, and the serving-maids'll waste days hunting for their lost pretty pet. You have my word you missed nothing at the Jubilee, if *that* is worrying you; it was a boring mess from beginning to end. Look at yourself, Granny Gableframe, you're just as you were—not a hair on your head is out of place."

She raised her index finger straight as a spike beside her temple, and she fixed him with a furious eye.

"You have tampered with my *person!*" she hissed. "You have tampered with my freedom! You have made a lower animal of a woman that was doing magic, and doing it with skill, before ever you were born! Don't you tell me you've done me no harm, you sorry piece of work—and you'd of done more if you dared. A Magician of Rank, using his Formalisms & Transformations against an old woman—phaugh, it'd make a worm puke for shame. Now stand aside!"

And she marched out of the room, with him following her at a discreet distance and feeling that it wasn't going well, and down to the parlor where the Family had gathered for coffee and ginger cake. They sat up nervously when she sailed into the room, he noticed, and Dorothy—now Princess Dorothy—began to bawl.

Delldon Mallard spoke up first, his voice warm and sticky with his confidence in his own righteousness, and bid the Granny good afternoon.

"Sit down and have some coffee and some of this good cake with us, Granny Gableframe," he said. "We have a lot to tell you, now we're home."

"I wouldn't sit with you," said the Granny, "if both my legs'd been removed. *Which* you might very well direct your toy Magician of Rank over there to do next, I reckon!"

"Now, Granny," said Delldon Mallard, "when you hear what we have to tell you, you'll forget all about your mad. You'll be sorry you didn't go along to be part of it all, and you'll be proud of this Family. Sit down, Granny, and let us tell you about it."

"Don't you put yourself out to tell me anything," she spat at him. "I know all about what happened—and you know who told me? A *Mule* told me, in your own stables, that's who! A Mule won't stoop to mind-speech with a human being, but it's perfectly willing, I discovered, to share minds with a cat—and I know all about it. Ever hear a Mule laugh, Delldon Mallard? They haven't left off laughing since you made your speech!"

"Granny Gable—"

"You hush!" she declared. "Don't you talk to me, you pitiful excuse for I declare I do not know what! And as for you females, you'd best really settle in to your weeping and your wailing, for you've got a lot of it to do down the road, and a long and lonesome road it is, mark my words. I'll not stay under this roof another night, just for starters; not one night. I'm a decent woman, raised decent, lived decent, and plan to go on the same way; I'll not cast my lot with such trash as you—cover your worthlessness with royal velvet, will you? Might as well go crown the goats! You pitiful females, you hear me now—there's no velvet heavy enough to cover you, ever again!"

"Granny," Lincoln Parradyne objected, "you're frightening the women."

"Am I? Am I? I should surely *hope* I am! They know their duties in this world, and well they know what they've done—oh, Dorothy of Smith, don't you shake your head at me, your crown'll fall off; and I raised you my own self, don't you *dare* tell me you don't know what you've done. Shame on you!"

"Granny, please listen for—"

"Silence!" she thundered, and struck the floor with her cane so hard she dented the planking; and they made not another sound.

"You think you're a sovereign Kingdom now, do you, with a royal court, and a King and a Queen, and a Crown Prince and a Royal Princess and a passel of Royal Whatnots and Flumdiddles . . . and all of it blamed on First Granny, bless her soul as is whirling somewhere, I can tell you! And here you sit, on the southwest corner of Oklahomah, sharing this continent with Castle Clark and Castle Airy, neither one of which'd give you a crossclover leaf to play at casting Spells with. It's many a long and weary mile to Kintucky and Tinaseeh, clear across the Ocean of Storms— and there'll be no help for you from either Traveller or Wommack, they'll have their hands full and running over with their own troubles."

"Granny Gableframe," put in Marygold of Purdy—and then waited a minute, till she was sure the Granny planned on letting her speak—"that makes no special difference. It's no more than a step over to Arkansaw, no more than half a day's flight by Mule from here to Castle Guthrie. We've near neighbors, and near friends."

Granny Gableframe sniffed. "Marygold, you pay as much attention to what goes on in this world as the squawkers do, you know that? You needn't expect help from Castle Guthrie, nor yet the Farsons . . . Might could be the Purdys would be willing to help, seeing as you're their close kin, but they won't dare. Guthrie and Farson are feuding, and Purdy's caught in the middle playing looby-loo and trying to keep their skirts out of both puddles. They'll have nothing to spare for you for a very long time. I think you're about to find yourselves mighty lonely, you Smiths— thank the Gates, Lincoln Parradyne, I am a Brightwater by birth and not one of this line. Envy me that, don't you?"

"Granny Gableframe," said Delldon Mallard, brushing ginger crumbs off his smocked velvet trousers, "I know you feel obligated to granny at us, and I . . . uh . . . must admit you're doing a right fine job of it. But there are things you don't know—things we *men* know. There's nothing that the other Kingdoms ever did for us we can't do for ourselves, and I'm not all that willing to humor you any longer in your tirade at these innocent women. It's not . . . uh . . . called for."

His brothers the Dukes allowed as how they agreed, and the women looked at the floor, and the Granny just looked amazed.

"Part of that, the part about humoring me, I'll ignore," she said disgustedly. "It's not worth my time. But I suggest you think again about your claims to being so sufficient. *True*—you'd be hard put to it to remember calling on most of the other Families for anything. You've never had to. Never been any need, so long as you all had Castle Brightwater for a sugartit to do everything for every last soul on Ozark—all the rest of you,

you've just hung there, hundreds of years now. You've forgotten all about what Brightwater's been doing for you, same way you don't think on what the sun does for you, nor the air . . . Well, Brightwater'll do for you *no* more, pretty ladies, fine gentlemen. *No* more!"

Lincoln Parradyne could see by their faces that not a one of them knew what the old woman was talking about. Possibly Dorothy might of had a glimmer, since as eldest daughter she had more to do with the Castle accounts than any of the others, but she was so wrapped up in her own hysterics he doubted she'd even heard the Granny's words, much less understood them.

"Granny Gableframe," he said at last, leaning against the wall and crossing his arms, "you're wasting your breath on this group. They don't follow you, my dear lady."

"I am not your dear lady, nor never was, nor never will be," she informed him, and he begged her pardon.

"Nevertheless," he said calmly, "*I* am here. And what this Castle can't obtain by trade agreements from the other Kingdoms, I can produce for them myself."

The Granny stared at him, flabbergasted, and shook her head slowly from side to side.

"The *depths* of your ignorance!" she breathed. "It's a bottomless well, a pit with no end to it! You see yourself, do you, using Insertion Transformations to feed and clothe and heal and otherwise provide for the needs of every man jack of this Kingdom? Is that what you mean, Lincoln Parradyne Smith? You that it takes half an hour's preparation and an hour's restup to come up with one little old peachapple for a demonstration, when the Tutors call you in to show the little boys what a Magician of Rank can do? You see yourself materializing tons of grain, and bales of herbs, and . . ."

Her voice trailed off into silence, and then what was clearly a snicker, and Lincoln Parradyne felt a small twinge of uneasiness. It was true, he'd be busy, but he'd had no doubts of his ability to handle whatever the ordinary economic processes wouldn't be adequate for, no doubts of his ability to bring the Kingdom through this brief period of adjustment. And he had no doubts now, really. It was just the way the Granny was looking at him, as if she knew something he didn't and had no mind to tell him what it was. He turned his back on her and stared at a painting of some ancient Smith, hanging on the wall; he'd had all he chose to take from the old crone. Let her rail and rant at the rest of them; he was through listening.

She had one question left for him, however, and she didn't mind directing it to his backside.

"Think on *this*, Lincoln Parradyne!" she said. "You plan on taking a great deal out; what do you plan on putting back *in?*"

Dorothy stopped her blubbering for a moment, and spoke to her father.

"Daddy," she started out, and then when he cleared his throat and frowned at her, she began again with, "*Sire,* I mean to say—"

The Granny clapped her hands. "Sire, is it?" she cackled. "Sire? Such as the goats have, and the Mules? And you plan on addressing your mother as 'Dam,' do you?"

Dorothy could be stubborn, too; she ignored Granny Gableframe and put her question. "Sire," she said doggedly, "you heard what Granny Gableframe just said to Lincoln Parradyne. I would like to know what it *meant.*"

The Granny snorted.

"While he tells you, Your . . . uh . . . Highness," she said, "while he tells you all the marvelous things the *men* know that are going to be such a comfort to you, I'll be getting my Mule saddled and bridled—I've earned that much for my services here—and I'll be on my way. I don't want ary thing else from this Family, thank you very much—give it away, or burn it, or better still, keep it. When you run out of everything you can divide it up among you."

Marygold's voice was not much more than a whisper, but it was honest. "Granny," she said, "please don't you leave us. If I'd of known it would end this way, you leaving us, I never would of gone along with it all."

"And if you'd suspected the sun came up in the morning, no doubt you'd of pulled your windowblinds, Marygold of Purdy," answered the Granny. "What precisely did you *expect* I would do after this shameful carryon?"

"Well, the men were sure you'd see it their way after it was all over; even Lincoln Parradyne there, with his back to us all like he'd had nothing to do with it, he was positive you'd be pleased when you saw us be a true Kingdom, the way First Granny wanted it done . . ."

And Delldon Mallard ran it past her one more time, all about what First Granny had said, and how it had been a Proper Naming, and how now that the Kingdom was taking that road it couldn't help but prosper. "And so you see, dear Granny Gableframe," he wound it up finally, "there's no call for you to be going anywhere, and no call for you to be breaking Marygold's heart the cruel way you're doing. Your place is here, with your Liege Lord."

Lincoln Parradyne turned around at that; if the Granny burst, which seemed to him likely, he didn't want to miss it. And he bit his lip to keep his face straight; it wouldn't do to undermine the Liege Lord's confidence by laughing at it. It was going to be useful, having a King with no more sense than Delldon Mallard, but it was going to have its embarrassing moments.

"My place," said the Granny in a voice of silver needles and icicles, "is at Brightwater. And that's where I'm going, this minute."

The King leaped to his feet and struck the table with his scepter, making all the dishes rattle and dance and splattering coffee far and wide.

"You'll do no such thing!" he roared. "It's treason! I *forbid* it!"

The Granny looked him up and she looked him down, as if she couldn't believe her eyes or her ears, and Lincoln Parradyne rather expected she couldn't, when it came right down to it. He wondered when anybody had last forbidden Granny Gableframe, that was Bethany of Brightwater by birth, and a McDaniels by marriage, any least thing she chose to do. Eighty years or more, he supposed; he much doubted her husband had dared cross her, even before she was a Granny.

She didn't bother replying to the King's forbidding; she turned her back and walked right out the door into the hall, down the corridor and out the side doors that led to the stables, and they all heard the braying of the Mules not five minutes later. It seemed to Lincoln Parradyne that it would not be far off to say that the Mules were laughing.

After she was gone, he found himself facing a solid wall of glares; and a man that had been only one of the Smith brothers yesterday morning but was a Duke Hazeltine Everett of Castle Smith this afternoon stated it for all of them.

"You told us," said the Duke, "that the Granny would get over it. You allowed as how she'd be *mad*—and that's reasonable—but you never told us she'd leave."

The Magician of Rank bowed elegantly. "My apologies, Your Grace. The Granny has proved me mistaken—and given her temper, I'd say we're well rid of her."

"Would you, now?" The Duke did not seem soothed. He nodded toward his wife's swollen stomach, and asked: "What do you propose for us to do, Lincoln Parradyne, if my Duchess has a girlbaby? Who's to name her, now the Granny's gone? I never heard that anybody but the Grannys knew the ways of safe and Proper Naming, and Granny Gableframe was the one and the only Granny in this Kingdom!"

"I can't see either Castle Airy or Castle Clark," said his wife, her hands folded protectively over the shape of the possible girlbaby, "seeing fit to loan us a Granny when my time comes."

"Well, I can," said Lincoln Parradyne. "Charity of Airy would send aid to the Devil himself if she thought he needed it. Put it out of your mind, and should it prove necessary we'll send to her for help."

"I don't much like being beholden to Airy," said the King. "They're Confederationists to the last . . . uh . . . servingmaid, over there."

"You like the idea of an Improper Naming any better?" demanded his brother Hazeltine. "You like the idea of a curse such as hangs over Castle Wommack, and I don't know how many generations since the babe there was Improperly Named?"

"Allow me to point out," said the Magician of Rank, "now that you've brought it up, that particular error was made by a Granny. Are you quite sure, all of you, that the rule which says only Grannys can name female children is anything more than a superstition?"

Too far, too fast. Their shocked gasps and the thud of his Liege Lord's scepter falling right out of his hand onto the floor told him that.

"That Granny," said Dorothy of Smith, "*that* Granny, she was at her very first Naming, and it's known she was poorly at the time besides, with a woman in the Castle using illegal Spells against her and not caught until nearly two weeks after it all happened! Everybody knows that!"

"All the same," he shot back at her, "the Wommack Curse has lasted over four hundred years. The Granny's circumstances at the time do not seem to have been taken into consideration by the Powers—which makes very little sense. If even you can see that the Granny ought to have had allowances made for her, it does seem that the Holy One could have mustered up the same amount of wisdom!"

"Oh, Lincoln Parradyne," said the Duchess Linden of Lewis, wife of

Duke Whitney Crawford Smith and undoubtedly the most capable of the women there—which was saying very little—"you walk a narrow and perilous line!"

Which he most assuredly did. He was aware of that, and the beads of sweat stood clammy on his forehead. But he'd risked far too much to see it all go sour now for lack of courage to stay on that same dangerous line she referred to; it was the path he'd chosen, and the point of no return had gone by some time ago—he had no intentions of looking back. The biggest problem in this Castle for the next few months, he was willing to wager, would be morale; as the Granny had said, the Smiths were going to be mighty lonely in their pomp. And it was by no means certain that the people of this Kingdom, that for quite a while would find their new rulers as ridiculous as Granny Gableframe had, could be easily controlled. It would not take many crowds of laughing townspeople and farmers to drive the Royal Family to a shaky condition.

He wanted that, of course; it was his intention that *he* should rule this Kingdom, and that required a shaky King and a vaporish Queen, and all the rest to match, and the Gates knew he had promising raw material to work with. But they had to be able to at least put up some kind of front.

"I suggest," he said quickly, "that we put this out of our minds for now. We're all tired, and we've all been under a strain—and we've been cheated of three days' holiday by the dainty sentiments of the other eleven Families, with, I'm sure, a judicious amount of pressure from Brightwater and the rest of the Confederationists. This is no time to be debating policy, or philosophy, or any other subject. It's a time for changing our clothes and spending the rest of the day quietly relaxing. Tomorrow we'll have a great deal of work to do, and we'll be in no shape for it if we go on squabbling like this among ourselves."

"I'm not sure," said the King, pulling at his beard, "that I feel . . . uh . . . *safe* without a Granny in the Castle. There's always been a Granny here . . . I've never heard of a Castle that has no Granny, and I don't believe I like it. It's not . . . seemly."

"Maybe Granny Gableframe'll get over her conniption fit and come back," suggested one of the Duchesses.

"No she won't," snapped Dorothy. "No—she's made her mind up for good and all."

Firmness was necessary here, and confidence; Lincoln Parradyne provided both.

"I don't know that I can go along with your concern," he said casually, "or that I think being without a Granny is necessarily any problem. But I do see that it matters deeply to you, and I think I can set it right. I know of a Granny that has no Castle she calls home."

"There's no such Granny!"

"There is. Granny Graylady, her name is, and I know where she is to be found. Give me a few hours to rest, and I'll saddle a Mule and head out to where she's camped and ask her to join us. No doubt she'd be glad to be settled at last, like all the other Grannys, instead of living all alone. You leave it in my hands; I'll see to it."

They believed it. He could see their faces relaxing. And though he knew perfectly well that no inducement on this planet could have brought Granny Graylady into Castle Smith or any other Castle—she preferred the cabin she lived in the Wilderness Lands, and the role she filled there—he was equally certain he could find an old lady somewhere in one of the towns who'd be willing to play at grannying for a while if he offered her a large enough sum. All he needed was a female sufficiently old, sufficiently scrawny, and sufficiently venial; *anybody* could use the formspeech proper to a Granny, seeing as how everybody spent much of their lives listening to it.

As for himself, he had no reason to believe that a Granny was necessary to the safety of any Castle, or anything else. But he knew the power of superstition. It was power that worked in his favor, day in and day out, and he intended to accord it the proper respect.

11

"Frankly, Granny Hazelbide, I'm surprised at you," said Thorn of Guthrie. "A body'd think there was nothing to get done around here that required any attention from that girl . . . you realize what time it is?"

"I'm not yet addled," said Granny Hazelbide. "It's near on one-thirty by my reckoning."

"*And* mine," said Ruth of Motley. "Who ever heard of anybody not on their deathbed sleeping till one-thirty in the afternoon?"

"If you'd happened to drink the brew I sent up to Responsible last night, and had the servingmaid stand over you to be sure you drank it every drop down, you'd still be asleep, too, I guarantee you that."

"Oh, you potioned her, did you, Granny?"

"If I hadn't of done, she'd of worked all night long last night the way she has the past three. Since when do either of you, or anybody else around here, have to worry about Responsible pulling her weight? The problem's always been keeping her *from* working, not getting her to keep at it, as *I* recall."

"Nevertheless," said Thorn of Guthrie, "it's a purely disgraceful hour for her to be still in that bed! If you say she's overworked, I'll take your word for it, but she could at least get up and sit in a chair. She's fourteen, Granny, not fifty; she'd make it through the day."

"Fifteen," said the Granny, staring hard at Responsible's mother. "Fifteen years old on the eleventh of May—which it happens to be, this very day."

Ruth of Motley frowned at her daughter-in-law, and exchanged looks with Granny Hazelbide, and then she asked: "Thorn of Guthrie, did you forget that child's birthday again?"

"Third year in a row," observed the Granny.

"May have done," snapped Thorn, with a high flush on her cheeks that only made her more beautiful.

"I notice she always remembers *yours*."

"It makes no smallest nevermind to Responsible, and you know it,"

Thorn told them both. "Why you nag me about it when she's got no natural affections whatsoever, I cannot imagine, and I don't choose to listen to any such trivial clatter on a day like this, thank you very much all the same."

"Well," mused Granny Hazelbide, pursing her lips, "I suppose as a woman reaches your age her memory does begin to suffer a tad, Thorn. No doubt Responsible knows that—and as you say, it won't worry her a mite. *Not* a mite!"

The Missus of Castle Brightwater drew an exasperated breath, and the high flush flared higher still, but she was not about to take bait that obvious.

"*I* think," she declared, "that she should get up. And that's my last word on the subject."

"I'm pleased to hear you say so," answered the Granny, "seeing as how you've already said too many and some left over. You leave the girl alone; the staff's seeing to clearing up after that mob we had in here, and that's what we pay 'em for. No reason Responsible should be doing *anything*. For sure she's not missing anything in the way of inspiring conversation."

"Since it's her birthday," said Ruth of Motley pleasantly, "I'll side with you, Granny."

"You might just as well—because I'm letting nobody near her till she's slept out, and that's all there is to it. The load on that child's back is going to be mighty heavy from here on out, and I'm glad she's not having to think about it for a little while."

Thorn of Guthrie tightened her lips, but she held her peace, and only the speed with which her stylus scribbled at the diary page betrayed her.

As it happened, Responsible was not asleep. She was awake, and had been since a little past one; but she was not brimming with energy. She felt like she'd been drowned in honey and then had it harden round her— that would be the ebonygrass Granny'd put in the potion. It was rare stuff, and saved in the ordinary run of things for people that'd been through some hellish kind of experience. The little Bridgewraith's mother and daddy, for example—it would of been appropriate to potion them with ebonygrass, and Responsible hoped somebody had thought to do it.

She lay there, determined to move, thinking every minute she would move, and only sinking deeper into the languor that held her fast. Her conscience would never have brought her out of it alone; what finally did it, right around four in the afternoon, was the hunger gnawing at her stomach and the leftover taste of the potion. Her mouth put her in mind of the cavecat's den she'd spent some unanticipated and unpleasant time in back a few months, and that did at last drive her in search of her toothbrush.

When she'd first waked up, just for a second, she'd thought "Fourth Day of the Jubilee!" . . . Just for a moment she'd forgotten the shambles things were in. It would have been wonderful; just imagine, if things had gone the other way, if the delegates had told the Travellers and the Smiths to take their "free men and sovereign states" hogwash and throw it into the Ocean of Storms. There'd of been a party at Brightwater this night to end all parties; she'd set aside a quantity of strawberry wine, that's price would of fixed every comset in the Castle, against just such an outcome. Now they'd be able to put it down in the cellars as an investment; not likely it would get any less expensive. Perhaps King Delldon Mallard of Castle Smith would buy it off of Brightwater for his state dinners.

She spat into her basin, getting rid of the taste of the ebonygrass but not the taste that the thought of the Smiths brought to her mouth. Bitter, it was. And bitterest of all was the thought that nagged at her, that if she'd stayed home till the Jubilee and passed her time at her magic—instead of taking off on that fool Quest all around the Kingdoms—she might well have discovered what the Smiths were intending. She was *supposed* to find out such things, and make provisions to deal with them, she bore the label for that. But she'd had no slightest inkling.

Which she rather expected could mean only one thing. The Smiths had been truly, genuinely, wholeheartedly convinced that what they were up to *was not wrong*. How they'd managed that was a marvel to her, but given the awesome depths of their stupidity, might could be any kind of nonsense was possible for them. They surely had not been backward about turning up in their gaudy array before all the Kingdoms assembled, not any one of them, so far as she could tell. Ignorance, like innocence, was a powerful talisman.

And then there was the memory, rankling at her day and night, of how she'd sat still for it without a murmur when she'd gotten the letter from Dorothy of Smith saying it wouldn't be convenient for Responsible to visit Castle Smith on her Quest. It was just that she'd counted on

Granny Gableframe to keep things in at least rough order, and the idea
of a Magician of Rank actually turning magic against a Granny had never
entered her head. It was an unnatural idea, like a Mule playing a fiddle;
if it *had* entered her head no doubt she'd of thrown it right back out again.

"Things," she said to her own face in the bathroom mirror, "things
are entirely *out of hand* on this planet!"

And what was she to do about it? She doubted sleeping all day was
a productive way of tackling the problem.

There were times when she wondered if it wouldn't have been an
easier row to hoe if it'd been runaway technology she had to deal with
instead of runaway magic. They'd been so careful about the technology.
No robots, not even in the fields and the mines where robots could do
the work far more efficiently than human beings ever could hope to. No
nuclear *anything*; she doubted there were more than a score of human
beings besides herself who even knew the word. No chemicals in the
food or on the soil, no synthetics . . . Without Housekeeping Spells to
smooth the heavy wools and linens they wore, the women of Ozark
would of spent many hours with their irons. And they'd thought long
and hard before they allowed electricity, according to the Teaching
Stories, deciding finally that it was a natural thing with its roots in the
lightning—and even so, the Travellers wouldn't use it. Not in their
Castle, not in their Kingdom. They'd had to move clear to Tinaseeh to
escape its taint, and they'd done it with a grim enthusiasm—and believed
that it was magic that powered their comsets.

She smiled, remembering the way the Traveller delegation had
behaved about the switches that turned things on in Castle Brightwater;
she'd seen a mother smack her tadling's fingers for touching one, like
he'd put his hand into goat droppings.

No, they were pure as pure, using the power of sun and wind and
water and plain old-fashioned muscle—and magic. Which was where the
trouble lay. Magic. Common Sense Level, available to everybody unless
they just plain weren't interested, same as the times tables and the alphabet were. Middle Level, for the ambitious, or those as didn't care to be
overdependent on the Grannys. Granny Magic, for the Grannys only;
Hifalutin Magic, for the Magicians. And for the Magicians of Rank, the
highest level—the Formalisms & Transformations. Power there and to
spare—at least you could turn a robot *off!*

She decided she hadn't the courage to send down for tea at this hour of the day; it was twenty minutes till time for supper. She pulled on a plain blue dress, left her feet bare to irritate her mother, and padded on down the halls and stairways to the kitchen. She could ask for coffee, anyway.

"Evening, Miss Responsible," said the women when they saw her, and a servingmaid smiled and said she was pleased to see her looking rested.

"Thank you, Shandra of Clark—ladies. Do you suppose I could have a cup of your coffee?"

They settled her at the big kitchen table with a mug of coffee strong enough to make the spoon stand up straight in it, and she began to feel that she might be able to face the Family for supper after all. She'd rather far have stayed in the kitchen, or eaten in the staff's own diningroom— but that was for tadlings. And she was going on fifteen.

At which point in her musings, the Senior Servingmaid set down a long narrow basket in front of her and said, "For you, Miss Responsible, from all of us, and many happy returns," and she realized that she'd stopped going on fifteen and gotten there.

"Youall spoil me," she said, and it was true. They did. For all they had to take from her in the way of scolding about the dust on the furniture and the polish not being high enough on the floors and too much salt in the cornbread—they spoiled her all the same.

"Open it, miss," said the Castle Housekeeper, that somebody'd just brought in to see the event. "Go on, now."

The basket was new woven, with a handsome *R* worked right into the lid, and two strong handles, and she'd of been satisfied just to have that for her birthday gift; she looked up at them, surprised.

"Open it!"

She lifted off the lid and looked inside, and saw why the basket had had to be such a big one and needed a braced bottom. Inside was a little dulcimer, like the one she'd lost on her Quest, dropping it right off the Mule's back into the ocean—only much prettier. It had inlays of shell all along the sounding boards, three hearts and a rose with two leaves to it. Her old one had been just plain wood.

"The basket won't do to keep it in, Miss Responsible," said the Housekeeper apologetically. "We had to tip it to get it in there just for the giving. But I expect you'll find a use for a big basket like that all the same, and we wanted you to have both."

Responsible smiled at them, and turned red, and wished she could think of something to say. People being nice to her was too rare for her to have developed any skills in dealing with it; it always took her aback and left her foolish.

And even more, she wished that she could sing decently, but there was no use wishing that. Might as well wish for wings. She settled for taking the instrument out of the basket, laying it across her lap, and playing them three verses of the easiest song she knew.

"Ah, it has a sweet tone!" she said, then, while they clapped—spoiling her some more—and laid it to her cheek. "I thank you . . . so much."

"It pleasured us to do it," they said, and then the Housekeeper spoke up on the subject of what Thorn of Guthrie would do to them if supper was late to the table, and they scurried around the kitchen while Responsible sat and glowed at them.

"Sally of Lewis," she asked the Housekeeper, "just how did youall know I wanted another dulcimer?"

"The way you'd treasured that one the Granny had made for you when you were a little bit of a thing? And then losing it like you did? Why, miss, it didn't take all that much brains to puzzle it out that you'd be yearning after another one. It's small, but then so was your lost one. We did wonder about that. Might could be you'd rather of had a proper one, instead of a child's. But you were so fond of the other one . . ."

"You did just right," Responsible assured her. "I couldn't manage a bigger one. It's beautiful, and I love you one and all for thinking of me. It must have taken a precious long time to make it—and the basket, too."

"We all worked at it, miss," said Sally of Lewis. "It went fast that way."

"Bless your hearts," said Responsible.

"We'll need more than our hearts blessed," the Housekeeper told her, "if you don't get yourself on in to supper. They'll be waiting on you."

"Law! I'd forgotten all about it!" Responsible touched all the hands she could reach, tucked her dulcimer under one arm and the basket under the other, changed her mind and hid the dulcimer away in the basket again while Sally of Lewis fretted, and hightailed it for the diningroom.

And then as she went out the door the woman called after her suddenly, "Oh, miss!"

"Yes?"

"I didn't want to forget . . . one of the stablemen was up here not thirty minutes ago, saying as how that Mule of yours is acting up."

"Acting up, Sally of Lewis?" Responsible turned back and leaned against the doorframe. "He have any idea what was wrong with the creature?"

"No, miss—he'd had the Granny down to look at it; and he told me the Granny said you were to go see to the Mule yourself, after supper. I expect you'd best ask *her* what the trouble is."

Responsible nodded slowly, thinking, and stared at the floor.

"Is something wrong, miss? You look right peaked to me—and you're about to crush that basket."

"It's the potion Granny gave me last night," said Responsible quickly. "That and lying in bed this whole day long."

"I know what you mean—nothing makes a person feel more like leftovers than lying all day abed doing nothing. You go on in and get a good meal under your ribs, you'll feel better."

"And then she'll be turned around entirely," commented one of the servingmaids. "Sleep all day, you can't sleep that night . . . it goes on and on."

"Half a potion this night," agreed another one. "To straighten things out. You speak to the Granny, miss; and we'll see to it your tea's brought up as soon as it's light tomorrow morning."

Responsible thanked them, and they wished her a happy birthday one more time, and she thanked them for that, and then she headed with a pounding heart for the diningroom.

Granny Hazelbide, seated at Thorn of Guthrie's left hand, looked a little peaked herself, Responsible thought, as she slipped into her own place at the corner of the table where her left elbow wouldn't always be poking people as she ate.

"Nice of you to honor us with your presence," said her mother, tart as bad vinegar, and Ruth of Motley moved right in over that with "Happy Birthday, Responsible!" and the salutations ran round the table.

"Thank you kindly," she said.

"How does it feel to be fifteen?" asked her uncle Donald Patrick. "You find gray hairs on your head this morning?"

She was of the opinion that her hair would be snow-white by the *following* morning, if the message about her Mule was what she thought it had to be, but she didn't intend to tell him that.

"Just one," she said. "And I pulled it out."

Emmalyn of Clark, Jubal Brooks's wife, set down the forkful of fried squawker she'd had halfway to her mouth and shook a warning finger.

"I hope to goodness you *burned* that hair, Responsible of Brightwater!" Emmalyn declared. "No telling who might find it, you know."

The other women at the table avoided one another's eyes, and Responsible waited, wondering if her mother would be able to resist the chance to make a remark about how Responsible hadn't even been out of *bed* the whole day and couldn't therefore have found any gray hairs among the black ones. When her mother said nothing, she was pleased; perhaps, as time went by, she'd mellow.

"I took care of it, Emmalyn," she said courteously. "But I thank you for the reminder."

"You're welcome, I'm sure," said Emmalyn. "You can't be too careful these days. Such goings-on I'm sure I *never* heard of before as we've had since this year began. It makes me nervous."

"Emmalyn of Clark," said Granny Hazelbide, "you wouldn't be nervous if you didn't dwell on everything. It's not healthy, the way you do, and it's time you gave it up and had babies instead."

It wasn't especially nice of the Granny, saying that, seeing as how it was due to her judicious alterations here and there in Emmalyn's diet that she and Jubal Brooks were still without a single babe and them married almost six years now. But Granny Hazelbide was out of sorts, and Emmalyn irritated her rather more than somewhat.

"Now, Granny Hazelbide," put in Ruth of Motley, "I'm sure Emmalyn does the best she can."

"Emmalyn has *always* been delicate, haven't you, Emmalyn?" said her sister Patience of Clark demurely.

Emmalyn gloried in being called delicate, and while she was glowing with pleasure and Jubal Brooks was patting her hand to show he too appreciated her frailties, she forgot all about Responsible's one gray hair and the hazards thereof.

"Responsible," said Thorn of Guthrie, "you going to tell us what you've got there in that basket by your feet, or not? It's big enough to hold a morning's firewood, or a couple of babies set head to toe, if they scrunched up a tad. You can't expect us not to be curious."

Responsible hadn't realized she'd been so obvious with the basket; that showed how distracted she was, and Granny Hazelbide clucked her tongue.

"A birthday present from the staff," she said, and showed them all the lid with her initial worked in, and the dulcimer tucked inside.

"Law," said Thorn of Guthrie, "here I was so grateful when you lost the old one, and now you're all equipped again. They must be out of their minds."

The uncles chuckled, and Emmalyn fell in behind them, and Responsible gave the basket a shove with her toe to get it out of sight under the table. "I had no plans of singing to you, Mother," she told Thorn of Guthrie. "I believe you can stop worrying about it."

"Won't be caterwauling under my window in the middle of the night, eh?"

There went Thorn—prick and poke, poke and prick. Responsible had been six years old, and the dulcimer Granny'd given her brand-new, the year she'd decided it would be appropriate to celebrate Thorn's birthday by serenading her from under her bedroom window. It had not been a great success.

"No, ma'am," said Responsible. "Set your mind at rest."

Jonathan Cardwell Brightwater the 12th put his oar in then.

"Thorn," he said, "you are downright mean. I don't know what keeps you from pickling in your own juices, I *tell* you I don't. Pass your girl some food here before she faints away—that's the least you can do, I happen to know you forgot her birthday again—and stop your jabbing at her. Listening to you, I understand why Troublesome stays on top her mountain and won't come down; shows good sense on her part, if you ask me. You trying to drive Responsible off the same way?"

Ah, thought Responsible; the bosom of her family. However, at one hundred and nine a man had certain privileges, and Thorn of Guthrie apologized charmingly to her father-in-law, who responded that he should think she *would* be sorry.

"You get my message, young lady?" Granny Hazelbide asked, as if it had been maybe something about piece goods.

"I did," said Responsible. "And I'll see to it."

"You do that," said the Granny. "Pass the gravy, Emmalyn!"

Jubal Brooks was a swift eater; he pushed his plate away and concentrated on his coffee, and Responsible felt him looking at her from under his thick black brows.

"Something on your mind, Jubal Brooks?" she asked him. Might as well be helpful.

"Yes, as it happens," he said. "I'm wondering. You've had a day off now—don't remember you having one since that time you were taken so sick three years ago. And the Jubilee's over—for five hundred years or forever, whichever comes first. Now I'm wondering what you plan to do starting *tomorrow* morning."

"Well," said Responsible, "I plan to be busy."

"So Granny Hazelbide told us," said Ruth of Motley, "and she was right sharp about it, too."

"Details!" said Jubal Brooks. "That's what I want to hear."

Emmalyn smiled proudly. She fancied her husband something of a power in the Castle, especially when he was being forceful like he was now. And Responsible gave up pretending to eat.

"First thing that happens tomorrow," she told them, "is we cut back the comset power till it transmits only to the borders of this Kingdom. For example."

Both of the uncles whistled long and low, and Jonathan Cardwell swore a round oath, women or no women. "You don't plan on the grass growing under your feet, do you, missy?" he demanded. "You really think it has to be done that fast? Law, and I was calling your *mother* mean!"

"Has to be done," said Responsible, "and it won't be a whit easier next week than tomorrow. Whatever a whit is."

"But what will people do?" quavered Emmalyn. "How'll they get messages around and how'll they get the *news*? And what's going to happen to the lessons for the older kids, and—"

"Emmalyn," answered Responsible, "I don't have any idea *whatso-*ever what 'people' will do. That's 'people's' own problem."

"Responsible," said Donald Patrick slowly, "this isn't going to be much help to business, you know. Are you sure we oughtn't to have a kind of transition period here, while some other arrangements are worked out?"

Responsible stared at him.

"As I recall," she said coldly, "when the delegations of the Twelve Kingdoms began whooping and hollering their votes to dissolve the Confederation of Continents, you made no least move to stop them—though you were chairing at the time and the whole procedure was out of order. I don't recall you even saying 'point of order,' Donald Patrick."

"The sense of the meeting was *clear!*"

"It was that. And a part of the sense of the meeting was that there was to be no more central government, am I not right? And that we were, as of the moment that fool vote went round, twelve separate and sovereign nations, each to its own self. You correct me, Donald Patrick, if I'm wrong."

When he didn't answer her, she went on.

"I can't quite see how, without taxes from the other eleven Kingdoms, we could manage here at Brightwater to continue a planetwide communications system. You ask the Economist what it costs to run the comsets if you think it can be done for the price of eggs, dear Uncle. Furthermore, it appears to me that sending out comset broadcasts from *this* separate and sovereign nation into the other separate and sovereign nations would constitute interference in their national affairs. I surely wouldn't want to be guilty of that, would you? Downright unboonely. Sticking our noses in where they're not wanted."

"Responsible," said Donald Patrick, "when those comsets go dead, all over this world, there's going to be an uproar like . . . like . . ."

"They'll have to send their uproar by ship, Mule, or lizzy," said Responsible grimly. "They'll not be sending anything else by comset."

"Oh, now," said Jubal Brooks, still staring at her, and his coffee going stone-cold in his cup, "I object! There's no need to go off into *extremes* like that, and you never said a word of warning before the vote."

Granny Hazelbide saved her the trouble of answering.

"You mean to tell me," she demanded, beating her fork on the edge of her plate to point out her opinions, "you mean to sit there and tell me that a whole roomful of grown men, and those men trusted these past I don't know how many years with the governing of this *entire* planet, they needed to be told such baby stuff as that?"

"Well, Granny Hazelbide, I don't know that I care for your tone!" he protested. "We were fully cognizant of the political facts. *Fully* cognizant!"

The Granny snorted and went back to her eating, talking through the mouthfuls.

"Would of done you a sight more good to be just a tad cognizant—cognizant!—of the practical common-sense facts," she said. "I'm with Responsible; it never would of entered *my* head that you men all assumed the Kingdoms could pull out of the Confederation and put crowns on all their pointy little heads and still count on all the services to go on just like they always had. And no reason it should of entered Responsible's head, either—it was obvious to a plain fool. You men made your decision; now you can live with it."

"You can be certain," put in Responsible, "that Castle Traveller had thought of every one of the practical consequences. And were mighty careful not to point them out to any of the rest of the baa-goats in the room, *who*—I might add—it is not my place to lead by the hand and pick up after. Why didn't you *think?*"

"Responsible, you can't talk to Jubal like that," said Emmalyn, and then jumped as Patience pinched her under the table.

"I beg your pardon, Emmalyn," said Responsible, "but I suggest you consider carefully what your Jubal, and the rest of the Brightwater men present at the Hall—not to mention our so-called friends and allies—allowed to happen. Then, you care to speak sharp to me on their behalf, I'll listen to you."

"Responsible—"

"If," she went on, "*if* procedure'd been held to, as Donald Patrick had full authority to insist that it should be—he was Chair, remember?—if there'd been the rest of the speeches for and against, and the rebuttals, as the law calls for, then there'd of been time for these matters to be raised. One of the Lewis delegates, someone from Castle McDaniels or Castle Motley, *some*one among you distinguished gentlemen, would no doubt have asked the necessary questions. Such as: how did the others plan to get along without the comset system, that's been broadcast from Brightwater these many hundred years? Such as: what happens to supply deliveries, that have been worked out and run by the computers at Castle Brightwater since the day they were hooked up—and the only Kingdoms with ships large enough to serve as supply transport are Brightwater and Guthrie?"

"I do believe this is going to be interesting," said Thorn of Guthrie crisply. "And Responsible is quite right, Donald Patrick. If you'd not just stood there like a gawk—pardon me, *sat* there like a gawk!—and let that vote go by you, those questions would have been raised."

"And we would, I expect, have a Confederation this minute," added Ruth of Motley. "Not a happy Confederation, I daresay—but a Confederation. Jacob Jeremiah Traveller would of found it a good deal harder to get his point across if there'd been ample time to talk about just what it might *mean* to be boones."

"Castle Traveller," said Granny Hazelbide, "doesn't especially care about the comsets. Anything they want to tell, they just walk round the one town they've got and tell it. Not to mention that from their point of view the end of the broadcasts just means one less source of corruption for their tadlings. And I reckon they've been laying in supplies now for a good long time. Right, amn't I, Responsible? Yes, I thought I was!"

And she threw in something extra about lying in beds after people made them.

"The *Smiths* are to blame," Donald Patrick sputtered. "Youall make it seem to have been me—"

"Nope," said Responsible. "Not you by your own self, you can spread that blame around for a considerable distance. But you *were* Chair, mind—and you could have ordered the Smiths to sit down and shut up, as was proper, and gone on to conduct that meeting as it should of been conducted."

Donald Patrick Brightwater's face was a ghastly white, and sweat stood out on his forehead.

"I was taken completely by surprise," he said, almost whispering. "I was expecting everything to go in order, and then all of a sudden there stood Delldon Mallard in his purple velvet and his crown, and all those Attendants kneeling all around the room, and his wife up in the balcony being crowned a Queen . . . I swear I didn't know what was happening till it was over, and too late!"

It had gone far enough, and Ruth of Motley slid smoothly into the breach.

"Son," she said, "anybody would of done the same in your place. I recall you weren't feeling yourself that day anyway, and you shouldn't of *tried* to force yourself to go on with the chairing of that meeting."

"You know how Donald Patrick is, Ruth," added Patience of Clark.

"There's no way a person can get him to think of himself, not if he's convinced there's a duty to be done and his name on it."

"Responsible had no intention to criticize you, Donald Patrick." That was Thorn of Guthrie, adding her careful bit to the orchestration. "She's just upset that things went like they did."

They went on, soothing the men as automatically as they braided their hair in the mornings; and Responsible let them handle it. For one thing, she had no intention of pointing out to them that her purpose in cutting off the comsets so quickly was not revenge—it was just the most effective leverage she had for forcing the other eleven Kingdoms to fall to at once and get their affairs in order. They had to be weaned, and she knew no swifter means of doing it. If this pack of her relatives couldn't see that on their own, so be it; she had other things on her mind.

For example, she had a trip to make down to the stables—to see a Mule.

12

Responsible began by making it very clear to the Mule what she was pre-pared to tolerate.

"Sterling," she said, leaning over the front gate of the stall, "you give me one of those headaches you're so good at passing around, I'll give *you* one with a two-by-four. I hope that's clear?"

The Mule rolled her eyes and flattened her ears, but it was no more than a ritual response, the same way the two-by-four was a ritual chal-lenge. Sterling was breathing as easy as stirring thin soup—an angry Mule huffed and went on till you could hear it a hundred feet off.

"I *won't* have it," Responsible warned. "I *mean* that. I'll potion your oats and do an Insertion Transformation that'll mean things you never dreamed of in your tail; you hear me?"

The ears came up, and Sterling made a gentle whuffling noise.

"All right, then," said Responsible, and unlatched the stall. She went inside and went over to the Mule, and laid her face for a second—all any Mule would tolerate of such stuff—against its neck. And then she leaned back against the stable wall, noting it needed a new coat of whitewash, and waited.

THE OUT-CABAL CALLS YOU.

"*Drat* you, Sterling!" Responsible clapped her hands to her head. "What did I tell you? Gently, you ornery creature, gently! Human minds are not suited for that blasting away you do—*mindspeech,* we use! *Not* mindbraying!"

The Mule whuffled again, and thrashed its tail.

MY APOLOGIES, DAUGHTER OF BRIGHTWATER.

That was better, though not yet exactly pleasant. Responsible nod-ded her approval, and dropped her hands.

"Go on, then," she said. "And mind you don't forget."

THE OUT-CABAL HAS ASKED ME TO PASS ALONG A MESSAGE TO YOU, AND WHILE I DON'T LIKE THEM, NEVER HAVE AND NEVER WILL, I HAVE A CERTAIN REGARD FOR *YOU,* DAUGHTER OF BRIGHTWATER. THEREFORE I WILL TELL YOU WHAT THEY SAY.

"And tell them what I say in return," Responsible reminded her.

IT WOULD BE A WASTE OF MY TIME, OTHERWISE.

"All right, then . . . What do they want *this* time?"

The first time, she had been only ten years old, and she'd been scared half out of her wits. Like the Grannys and the Magicians, she had known the Mules were telepathic, but along with that knowledge went a stomach-twisting familiarity with the stories of what had happened to various foolish humans that had tried to take advantage of that fact. The Mules out-Ozarked the Ozarkers; they kept themselves to themselves, and they intended that everybody else should do likewise. When Sterling first mindspoke her, Responsible had waited, holding her breath, for her brain to be battered at and bounced around her head like a child's play ball. It hadn't been that bad, but it hadn't been any fun, either; the only good thing about that first time had been that it hadn't taken very long.

They were the Out-Cabal, they wanted her to know; they represented a group of planets called the Garnet Ring; their resources of magic were sufficient to simply remove Ozark from the sky like blowing out a candle, if they so chose—under certain conditions established by their laws, which it happened had not yet been met, lucky Ozark—and they were merely setting up relations.

The second time, three years ago, they'd directed her to call all the Magicians of Rank together at the Castle and put them through their paces. They'd wanted an idea of what, precisely, the abilities of "the current crop" were. And Responsible had gone outraged to Granny Hazelbide, and been told in no uncertain terms how to proceed. "You get those men here," the Granny'd said, "and you lose no time. *No* time!" She'd done it; and she'd lain near dying for eleven days afterward from the effects of their hatred. The Magicians of Rank didn't take kindly to a twelve-year-old girl in pigtails being able to call them in and set them to doing Formalisms & Transformations like you'd show off a fancy Mule team at a fair—and they took even less kindly to not knowing why they were unable to refuse her, or why they were unable to speak of it afterward. Nine Magicians of Rank, all concentrating their hatred on her over the course of the long day the Out-Cabal had requested . . . Remembering, Responsible shivered. She wanted no repetition of that pain, beside which the pain of deathdance fever was no more than a needleprick to a careless finger.

THEY PUT YOU ON NOTICE, said Sterling, THAT THIS PLANET IS NOW UNDER THEIR FULL SURVEILLANCE.

"It has *always* been under their surveillance, so far as I know."

FROM TIME TO TIME, SINCE YOUR PEOPLE CAME TO THIS LAND, THEY HAVE CHOSEN TO WATCH YOUR BEHAVIOR AND YOUR DEVELOPMENT. NOW, IT WILL NOT BE FROM TIME TO TIME. IT WILL BE AT *ALL* TIMES.

"Why? What makes us so much more interesting all of a sudden?"

YOU ARE A PLANET RULED BY THE LAWS OF MAGIC, NOT THE LAWS OF SCIENCE; THUS, YOU FALL WITHIN THEIR INFLUENCE.

"That has always been so," said Responsible stubbornly.

BUT OTHER THINGS HAVE CHANGED. UNDER ONLY TWO CONDITIONS DO THE LAWS OF THE GARNET RING ALLOW THE OUT-CABAL TO INTERFERE IN THE AFFAIRS OF A MAGIC-BOUND PLANET: WHEN THERE IS A PLANETARY CATASTROPHE, SUCH AS FAMINE OR PLAGUE OR WAR, THAT THREATENS TO DESTROY ALL THE POPULATION—

"I know the laws!"

DO NOT INTERRUPT ME, DAUGHTER OF BRIGHTWATER!

Stars danced before her eyes, but she knew she deserved it.

"Sorry," she said. "Beg your pardon, Sterling."

AND THE OTHER IS: WHEN THE PLANET IS IN A STATE OF ANARCHY. THAT IS TO SAY, WHEN HUMANS HAVE THE GOOD SENSE TO RUN THEIR AFFAIRS AS MULES DO. I FIND THIS SECOND CONDITION FOOLISH.

Responsible didn't doubt that for a moment.

"There are differences between humans and Mules," she said.

Sterling's silence was both eloquent and insolent, and Responsible longed to pull her braided tail.

PLEASE TELL THEM, she said instead, switching to mindspeech herself for discretion's sake, though she'd set wards before she came in, PLEASE TELL THEM THAT WE FACE NO PLANETARY CATASTROPHE. WE ARE WELL FED, WE ARE IN FULL HEALTH, AND WE ARE NOT AT WAR NOR HAVE WE EVER BEEN.

There was a moment's silence; then, I HAVE TOLD THEM, said Sterling.

AND TELL THEM, STERLING, ESTIMABLE MULE, THAT WE ARE NOT IN A STATE OF ANARCHY.

After the pause, the Mule stamped a front foot for emphasis.

THEY SAY THAT DOES NOT APPEAR TO THEM TO BE FULLY ACCURATE.

IT IS, said Responsible, A MATTER OF DEFINITION.

THEY DEFINE ANARCHY, the Mule responded, AS AN ABSENCE OF GOVERNMENT. YOUR GOVERNMENT WAS THE CONFEDERATION OF CON-

TINENTS, WHICH HAS NOW FALLEN. THEREFORE, THEY SAY, YOU ARE WITHOUT A GOVERNMENT.

THEY ARE IN ERROR, said Responsible. WE ARE NOT WITHOUT GOVERNMENT . . . UNFORTUNATELY, WE HAVE AN *EXCESS* OF GOVERNMENT.

The pause was longer than usual.

THEY WOULD LIKE AN EXPLANATION, said the Mule finally.

PLEASE TELL THEM: WE HAD ONE GOVERNMENT, THE CONFEDERATION OF CONTINENTS. THAT HAS BEEN DISSOLVED, LEGALLY AND BY DUE PROCESS. AND NOW THAT IT NO LONGER EXISTS, WE HAVE *TWELVE* GOVERNMENTS, EACH SEPARATE AND SOVEREIGN. WE ARE TWELVE TIMES AS GOVERNED AS WE WERE BEFORE THE CONFEDERATION FELL. PLEASE TELL THEM THAT, STERLING, EXACTLY AS I HAVE STATED IT.

She waited, then. A Mule in the next stall brayed in what she would have taken for sympathy in any creature except a Mule. Mules did not sympathize.

THE OUT-CABAL SAYS THAT THAT IS ONE POSSIBLE INTERPRETATION OF THE PRESENT SITUATION.

IT IS THE *ONLY* POSSIBLE INTERPRETATION!

THEY DISAGREE, DAUGHTER OF BRIGHTWATER. I TOLD YOU . . . I WILL TELL YOU AGAIN: THEY SAY IT IS ONE POSSIBLE WAY OF LOOKING AT THE MATTER.

AND?

AND WHAT?

AND WHAT ELSE? WHAT ELSE DO THEY SAY, STERLING? ARE THEY MOVING AGAINST US IN THE MORNING, DO WE HAVE THREE DAYS TO PREPARE, ARE WE ABOUT TO BE TURNED INTO A SMALL DENSE CUBE? WHAT WILL THEY DO NOW—WHAT IS GOING TO HAPPEN?

PLEASE BE STILL. I AM LISTENING.

BEG YOUR PARDON, said Responsible again.

DAUGHTER OF BRIGHTWATER, THEY SAY THAT YOU ARE NOW UNDER THEIR CONSTANT OBSERVATION. THAT IS HOW THIS BEGAN; I AM NOT IMPRESSED.

WHAT DOES IT MEAN? WILL THEY TELL YOU?

IT MEANS THAT THEY ARE WILLING TO CONSIDER THE POSSIBILITY YOU SUGGEST, BUT THAT ONLY BY WATCHING ALL DAY AND ALL NIGHT, EVERY DAY AND EVERY NIGHT, CAN THEY DETERMINE WHETHER YOU ARE RIGHT OR WRONG. THEY HAVE NO RESPECT FOR PRIVACY, THAT IS OBVIOUS.

THEY WILL SEE TWELVE ORDERLY GOVERNMENTS, GOING ABOUT

THEIR AFFAIRS. TELL THEM THAT. TELL THEM THEY CAN WATCH TILL THEY FALL OUT OF THE SKY, BUT THEY WILL SEE NO FAMINE, NO PLAGUE, NO WAR, AND NO ANARCHY. TELL THEM THEY HAVE MY WORD ON THAT.

DAUGHTER OR BRIGHTWATER, I APOLOGIZE . . . THEY ONLY REPEAT THEMSELVES. THEY SAY THEY WILL BE WATCHING. AND THAT IS ALL THEY SAY. THEY HAVE NOTHING TO ADD.

Responsible braced herself; the Out-Cabal liked to end their conversations with a little exhibition of the potency of their arcane skills, and there was no predicting what form it might take.

ALTHOUGH THEY HAVE SAID THEY HAVE NOTHING TO ADD, Sterling said disgustedly, THEY HAVE ADDED SOMETHING.

YES?

THEY SAY NOT TO WAIT—NOTHING IS GOING TO HAPPEN. THEY SAY THAT THEY ARE NEITHER CRUEL NOR UNREASONABLE AND THAT YOU ALREADY HAVE TROUBLE ENOUGH ON YOUR HANDS. THEY SAY THEY FEEL NO NEED TO ADD TO THAT.

She refused to thank them; she closed her mind firmly so to indicate. But she was nevertheless grateful. Once it had been a whirling column of lightning that had chased her all around the stable; the second time it had been towers of flame ringing her in, burning up just to the distance where the heat began to be torture, burning just long enough to cause her genuine fear, and then flickering out and leaving no mark behind. Not a charred spot, not a singed stalk of grain. Only the stinging of her skin and the heat of her clothing. If they felt obliged to be more spectacular each time, she couldn't bring herself to look forward to it. Not that either of their displays so far had been anything she couldn't of done herself. It was the things she'd heard they could do, and not knowing what to expect, nor how far they'd go, that made it uncomfortable.

She marched back to the Castle, getting angrier with every step she took—she was halfway there before she remembered the wards, and had to go back and take *them* off—and went to find Granny Hazelbide.

Who had, she discovered, acquired a partner.

"Hello there, Granny Gableframe!" she said, almost surprised out of her mad. It wasn't like Grannys to go visiting; they didn't have time.

"Evening, Responsible," said the Granny.

"Granny Gableframe," explained Granny Hazelbide, "is asking for our hospitality."

"Only for a little while, mind," put in the other. "I've been Granny-in-Residence at Castle Smith now over thirty—law! over forty—years, and it's been nothing but outlandish misery the whole time. What I fancy now is a little house in a near village, if you can spare one, where I can granny for decent folk for a change, instead of that pack of . . . unspeakables . . . at Castle Smith. Seems to me Granny Hazelbide needs no help here."

"You're welcome ten times over, Granny Gableframe," said Responsible. "And as for your settling, that'll be no problem. There's no such thing as too many Grannys in a Kingdom. I'll send the word around, and we'll have the Magician take you to see the towns that apply for your services, and let you choose at your leisure."

"In the meantime," said Granny Hazelbide, "I've told her we can use her here—if she can abide our plain ways, that is. We're a tad short on scepters and crowns and suchlike."

"You've a wicked tongue and a cold heart, Hazelbide," said Granny Gableframe, "and you'll live to regret it."

Granny Hazelbide chuckled, and patted her friend's knee, and then turned serious.

"They'll quiz you to a nub, come breakfast time," she warned. "Thorn of Guthrie will want every last smidgen, every last *de*tail, and those two boys of Ruth's are more curious than's healthy . . . and Jonathan Cardwell Brightwater is worse for gossip than seven old ladies not fit to granny. You want to keep to your room and put all that off awhile?"

Granny Gableframe hummphed; and then did it louder.

"*No*-sir," she said, tart enough to pucker metal. "I have no intentions whatsoever, just *no* intentions, of furnishing that lot with the tale they're after. Here I am, and that's the end of it, and if they won't have me on that basis they can throw me a pallet in the stables with my Mule. I'll not discuss it, I put you on notice here and now. And you needn't go to any effort to prepare them for it, ladies, for I'm fully capable of telling them where to take their nosy questions when the time comes. Just leave it to this old Granny, thank you kindly."

"You sure?"

"Sure as sure, Responsible," declared the old lady. "It'll be a day to remember when I can't manage a few Brightwaters with their mouths flapping."

"Fair enough," said Responsible, "and I'll enjoy the spectacle. Now has anybody seen to your rooms?"

"Sent a servingmaid to do that, it'll be half an hour ago now," said

Granny Hazelbide. "There's an empty room two doors down from me, looking out over the meadow and the creek, and has its own bath and a nice little old fireplace in a corner. Just the thing. It'll be ready whenever Gableframe cares to go up there."

"All taken care of, are you?"

"That I am," said the Granny, "or do seem to be. Depends of course on how clear Hazelbide's instructions were, and whether she fancied a mudtoad or two under my pillow as a welcoming gesture."

Responsible smiled; they were going to enjoy themselves, those two, and perhaps with a little time to recover from whatever outrage Lincoln Parradyne Smith had perpetrated on her, Granny Gableframe could be cozened into staying at the Castle permanently. She'd be company for Granny Hazelbide, and the idea of two Grannys on call at all times appealed to Responsible in the strongest terms just now.

"Want to give me a bit of advice, you two?" she asked suddenly.

Granny Hazelbide jerked her chin toward the other Granny.

"Already told her about it," she said. "We've just been waiting on you to ask."

"What do they want, blast and blister them?" asked Granny Gableframe. "I do believe they are the most . . . Hmmmph. I wish they'd mind their own business."

"Almost said a broad word, did you, Granny?"

"Never you mind. What'd they want?"

"Well," said Responsible, "we had a little talk, by way of my Mule. It *does rankle,* you know—having to use a Mule for interpreter. Lacks a certain dignity."

"You be glad the Mule is willing," cautioned Granny Gableframe. "You thank your lucky stars and comets for that small favor in a cold world! Cause there is *no* way that the human being could pass mindspeech directly with the members of the Out-Cabal and stay sane! It's been tried, and what was left over afterwards was not pretty to look upon."

"Died in a locked room, she did," said Granny Hazelbide, nodding her support, "and nothing any level of magic could do for her. Crawled around in her own filth and howled, day and night, and just plain luck that the next Responsible was already nine years old at the time and able to get through the muck that was left of her mind when it was needful. You *appreciate* the Mule filtering that down for you, hear? You want your brains burned right out of your head?"

"The *point*," said Responsible, "is that it makes it look as if the Mules are more stable of mind than we are. I don't fancy that."

"Faugh!" said Hazelbide. "It's not that atall. The Mule's just closer in its perceptions to the Out-Cabal than humans are, and the sharing seems to be no strain for the creature. Might could be they're Mules themselves, in which case we've no call to be embarrassed. Now what did they want, or you plan to sit there going on about your dignity all this night?"

Responsible told them, and they put in the necessary Granny noises at all the proper places, and approved of the stand she'd taken.

"Handled it right well, I'd say," said one; and the other allowed as how that was accurate.

"Got 'em on a *neat* point, didn't you, missy? I'm proud of you."

Responsible thanked Granny Hazelbide for the compliment, pulled up a rocker, and began to rock. She was still mad, and the distraction provided by Granny Gableframe's sudden arrival was beginning to wear off. The chair started to creak in protest at her speed, but she didn't care; if it fell to pieces, it might relieve her feelings some.

"Responsible," observed Granny Hazelbide, "why don't you just take an ax to that rocker? It'd be quieter and quicker."

"Why've you got your dander up, anyway?" asked Gableframe. "Seems to me you bested them; aren't you satisfied?"

"No, I am not!"

She rocked harder, which wasn't easy.

"Law, she'll take off any minute and fly chair and all out through that window!" said Granny Gableframe. "Girl, what *is* your complaint? The Mule give you a headache?"

Responsible stopped rocking so suddenly that she nearly fell out of the chair. "I just don't understand it," she announced. "And what I don't understand, I purely *despise!*"

"Well, you're not the first," said Gableframe. "Nor will you be the last. The time comes the Out-Cabal lets four five years go by and no message sent, then I'll begin to fret—we'll know then they're up to some devilment."

"We don't know, and we wouldn't know," Responsible said, flat out, and struck the rocker arm with her fist. "We just *assume!*"

Granny Hazelbide sighed, and shook her head.

"There she goes again, Gableframe," she said. "Been through this with her I don't know how many times now, and her only ten years old the first time, and her pigtails pulled back so tight they made her ears stick out—and she's not changed since. My, but she's stubborn!"

"I say," said Responsible, "and there's nobody to say me nay, either, that we have no proof the Out-Cabal can do anything they claim. No proof there's any such group of planets as the Garnet Ring. No proof that there is any such thing as the *Out*-Cabal, far as *I* can see, and I'm not exactly shortsighted!"

"Now, Responsible——"

"Never mind your 'now-Responsibles'! You give me one bit of evidence, one solid piece of anything to show me I should believe in all this stuff; I'll back down. So far, you've had nothing to say that sounded any more sensible than Emmalyn of Clark prattling about umbrellas inside the house and spitting when you see three white Mules, and I'm purely sick of it."

"You recall that other young woman, Responsible, if you want proof—she had the same problem you have, and bad cess to the Grannys advising her that they couldn't keep her from pushing it to where she did! Her mind didn't leave her on account of fairy tales, Responsible of Brightwater, and she did no more than insist that they speak directly to her and not through the Mules. She didn't defy them, nor question their existence!"

"And what about that lightning they chased you with, and the fire all round your pretty little feet last time? *Not* to mention they know *everything* as happens here on this planet, when and as it happens! You forget that?"

Responsible drew a deep breath, and began to rock again, careful to keep it slow and sensible.

"Look here," she said to them. "Let's just look at what you say, and no more of this carryon, fair enough? I don't know about that other Responsible, though I'm for sure sorry about her; that's been two hundred years ago or more, and the circumstances that went with it wrapped up in more mysteries than an onion has layers—I don't consider that evidence. Being that nobody but the Grannys and one lone woman in every generation *knows* about the Out-Cabal, it's understandable that we don't have much in the way of details on the subject . . . but for all we really know she just had too hard a row to hoe and wasn't strong enough to bear it. As for their fancy effects—I've got *Magicians* as could do everything I've seen them do, and Magicians of Rank that make their magic look like baby fooling. Knowing what goes on on Ozark'd be cursed easy if you just happened to *be* on Ozark, let me point *that* out! And if they're so all-fired omnipotent and powerful, if their magic's as far superior to ours as a spaceship's superior to a river raft, like they claim, then why haven't they shown us some of it? Why haven't they rattled things around a bit? Moved some mountains? Canceled some of our weather? Ruined some of *our* magic, at least? *Shoot!*"

The two Grannys traded glances and allowed as how that was quite a speech, fit to try the patience somewhat more than somewhat, and added a half dozen more platitudes to the broth, until Responsible got disgusted with them, too.

"I made you a speech," she said wearily, "you could at least make me an answer. Two of you—you ought to be able to work up something."

Granny Hazelbide rocked and knitted, and rocked and knitted some more, and they all waited, and then she said: "Let me ask you a question, Responsible of Brightwater."

"At your service."

"Say there's no Out-Cabal. Say there's no Garnet Ring, no group of planets all bound by a single system of magic and out to add to their numbers. Say that long-ago Responsible *did* scare her own self insane. Say all the things you propose are true. But then answer me this: if it's not them, if it's no Out-Cabal, then who or what *is* it?"

"Someone on this planet," Responsible muttered. "Somebody right here on Ozark."

"For hundreds of years? Child!"

"For just as many hundreds of years," insisted Responsible, "we've managed to keep all this secret not just from the people of Ozark but even from the Magicians and the Magicians of Rank. That's every bit as hard to believe, but we've done it."

"Well, who do you suspect, then?" Granny Hazelbide demanded. "Speak right up, there's nobody here but us!"

Responsible said nothing. She'd run it through the computers on run-and-destroys till she was blue, and it kept coming out with a whole passel of choices. Might could be it was a Magician of Rank—or two or three of them—passing it along to new ones carefully chosen as they grew old, and enjoying themselves tremendously at what they put the women through. Might could be it was the Skerrys—nobody knew anything about the Skerrys, what they could or would do, hidden away in Marktwain's small desert and not seen once in a hundred years—could *certainly* be the Skerrys. Could be the Mules themselves, and wouldn't *that* be a fine howdydo! She'd had some experience with what a Mule could do if it took a fancy to, and might could be they were not all that happy having their tails braided and their backs saddled and bridled and behaving in general like the Mules of Earth; might could be they'd been getting their own back, in their own way. It wasn't unreasonable; it was so far from unreasonable that she shivered.

"Look at the child! She's all aquiver!"

"I'm all right, Granny Hazelbide."

"All right, are you? Take a closer look at yourself, missy—you that has no trouble whatsoever facing down the whole crew of Magicians of Rank assembled, and knows more than all nine of them put together. You that knows more than all twenty-nine of us Grannys and sees the web of the universe laid out clear and clean before you like a tadling does a fishing net—*you*, Responsible of Brightwater! And you've done no more this night than send six seven sentences back and forth between you and the Out-Cabal, filtered through the mind of a Mule to keep it easy for you, and I do believe you'll have to be carried up to your bed! What's that, Responsible, if not proof the Out-Cabal's real?"

"You speak mighty plain," said Responsible. "Guard your tongue!"

"There are times," answered the old woman, "only plain speaking will do the job. Think I want to see *you* with your mind destroyed? Just because I failed to speak up plain when my turn came? I'm not such a shirkall as that, nor yet such a fool. You *can't* walk, *can* you? Now *can* you?"

Many things were not clear to Responsible at that moment. It seemed to her, for example, that even the Grannys should realize that all that power and wondrous knowledge they claimed she had was being carried around in a head that had seen only fifteen summers go by, and half the time didn't know what to do with what it knew. It seemed to her they'd realize that her loneliness was a torment, an awful and awesome burden like the whole sky down upon her two shoulders, with no living soul to ask any question of. It seemed to her they'd know so many things; and it seemed to them—that at least was clear—that she knew so much more than she did.

And she could not afford to have them think any differently. Not the Grannys. Not and keep this planet stable, and all the Magicians of Rank in order, while she waited for what she knew to come to *mean* more to her. She had to make a show of strength for these two.

"If there's anything wrong with me," she said to them crisply, drawing on a source of energy she'd have to pay back in a painful coin later, "it's the potion I was given twenty-four hours ago. Wonder you didn't kill me with it, Granny Hazelbide!"

And she stood up and walked straight out of the room, steady as the stones of the Castle walls, and left them looking after her in comfortable silence.

13

All the way back on the ship, Gilead worried about her father. Jacob Donahue Wommack sat through the days, staring out over the water; at the ship's table he made little pretense of eating, picking absently at his food. And in the night she often heard him in the next cabin, pacing, hour after hour; when he slept, which was not often nor for long, he moaned like a creature wounded to the heart. Gilead herself grew thin from the nights she spent listening to him, catching only a few minutes of exhausted sleep toward morning, and the Grannys fussed at her incessantly. Did she think, they wanted to know, that she could help her father by wasting away to a stick and wandering around with two eyes like burnt holes in her face?

"I can't sleep, while he's like that," she told them.

"You do him no service, listening to him and brooding over him!"

"I cannot *help* it," she insisted.

"Then shame on you," Granny Copperdell rebuked her, "for if there's something serious wrong with your daddy he'll need your strength later, and precious little you'll have to offer him! You'll have young Jewel with that on her back as well as the minding of her brother—and that's unfair, Gilead of Wommack. Just *unfair!*"

Gilead turned her head away, and the tears burned in her eyes.

"It's just that I love him," she said, almost choking on the words. "Aren't I supposed to love him?"

"Fine kind of love that is," the Granny went on, grimly. "You do your duty, we'd have a sight more respect for your 'love.'"

"It's my duty to *sleep,* while my daddy suffers?"

Granny Copperdell turned her back on Gilead, a gesture as eloquent in its contempt as a slap would have been, and harder to bear; when the young woman pulled at her elbow she would not even look at her.

"What is it you're after me for now?" she said, rigid as a rail.

"Granny, I don't blame you for what you're thinking, I know I'm not much of a woman."

"That you're not. I'm ashamed to have had the raising of you."

"Say whatever you care to—but can't you potion Daddy?"

"He won't have it."

"You've tried, then—you've already tried?"

"I have tried, for sure," said Granny Copperdell. "Granny *Goodweather* has tried. We know our business, Gilead, we've been at it more years than you've been on this world. And your daddy has sent us both packing, as is his privilege. He's neither a tadling to have his nose held and the potion poured down him, nor yet an addled old one gone child again. He is a strong man in the flower of his manhood, and if he doesn't choose to be potioned he doesn't have to be."

"I can't bear it," lamented Gilead of Wommack, "I can't! Daddy like he is, and both of you Grannys ice and steel to me, and Lewis Motley behaving like a lunatic and driving Jewel distracted, and all the children upset—"

The Granny gave her a look, shook off her hand, and walked off and left her standing there, muttering about worthless females, and for the rest of the trip both Grannys made a point of avoiding her. When they reached Castle Wommack, they shunned her still.

"Don't pay them any mind," Lewis Motley told her once, seeing them pass her as if she'd gone invisible in the night. "What do you care for the opinions of a pair of creaking old women like that?"

"They're *Grannys*," said Gilead. "You don't understand."

"No, I don't. Jewel has told me a mess of nonsense that's supposed to explain it, but I don't understand that either. You have a right to be worried about Jacob Donahue—I'm worried about him myself. I see no reason why you should be treated like they're doing you, just for that."

There is no harsher judgment in all this world, thought Gilead, than that of an Ozark woman for a female that can't cope. But she didn't say it aloud, it wasn't the kind of thing you said to a man; and Lewis Motley went off shrugging his shoulders.

On the morning of the second day of their return, Jacob Donahue was dead. The Attendant who took his coffee up came back swiftly, looking white and stunned, and had the Grannys go back up with him to be sure. He was down again, fast as he'd gone up, and off to the stables like he was in a hurry to get to them. The Grannys were upstairs a considerable time, doing what was necessary, and would let nobody in until they were through. Even then, it was only for long enough to see the dead man laid neatly on a fresh counterpane with his eyes closed and his hands folded and a single candle lit beside his bed, and they shooed all the others away, scolding. "Leave him in peace now, get on with you!"

The staff were satisfied, saying, "All's been done proper; trust the Grannys," and they went back to their work, taking just time to tie a band of black cloth on their sleeves from a supply the Grannys kept handy. And then the Family went to the meetingroom and took their places round the table, leaving the Master's chair empty.

"He left a letter," said Granny Copperdell, without preamble. She reached into the pocket of her apron and pulled out a sheet of heavy paper folded in thirds, and slapped it down before Gilead. "With Gilead's name on its outside."

"Oh, no, Granny," breathed Gilead, "I can't—"

"Say you can't bear it one more time," Granny Copperdell cut in, "just one more time, and I'll send you from this meeting like you weren't yet weaned, you hear me? Now that's your *father's* letter, the last words he wrote, and they are addressed to you. I'll thank you—we'll *all* thank you—to read them in a dignified manner, as is suitable to his memory."

Gilead picked up the sheet and unfolded it, staring at the Grannys, and she asked, in a voice that nobody recognized: "Does this mean that Daddy killed himself? Does it?"

"You know anything else it could mean?" snapped Granny Goodweather. "Now will you leave off, and read what's written?"

> My dearest family and my beloved friends,
>
> I write these last few words to you, not because I mean to excuse what I am about to do, but because I would like to try to explain. Perhaps then you will find you can forgive me.
>
> My life has never been a hard one; excepting the loss of my dear wife, everything has been made easy and smooth for me, now that I look back on it. My memories are good ones, and for all that you have done to make that true, I leave you my thanks.
>
> But I've come now to a place where I find myself too much a coward to go on—and that surprises me; I never knew I was a coward. I always thought I was a brave man—but I can't face what life will be like now, nor bear the shame of

my part in making it so. Of all the delegates to that doomed Jubilee, only one was of my generation in both years *and* mind. Only that fanatic, Jeremiah Thomas Traveller, who so well lives up to his name. We are told, you know, that Jeremiah was a prophet of doom, and that Thomas was a doubter—that's Jeremiah, and I have known him many a long year. For the younger men and for the foolish ones there is maybe some excuse; there is none for either Jeremiah or for me. I leave it to the Holy One to punish him for the wickedness that rots his soul; no doubt I will be punished, too, for dying a coward's death, and a death of shame. It is a bitter legacy I leave you—never think I didn't know that.

One question will come up now, and perhaps be a source of discord. I can do at least this much for you; I can settle that question. My sons will be fine men, but they are very young; my daughter Gilead is dear to me, but she is not a strong woman. I therefore direct that the title of Master of Castle Wommack be passed on not to any one of my children, but to my brother Lewis Motley Wommack the 33rd. I make this choice without any hesitation; I know my brother. He is called a wild young man—I leave the conduct of this Kingdom and its people in his hands, knowing he will lay aside that wildness as easily as he would lay aside a cloak. Let there be no dispute on this matter, as you respect my memory. Help him, as you have helped me; support him, as you have supported me; honor him, as you have honored me.

As I look back over what I have written, I see that I have failed in this as well—I have *not* explained. And I cannot, I have no more strength than I have courage. Forgive me then, my dear ones, for love of me alone.

I bid you farewell.

Jacob Donahue Wommack the 23rd

"There! I read the awful thing!" Gilead threw the sheet of paper from her, white-lipped and shuddering.

"Thank you, Gilead of Wommack," said Granny Goodweather. She reached out and set the letter in order again, and laid it down in the center of the table. And she looked round at all the children with a pitying eye. Gilead, the eldest. The two young boys, Thomas Lincoln the 9th,

and the father's namesake, Jacob Donahue the 24th. Gilead's sisters, and
their husbands, and the grandchildren with their eyes like saucers. Jewel
of Wommack, crying openly but without a sound, the tears pouring in
rivers down her face. All these people, and the 14,000 souls—give or take
a dozen—who were the people, all in the hands of Lewis Motley
Wommack the 33rd.

One of the sons-in-law opened his mouth, and the Granny knew
what he was about to say. At twenty-four, it wouldn't be easy for him to
accept the younger man as Master of this Castle.

"There will be *no dispute!*" she said. "He lies dead, sudden, taken in
the prime of his life and by his own despairing hand; you'll not dishonor
him more by moving against him now, when he cannot compel you to
obedience. You put any such ideas right out of your mind, for I won't
countenance them, nor will Granny Copperdell, nor will the Magicians
of this Kingdom."

"That's well put," added Granny Copperdell. "Anybody as cares to
question it, they'll rue it. Mark my words."

The son-in-law closed his mouth and settled back with a look of resignation, if not acceptance, and the silence went on and on.

"Why?" Gilead ventured finally. "I don't understand why."

"He told you," snapped Granny Copperdell.

"No! It was riddles!"

Her sister Sophia agreed, and the concord ran round the table along
with the questions.

"What's any of this got to do with the Travellers?"

"What'd he mean, he was ashamed?"

"What'd he mean, he couldn't face what life's going to be now?
What's going to happen?"

In the middle of the questions and the complaints, Lewis Motley
Wommack silenced them all. He got up from his chair, far to the foot of
the table beside Jewel's, and he walked right to the head and took the
Master's chair.

"Law!" breathed Gilead in the sudden hush. "Law, that does look
strange!"

"Makes no nevermind how it looks," said Granny Goodweather.
"It's as your daddy ordered it, and no doubt he had his reasons. You got

a few words to say to us, Lewis Motley, before we leave this room and
turn properly to mourning your brother?"

"First," said Lewis Motley, "I'll settle the riddles for you—those as
seem fit for settling, in my own judgment."

"You'd do that, would you?"

"Yes, Granny, I would and I will. Jacob Donahue Wommack saw
that the end of the Confederation meant the beginning of chaos, and he
couldn't face that. He's had order all his life—and there'll be no more
order. That's one riddle answered. As for the shame, he knew it was his
place to stand against that foolish ending set in motion by the Travellers
and carried to its fruit and harvest by the Smiths. He was no young man
to be carried away with the excitement of the moment, nor any fool like
the Brightwater that was Chair and let the meeting be run away with and
said not one word to stop it—he was a man in the wisdom of years, and
a man that saw clear. He knew what it would be like, and he knew he
should speak, and he said nary a word, just for fear of the fuss it would
make. That's the shame he writes of, and a shame I share."

"You tried to speak up!" Jewel protested. "I saw you, from the balcony. You were hollering for them to let you speak."

"So I was," said Lewis Motley bitterly. "I stood there, and I hollered.
The proper thing to do, once I saw nobody else was going to, would of
been to snatch the crown off Delldon Mallard's fool head, take away his
scepter, and use it to beat some sense into as many idiots as I could get to—
starting with the Chair. I did *not* do that, you notice; as my sister tells you,
I stood there hollering for somebody to listen to me, like a nanny goat.
The only person at that meeting as did anything honorable—the one and
only person—was Troublesome of Brightwater. A *woman!* We deserved
every word she said, we deserved to be driven from Confederation Hall
and have it locked against us, and we deserved the look of her back as she
rode out of town."

"Accurate," said the Grannys together.

And Granny Goodweather checked her pocket. She'd taken the tall
glass that sat on the table by Jacob Donahue's bed, rinsed it carefully to
be sure certain every last dreg of the poison he'd used was gone, and
smashed it to bits at the back of his fireplace. But she'd kept one shard
for herself, a good-sized one with a trace of a berry vine etched on it, and

given another like it to Granny Copperdell. It wouldn't do to lose that shard. Such things were very useful, and not often come by; and she had a feeling they might be needed more often in the days to come than they'd been in the past. The sharp bit was still where she'd put it, lying between a shammybag of herbs and her long scissors.

"Well? Is there more?"

That was the son-in-law again, and Lewis Motley gave him a long considering look, what was called a "withering glance" in that Castle, and much feared. Sophia caught her lower lip between her teeth, and moved closer to her husband, that'd made so bold as to challenge the heir.

"I'm still on the riddles," he said coldly. "When I've finished, I'll say so. That suit you?"

"It suits me."

"Consider our situation, then: say you don't worry, as my brother did, about lack of political order. I'm willing to grant that's not an issue likely to grip everybody's mind as it did his, and does mine. But we are the *Wommacks,* I remind you. We are alone, fourteen thousand-odd of us, in the middle of a wilderness barely cut back from its original state, surrounded by a great ocean known for its storms. And to comfort us? We have the Wommack Curse."

"Lewis Motley—"

"No more comsets to provide us easy company, tie us tight to the other eleven Families at a push of a button. No more freighters pulling in to our dock with the latest gewgaws from the cities. Not likely we'll have visitors flying in by Mule, anxious to see the beauties of our wilderness and our inhospitable coasts. We are going to be *alone* now, in a way that no Ozarker has ever been alone before. That, now, I reckon you can understand, whether you're interested in politics or not. And it's that that's got to be dealt with."

He looked at them all, long and hard, and rubbed at his beard with both hands, fiercely, like it tormented him.

"As for me being Master of this Castle," he went on, "that's a piece of foolishness, and brings me to the end of the riddles and the beginning of business. I told you I'd let you know—what I am about to say is the urgent business of this day."

"Now, Lewis Motley?" demanded Granny Goodweather. "You think that's fitting?"

"Now," said the young man. "Right now."

"Then I'll have the tadlings sent out of here, and the staff told to feed them and cosset them and put them to bed. This is no place for children."

"Fair enough, Granny Goodweather," he told her, "fair enough. I've no special desire to bore them, and nothing to say that would interest them. But anybody that's reached the age of twelve stays—that's no child. Not any longer, if ever they were. Jewel of Wommack, you'll stay. And you, Thomas Lincoln. And while you're sending the rest out, Granny, I'll say my say.

"I understand," he said, "all the fire and brimstone you Grannys are putting out about not crossing Jacob Donahue, and it strikes me very odd, seeing as how you never scrupled to cross him ten times a day and twice that on Sundys while he lived. But I'm not afraid of either one of you— let us have that straight and no question in your minds about it—and I'll *not* be Master of Castle Wommack. Master! The very thought turns me sick." He saw the Grannys' mouths open and he shouted at them, "Hear me out!"

"Very well," said Granny Copperdell, and Granny Goodweather nodded. "But what you say had best be carefully thought out aforehand, young man. Custom is, the Master of the Castle names the heir; you plan to go against that, you lay your reasons out mighty plain."

"This is no time," said Lewis Motley grimly, "for the people of Kintucky to be asked to accept me as Castle Master. Nineteen years old, known—as my brother pointed out—to be wild; and far less willing than he thinks to be any less so. That may be romantic, but it's not good sense. I'll have no part of it. But I'll compromise, for the sake of your sacred damned customs, and not to scandalize the countryside further, and because I care for the Wommack name. I'll not be Master; but I'll be Guardian."

"Explain yourself!"

"Granny, if you'd leave off interrupting me, I might be able to do that."

"Get on with it, then."

"The proper heir, and proper Master, sits there beside you—Thomas Lincoln Wommack the Ninth, my brother's elder son. He's his daddy all over again, and he'll make a fine Master; he just needs a little time. I propose to give him that time. I'll be Guardian for this Castle, and him at my side to learn what there is to do—precious little that is, by the way, in case you females think I haven't noticed. I'll do the tasks left to the Master, and do them with my whole heart and my whole strength—until the day Thomas Lincoln reaches an age and skill suitable to let him take it on, and *that* day, ah, that day, I shall be free of this particular set of fetters my dear brother saw fit to leave me."

"Shame on you," said Gilead. "Him not cold yet, and you speaking of him that way! You're a hardhearted man, Lewis Motley Wommack, and not a natural one. He was your brother, and he stood as father to you, as best as ever he could!"

"That does not oblige me to be grateful, Gilead, when he hands on to me a task he tells us he couldn't face his own self, and not only am I not grateful, I resent it. You hear me? I resent being *used,* and I resent years of my life being taken from me, and nothing but my loyalty to this Family keeps me from handing this over to Chandler over there, that's just chafing at the bit to have the job! Or Jareth Andrew Lewis, hiding behind Sophia, that's already challenged me twice!"

Granny Goodweather raised her finger beside her temple for silence, and waited till she had it, and then she spoke straight to Thomas Lincoln.

"You understand, boy, what your uncle is saying?" she asked him. "You agree to it? It's your right to object, and your right to *insist* on Lewis Motley following your daddy's wishes right to the smallest letter. And though he claims he's not afraid of a Granny or two, I give you my word on it we have ways of making him take *that* back in a hurry! What's your feeling on this, Thomas Lincoln?"

The boy threw his head up and gave her a casual look that was so like Jacob Donahue it made Gilead catch her breath.

"I think it shows good sense," said Thomas Lincoln, "and I stand behind it. And if it'll make Lewis Motley feel any better, there won't be many years taken from him, as he puts it—the sooner the better, to my mind."

The Granny sighed, satisfied. "That's settled, then." And she pushed her chair back, and smoothed her skirts, ready to leave the room and be about her business.

"Please sit yourself down, Granny Goodweather," said Lewis Motley, "I'm not through yet. There's just one more thing. We have ahead of us a long time of hardship and lack and terrible loneliness. And through that time, our people will need something to rally round, something to look to as a stable center. The Travellers have their faith to carry *them;* we have nothing but our Curse, and it makes a poor companion. Delldon Mallard Smith's an idiot, and the day will come he'll wish he'd never heard the word 'King,' but he has one thing worth copying. What we need, all alone out here, is magnificence. Pomp and circumstance. Ritual and pageantry. And lots of it. And as it happens, we have a perfect excuse for it."

"Whatever in the world?" demanded Granny Copperdell. "Whatever in this wide world?"

"We have the problem, now there's no comset, of educating the children on this continent. No more sitting them down every morning to learn what the computers served up from Brightwater; and the Grannys and the Tutors can't be expected to take them on more than a year or two past the seven years old they are when they finish with them now. They don't have the time, nor the training. And we have Jewel of Wommack."

He rubbed his hands together, and nodded politely at his sister, who was staring at him, feeling a chill in her bones. Whatever it was he had in mind, she could be sure certain it meant another burden for her.

"We'll have a Teaching Order," said Lewis Motley with satisfaction. "And Jewel will head it—whether she fancies it or not! She knows chemistry, she knows physics, she knows biology, she knows music theory, she knows painting, she knows history, she knows linguistics—what don't you know, my much indulged little sister? Always at the comsets, and Jacob Donahue so proud of your learning, saying you were to be let alone and somebody else could peel the vegetables . . . The day's come to redeem that favor, Jewel! We'll need a suitable *habit* for you, something splendid and yet dignified, something that will draw attention and inspire respect; and we'll send you with two Senior Attendants and a serving-maid for escort, all round the towns, to find and bring back here other young females with qualifications like yours. We'll house all of you in the north wing of this Castle—not a room of it's in use, except for one library, and that fits neatly—and you will be Senior Teacher. Teacher Jewel, we'll call you, and we'll send the other Teachers you train out over this scratched patch of living for people to be in awe of. One in every town, to be their own bit of pomp and majesty. Gilead, you're clever with the needle—you'll help me gown her properly."

"Not today!" Gilead cried. "Not today, nor tomorrow!"

"No—but the day after. And you, Jewel, close your mouth. You have the skill, you have the knowledge, you have the beauty, you'll have the elegance once we've garbed you; and most important of all, you have the will. You can command, and you're not afraid to. You'll do it beautifully, sister mine! You hear me?"

Jewel of Wommack had planned on a husband and half a dozen babes for herself, to add to the ones already making the halls noisy at the Castle. She'd planned on a suite of rooms nobody else had seemed to care for, a corner suite with a window looking out into a tangle of huge old trees, where a tadling could step right from the windowseat onto a treelimb and back again. Three girls and three boys, she'd planned on, all raised loyal to the Confederation, fallen or not.

She set that aside, now. As she'd set aside the idea of being a child, when her parents had drowned, and taken up her post as the woman that'd have to do for her brother.

"I hear you, Lewis Motley," she said.

She had some idea what a habit would be like. There'd been little room on The Ship for pictures of such stuff, but there were a few in the library her brother had mentioned, and she felt the weight of the wimple on her forehead already. And that brought a thought.

"I'll not cut my hair," she announced to nobody in particular. "You put that out of your mind."

"Is that where your learning is?" asked Lewis Motley. "In your hair?"

The Grannys clucked their tongues, and Goodweather spoke up.

"Too much has happened for one day," she said, "and all of us are in a sorry state. You there, making jokes at a time like this; and Gilead, about to faint on us. I believe you have the right of it, young Wommack, with your Teaching Order, I do believe that is exactly what we need, and I can see it down the way—it'll be a thing that comes to matter. But for now, enough. Enough and a right smart piece left over. This meeting's closed."

And then she thought of one more thing.

"Lewis Motley?"

"Yes, ma'am?"

"I'll be expecting you in my room shortly, about that earache."

"Granny," said Jewel, "that's a waste of your time. I've been trying to send him to you about that for days now, and he takes my head off every time I mention it. He's *got* no earache, you care to listen to him, nor no headache either. You can tell him all you like how many times you've seen him, wincing like somebody stuck him with a pin again, rubbing at his head and scowling—it won't do you a scrap of good."

"Lewis Motley!" objected the Granny. "You've got your work cut out for you for a good time to come, and no quarter anywhere. This is no time to be distracted with a misery, you need to be the very best you can be! You come and see me and let me—"

He cut her off with a sudden chop of both hands in the air.

"Like you said, Granny," he told them, looking right through them all and biting the words off one by one, "this meeting's closed."

14

At Castle Smith the sovereign was fretful, despite the fact that that very morning the new Granny'd flown in behind his Magician of Rank on his Mule and taken up residence in the Castle. She looked mean enough, and she talked the formspeech in a way that was a consolation to ears long used to hearing it, and having her there filled a hole that'd been gnawing at him. But he was not happy. He sat on the throne set up for him in the Castle Ballroom, now known as the Throne Room, and fidgeted, while his Queen watched him distractedly.

"She can't do it," said King Delldon Mallard Smith the 2nd. "I don't *believe* she can do it!"

"She's done it," answered Lincoln Parradyne.

"She's got no *right!*"

"On the contrary, Your Majesty—she has every right. Or, to be more accurate, Brightwater Kingdom has every right."

"There has *always* been the comset network on Ozark, Lincoln Parradyne. From the very . . . uh . . . first. The comsets supply our news. They carry our messages. They provide our education and our entertainment. They are everything that on Old Earth had to be done by a mail service, and a telephone service, and a television service, and a radio service, and a—"

"Your Majesty," interrupted the Magician of Rank, "I am familiar with the history of Earth. And I assure you that the comsets have done far more than all the services and media of that misbegotten planet combined. We will be greatly inconvenienced without them."

"Then—"

"*But,* Your Highness, Responsible of Brightwater is as much within her rights to restrict the range of the comsets to the Kingdom of Brightwater as she would be to keep its buildings there, or its Mule herds there, or anything else that belongs to it. Brightwater provided the comset service to the Confederation, not to the Kingdoms—and the Confederation is no more."

The King pulled at his lower lip, and blew out a long breath. "You didn't mention this point to me before the Jubilee," he said accusingly.

"On the contrary again, Your Majesty. I did."

"I remember no such thing."

"He did," put in the Queen. "I was there at the time, and for sure he did. You laughed at him. You said he was talking nonsense. You told him not to bother you with stories meant to scare tadlings, when you had important business to discuss. I remember *most* distinctly."

"Well, whatever happened—not that I'm admitting it, you . . . uh . . . understand, I tell you nobody mentioned it to me!—but isn't there a law? Can't she be stopped?"

Lincoln Parradyne raised his eyebrows.

"Your Majesty," he protested, "the comset stations, and the equipment, and all the transmitters and relays, *all* those things, are the property of Castle Brightwater. The reply that was given to me yesterday by Jonathan Cardwell Brightwater—saying that to continue comset transmission would be an act of interference in the internal affairs of the sovereign Kingdoms—was absolutely right. Not to mention the expense, of course."

"Even if the sovereign Kingdoms desire to be interfered with?" demanded Delldon Mallard, ignoring the part about expense. "In that one way only, of course."

"Really, Your Majesty!" said Lincoln Parradyne. "Think what you are saying. Either we are independent, or we are *not*."

"Perhaps," ventured the King, "Responsible of Brightwater has a price."

"I doubt that," said Marygold flatly.

"Even if she did—where would you *get* that price? You have not yet established a Royal Treasury, and it's not because I haven't reminded you."

The point was a sore one with the King, who'd been putting off by every means possible the inevitable moment when he would have to inform his subjects of the new realities of taxation, and explain to them just what services they would be receiving from him in return for their funds. He did not have that worked out to his satisfaction as yet, and he was not so thick-headed that he did not realize it might take some fancy talking to bring it off. Taxes in the past had gone to Brightwater, and the services provided had been both obvious and welcome; things would be different now.

"Lincoln Parradyne?"

"Yes, Your Majesty?"

"How about our building . . . uh . . . our own comset rig? It's not secret how it's done, is it?"

"No, it's not secret. It was part of the information brought along when we landed here; it's available to anybody."

"Then let's do it!" It seemed very obvious to the King.

"All of the Kingdoms," said the Magician of Rank, "now that the Confederation has finally been dissolved, will have to consider that option. They might each build their own networks . . . they might go back to sending information by riders on Muleback . . . they might take up some of the devices of Earth. But it will take some time, Your Majesty. The decision must be made in each case, separately. The funds must be found. The necessary *technicians* must be found, or hired from elsewhere. A communication network requires experts, and money, and time."

"Do we have the people we need, here in this Kingdom?" asked Queen Marygold practically. "Seems to me that's the first question."

"No, Your Majesty."

"Then where do you reckon—"

"Marygold of Purdy!" said the King. "I have asked you, now that you are a Queen, to be more careful of your speech. If the Magicians of Rank can manage to talk without sounding like Grannys, surely you can do the same!"

Lincoln Parradyne forbore to mention the pitiful weakness of that argument, and answered his Queen directly.

"Madam," he said respectfully, "so far as I know they are all to be found on Marktwain—in Brightwater."

"*Curse* that female!" shouted the King of Smith. "*Curse* her!"

"Delldon, you have no way of knowing that Responsible of Brightwater is the one that ordered the comsets cut back," said his Queen. "It was Jonathan Cardwell Brightwater that spoke to Lincoln Parradyne when you sent him inquiring, not that girl."

The King sputtered helplessly about the ignorance of women, and his Magician of Rank moved to smooth the waters.

"I am much afraid, my dear Queen," he said, "that the King is correct. Whoever may *speak* for Brightwater, it is Responsible that holds the reins of power."

"That's very odd," commented Marygold of Purdy. "I don't understand it at all, and I don't see it as proper or fitting. How can a girl of fifteen be running a whole Kingdom?"

While Delldon Mallard was explaining that it wasn't that way at all, it was just that as was entirely suitable the Family at Brightwater saw fit to leave a lot of trivial detail work to the elder daughter, in the same way that he and Marygold left such stuff to Dorothy of Smith, the Magician of Rank mulled over the question. Not for the first, nor yet for the thousandth time. If he had the answer to that question, he would have the secret to all the mysteries. But seeing as how he didn't have, and no number of Formalisms & Transformations tried by him or any of the other Magicians of Rank would yield it up, there was little point in fretting over it. And so he smiled and spread his hands to indicate that he was as puzzled by it all as Marygold was.

"There is always a Responsible—though not always of Brightwater," mused the Queen, leaning her chin on her hand. "And there always has been, so far as I know . . . and always she has had some special place. And yet she is not a Granny, and not a Magician, and not a Magician of Rank . . . And if you try to talk about it when you're little, the Grannys tell you it's not polite and shush you right up." She stared up at the ceiling, high above her head, and concluded: "I wonder how it *works?*"

"On Earth," grumbled the King, "people did not understand science —and we know . . . uh . . . where that led. Here, we do not understand magic. And who's to say it won't lead to the same place?"

Lincoln Parradyne Smith was taken aback; it was a very perceptive thing to say, and sounded as odd in his sovereign's mouth as a bray would have. He hadn't thought the man had it in him.

"Nicely put, Sire," he said with great formality, bowing low. "Nicely put."

15

Silverweb of McDaniels found her refuge, finally, high up in the Castle, at the end of a tiny passage down which two people couldn't have walked side by side. It was a room smaller than the one in which the Castle linens were stored, but it was big enough for her purpose and clearly not wanted by anybody else; the dust and the cobwebs lay thick enough to show that it got no attention but the yearly spring cleaning, and the one window was so dirty that she could see nothing through it but a weak and murky light even at high noon.

She began by throwing out everything that was in the small space, carrying what was worth saving into the Castle attics—a simple task, since they opened on the passage, and there was no lugging up and down stairs to be done—and putting all the rest down the garbage chute on the floor below. There wasn't much to dispose of. A narrow bedstead with neither spring nor mattress nor hangings, not even a straw tick; a wardrobe that couldn't of held more than a half dozen garments, with a tarnished mirror on its single door that gave her back a crazed wavery image of herself; one low rocker, in need of polish but worth keeping; a threadbare rug the size of a bath towel and rank with mildew; and a pair of curtains that fell apart in her hands when she touched them—how long they had hung there she didn't know, but it had to of been many years.

When the room was empty she put on one of the coveralls the serving-maids used for heavy cleaning, and wrapped a kerchief round her hair. She scrubbed the floors first, till the boards had a soft gray gloss and were satiny to the hand; they had never been varnished. She scoured the walls and ceiling, stripping away from the wall where the bed had been an ancient paper that might of been roses once upon a time. And when she had the wood bare, broad boards vertical up the walls and then crossing the low ceiling, she rubbed into it a sweet oil made from the crushed fruit of a desert bush. It took days, but when she had it done the room had a faint delicate odor that was nothing you could put a name to; she liked it because it made her think of early morning, or high grasses after a soaking rain. The doors and moldings, inside and out, got the same treatment, and it was thorough. Silverweb was as strong as any average man her own age, and she put her sturdy muscles to good use with the rags and oil.

There was the window. She made it clean, till the old glass sparkled with an almost imperceptible tint of yellow, and looked out. If she looked down she could see all the way to the coast, and even make out the white curl of low breakers against the sand. But looking out, she saw only the Holy One's bright clear sky, and that was as she wished it to be. Trees, rooftops, mountains—any of those would have been a distraction, and Silverweb wanted no distractions.

Then came the very last thing. She worked on a table in the attics, finding her materials in broken vases and cracked or chipped glass things of all kinds. There were punchbowls there, and oval plates with nests for stuffed eggs, pitchers meant to hold tea for twenty or more, great glass trays for passing sandwiches, and as in any good Ozark household there was a bin of glass shards and chips kept for the principle of thrift and because the tadlings liked to use them for playing house. The leading was the only thing she lacked, and she found it easily enough in the town.

She cut and fit the pieces carefully, measuring and remeasuring, checking after each added bit to be certain there was no mistake; and when she was through she was flushed with pleasure. For her labors she had a pane of glass that fit into her single window, formed of every shade of yellow, from the palest lemon to a deep color that almost lapsed into orange. She set it firmly into the window frame, over the old glass, and made it secure, and she had perfection. In the early morning and all through the day till midafternoon the air in the room was golden, glorious yellow; then as the sun grew lower it took on a paler tint, the light of afternoons in winter when the lamps are on but the curtains are still open. Still a golden light, though it lacked the splendor of the morning.

"It is my place," she said when everything was ready and she stood looking round her. "*My* place." Her brothers would not think to come here, nor be interested if they did. There was nothing here for them.

Grateful, overwhelmed at the mercy the room offered her, Silverweb of McDaniels dropped to her knees on the bare gray-white floor, raised her eyes to the flood of golden light, and folded her hands—not in the prim steepling of the Reverend and the Grannys and the Solemn Service, but clasped together and round one another as if something beyond price were sheltering inside them.

Her lips moved, but she made no sound; the words were not intended for any human ear.

> *Holy One,*
> *Hail and all hail!*
> *Hosannah!*
> *Hosannah, glory in the highest!*
> *Allelulia!*
> *Amen.*

The prayer moved through her; as it was repeated again and again it was no longer Silverweb praying the words, but the words praying her. Love unbearable caught her up and surged in her, a touch that carried bliss for which no words would ever be adequate, and she became a part of the golden light. She was a crystal that rang to the touch of a Thing unseen but more real than the floor under her knees, a crystal burning in a constant fire that would one day—the Holy One grant her that grace!— burn away every last flaw and let the light pour through her as it poured through her window. And she, Silverweb, would disappear.

Oh, the flesh of her might move around, it would carry her through days and speak the necessary phrases and lie in a foolish bed at night and put food and drink into its mouth—but *she,* the real Silverweb of McDaniels, would not be there. She would be caught unto the One and radiating the glory of the universe; that would be her privilege and her life.

Soon there was only the one word left, and even her lips ceased to move. Looking at her, you might have thought she was not breathing, but she was. Her breath was the Allelulia! and all the rhythms of her blood and breath had set themselves to its measure, and she was aware of nothing else.

Anne of Brightwater knew that her daughter was occupied deeply by some project. Every day Silverweb ate breakfast with her family at Castle McDaniels, did the chores set her with her usual serene efficiency, reappeared again at supper—rarely at the noon dinner, but always at supper —read with them in the evenings, or sang for them in the clear strong voice that was the backbone of the Reverend's choir. Whatever was asked of her she did willingly, while the eight brothers tried in vain to shake her calm and she smiled at them. She would peel pan after pan of vegetables: given a basket, she'd go off and gather fruit or nuts; she would milk goats and bring the pails back brimming, not a drop spilled; hand the girl a pile of the most boring sort of stuff to mend—her brothers' stockings, or the heavy linen napkins and pillowslips—Silverweb took up her needle, found a chair, and shortly the work was done. She complained never, argued rarely, and spoke only when she was spoken to.

It was unnatural, and Anne knew it. No healthy young woman of sixteen, soon to be seventeen, behaved like that. She should have fussed, the way chores had been loaded on her in the last few weeks, testing for some response; she should of been complaining bitterly—and with justification. The Castle had servingmaids in abundance, and Silverweb had a mind glittering in its brilliance, a mind that had terrified the Grannys and impressed whatever crevice it was in the computers that set her lessons and graded them once she outgrew Granny School. Silverweb had finished every course offered, before her twelfth birthday; and someone—a human someone—had come to apologize. They were extremely sorry, he told Anne of Brightwater and Silverweb's father, Stewart Crain McDaniels the 6th, but there was nothing left to teach the girl.

"Youall could of course bring in a human teacher," the man had said, hesitantly, almost as if there were something impolite in the suggestion. "There are specialists that know many things we've never seen any need to include in the programs . . ."

Stewart Crain had been firm in his response; Silverweb knew far too much already to suit him. A young woman that'd turned down four young men he'd offered her for husband, one after another, with the same fool reason—she didn't "choose" to marry? A young woman that'd run away from home to try to join Responsible of Brightwater on her Quest, and had to be sent clear to Castle Airy for the three Grannys there to punish? He'd not have her taught more things she might use as warp or woof for her stubborn and always unexpected behavior; oh, no. He sent the man away, thanking him brusquely for his concern, and that was the end of it. Thereafter, Silverweb relied on the libraries.

But now she did not do even that. When she first began disappearing, slipping away as soon as the mountains of household and garden tasks set her were finished, showing up again only when her absence would be remarked upon, the libraries had been Anne's first thought. After all, through the brief days of the Jubilee, while the other young ones spent their time at the plays and the fairs, Silverweb had moved inflexible between their rooms and the libraries of Brightwater. But she had not found her daughter among the books. Not in the Castle's own very respectable room of volumes and microfiches; not in the town library with its banks of machines making available all the books of the world and facsimiles of some from Old Earth; not in the ample and specialized library of the Reverend.

And then she had had a thought that she almost dared not entertain: was it possible Silverweb was slipping away to meet some young man? Anne would of been obliged to make a show of stern disapproval for that, but in her heart she'd of been overjoyed. A girl not married at Silverweb's age, and showing no sign of any interest in the state, was a rare creature on Ozark. Anne didn't mind having a rare creature about, precisely, but she'd rather have had grandchildren, and the boys were still far too young to provide them.

She set the servingmaids, a few that she knew to be trustworthy, to watching, then. And they came back with just the news she'd feared. There was not, so far as any of them could find out, a young man in the picture.

At last, when she'd made up her mind to confront Silverweb and demand an explanation—an awkward thing at her age, and with her behavior so sickeningly perfect that it allowed no smallest chink for objection—the mystery was solved for her. Among the Castle staff there was a very old woman, well into her nineties, that'd been there all her life, born in the bedroom of her mother, also a McDaniels servingmaid. She was not expected to do anything now but sit and rock; though she insisted she could still outwork any woman in the Castle, she made no attempt to prove it.

Joan of Smith came to Anne's workroom to tell her, leaning on the cane she swore she didn't need—and would *not* have needed if she'd allowed modern magic to help her. She had an awesome stubbornness.

"I know where the young miss has been getting herself to, my lady," said Joan of Smith. "A long walk it was for me, but I checked before I came—and sure enough, there she was."

Anne stood up, heedless of the yarns slipping off her lap onto the rug, asking, "Well, *where?* Not in this Castle, surely!"

"Yes, indeed," said Joan. "Right here in this Castle. She's not a child to go gallivanting, not Miss Silverweb."

"But we looked everywhere—we even sent staff up to the attics, and they found her there once or twice fooling with bits of glass, but not after that . . . We looked this Castle up, down, and sideways!"

"Missus," said Joan of Smith, "there's a place you didn't look. I've been here all my life, and I've seen it only once or twice, and would of had no idea what it was intended for. But my mother'd heard of it from her mother . . . My lady, there's a room beyond the attics."

"Joan!" Anne of Brightwater settled the old lady into a chair and saw her comfortable, fussing over her till she was sure the pillows at her back were as she liked them, and talking the whole time. "I have not been here all my life, for sure, but I've been here a considerable number of years, and I have been over every inch of this Castle. There's no room beyond the attics—there's no 'beyond the attics' at all!"

"Oh, yes, Missus, there is. A few of the maids know of it, those as are truly honest about their work; they clean it once a year. But it never entered their heads the young miss'd go there, seeing as how they're scared to death of the place their own selves. Come cleaning time, they draw lots for who'll do the job, and it's always *two* of 'em, and garlic in both their pockets. Ninnies!"

"Well!" Anne sank down in a chair and pulled it close to Joan's, whose ears were no longer what they had been. "So there's a secret room in my Castle, and everybody knows about it but me, is there? You don't seem to be afraid of it, Joan of Smith . . . You know something the others don't?"

"As I said, Missus, *I* heard of it from my mother, that heard of it from hers. In my grandmother's day—that'd be more than a hundred and fifty years back, mind—the Magicians were few and the Magicians of Rank even fewer. It wasn't like it is today, ma'am. Times there were when a Magician of Rank couldn't come when you sent for him, good will or not—even such a one can't be in two places at once, and it was a matter of choosing among the emergencies which was the worst. That left only the Grannys—and *they* were not so many in those days, either!—to do all the healing. And so it would sometimes come about that there'd be somebody taken sick as was *catching,* and it something the Granny couldn't manage, and might could be days before anyone from the higher ranks could come to the Castle. And a person like that, they put 'em up in the room back beyond the attics, with just a Granny to nurse them—or sometimes just a willing woman, if no Granny was to hand either. And there they stayed, for so long as was needful. It's a *tiny* bit of a room, Missus. Just a *tiny* one!"

"And you've been up there?" marveled Anne, staring at the aged woman with little but a quaver left for a voice, all bones and wrinkles, and a fine trembling to both her hands if she didn't keep them clutched tight to her cane. "Up to the *attics?*"

"I didn't care to disappoint you, Missus," said Joan. "If the room'd shown no signs of anybody being there, you see, I'd of said nothing. Hate to spoil the only thing that gives the young females on the staff any pleasure at spring cleaning. So I checked, first."

"Law!" said Anne of Brightwater. "Well, I thank you . . . And what's she got up there? A lovers' bower? A . . . I don't have any guesses, Joan; what is it? A place to get away from her brothers, that's clear, and nobody could fault her for *that.* But is there more to it?"

"You'd best go see for your own self, dear lady," said the old woman, giving a wave of the cane. "That'd be the way."

"I'm willing; tell me how to get there."

"Go all through the attics, to the furthest one, yonder on the east tower . . ."

"Yes?"

"There you'll find a old blanket tacked up on the wall. Looks like somebody just put it there to cover might could be a cracked place, or a stain where rain'd got in. Tacked just at the top corners, it is. You pull that aside, and back of it you'll find a kindly hall about wide enough for one person with her elbows pulled in real careful. And the room's at the end of that."

"I've seen that old blanket!" Anne declared. "I never thought . . . Isn't there a trunk pushed up against it?"

"Used to be. But not this moment. I expect Miss Silverweb shoves that trunk back there when she comes downstairs."

"Do the boys know about this room?"

The old lady chuckled. "Think the women as keep this Castle are pure fools, Missus?" she demanded. "*No* male person—less he was too sick to know where he was!—has ever known about that room. Bad enough that people have died in there, and people laid moaning while they waited for help. Bad enough with all the bedclothes having to be carried out and burned out behind the stables, right down to the mattress —*none* of us had ary interest, my lady, in little boys as would think it fearsome fun to wrap up in bedsheets and hide in the old wardrobe in there, and jump out at you when you went in to clear away the dust! No, no; the boys have no least notion."

"Then how did Silverweb find out, when even I don't know?"

"Ah, Missus," said Joan of Smith, "I'll not speak to that question. What a woman can do provided she's driven sufficiently—now that's been a wonder since the beginning of time. Every inch, as you put it, the youngun must of searched—just every inch! And not to be fooled by holes with a blanket hung over 'em, either. As I said—you'd best see for yourself."

Anne stood up and hesitated, half afraid to go see what her tall grave daughter was up to, wholly afraid not to, and Joan of Smith said, "The reason for that blanket and trunk, you see, that was so as nobody'd wander into there by mistake and catch whatever it was the person sick there had at the time. You see how that would be."

Anne saw. "You sit here and rest," she told Joan, "just as long as you fancy it. Up to the attics, at your age, and all those stairs! I'd fuss at you if I had the time, Joan of Smith, I declare I would—but I'm going up to see what's to be seen, before she comes down."

"That's wise," said the other. "And I can climb as many stairs as you can, or any other soul in this Castle, you keep that in mind, ma'am! I'm no invalid, and I'll be climbing stairs here when—"

Anne knew from experience that this would go on a long time before the old lady wound down at last and was satisfied with her disclaimers. She leaned over and patted the frail hands holding the battered cane— absolutely, she must be made to have a new one, if they had to send in the Grannys to make her give in to the change, this one was falling to pieces and would give her a broken hip one of these days!—and she slipped out and left her still at it, and headed for the eastmost attic.

The room was there; she found it easily enough. She found her daughter, too. Three knocks she made at the door, clucking her tongue at the sheen it had—she knew how many coats of polish that meant, and how much rubbing, and the servingmaids had never in a million years done *that,* or her name wasn't Anne of Brightwater—and there'd been no answer. She'd hesitated; a person of Silverweb's age had a right to her privacy, and clearly this was a very private place. Then her mother's concern had triumphed over her manners and she'd turned the knob and stepped inside, saying smartly, "Silverweb?" so the girl couldn't claim she'd been sneaking up on her.

It wouldn't have mattered if she'd come in with a brass band; she saw that at once. She went forward to where her daughter was kneeling, tiptoeing for no reason that she understood, and said the name again. Silverweb neither saw her nor heard her. Not at all.

Anne ran, then. Down the tiny hall, scraping her arm painfully on its walls in her panic, through all the attics one after another, down the flights of stairs—and came to a full stop. At the bottom of the first staircase, Joan of Smith stood waiting for her; that meant three flights the old lady had toiled up *again* this day. She would be weary and aching tonight, and Anne thought distractedly that she had to remember to have someone see to her.

"Found her, did you?"

"Yes, I did—and I don't like it!"

"Thought you wouldn't, child; that's why I'm here."

"What will I *do?*" She knew she looked foolish, wringing her hands and rubbing at her scraped arm—if she hadn't Joan would never have called her "child"—but she didn't care. She was frightened.

"Do? You can leave her be," said Joan. "You're Missus of this Castle, and a fine lady, as it's a privilege to serve under. You're mother of nine, and my womb never quickened—Aye, I'll go virgin to my grave, if you want to know the truth of it! Never could bear the idea of a man . . . doing as they do. But I have been walking this earth more years than you and all your babes combined, and I know a thing or two. Anne of Brightwater—leave her be."

Anne leaned against the wall, too weak suddenly to support herself.

"Oh, Joan," she wailed, "it's not natural! You know what it is, don't you? You saw her—you know what it is?"

"*Rap*ture, it's called," said Joan calmly. "And ecstasy, sometimes. I do believe rapture has a better sound to it, though I've always thought both were ugly words."

"And you say leave her be?"

"I do."

"I'll talk to the Reverend!"

"Do that, and he'll drive her away," came the warning. "She would be just as satisfied with a bare cave in the desert, or a hut out in the Wilderness Lands, as she is with that room up there. You care to keep her home, you say nothing at all to the Reverend. I've seen him, how he looks sharp at her when she sings in the choir on Sundys; he's suspicious already, and a word from you about this would be the last dot on the *i*. He wouldn't tolerate it."

"But what will become of her? What will she do, where will she go? On Earth she could have gone into what they called a convent, lived in a bare cell and prayed all the days of her life back of bars if she chose to— we've no such things here! She will be so terribly alone!"

Joan of Smith shook her head firmly, and then again.

"Oh, no!" she said. "There's nothing of this world as Miss Silverweb wants or needs, Missus, and nothing she lacks. She has the Love of Loves, beside which all else is no more, they say, than dry husks and ashes. Such things happen for a purpose, and hers will be clear in time—we will know, and the Twelve Gates grant these eyes live to see it!—we will know what that purpose is. Until then, there are two things to do."

"And they are?"

"Wait, in patience and in humility, if you'll pardon my using the word, as has no right. That's one. And give her hard work aplenty. Chores! To make a balance. Rapture's all very well, but madness lies just the other side of it. See to it she's in the kitchen and the garden and the orchards, make her *sweat,* to tie her safely to this earth in its *wholesome* parts. You've been doing that, I've had my eye on you; your woman's knowing, your mother's knowing, has been directing you as proper as you could be directed. See you don't stop that, now—I'd make it harder on 'er, were I you."

Anne nodded, numb to the core. It was right—every word of it— though how the old creature knew it she couldn't imagine. Perhaps it was the fabled wisdom of age, perhaps it was an experience Joan of Smith didn't care to speak of or had forgotten entirely . . . but it had the ring of rightness. Nevertheless, she was blind with anger. That this should happen to her daughter! All that blond ripeness, the heavy braids always wound in their figure eight like a crown! She had seen the pale down on Silverweb's breasts, and the way they strained at the fabric over them, and the long line of spine when she bent to weeding. And those good hips, meant for babies, designed for them! The waste of it, the utter heart-breaking waste . . . Anne could have cursed the deity that had stolen away her only daughter and denied the motherhood that daughter was fashioned for in every last detail.

Except the spirit. The spirit was—

"Warped!" she said aloud, defying the Powers to do their worst. And then, "Maybe she will grow out of it."

"That happens sometimes," said the old woman. "Might could be."

But Anne of Brightwater had seen her daughter's face, and she knew she spoke a lie, and that Joan of Smith humored her in it. Silverweb would not, would never, grow out of it, and the time would come when it would ripen to a terrible purpose that had nothing at all to do with the ripeness of the flesh, and there was no least thing she could do to stop it, or slow it, or turn it aside. It was like so many other things—it was to be endured.

16

Responsible's list of tasks had been reduced considerably by the turn of events. The project for spreading the Purdy girls round the Kingdoms to break the hold of the "you can't do anything right because you're a Purdy" idea would have to be postponed; at the moment, Brightwater had no kind of relationship with Castle Purdy to even suggest such a thing. She could also draw a firm line through the item that instructed her to see to the Arkansaw feuds; Farsons, Guthries, and Purdys could now go at one another with broadswords and bludgeons, free from all interference—the advantages of sovereignty. The matter of holding a day of celebration in honor of the alleged Skerry sighting had become irrelevant, even if there really had been a Skerry. The penalty for failing to celebrate was bad luck, and that had already arrived in ample measure. And the superstition at Castle Wommack?

Responsible thought about that one awhile. No question about it, she would of welcomed any sort of excuse to visit Castle Wommack, seeing as how that was where Lewis Motley Wommack the 33rd was to be found. Her sleep was filled with dreams of him, far too vivid to be restful, and she woke from them drenched as she had risen from his arms. Once awake, she guarded her mind rigorously, stamping out any thought of him the same way she'd have stamped out fire in dry grass, but her nights were a scandal. The advantage, of course, was that they required no effort on his part and only she was troubled by them; she would heartily have enjoyed a chance to let him share the occasions.

But the Wommacks had done no more to save the Confederation than any of the other Families had, and had left Castle Brightwater as rapidly as everybody else, and they'd left no invitations behind them. While the Confederation stood, she'd felt comfortable touring the Castles; now, for all she knew, they'd bar their gates against her and shout Spells. She'd best leave Castle Wommack alone.

Some of the Families had been prompt in their actions, praise the Gates. Castles McDaniels, Clark, and Airy had sent bids for alliance, obviously written as fast as Family meetings could be held, votes taken, and

Mules saddled to fly the documents to Brightwater. Castle Motley had sent its own Magician of Rank, Shawn Merryweather Lewis the 7th, to let Brightwater know that Castles Motley and Lewis would remain allied with Brightwater for so long as it was possible to do so.

She looked up at the map above her desk; the tiny continent of Mizzurah had all of Arkansaw between it and Brightwater, and looked more like an island off Arkansaw's coast than a nation of two Kingdoms. It was brave of Lewis and Motley to send the message, and a bit of good fortune for them that they had a Magician of Rank to SNAP it on to Brightwater; but they were very isolated now, just the same. When their supplies began to dwindle, which wouldn't be all that long a time off, she was reasonably sure they'd have no choice but to turn to Arkansaw for help—and that would be the end of their ties to Brightwater.

There'd been no word from Castle Smith, now surrounded by Brightwater allies but only a brief flight away from Castle Guthrie, just across the narrow channel between Oklahomah and Arkansaw. Presumably they were debating their options . . . or might could be Delldon Mallard Smith was really fool enough to think he could go it entirely alone.

She turned back to her list, it being pleasanter food for thought than the blamed Smiths. There was the question of whether Una of Clark had acted alone in using magic against Brightwater to scuttle the Jubilee— she'd waste *no* time on that one! The Jubilee, and all that went with it, was over, and she intended to put it behind her, thought *and* deed, like any dead and dishonored thing.

But there was one task that had now become not just one more promise, one more duty postponed, but a matter of urgent necessity. She had given the Gentles her word. Whatever happened to the Confederation of Continents, stand or fall, they would not be involved in the results. For thirty thousand years of recorded history they had lived in the caves of Arkansaw; they had granted the surface of the land without stint or hesitation to the humans, by treaties that guaranteed them the right to go on with their own lives as they always had. And now they were smack in the middle of the feuds. Might could be the Farsons and the Guthries, and the Purdys following along, would hold to the treaties for the sake of simple decency; she would have liked to think so. Might could be, on the other hand, they'd take the position that the old treaties were Confederation agreements and no longer bound them. The Gentles would of been safer, all in all, at the hands of the Travellers, obsessed as they were with right-eousness. No telling *what* the Arkansaw Families might do . . .

It was going to be a curious situation, grant that right off. The Granny had been discussing it that morning at the breakfast table, and Granny Hazelbide had laid it out for the rest of them with absolute accuracy.

"It'd be one thing," she'd said, glaring over the top of her coffee cup, "if the very minute of First Landing we'd divided this world up twelve ways and sent everybody off to their own homeplaces and stayed that way since. That'd be *one* thing! As it is, that is *not* what we have on our plat-ter, not in any degree whatsoever. We're all scrambled and mixed and conglomerated . . . why, there's not a place on Ozark that's not got folks all settled in from every one of the Twelve Families!"

"Travellers excepted, might could be," said Granny Gableframe. "I misdoubt there's anybody on Tinaseeh but Travellers, Farsons, and Purdys—maybe a Guthrie or two. No more."

"Tch!" went Ruth of Motley. "That's not even decent."

"If we'd gone the way Granny Hazelbide was mentioning," Jonathan Cardwell Brightwater pointed out, "we'd of been inbred worse than the goats long before this."

"Jonathan Cardwell! Such talk!"

"May not be elegant, m'dear, but it's accurate," he answered her, and bent to kiss her cheek. "It's a right good thing the Families had sense enough to mix it up, and plenty of other family lines represented among them at the beginning."

"So it is," said Granny Hazelbide, "so it is. But it leads to a pure *mess* now. Take Brightwater, seeing it's so handy—is there any Family we don't have among the folks living here, Responsible?"

"No Travellers," she said. "Nary a one."

"Well, they don't count anyway. If they lived here they'd have to worry all the time about their precious souls, what with our wicked elec-tric lights and our evil lizzies and far on into the night. You can't count them."

"Everybody else, though," Responsible agreed, "we have passels of. I know what you mean, and I don't know precisely how they'll do. Say you're a family with Smiths in all directions, living here in Brightwater, then what? That make Delldon Mallard your King, or not?"

"It has always been true," said Patience of Clark gravely, "that a woman gone to live in the house of a man considered herself a part of *his* family, from that time on, or went back to her own place. And the same for a man."

"True," said Thorn of Guthrie. "But that was when it didn't matter, if you follow me. That was when we were all one Confederation. There might be squabbles among us, and some Families more annoying than others, the way one of the tadlings in a house'll be more bothersome than all the rest put together. But in the ways that mattered, we were all *one*."

"Bless my stars," muttered Granny Hazelbide, "if Thorn's not begun to learn politics in her old age! Never thought I'd see the day."

Thorn of Guthrie curled her perfect lips and looked scornful, and allowed as how a question that related to the real world was worth noticing and she wasn't such a poor stick she *couldn't* notice it, thank you very much.

"It's a skein that'll be a long time unwinding," observed Patience of Clark. "I'm not all that comfortable about it."

"*Nor* me, child," said Granny Gableframe. "I've got a feeling in my bones."

"People will have to make up their minds, I suppose," said Jubal Brooks. "Do they go by lines drawn on a map, when it comes to their loyalties, or do they go by blood? And say you're a Farson man married to a McDaniels, and the both of you living in Kingdom Motley—if you *did* want to go back to your own kind, which one'd take precedence? Farson or McDaniels? And the children, would they want to go or would they consider theirselves Motleys by having been born there?"

"It's Old Earth all over again," said Granny Hazelbide grimly. "Next thing you know we'll have people starving one side of a line that doesn't exist, and people fat and sleek on the other, burning their garbage. I can just see it coming. Just see and *hear* it coming!"

"This world once more," Granny Gableframe declaimed, "and then there'll be fireworks." Whatever that might mean.

It had put something of a pall on breakfast.

And thinking now, musing over the Families, scrambled or not, Responsible felt a good deal less than comfortable herself. She was *worried* about the Gentles.

Nothing she knew of the Guthries, for all that they were her close kin, led her to be optimistic about their behavior; they were sharp of wit, but they were by and large outrageous. The Farsons had a kind of elegant devious charm that was more dangerous than any of the right out front stupidities the Smiths had carried through. And the Purdys! Prejudice or not, you could *not* trust the Purdys. They didn't even trust one another. And there sat the Gentles, relying on the sworn word of Responsible of Brightwater, completely surrounded on all sides by the three of them. And not knowing, might could be, that anything had changed.

Her mind was made up. Anything that might come up here at Brightwater for sure didn't require *her* attention; there were a Magician of Rank and two Grannys under this roof. Already, she was pleased to remember, the Grannys had settled the Bridgewraith, and with the two of them working together it had taken hardly any time at all. She would go this very night, no more excuses, soon as it was dark enough to travel easily, and she'd see to the warding of the Gentles. The supplies she'd gathered that night Lewis Motley Wommack had made such a sorry showing trying to follow her were adequate for the task, if she was. It was near on nine o'clock this minute; if she planned to see to the matter tonight, and for sure she did, it would take her all the rest of the day and a hard push to get ready in time. Starting with locking her door and sending down word that she was to be left alone and not bothered even for meals. That would give the Family something else to talk about at the table, at least.

Two hours later, purged of her breakfast—and thank the Twelve Corners the conversation that morning hadn't been the kind that made for a good appetite—and as clean as the three ritual baths could make her, her skin sore from the crushed herbs, she sat in her blue rocker and considered the problem. It was a nice one, and the more she thought about it the more complicated it became.

How, precisely, did you accomplish a task that could only be done by magic, on behalf of a large population that considered magic to be not only barbarous and primitive but unspeakably evil? How did you go about keeping a promise that had been a lie to begin with, on behalf of a race that so far as anyone had been able to determine was not capable of lying? For she had sworn she'd use no magic, when the complaint was made to her. And no way did she dare call in anyone for advice; as Granny Hazelbide would have said, she had a funny feeling.

She went over and pushed the computer access numbers for POPU-LATIONS, INDIGENOUS, which produced three entries: SKERRYS, GENTLES, MULES. That always made her nervous, finding the MULES on the list, but the computers were very firm about it. From among the set she chose GENTLES, and requested a full data display. The comset made none of its usual crotchety noises; the reduction of the broadcast area to one small Kingdom had improved its performance enormously. It hummed softly, and gave her what she asked for:

> GENTLES, INDIGENOUS POPULATION OF PLANET OZARK—
>   HUMANOID
> ESTIMATED NUMBER OF YEARS ON PLANET, FIFTY THOUSAND
> ESTIMATED NUMBER OF INDIVIDUALS, ELEVEN THOUSAND
>   (CAUTION, THIS FIGURE BASED ON INADEQUATE DATA)
> LOCATION: CAVES UNDER WILDERNESS LANDS OF CONTI-
>   NENT ARKANSAW, BOUNDED ON NORTH BY KINGDOM
>   PURDY,ON EAST BY KINGDOM GUTHRIE, ON WEST BY
>   KINGDOM FARSON, ON SOUTH BY OCEAN OF STORMS
>   (NOTE NO EVIDENCE AREA INHABITED BY GENTLES
>   EXTENDS TO OCEAN, DATA INSUFFICIENT)
> PHYSICAL DESCRIPTION: MALES AND FEMALES, APPROX
>   THREE FEET TALL, WHITE FUR ON ALL BODY SURFACES,
>   EYES DARK PURPLE ON YELLOW, FELINE PUPILS PRESUM-
>   ABLY FOR SEEING IN DARKNESS OF CAVES
> PHYSICAL STRENGTH ONE FOURTH HUMAN APPROX (CAU-
>   TION, DATA INADEQUATE)
> INTELLIGENCE PRESUMED EQUAL TO HUMAN (CAUTION,
>   DATA INADEQUATE)
> PSIBILITIES UNKNOWN
> GOVERNMENT: OLIGARCHY OF THREE ANCIENT FAMILIES
> RELIGION UNKNOWN
> CUSTOMS UNKNOWN
> HISTORY: CEDED ARKANSAW SURFACE TO HUMANS BY
>   TREATY ON SETTLEMENT
> (CAUTION, REPEAT CAUTION—GENTLES CONSIDER ALL
>   MAGIC SINFUL, HAVE BEEN KNOWN TO SUICIDE FOR
>   "DISHONOR OF MAGIC"—APPROACH WITH CARE)
> DATES OF CONTACT: NOVEMBER 11 2129; APRIL 4 . . .

The list went on, showing some sixty-odd contacts in one thousand years—those would be the reported ones, and there'd be twice as many unreported, she didn't doubt—and then there were a few names with a handful of data attached to each, and the display winked out.

It was a pitiful fragment of knowledge to have about a race you shared a planet with. On the other hand, it was a tribute, after a fashion, to the Ozarkers. They'd made no attempt to investigate the Gentles, as they'd made none to seek out the Skerrys, about whom far less was known. If there was one thing an Ozarker did understand, it was a request for privacy.

Responsible prayed rarely. She had an idea that she ought to pray more often, but she kept forgetting. This, however, was a situation where prayer was indicated forcibly enough to override even her desire not to be beholden. She found herself faced with the fact that if she did not use magic to protect the Gentles they might well be destroyed by the misbehavior of the Families of Arkansaw—not that they'd harm them on purpose, she wasn't ready to consider any such thing as that, but that in the course of tearing around the continent disputing with one *another* they were almost guaranteed to grow careless of what they tore up and who got discommoded in the process. And if she did use magic, and the Gentles should discover that she had, the whole population might well feel obligated to ritual suicide. Talk of being between a rock and a hard place! She prayed, and she prayed from the heart, and she prayed at length, though she didn't kneel; the idea that the Holy One had any special admiration for one posture over another, so firmly held to by the Reverends, struck her as ridiculous. The point was the praying, not how your legs were bent, nor how uncomfortable you could manage to get.

When that was done, she sighed, wishing she felt more confident and all charged with divine fire or some such, and not feeling that way at all, and she began taking things from her magic-chest. She drew out the gown of fine lawn and pulled it through the golden ring that fit her little finger; it went through without hindrance or snag, and she slipped it over her head. Her hair went into a single long braid down her back, bound by a clasp handed down from one Responsible to another since First Landing; she was always terrified she'd lose the fool thing and bring on some unspecified catastrophe, but so far she'd hung on to it. Next there were the shammybags that held the holy sands, to be hung from the narrow white belt that went round her waist, and the flagons of sacred springwater, bound together on a cord braided of her own hair and fastened to that same belt. A pouch of gailherb hung round her neck and slipped between her breasts to be warmed. On her bare feet went low boots of Muleskin made soft as velvet; over all, a hooded cloak of the same supple stuff. And she was ready.

She went lightly equipped, by Granny standards. They'd of thrown in two saddlebags of herbs, and put amulets and talismans all over her, and hung strings of garlic and preserved lilac from one end of Sterling to the other; there'd of been feathers and asafetida and probably conjure poppets . . .

Responsible grinned. By Granny standards she was off to a war naked and barefoot and blindfolded. She'd make very sure neither one of them caught sight of her, prowling the Castle in the night as was their habit. The thing was, the less of that truck she had on her person, the less likely she was to be spotted and seen to be engaged in magic if she had the awful fortune to be seen by one of the Gentles. And she'd not have used it anyway; this was a task requiring Formalisms & Transformations, not dolls and herbs and doodads.

As the sun started going down she began to get hungry, but that was to be expected. She ignored her stomach, and watched the line of Troublesome's mountain out through her window. When the sun was tucked exactly in the notch that marked the highest ridge, it would be time for her to go.

And what, she wondered idly, would Lewis Motley Wommack the 33rd have had to say if he'd seen her SNAP from her own windowsill without benefit of a Mule?

Law, there she *was,* thinking of him again! She clicked her tongue like a Granny, disgusted with herself. Sure enough, it had been a kind of peace, a kind of wondrous *rest,* being with someone whose mind she could share as easily as she shared ordinary speech with everybody else. Like moving around in a place of columns and soft wind and—She brought herself up short. If there'd been words for what it was like, it wouldn't have been what it was; she was just translating perceptions that had no counterpart into perceptions there were names for, and a mighty poor job she was doing of it. Nothing in the dictionary, so far as she knew, would cover an endless space confined in a finite one, nor label for her tongue a corner that you could not go round because it came back upon itself . . . She rubbed absently at the aching place just above her right eyebrow, that spot back of which the Immensity began, a golden Immensity swept by—

"Responsible of Brightwater, *stop it! Now!*" she said aloud, sharp as she knew how. A fine shape she'd be in for what lay ahead of her if she went on like this! Think of Una of Clark, rotten to the soul with the sickness of Romantic Love, and how she'd despised her, taunted her, for that! Then think of *her,* Responsible of Brightwater, mooning here at her window over this man she'd lain with twice, and neither time blessed by either Reverend or custom . . . Was she any better than poor Una?

It was just that until he came she had thought there was nobody else like her in all the world. It was a kind of loneliness that was not eased by sharing mindspeech with a Mule, nor what the Magicians of Rank thought passed for mindspeech. And he had eased it, unbraided her mind for her where the knots were tightest and most tangled . . .

Nevertheless, Responsible, there was such a thing as seemliness.

She stepped to her window, set one foot on the sill, made certain the picture she held firmly in her mind's eye was the proper one, so she wouldn't end up in some Arkansaw goatbarn by mistake—and SNAPPED.

On Kintucky, where it was daytime, the Guardian of Castle Wommack sat at *his* desk, going over again the specifications for his Teaching Order. He was pleased with the habit the Grannys and Gilead had designed; a long gown, high-necked and full of sleeve, hem right to the ground, with no sewn waist. It was caught round by a cord, from which could hang a useful pouch or two with the things a Teacher might need to carry. The cut would be useful; when a Teacher raised her arm to point to a map or a drawing, or just to get the attention of her pupils, the sleeve, narrow at the top and tapering out the rest of its length, would be dramatic. It would form a triangle, with its point below the Teacher's knees.

Choosing the color had been difficult. The Wommack colors were sea-green and gold, but neither of those had the solemn dramatic quality he was after. Finding a color not taken by any of the other eleven Families, now that the Smiths had added purple to their traditional silver and gold and brown, had seemed impossible. Black was surely dramatic and solemn enough, and the drawings of nuns after which the Grannys had modeled the costume showed that they had been black—but black was the mark of a Traveller. Lewis Motley would not have his Teachers in black. They had settled at last on a shade of blue; not the medium shade worn by the Guthries, nor yet the Lewis azure—but a deep, dark, vibrant blue that was exactly right, and belonged to no one.

The headdress, the wimple and coif that Jewel had dreaded the weight of, the Grannys had modified only a little from the drawings. They had made it one piece and all of the same blue; it showed only the face, coming straight across the forehead just below the hairline, and falling to a point at the waist in back. And round the neck, the only ornament; a medallion with the Wommack crest, on a leather thong.

There was nobody cared to point out to him that the color of the habits was exactly the color of his eyes. And no one of the women would have mentioned to him how the cut of the gown was the same as a woman wore that achieved the rank of Magician; it was, after all, a very different cloth, and it was not subject to the requirement that it be possible to draw it without hindrance through a gold ring that fit the woman's smallest finger. The women held their peace.

Already the first habit had been sewn up. He had trusted that task only to Gilead, whose fingers were famous for their skill with the needle. A ceremony had been put together—not hastily, either, for he'd done it himself, and he'd weighed every syllable and every gesture—and Jewel had donned the habit and the headdress and dedicated her life forever to the service of the Order. She rode out on Kintucky now, with the Attendants and servingmaid, the Mules walking every inch of the journey so that the people could see them pass by in search of other learned virgins, and she would bring them back to him at Castle Wommack.

The plans for the wing where the Order would be housed were before him, and he meant them to have his full attention. Until a few moments ago they had had it. But now he shook his head in that gesture the Grannys and Jewel noticed more and more often lately, and cursed bitterly, lengthily, obscenely, pounding his fist upon the surface of his desk till the knuckles bled.

Damn her, *curse* her, oh, the devils all take her and torture her, why could she not have the decency to stay out of his *mind?* Within him, something squirmed, and he was sick with a more than physical nausea; he knew now what the price of a witch's virginity was, without asking.

The question he could not answer was how long it had to go on being paid, and whether he would ever be free again.

He was an Ozarker; violence was something foreign to him. When he used his great physical strength he did it without violence, because it was a force that happened to be needed at that time and place. But so tortured was he now by this woman he had thought to make a pastime of . . . if he could have reached her at that moment, he would have killed her with his two bare hands.

If she could be killed. Could she? He did not know even that, and he laid his forehead on his arms and wept with rage and the despair of utter frustration. He might as well of wished to rid himself of his heart! No—that at least he could have torn from his breast. He did not know where the place that Responsible of Brightwater befouled within him *was*.

Responsible stood quietly in the darkness, alert for any sounds that might mean someone had seen her SNAP out of nowhere and would be coming along to demand an explanation.

It wasn't likely; she stood in a tangle of trees and briars so thick she could not see her hand when she held it up before her eyes, and in her dark cloak and boots she would be invisible unless somebody stood almost within touching distance. Still, this was no time to take chances.

Nothing but nightbirds, used to her now and gone back to their singing, and something making a soft croak in a tiny creek that was running behind her just within hearing. And that was as it should be; there was no honest reason for anybody to be lying out here in the Wilderness Lands of Arkansaw in the middle of the night. The only possibility was a party of hunters—not probable in a tangle like this, it'd make a poor campsite—or the one thing she really feared, a Gentle standing watch. Not that she knew whether they stood watch or not! Ethics, that eternal millstone round her neck; not to interfere, as promised by the treaties, meant not to observe, either; and so she knew almost nothing about the people whose peace and tranquillity she had come to preserve. It was not an ideal situation in which to work, and she considered, briefly, the idea of using a Spell of Invisibility as a means of making certain that the ignorance stayed mutual.

No, she decided. Spells were not a part of Formalisms & Transformations, they fell into Granny Magic, and mixing levels was a sure way to get into a mess. She'd just be *powerfully* cautious.

Her eyes were getting used to the darkness now, as far as that was possible in this tomb of branches and thorns and roots, and she unrolled the pliofilm map, no bigger than her palm, that she was carrying in the left-hand pocket of her cloak. It showed all of Arkansaw, but that didn't concern her; the part that interested Responsible was the part that glowed dimly, barely above the level of darkness. A line, running round and bordering off the Wilderness Lands; and then eleven tiny x's, marking each of the entrances to the territory that was the rightful domain of the Gentles. She must ward each and every one of those entrances.

Technically, she could of done it by Coreference alone, working with the tiny map. But equally technically, it shouldn't have been required at all. The Gentles should have been safe from the Families for all time, just because they were Ozarkers, and their word pledged. Just because of *privacy*. The Gentle T'an K'ib, coming to Responsible in the night to present her complaints, had not felt that to be any guarantee of the security of her people.

No, she would ward each entrance on the actual spot it held on the surface of the land, all eleven one at a time, SNAPPING from the first to the last. And it was time she began. The Twelve Gates grant she did not land right on top of some Gentle, out doing whatever it was that Gentles might do in the darkness, or find herself sharing a bedroll with an astonished hunter. Accuracy was not going to be a simple matter in this murk and with the limited information she had available.

Three hours it took her, moving from x to x, carefully, silently, until she had completed the circle and stood at the first one once again. Now each of the entrances was marked by the asterisk that means FORBIDDEN, laid in six overlapping lines of the holy sands. Three lines of white sand, three lines of ebony, alternating to form the six-pointed star, so: ✶ . That should cause any ordinary citizen, happening to approach an entrance either accidentally or deliberately, to feel a sudden disinclination to move one step closer that could not be overcome by any effort of will.

And then, against not the ordinary citizen but some Magician or Magician of Rank bent upon mischief, or made curious by the repelling effect of the asterisk, she had set yet another ward at each—the double-barred arrow of the Transformations, slashed through with a diagonal line. Golden sand for the arrow; silver sand for the slash that said THE TRANSFORMATION DOES NOT APPLY and would keep anybody skilled in magic from removing her asterisks by a Deletion Transformation.

Over all the devices of sand she had poured sacred water from the flagons, so that they sank into the earth and could no longer be seen, but were bound there irrevocably by the power of the waters. Perhaps the Out-Cabal had ways of undoing such a warding—they claimed to have, bragging and threatening through the Mules, calling the Ozark magic bungling and primitive. But it was not against the Out-Cabal that she had promised to protect the Gentles, and no Ozarker, whatever his or her level of skill at magic, could undo what she had done. And nobody had seen or heard her, neither human nor Gentle. If the small people, down in their caves, had somehow heard her moving about and were to come up in the dawn to investigate the sound, they would find nothing; there would be nothing to see, nothing to sense. The wards were set *for* them; they would not be affected by their presence in the earth.

She tried to think; had she forgotten anything? There was a last step, but once it was done she would no longer have the power to make changes if anything had been neglected.

She checked it off on her fingers. Eleven entrances, eleven asterisks, eleven signs that said FORBIDDEN. Eleven entrances, eleven slashed arrows, eleven signs that said THE TRANSFORMATION DOES NOT APPLY. Twenty-two signs; water from the sacred desert spring poured over every sand-grain that formed them, the whole branded into the land. She could not see what else there could be to do, and she was tired; when she had first planned this, she had never considered that she'd have it all to do by herself alone. She'd thought a few of the Magicians of Rank would be with her, giving her aid, making it a minor effort.

That was before the discovery that a Magician of Rank could turn his magic against a Granny. It was natural that they should attack her, Responsible of Brightwater, they had reason to hate her—but harm a Granny? It was unthinkable, it was a tear in the fabric of magic, and she trusted them no longer. And she was weary, weary . . . which was no excuse for carelessness. Deliberately, she pinched the sensitive skin at the base of her thumb till she was certain beyond question that she was alert.

And then she moved to the final act that would complete her task and some left over. One flagon of water she still had, one small shammybag of sand all of silver. Carefully she prepared her Structural Index, using the little map with its glowing border and its eleven x points. Scrupulously, she prepared the Structural Change, specifying all eleven points of Coreference rigorously. The sharp point of her silver dagger cut it all into the earth at

her feet, laid bare of its layer of thick leaves and protesting tiny crawlers
and wigglers. In the glow of the map she made sure there was no character of the formal orthography not cut clean and clear and deep. The weariness moved over her in sluggish waves as she worked, and she knew there
would be no SNAPPING back to her room until she had rested. She would
be lucky if she had strength enough to get her over the water and onto
Brightwater land, under some convenient bush that would hide her while
she slept a little while.

Responsible of Brightwater stood then, and traced the double-barred
arrow in the air, where it hung, quivering and golden, throbbing with
its stored energy held back only by her skill, between her two hands.

"There!" she whispered, and released it.

It was a Movement Transformation; the arrow sped straight for the
line that bordered the Gentles' holdings and raced round its perimeter in
a blinding streak of gold, faster than the eye could follow it, out of her
sight. She knew where it was going, though she could no longer watch
its progress; a few seconds later she saw it again, coming back, and it
plunged to the ground at her feet and winked out in the darkness.

Now, it was done. Well and truly done. Not only had she warded
the entrances themselves, so that no Ozarker would be capable of passing
them, but she had linked the wards one to another to make of them a *ring*
of wards. If that was not invulnerable, if it did not represent a full keeping of her promise to T'an K'ib, then doing so was beyond any skill known
to Ozark. It *should* be invulnerable, and no way for any Gentle ever to
know that what guarded them was the magic they so abhorred. There was
nothing left to give the secret away, and there was no living soul that knew
what she had done, to tell them. It was done, over, accomplished.

If all her blood had been drawn from her veins she could not have
been more weak, but she must get safely off Arkansaw before she let herself rest. She was aware that she shivered in the warm summer night and
that she had bitten nearly through her lower lip, forcing herself not to
fall, not to close her eyes.

She SNAPPED, sorry now she had not brought a Mule, clearing the
coast of Marktwain but not reaching the borders of Brightwater, and fell
unconscious in a patch of brush back of a goatbarn somewhere inside
McDaniels Kingdom. She was past caring if the farmer found her there
before she woke.

17

The Magicians of Rank SNAPPED in one by one on their Mules, even the four from Castle Traveller, not more than half a dozen minutes apart. They made a spectacle in the courtyard of Castle Wommack in their elaborate robes of office; and the nine Mules were not your average Mule. The stablemen that led the animals off to be rubbed down and watered and fed did so with a wary eye and a delicate touch. Feisty creatures these were, and accustomed to special treatment, *in*cluding a ration of dark ale with their grain. Treated with anything less than the respect they considered their due, they'd been known to kick an unwary staffer right out a stable door with one contemptuous stroke of a back hoof. The men circled them gingerly, doing their best to stay out of range while at the same time accomplishing all the necessary attentions. The fact that the Mules were obviously hugely amused by it all didn't make it any easier.

When it was all over, and everybody safely out of the stables, the men had much to say about animals getting above theirselves, and how a whack with a two-by-four right between the ears would of done this or that one a lot of good—but they waited till the Mules were safely stalled and the stable a hundred yards behind them before they let any such talk escape them.

"Howsomever," pointed out one of the men, "I'd rather deal with the Mules than with *that* lot." And he jerked his head toward the Castle entry, with its doors thrown wide, where the nine distinguished visitors were still standing in a huddle waiting for things to begin.

"Right you are," said another. "They give me the shivers, the whole nine of 'em. And the sooner we're out of their sight the better, I say. Unless there's one of youall as fancies getting changed into a billy goat, or SNAPPED off to Castle Purdy 'cause they don't like the look of him."

"What are they doing here anyway?"

The man that had expressed the strong preference for Mules over Magicians of Rank shrugged. "Can't say," he answered, "but Lewis Motley Wommack sent for 'em. Sent an Attendant off on a Mule to Mizzurah, that's got a Magician of Rank of its own, and got him to SNAP the invitation round to all the rest."

"And they came?"

"Well, you *see* 'em there, don't you? Like a pack of fancy birds, to my mind, more'n men."

"You'd be better off to watch your mouth," said the oldest. "You know if they can hear you out here? *I* don't."

"I just don't understand why they came," the first one muttered. "Who's Lewis Motley that they should come when he calls 'em? Now, I ask you, how do you explain *that?* He's not even Master of a Castle!"

The Magicians of Rank were a tad surprised their own selves, most of them having been convinced almost to the last minute that they would ignore the whole thing. They were busy men, important men, and they had images to maintain. But when it came down to the wire, not a one had been able to resist the invitation from the young Guardian; the wording had been irresistible. He needed their help, it had said, "in a matter involving Responsible of Brightwater, a matter that can only be attended to by Magicians of Rank, and that requires the utmost secrecy." And here, only slightly embarrassed, they were.

They saw one another rarely, but that didn't keep the four from Traveller from commenting that the rest looked like a passel of females, or the passel so addressed from replying that *they* looked like a quartet of carrionhawks.

Veritas Truebreed Motley made a slight change in an ancient hymn. "How many points do you *expect,* gentlemen," he asked them, "for darkening the corner where you are?"

Feebus Timothy Traveller the 11th didn't hesitate a heartbeat.

"One *dozen,* dear colleague!" he gave it back. "One dozen exactly!"

"Darkness," added Nathan Overholt Traveller the 101st gravely, "is a prerequisite for the perception of color. If we four weren't here, you five could not be seen at all."

The two Farson brothers, Sheridan Pike the 25th and Luke Nathaniel the 19th, smiled that very limited smile that Castle Traveller allowed its residents, and moved closer to the other two. They had the solidarity that comes of fanaticism, and would be formidable if they chose to be. The other five, lacking that useful characteristic, moved uneasily away from them and pretended to be very busy discussing matters of great importance.

So it was that when Gilead of Wommack came down the steps to invite them up to the Meeting Room, she was treated to the sight of two clusters of magnificently garbed males. The Traveller contingent in its deadly black relieved only by the silver clasps that caught the folds of their robes at the shoulder. And the other five bearing the colors of their Family lines—Smith, Motley, Lewis, Guthrie, and McDaniels. But Gilead of Wommack was not interested in their costumes, not even in the Farson brothers' strange acceptance of the Traveller black instead of the red, gold, and silver that was rightfully theirs by birth. She knew more about Magicians of Rank than that—it was their hands that you watched, their clever swift fingers and their supple wrists. That was where the danger lay, and where it would of stayed if you'd dressed them in feedbags and put milkpails on their heads.

"Welcome to Castle Wommack," said Gilead briskly, determined not to appear intimidated. She'd seen them all at the aborted Jubilee, and they hadn't eaten her alive; no reason to think they would do so here under her own roof.

"Thank you, Gilead of Wommack," said Shawn Merryweather Lewis the 7th of Castle Motley, him that'd been kind enough to carry the message to the others. "We are ready to see your . . . Guardian . . . when he is ready for us—but would you remind him that we are busy men? We'd like to get on with this."

"Follow me, please," Gilead replied. "He's waiting upstairs in the Meeting Room."

"We're your guests," put in Feebus Timothy Traveller, "but there's something that must be said. This innovation—this title of 'Guardian' rather than 'Master' as custom dictates—we don't approve of it, not one of us. A Castle without Master or Missus; that's not proper, Gilead. Granny Leeward has asked that we express her objections in the strongest terms, and we concur."

Gilead was not a formidable woman, and she still bore the silent displeasure of the two Grannys; but she was no coward, and she was a true Six—her loyalty to her Family and her devotion to its members were her ruling qualities. She faced the Travellers, all nodding their solemn agreement, and she spoke up clear and confident.

"At least," she said, looking them straight in the eyes, "this Kingdom will never have a *Pope*."

They drew back from her, white and furious; that had struck home, and it told her a few things worth passing along to the Grannys later. Jacob Jeremiah Traveller, all alone at Booneville on Tinaseeh with nobody to challenge his authority for thousands of miles, and no comset to grant anybody an occasional peek at his doings, must be busy demonstrating to the people of his Kingdom what a heavy yoke a burning faith could be.

"And how are we to address this . . . youngster?" spat Feebus Timothy.

"Try 'Mister Wommack,'" she said pertly. "Or just 'Lewis Motley'— he doesn't suffer from delusions of grandeur, gentlemen."

And she turned her back on the two groups before the tension could grow any worse, or her traitorous knees fail her, and led them after her, feeling ice between her shoulder blades at the idea of what those nine pairs of hands might be doing that she could not see. Just as *well* she could not see, if they were in fact about their mysterious flickering business; she wouldn't see it coming, whatever it was, and she'd no desire to.

But nothing happened; and they were at the Meeting Room door, where one Senior Attendant stood casually with folded arms, waiting. "Here," Gilead said to him, "are the nine Magicians of Rank of this planet, come to see Lewis Motley. Will you take them in, please?"

Lewis Motley Wommack sat at the head of the table, smiling at them as they came through the door. He wore the Wommack sea-green, a color that was as appropriate to his copper hair and beard as it was to the sands of the beach. The long narrow robe was of a soft woven stuff suitable for the summer heat; it had no collar and no cuffs, just the elegant sweep of a well-cut and well-sewn garment, and the Wommack crest on a heavy enameled pendant hung round his neck on a leather thong. On his right hand was a gold ring with the same crest, and his feet were clad in plain low boots of green-dyed leather, narrow-cuffed. He sat in a worn heavy chair at the head of a small round table, and that was all. And the sum of it was wholly regal.

It was not what the Magicians of Rank had expected.

"Should you lose your youthful figure, Lewis Motley Wommack," said Sheridan Pike Farson the 25th to break the speculative silence, "that garment you wear will become something of an embarrassment."

The young man gave him a long considering look, and Sheridan Pike was astonished to discover that he felt rebuked. He had not experienced those eyes before; Responsible of Brightwater could have told him something about the dangers they posed.

"Be seated, gentlemen," said the Guardian, as if the remark had not been made. "Anywhere you like, please. There is wine there, and ale for those who prefer it. I thank you for your courtesy in responding so promptly to my invitation, and for taking time from the pressure of your duties to come to my aid."

The Farsons glanced at each other, and Sheridan Pike touched his brother's hand with his fingertips, like moths lighting, spelling out in the ancient alphabet of bones and knuckles the single message—"Beware his eyes." And Luke Nathaniel Farson spelled back—"And his speech."

You could tell a person's station on Ozark by their speech. There was the formspeech of the Grannys, a carefully artificial register of exaggerated archaic vocabulary and intonation—especially intonation. There was the speech of the ordinary citizen, that had undergone all the normal processes of language change, but whose speakers prided themselves on its roughness and its lack of pretension; they spoke as boones, however crowded they might live. There was the flowing mellifluity of the Reverends, required of them only in the performance of their duties, but often taken up for all purposes as a man grew older in the profession. And then there was the speech of the Magicians of Rank, restricted to those nine, laboriously learned along with the Formalisms & Transformations, intended to force respect by its elegance and elaborate usage, as artificial in its way as the mode of the Grannys. Lewis Motley Wommack the 33rd had spoken only a few dozen words, and they might indicate nothing more than his excellent brain and even more excellent education; on the other hand, there was a suspicious ring to them. The mode of the Magicians of Rank, unlike that of the Grannys, ought not to be easy to assume; most citizens had no contact with a Magician of Rank in all their lives.

"Gentlemen?" The Guardian of the Castle was waiting, and they took their chairs, with a mild scuffle over who should be at the dividing line between the Travellers and the others, and that dubious honor falling at last to Lincoln Parradyne Smith. Lincoln Parradyne was uncomfortable; the contrast between the self-made King he had at home and the utter elegance of this youth was striking. When he returned to Castle Smith he thought he might try some fine-tuning . . . perhaps convince Delldon Mallard to remove some of the gems from the crowns and settle for less sumptuous robes at least around the Castle and on non-state occasions.

"I will not waste your time," said Lewis Motley, "I am well aware that your duties call you, and that your leisure is limited. I call you here only because I have nowhere else to turn, and I have reached the out-most limits of my own endurance in this matter. The task of rendering assistance to me in my quandary is appropriate only to your group; there-fore, I have called upon the nine of you for succor. You are the sovereign remedy, so to speak."

That settled it, if what came before had not; he *was* using their regis-ter, the speechmode of the Magicians of Rank. It was a subtle declaration—but of what?

"Your manner of speech, sir—" began Feebus Timothy Traveller, ready to express the displeasure felt by all of them, but Lewis Motley cut them off.

"The 'sir' is not called for," he said. "Nor will it ever be—I have no interest in such things. As for my manner of speech"—he smiled again, and looked all round the table—"it is said that imitation is the sincerest form of flattery.

"And now," he went on, "if you are all comfortable, I would be pleased to present my problem. It is, as I told you in the invitations, a matter regarding a woman—Responsible of Brightwater."

That changed things. A moment before the only emotion in the room had been the chill of disapproval and angered pride; now the nine leaned forward as one man, their pique forgotten. If there was one thing that united them, other than their shared duties and privileges, it was their hatred of the woman he named; perhaps the most difficult task Veritas Truebreed Motley had to deal with, living as he did under her very nose, was hiding that hatred from everyone except her. He knew it was use-less to try to fool Responsible, even if he had cared to. The Magicians of Rank were like preybeasts that have caught a scent; they had been nine, now they were one.

"You are not fond of the daughter of Brightwater," mused the Guardian, watching them. "That is indeed curious; except for you, Veritas Truebreed, I should have thought you would of had no dealings with her to arouse your emotions. I am astonished, gentlemen, at the way in which one mystery often lies behind another, only to reveal a third and a fourth beyond."

"You assume a great deal," said Michael Stepforth Guthrie the 11th, he of Castle Guthrie itself, known planetwide for his skill and for his delight in elaborate mischief. There was no mischief in his voice now.

"Where there is knowledge, one need not make assumptions," said Lewis Motley calmly. "Is that not a general maxim, gentlemen?"

He took the medallion bearing his crest in his fingers, stroking it lightly, smiling at them, that maddening constant smile, and waited; and Michael Stepforth Guthrie spoke again.

"What is your problem with Responsible of Brightwater?" he asked roughly. "She is Thorn of Guthrie's daughter. The Mistress of my Castle, Myrrh of Guthrie, is her grandmother. I know her better than anyone here except perhaps Veritas Truebreed, who has the misfortune to share her roof—and I know no reason she should have drawn your notice. She is not even a pleasure to a man's eye, Lewis Motley . . . and less by far to a man's ear. What have you, an ocean and two continents away, to do with Responsible of Brightwater?"

The Guardian's face hardened, and for a moment they saw not a youth of nineteen but a glimpse of the man he would one day be, when he had more years to his credit.

"You have said she is no pleasure to the eye or ear of a man," he said grimly. "I am a good judge of women; I am in full accord with that judgment. She is an awkward, scrawny gawk of a girl; her face is too bony, and her breasts are too small. She runs when she should walk, interferes when she should refrain, and speaks when any decent female would keep silence. But I will take it a step farther than eyes and ears, gentlemen! A *large* step farther . . . Had I only the sight and sound of that accursed young woman to deal with, I would not have needed you. The distance of which Michael Stepforth speaks would of solved my problem."

"And it does not?"

"She is not bound by distances," said the Guardian flatly. "Not in space; not in time. So far as I know, unless you nine have the skill to restrain her, she is bound by nothing in this universe but her own whim. And her whim is to make of my life an unspeakable hell."

A stir went round the table; they were more than interested, they hung on his words.

"Explain yourself!" ordered Michael Desirard McDaniels the 17th, Magician of Rank in residence at Castle Farson. "We cannot help with riddles—save those for the Grannys, and do *us* the favor of plain speech."

"And promptly," said another. "Enough of this dawdling."

"Responsible of Brightwater," said Lewis Motley, "offends the eye and the ear; in my case, she does not scruple to offend the mind as well."

"The mind . . . *how* does she offend your mind?"

"I thought a long time before I called you," said Lewis Motley slowly. "It is not pleasant to be telling tales on a female not much more than a child—for a long time I was determined I would not. But she has gone far beyond that limit at which the scruples of ordinary decency and honor apply to her; she no longer merits any of those scruples, and my conscience is clear. To betray evil—monstrous evil—I owe her no hesitation. Not any longer."

"What in the world," breathed Veritas Truebreed, "has she *done* to you?"

"Done? Not only done, but *does!* Every day of my life."

"Lewis Motley—"

"She will not leave me in peace," he said simply. "As another female might tag after you day and night in the ordinary world, forever after your attention, always there wherever you look, her voice always in your ear, Responsible of Brightwater tags constantly after my mind. *I want it stopped.*"

The last four words fell like four stones into a pool of silence.

"Well?" demanded the Guardian. "Can you or can you not control her? Do you or do you not command this world of Ozark and all that moves upon it? Is this a simple matter for you, a mere child's trick—as I have been led to believe—or are you a pack of *frauds?*"

The Magicians of Rank were in a state that did not inspire confidence, all trying to speak at once, and their fingers flying under the table like frantic insects. It was a discomfiting sight, and Lewis Motley shoved back his chair from the table and stared at them with frank wonder.

"Answer me, gentlemen," he said, and still he did not raise his voice. "I am surprised—I admit that frankly. Your behavior is . . . bewildering." And he added, "If the people of the six continents could see you now, they would never be in awe of you again, not if you sailed a thousand golden ships with silver sails, not if you SNAPPED from here to the stars and back!

They would laugh at you, as they laugh at Lincoln Parradyne's puppet of a King—and they would be fully justified in their disrespect. Be glad, gentlemen, that there is no one here to see you but myself!"

Nathan Overholt Traveller was the oldest of the nine; Lewis Motley's words brought him instantly out of his disarray. He had not been spoken to in that way since he donned the garments of his profession, and he didn't care for it.

"That will do!" he declared. "You may be of some importance in this backwater, you may be Guardian of this Castle—whatever that means—but know that we can make you a *dead* Guardian, without moving from these chairs! Guard your *tongue,* Guardian; or you will find your tenure short, I promise you."

Lewis Motley sighed and pulled his chair back into its proper place.

"Now that," he said with satisfaction, "is the sort of thing I expected. Thank you, Nathan Overholt; you have restored some portion of my confidence."

Veritas Truebreed cleared his throat. "Lewis Motley Wommack," he said carefully, "do we understand you to mean that Responsible of Brightwater uses mindspeech with you? Is that your claim, or do we misunderstand? Be careful, now—you realize that it's a grave charge you are making. That goes beyond mere illegality, for a woman; you charge her with blasphemy. Be certain!"

"Mindspeech . . ."

"Well? Is that your claim?"

"Almost," said Lewis Motley. "Almost. It would be more accurate to say that she uses it *at* me than with me . . . I certainly have no means of making reply. And she does not confine herself to speech; she does not scuple to—" He caught himself, and a muscle twitched, suddenly, in his cheek. "I will not speak of that," he said, with a determination that had all the finality of a Castle gate swinging shut and its bars falling into place. "There are obscenities that a man keeps to himself. Just see that she respects the privacy of my mind; I ask nothing more than that. You can do that?"

"The problem," said Nathan Overholt, "was not whether we could; it was a question of whether it was permitted to us . . . whether it was justified. You have answered that question for us."

"Good," said Lewis Motley. *"Good!"*

It was clear to the Magicians of Rank that Lewis Motley had no idea what lay behind their temporary confusion, and there was no particular reason why he should have. Mindspeech on this planet was supposed to be confined to them, to a rare and exceptionally talented Magician, and—for some unknown and outrageous reason—to the Mules. A Magician not sufficiently skilled to be a Magician of Rank, but beyond the ordinary, could mindspeak in a clumsy fashion, one or two semantic units at a time, with great and exhausting effort—it was a rare thing. Leaving out those exceptions, the Grannys and the Magicians had empathy to spare, but could go no further. As for Responsible of Brightwater, the news that she could use mindspeech, and his hint that there was more to it even than that, went beyond revelation. It was the Twelve Towers crashing down about their learned heads. He could not know that, but they did, one and all.

"Perhaps," suggested Michael Stepforth Guthrie carefully, "it is only your imagination, Lewis Motley. You have been under a great strain lately, and the pressure of your new duties, isolated as you are here, and your brother only a short time in his grave, must be extreme. Please consider once again: are you *certain?*"

And then there were nine Magicians of Rank leaping with varying degrees of nimbleness out of the way as the Guardian of Wommack threw the heavy table over into their laps.

"*Months* I have lived with that witch prying and poking about in my head!" he shouted. "*Months!* At first it was only a moment, only a nudge now and then . . . then it was every day . . . soon it will be every hour of every day! Why she leaves me in peace in the nights now I cannot imagine, but I know it will not last . . . And you dare ask me if it is my imagination! *Imagination!* I may be imagining *you,* gentlemen, I may be imagining the beat of my own heart, I may be imagining this room and this chair and this table—but I do not imagine the liberties that Responsible of Brightwater takes with my mind!"

The Magicians of Rank, back against the walls and the door, began to feel almost warm toward this arrogant stripling, for all that he had shown them less deference than he had shown their Mules. If what he said was true, and by his words it surely must be—if he had been mad they would have known at once; his mind was harried and fretful and fractious, but it was sound—if it was *true,* then at last they had their chance to revenge themselves! Even with one another, whatever it was she used to bind their lips held; they could not speak of the experiences they had shared. But they knew, every one of them knew, and for the opportunity to pay her back as she should be paid there was almost nothing they would not have offered.

Lewis Motley was breathing hard, and staring round him like a Mule stallion with a threatened herd. When the Magicians of Rank began moving toward him, speaking to him with the voices they used for the ill and the frantic, he had only one thing to say to them.

"Can you make her stop it?"

He had no interest in anything else they might be able to do, to him or for him.

"Can you?"

They were grinning at one another in a way that lacked dignity, but had enough of malice and sheer unfettered glee to make up for it. For a man to use mindspeech, unless he were a Magician, was illegal. For a *woman* to do so . . .

It would take all of them, and for once in their lives they would have to work together. But it was allowed. Her offense was monstrous.

"Yes, Lewis Motley," they said, "we certainly can."

They were nine ecstatic Magicians of Rank, and they could already taste the sweetness of revenge in their mouths.

18

Shandra of Clark was out of breath; first, there'd been dropping the eggshells into the batter for that morning's cornbread and having to make a whole new batch, and the cook down on her for that; and then there'd been tripping over somebody's small boy as had *no* business being in the staff hallway down the side of the Castle . . . and then going back for another pot of tea to replace the one she'd half spilled on Miss Responsible's tray, and the cook down on her for *that.* She was determined this time to get up the stairs and down the corridor, and the tea delivered with no further mishaps.

"Keep on as you've been, Shandra of Clark," she muttered to herself as she went along, "and you'll spend the rest of your life stuck in the back kitchen of this Castle peeling things and taking dressdowns from the rest of the staff, see if you don't." That wasn't her plan for her life; she intended to work her way out of the kitchen and into the affections of a certain young man with good prospects—but first she had to get out of the kitchen.

Responsible's door . . . there! She stopped, balancing the tray carefully on one hand, and smoothed her hair down, and then she knocked softly three times.

"Your tea, miss, and good morning with it," she said, hoping she sounded more agreeable than she felt. The cook had been *really* mad at her, and considering it was two dozen squawker eggs wasted, that was reasonable.

She waited for an answer, and passed her time admiring the door. If ever she did have a house of her own, she wanted just such a door. Boards of ironwood, set vertical, and the top arched to a high peak, and then the whole thing painted a proper blue. And the doorknob had set in its center a Brightwater crest—she wouldn't have that one, of course—in glorious bright colors you could near see in the dark. And the horseshoe nailed above the door was a dainty thing of silver, no rough and (admit it!) rusty iron such as she had over her own door on the Castle's top floor. Time she polished *that,* for sure.

"Miss Responsible?"

She knocked again, and frowned. Miss Responsible was an early riser, saving always that day after the Granny'd potioned her, and lately she'd been up so early that several times she'd come down after her own tea and caught the staff just coming into the kitchen. Shandra fancied having her own house to run, but she didn't envy Responsible of Brightwater the managing of this great hulk of a Castle, thank you, not one bit she didn't.

She knocked sharper, and then clucked her tongue, irritated. Now she'd be getting it in the kitchen for being gone too long right in the middle of making breakfast!

If it'd been some doors, she'd of opened it—not looked in, of course, but just opened it a crack—and called right into the room. But nothing would have brought her to that at this door, or either of the Granny's, nor the Magician of Rank's either. Warded doors she'd keep her hands off of unless invited, now and forevermore, and she had no intentions of having Miss Responsible do . . . something. She wasn't sure just what Miss Responsible could do, but she gathered it wouldn't necessarily be pleasant, and she had no desire to test it out. It was said Miss Responsible was right clever with Charms and Spells.

There being nothing else to do, she took the tray back to the kitchen one more time, and told the others that Responsible of Brightwater wasn't answering her door this morning.

The cook set her arms akimbo and made a fuss like she'd made over the eggs, only more so. "*Are* you for sure of that, Shandra?" she demanded. "Seems to me your mind's dead set this morning on seeing if you can't do the day backwards and hindside *to*. Did you knock? Loud enough so as you could tell somebody was knocking?"

"Three times three times, I did! And loud, the last time. *And* I called out. And it's cruel of you going on and on about the eggs like I did it on purpose—"

"I'll have none of your sass," said the cook, and Shandra closed her mouth abruptly. She stood a head taller than the cook, and likely outweighed her by twenty pounds, but Becca of McDaniels was a true Five, she'd as soon take your head off as look at you, and she ran the Brightwater kitchen the way her husband ran its stables. No sass, no slack, and no time to breathe from the minute you got there till you were through *by the clock*.

"Yes, ma'am," said Shandra of Clark. "Begging your pardon."

"You knocked, and you called, and no answer, you say?"

"Yes, ma'am."

"Then you take that tea, which is strong enough now for goat-dip, I expect, and you go straight to one of the Grannys and you tell them what you just told me. They aren't as impressed by wards as we are."

"Nice having two Grannys in the Castle, don't you think, Becca of McDaniels? It makes a person feel safe."

"If you don't hightail it, and right this instant, it'll take a sight more than a couple of Grannys to keep you safe, young missy!"

Shandra gulped, and followed instructions. Down the hall again, up the stairs again—only one flight, praise the Gates, the Grannys were both on the second floor—down *that* hall, and she almost ran into Granny Hazelbide coming out to breakfast already.

"Oh, Granny Hazelbide, I'm glad to see you!" said Shandra. "You'll pardon me for holding you from your breakfast, I hope, but I've knocked and knocked and I can't rouse Miss Responsible, and the cook said as I was to come tell you and you'd see what was up."

"She did, did she?"

"She did. If you'd be so kind, Granny Hazelbide."

"Nothing that pleasures me more of a morning than traipsing up and down the stairs with the servingmaids," said the Granny, "you tell Becca of McDaniels that. *I* have nothing better to do with my time."

"Yes, ma'am, Granny Hazelbide. And thank you kindly, ma'am."

"You were any more humble, you'd disappear altogether, you know that?"

"Yes, ma'am."

The old woman humphed, and gave the floor a good one with her cane, but she followed Shandra briskly enough, grannying at her all the way, and the girl managed to keep her face straight even through the part about the epizootics, till she stood once again at Responsible's bedroom door and gave it three knocks.

Back at her came the silence, and she turned to the Granny. "You see?"

"Where's that girl got to now?" grumbled Granny Hazelbide, and she reached right out and grabbed the doorknob that Shandra of Clark wouldn't of touched for ten dollers, nor for fifty either. And then Shandra did feel strange, for the Granny snatched back her fingers as she would have done from a live flame and cried out "Double Dozens!" like her voice was scorched, too.

"Granny Hazelbide? Is something the matter?" quavered Shandra of Clark.

"Girl, you set down that tray—right there on the floor'll do—and you go get Granny Gableframe, fast as you can hoof it, and send her here to me! Go!"

Shandra did, fast as she could as instructed, and then she fairly flew down to the kitchen to tell, stopping only to grab the tray as the two Grannys disappeared into Responsible's room.

"The Grannys sent me away!" she said, right out, before Becca of McDaniels could have at her again, and she set the tray of tea down on the big kitchen table so hard the teapot rattled. "They said for me to *scat!*"

"And?"

"And they both went into Miss Responsible's room . . . and they did *not* close her door behind them. Which means they were afraid to touch it, seeing as how it burned Granny Hazelbide the first time!" Shandra clutched herself tight with both arms and wailed, "Oh, Becca of McDaniels, I'm plain terrified!"

She had to tell it all, then, and everybody gathering round to hear, until the cook shushed her in no uncertain terms. "It's none of our business," she said, grim of eye and lip, "but the breakfast is. And if we're to know what's going on, we will; and if we're not, life'll go right along just the same. Now turn to, and no more nattering and lollygagging."

"But if—"

"Turn *to!*" thundered the cook, her hollering twice as big as anything else about her, and that was that. If they died of curiosity, they'd just die of it. And Shandra berated herself for an idiot; if she'd "forgotten" that tray she'd of had to go back up after it and she might of been able to find out something, and as much trouble as she was in already it wouldn't have made a scrap of difference. Trust her to make a mistake when all it got her was broad words, and then do a thing right when the mistake would of been worth it!

Up in Responsible's room, the two Grannys stood, one on each side of her bed, and pondered.

"She's breathing," said Granny Gableframe.

"Barely. *Just* barely. There's none to spare, Gableframe."

"The mirror clouded over."

"But see her bosom? Still as my own hand—not a move, not a flutter."

Granny Hazelbide laid her fingers to the girl's throat and pressed, hard, below the joint of the jaw.

"Pulse *there*," she declared. "It's not thumping and pounding, but a pulse it surely is. She's breathing."

"Tsk!" went Granny Gableframe. "Now what*ever* do you suppose?"

"You? You're senior to me—what do *you* think?"

Granny Gableframe pinched her lips tight and shook her head.

"I don't know," she said slowly, "I surely don't. But the wards on that door weren't put there just to keep out the servingmaids, I can guarantee you that . . . see that mark on your palm where you gripped the knob? Looks like you'd gone and picked a handful of coals up out of a fire!"

"Coals," said Granny Hazelbide dryly, "don't leave an asterisk when they burn," and she turned up her palm, where the little scarlet star glowed sullen and sore.

"Law!" breathed Granny Gableframe. "Will you just look at that!"

The two old women stared at Responsible, and they stared at each other; and then Granny Gableframe said "Do you *suppose?*" and pulled the pillow gently from beneath Responsible's head.

There was nothing gentle about the way she first ripped off the pillowslip and then tore the ticking right down the way she'd of made cleaning rags.

"It's there!" she cried. "You see that, Hazelbide?"

And she plunged her hand into the pillow and pulled it out, triumphant, holding the thing she found there gingerly with the tips of her fingers, and let the ruined pillow fall to the floor.

Granny Hazelbide whistled a little tune under her breath.

"More of 'em, I wonder?" she said, when she got to the end of it.

"I misdoubt that—one's more than enough."

Granny Hazelbide looked again at the asterisk branded into her palm, and then she took the other pillows and patted them all over, muttering that she'd never seen such a girl for pillows and how many times had she told Responsible she'd end up with a double chin, and then she got to the last of them, and said: "Sure enough. Sure enough, there's one in here or my birthname adds up to a minus Two and yours along with it. Look here, Gableframe, just look here!"

"Well, who the Gates'd want to put *two* feather crowns in the pillows of one scrawny girlchild?" demanded Granny Gableframe.

"More to the point, seeing as how it's this *particular* scrawny girlchild," said Granny Hazelbide, "who *could?*"

Who could put burning wards on the door, and feather crowns in the pillows, of Responsible of Brightwater? It was a nice question, and both Grannys pressed their fists to their top teeth, thinking on it.

"Well, she won't wake," observed Granny Gableframe in the silence. "We'd best brush out her hair and make her tidy."

"You're sure?"

"Not for us, nor for any Granny Magic, she won't. We'll get the Magician of Rank in here—maybe for him. But I'll have her neat first, afore he sees her."

"And these nasty pieces of work?"

Granny Gableframe looked with disgust at the feather crowns. They were squawker tailfeathers, tips together and fanning out from the center, making a circle big as a feast-day platter.

"Notice," said Granny Hazelbide, "how the feathers go? Widdershins, both of 'em."

And so they did. Counterclockwise.

"I'd burn them both," said Gableframe, "except that might could be they'll be needed later on to get to the bottom of this."

"Or pay for it."

"Ah, yes . . . there's that."

"Give me the one you have," said Granny Hazelbide decisively. "I've already crossed those wards, might as well go whole hog. I'll stand here and hold them, and keep my eye on that child—for all the good it'll do— while you get Veritas Truebreed Motley the 4th in here, and then I'll give them into *his* keeping. This is a tad past me, I don't mind admitting."

"*And* me," said Granny Gableframe; and she handed the feather crown to Granny Hazelbide and set to brushing Responsible's hair and straightening her nightgown. "And it's good fortune you have a Magician of Rank here . . . I don't like the look of her."

"Will you hurry then, Gableframe? We've been standing here, gawking and gabbing, it'll be near half an hour."

"Peace, Granny Hazelbide," said the other. "You know as well as I do, there's no chance of her dying. They could of put a *dozen* feather crowns in her pillows, bad cess to 'em whosoever they may be, and she'd still be in no danger of dying. Not so long, Granny Hazelbide, as there's no little girl in a Granny School on this round world as is named Responsible—and there's none."

"One misnamed again, maybe?"

"*No*-sir!" Granny Gableframe shook her head. "I'd know, if there were—there's nobody senior to me excepting Golightly at Castle Clark—I'd know. My word on it. But I'll get Veritas Truebreed, because there's far too much here as I don't know any more about than that servingmaid did—and I will hurry."

It was all over the town and out into the countryside before the day was over, and the ban that Jonathan Cardwell Brightwater had set on the comcrews as to how they'd be jailed for treason if they put one word out on the comsets hadn't slowed it down one bit. It was that sort of news.

Responsible of Brightwater, people were saying, lay on her bed like a poppet made of ivory wax, just barely breathing, her eyes closed and her lips sealed and making no response even when she was pinched and stuck with a sharp needle. And under her head, in her pillows, they said, there'd been two—not one, but two, and *that* never had happened before!—two feather crowns found, and both of them made widdershins! And they'd called in all the Magicians in the Kingdom, and the Magician of Rank as well, and not a one of them as could do anything for her, or even explain why not. And to send shivers up and down your backbone, if all that wasn't enough, it seemed that as Veritas Truebreed Motley the 4th marched out of Responsible of Brightwater's bedroom door, throwing up his hands and declaring himself helpless, the bright silver horseshoe nailed over the door flew off the nail that held it, all by its own self, and struck him right between his shoulder blades!

"It fair curdles the blood in your veins," they were saying. And "It's not natural." Mothers caught a suspiciously quiet clump of tadlings playing at making feather crowns and put an end to *that*—every one of them sent off to find a perfect willow switch, take off every leaf, peel it down to the lithe core, and bring it back for application where it would do their characters the most good. You didn't switch a child often, nor lay a hand to one in anger; but there were some things that had to be made so clear they'd never be forgotten. This was one of those things.

There were no places on Marktwain given over entirely to drinking, as there'd been on Old Earth. Whiskey, made powerful as gunpowder, was kept as a medicine, made from the tall red Ozark corn; beer and wine were served in the home on festive occasions, and that was the end of Ozark drinking. But there were three hotels in Capital City where a man could get a glass of berry wine, or a strong dark ale, for a *private* occasion—be it feast or distress—and they did a heavy business in beverages that night.

The men discussed it logically, gathered at the long tables set in the hotel diningrooms. Gabriel Micah Clark the 40th had offered as opener that it was his opinion the ruckus at the Castle was an example of pride going before a fall.

"That Brightwater girl has called down the wrath of the Powers on herself," he announced. "That's how *I* see it." And he blew the head of froth off his ale. "Been tempting fate now fifteen years—"

"Oh, come off that, Gabriel Micah," snorted his left neighbor, a lawyer of the McDaniels line and given to nitpicking by trade. "You can't accuse a one-year-old babe of pride; a tadling's not even civilized till it gets to be three."

"You know what I mean," Gabriel Micah protested.

"Put it clear or don't put it at all," insisted the lawyer.

"Near on ten years at least, then, that split the hair fine enough for you? I mind her *very* well, I was working in the stables at the Castle then, and she but five years old, and you talk of *pride!* Why, she'd come right down to the stables and give us all what for about the tackle not being hung right, or the straw not clean enough on the stall floors. And ten minutes later you'd hear her in the Castle, like she was Queen of all the Shebas, ordering the servingmaids around and telling them where she'd found more dust than suited her fancy. You can't tell me *that's* natural!"

"Well, some of that should be laid to the account of Thorn of Guthrie," put in another. "If she'd been doing her job as mother—"

"Thorn of Guthrie?" Gabriel Micah was amazed. "All that woman needs do to fill her role in life is breathe in and breathe out and let the rest of us have the privilege of looking at her."

"That may well be, but it makes for sorry mothering."

"*For* example, let's consider Responsible's sister Troublesome!"

"For example, let's not." The Reverend was a tolerant man, considering, and he didn't scruple to spend an evening here with the male members of his flock, listening to what they had to say and getting a certain perspective on the turn of their minds at any given time—but he had his limits.

"Sorry, Reverend."

"I should hope."

"Like I said, Reverend, I beg your pardon for mentioning that one. But Responsible's another matter, and I say she's meddled and poked her nose where it wasn't wanted, and wasted good money on folderols till the time came when even the Holy One couldn't stand her any longer. And this is what it comes out to."

"There was that Quest of hers—talk of wasting money! Every Castle on this planet—always excepting those fool Smiths, and I don't doubt they were up to something as wouldn't bear the light of day or they'd of been in on it too—every Castle put on some kind of to-do for the 'daughter of Brightwater'! I've heard it said it was the Grannys as ordered that, but I can't see it. Can youall?"

Everybody agreed that they couldn't; it didn't sound like the Grannys.

"And there was her traveling outfit—you recall that? Three hundred dollers, good Kingdom money, that all cost, or I mistake myself!"

The Reverend set his ale mug down with a thump, shaking his head. "How much, then?"

"Excepting the whip and spurs, that have been in that Family now over three hundred years and didn't cost any of *us* a cent, though they may of been a strain on some of our grandfathers, that costume came to precisely sixty-three dollers and twenty-nine cents. I happen to know."

"Magic in it, then," said the lawyer.

"A needle goes a sight faster with a Granny pushing it," agreed the hotelkeeper, filling glasses and mugs all round.

"And then, there's all the money—Reverend, you can't tell us it wasn't enormous sums of money!—as was spent on that fool Jubilee!" Gabriel Micah snickered. "What's the opposite of 'Jubilee,' Reverend? A wake?"

The Reverend gave him a chilly look.

"*You*, Gabriel Micah—if I remember correctly, and I believe I do— you had a good time at the Jubilee such as you've not had since you were caught that time down by the creek, with—"

"I recollect that, Reverend," said the man hastily. "No need to review."

"Well? Are you trying to tell me that all the people in this Kingdom, and many a dozen more that were our guests, didn't have a fine time at the Jubilee? Didn't enjoy the fairs, and the picnics, and the competitions, and the plays, and even—one or two of you—the sermons, and all the rest of it? I'll grant you Responsible didn't have much fun out of it, but I didn't hear any of the rest of you complaining as it was going on."

"No," said another, "it was a right fine celebration. Fair's fair, Gabriel Micah—and the rest of you, too. Not to mention, long as we're talking her up, that it was Responsible of Brightwater as ordered five days' wages paid to every last one of us out of the Castle funds so we wouldn't have to work during the Jubilee."

"That was our own money—tax money!"

"Howsomever; there's a lot of other things it could of been spent on that we'd never of had any good from. And there was nothing to make her do that, you know. They could just as well of said work as usual and find time for celebrating after, if you've any energy left—and spent the tax money on theirselves. And you know it very well."

"Well, if she's such a fine lady," demanded Gabriel Micah, determined now to be spokesman for his position if he died trying, "then how *come* she's lying up there now, as near dead as makes *no* nevermind, and nothing any of the Magicians can do to bring her out of it? That sound like some mark of heavenly favor to *you?*"

The Reverend listened to them grumble and fuss for a while, and then left, clapping each one in his reach on the shoulder. He was satisfied that the doings at the Castle weren't worrying the men much; if anything, they were pleased to have something new to talk about. The fall of the Confederation had made no difference in their lives up to now, since they were of Brightwater Kingdom and enjoyed every privilege they ever had, with the added advantage of not having to put up with the Continental Delegations coming in one month in four and filling up the hotels.

The men of Brightwater were in no way worried; curious, distracted at worst, uneasy perhaps that the Magicians and Magicians of Rank seemed not to know what was going on. But not worried.

It was the women that worried. At home in their houses, they were white-faced and tight-lipped, and they had just one question: what was going to happen now?

The Grannys and the Family had asked Veritas Truebreed Motley the same question.

"Now what, you hifalutin fraud?" Thorn of Guthrie'd thrown at him, speaking for a number of them that wouldn't have dared say the words. "You and your high-and-mighty magic! What's going to happen now to my daughter?"

The Magician of Rank had smiled and expressed his approval of the first concern for her child he'd ever heard from her lips, and Thorn of Guthrie had come near spitting at him. "I'm *not* concerned for my child," she said, tossing that Guthrie hair, "not so much as my little finger-end's worth! My child, from what I can determine and from what you tell me, is resting comfortably. I am talking about the effect of her condition on all the rest of us!"

Veritas Truebreed raised his eyebrows, and then he bowed his head, ever so slightly, and clasped his hands behind him.

"My dear Thorn of Guthrie," he answered her, "I think 'all the rest' of you have no cause for concern. Responsible attended to a thing or two in this Kingdom, and meddled a good deal more than was appropriate in things elsewhere, but there's nothing she did that can't be handled by others. Your Economist can see to the accounts she kept, the staff can—"

"Veritas Truebreed!"

"Yes, Thorn of Guthrie! I am not deaf, you know!"

"I am not referring to the things Responsible did that could be handled by the servingmaids! You'll push me too far, even for a Magician of Rank! I am referring to her *other* duties!"

He looked her right in the eye and assured her that there was nothing —*nothing*—that Responsible of Brightwater ordinarily saw to that couldn't be handled just as well by the nine Ozark Magicians of Rank.

"You're sure of that?"

He was sure of it, and so were his colleagues. In the time it had taken them to accomplish the task of putting Responsible into pseudocoma—and that had turned out to be somewhat more of a project than they'd anticipated—they'd come to an agreement on that. The idea that the existence of a female, duly named and designated Responsible, in every generation—the idea that that was somehow essential to the well-being of Ozark—had been thoroughly discussed and set aside for what it was. Mere superstition.

EPILOGUE

It was eight o'clock in the morning on Tinaseeh. Morning prayer, morning chores, and the essentials of the body were out of the way; now it was time for teaching. The Tutors, though they came from the ranks of the Magicians, wore nothing to distinguish them from any other Traveller male. Their charges—exactly twelve per Tutor—were miniature versions of themselves. Black trousers, black shirts, black jackets, black shoes, black hats; the only concession made to childhood was the absence of the tie. In Booneville there were six little boys that didn't have to go to Tutorials, because they were waiting for six more little boys to reach the age of three and bring their group up to the required dozen. The boys in the Tutorials hated them, because they were still free to play; the boys left out hated and envied the others, and felt deprived because they could not attend and would be late starting.

There were no problems of curriculum on Tinaseeh. Each Tutor had a heavy book he carried with him, laying out the content of each of the twelve hundred teaching days he would have with his pupils. Four years, from the third birthday to the seventh, he would have them, for three hundred days of the year. And there would never be a day in that twelve hundred when he thought to himself, "Now what shall I do today?" That's not how it was done on Tinaseeh.

On this particular day, the subject was "Governments of Our World."

"Boys?"

Tutor Ethan Daniel Traveller the 30th tapped his ironwood pointer once, for order, and was rewarded with instant silence. He was an experienced Tutor—weary of it, if the truth were known, and hoping this year's examinations in magic would free him of the role—and his charges gave him no problems. They wouldn't have dared.

"You'll look at the map now," he said, and raised the pointer to touch each continent as he spoke.

"Kintucky!" he said first. "Up here in the left-hand corner, with the

Ocean of Storms all around it. Kintucky, settled in—" He waited, with the ironwood poised.

"Twenty-three thirty-nine!" they shouted, and he nodded approval.

"Kintucky is held by the Wommack Family, and it is a mite different from the other Kingdoms. It's governed, right now, by a man called a Guardian, the uncle of the rightful Master of Castle Wommack, just until the boy is old enough to take his place. The name for such a government is a *regency*. You will remember that."

"Yes, Tutor Ethan Daniel."

"Mizzurah, across the Ocean of Storms and off the coast of Arkansaw, was settled in twenty-three thirty-two. It's a very small place, as you can see, but it belongs to two Families—the Lewises and the Motleys. They are both democratic republics—as Kintucky will be, one of these days—and that means their government is a kind of council, that elects its leader. But it has never happened on Ozark that that leader was not also Master of the Castle in that Kingdom. And so the government of Mizzurah is led by the Masters of Castles Lewis and Motley. Is that clear?"

"Yes, sir," chorused the boys. Those old enough to write made notes with their styluses, and the three- and four-year-olds said it over and over under their breath to help themselves remember.

"Moving on, we have the continent—a continent, boys, is a large body of land completely surrounded by water; you will remember that—we have the continent of Arkansaw. Cletus Frederick Farson? Are you paying attention? Look at the map, Cletus Frederick, not the ceiling; there is nothing written on the ceiling!"

The other eleven boys laughed and nudged each other; and Cletus Frederick, supremely uninterested in the topic of "Governments of Our World" but not so stupid as to let it be known, fixed his eyes firmly on the point of the stick and stared at the map.

"The continent of Arkansaw, with the Ocean of Storms on the west and the Ocean of Remembrances on the east, was settled in—"

"Twenty-one twenty-seven!"

"Twenty-one twenty-seven, quite right. It is held by three Families: the Farsons, the Guthries, and the Purdys. The Farsons and the Guthries have Kings, and are called—*monarchies*. You will remember that. Now Kingdom Purdy is a little different: it does not have a King, but it is not a democratic republic. It has a group of three men ruling it, that are called

Senators; they rule together. This kind of government is called an *oli-garchy*. Say it after me."

"*Oligarchy!*"

"Again!"

"*Oligarchy!*"

"That's it. Now, crossing the ocean, still going clockwise, we come to Marktwain, the continent where First Landing happened in the year twenty twenty-one. For six years all of the Families lived together on Marktwain, which—as you can see—is small, almost as small as Mizzurah. It is shared by two Families—the Brightwaters and the McDaniels—both Kingdoms are democratic republics."

"That's where the comsets are!" piped one very small boy.

"That's true, James Thomas," agreed the Tutor. "But we don't want the comsets, do we, boys?"

"No, sir!"

"And why don't we?"

"Because they are evil!"

"So they are, so they are. And what else is there on Marktwain, in the Kingdom of Brightwater, that is evil?"

The boys looked at each other, not quite sure what he wanted. There was so much evil everywhere.

"James Thomas?" said the Tutor sharply. "You brought up the comsets—how about you telling us the answer to my question?"

"Responsible and Troublesome," mumbled the little boy very fast, looking at his feet and hoping.

"That is *exactly* right!" the Tutor thundered. "Exactly! Two evil women. Troublesome of Brightwater, exiled now for years to the top of a far mountain also called Troublesome, where decent people will not have to be around her! And Responsible of Brightwater?"

"She's asleep!"

"Yes; she's asleep. She was so wicked that the Holy One struck her down, putting her into a sleep like unto death—and she has been that way now for ten months, two weeks, and three days. You *see* where evil leads?"

They assured him that they did, until he was satisfied.

"Now," he said, "you see the Outward Deeps there, off to the east of Marktwain? We don't know anything much about the Outward

Deeps. But to the south of Marktwain is the continent of Oklahomah, settled in twenty-one twenty-seven jointly with Arkansaw. That is, an expedition moved from Marktwain in two parties; one to Arkansaw, one to Oklahomah, at the same time. That is called a *joint expedition*. You will remember that.

"On Oklahomah," he went on, "there are three Families. Two of them are democratic republics—the Kingdoms of Clark and Airy. One, Smith Kingdom, is a monarchy, which means that it has—"

"A King! A King!"

"Good. A King. And finally, we come to"—he swept the pointer around to the bottom left-hand corner of the map with a flourish, and the boys cried—"*Tinaseeh!*"

"Settled in—"

"Twenty-three forty-nine!"

"Good boys! Tinaseeh is the largest of all the continents, and it is the only one to have an inland body of water large enough to be called a sea. That is our *Midland* Sea. And its government is?"

"A *Holy* Republic!"

"So it is. And do we have a King?"

"No!"

"Why not? Why don't we have a King?"

"The Holy One is our leader!"

"And the Holy One's representative on this continent, that interprets the laws and says how we must behave?"

"Jacob Jeremiah Traveller, Master of Castle Traveller! Hurrah!"

Cheers from all directions; the Tutor allowed that for a minute or two. They were, after all, very young. And enthusiasm for Jacob Jeremiah Traveller was a sentiment to be encouraged.

"Now, are we through?" He asked finally, quieting them.

"Yes!"

"No; no, we are not. First, there is a very important question. Remember that there are six"—he held up six fingers—"*six* Kingdoms on Ozark that call themselves democratic republics. Those six—Brightwater, McDaniels, Clark, Airy, Lewis, and Motley—are joined as the Alliance of Democratic Republics. You will remember that. Now—does anybody know what the important question is?"

He didn't expect them to know, so he did not wait, but went right on. "What," he asked, "is the difference between a *democratic* republic and a *Holy* republic? Well?"

Silence. The Tutor tapped the pointer. Tap. Tap. Tap.

"Think!" he said. "Think how they are ruled; isn't that what we've been talking about all morning? How the Kingdoms are ruled? Now, *repeat after me*. A democratic republic is ruled by a man, but the Holy Republic is ruled by the Holy One! All together, now. . ."

He made them say it three times.

It didn't matter how many girls there were to a Granny School; a Granny took as many as happened to be there. And since, on all of Tinaseeh, the only Granny was Granny Leeward, it was a large group of little girls she faced that same day. But she had no more concern about what they must be taught than the Tutors did for the boys, and she needed no book to keep it straight in her head.

"Men," she was saying, "are of but two kinds: splendid, and pitiful. The splendid ones are rare, and if you chance on one you'll know it. What I tell you now has to do with the *rest* of 'em—as my Granny told me, and her Granny told her before that, and so back as far as time will take you. . ."

And Then There'll Be Fireworks

1

The child struggled under his hands; and he blamed it not at all. The sight of the Long Whip rising and falling on the naked back of ten-year-old Avalon of Wommack made his own stomach churn. Avalon was a slight and scrawny child, narrow of shoulder, the copper Wommack hair gone dark now with the swift-pouring sweat of her agony and clinging in a drenched coil along one frail shoulder blade. Something about the nape of her neck, where a babyish curl nestled all alone, tore at him worse than the blood.

"Look you well," hissed Eustace Laddercane Traveller the 4th through clenched teeth, holding his youngest son's head as every parent in Traveller Kingdom had learned it must be done. Not just the iron grip that kept the small head from turning away, but the little finger of each hand jabbed cruelly into the corners of the child's eyes, drawing the eyelids back taut against any possible hint of their closing.

It hurt, of course; but not so much as the smack of that Whip would hurt, should one of the College of Deacons see the child avoiding its present duty: to watch the public whipping of Avalon of Wommack. And one day this boy he held so tightly now would perform the same service for the babe that swelled his mother's belly this very moment, as his older children held their younger brothers and sisters all around him. His wife had not been spared, either, though Eustace Laddercane had requested it; her time was very near, and it a tenth child—this whipping was enough to set off her labor and see his tenth-born arrive in the public square. But the Tutor had been absolutely adamant about it. Should that happen, he'd told him, it would be a blessing for the newborn, its first sight in this world one guaranteed to further its moral education and set it on the straight path for life.

Should that happen, thought the father, he'd blind the babe with his own two thumbs before he'd let that be its first sight of the world . . . the Holy One grant that it *not* happen.

Avalon of Wommack was well shielded from any lustful eyes. The

Whipping Cloth hung foursquare from its hooks above her head to her bare feet, with only the narrow space cut away at the back to allow the Whip room. But it did nothing to shield her screams. Eustace Laddercane hoped they hurt the ears of the Magicians of Rank that stood one at each corner of the cloth, twelve inches between them and their pitiful victim.

The whipping itself, now—no man could have done that, though not one had courage enough to stop it. It was Granny Leeward of Castle Traveller, her that was the own mother of the Castle Master, that wielded the Long Whip.

She'd explained Avalon of Wommack's grievous sins to them all carefully before she began the chastisement, looking all around her with those measuring eyes, counting. She knew precisely how many people should be there on the walkway that bordered the square, did the Granny. Ninety-one excused by the College of Deacons for illness near unto death, a sign of sure wickedness in those ninety and one; and seven hundred thirteen that left to be counted. Eustace Laddercane was certain that Granny Leeward was able to count each and every one of the seven hundred thirteen, and would have known if even one had been missing. They lined up by household and by height, the tallest at the back.

There still was not room for all of them within the Castle walls, and it had been necessary to lay out this whipping ground outside, burning away every last sprig and blade of growing life, grading it flat as the top of a table, anchoring down the board walkway that bordered it with spokes of ironwood hammered into chinks blasted out of the Tinaseeh rock. But that was changing. The people of Tinaseeh, they were dying with a terrifying speed, ten and twenty and more now in a single day . . . soon they'd be able to take their Whipping Cloth inside one of the courtyards, right into Roebuck . . . might could be soon they'd have ample space in the Castle Great Hall itself, and be hard put to it to find anybody left to whip.

Avalon of Wommack had sinned doubly. First she had sinned against the cause that bid the Chosen People of Tinaseeh repopulate this land, to replace the dying who by their very deaths had revealed the vileness of their souls. Avalon's father had brought her home a husband, a man of seventeen, and Avalon not only had not welcomed her bridegroom tenderly and obediently as was expected of her, not only refused to go willingly to the marriage bed where this male twice her size and near twice her age might do her the favor of placing his seed in her womb—Avalon had tried to hide herself away. They had dragged her from a granary, half suffocated already on the grain and on her terror. Despite the fact, Granny Leeward had hammered the point home, that Avalon's womb had been through two full cycles. And secondly, there was the additional fact that Avalon of Wommack was a Two, and a female whose name came to the numeral two was intended by destiny to be passive and submissive and weak. The girl had also sinned against her Naming.

That, the Granny had said, was the greater sin of the two. A young girl, modest and timid as was fully appropriate, might be leniently treated for fearing the wedding bed and the inevitable childbed that followed it. She might well of had only a token stroke or two of the Long Whip for that, provided she went then and did her duty ever after.

But to rebel against her Naming was not just to rebel against Jeremiah Thomas Traveller's orders to marry and be fruitful, the orders of a mere man. It was rebellion against the path laid out for her by the Holy One; a fearsome evil, a defying of the divine law.

And so the number of lashes had been set at twice twelve. A memorable number. Eustace Laddercane remembered only one other unfortunate to earn so high a number as that, and that time it had been for stealing food from the common stores and gorging on it. And that time the Whip had fallen on the broad back of a man full grown.

The Long Whip whistled through the air—stroke seventeen. The Magicians of Rank put themselves to the trouble of calling out the number each time for the watchers, that they might not lose track and think that surely it had to be almost over.

At his side he felt a long shudder take his wife's body, and he dared a quick look, sure it was the birth pains, but she knew his thought as soon as he did, and without turning her head she murmured to him not to take foolish chances, that she was all right. All right, she said, but for the whipping.

Avalon of Wommack did not scream again after the nineteenth stroke, but Granny Leeward took care not to leave the people wondering what was the point of laying five more strokes on a body already dead.

"Praise be," said the Granny solemnly. "The household of this youngun can go tranquil to its beds this night. Avalon of Wommack has paid in full the debt of her wickedness, and she stands now in eternal bliss, smiling and singing at the right hand of the Holy One Almighty. Praise be!"

The Magicians of Rank raised their long shears as one man and cut the loops that held the Whipping Cloth to the hooks, and there was nothing then to see but a pile of bloody linen, very nearly flat, upon the stained ground.

Somebody's child, walking the edge of hysteria, screamed out over and over: "Where did Avalon of Wommack go? *Where is she?*" And there was the ringing smack of a full blow across that child's face as its mother moved desperately to offer up a penalty before the College of Deacons could prescribe one.

And Granny Leeward's voice rose strong and sure—and why not, seeing as how she was little more than sixty and mighty young for a Granny—leading them in the hymn that had been chosen to end this particular whipping. It was seemly; its title was "Divine Pain, Willingly Endured." Except that Avalon of Wommack had not been willing.

The members of the College of Deacons moved along the walkway, their arms folded gravely over their chests, watching and listening for any sign of somebody singing with anything less than righteous enthusiasm. It was, after all, an occasion for celebration, what with Avalon of Wommack's eternal bliss and her family's tranquillity and all; and the College of Deacons was fully prepared to see to it that a suitable explanation was provided for anybody present that couldn't understand that on their own.

The little ones sang their hearts out, and the older ones sighed and released their grips upon the small heads just a mite. The children knew already; sing, sing loud, and sing joyful. Make a joyful noise . . . they knew. Or there'd be a smaller version of the Long Whip waiting at home, and the mother assigned a specific number of strokes to be laid on, by the Deacon that'd spotted the wavering voice. It made for hearty music.

Eustace Laddercane Traveller the 4th believed, really believed, in the Holy One Almighty. And there had not been a whipping yet that he had not raised his own voice in the closing hymn, almost roaring out the words, waiting for the divine wrath to reach the limit of Its endurance and strike Granny Leeward dead before his eyes. It had not happened yet, but his faith that it would was a rock on which he stood, and a comfort to him in the nights when often he dreamed it was a child of his loins that cringed and screamed and twisted under the strokes of the Whip.

"It went well, to my mind," said Nathan Overholt Traveller the 101st. "No faintings, no foolishness, and no punishments to pass out afterward— all very satisfactory."

The other three nodded, and agreed that it had gone well enough.

"Well enough, perhaps." That was Feebus Timothy Traveller the 6th, youngest of the Magicians of Rank on Tinaseeh. "But the child ought not to have died."

The two Farson brothers, Sheridan Pike the 25th and Luke Nathaniel the 19th, looked at each other. There were times when they wondered about Feebus Timothy, finding him a tad soft, wondering if there wasn't a slight taint of Airy blood there somewhere to account for what came near at times to romantic notions. Times when they felt he'd profit from a stroke or two of the Long Whip himself. He sorely needed toughening up.

"There is no room on Tinaseeh for a disobedient child," said Nathan Overholt harshly. "The subject is closed."

"There was a time," persisted Feebus Timothy, "when we could have saved her, any one of us, no matter how many lashes she had taken."

"There was a time," said Sheridan Pike reasonably, "when we could cause the Mules to fly and carry us on their backs, and a time when the winds and the rains and the tides obeyed us. And that was that time, and it is gone. We deal now with *this* time."

The mention of the powers they had lost silenced them all. It was not something you got used to. Once you had been someone whose fingers could make a casual move or two and a cancer would shrivel and disappear inside the sick one's body, leaving no trace behind. Once you had been someone that could SNAP through space, moving from the Wilderness Lands of Tinaseeh, across the vastness of the Oceans of Remembrances and of Storms, to land less than a second later in the courtyard of any of the twelve Castles of the planet Ozark. Once you had been someone who saw to it that the rain fell only when and where it was needed, and that the harvests were always bountiful, and that the snow fell only deep enough and often enough to be an amusement for the children and a change for their elders . . . once.

Now, on the other hand, it was as Sheridan Pike had said. Now they had to deal with *this* time. Four Magicians of Rank, their titles as hollow as their stomachs and their gaunt faces, garbed in a black grown shiny with wear, and their only power now the power of fear. It was a painful comedown, for they had been truly mighty.

Luke Nathaniel Farson had been picking idly at his front teeth with his thumbnail, a maddening little noise in the silence; and then he stopped, just before they could demand for him to, and asked: "Do you suppose it's true, that rumor about the Yallerhounds?"

"Luke Nathaniel!" Even Feebus Timothy got in on the outrage.

"I don't know," mused the other man. "They're hungry. We're hungry, here at the Castle . . . think of the people in the town. A Yallerhound, or a giant cavecat, that's a sizable quantity of meat. And though it's true I can't think of any of the men with strength enough left to take a cavecat, you know as well as I do that a boy of three could catch a Yallerhound. All you have to do is call the creature, and it will come to you."

"Nobody," said Sheridan Pike, "nobody at *all,* would eat a Yallerhound. They would starve first."

"They will, then," said Luke Nathaniel. "Those that haven't already."

"Change the subject," ordered Sheridan Pike flatly. "Can't any of you think of *something* that's not intolerable to talk about? You've lost your magic powers, but I wasn't aware that you'd lost your minds as well."

"Well," said Feebus Timothy, "we could discuss today's scheduled urgent and significant meeting. That's not intolerable, just useless, and silly, and stupid."

"Your sarcasm is very little help, Cousin," said Sheridan Pike.

"All right, then, I'll ask seriously. What *is* on today's agenda?"

"A discussion of the situation."

"Again?" Feebus Timothy was serious now, serious and flabbergasted. "Whatever for? We have had nine hundred and ninety-nine 'discussions of the situation' and we have yet to arrive at a single—"

Sheridan Pike cut him off. "Jeremiah Thomas Traveller is Master of this Castle, master of the four of us, son of Granny Leeward, and representative of the Holy One upon this earth. If he says we are to discuss the situation yet one more time—or one hundred more times—then we will discuss it."

Feebus Timothy snorted. "The only thing in all that that impresses *me,* Cousin, is the claim that he's Leeward's son. *That* I believe, it being a matter of record; and *that* I'm impressed by. As for the rest of it . . . if you'll pardon a phrase from the formspeech . . . cowflop."

"You talk a good line," said Luke Nathaniel Farson. "But I have yet to see you do more than talk."

Sheridan Pike moved smoothly to cover the charged silence, and observed that another discussion was not necessarily a waste of time.

"Each time we meet," he said, "there is the possibility that we will hit upon something we have overlooked before, colleagues. Somewhere there is a clue to be found, if only we were wise enough to spot it."

"The clue you seek," retorted Feebus Timothy, "lies in pseudocoma on a narrow bed at Castle Brightwater. Where we put her, we wise Magicians of Rank, these sixteen months past."

"Nonsense!"

"Not nonsense," said Nathan Overholt, knowing he plowed ground already furrowed to exhaustion, but too tired to care, "not nonsense at all. Feebus Timothy is somewhat confused, and somewhat overdramatic, but the facts of the matter are obvious. While Responsible of Brightwater went about her interfering and infuriating business on this planet, we were truly Magicians, with the power of Formalisms & Transformations at our command. From the moment we laid her in pseudocoma on that bed my cousin refers to so poetically, our power began to wane . . . and now it is gone. Entirely, completely, wholly gone. *Magic* is gone . . . and on Tinaseeh we have no science. The question is: *why?*"

"We have no science because we never needed it," said Sheridan Pike disgustedly. "Magic was a great deal faster than science ever hoped to be, and far more efficient."

"No, no . . . that was not my question! And you know it, don't you?"

"Of course I know it!"

"Then stop playing the fool!"

"He is not playing the fool," said Luke Nathaniel wearily, "he is just cross, like the rest of us. And we have considered that question so many times already."

"Magic," said Nathan Overholt, "is a great web, a great web in always changing equilibrium. Touch it anywhere, change it anyhow, and you affect the whole. When we removed Responsible of Brightwater from that web—"

"We haven't removed her. She's in better health than any of us. In pseudocoma you don't *need* to eat."

"In a sense," Nathan Overholt went on, "we removed her. We changed her from an active principle to a passive one . . . and yet she is a female. How can a female represent an active principle?"

"Granny Leeward is exceedingly 'active' with the Long Whip," observed Luke Nathaniel. "And she is female."

"She is not a *principle*—she is only an item."

Feebus Timothy longed to lay his head, still aching from the screams of Avalon of Wommack, down on the table, right then and there, and go to sleep. They had been over it. And over it. The difference between an item and a principle. The difference between substitution of a null term and substitution of a specified term. The degree of shift in an equation sufficient to destroy its reversibility—or restore it. And over and over . . . what role had Responsible of Brightwater, a girl of fifteen like any other girl of fifteen to the eye, played in that equation, such that the cancellation of *her* input had been enough to destroy the entire system?

There were never any answers. That she had known a little magic, some of it more advanced than was suitable for a female or even legal, they all knew. The four of them had been present when Responsible fell into Granny Leeward's trap and changed the old woman's black fan into a handful of rotting jet-black mushrooms before their astonished eyes. Jeremiah Thomas Traveller had been mightily impressed by that, as the Granny had intended him to be.

But *they* were Magicians of Rank. It was a Transformation, certainly, and the girl should not have been able to do it, but it was trivial. It was a baby trick, such as any one of them might of done—in a less ugly way—to entertain guests at a celebration of some kind. It was probable that it had been as much blind luck as skill, and mostly the product of the girl's rage; for she had lain in torment while they watched her and mocked her misery, suffering from the gift of Anderson's Disease, the deathdance fever that Granny Leeward had ordered them to impose as punishment for her scandalous behavior. And she'd shown no sign of any talent for things magical but that one . . . nor had she been able to stand against them when the nine Magicians of Rank had chosen to impose pseudocoma upon her or during the months that had dragged by since. If there was something special about her, why had she not leaped up from that bed and laughed at them and put all of *them* into pseudocoma?

It was hopeless.

"It's hopeless," he said aloud. "Hopeless."

The others looked at him, suddenly caught by the nuance of his voice. He was young, and he was inexperienced, but he had been a skilled

Magician of Rank. Now they detected something . . . a note of petulance. Petulance?

Nathan Overholt Traveller reached over abruptly and laid his hand on the younger man's forehead and swore a broad word.

"He's burning up with fever!" he said. "One of you get the Granny, and tell her to lose no time coming down here!"

It had been bound to happen sooner or later. Sickness, the Master of this Castle had been telling everyone, sickness and death, were nothing more than the marks of wickedness and sin made visible in the flesh. Only the Holy One culling the rotten fruit from the crop and leaving the sound and the wholesome behind. It made an entertaining sermon, and perhaps dulled grief for some . . . after all, if those that suffered and died deserved their fate, then what was there to grieve over?

But the Magicians of Rank had been uneasy, listening. For if one of them, one of the Magicians of Rank, one of the Family, were to fall sick or, the Twelve Gates forbid, to die—how was that to be explained? The urgency of preventing that had provided them with a shaky justification for the extra rations they shared in secret in the Castle, while tadlings cried with hunger in the houses of the town. *Eggs,* they had been eating . . . it was safe to assume that no one else on Tinaseeh had seen an egg in six months or more, much less eaten one. And now this? It must not happen.

"Why call the Granny?" demanded one of the others, and Nathan Overholt took time from rubbing the temples of his brother's head to give him a look of contempt.

"We have no magic now, you benastied fool," he spat, beside himself with worry, and his elegant manners and speech forgotten for once, "and no medicine either. We have *nothing*—except what the Grannys know. The ancient simples. The herbs and teas and potions and plasters of the times *before* magic, the Holy One have mercy on us all! Now *get* her!"

"Nathan Overholt—"

"You think," shouted Nathan, "you think that if one of us falls to a fever we will be able to stand on the whipping ground and convince the people of Tinaseeh that we order that Whip laid on out of our own innocence of all sin? You think that Granny Leeward would scruple to set that Long Whip to your back, or to mine, if that seemed necessary to further the cause of the Chosen People? Dozens, man, don't you realize that

if Feebus Timothy has it we may *all* be in the same fix, whatever it is—
and it could be *anything?* Now go!"

He went around behind his brother and clasped the young man's
head in his hands, closing his eyes, concentrating fiercely. It was an act
he knew to be only superstition. But perhaps. Perhaps there was still some
fragment of healing in it. He could not do nothing at all. He had no desire
to die like Avalon of Wommack had died; nor did he want to learn how
many strokes of the Long Whip it would take to kill a strong man in reasonably good condition.

2

Mount Troublesome was not much, as mountains go; it peaked at a tad past four thousand feet, and it hadn't a glacier or a crevasse to its name. On the other hand, though it didn't live up to the "Mount" part, it more than made up for that in its fidelity to the "Troublesome" part. It missed no smallest opportunity for ravines to get stuck in and caves to get lost in and vast thickets to be scratched ragged in; and it was abundantly generous in poisonous ivies and creepers winding along the ground and up around the trees to hang down and smack you in the face. Springs were everywhere, trickling along under matted undergrowth that looked solid as a stable roof, till you set foot on it and sank in icy water up to your knees. There were waterfalls enough to go around, pretty white water gushing over sheer rock faces into pools circled by ferns and nearwillows. The pools were tempting to the eye, and might of been pleasant-feeling, but you waded them at your peril and the pleasure of dozens of small ferocious yellow snakes with ingeniously notched teeth. It did happen to be a fact that Mount Troublesome was the tallest thing on the entire continent of Marktwain.

The seven old women toiling their way up its tangled sides were more than satisfied with the obstacles it presented. If it had been any worse, there was considerable doubt in their minds that they could of made it to the top at all.

"Drat the ornery female!" Granny Sherryjake had declared after the second time a whole hour had to be wasted finding a way round a berry thicket as impenetrable as solid rock and twice as unpleasant. And she went on to expand on that, and elaborate on it, and weave variations on it, as the hours went by and it became obvious that there was no way they could reach the top before nightfall. They'd be overnighting out on the mountain.

But Granny Hazelbide, that was in residence along with Granny Gableframe at Castle Brightwater, had taken exception to that. It was *fully* appropriate, she'd said, slapping back at a branch that had slapped her first, for a woman named Troublesome to choose a mountain named Troublesome when she went into exile.

"Fully appropriate, and seemly," said Granny Hazelbide. "I'd of done the same exact thing, in her place."

"Well," grumbled Sherryjake, "there may be something to what you say."

"I should hope and declare there is. Naming is *naming!*"

"But," went on the other doggedly, "I do *not* see that there was any special merit to be gained from her establishing herself at the very most tip *top* of this accursed hump of dirt and rock. She was not named *Peak* of Troublesome, you know. Halfway up would of done it, seems to me. Quarterways up."

"Troublesome of Brightwater was instructed to take herself as far away from the rest of the population of Brightwater as it was possible for her to get," said Granny Frostfall firmly. "I hold with Hazelbide; she did what was proper. But I surely do not find that it makes for a pleasant little stroll."

"Time was," fussed Granny Gableframe, "this would of been no more than that, for any of us."

"And in such a time," snorted Granny Frostfall, "we'd none of us of crossed a city *street* to pay a call on Troublesome of Brightwater. Can't say as how I see that it applies, Gableframe."

Granny Gableframe didn't bother to argue, but sighed a long sigh and took a firmer grip on her walking stick with her thin old fingers. It wouldn't do to lose it.

Grannys had always been thin, that went with the territory; but these seven were thin to the bone, and those bones pained them. Grannys had always been old; but up till recently they'd been protected from the usual miseries of old age by their own Granny Magic, and from its more *un*usual miseries by the skills of the Magicians and the Magicians of Rank. Without that protection, things had changed for them. Angina and arthritis, gallbladder colic and kidney trouble, ulcers and headaches and high blood pressure, all the bodily discomforts taken for granted as the lot of any aged woman on Old Earth, had struck the Grannys of Ozark. It was even said that at Castle Clark—though she denied it fiercely—Granny Golightly was developing a cataract in her right eye.

Under the circumstances, when Granny Gableframe first proposed that the seven of them should go up to the mountaintop and talk to Troublesome of Brightwater, the hilarity had been like a squawkercoop with a serpent inside, and two servingmaids had come running to find out what the commotion was.

"You are daft, Gableframe," the other Grannys had said with a single voice, and they'd sat in their rockers and cackled and held their aching sides at the very idea. Seven creaking old ladies, half blind and half deaf, feet too swollen to go in their shoes and bones so brittle they barely dared move them—and they were to trek up the meanest mountain on Marktwain in the middle of the autumn? It was a fool idea to top all fool ideas.

"That does take the rag off the bush, Gableframe," they'd said, and it was unanimous.

"And what *do* you propose to do, ladies?" Gableframe had challenged them, standing there arms akimbo and her sharp chin stuck out ahead of her. "You propose to just sit here, do you? While the crops all die and the animals sicken and the people do the same, and Responsible of Brightwater lies month after weary month on that white counterpane, so still the only reason I can believe she's alive is that her body has yet to *mortify?* Well, ladies? You laugh right prompt, real quick to make fun, *you* are! But I don't hear you offering any plans of your own."

They did know two things, there was that. In the first months after Responsible had been struck down, while the power of magic was waning but not yet exhausted, the Grannys had managed to learn two small pieces of information. They'd read tea leaves, they'd swung their golden rings on long black threads, they'd stared into springwater till their eyes were red and weeping, night after night. And back at them had come two scraps.

The reason behind the trouble, the reason behind Responsible's death-like interminable sleep, was "an important man." That had come first, and after much labor, and had irritated them considerably. Then there had been the search for that man's location in this world, holding the golden rings over the maps, holding their breaths as well, waiting for one ring to begin its telltale swinging and circling. All atremble like they were, it took a sharp eye to tell when the movement was of its own self and when it was just the doings of a Granny whose hand was no longer steady.

And then there'd been argument. The Spells were so little use by then, the movement of the rings so near no movement at all, and so

ambiguous—was it Tinaseeh or was it Kintucky? All of a week they'd
nattered over that, half for one and half for the other, knowing that if
they made the wrong choice there'd be no second chance. There weren't
resources enough for trying twice, for one thing. And for another, if anything was to be done it had to be done swiftly; there was nothing in the
way of extra resources of *time,* either.

Grannys Gableframe, Whiffletree, and Edging had been strong for
Tinaseeh, swearing it was Jeremiah Thomas Traveller that was the "important man." Did he not, after all, rule that continent with a fist of iron, and
hadn't he always? And hadn't he always hated Responsible of Brightwater
and everything she stood for?

"Hmmph," said Granny Cobbledrayke of Castle McDaniels, "it's not
Jeremiah Thomas as rules Tinaseeh, it's his mother, her that took Leeward
as her Granny Name and is about as much like a leeward side in a storm
as a lizard's like a bellybutton. Don't give *me* Jeremiah Thomas Traveller
for an 'important man'—he's a mama's boy, and always was."

She, and the rest of the Marktwain Grannys, had been set on
Kintucky, and Castle Wommack. Hadn't Responsible herself, they argued,
run away from Castle Wommack—her that wasn't afraid of anything living or dead—run *away,* rather than face Lewis Motley Wommack? And
wasn't it Lewis Motley Wommack that now governed all of Kintucky?

"He is barely twenty-one years old . . . *wouldn't* be, not quite yet,"
Gableframe protested. "A *boy* yet, last time we saw him! Here for the
Jubilee, remember? With his little sister Jewel set to tag around after him
and keep him out of mischief? How can that one be the 'important man,'
I ask you?"

"He is important on Kintucky," said Sherryjake.

"Well, we don't know how that came to be," grumbled the others.
"We don't know atall. Way our magic was working in those last months,
for all we know the messages we got were plain scrambled . . . might
could be Jacob Donahue Wommack the 23rd's still hale and hearty and
Master of that Castle and the whole tale about it being Lewis Motley in
charge is no more than a puckerwrinkle in a puny Spell. Who'd be fool
enough to put a wild colt like that one in charge of a Kingdom? Now I
ask you . . ."

But the time had come when the decision had to be made; and for
want of anything better to base it on they'd deferred to Granny Hazelbide,

seeing as it was Hazelbide had had the raising of Responsible of Brightwater and knew her best of any of them.

Now, fighting the thorns and the vines and the poison weeds, keeping a sharp eye for the false earth over running water, making a hardscrabble way up through a drizzle that threatened to be a rain and praying they'd find at least an overhang to shelter them through this night, they hoped they'd decided rightly. Everything rode on this one throw of the dice, and Granny Hazelbide shivered with more than the fever that plagued her now every day of her life, thinking what she'd done if it was the wrong choice and she had convinced the others of it. And what they'd do to her . . . law, *that* would be a production!

"Ah, Hazelbide," said Granny Willowithe, her that almost never spoke, and had done her grannying in the farther reaches of the Kingdom where there were few to bother her, "if you are *wrong!*" It was always that way. Those as spoke rarely, when they did speak it tended to be significant and to be what everybody else was thinking and hadn't gotten up gumption to give voice to.

Troublesome of Brightwater woke to a wind howling round her cabin doors and windows, and that was ordinary enough. She woke also to a downright infuriated rapping on her cabin door, and that was distinctly *not* ordinary. Over ten years she'd been here now, and she'd never had a visitor but her little sister, and that only three times. It could not be her little sister this time.

She listened again, and stretched in the warmth of her bed, wondering if it had been maybe something blown by the winds, or something in a dream, half a mind to go back to sleep. And then the hollering came: "Troublesome of Brightwater, *will* you open this door? Or have you taken to murdering old ladies along with the rest of your wicked ways?"

That brought her up out of her bed in a hurry. Old ladies, was it, on her doorsill? She went to the door just as she was, and stood there before them mothernaked and barefoot, with no cover but the heavy black hair that tumbled almost to her knees. She held the door with one hand and set the other on the curve of her shameless hip, and she sighed a sigh of sheer wonderment.

"Whatever in all the world?" breathed Troublesome of Brightwater, looking them over. "Whatever in all the wondering twelve-square world?"

The Grannys were a sight to behold, for sure. They were wet and they were dirty and they were nettlestung, and they were cold and wrinkled and miserable. With no more Housekeeping Spells to use, and nothing around for a tidy-up but one stream the width of their hand trickling over slabs of bare rock, they were as pitiful a representation of seven old ladies as had ever met the eye.

"Out of my way, trollop," announced Granny Gableframe, and would of pushed right past Troublesome into the welcome warmth of the cabin; but the young woman barred her way with one sturdy arm.

"I'm no trollop, Granny Gableframe," she said. "I'm virgin as I came from my mother's womb—and that's more than any one of you here can say back at me, as I recollect. As for my costume, I don't recall sending out any invitations. You've gotten potluck, Grannys."

"Law, the creature's enjoying it," muttered Granny Hazelbide. She'd had the raising of *her,* too. "Troublesome," she demanded, "will you for the love of decency drop that arm and let us in? We are tired near to death, we spent all yesterday on this mountain and all last night in a cave full of varmints and dripping water, and we've no magic any more to ease the toll all that has taken. Would it pleasure you to see one of us drop dead right here before your eyes, you dreadful female?"

Troublesome dropped her arm at that and let them by, saying: "Well, that's more fair. A trollop I'm not, but a dreadful female I'm willing to admit to. Do come in, and I'll put the kettle on and stir up the fire. I don't suppose youall'd take your clothes off and let me hang them to dry, would you?"

That met the frigid silence she'd anticipated, and she nodded her head in resignation.

"Stay cold and wet, then," she said, "and die of pneumonia, not on my doorstep but on my hearthstone—but don't you lay it to my account. There's not a one of you as has anything different to her body than I have myself, and I do believe I could bear the sight of your old skinny-skin-skins . . . for sure I would not lust after you! But if you rank your modesty higher than your misery, so be it; I'll not squabble with you."

The cabin was small and bare, and even after Troublesome got the fire crackling in the fireplace the best she could do was pull up a rough board bench with no back to it for them all to sit on and try to bake the damp from their bones. Troublesome had no rugs, and no curtains; her bed was a pallet laid on a rope frame in the corner, she had one straight chair and one rocker and one low stepladder and a small square table and a cookstove. And except for a bucket or two and a shelf here and there, that was it. The Grannys were bemused by it, even with their teeth chattering.

"Don't have eight cups, do you?" asked Granny Sherryjake.

Troublesome chuckled, and admitted she didn't, and served them up the scalding tea in an assortment of jars and ladles and whatnots that was ingenious, but not elegant.

"Never needed more than three before," she told them. "One to drink with, one to measure with, and one in the dishpan soaking."

"I can't say as you exactly . . . do yourself *proud,*" commented Granny Frostfall, and a kind of snort of agreement ran down the bench.

"No, I don't suppose I do," Troublesome agreed.

"Tain't natural," said one, and Troublesome's eyebrows rose.

"You expected things up here to be natural?" she asked.

The Grannys sighed all together, seeing it was a hopeless case, and Troublesome went to a row of three pegs on a wall by her bed and took down a long dress all in a soft scarlet wool and slipped it over her head.

"There," she said, "now I'll not be quite such an offense to your eyes." And her long fingers were almost too quick for those same fourteen sharp eyes to see as she put the mass of hair into a braid and wound it up around her head and fastened it tight.

It was unjust that anything so wicked should be so beautiful, or so clever, or so serene, or so happy with her lot—especially the last—and the Grannys stared glumly into the fire and pondered on that.

"Well, ladies," Troublesome said at last, sitting herself down on an upended bucket with her arms wrapped round her knees, since it wouldn't of been mannerly to take a chair while the old women huddled on that bench, "now you're a bit warmer and dryer, maybe you'd tell me what I'm beholden to for the pleasure of your company?"

"Maybe you might offer us a bite of breakfast first!" snapped Granny Gableframe. "*If* you care to spare it!"

"It's already cooking," said Troublesome calmly, "but I can't do anything much to hurry it along. And while we're waiting on it—no, I don't have eight plates either, but as it happens I *do* have eight spoons—while we're waiting on it I see no reason not to make the time go by speaking up on the reason for this visit. I'm afraid I'm not much for visitors."

The Grannys allowed as how they never *would* of figured that out if she hadn't mentioned it, and she chuckled again.

"Earn your keep, you dear old things," she teased them, brazen as brazen, "earn your keep. What brings you hanging round my door all unannounced and unkempt, with snow before the week's out or my name's not Troublesome of Brightwater? You should be home, each in your rocker with your knitting, by your own fire, telling terrible stories to the tadlings."

Granny Hazelbide was embarrassed; true, this one was properly Named, and her outrageousness came as no surprise to anybody, but it *had* been her, poor Granny Hazelbide, that had tried to keep some control over her when she was a little girl at Castle Brightwater.

"Troublesome," she said sadly, "have you no feelings atall?"

"Probably not," said Troublesome promptly. "Feelings about what?"

"Times are *hard,* young woman," said Hazelbide, "times are fearsome hard! You talk of sitting by our fires . . . there's precious little left to lay a fire *with,* down in the towns. People are suffering, and your own sister lies near death in the Castle. How can you sit there and face us and make jokes over it all?"

"Would it help," Troublesome put the question, "if I moaned about it instead? Would it ease anybody's fever, stop anybody's bleeding, or put food in anybody's stomach or fire on their hearth? Would it wake my sister—who is *not,* by the way, anywhere near death. Not as near as the seven of you, I assure you."

"Ah, you're heartless," Granny Hazelbide mourned. "Just heartless!"

Troublesome said nothing at all, but waited and watched, and they began to smell the porridge on the stove and their stomachs knotted.

"Well, we want you to make a journey," said Granny Gableframe when it finally became clear that they'd get no more out of the girl. "A long and a perilous journey. And that's why we're here . . . to ask you. Politely."

Troublesome stared at her, black brows knit over her nose, and gave a sharp "tchh" with her tongue.

"A journey? Go on a trip?"

"Yes. And a good long one."

She stood up and went to the stove and began passing the porridge over to them, warning them to use their shawls to hold on so they'd not burn their fingers.

"Certainly can't hurt the shawls, the state *they're* in," she said.

She watched them while they ate; and seeing that they were truly hungry, she didn't bother them, but busied herself pouring more tea and serving more porridge until it seemed to her that everybody was at last satisfied and she could gather up the motley collection of serving things in her apron and put it all into a pan of hot soapy water.

Whereupon she sat down, shaking her hands to dry them, and said, "No more excuses, now. You're dry, and you're warm, and you're fed and watered. It's too cold for you to be taking baths at your age, so you'll have to stay dirty, and I've no remedies for your other miseries; I've made you as comfortable as I'm capable of. Now I'll have you tell me about this journey, thank you kindly."

"We want you to go to Castle Wommack," said Granny Hazelbide, and Troublesome almost fell off her makeshift stool in astonishment.

"To Kintucky? Granny, you've lost your mind entirely! However would I get to Castle Wommack?"

"On a ship."

"Granny Hazelbide, there's no ship goes to Kintucky any more, and no supplies to last the journey if there were. You've been nibbling something best left on its stem, *I* say."

"We have a ship," said Hazelbide, putting one stubborn word after another, "and a crew—not much of a crew, but it'll serve in this instance —and supplies enough to get all of you to Kintucky and back. Including the Mule you'll be taking along to get you from the coast to the Castle."

"Dozens!" said Troublesome. "I'd of said that was impossible."

"It wasn't cheap."

"It took all we had," put in Granny Whiffletree, "and all that the Grannys had on Oklahomah, and a contribution or two—not necessarily voluntary, if you take my meaning—from a few useless Magicians and Magicians of Rank. But we did it."

"Bribed the ship captain, did you? And bribed the crew?"

"That we did."

"And you think they'll stay bribed!"

"We do. The captain's a Brightwater, and all but one of the crew as well. And that one's a McDaniels. They'll stay bribed."

"Supposing," hazarded Troublesome, leaning forward, "that I was such a lunatic as to go gallivanting off to Kintucky in the middle of the autumn . . . just suppose that, *which* I'm not . . . what precisely is my goal,

other than to drown myself and the captain and the crew and that poor
Mule?"

They told her, and they watched her face go thoughtful, and Granny
Gableframe pinched the next Granny down on the bench, gently; they
knew then that they had her.

"I agree," said Troublesome slowly, "that it's sure to be Lewis Motley
Wommack the 33rd. I do agree on that. Not a thing Jeremiah Thomas
Traveller could have done that would account for what's happened, but
that Wommack boy is something else again, and I do believe he lay with
Responsible while the Jubilee was going on."

"So *that's* who it was!" exclaimed Granny Hazelbide. "How did you
know?"

"Ask me no questions, Granny, I'll tell you no lies," said Troublesome.
"It makes no nevermind how I knew. But you've chosen right, for sure
and for certain. However . . . you've nothing here but missing pieces."

"Explain yourself!"

"*Did* you learn, before your magic wound down, that if somebody
went to see this 'important man' it would make some difference in the
course of events on Ozark?" Troublesome stared them down, and they
had to admit that they hadn't.

"And *did* you learn that just because he's the cause of Responsible's
hearty nap he knows how to wake her up again?

"And *did* you learn that even if my sister *was* awake again, she'd be
able to do something about all this tribulation we suffer from? Did you?"

It was no to both, of course, and they had to admit it.

"But you'd send me half round the world on a wild goose chase, on
the slim tagtail of a chance that there *might* be some use to it?"

And they agreed that they would.

"Well," said Troublesome. "I never heard such nonsense."

"Sass!"

"No, I never did. Unless it was youall coming up here like you did,
risking pneumonia coming up and breaking every bone in your bodies
going down—'cause you pay me mind, now, if you thought you had a
hard time getting up here, you just wait till you try getting back down!
It's a heap faster, but it's not a safe trip. No way, no way in this world,
am I going to take any part in such a fool project, and you should of
known better than to ask me."

"Your sister lies——"

"Tell me no more about how my sister lies!" shouted Troublesome. "And tell me no more about the suffering of the people down there below! Wasn't it those very same people that would not *heed* my sister when she tried to warn them, and voted away the government that was holding them all together? Wasn't it?"

"Troublesome——"

"And for all my sister had done for them, was it not those very same people that showed her no more gratitude than they would a stick? That's the people we're talking about, amn't I right, Grannys? Don't you ask me to feel sorry for those people—I despise them for a pack of contemptible ignorant two-faced good-for-nothing belly-creeping *serpents,* do you hear me? If their stomachs hurt them and their backs pain them and their hearts are broken, they've asked for that, and no call to come whimpering to me! They made their beds, let them wallow in them and cry in their pillows."

"And your sister?" said Granny Hazelbide, ever so carefully, in the hush. When Troublesome got going, she gave a spectacular performance, and even the Grannys were impressed just a tad.

"It is well known," said Troublesome of Brightwater in tones of ice, "that I have no natural human feelings. My sister can rot there for all I care—not that she will, that doesn't go with it, but she's *welcome* to—and you know it perfectly well. Ask any man, woman, or tadling on Marktwain about the compassion and the warm heart of Troublesome of Brightwater and see what you get back, if you don't know it already!"

Troublesome wasn't out of breath, but she was out of patience and way beyond out of hospitality. She stood up then and ordered them off, ignoring what they said about needing to rest, stuffing a careless handful of peachapples in a sack with some cold biscuits and shoving it at them for food on the journey home, telling them where the water was safe to drink and which paths to stay shut of. Warning them of a place where the snakes were thick this time of year because of a rock that got warm each day in the sun, and all but slamming her door behind them. They were back out in the weather and the downhill trek ahead of them before they could catch their breaths, and they heard the thump of that bucket as it hit the wall when she gave it a toss across the room.

"Well!" said Granny Frostfall. "I've seen manners, and I've seen manners . . . but she does beat all. She is every last thing she's made out to be, and some left over, and I'll wager she eats nails for breakfast when she's got no company to see her."

"She has a reputation to maintain," pointed out Granny Hazelbide.

"What's important," said Granny Gableframe, "and all that matters now except for getting down this dratted mountain, is that she'll do it."

"We're sure of that, Gableframe? I don't see it!"

"Oh, we're sure," said Gableframe; and Granny Hazelbide and Granny Sherryjake agreed. "We had her the minute she asked us to tell her about it, don't you know anything atall? If she'd turned us a deaf ear, now, and refused to even listen, and sent us all packing without so much as letting us tell her why we were here . . . well, that would of been Troublesome's way."

"Oh, yes," said Granny Hazelbide. "We've got her fast, the Twelve Corners preserve us all."

"But how'll she know where to go? How to find the ship?"

"I had that all on a slip of paper before ever we started up this overblown hill," sniffed Granny Hazelbide. "And tucked away safe in the pocket of my skirt. And it's tucked away safe now in her own hand, everything she needs to know. She gave that bucket quite a fling, there at the last, and she may well pitch the bench we sat on into her fire—but she'll keep that piece of paper safe. Every last *de*tail she needs to know, it's on there."

"Law, Granny Hazelbide," said one or two. And "My stars, Hazelbide."

"Well, I know her," said the Granny. "I know her well."

"Can't say as I envy you that."

"I don't envy my *self* that, but there's times it's useful," said Granny Hazelbide. "And now let's us head for home. Might could be we'll make it before dark. Like Troublesome said, it's a sight faster going down than coming up."

3

Smalltrack was neither a supply freighter nor a pleasure craft. The smell aboard, in spite of a powerful scrubbing, made you instantly aware that it had been a fishing boat for a very long time. Having the Mule aboard didn't improve matters, since Dross had no respect whatsoever for a human being's ideas about waste disposal; she added a new fragrance to the prevailing reek of blood and entrails and ancient slime. The captain and the four men of his crew had been on workboats of one kind or another all their lives; if they noticed the smell atall, they paid it little mind. They knew themselves fortunate that it was wintry weather, and no hot sun broiling down to bring everything to a constant simmer and perk. As for their passenger, if she found conditions not to her liking, they didn't mind that atall.

If pushed, all five would have acknowledged a relish for the idea that Troublesome of Brightwater might not be all that comfortable crossing the Ocean of Storms to Kintucky in their racketydrag old boat. They didn't precisely want her to suffer, being good-natured men, but they were in mutual accord that she had a trifle discomfort coming to her. If the mechanisms of the universe saw fit to provide that discomfort without any call for their hands meddling in it, why, they found that positively Providential. It spoke to their sense of the fitness of things.

They were Marktwainers—four, including the captain, being Brightwaters by birth, and a single McDaniels finishing up the party— and they were conscious enough that the woman who spent her time silent on an upturned barrel in the stern, looking out over the rough water, was their kinswoman. It comforted Gabriel John McDaniels the 21st that he was just a tad less related to her than the other four, but they all recognized it as a burden to be borne. Relations, like poison plants and balky Mules and the occasional foolfish spoiling a catch, were part of the territory; wasn't anybody didn't have kinfolk they'd just as soon *not* of.

They'd had their instructions from the Grannys: "You leave her alone, she'll leave you alone." Same instructions as for most pesky and viperous things in this world, and they'd proved accurate enough. She sat there on her barrel by the hour, peering through hooded eyes they none of them would of cared to look into directly. If she wanted a drink of water, or something to eat, or a blanket to wrap round her strong thin shoulders, she got it without bothering any of them. If there was anything she wanted that she didn't have—and likely there was, though it was said she lived a spare and scrimped existence on her lonely mountaintop—she didn't mention it. And if a line fouled near to her, or a solar collector was wrong in its tilt, she fixed whatever was awry, without fuss and without error and with no assistance from the crew.

"Uncanny, she is," muttered Haven McDaniels Brightwater the 4th, some six hours out to sea. "Just *uncanny!*" He cleared his throat and stared up at the gray flat lid of the sky as if he was indifferent to the whole thing, just mentioning it in passing. "Can't say as how I wouldn't rather of had something else along . . . say a serpent, or maybe a Yallerhound."

Gabriel John McDaniels spat over the side to signify his disgust and demanded to know what Haven McDaniels had come *along* for, if that was the way he felt about it.

"What'd you expect?" he asked, jamming his hands into his pockets and setting his feet wide against the roll of the boat. "You expect a fine lady sitting on a tusset? With needlework to her hand, maybe, and a kerchief to her delicate little nose? That is Troublesome of Brightwater back there, just as agreed upon with the Grannys, and exactly as advertised."

"I know it," said Haven McDaniels sullenly. "You think I don't know it?"

"Well, then," Gabriel John answered him, "there's no call to comment on it. I strongly misdoubt the Grannys would of offered each of us the sum they did if we'd been taking a Yallerhound to Kintucky. We're being paid for the hazard of the thing . . . and she's rightly named, is Troublesome! Rightly named, her as could fry your heart in your chest with no more'n her two blue eyes, if she'd a mind to."

The captain heard that, and it didn't surprise him. He'd heard the rest, too, but he'd been ignoring it. One of the advantages to captaining so small a boat was that neither crew nor anybody else aboard could keep anything from him. He spoke up sharp and quick.

"That's enough of that, Gabriel John McDaniels," he rapped out. "*Days* we've got ahead of us, this trip. Bad weather and poor food and none of us truly fit . . . last thing we need here is superstitious claptrap fouling the air."

"Now, Captain—"

"I said it was *enough*. You hear me? I can speak louder, should there be call for to do so. You look to the weather, Gabriel John, and to this leaky woodbucket we travel in so precariously, and leave the tall tales to the tadlings and the Grannys. I'm purely astonished, hearing such stuff from a full-grown man, and him with four years' full service now on the water."

Gabriel John McDaniels was not impressed, and he was not about to drop his eyes to the captain. He'd not spent his own childhood roaming the Wilderness Lands of Marktwain with the man, but his *daddy* had; and many a night he'd seen the two of them with more whiskey in them than had pleased his mother. He held Captain Adam Sheridan Brightwater the 73rd in no awe.

"You're obliged to take that stand," he said, speaking right up. "We know that, all of us. But there on that nailbarrel sits the Sister and the Mother and the Great-grandmother of Evil, the Holy One help us all, and we all of us know *that*, too! If she so chooses we'll have storms and leaks; and if she don't so choose we'll have an easy journey of it. That's no tale for tadlings, now—that's same as saying the sun's more use to solar collectors than snow is."

There were two Michael Callaway Brightwaters standing near, one of them a 40th and the other a 37th, something of a nuisance in such close quarters. They hadn't much use for one another, or for Gabriel John, but they shook their heads like one man now and allowed as how he was absolutely right and the captain could leave off *his* tales any time.

"We're not fools," said the one they called Black Michael—not that his hair was any blacker than Michael Callaway the 37th's, that was called simply Michael Callaway in the ordinary fashion, but you couldn't be having them both speak up every time one was wanted. And Michael Callaway nodded, saying: "We came for the money, same as you, Captain. And what trouble we've got on our plates is trouble we bought ourselves. Complaining about it, that's not seemly; I agree to that. Howsomever, Captain, you'll do us the favor of telling us no lies, thank you very much."

The captain stared at the three of them, considering, and at the eloquent back of Haven McDaniels Brightwater the 4th, pretending to be fooling with a sail—him that had started all this—and he shrugged his shoulders.

"All right," he conceded. "I'll not dispute youall on it. I don't care for her myself . . . they say she was a child once, but I'm hard put to it to believe it. But I'll not listen to *prattle* over the matter, either, mind you. As Michael Callaway rightly says, this is our own doing, of our own free will, and talk'll change nothing. Furthermore and to go *on* with, such talk heard at the wrong end of the boat might well provoke the lady. You'll do *me* the favor of not chancing that. That's my last word!"

Truth was, he thought as he turned away from them with a set jaw intended to impress them with his firmness of purpose, the sight of her made his blood run colder than the seawater. No woman should stand six feet tall like she did; no woman should fit to a fishingboat like she'd been born on one, when she'd spent her whole life in Castle and in mountain cabin; no woman should have the dark fierce beauty that somehow flamed around her, putting him in mind of the black roses that grew near the edge of Marktwain's desert in deep summer.

Anybody'd described her to him, and him not knowing, he'd of thought she'd stir his loins. Especially out on this b'damned ocean with no other woman for many a mile and many a long lonely night. Yet when he looked at Troublesome of Brightwater, for all the sweet curve of her breasts and hips and the perfection of her face, he would of sworn he could feel his manhood shriveling in his trousers. He'd as soon of bedded a tall stake of Tinaseeh ironwood.

That didn't mean he'd tolerate a dauncy and fractious crew, whatever the feelings she raised in him or in them. He'd keep the men too busy to have time left over for mumblings and carry-ons. He wanted to get this fool trip over with—he needed the money the Grannys had come up with, and how they'd done it he couldn't imagine, but it was none the less a fool trip for all that—and he wanted to find himself back in his own bed, cosy with his own wife, that was a soft round woman more his style. With a voice like the call of an Ozark housedove just as the sun was coming up, and no more like that female in the stern than if they'd been different species altogether.

"You turn to," he barked over his shoulder at the men, "and I'll do my share, and we'll get this out of the way and be home to brag on it before we have time to think."

Nobody said "*if* we get home"; they weren't whiners. They'd been offered a fair sum of money badly needed, and they'd do the job it was offered for. Still, it was a sorry time of year to take to sea in a boat this size and age, Troublesome or no Troublesome. Had the boat been newer, that would of been a help; had it been larger, they couldn't have handled her with only the five, and that would *not* have been a good thing. It would cause a certain amount of fuss and feathers to drown five good men, for sure—but if they drowned a daughter of Castle Brightwater they'd set every Granny on Ozark whirling like a gig . . . that happen, they'd better hope they all drowned with her. It'd be more comfortable in the long run.

Behind the men, Troublesome chuckled under her breath, and Gabriel John jumped like he'd been pinched.

"Knows what we're thinking, that one does," he said flatly.

"And so does the Mule, and that doesn't bother you."

"*She* bothers me," insisted the man doggedly, "considering what I was thinking just then when she laughed."

The captain turned back and grabbed Gabriel John's shoulder in his fist. "That's one word too many," he said through his teeth. "*One word* too many! You guard your thoughts and keep 'em proper; and you sail this boat and keep your mind on your business. I don't intend to have to say any of this again."

As they'd said, there were certain stands he was obliged to take.

It happened that Troublesome did know what they were thinking. But not because of any telepathic powers, such as the Mules had, or the Magicians of Rank. No special powers were required to read those stiff backs with the muscles knotted round the necks—whopping headaches they were going to have, later on!—or the rigid shoulders, or their muttering back of their hands and out of the corners of their mouths. It amused her mightily to think that they could believe she had special skills and still be fretting about their hides; it showed a lack of common sense. After all, if this boat went down, she'd go down with it. Or perhaps it was their souls that they were really worried about, and not their hides; perhaps they thought the wickedness might blow off of her in the sea-wind and stick to them forever and ever more. She chuckled again, and watched the muscles in their backs twitch to the sound, before she turned her head to look out over the water.

She wasn't sure of what she'd seen out there, not yet. Might could be it'd been only a trick of the light slanted on the water, such as had ages back made men think dragons swam in the oceans of Old Earth. Might could be it had been the squint of her eye against that light, or her irritation of mind. There was not a single reason to believe that a creature never seen since First Landing—seen then by a group of exhausted people that might have been over given to imagining—should choose to show up a thousand years later and swim alongside her to Kintucky. It was as unlikely a happenstance as had come her way within memory, and she wasn't going to assume it for gospel too quickly.

First, she'd wait for another sight of that great tail split three ways. And then probably she'd wait for the royal purple of the thing's flesh to show up clear in the gray of the sea. And when both had happened, assuming they did happen, she'd think it over—and might could be she'd go below and swallow a dose to cure her of her mindfollies.

The Teaching Story had not one word extra to spare on the subject of the creature she half thought she'd seen. The fuel on The Ship had gone bad. Every last thing had been going from bad to worse. The time had come when it was land or die; and then just as they made a desperate plunge toward the planet below them the engines gave up completely and The Ship fell into the Outward Deeps. At which point, as the Grannys taught it:

> Even as the water closed over the dying ship and First Granny told the children to stop their caterwauling and prepare to meet their Maker with their mouths shut and their eyes open, a wonderful thing happened. Just a wonderful thing!
> Forty of them there were, shaped like the great whales of Earth, but that their tails split three ways instead of two. And their color was the royal purple, the purple of majestic sovereignty. They met The Ship as it fell, rising up in a circle as it sank toward the bottom. And they bore it up on their backs as easy as a man packs a baby, and laid it out in the shallows, where the Captain and the crew could get The Ship's door open, and everybody could wade right out of there to safety.
> They were the Wise Ones, so named by First Granny; and it may be that they live there still in the Outward Deeps. . . .

And it may be that they don't. A thousand years ago, that was, that First Granny had looked into the huge eye of one of them and seen there something she claimed at once for wisdom, and no least sign of them since in all this long time. They could certainly all have died—long, long ago. If ever they were real, that is, and not an illusion born of desperation and nourished on Grannytalk.

No other Teaching Story made mention of them, and no song; not even a scrap of a saying referred to them. It made them *most* unlikely traveling companions! Why, even the creatures of Old Earth, those left-behind ones that nobody'd seen since before the Ozarkers left their home planet, came up now and again in sayings. Take the groundhog; what a groundhog might be, Troublesome couldn't have said. There was nothing whatsoever in the computer databanks about them, nor anywhere else. But she knew easy enough from the roles groundhogs took in daily converse that they couldn't of been any kind of *hog*. "Quick as a groundhog down a hole!" the Grannys would say. "No bigger'n the ear on a groundhog!" "Saw its shadow and popped under like a groundhog!" Had to of been little, and quick, and somehow significant; you could figure that out from the scraps. But the creatures of the Outward Deeps? They were mentioned nowhere at all, and what mysterious purpose might bring one to be her escort now . . . She sighed. It wasn't reasonable; but then her ignorance was great.

Troublesome turned her head to the wind and took a deep breath of the salt air to drown out some of the fish stink, and gathered her shawls closer round her, wrinkling her nose as the blown spray spattered her face. It would come up a rain shortly, she was sure, and the men would be blaming her for it. Law, what wouldn't she give to have had the weather skills they were willing to lay to her account! Now *that* would of been of some use. Dry fields she could of watered, and high winds taking off the good topsoil she could of tempered, and where the rivers were bringing sullen rot to the roots of growing things she could of driven back the clouds and let the sun see to drying them out. There'd of been a good deal less hunger on Ozark if she'd been able to turn her hand to such work as that.

Instead of which, she thought, reality falling back over her with a thump, she was off on the wildest of goose chases, set her by seven dithering Grannys. Off to see the Lewis Motley Wommack the 33rd.

No special wonder her sister had lusted after the man and taken him so willingly to her bed. There was no prettiness to him, no softness anywhere, but he was a man to feast the hungry eyes on, not to mention a

few other senses. He gave off a kind of drawing warmth that naturally
made you want to shelter in it, male or female—as she herself gave off a
cold wind that said, *Stand Back!* If lust had been one of the emotions
known to her she might very well have fancied him her own self; in a
kind of abstract fashion, she could see that. But handy though he might
be in a bed, the idea that some act of his lay behind Responsible's sorry
condition, or that he could do anything to improve it . . . ah, that was
only foolishness. Troublesome had no hope for the journey's end; she
traveled to Kintucky for the excellent reason that she'd never been there
and might never have a second chance, and because curiosity *was* one of
the emotions she was familiar with.

There were times, in point of fact, when she found herself so curious about the workings of this world that the lack of any source to ask
questions of was almost a physical pain. At such times, there being no
purpose to such a feeling, she was grateful for the mountain to take out
her energies on, and she welcomed the work given her to do though she
understood it scarcely at all. She would go at her loom then with a
vengeance, making the shuttle fly, singing ballads so old she didn't know
what half the words meant. Unlike her sister, she could sing to pleasure
even the demanding ear, and when her audience was only birds and small
creatures she didn't mind doing it. There was nobody on the mountain
to wonder at a female singing out "I go to Troublesome to mourn and
weep" when the word was her very name, nor to pity her for the next
line all about sleeping unsatisfied, nor to wonder as she changed tunes
where Waltzing Hayme might be. She loved the queer ancient songs and
valued them far above such frippery as was sung these modern days.

Thinking of it, she very nearly began to sing, and then remembered
the five men—it would not do to have them hear her singing and carry
the tale of it back to Brightwater. She closed her lips firmly on the riddling
song she'd almost let escape, and resolved to close her mind just as tight to
the questions running round there. She'd get no answers to them in her
lifetime, and might could be it wasn't meant that humans should have those
answers. Might could be, for instance, that they were the proper knowledge of the Wise Ones, kept in trust against a time when they might be
needed. . . .

Granny Hazelbide, commenting to the little girls on the Teaching
Story about the saving of the Ozarkers at First Landing, always said the

same thing: "First Granny looked right into the eyes of one of them, just *right into its* eyes! And she said then and there, no hesitating and no pondering on it, 'They are the Wise Ones,' and no doubt that is so."

Perhaps, thought Troublesome. Perhaps. She'd seen eyes to creatures that looked to contain all the secrets of the universe. The feydeer, for example, along the ridges above timberline. They had eyes you could gaze into forever, and they had minds as empty as a shell left behind by its tenant and scoured out by a determined housewife. Rain gave them a fever that became a pneumonia and kept them few in number, but they hadn't sense enough to go down a few feet on the mountain where they could have stood beneath a tree or under a ledge out of the weather. They just waited, shaking and bedraggled, for the rain to kill them off. It gave the lie to those eyes, for all they looked so knowing.

She had a firm intention, if there was indeed a Wise One keeping this dilapidation of a boat company for some purpose of its own; and it was that intention that kept her here with her eyes fixed to the water, hour after hour. She wanted to look, her *own* self, "right into" the eye of the sea creature. It would be an eye to remember, if it were no more a gate to wisdom than the feydeer's! Judging by the tail she thought she'd caught a glimpse of, be the animal truly wise or truly foolish it was as big as this boat. The eyes would be . . . how big? The size of her head, with a pupil to match? Might could be. Law, to see that, to give it a look as it rose to dive, and to get a look back! That would be a thing to remember all her days and all her nights, and she had no intention of missing it if it came her way. She had no other chores; she would sit here and watch over the water for that exchange of glances, all the way to Kintucky and all the way back if need be.

The men turned surly eventually, as was to be expected. And after they'd seen Troublesome well onto the land the captain thought it prudent to let them talk it out of their systems while the boat rode at anchor.

They went on awhile about the various disgruntlements, allowing as how they were sorry they ever let the Grannys tempt them to this forsaken place. Allowing as how they'd never before seen a Mule swim the sea with a woman on its back and they called that witchery and they'd like to hear the captain deny them *that*. And they did a ditty on the short rations—as if they were any shorter than they'd been ashore—and another on the constant drizzling rain that had pursued them all the way and looked likely to pursue them all the way back, and they'd like to hear the captain deny them *that!*

Adam Sheridan Brightwater was wise in the ways of surly men; he denied nothing, made uninterpretable noises when they drew breath and seemed to expect a response, and let them wear themselves out. Only when they were reduced to muttering that if she hadn't been a woman, by the Holy One, they'd of gone off and left her and her bedamned Mule to fend for themselves did he add anything to the conversation. Seeing as there was no knowing how long they'd be there waiting for her, he thought it might be better to turn their minds from the idea of abandoning her in the Kintucky forests and heading for home.

"What do you suppose she was *looking* at back there all that time?" he threw out, rubbing at his beard. "That has got to be the lookingest woman ever I did see . . . and nothing to look at but water, water, and still more water. Thought her eyes would drop right out of her head."

"I don't know what it was she was staring after," Gabriel John answered him promptly, "but I know one thing—it never turned up, and she's given up on it."

"*How* do you know that?"

"Heard her. This is a mighty small boat, if you hadn't noticed that already, for keeping secrets on."

"What'd she say?" demanded Black Michael, and when Gabriel John told them they whistled long and low.

"No woman says that," declared Haven McDaniels Brightwater.

"She *did*." Gabriel John was staunch as staunch. "Right in a string, she said it, three broad words such as I never heard before at one time in the mouth of a *man*. *And* I saw her give the gunwales a kick that I doubt did her foot much good. In a right smart temper, she was!"

"We could ask her," Michael Callaway proposed.

"Ask her? You enjoy being dogbit, Michael Callaway?"

"There's no dogs on this boat, you damned fool! Mules, but no dogs. Talk sense, why don't you!"

Black Michael gave him an equally black look and smacked his thigh with the flat of his hand and called *him* a damned fool.

"You ask her a question," he said, "she'll take your head right off at the armpits! Dogbit's not a patch on it, *I* can tell you. Why, I had the uppity gall to ask her highandmightyness could I help her with a jammed *hatch,* Michael Callaway, and I near lost part of my most valuable anatomy when she flung it back at me . . . you'd of thought I'd offered to toss her skirts up and tumble her, tall scrawny gawk that she is, and I meant her only a kindness! Huh! I say leave her alone, as the Grannys directed, and be grateful if she follows suit. *W*omanbit, that's what you'll be otherwise . . . or womankicked, or womanstung, or worse!"

Captain Brightwater nodded his agreement with that as a general policy, it being somewhat more than obvious, and the nods went slowly all round.

"Maybe she'll sight whatever it was on the way back after all," he said easily. "And maybe that'll make her pleasanter to be around. We can hope."

Troublesome, doing her best to keep the branches from whipping Dross into a refusal to go on through the Kintucky Wilderness, was not expecting any such thing. The tail she'd seen again, a time or two, and a flash of purple. Sufficient to prove that the animal was there and as real as she was. But had it meant her to see anything more, had it intended a shared glance, it would have happened by now, and she'd resigned herself to that. She'd not be staring over the water on the trip back, yearning after what she was not to have.

She only hoped they'd *make* it back to Marktwain. Glad as she was that they hadn't seen their huge companion, those stalwart sailing men, and determined as she was to let slip no careless word now or later, she was astonished. It seemed to her that they might well have trouble even finding Marktwain again, it being no bigger than a continent. What kind of sailors were they, that an animal the size of their boat could swim alongside them from one side of the ocean to the other, and them never even notice it? Come time to land again, she might have to point them out the coast or they'd sail right on past.

"*Dis*gusting," she said to Dross, who said nothing back, but whuffled at her in a way Troublesome was willing to take for confirmation. "Plain disgusting!"

4

"I say we should use the lasers, and the devil take the treaties." The King of Farson Kingdom took a look at their faces and shivered in the cold, and he said it over again, louder and clearer, to be sure they'd heard him.

There'd been a day when a statement like that, all naked and unadorned and enough to shock the whiskers off a grown man's face, would have been cushioned somewhat by the rugs and draperies and furnishings of Castle Farson. No longer. The Castle had been stripped of everything that had any value, and it was nothing now but a great hulk of stone in which every word echoed and bounced from wall to wall and down the bare corridors. Any citizen choosing to look in the windows at the royal Family might do so; no curtains hung there. And the chair where Granny Dover sat pursing her lips at the King's scandalous talk was the only chair they had left; a rocker for the Granny in residence, and a courtesy to her old bones. As for the rest of them, they sat on the floor and leaned against the wall, or dragged up the rough workbenches that had once been out in the stables and now served for eating meals. When there *were* meals, which was far from always.

"Jordan Sanderleigh Farson the 23rd," said the Granny grimly—she'd never said "Your Majesty" to him nor ever would—"you've been hinting at that, and tippytoeing around that, these last three days now . . . but I never thought I'd live to hear you come right out and say it in so many words."

"And only blind luck that you *have* lived that long," the man retorted.

"No," said the old lady. "Many a thing as has changed in these terrible times, *many* a thing. Kings at Farson and Guthrie, 'stead of Masters of the Castle, as has been since First Landing and is decent and respectable! Three old fools at Castle Purdy calling themselves *Senators,* if you please, and splitting the Kingdom's governance three ways, when they never could run it even when it wasn't split and they had tradition to give 'em a clue what to do every now and again!"

"Granny, don't start," begged the King, but she paid him no mind whatsoever.

"But the day's not come yet," she went on, "when an Ozarker—always excepting the filthy Magicians of Rank, that, praise be, have had their teeth pulled anyway—when an Ozarker would raise a hand to harm a Granny. I'll be here a while yet, if we do live on weeds and bad fish. I'll be here a while."

Marycharlotte of Wommack, huddled against the draft in a corner more or less sheltered from the wind, challenged her husband and drew her shawl tighter round her shoulders.

"We gave our word," she flung at him, "as did Castles Guthrie and Purdy! We aren't degraded enough, living worse than animals in a cave—at least they have fur enough to keep them warm, or sense enough to sleep the winter out—we aren't degraded *enough?* Eating thin soup three times a day, made like the Granny says out of weeds and roots and one bad fish to a kettleful, and the Twelve Gates only knows what people not at the Castle must be living on! That's not enough for you yet? All the animals slaughtered, all the children and the old people sick, and the young ones fast joining them, that won't satisfy you men? Must we be liars and traitors as well, *before you've had enough?*"

Jordan Sanderleigh Farson turned his back on his Queen and spoke to the wall before him, down which a skinny trickle of water ran day and night from the damp and the fog.

"We cannot go on like this," he said dully.

"There's a choice?"

"We cannot go on fighting a war," answered the King, "grown men from a time when ships can travel from star to star and computers can send messages over countless thousands of miles . . . fighting a war with sticks, and boulders, and knives, and a handful of rifles meant for hunting or taken out of display cases at the museums. You should *see* it out there, you two . . . you're so smug, you should go take a long look. It's a giant foolery, entirely suitable for the comedy at a low-quality fair in a Purdy back county. Except that people are not laughing, you know. People are dying."

"I thought that's what you wanted," said Marycharlotte. "People dying."

"You made it right plain that was what you wanted, all you men," Granny Dover backed her up. "No question."

The man leaned against the wall, whether it was despair or exhaustion or both they did not know, and shouted at the two of them.

"We never had any intention that it was to drag on and on and *on* like this!" he roared. "A week or two, we thought, maybe a month or two at worst and a few hundred dead, and then it would be *over!* This isn't what we meant to have happen . . . oh, the Holy One help me in a bitter hour, it was never what was intended, never!"

The two women, the one near a hundred years old and the other in the full bloom of her years, but both little more than bones wrapped in frayed rags, they kept their silence. He looked to them for the smooth moves to comfort that he expected, the reassurance that of course it wasn't his fault and he had done all he could and more than most would of been able to; and none of that was forthcoming. They didn't *say* to stop his whining . . . but he heard it nonetheless. Jordan Sanderleigh, raised on the constant soothing words and hands of Ozark women, felt utterly abandoned. This was indeed a new day, and a new time altogether, when the women of his own household looked at him like they would a benastied three-year-old.

"Jordan Sanderleigh," said the Granny, and she measured her words out one by one and hammered them in with the tip of her cane, "when this war began, a Solemn Council was held. All the Families of Arkansaw, there assembled. And it was agreed that we were Ozarkers, not barbarians such as we left on Old Earth because we despised them worse than vermin! And it was agreed that in the name of decency, *to* which we still lay claim, I hope, no Arkansawyer would use a laser against another or against another's holdings. Signed it was, and sealed. And we'll not be the ones as goes back on it."

The man flung himself down on the nearest window ledge and closed his eyes. He remembered the occasion well. Himself, King of Farson; James John the 17th, King of Guthrie; the three Purdy Senators . . . the Granny was right that they were fools, all they could do was squabble among themselves, but they'd had dignity that day, the Purdy crest on their shoulders and their staffs of office in their hands. And the women, all absent to show their disapproval, but willing when it was over to admit that if there had to be a war it was a considerable improvement over the ancient kind for them to meet before it and set up its conditions. He had not been ashamed that day, and he had not been poor; he had been eager to get at the war, to settle once and for all the question of who should be first on Arkansaw, to be done with it and take up their lives once again. And he had been more than willing to sign that treaty banning the lasers . . . it was civilized.

"We all die, then," he said aloud. "Slowly. Like fools and lunatics."

The Granny hesitated not one second.

"So be it," she said.

"Ah, you women are hard," mourned the man.

"Ah, you men are fools. And lunatics." Marycharlotte of Wommack mocked him, matching her tones exactly to his. And he said nothing more.

Out in the ravaged Wilderness Lands of Arkansaw the struggle went on, as it had for near twelve months now. First there had been the preliminary squabbling, as each of the Castles moved to lay out that *it* should rule over all on Arkansaw henceforth, and be first among the three Kingdoms, and had thought to do that with words and threats and strutting about. There'd been no idiot behavior such as had disgraced Castle Smith, no purple velvet and ermine and jeweled scepters and Dukes and Duchesses—a King and a Queen, dressed as they'd always dressed, that had sufficed. But it had never occurred to either Farson or Guthrie that the two other Castles would argue about their obvious and predestined supremacy on the continent.

And then when it became obvious to everybody that neither Farson nor Guthrie would ever accept the other, and that Castle Purdy would never do more than wait to see which was the winner so that it could join that side, there had been the period of drawing back to the Castles to decide what was to be done. There had been the shameful ravaging of the tiny continent of Mizzurah off Arkansaw's western coast, both the Kingdoms of Lewis and of Motley, so that that land which had been the greenest and fairest of all Ozark now looked like the aftertime of a series of plagues and visitations of the wrath of some demented god. Not that Mizzurah had wanted any part in the feuds of Arkansaw, but that Arkansaw had been desperate for even Mizzurah's pitiful resources.

And then the war had broken out—with the dignified meeting first, of course, to lay down the rules—and it dragged on still. Civil war.

When the citizens of Mizzurah had been ordered to join in the fighting on Arkansaw, they had made it more than clear that no amount of harassment would bring them to any such pass, so that it had been necessary for the Arkansawyers to take the Masters of Castles Motley and Lewis and hold them hostage at Castle Guthrie as surety against their people's obedience.

And now the men of Mizzurah fought alongside the men of Arkansaw, divided up three ways among the three Castles as was fair and proper, since it was that or see the hostages hung, or worse; but they spoke not one word, and they never would. In silence, they drew their knives, that had been intended for the merciful killing of herdbeasts, and used them on other Ozarkers as they were commanded, excepting always the delicate care they used to be sure they raised no hand against another Mizzuran. In the same silence they dropped great boulders from Arkansaw's cliffs down on columns of climbing men, and threw staffs of Tinaseeh ironwood to pin men against those cliffs for a death not one of them would have inflicted on *any* animal. The officers had the few rifles, and no Mizzuran was an officer, which meant they had no shooting to do, and that was probably just as well. The Lewises were without question the best shots on Ozark, having always fancied the sport of shooting at targets, and keeping it up over the centuries when most of the Families had let the skill fall away into disuse.

The Mizzurah women fought beside their men, those not required back at home to care for tadlings and babes. "If the men must go, we go also," they'd said, and the women of Arkansaw, that would have nothing to do with the civil war among their men themselves, had nodded their heads in approval. It was fitting, and they would have done the same, had the situations been the same. They had been much embarrassed when a Purdy female, a tad confused about what was after all a complicated ethical question, took up an ironwood staff and marched off to join her older brother in the Battle of Saints Beard Creek; and it was the women of Castle Farson, happening to be closest, that had gone out and got the fool creature and brought her back to a willow switch across her bare buttocks, for all she was sixteen years of age. If that was what it took to make things clear at Castle Purdy, that was what it took, and they had not scrupled to do it.

Thirty men, two of them Mizzurans, were dug in at a mine entrance near the border of Farson Kingdom under the command of Nicholas Andrew Guthrie the 41st, on this day. Three days they'd been there now, and though water was plentiful it was fouled—that'd be the work of the Purdys, upstream—and the food was gone since the night before.

Their leader stared sullenly into the drizzle, and sat in the slimy packed layers of wet leaves at the mine-mouth, and would not be persuaded to go inside where it was at least dry.

"The sentries have to stay out here," he pointed out.

"You're not a sentry."

"All the same."

"It's foolishness," objected another Guthrie, close kin enough to offer open criticism regardless of rank. "What'll you gain that way, except pneumonia?"

"Pneumonia," said Nicholas Andrew Guthrie. "And I'll welcome it. Rather die that way than most of the other possibilities . . . at least it's an honorable death."

"Not if you leave your men without a leader by catching it, you blamed pigheaded fool!"

Nicholas Andrew Guthrie didn't even turn his head.

"What you talk there is the talk of a war that's real," he said, and spat to show his disgust. "This is no real war, and I'm no real leader, and youall're no real soldiers. And you'd be no more leaderless without me than you are while I sit here and court the passing germs, so shut your mouth."

"That's inspiring talk," said his cousin. "Really makes us all feel like throwing ourselves into the heat of battle, let me tell *you*."

"You want inspiration," said Nicholas Andrew, "you go home and get some. You'll get none out here. Here, you've got nothing whatsoever to do but wait for a Farson, or might could be some pitiful Purdy, lost as usual, to show up, so you can stick him through the gut with whatever's handy, or him you. Might could be you'd even have the privilege of doing your gutsticking on a Mizzurah woman, just for the variety of the thing. And everybody can cut one more notch on the timber nearest them to signify the occasion. That inspire you? It doesn't inspire me, not the least bit."

There was a long silence, broken only by the constant nameless noise the drizzle made. And then a man spoke from behind them. "How many do you reckon there are left of us?" He had a festering sore on his leg, that would get no better in this damp, and a bandage to his shoulder, and he leaned against the mine wall to keep from falling. "How many, sir?"

My brave and stalwart company, thought Nicholas Andrew wryly. *My company of walking dead. Flourish of trumpets, roll of drums, off left.* Aloud, he said he didn't know.

"What with the bad food, and the sickness there's neither magic nor medicine to treat, and what with the cold, and this bleeding twelvesquare excuse for a war . . . there might could be two thousand of us, all told."

"Two thousand, Nicholas Andrew Guthrie!" The man staggered and clutched at nothing, and somebody moved quickly to grab the shoulder that wasn't hurt.

"Come on, now," said the kinsman hastily, "you don't mean that, and it's a downright cruel thing to say."

"Well, I stand by it," snapped Nicholas Andrew. "And if only a Purdy or a Farson'd come by this place, might could be we'd be able to make that one thousand nine hundred and ninety-nine."

There was silence behind him again, and he hoped it would last this time; he had no heart for talking to them. The figure he'd named was a blind guess, but it could not be much more than that. Taking it in round numbers, there'd been ninety thousand of them when this began; fifty thousand Guthries, twenty thousand Farsons, and twenty thousand Purdys. At least sixteen thousand Lewises and Motleys combined, he'd hazard. And what was left would hardly make one good-sized village . . . and nothing gained for it, nor nothing *ever* to be gained. Over those centuries when violence was just something in stories and songs around the fire, and an evil something at that, the Ozarkers had forgotten what their native stubbornness would mean if it were put to violent purposes.

It meant nobody would ever yield. It meant nobody would ever give up, ever say, "All *right,* let's stop before every last one of us is dead in this mess. All *right—you* can be the winner, if that's what it takes to stop this!"

It would never happen. When only two Arkansawyers of different Kingdoms still remained alive on this land, they would be fighting hand to hand—with two rocks, if that was all they had left to fight with, as seemed likely. And it would be a fight to the death. It seemed sometimes that somebody ought to of remembered, when it started, what a war would be like when there could be *no giving up ever* . . . but nobody had.

The Gentles had no doubt gone deep into the bowels of the earth; not one had been seen since the first day of the fighting. And if they simply waited there long enough, they would have Arkansaw back for their own again, what was left of it, without a single Ozarker to trouble them.

"I think I hear something," whispered a boy at his side, crawling up close to whisper it in his ear. "Want I should go take a look?"

"You step outside this mine-mouth," said Nicholas Andrew flatly, and right out loud, "and provided you did indeed 'hear something' you'll be picked off before your beautiful blue eyes can blink twice."

"Oh . . . I thought I could get out there, quick-like, and scout around."

Nicholas Andrew was so weary of explaining what two and two added up to, and explaining it to babes barely out of their diapers . . . He drew a long breath, and tried to sound patient.

"Supposing you did hear something, son," he said, "and supposing it was a human being and one fighting against us. Either he'll stay where he is, which'll do us no harm, or he'll come out into the open where we can pick him off from here—which'll do us no harm. If he made a noise, you can be sure the idea was to get one of *us* to come out and be picked off. Otherwise, he'd of kept quiet. You follow all that?"

"Yes, sir," said the boy. "Yes, sir, I do. I expect I'm mighty ignorant."

"I expect you're mighty young," said Nicholas Andrew. "Now get back inside where it's safer."

Ignorance. He thought about ignorance. His own military training had been composed of a speech made to a couple dozen like him. They'd all been told that war wasn't much different from hunting, always excepting what the quarry was, and that they'd been picked for their natural qualities of leadership and their good health, and that they were expected to use their common sense. That had been the sum total of it.

At Castle Guthrie the state of despair was not quite so complete as it was out in the Wilderness Lands or at the other two Castles. Castle Guthrie had been richest to begin with; it was richest still, though its poverty was astonishing. And it had the two hostages, two living symbols that some real action had once been taken—Salem Sheridan Lewis the 43rd, and Halbreth Nicholas Smith the 12th, him as was husband to Diamond of Motley and Master of Motley Castle. Whether he would have stayed on as Master there after the Confederation of Continents was dissolved, or gone back to Smith Kingdom to join his kin, there'd not been time for anybody to find out. Before the issue could be resolved, he'd found himself hostage here; and might could be there were times when he was thankful for the curious chance of it. It would not of been easy for him to choose between his own household—his wife and his children—and his kin. Especially when his kin were known to out-Purdy the Purdys for stupidity.

Around the one fire they had burning in the Castle, the Guthries sat in Council. James John Guthrie the 17th, another threadbare King; Myrrh of Guthrie, his sixth cousin and his queen as well; Michael Stepforth Guthrie the 11th, Magician of Rank (for all that signified these days); three older sons and an odd cousin or two.

They were not discussing the possibility of bringing into this war the cruel and efficient lasers, of which every Arkansaw Family had a plentiful supply, used to shape Tinaseeh ironwood and work Arkansaw mines and quite capable of cutting a man into strips no thicker than a sheet of pliofilm. They were not yet reduced to considering such measures, unlike the Farsons, for they had one hole card left to them still. They were discussing the question of whether a Guthrie ship might be put to use.

"We only have men enough left to send one medium-sized ship, maybe a Class C freighter," Michael Stepforth was saying, "but one is all we ought to need, and a Class C quite big enough. We send it in to Brightwater Landing, we take the Castle, we get ourselves a computer and a comset transmitter and three or four technicians that know how to assemble and run those, grab whatever they tell us we have to have in the way of equipment—and back we come. Why not?"

"You think Brightwater'd let us get away with that?" demanded Myrrh of Guthrie. "It's a far sight from being what I'd call a *secret* operation."

"We don't have any reason to believe Brightwater even knows there *is* war on Arkansaw," said her husband. He gave the high stone hearth an irritated kick with the toe of his boot, and then did it again for good measure. "For all they know, we're fat and prosperous over here, living peacefully and respectably, sitting round the tables tossing off strawberry wine and reminiscing about the olden days."

"Goatflop," pronounced Granny Stillmeadow. Elegance had never been her strong suit. "I suppose they think snow doesn't fall here, nor diphtheria touch the babies, nor rivers ever go to flood, nor any *other* such ordinary human catastrophes. I suppose they think we Arkansawyers are immune to all such truck. Goatflop!"

"All right," said the King, "I'll grant you that's not reasonable. I'll grant you that wasn't the brightest speech I ever made."

"That's mighty becoming of you," snorted the Granny. "Seeing as how it was beyond question the *stupidest* speech you ever made, and not for lack of other examples to choose from."

"Granny Stillmeadow," said the man, "you can granny at me all you like, and no doubt I deserve it. But it still holds that they have no reason, none whatsoever, to be suspicious of one of our ships at their Landing. If they think we're starving over here, they'll be just that more likely to think we've come to beg for food, and I say *let* them—just so as we get inside the Castle."

They thought about that a while. It was true, there'd been no communication between the other continents and Arkansaw—it was barely possible that, with the comsets out and the Mules not flying, the war on Arkansaw was as much a secret to the Brightwaters as conditions on Kintucky were to the Families of Arkansaw. It was not something you could test, one way or the other. The war took up so much of *their* minds that there was a sneaking tendency to consider it the major preoccupation of everyone else on Ozark as well . . . but that was clearly foolish. Childish. Might could be everybody knew, and what they thought of it would not be anything to pleasure the ear. And might could be nobody knew except the sorry citizens of Mizzurah, that had suffered its effects directly. There was no way of knowing.

And it was true that nobody but Brightwater and Guthrie had had ships of a size adequate for ocean transport, and Guthrie still had its ships; putting one of them to use was something open to them, however much it might strain the last fragments of their supplies and energies.

"Think, Granny Stillmeadow," said Michael Stepforth Guthrie. "Think what it would mean, if it worked."

"With computers, and computer technicians to run them, we'd have just enough of an edge," put in one of the sons. "Just enough to turn things around, Granny."

Yes. They would be able to offer the remnants of the population of Arkansaw quite a few things, if they had the computers. And *do* to them quite a few things, if they seemed reluctant to accept the benefits offered.

"It's everything wagered on one throw," said Granny Stillmeadow, "I remind you of that. We might send a ship once; we might get into the Castle once . . . but there's only the once. And I remind you that even that piddling chance is a matter of pure ignorant luck, no more! We've not so much as a Housekeeping Spell to set behind it as a prop-up, don't you forget that!"

"So? Our luck is not as good as anybody else's?"

The Granny made a noise like a Mule whuffling, and brought her knitting needles to a full stop, and stared at him in a mixture of contempt and disbelief that had an eloquence words would be hard put to it to match.

"Coming from you, Michael Stepforth," put in Myrrh of Guthrie, "that *does* sound half-witted. I'll back the Granny on that. We may all have started even, so far as luck was concerned, when we began this— everything fair and square. But when we brought the Masters of Lewis and Motley into this Castle and put them under guard, them as had no quarrel with us nor ever wanted any, nor ever raised a hand against any Arkansawyer . . . then we changed that luck considerably."

"Purdy and Farson were in on that, too!"

"Purdy and Farson don't have the hostages—Castle Guthrie has them," said the Granny grimly. "A Guthrie stands guard by their doors. A Guthrie takes them their rations, and checks to be sure their bonds are adequate. Not a Purdy, my friends, not a Farson—that is our *personal* contribution, done on our own resolve, and volunteered for, as I recollect. Nobody forced it on us. And for *that,* you mark my words, we will pay."

"We *have* paid!" James John Guthrie looked more a madman than a monarch, roaring at the Granny and shaking his fists. But she was not impressed one whit.

"And we will pay more," she told him. "I wouldn't send a rowboat across a rain puddle myself, the way the Universe is stacked against this Family at this particular point in time. As for taking all the men we have left as are strong enough to fight, and all the supplies called for to last them to Brightwater, and sending them off in a ship across the Ocean of Remembrances? Pheeyeew! Why not go dig up a Gentle and shoot it, James John Guthrie? Why not jump off the Castle *roof,* for that matter, and be done with it? It'd be quicker and cleaner."

The Granny shoved her rocker back and stood up, very slowly and carefully. Her arthritis was tormenting her, and she had a crick in her neck that was about to drive her wild, from staring up at the Guthrie men while she tongue-lashed them.

"You think it over good and long before you decide," she said, trying not to let the pain overrule the contempt in her voice as she struggled to straighten her spine. "You think it over good and long and thorough.

Might could be you ought to pray over it, too—I know *I* would. Take yourselves down to where Salem Sheridan Lewis the 43rd, that good man, that *honorable* man, sits a prisoner in your Castle, and ask him to pray with you. . . . I reckon you've forgotten how, these many days past. And when your minds are made up, do me a favor—keep it to your own selves. If you decide on any such folly as that expedition off to Never-never Land, don't you tell me about it; I don't care to know."

"Granny Stillmeadow," sighed the King of Guthrie, "you're no help at all, you know that?"

"I should hope I am not any help to you, I never intended to be for one *instant!* Myrrh of Guthrie, you plan to sit there and listen to these idiot males go on with their claptrap, or you want to come with me and see if there's maybe some small thing we can do upstairs for that tadling down with the fever?"

Myrrh of Guthrie looked around her once, and then she didn't hesitate.

"I'll be right with you, Granny," she said.

"I'll go on ahead," said Granny Stillmeadow. "The air's cleaner outside this room."

And with that she turned around and stalked out, leaning on her cane and striking the floor with it every step like a stick coming down hard on a drumhead. There was no possibility of mistaking the Granny's opinion of them. Even with nothing to go on but the sight of her aching back.

5

Lewis Motley Wommack the 33rd was feeling reasonably content with his lot. He would have gone to some pains not to admit it, since the rest of the population was of a much different mind, but he found the current spartan regime exactly to his taste. The rooms of Castle Wommack—all four hundred of them—had always given him a vague feeling of claustrophobia; he knew why now. It had been all that furniture. The massive benches lining every hall, and the huge tapestries behind them. The draperies that you could have easily made a tent for five or six people out of, with the green velvet with twelve inches of gold fringe . . . and the occasional variety of *gold* velvet, with twelve inches of green fringe. The vases of flowers and the paintings in their heavy frames, and the thick carpets, all four hundred of *them* . . . no, he took that back. There had never been carpets in the kitchens. Make it three hundred and ninety-seven carpets. He had been smothered by all that, but he hadn't realized it; after all, in rooms thirty feet square, with fourteen-foot ceilings, the furnishings had been scattered around in a lot of empty space—as he recalled, there'd been a deliberate effort expressed by his cousin Gilead to keep the Castle's decoration "spare." That had been her word, and he'd assumed it had some congruence with reality.

But now that it was all gone he realized that he could at last breathe freely. He liked the feel of the bare stone floors under his feet, and the look of the arched high windows open to the air and sky. He no longer felt that he had to go out and pace the balconies in the middle of the night, he was contented to pace his own almost empty room instead.

As for his once elegant wardrobe, now only a memory, and the diet of grains and root vegetables and ingeniously concocted soups that had replaced the roasts and stuffings and steaks and lavish desserts . . . he had never cared about such things anyway.

And at the moment he had several specific things to be happy about. There was, for instance, the blissful ease of his mind. At first he had been like the man with a toothache that comes and goes, always braced for the next twinge out of nowhere. Now, enough time had gone by since the last intrusion from Responsible of Brightwater that he felt *secure* in his privacy. She had been a parasite coiled in his head, never mind how many hundreds of miles of physical space separated them, and he had lived in constant dread of the stirring of that . . . thing . . . within him; it was gone, praise the Twelve Gates and the Twelve Corners, forever.

And there was the fact that Thomas Lincoln Wommack the 9th was now Master of this Castle, and had lifted from Lewis Motley's unwilling neck the burden of Guardianship that had chafed it so mightily since the death of Thomas Lincoln's father. He had detested being Guardian, and everything that went with it—all that constant fiddling detail—and he was firmly determined that never again would he have to administer so much as a dollhouse, or be responsible for anything more than his own person. His sister Jewel had the Teaching Order that had replaced the old comset educational system well in hand, and showed a natural talent for administration that he recognized as invaluable. He didn't even have to worry about *that*.

Bliss, basically. Impoverished bliss, perhaps, and a nagging concern for the problems of sickness and crop failures and the like that plagued Kintucky—but it had to be admitted that all of that was out of his hands and beyond his power to alter in any way. What he could do, he did; mostly, it amounted to encouraging Jewel of Wommack and her flock of Teachers in *their* efforts, all far more productive than his could have been. The ways they found to stretch supplies, and the things they thought of when there was pain to be eased . . . He admired it, loudly and openly and enthusiastically. And he thanked the Powers that none of it required anything more of him personally than that unflagging enthusiasm. Enthusiasm, he could always produce.

Thinking about it, a bowl of hot oats and half a cup of milk comforting his stomach, he leaned back in his chair and put his feet up on his desk, folded his arms behind his head, and sighed a long sigh of satisfaction.

At which point, his door flew open without so much as a warning knock, and he found himself facing a woman taller than he was, thinner than he was, and looking much the worse for wear, though it was clear she was beautiful underneath the scrapes and the grime. It took him only a couple of minutes to recognize Troublesome of Brightwater—there was only one woman on the planet who looked like she looked—and that was such a shock that he leaped to his feet and knocked his chair over in the process.

"Uhhhh . . . Troublesome of Brightwater!" he managed, and bent to pick up the chair and set it right.

"As you live and breathe," she said.

"Well, I know it wasn't exactly a fanfare and a red carpet, Troublesome, but you took me by surprise. I thought you spent all your time on top of a mountain and never came down except for emergencies . . . like clearing a pack of rats and weasels out of Confederation Hall, for example. Not to mention that however in the world you got *here,* all the way from Brightwater, is beyond me. Surely you didn't expect me not to be surprised?"

"May I come in or not?" Troublesome demanded. "Finding you wasn't easy, young man, and I'm sick of prowling your halls in search of your august presence."

"Please do come in," said Lewis Motley readily enough. "I'm . . . well, no, I can't say I'm delighted to see you. We'll no doubt end by regretting that you dropped by, I'm aware of that. But I am most assuredly *interested* to see you. . . . Do come in, and sit down."

Troublesome's eyes flicked over the room, and she clucked her tongue in amazement.

"What is it?"

"All this furniture." She stepped inside and closed the door behind her. "Brightwater's got a rocker for the Grannys, and beds all around, and that's about it. Everything else has gone for firewood long ago."

"I was just thinking how *bare* it was. And how much I liked it bare."

"A matter of your point of view, I expect," said Troublesome. "It looks mighty grand to this pair of eyes."

"You're on Kintucky," he reminded her. "How, I don't know— we'll come back to that. But on Kintucky we could burn fires day and night for a hundred years and we'd still only have cut down the undergrowth. If we could eat trees, we'd be well fed here."

Troublesome reached for the offered chair, turned it backwards so she could lean her arms and chin on its back, and stared at him until he began to feel uncomfortable. And then it dawned on him why he felt that way, and he hollered till he got a servingmaid's attention and told her to bring up some food and drink.

"Not that it'll be much," he warned her. "Bread, I expect. And coffee, if we're lucky and Gilead's set some by for the odd special occasion."

"Considering it's been near on two days since I've had anything but water . . . and you do have glorious water on Kentucky, I meant to comment on that . . . I'm not likely to complain. And the Mule I left in your stable was not the least bit ungrateful for what he was getting there."

"The Mule," mused Lewis Motley Wommack. "You came in by Mule, did you? Now, Troublesome, I don't mean to seem to doubt your word, but—"

"Just from the coast," she sighed. "One leg after another, solid on the ground. The rest of the trip was in a pathetic beerkeg that's got the nerve to call itself a ship, and for which the only good word I've got to offer is that it didn't sink on the way over here. No doubt it'll make up for that oversight on the trip back, always providing it'll still even *be* there when the Mule and I trek back down to the shore. No, Lewis Motley Wommack, I am not claiming I can get a Mule to fly; I had trouble enough getting it to move at all."

"Well, it might have been that you could. Considering your reputation."

Troublesome let that pass, and he went on.

"*Will* you tell me why you're here and how you got here?" he insisted; he was rapidly running out of patience. "It's about as likely as a goat playing a dulcimer, you know. I think I'm entitled to an explanation."

"Passel of Grannys sent me," said Troublesome. "They near killed themselves, poor old things, getting up Mount Troublesome to talk me into it and then back down again. And they used up everything they had left in this world to bribe the captain of that purely pathetic boat and his patheticker crew, and putting together supplies enough for this carry-on. The supplies they meant me to have while I rode the Mule here, those *I* left for bribe, along with a trinket or two, to keep my trusty friends from heading back to Brightwater and stranding me here. And the Holy One defend them if they do strand me . . . if I have to *swim* back, I'll find them, every last one of them, and they'll rue the day they ever did any such a misbegotten trashy thing."

"Oh, they'll be there," said Lewis Motley.

"You think so?"

"You put it very well," he said, looking at the ceiling. "I doubt very much they'd care to have your lifelong vengeance on their coattails, Troublesome of Brightwater."

"Let us hope you are right," said Troublesome grimly. "For their sakes, and everybody else's."

"How does everybody else figure into it?" he asked, and she passed along the Grannys' tale to him, while he sat there shaking his head. For a while it was his wonderment at the Grannys going to all this trouble and expense, and Troublesome going along with it, for no more motivation than some old tea leaves and a gold ring on a thread in a stray wind. And then when it began to be clear to him that it had to do with Responsible of Brightwater, it was his dis-ease at the position he was being put in. True, this was Responsible's infamous sister; and true, if there was anything bodacious to do, she'd either done it or invented it. But there was such a thing as tattling, and there were certain kinds of tattling that were even more despicable than other kinds, and he felt like a skinnywiggler on a hot rock before she got to the end of it.

"Hmmmmm," he said, by way of response, and fooled around with his beard some. And then "hmmmm" again.

Troublesome gave him a measuring glance, and cleared her throat. "If it's your gallantry as is causing you pain, Lewis Motley, you can set that aside. The Grannys already told me Responsible lost her maidenhead during the Jubilee, and seeing as how you were there at the time and footloose, and seeing as how you are the most spectacular example of manflesh *I* ever laid eyes on, I do believe I can add up two and two and come out with four. And if I already know you were bedding my sister, we can perhaps just acknowledge that and move on to something more significant."

Lewis Motley cleared *his* throat, and blessed the fates that had put this female on Brightwater and him clear across an ocean away from her.

"Well?" she asked him. "Does that simplify matters for you some?"

"It does," he began, and was much gratified that the serving-maid came in just then with the bread and the coffee and gave him a chance to collect himself.

"Yes," he said again, when he'd got his breath back. He took a drink of the coffee and made a face; it wasn't much more than troubled water, weak the way they made it to stretch the last of the beans, and grain added in with a liberal hand. "That was abrupt, but it did ease my mind. I wouldn't have felt justified in telling you that, but if you know it already we've cleared the air. Now what *exactly* is the question the Grannys think I know the answer to? Because I warn you, Troublesome of Brightwater —I doubt it."

Over her shoulder he saw the flash of a long robe in the hall, through the door the servingmaid had left decently open instead of shut tight as she'd been shocked to find it, and he called out for his sister to join them. He knew the look of that robe, though he wasn't aware it was exactly the color of his eyes, by a frayed place at the back of the hem that came from too many hours spent on Muleback. It would be useful to have his sister here as a buffer between himself and Troublesome, now the indelicate part of the conversation was past; furthermore, he enjoyed showing her off.

"Jewel!" he called to her. "We've got company—come see!"

"Company?" She stepped in the door, one hand on the sill, the long sweep of her sleeve falling almost to the floor. "Are you wasting my time with foolishness again, Lewis Motley?"

Troublesome gasped, and clapped both hands to her mouth, and through her fingers she said, "Jewel of Wommack, I declare I never in all this world would of known you!"

The grave eyes of a woman grown looked back at her, that had been a child's eyes so short a time ago, calm, and possessed of a natural authority. The copper hair was hidden away completely under the wimple, and most of the face as well, but Jewel was all the more beautiful for the mystery the Teacher's habit lent her. For the first time she could remember, Troublesome of Brightwater was uncomfortably aware that she herself could do with a change of clothes and a tidy-up.

"Troublesome of Brightwater," said the Teacher, the first of all the Teachers. "I never thought to see you again, and now here you are. . . . What brings you here?"

"She's just about to set me a question," said her brother. "Sent here by the Grannys of Marktwain assembled, on a mountaintop no less, for that precise purpose. You sit down with us, sister mine, and have a cup of this terrible coffee, and if I can't answer the question perhaps you can help me a tad.

"It has to do with Responsible of Brightwater," he added, as if it were an afterthought of an afterthought, and he watched Jewel's lashes drop to shield her eyes as she took the third chair and poured her coffee.

"The Grannys know full well," said Troublesome, seeing no reason to waste time, "that the magic they were able to do was done on mighty puny power. But they were sure enough they were right to put this expedition of one together, and sure enough to convince me to try it. Jewel of Wommack, they are of the opinion that your brother knows how it came about that Responsible of Brightwater has been in a sleep like unto death these past two years. And if he knows that, they believe, it just might could be he'll also know how she can be waked up."

She looked at the man, in a silence so thick she could have stirred it with her coffee spoon, and then at his sister, and her heart sank.

"Ah, Dozens!" she said despairingly. "Dozens! You didn't even *know*, did you? I can tell, just looking at you! Without the comsets, and Kintucky out here on the edge of nowhere, and no travelers anymore . . . I suppose nobody on Kintucky knows. Ah, the waste of all this! Bloody Bleeding *Dozens!*"

Lewis Motley was so taken aback he couldn't have spoken a word, or moved, but Jewel of Wommack reached over and took the other woman's hand in both of hers.

"Tell us," she said, in the voice that every Teacher was trained to use, or sent to do research and keep out of the classrooms if she couldn't. It was a voice that could not be disobeyed because it left no possible space for disobedience.

"My sister," said Troublesome, and because the exhaustion in her face frightened both the Wommacks, Lewis Motley shouted again for a servingmaid and demanded the last of their whiskey, "just into summertime, after the Jubilee, fell into a kind of sleep. Or a coma. . . . To look at her, you would think she was dead, but she has no sickness, and the name Veritas Truebreed Motley puts to it is *pseudocoma*. Just a sleep that does not end and cannot, so far as we've been able to tell, be ended. And since the day it began, everything has gone from bad to worse on Marktwain and Oklahomah; we hear there is *war* on Arkansaw. What may be going on in the rest of the world nobody knows . . . or even if there is a rest of the world any longer. Since the trouble started with whatever happened to my sister, the Grannys are convinced that there's a connection there—that if we could wake Responsible there would be hope for Ozark again. And they were certain—certain sure!—that Lewis Motley Wommack had the key to it. . . . Law, but they're going to be in a state over this, and I don't blame them, I don't blame them one least bit!"

"Just a minute, Troublesome," said Jewel.

"If Lewis Motley Wommack didn't even know about this," insisted Troublesome, "then the Grannys have made a mistake to end all mistakes, and a minute—nor a dozen minutes—won't change that."

The servingmaid came running with the whiskey, and Jewel poured it out with a level hand and passed Troublesome of Brightwater the glass.

"You drink that," she said calmly. "And then, let's us *ask* him. Before we decide to speak of mistakes and waste and the end of the world, let's just ask him. Might could be he knows more than you think he knows, provided the questions are put to him properly."

Lewis Motley had his whole face buried in his hands, and they could see the muscles of his arms straining under the cloth of his sleeves.

"Never mind throwing chairs, dear brother," warned Jewel emphatically, keeping a wary eye on him. "This is not the time nor the place."

"Curse them!"

The bellow shook the lamp hanging above their heads, and although neither Troublesome nor Jewel jumped, they both had to grip their chairs not to.

"Curse them all, the *idiots!* I never had any such thing in mind—they must all have been crazy! Oh, if I could only get my hands on them, if I could just—"

Troublesome looked at Jewel of Wommack. "He knows something," she said, over the din. "He knows something after all."

"He knows everything, from the sound of his conniption fit," said Jewel coldly. "Now it's just a matter of getting it out of him . . . once he's worn himself out. Talk of *women* having hysterics!"

"I've been a damned fool," said her brother.

"Not for the first time, nor yet the hundred and first."

"But this time is exceptional."

"Then the sooner it's admitted to, the sooner we'll know if it can be mended. I suggest you tell us what you've gone and done, Lewis Motley."

"Can I have some of that whiskey?"

"You can *not*. That's for medicine, and precious little we have left of it! There's nothing wrong with you but temper, and if you haven't died of temper before this you won't die of it today. Just speak up."

Lewis Motley sighed a long sigh, and began. "Your sister," he said to Troublesome, "was causing me a good deal of . . . misery."

Troublesome was dumbfounded.

"Misery? In what way, causing you misery? She was clear back on Marktwain, you were all the way over here on Kintucky."

"I hesitate to say it of her—"

"Say it!" commanded Troublesome.

"Your sister would not grant me privacy of mind," he said then, and the words fell, quaint and formal, in the stillness of the room.

"Lewis Motley," said Jewel simply, "you are either mocking us or you are stalling for time, and whichever one it is, it's not to be borne."

"No, I am not!" he protested. "Responsible of Brightwater *mind-spoke me*"—she had gone far beyond just mindspeech, but he would not talk of that before two women, even to defend his actions—"every day, day after day after day, till I was nearly mad with it. I would be sitting working, I would be eating, I'd be seeing to a problem in the stables, I'd be talking as I am now, with one of the Family . . . and suddenly she was there, in my mind." He shuddered. "There've been many females that tried to tag along after me, but they had at least the decency to do it in the flesh, where a person could see them and have a fair chance at getting away. Not Responsible of Brightwater! Oh no—not that one."

"And so you did what?" Troublesome held her breath, waiting.

"I sent for the Magicians of Rank, and asked them all to come here on a matter concerning Miss Responsible of Brightwater, which they were willing enough to do, let me tell you; and I told them what she'd done—because she'd gone far, far *past* the bounds of decency—and I asked them to make her stop. *That's* what I did. But not for the smallest wrinkle of time did I intend anything of the sort you've described to me, Troublesome. I meant them to reason with her, threaten her perhaps, set a small Spell on her . . . just stop her unspeakable mucking about in *my mind!* Never did I mean them to hurt her. . . . Jewel, tell her. Little sister, explain to this woman that I never meant them to do her harm."

Jewel of Wommack nodded, her eyes the color of river ice in late afternoon.

"He is mischief incarnate," she said slowly, in grave agreement, "but he would not do anybody deliberate harm. He simply does not *think*— he never did. And now, because of his selfish temper, if the Grannys are right we have this dreadful time of trouble all to be laid at my brother's feet. For all time. Congratulations, to the Wommack Curse!"

Troublesome gnawed at the end of her thick black braid, dust and leaves and all, a gesture Thorn of Guthrie had tried in vain to break her of.

"Lewis Motley Wommack," she said carefully, "what did Responsible say to you when you asked her to stop it? Did she just refuse, say no, flat out with no explanation? That's not like her . . . not that any of it is like her . . . but what did she *say* to you?"

The man's face went cold and hard, and now it was Jewel's turn to clap her hands to her mouth, because she suddenly understood, before the answer came.

"I never asked her," he told them, voice like granite and a face to match. "She was *in* my mind; she knew how it repulsed me. . . . It would have been a very cold day in a truly hot place before I stooped to beg that vile little—before I stooped to ask Responsible of Brightwater to stop her foul behavior. *Ask* her, indeed—what do you think I am?"

Troublesome stood up and went over to a window, turned her back on him and on the Teacher, and stood staring out into the tangled woods beyond. She was shaking from head to foot, and her teeth gritted to keep them from chattering, in spite of the whiskey, and not until she had it under control did she turn round again, even through the spectacular bout of tongue lashing that Jewel of Wommack turned on Lewis Motley with. He had been told in baroque detail what an utter, despicable, pathetic, unspeakable, pigheaded, stupid, fool *male* he was, with elaborations and codas and emendations to spare, before Troublesome said another word. And when she did speak, her voice was hoarse with rage restrained.

"Lewis Motley Wommack," she said, "I cannot explain this, and I shan't try. I have no way of knowing the truth of it; I never knew even that Responsible had the skill of mindspeech. But I swear to you, and I know whereof I speak: my sister would never have knowingly done what you say she did. If she did it, she was bewitched, or mad, or anything else you fancy—but she would not have *done* that. Saving only Granny Graylady, there's not an Ozarker alive more scupulous about privacy than my sister. And you . . . you never even asked her. You couldn't *stoop,* to one small question. Lewis Motley, I would not be you and bear the burden of guilt that you will bear. Not for any power in this Universe."

"I tell you—" he began, but Jewel's hand came down hard on his arm and silenced him.

"You've told us," said Troublesome. "You've told us all I care to hear from you. You've answered the question I came to ask, and the Grannys were right. It took all the Magicians of Rank to put my sister to sleep, apparently; it will no doubt take all of them together now to wake her up. *All* of them; now when the ships are not running the oceans, and the Mules are not flying, and the Magicians of Rank are scattered to the four corners of the world . . . four of them somewhere in the wilds of Tinaseeh, if they still breathe. And somehow, we will have to get them all together at Brightwater and have them undo this awful thing. And I'd best get on with it. The crew was half mutinous all the way here. Not a cloud came up they didn't charge me with having caused it just by being on their leaky old rowboat—I'm not anxious to leave them waiting for me any longer on your coast."

"I'll ride with you," said Lewis Motley at once. "I know the shortest ways—we'll save time."

Jewel of Wommack stood up, put one slender finger in her brother's chest, and pushed. It was a measure of his state of mind that it brought him to a full stop; ordinarily, he was about as easy to stop as an earthquake.

"You will not," she said flatly. "You've done enough. You've done so much more than enough already, my beloved brother, that your name will go down in history—be satisfied with that. You may well have destroyed an entire world for the sake of your pride—be satisfied with that. And I will ride with Troublesome of Brightwater to the coast to see if her ship has waited for her. And if it hasn't, I will see to it that a way is found to get her home, if I must call in every man still able-bodied on Kintucky to turn his hand to shipbuilding."

"I would feel better if—"

"No doubt you would!" she cut him off. "I haven't any interest in you feeling better. You have a lifetime ahead of you to spend trying to ease your guilt, but *I'll* not help you! And besides that, they wouldn't obey you, Lewis Motley. Not as they will me, if that proves needful."

Lewis Motley closed his eyes and made no more objections. She was right. Not a man on Kintucky that would not, if a Teacher asked it of him, build a ship or a cathedral or a rocket or anything else she might demand. It had been planned that way, and it had gone according to plan; the Teachers were not just respected, they were reverenced. He could not command that sort of loyalty.

And then . . . there was the way his head was whirling. It could not be true, but what if it were? What if Responsible had not known, really had not known, what she was doing to him? And he had not even given her the chance to stop?

He had seen it himself, it was what had led him to her bed, scrawny plucked creature that she was; there had been something special about her, and he had been determined to investigate it. Was it his curiosity, and his pride, that had made Ozark a wasteland . . . and how many deaths lay at his door?

He could not have ridden to the coast, he realized, as the two women left the room and slammed its door behind them. He could not, at that moment, have risen from his chair.

6

It was cold at Castle Brightwater; bitter bone-stabbing cold, the cold that comes when the skies are full of snow that refuses to fall; and the sky was a leaden sorrowful gray. No fires burned in any of the Castle fireplaces. The people in the towns and on the farms were better off by far than those at the Castle, because it had been for the most part a clear and sunny winter, and the solar collectors on their roofs had been adequate to carry them even through days like this one. The problems of keeping warm a hulking stone Castle designed with all the traditional drafty corridors and stairways were considerably more formidable.

Troublesome had gone through the gloom of the Castle like a wind added to the drafts that already whined there, with a fine disregard for the staff scuttling out of her way and the just-barely tolerance of the Family, shouting for Veritas Truebreed Motley the 4th, the Castle's very own Magician of Rank. "Where *is* the man?" she had demanded as she tore up and down the halls and through the parlors, and "Where has he *gotten* to?" She got nothing for her troubles but shrugs and raised eyebrows, but she was accustomed to that; ten years' practice being shunned toughened you up some.

She found him at last, by the simple expedient of looking everywhere there was, up on the Castle roof rubbing his hands together and cursing fluently in a spot where a tower kept off the wind but let the dim light by.

"It's a fine thing," he observed, glaring at her, "when it's warmer outside the place you live in than it is *inside,* in the dead of winter. I've a good mind to move into that hotel down by the landing—I'd be more comfortable there, and I'm sure the company would be better. How did you find me, anyway?"

"Used an algorithm," said Troublesome.

He made a face, not appreciating that word in her mouth, and went on as if she'd not used it. "And it's finer *yet,* when a man can't even find privacy on the bestaggering roof of a bestaggering *Castle!* First, it was one of the Grannys; and then it was Thorn of Guthrie—curse her narrow pointy little soul—and now, the Twelve Gates defend us all, it's *you!* What's next, ghosts and demons?"

"Morning, Veritas Truebreed," said Troublesome calmly. "Nice to see you, too, I'm sure."

"What do you want with me?" the Magician of Rank demanded, cross as a patch. "Whatever it is, the answer is either no, I can't or no, I won't—there aren't any other answers at the moment."

"Might could be you're right," she said, "and might could be you're wrong. Long as we're being all binary here."

"Troublesome, you'll provoke me," he warned her, and she let him know how alarmed she was at that prospect.

"Besides which," she added, "you were already provoked before ever I set foot on this roof. And you may go right on being provoked till you choke, for all I care."

"Well?" Veritas Truebreed was blue with cold and purple with outrage, but he knew quite well she could outlast him. "Speak up, woman; what are you here tormenting me for?"

Troublesome looked him up and down, noting that he'd abandoned the elegant garments of his station for something that looked more like a stableman's winter wear. Something nubby and bulky, with a thick lining and a narrow stripe and a capacious hood. It showed good sense on his part.

"I want you to wake up Responsible," she told him.

"You want me to what?"

"I've been to Kintucky and back, Veritas, and I —"

"You've been to *where?*"

"*As I said,* Veritas Truebreed, I've been to Kintucky and back— never you mind how, just let me tell you it wasn't easy and it was hardly what you might call a holiday excursion—and I've heard the whole sorry tale from the lips of Lewis Motley Wommack the 33rd his very own self, and you'd best hop it. Time's awasting."

The Magician of Rank stopped rubbing his hands together then, and blowing on them, and he leaned back against the stone of the tower, closed his eyes, and groaned aloud like a woman birthing.

"Only you could have brought this upon me, Troublesome of Brightwater," he said at last through clenched teeth, when he'd done with his groaning, "only you! We don't have trial and misery enough already; now we have to have *this*. Oh, for the power to do just one tiny Transformation. . . . I'd turn you into a slime-worm, with the greatest of pleasure, I'd step on you with my shoe heel . . . no, I'd set *fire* to you, right at the tender end where your little yellow eye was, and then—"

"Demented," said Troublesome.

"What?"

"You're demented. Mad. Plain crazy. And I've heard enough and a few buckets left over from you. I'm not *interested* in the twisted inventions of your imagination, Veritas Truebreed. I am interested in having you wake up my sister—bringing in all the other Magicians of Rank you need to help you at it, if that's required, and I suppose it is, though it's mighty curious that it takes nine-to-one odds for one small female like Responsible—and I'm interested in seeing if the Grannys are right that that will improve things around here a tad. Either you leave off your drivel and come along to get started on that, or I'll push you off the roof—how's that for managing without Formalisms & Transformations? Nothing fancy, O Mighty Magician, just shove you right off and let you try the effect of the stone down there in the courtyard on the very same body you came into this world with. You'll squash, I expect, and the Holy One knows you deserve it."

He opened his eyes and sighed, and she wondered impatiently what was next. There are only just so many meaningful noises in the sigh & moan & grunt & groan category, and he was running through them at a great rate.

"It can't be done," he said simply, and that surprised her. "I'm more than willing, but it—cannot—be—done. Don't you think we *tried?*"

Troublesome hunched down beside him and regarded him seriously. This didn't look to be at all funny, if he spoke the truth.

"You explain," she said. "*Right* quick."

"When we realized what we'd done," said the man, making vague hopeless gestures, "we tried right away to undo it. The Mules weren't making more than about ten miles an hour by then, some of the boats were a knot or two faster, whatever was left of the energy that had been fueling the system was winding down fast . . . but since it had taken all nine of us to put Responsible into pseudocoma we had a feeling it would take all nine to get her back out again. We all got here; and since you were yammering about the difficulties of your jaunt to Kintucky, allow me to observe that there was nothing easy about *that*—but we did get here somehow. And in the dead of night we stood round her bed and we did everything we knew, and made up a sizable amount of stuff that had never been tried before . . . and we kept at it until there was barely time for some of us to get out before people saw us leaving. Whether everyone got back home again, I don't know . . . and I'm not sure I care. But we *did try*, Troublesome."

"And what happened?"

"And nothing happened. The only difference between pseudocoma and real coma is that the victim of pseudocoma does not deteriorate physically or mentally. Otherwise, it's exactly the same—and we did a good job of it. Oh yes; that's a downright magnificent pseudocoma we put her into. She went right on just as she was."

"Do you understand it?" Troublesome asked gravely.

"No, of course we don't understand it, curse your insolence for asking! We *ought* to understand it . . . do you have to rub my nose in it? Does that give you pleasure?"

"That's my sister," she reminded him. It was no time to make her ritual speech about having no human feelings.

"And the hope of the world."

To her amazement, she saw that there were tears on his cheeks, running in rivulets down into his beard; it wouldn't do to let him know she saw that, and she devoted her attention to watching a seabird wheeling above them. It must have gone demented, too, she thought absently.

"We were so careful," he mourned beside her. "One thousand years of being *so careful*. Keeping the population small, so that there was always abundance. Balancing every substance that went into the soil and the water and the air, and every substance that came out, to guard its purity. We made a paradise . . . no crime, no war, no disease, no crowding, no hunger, no—"

"I remember, Veritas Truebreed," Troublesome cut him off. "I was up on a mountaintop a good deal of the time, but I do remember. And I'd rather hear explanations than memorial services, if you don't mind."

"We have some guesses."

"Guesses? What kind of guesses?"

He didn't answer her, and she turned to look at him, tears or no tears.

"I said, what *kind* of guesses?"

"They ought, by rights, to be secret. . . ."

"Oh, hogwallow, you fool man! Secrets, at a time like this!"

"Maybe you're right," he said, "and I'm too tired to care any more . . . and nobody'd believe you even if you weren't too mean to tell, so what does it matter? We assume—just assume, mind you, we've no proof—that there was something about Responsible that was essential to the functioning of magic. She had no *powers,* of course, beyond those of any other female; don't misunderstand me."

"You're a liar, Veritas—I told you I had the whole story from that poor piece of work at Castle Wommack, and he had a few words to say about Responsible's powers; seems as how he mightily disliked being subjected to them."

"Even on Old Earth," said the Magician of Rank stiffly, "in the times of utter ignorance of magic, there were rare individuals capable of mindspeech—as there were rare individuals seven feet tall. Your sister is a freak, as those were freaks, with no knowledge or control of her abilities. But she is something else, something . . . a catalyst, perhaps? Somehow, whatever she was, taking her out of the system of magic brought it to a full stop. And pseudocoma *takes* magic—you can't put someone into it, nor take them out of it, with solar energy or electrical energy or any other kind. By the time we realized what had happened, there was no energy left—without her—for us to use to cancel the coma. So far as I know, that's the way of it. And if you could get all nine of us together in her bedroom again, which I doubt, since the ships aren't sailing and the Mules aren't flying, it would be the same as it was. Just the same as it was. . . ."

"You were fools," said Troublesome. "Plain fools."

That long groan again . . . it was getting boring, especially since he was in no pain.

"You were, you know," she said, happy to twist the knife.

"We didn't *realize,*" he protested. "We had no idea that she mattered that way. . . ." And if someone had told them, he thought to himself, if they'd been warned, it would have changed nothing. They wouldn't have believed it. They had hated Responsible of Brightwater so much, and they had so welcomed a legitimate opportunity to punish her for humiliating them, he knew that no amount of warning could have held them back.

"You do not know the hours," he said slowly, "the countless hours I have spent standing beside her all by myself . . . trying things. Hoping I'd jog something loose, find the right thread accidentally. Because whatever it is that she is for, *that* is still intact. *That's* still there, if I could only get at it."

"How do you know that? How can you possibly know?"

He raised his eyebrows at that, and he admonished her to think. After all, he pointed out, she had a reputation for wisdom as well as wickedness. And, goaded like that and held in the fierceness of his eyes wanting to get back at her for the way she'd spoken to him, she saw it.

"Ah," she breathed, "you're right! Otherwise, if it were *other*wise, she'd be like someone in true coma . . . she'd be curled tight and wasting away and—"

"And all the rest of it. Yes. And she's not. She looks exactly as she looked the hour we did our work, and that can mean only one thing— all that is left of the energy of magic is concentrated there in her, keeping her from ever changing."

Something in his tone caught her attention, and she looked at him close, and marveled at the way of the world. Revelation followed upon revelation.

"You hate her," she said. "She's your own kin, grew up here under this roof playing on your knee and riding piggyback on your shoulders— and you hate her worse than sin! Why?"

Veritas Truebreed squared his shoulders, and he met her eyes, but he said not one word. No one not a Magician of Rank was ever going to know the answer to that question, not from his lips. Not ever.

"It must have been hard," murmured Troublesome. "All those years, pretending to be helpful . . . playing at being loyal."

"It was."

Troublesome went back down into the Castle, her breath making little white puffs in the air, and she found Grannys Hazelbide and Gableframe, and told them.

"It seems," she wound it up, "that you went through all of this and gave up the last of your treasure things—not to mention a certain amount of discommodance on *my* part—all for nothing. It's a shame."

"No," said Granny Gableframe firmly. "It wasn't for nothing, young woman. In *no* sense of the word. We traded an ignorance big as this Castle for a whole *pot* of knowledge, bubbling and simmering this minute. I'd say as it was a fair trade. We're not out of it, mind you, not by many a mile, but we at least know how we came to be where we are."

"Knowledge," said Granny Hazelbide, "is for using. Now we have some, the problem is how we put it to use. And for that, Troublesome, we don't need you. No call whatsoever to keep you from your home-place any longer, and we're grateful to you for what you've done, how-ever much it sticks in my craw to say it. We're beholden to you."

"Hazelbide, you exaggerate," said Granny Gableframe.

"You know any other living soul on this earth as would of done what Troublesome did?" demanded Granny Hazelbide. "Gone off in the cold and damp in a leaky boat with a bribed crew, on what was ninety-nine-to-one a wild goose chase? Gone off and chanced being stranded forever in a wilderness, dying all alone in some Kintucky briartangle? Just because we asked her to, and no other compensation offered?"

"Flumdiddle!" said Gableframe. "The fact you raised Troublesome's addled your brain—*which* it can't tolerate much of, I might add. That's her own sister as lies in there, and it's her own people as are suffering. She had as much to gain from this as any of us, and more than some, and I'll be benastied before I'll say we're beholden to Troublesome of Brightwater! The *idea!*"

"One more time, Gableframe," said Granny Hazelbide, tightlipped. "Just *one more* time, I'll tell you. . . . Troublesome has no natural feelings. Responsible could die this minute, putrify right there on her bed, and her sister's only complaint'd be the smell. And that goes for every sick baby and hungry tadling and suffering human on the face of this world, you have my word on it. If *she* helped us, we're beholden. You care to be benastied as well, that's your choice."

Troublesome chuckled, and Granny Hazelbide said: "See there?"

They were sitting there together, the two old women rocking quick and hard to show their irritation, and Troublesome still grinning, when the Mules began to bray in the stables, and Granny Gableframe said, "There's somebody coming—listen to that racket!"

"Probably Lewis Motley Wommack the 33rd," observed Granny Hazelbide. "Swam all the way here for penance, and crawled the rest of the way when he ran out of water."

"For sure it's a strange Mule to bring all that on," said Granny Hazelbide. "That's all we need now, when we should be setting our minds to how to use what we've learned—company. Botheration!"

"Don't you get awfully tired of that?" asked Troublesome.

"Tired of what?"

"The formspeech. Having to go 'botheration' and 'I swan' and 'flum-diddle' and 'mark my word' and all the rest of it. Do you keep it up when you're all by yourselves and nobody around to say, '*Eek!* I heard a Granny talking normal talk like anybody else'?"

The Grannys drew themselves up in outrage, right together like they'd practiced it, and Troublesome chuckled some more. There was nothing more fun to tease than a Granny.

"Troublesome of Brightwater," said Granny Hazelbide stiffly, "just you go and see who's come—or *what's* come, might could be that's more near the mark! I wish to goodness it *would* be young Wommack, I'd pull every hair of his beard out one at a time . . . but we'll not be that lucky, it'll be somebody useless, or worse. You've had your thanks, missy, and we've had your sass, and now we're even—make your young bones use-ful and see what's come to pass."

But Troublesome didn't have a chance to more than straighten up from her chair before a knock came at the door; and when they called, "Come in!" it was a servingmaid of Brightwater and an Attendant from Castle McDaniels, the latter looking as if he'd fall over if you blew on him.

"I'm here," he blurted out, "with a message for Miss Troublesome. Law, but I was scared to death she'd be gone before I got here. . . . Miss Troublesome, I'm pleasured to see you."

"First time in her life she ever heard *that!*" said the two Grannys together, and Troublesome allowed that it was, and the young man hur-ried to explain himself.

"I don't mean as how I'm happy to see *her,*" he said hastily, stum-bling into the doorframe and causing the servingmaid to put a sturdy hand to his elbow to help him out. "Don't misunderstand me; it's that I'm happy to see she's not *gone* yet. If you see what I mean."

"The distinction's a mite subtle," said Granny Gableframe. "But we won't hold it against you, whatever it might mean, seeing as how it's clear you've had a hard ride and a long one and can scarcely stand on your feet, much less orate and do declamations. What are you after with Troublesome of Brightwater, young man?"

"Message from Castle McDaniels, ma'am," he said, bobbing his head. "And it's urgent."

"Then *deliver* it," snapped Troublesome, running out of patience. "*Before* you fall over. It'll be more practical that way, by a good deal. And don't mumble. When I get urgent messages brought in to me at a last gasp like this I like them to be turned over with *clarity*."

"Troublesome!" Granny Hazelbide was fairly quivering. "*Will* you not tease the poor young man, for all our sakes!"

"Oh, that's all right, Granny Hazelbide," said the Attendant from McDaniels, trying not to lean on the servingmaid. "I've been warned about her already, at some length. Missus McDaniels, her that was Anne of Brightwater, she talked to me about Miss Troublesome for it must of been a good hour and a half. I expected horns and a tail on her, if you want to know the truth of it."

And Troublesome chuckled some more. For a day that had begun with spoiled food and bad water and a crew of sick and surly men on a leaky boat, this one was turning out to have its good parts.

"Well, then," she said. "You've seen me, and you're disappointed I don't live up to your expectations. That's clear. Now pass on the message, and you can be on your way and get some rest. Just speak right up."

"You're to stay here," said the Attendant.

"I'm to stay here? That's it? That's your urgent message?"

"Because Miss Silverweb's coming," he told her. "She wasn't quite ready to leave when I was, and she couldn't of kept up with me if she had been, I'm sure—I was told to ride hard all the way and not spare the Mule or me either one. But she says you're to stay right here until she gets here, never mind how anxious you are to leave, and never mind how much there's people encouraging you on your way."

"Miss Silverweb said that?"

"Yes, miss. And her mother as well."

"Hmmmph."

Troublesome gnawed on her braid, and the Grannys stopped their rocking, and Granny Hazelbide pointed out that considering the number of days she'd lost already another one couldn't do much harm. Or another two.

"Did she say *why?*" Troublesome asked the Attendant.

"Miss?"

"Did either of those women say *why* I was to wait?" asked Troublesome impatiently. "I can't see much point to it myself—I don't even *know* Silverweb of McDaniels, except that I believe I changed one of her diapers once. She for sure does not know *me*. Why should I wait for her?"

"Well," said the Attendant, "I can't say as I understand it. But I can tell you what they said to me."

"You do that, then," said Troublesome.

"Miss Silverweb, she said I was to tell you just this: you stay here, because she knows how to wake up Miss Responsible, but she needs your help to do it. And that's all."

The silence went on and on, and the Attendant leaned more and more obviously on the servingmaid, who fortunately showed no sign of collapsing under the strain, and when Troublesome spoke at last her voice was hesitant.

"You say that Silverweb of McDaniels knows how to wake my sister. . . ."

"So she claims, miss. I'm just passing it on, as I was bid."

Troublesome turned to the Grannys.

"Well?" she asked them. "Is it likely? You know the girl . . . any reason she should know what nine Magicians of Rank *don't*?"

"Miss Silverweb'll be here by morning at the latest," pleaded the Attendant. "And if I've got here and told you, and you're gone on anyway, I won't dare go back, I can tell you. Missus Anne was *most* particular about that. 'If she doesn't wait for Miss Silverweb, don't you bother coming back here,' she said to me. And I've worked there, and done my job *right*, more'n six years now. Shows where hard work won't get you."

"Troublesome," said Granny Gableframe, speaking right up, "I can't say honestly I know any reason why you should stay. Rumor is, Silverweb of McDaniels' gone some kind of religious lunatic, shut up all the time in an attic praying and carrying on. Not that I don't hold with prayer, mind you, indeed I do, in its place—but they say Silverweb carries it to and beyond extremes. On the other hand, reason or no, what's the harm? What's one more day to you? You've got no appointments to keep on your mountain, what's a few hours more or less at Brightwater?"

Troublesome gave it a minute or two for real, and a minute or two for tormenting them, and then she nodded slowly, and the Attendant went limp with relief and very nearly did fall down.

"All right," said Troublesome. "I don't suppose it can make any difference; and I don't mind admitting I'm curious. I'll wait for the child. Pray with her if need be."

"She's no child, Miss Troublesome," said the Attendant, very serious in spite of his exhaustion. "You wait till you see her—that's no child, nor ever will be again. Nor no woman, either."

"Well, what is she, then?"

"You'd best wait and see for yourself," the Attendant said, and that appearing to be all he could manage, the Grannys motioned for the serving-maid to take him away. Which she did, murmuring soothing words to him all the way down the corridor.

"Youall don't know anything about this?" demanded Troublesome, arms akimbo. "This is no Granny mischief, cooked up between you?"

"Honestly," said Gableframe. "How you talk."

"Your word on it or off I go this minute," declared Troublesome.

"Phooey," said Granny Gableframe right back at her. "It'll be a fine day when I give you my word on anything. As soon give my word to my elbow. And who are *you* to doubt a Granny's word?"

"Troublesome," put in Granny Hazelbide hastily, "I'm with Gableframe on that. But you said you'd stay. And you know this is no scheme we planned for you—we've got no heart these days for schemes. Leave off your nonsense, now, and keep *your* word."

"And so I will," said Troublesome. "I beg your pardon, I forget sometimes the way things have changed in this world. Up on that mountain . . . I don't see it the way youall have to."

"Understandable," said Granny Gableframe. "Not natural; but understandable."

"I suppose they'll make me sleep in the stable," Troublesome fussed.

"I'll put you up in my own room if they try it," said Granny Hazelbide. "I'm not afraid of you, and the Twelve Gates knows I'm *used* to you."

"I'd rather stay in the stable."

"Suit yourself. Just so's you stay."

"*My* word on it, to you and to my elbow," said Troublesome solemnly, crossing her heart elaborately with one finger. "I'll wait for little Silverweb and see what she's got to offer."

7

There was no order to it, when it happened—it happened everywhere, all at once, all at the same time. Twelve Castles there were on Ozark, and not one was overlooked or granted a delay. Nine Magicians of Rank as well, spread around over the planet, and they were stricken all together, with a unity that they had known before only on that single occasion when they had joined forces against Responsible of Brightwater.

Veritas Truebreed Motley the 4th was the only Magician of Rank on the continent of Marktwain, and the course of events was so swift that he heard only the first scream from outside the Castle walls before he was literally thrown to the floor with his hands pressed desperately to a head that he was sure would burst . . . he could hear nothing more after that but the message exploding there.

The ordinary citizens and the Grannys were spared that penalty; the Magicians felt only a sudden nagging headache, nothing out of the way. For them, unlike the Magicians of Rank, the problem was not what was in their heads but what was in the sky.

Above Castle Brightwater, suspended well out of reach of ordinary weapons but easily within sight of the eye, a giant crystal had appeared, spinning slowly on its point for just a moment before it stopped and hung there motionless above them.

It looked to be one hundred feet from tip to tip, stretching straight up, though it was hard to be sure without knowing exactly what its distance was from any object of reference. And it was in the shape of a flawless diamond, perfect in its symmetry, perfect in its utter transparentness. It would have been invisible, in fact, except that from some angles it acted as a prism and cast huge rainbows over the land and buildings beneath it, turning the countryside to a fairyland of glorious color. It made no sound at all. It came from nowhere and nothing held it in its place, nothing that could be seen. It was beautiful, and mysterious, and wholly terrifying.

The Grannys heard the screaming and ran out onto a balcony to see what the commotion was about *this* time, took one horrified look at the thing, and ran even faster after Veritas Truebreed. By the time they reached him he was aware that similar scenes were taking place at every one of the Twelve Castles, and he wished himself anywhere else in the Universe . . . preferably at the bottom of the sea. Any sea.

"Veritas Truebreed Motley," fussed Granny Gableframe when they found him, "whatever in this world are you doing? A lot of help *you* are, rolling on the floor and carrying on with that carry-on! You have colic or what? Get up and come see what's arrived this day to brighten the corners where we are . . . might could be you could be of some use at last!"

When that didn't budge him from the niche he had managed to thrash his way into, or bring him out of the position of tight-coiled agony he was twisted into, the Grannys knelt beside him and began an expert probing. He screamed louder, and begged them not to touch him, and if he had not been paralyzed with pain they would not have been able to stop his frenzied efforts to smash his brains out against the stone walls of the Castle.

"Men," said Gableframe. "Always there when you need them."

"Veritas?" Granny Hazelbide stood up and poked him with her shoe. "You stop that caterwauling, you hear me? I know you can hear me, don't you make out you can't!"

As a matter of actual fact, he could *not* hear her over the din in his head. He could see her mouth moving, and his long experience with Grannys gave him an excellent idea of what the two of them must be saying, but they might as well have been in the next county for all that he was able to hear of their bad-mouthing. There was only *one* sound, and it filled all his perceptions, and it was surely going to be the death of him unless he somehow got help. He had time to wonder, through his agony, how Lincoln Parradyne was faring at Castle Smith, where the "Granny" in residence was only an old woman hired by the Magician of Rank to placate the Family when Granny Gableframe walked out on them to move to Castle Brightwater. Veritas Truebreed had sense enough left to know that nobody but a Granny was likely to be able to help any of them.

One word, Veritas, he was screaming at himself silently, trying to get through the unbearable waves of noise, *you've got to say one word! Only one word!*

Granny Hazelbide poked at him again disgustedly with the tip of one pointy-toed black high-heeled shoe, and was just getting ready to draw back her foot for an actual kick when he finally succeeded in croaking out that word. And it brought both old women to rigid attention as if it had been a Charm and a Spell and a Transformation all combined into one. The sound that had come out of Veritas' mouth, strangled and deformed but comprehensible, was the word "Mules!" And once again, before he went back to the howling that was completely unlike the cries from outside—those were only terror—he said it: *"Mules!"*

"Mules," repeated the Grannys, looking at one another. "Do you suppose . . ."

"I do," said Granny Gableframe. "What else could do that?"

"Maybe that thing hanging over our heads," said Granny Hazelbide grimly, pointing up at the ceiling and tapping her foot to a smart beat. "Two sharp ends it's got like a double needle, and no knowing what it can do."

"Well, we can't talk to *it*, Hazelbide," snorted Granny Gableframe, "that's for sure. And the Twelve Gates only knows what will happen if one of those scared sick lunatics out there takes it into his head to shoot at the thing with a laser . . . likely to mean the end of all of us, and nothing left where Ozark was but a puff of dust, if that happens. The Mules, on the other hand, we could talk to."

"Gableframe . . ."

"I said *talk* to! Not either one of us is equipped to do any mindspeaking, and the Mules know that full well. I mean *talk*, ordinary tongue-and-mouth-and-teeth talk."

"What makes you think they'll listen?"

"Hazelbide, you have brains in that head or pudding?" Granny Gableframe was clear out of temper. "Stand there and go wurra-wurra like that poor fool on the floor if you like, but any ninny can see there's no way of talking to that . . . creation . . . up in the air, and the only clue we've got is what Veritas said, and I intend to hightail it for the stables!"

Granny Hazelbide knew sense when she heard it; she followed the other without a word, and without a glance behind her for the Magician of Rank in his awesome misery. She was only sorry there wasn't time to look for Troublesome and make her go along with them.

At the stables, they found the Mules standing in ominous silence. If the expressions on their faces could be interpreted in any human framework, they looked both grim and determined. In any framework, they had their attention fully occupied with something.

Granny Gableframe marched up to Sterling, the best creature in the stable, and said howdydo and she'd like it to listen to her. And when that had no effect, she whacked it smartly right between the eyes.

"You, Mule!" said Gableframe. "I want a word with you, and I *do* know that you can understand me just fine!"

Sterling rolled her eyes and laid back her ears, and Granny Gableframe whacked her again. She'd never thought to see the day she'd be dealing with a hysterical *Mule*.

"You want to listen polite-like and of your own free will, that's fine with me," said the old lady. "I'll be polite, too, as is proper; it pleasures me not atall to abuse any creature. But if you'd rather do it the hard way, I'm prepared for that, and I *do* intend to have you hear me."

"You think that'll work?" asked Granny Hazelbide, tapping her nose with her pointing finger. "It was always Responsible as talked to the Mules, and she had a mighty different approach to it."

"You have a better idea?"

"*No*-sir, you go right to it. And I'll try another one," said Granny Hazelbide, and went off to make her word good.

"Sterling," said Granny Gableframe, "I have reason to believe you're trying to mindspeak poor Veritas Truebreed, and I'm here to tell you that if that's what you're up to you're pouring sand down a rathole. He's curled up in a hole in the wall like a puking babe, howling and begging to be shot or poisoned a one, he doesn't care which, and a less promising mode of communicating I've never come across in all my born days! Now if you have something you'd like to get across to the Magician of Rank, m'dear Mule, I'd suggest you turn down the power somewhat more than a tad. You are addressing a human male, not Responsible of Brightwater, and he is most surely not up to taking in what you are putting out. Do you hear me, Sterling?"

The Mule gave her a look down its nose, and raised its ears one notch, and the Granny said it all over again, with more emphasis in the hard places.

"Tone it down!" she admonished Sterling, winding it up. "Tone it down or you might as well leave off entirely! That man's mind is frail as a flower petal up there, you can't just go banging around in it like some kind of natural disaster!"

Sterling whickered and ducked her head, and the Mules all around joined in.

"You suppose, Granny Hazelbide," said Gableframe then, out of breath entirely, "you suppose that means we got it across?"

"If we didn't, we probably can't," came the answer, "and the only way I know to find out is to go see what's left of old Veritas Truebreed." She brushed down her skirts and sneezed twice at the dust and remarked on stablemaids and how they got lazier every year, and Gableframe did the same, and then they looked at each other.

"You ready?" said Hazelbide.

"I'm not ready to go out and walk under that *thing* hanging in the air over my head; nor am I ready to see every last soul running around and screaming like their tails was caught in a door when it hasn't yet done any of 'em ary harm *what*soever . . . and I for sure don't want to go stare at that pitiful excuse for a Magician of *Rank*. But I will, Hazelbide, I will. Let's get at it."

"Fool Mules," Granny Hazelbide grumbled. "*Now* what?"

And all the way back to the Castle door and up the steps, she grumbled. It was one thing for the Mules to mindspeak the Magician of Rank—the Magicians had always known the Mules were telepathic, and vice versa—but the *Grannys* weren't supposed to know all that. But Granny Hazelbide was ready to bet twelve dollars to a dillyblow that when the Mules *did* turn down their power of projection to accommodate the limitations of Veritas Truebreed's mind the very first thing they'd done was inform him that the Grannys had told them to do so. And *that* was going to be a fine kettle of fish.

Things were a mite less chaotic . . . the townspeople had recovered from their first shock at the sight of the giant crystal and were gathered in clumps, talking and shaking their heads. This was not exactly the normal order of the day, but the Grannys found it an improvement on the original running around in circles and screaming. They hurried past a group of Attendants and servingmaids that looked ready to head them off, and went straight on up to Veritas Truebreed to see if their trip to the stables had been a mission of mercy or a red herring.

They found the Magician of Rank much the worse for wear, white as a sheet and soaked with cold sweat, still rubbing his head and trembling all over. But he was able to talk.

"According to the Mules," he said gruffly when they came through his door, "I've you to thank for an end to that unspeakable torture. And

I *will* thank you—because if it had not stopped I would be dead—and then I would appreciate an explanation."

Granny Gableframe didn't miss a beat. She reminded him that the Mules' telepathic ability was a pretty open secret after all these years. And she reminded him that *he* had been the one bellowing "Mules!" and they'd only followed directions. "And as for mindspeech," she finished up crisply, "we Grannys don't have it, so you needn't go searching for revelations there. We went down to the stable and whacked the Mules over the head and told them—out loud—that if they were trying to talk to you they were hollering themselves into oblivion . . . and then we came back to see what happened. You appear to be recovered—"

"I will *never* be recovered from that, thank you very much!"

"Never mind, Veritas Truebreed, you are at least on your feet and talking 'stead of howling, and we'll accept that for now. The question is: what have the Mules been telling you?"

The Magician of Rank swallowed and stammered, and Granny Gableframe threatened to kick him with her shoe the way Granny Hazelbide had.

"Speak up," she said, infuriated. "Time's a-wasting! The Mules never tried mindspeaking you before, and there's never been a gigantic humungus *bo*dacious chandelier-bobble hanging up in the air before, and I for one am inclined to believe there's got to be a connection! What did the Mules want with you?"

"It's a wild tale," said Veritas Truebreed.

"It's a wild *sight*," said Granny Hazelbide. "You take a look?"

"I looked. I saw . . . it. One of the basic primordial shapes."

"Primordial shapes be hanged, do you know anything *use*ful?"

"Careful, Hazelbide, you'll have a heart attack," cautioned Granny Gableframe. "And a lot of help that'll be."

"Well, the man's *mad*dening!"

"And if I had four wheels I'd be a tin lizzy. Calm down and let him talk . . . he'll get around to it. Eventually."

He did.

"It seems," he said slowly, "according to the Mules, it seems that thing you refer to as a chandelier-bobble is a kind of mechanism for the focusing of energy. It pulls in energy and concentrates it . . . and stores it."

"To do what with?"

"Just a minute. . . ." Veritas Truebreed wiped his brow with the back of a shaking hand. "I've got to sit down."

Granny Gableframe clucked her tongue and told him not to be such a sissy, but he sat down all the same.

"The Mules tell me," he said when he was settled, "that there is a group of planets not too far away from here that is called the Garnet Ring; and that their representatives—something called the Out-Cabal, and according to the Mules you'll be able to fill me in on that, and I will assuredly be interested in knowing *why*—that their representatives have been keeping an eye on us for some time. The crystal out there is sent by the Garnet Ring, on the basis of information reported back by this . . . Out-Cabal . . . and the Mules say there's one just like it over each of the Castles of Ozark."

"Ohhhh dear!" cried Granny Hazelbide. "Oh my! That is a predicament, for sure and for certain!"

"Indeed it is," echoed Granny Gableframe. "They tell you anything more, Veritas Truebreed?"

"I got the distinct impression," he snapped at her, "that you two knew more about this than they did."

"Not accurate," said Gableframe. "Not precisely."

"*Isn't* it? According to the Mules—"

"You believe a passel of pack animals, Veritas, or you believe two respectable Ozark Grannys?"

"After what they did to me? Those 'pack animals' you mention? I believe *them!*" The Magician of Rank was furious, and beginning to feel more himself. "It's more than clear that some very important information has been kept from the Magicians of Rank by the Grannys of Ozark for hundreds of years—information that might well have been crucial to the running of this planet—and I want you to know that I resent it, and that *steps will be taken!*"

"You don't say?" Granny Gableframe said. "What do you have in what's left of your mind, Mister Highandmighty? You without so much as a Housekeeping Spell on hand! You get your powers back . . . such as they were, such *as they* were . . . and then you can prattle about taking steps. In the meantime, you mind your mouth."

"*You* are an unpleasant old woman," said the Magician of Rank.

"Grannys are supposed to be unpleasant old women," retorted Gableframe. "You want something young and willing, you don't go looking for a Granny. Now what I'd like to know is how long that thing's going to be a part of our sky out there and what it's intended to do to us. If you know, we'd appreciate you spitting it out."

And then she muttered, "Oh, law, it heard me!" as a sudden pulsing . . . not exactly a sound, more a kind of powerful vibration that thrummed in the stone walls and floors . . . began. "I suppose that's it, warming up," she said.

"I suppose so too," said Veritas Truebreed. "How would I know? Until this accursed day, I had never heard of an Out-Cabal. Nor a Garnet Ring. You ladies have minded *your* mouths admirably."

"It was our duty to do so," said Granny Gableframe. "Quit your complaining over things you admit you don't know any more about than the doorknob does."

"The Mules say," Veritas Truebreed sighed, "that this planet is about to be taken over by the Garnet Ring. We are, they tell me, now 'eligible' —that's the way they put it—to be so treated. The crystals will remain where they are, doing whatever that is they're doing, until they are fully charged. And then, I am assured, we will be unable to resist this Garnet Ring. And I suppose it's true?"

"Could we do anything like those crystals?" asked the Grannys in one voice.

"They might could be only an illusion," added Granny Hazelbide. "I've seen you Magicians of Rank do some fancy things along that line, in my time."

Veritas Truebreed shook his head. "The Mules tell me they're real, and that they're as powerful as the Out-Cabal says they are, and that they can do what they claim. Now *you* tell *me* if the Mules are likely to know what they're talking about."

"Well, it's misery," said Granny Gableframe, "just plain misery—but we have no reason to think they don't. And plenty to think they do."

"Then we know where we are," he said wearily.

"Do we know how much time we have?"

"We have whatever time it takes until those things are 'fully charged,' like I said before. That's all the Mules knew."

"Well," asked Granny Hazelbide, "what do you plan to do?"

"Me? I plan to go lie down and not move my head until the Out-Cabal comes to cut it off."

"My, *that's* impressive!" scoffed the Granny. "You expect a medal for that, do you?"

"Be reasonable!" shouted the Magician of Rank, and winced at what it did to his aching head. "As you so politely pointed out to me, not three minutes ago, I haven't a Housekeeping Spell to my name. What do you *expect* me to do?"

"There are a lot of people out there," said the Granny, "as are frightened half to death. They're not as accustomed to wonders and marvels as you are, not by a long sight. And they respect you, magic or no magic. I'll thank you to go get on the comset and spread the word—in some suitable form. I don't believe I'd tell them what you just told us, not quite yet. Just get on there and tell them that there's no reason to be afeared right at this very minute, which is true. And that we'll get back to them, which is true. And that we're working on the problem—which is true. I do believe you could handle that, Veritas, and I believe you're obliged to. *Right* now!" She did not say scat, out of politeness.

On his way out the door, moving as fast as his condition would allow, and making other allowances for the unsteady feeling the whole Castle had with that low vibration running all through it, he very nearly ran right over Silverweb of McDaniels.

"Silverweb—" he began, but the Grannys, right behind him, gave him a push.

"Not *now*, Veritas Truebreed Motley, not *now!*" fussed Granny Hazelbide. "Whatever Silverweb of McDaniels needs, it won't be anything as concerns you, and you're needed to stop the panic out there in the town and all around the countryside. We Grannys'll see to Silverweb!"

But Silverweb needed no seeing to at all. She was as radiant as if she'd been living on strawberries and thick cream, as beautiful as ever, and as serene as if this were the most ordinary of days. She was there, she announced, to get Troublesome—and the Grannys realized they'd seen no sign of Troublesome of Brightwater through all of this, which was becoming of her and showed a proper consideration—and then Silverweb went on to say that she and Troublesome were going to take

Responsible of Brightwater out into the desert of Marktwain to the sacred spring.

"We'll hitch a Mule to a wagon," said Silverweb, her voice like rich melted butter running over in the dish, "and spread it with a comforter and a pillow to make Responsible lie easy. And Troublesome and I will lay Responsible inside, and we will take her away."

"But, child," hazarded Granny Hazelbide, touching the arm of the creature—as the Attendant had said, not a child, and not precisely a woman, either, but the Granny had the privilege of her years—"this is no time for such a trek! Don't you know what's happened?"

"What has happened," said Silverweb of McDaniels, "is that the Holy One has spoken to me and told me that I must get Troublesome, and that she and I must take Responsible out into the desert. That is all that I need to know, Granny Hazelbide."

"But—"

"There's Troublesome now," added Silverweb. "Right on time."

Troublesome had her sister gathered up in her strong arms, a comforter wrapped round her, and no more trouble than a tadling; she wasn't even out of breath, despite all the stairs.

"You lead on, Silverweb," said Troublesome, "you're the one as knows how this is supposed to go. And I'll follow. Can you hitch up a Mule? If you can't, I can."

Silverweb laughed. "I can hitch a Mule," she said. "I can hitch up any living thing that walks this planet, and I can do a sight more than that. You just come along with me—and I thank you kindly for waiting for me."

It took the Grannys' breaths away. They stood there in silence—not the usual way of things—as the two young women left with their sleeping charge. And then they watched from the balcony as the gates were opened and the wagon that carried Responsible was pulled out of the Castle yard by a prime Mule.

"That'll be Sterling," said Granny Hazelbide, and Granny Gableframe nodded.

"It would be."

"Whatever do you suppose is going to happen? There's nothing out there in that desert to eat nor to drink, and those two didn't gather up so much as a peachapple before they left here. . . ."

In the streets the people drew back, whispering under their breaths, to let the wagon through, and the parents held the tadlings up high to see. And above them, the crystal had lost its transparent clarity and was beginning to take on a pale garnet color, that pulsed along with the thrumming in the stone and in the air.

It was beginning to accumulate its charge.

8

Marktwain's desert, the one and only desert Ozark had, was something of a mystery. For one thing, the rest of the continent would have led you to believe there could be no desert there; Marktwain was lush green farming land, surpassed only by the emerald richness of Mizzurah, all the way to its coasts in all directions. That you could go through the pass between Troublesome's mountain and the others in its chain (not really much more than high hills, but the Ozark Mountains of Old Earth had not been towering peaks, either, and there was thus a precedent for it), and suddenly find yourself heading smack into a real desert—that was always a surprise.

It wasn't large, and was called simply "The Desert"; if you've only one, there's no special need to name it. The technology and the knowledge necessary to bind its sands with plant life and turn it green as the rest of the continent had been part of the Ozarkers' equipment even at First Landing. When Marktwain's population passed sixty thousand, the two Kingdoms of Brightwater and McDaniels all parceled out in towns and farms, the idea of keeping a desert for its unique character ceased to be anything but romanticism. But it was left alone, nevertheless, and it was a rare day when anybody did more than go to its border and glance out over its emptiness. The desert belonged, by treaty signed on First Landing, to the Skerrys.

Troublesome of Brightwater and Silverweb of McDaniels headed out into the desert, walking one on each side of the wagon, and the few people that had followed them that far turned back and let them go on. It was one thing to be those two and go trifling with the Skerrys; ordinary folk had best mind their own business.

And it was as well they did. Troublesome and Silverweb had hardly crossed the first smooth ridge of sand, talking idly of the foolishness going on in Smith Kingdom with its clown of a King and its dithery females, and on down the ridge's far side, before they saw ahead of them a group of Skerrys standing and waiting.

"How many do you think, Silverweb?" Troublesome asked softly, abandoning the ridiculous tale of the Smiths.

"I was told there would be forty-four," said Silverweb. "It is a number significant to them."

"Forty-four Skerrys!" Troublesome blew a long breath.

Not since First Landing had any Ozarker ever seen more than one Skerry at a time, and to sight one was so rare that it obligated the whole Kingdom where it happened to spend a day of celebration and full holiday in the Skerry's honor. Just what the sight of forty-four might have meant in the way of obligations was difficult to imagine. It surely would have been a heavy burden of worry and debate, and Marktwain's citizens had more than enough of worry on their plates at that moment.

Sterling stopped dead when *she* saw them, and would not take another step, and the two women hesitated, not sure whether to try forcing her on or not.

"What do you think, Silverweb?" Troublesome asked, measuring the animal with narrowed eyes. "Shall I encourage this blamed Mule a tad?"

Sterling's ears went flat back, and she walled her eyes, to indicate what she thought of the idea, but Troublesome was not impressed. "You care to find out who's meaner, you or me," she told the Mule, "I'm ready any time."

"I think I'd wait," said Silverweb, "and see if we get some kind of sign."

"Like forty-four Skerrys at once? Like a giant crystal over our heads?"

"I had something less outlandish in mind," Silverweb answered. "For example . . ." And she pointed, doing it discreetly with the tip of her chin as befit a situation where the fine edges of manners weren't well known, toward the Skerry that had separated from the group and was heading toward them.

"Is it male or female, I wonder?" Troublesome said softly.

"We don't even know that there *are* male and female to the Skerrys," Silverweb reminded her. "We know only that they are more beautiful than anything else that we have ever seen."

And that was true. The one approaching them, moving over the sand with a gliding step like someone on ice, and at ease on ice, was blinding in its beauty. Much taller than Troublesome, who missed six feet by only a quarter of an inch, copper-skinned and its silver hair like a fall of water in the sun well below its waist, with eyes of purest turquoise, it lacked only wings to make it Angel. Angel of *what* was the question . . . and nobody knew.

As nobody knew what substance of bone must be required to support the slender muscular bodies of a race that claimed eight feet as its *average* height. Or how many there were, or what they ate, or why it was they hated all water except the narrow trickle they held sacred.

Another time, Troublesome would have been adding up the bits of data, storing them in her mind to puzzle over later, as she did faced with any mystery. But not now . . . not when the Skerry smiled at them, leaned over the wagon, and lifted Responsible up in its arms and against its slender body, leaving the comforters and pillows behind in the bottom of the wagon; and then it turned, motioning with its head for them to follow.

Troublesome didn't like that at all, and it distracted her attention completely. That was, after all, her own kin being galloped off with by a being that nobody knew whether it might eat her alive or keep her for a pet or skin her for her hide. But she hadn't much choice, either, distracted or not; they were outnumbered many times over, even if they'd known what manner of living thing they dealt with . . . and they didn't.

The voice in her mind was gentle enough, but it was firm.

DAUGHTER OF BRIGHTWATER, YOU THAT ARE NAMED TROUBLESOME, it said, LEAVE THE MULE AND THE WAGON WHERE THEY ARE, AND FOLLOW US. NO HARM WILL COME TO YOUR SISTER OR TO ANY OF YOU— HOW COULD YOU THINK SUCH A THING?

Troublesome was not accustomed to mindspeech, and she didn't like *that,* either. Two of the indigenous species of Marktwain were telepathic, then. It made sense, when you thought about it . . . how else could the treaties have been negotiated? For sure, First Granny and the others had not landed speaking "Skerry," nor would the Skerrys have been fluent in Ozark English. She'd never thought about it before, and it was only that she was so flustered that she thought of it now. It kept her mind off the possibilities up ahead, that she could in no way predict. But it was said that when the Mules mindspoke anybody they nearly destroyed that person's mind in the process. The Skerry's voice in her mind only made her think of bells, chiming. Deep bells.

THAT IS HOW YOU TELL, came the voice again, and she judged that there was laughter in it. THE DEEP BELLS ARE THE MALES, THE MIDDLE

ONES OUR FEMALES, THE MIXED ONES THE SHEMALES, AND THE HIGH CHIMES ARE OUR CHILDREN, WHO DID NOT COME ALONG WITH US TODAY.

"Oh, now, that's not likely!" Troublesome protested aloud. She was impressed, but she would push just so far and no farther. She had no intention of just *thinking* at anything, if it did stand eight feet tall.

YOU ARE QUITE RIGHT, said a different voice. IT IS A CONFUSION OF TRANSLATION. MY FRIEND MEANS THAT THAT IS HOW YOUR HUMAN MIND INTERPRETS OUR COMMUNICATION. YOU HAVE BELLS AVAILABLE TO YOU AS A MODE OF PERCEPTION; WE MAKE USE OF THAT MODE, FOR ITS CONVENIENCE . . . OTHERWISE, YOU WOULD HEAR . . . UNPLEASING NOISES.

"Botheration," said Troublesome, and hurried her pace to keep up. Beside her, Silverweb called ahead to the Skerry.

"She is one that would prefer privacy of mind," said Silverweb. "You are distressing her with your invasions."

"I'd live through it," said Troublesome crossly. "I've lived through worse, and I don't need mollycoddling."

"There's no need for it," Silverweb answered. "I am here, and if they want to use mindspeech they can do it through me. I don't mind it."

"Not at all? Having your whole mind naked like that?"

Troublesome said it before she thought; and then she knew a deep shame, remembering the way she had lambasted Lewis Motley Wommack the 33rd for expressing a similar dislike. And he had had it to bear, if he spoke the truth, over months—not just a few moments, as she had. It might very well be different with another human, instead of this alien creature; nevertheless, she was ashamed. She had not known what it would be like, nor had she made any attempt to *imagine* it.

"Not a scrap," said Silverweb of McDaniels. "Anything in my mind, they are welcome to. My only problem is keeping up with youall in this sand—I'm not exactly short, but the rest of you are a good deal longer of leg than I'll ever be." She was silent a minute, and then nodded. "They tell me," she went on, "that it is absolutely necessary for us to hurry— that the crystals charge quickly and we have no time to spare."

All the Skerrys had in fact gotten far ahead of both the Ozark women, who had had no practice walking over dry sand and were floundering as much as they were stepping.

"If we don't hurry it up, Silverweb, I'll wager they'll just pick us up and carry us, too," fretted Troublesome, "like a couple of armloads of kindling. You fall down, I'll smack you, so help me."

"Your bark," observed Silverweb, "is much worse than your bite. Why *do* you go on like that?"

Troublesome had the usual answer ready. "I have a reputation to maintain." She needed it embroidered across her chest.

"Worked hard building it up, too, as I recall."

"Far too hard to throw it away now, in the middle of a desert."

Silverweb laughed, and stumbled, and hurried on as best she could. The Skerrys were leading them eastward, toward a line of rocks humped up on the horizon. Darkest gray, almost black, some of them *jet* black, against the sand. Where the sun struck them, rays of light split out like spears. It was hard on the eyes; what would it be like if this were not wintertime?

"The spring is there by those rocks," said Silverweb. "Or so I have been told." Her yellow hair was coming down from its usual elegant figure-eight of braid, something Troublesome had never seen happen before; she found that it worried her, and she stopped to coil the heavy weight of it back again, tuck in the stray ends, and anchor it firmly with the ironwood pins.

"Careful, Troublesome of Brightwater," Silverweb teased her. "It begins with tidying up a friend in the desert, and first thing you know you are seized with a lust for helping people and taking in stray tadlings."

"Nonsense—I just can't abide mess."

Silverweb only laughed at her. "That's Responsible's line, my friend," she said, "not yours. You should see yourself."

"Silverweb?"

"Yes?"

"What happens when we get there?"

"Whatever happens. Don't dawdle, Troublesome."

"It's farther than it looks."

"Save your breath, then!"

It was wise counsel; Troublesome hushed and concentrated on closing the gap between them and the rocks. And at last they were there, a few minutes behind the party of Skerrys.

When she saw what they were doing, she would have rushed forward to stop them, but Silverweb had a firm and astonishingly powerful grip on her arm, and the voice of a Skerry rang, equally firm, inside her head.

WE ARE SORRY, it said, TO BE DISCOURTEOUS . . . IF ONLY WE HAD MORE TIME, WE WOULD OBSERVE YOUR PREFERENCES, BUT THE CRYSTALS ARE GORGING ABOVE YOUR CITIES. THERE IS NO TIME LEFT FOR NICETIES. TROUBLESOME OF BRIGHTWATER, SILVERWEB OF MCDANIELS, THIS IS WHAT MUST BE DONE . . . PAY CLOSE ATTENTION, AND DO NOT FORGET ANY-THING THAT WE TELL YOU. TROUBLESOME, YOU SEE THAT ROCK, THERE WHERE THE WATER OVERFLOWS ITS BASIN?

The rock. Where the water overflows. Where her sister now lay naked, her hair loose in the water and her head pillowed on another rock set gently under it, where the water bubbled up out of some hidden source and poured over the still and lovely body. So frail, she looked!

"I see it."

TAKE YOUR PLACE THERE, came the voice. WE SKERRYS WILL FORM A . . . YOU HAVE NO SEMANTIC CONSTRUCT FOR IT, IT IS A SHAPE OF POWER . . . HERE AROUND THE HOLY WATER. YOU ARE TO SIT BESIDE YOUR SIS-TER, ON THAT ROCK. SILVERWEB, YOU OF CASTLE MCDANIELS, YOU WILL KNEEL UPON THE SAND, AND YOU WILL CALL DOWN THE LOVE YOU HAVE LEARNED TO DRAW UPON. YOU WILL ASK THAT THE SLEEPER WAKE, SILVERWEB OF MCDANIELS, WHILE WE SKERRYS SING FOR YOU. PLEASE, TAKE YOUR PLACES!

"I'm dreaming this," said Troublesome, too worried to be anything but cross and rude, but she did as she was bid, and she went and settled herself on the boulder near Responsible's head. Behind her, she heard the soft hiss of movement, and she looked over her shoulder and saw Silverweb kneeling on the sand with her arms raised to the sky and her eyes already rapt, even in the scalding sunlight and the constant battering of rays struck from the rocks. The Skerrys had taken up positions that looked to her to lack pattern of any kind, but she was willing to believe it was a congruent shape for them. She was willing to believe almost anything.

And now they were going to sing.

And Silverweb was going to pray.

"But what am I supposed to do?" she asked hoarsely; there was sand in her throat. "Outside of keeping this child from drowning, that is."

SHE WILL NOT DROWN, came a voice Troublesome felt was new. Not that it mattered. Bells are bells. THE WATER IS NOT DEEP ENOUGH OR SWIFT ENOUGH. THAT IS NOT THE DANGER.

"Tell me, then!"

IF SILVERWEB OF MCDANIELS IS SUCCESSFUL, IF THINGS GO AS WE

EXPECT THEM TO GO, THERE WILL BE . . . SUDDENLY, WITH NO WARNING
. . . A KIND OF TEAR IN THE FABRIC OF THE UNIVERSE. AT THAT INSTANT,
WE BELIEVE THAT YOUR SISTER WILL WAKE. AND AT THAT SAME INSTANT,
THERE WILL BE A CHANCE FOR SOMETHING EVIL TO COME THROUGH THE
TEAR WE HAVE MADE, SOMETHING THAT WAITS ALWAYS FOR JUST SUCH
AN OPPORTUNITY, THROUGH AGES UPON AGES OF TIME. YOU ARE TO PRE-
VENT THAT.

Troublesome felt terror in her somewhere; she would have sworn
there was none left in her.

The voice went on, confident, urgent, soothing her.

YOUR ROLE HERE, THE ROLE FOR WHICH YOU HAVE BEEN LEARNING
ALL YOUR LIFE LONG, IS TO RECOGNIZE THAT EVIL THING HOWEVER BEAU-
TIFULLY IT MAY BE DISGUISED, AND TO STOP IT FROM ENTERING THIS
SPACE AND THIS TIME. THAT, TROUBLESOME OF BRIGHTWATER, IS WHAT
YOU ARE FOR IN THIS WORLD—WE NEED AN EXPERT IN EVIL.

Troublesome felt the terror go, and in its place a fragment of knowledge, as of something forgotten long ago and now remembered for a fraction of time. From the breadth of that scrap of remembrance, she
straightened and stared at the Skerry she thought was speaking.

"Silverweb!" she cried out, taut as a bowstring. "What about
Silverweb? You know what you leave her open to?"

SILVERWEB OF MCDANIELS IS PROTECTED. THERE ARE FEW SHIELDS SO
INDESTRUCTIBLE AS PURITY AND VALOR IN COMBINATION. SHOULD ANY-
THING GET NEAR HER WITH STRENGTH ENOUGH TO PASS THOSE SHIELDS,
WE ARE MORE THAN ABLE TO DEAL WITH IT—AND IT IS NOT LIKELY. BUT
ALL OUR ATTENTION, AND ALL OF HERS, MUST BE FOCUSED ON A SINGLE
POINT. YOU ARE THE ONLY ONE, TROUBLESOME, WHO CAN PROTECT
YOUR SISTER. BE READY, NOW! DON'T WATCH US; WATCH THERE, CLOSE
BY HER HEAD, WHERE THE ANCIENT EVIL WILL TRY ITS BEST TO BREAK
THROUGH. . . . IT IS WEARY PAST BEARING OF LYING TRAPPED BENEATH
THAT SACRED SPRING!

Troublesome understood that well enough; she turned and set her
eyes to watch, holding her breath, her lower lip caught between her teeth
and her strong hands at the ready for . . . whatever might come.

And the Skerrys sang.

It was not precisely music, as Troublesome understood music.
Nothing to it of fiddle or dulcimer or guitar, nothing of melody or harmony either; not even rhythm. She could make no sense of it, but it rose

over the sand and the rocks with an unmistakable power. It was a call to that same Source that Silverweb called upon, and it supported her call, bore it up and carried it on what must have been notes and chords, focused it as Troublesome strained her eyes for anything—

There it was! Lovely in the water, a rose that rocked gently on the surface of the clear water, a single perfect yellow rose the size of her two cupped hands, with a scent that was as seductive as wickedness ever had been in all of time. Troublesome would have known it anywhere. She had it instantly, before it could drift one inch closer to the sands that were its first goal, crushed between her palms, and all her muscles knotted as she struggled with a loathsome squirming Unknown desperately determined to make the world its territory for a change.

"Nasty piece of work that you are," shouted Troublesome of Brightwater, laughing and exultant, "begone to wherever you came from, crawl back in your hole, you're no match for me, nor ever could be! Squirm all you like, and foul me all you care to . . . not even *trained,* are you? Ah, you're a sorry excuse for a Holy Terror, let me tell you; I was expecting more of a challenge!"

Occupied as she was, she had no way of knowing that the long silver hair of the Skerrys, and the tunics they wore, were being whipped and buffeted in a wind against which—for all their lives spent in this desert—they could scarcely stand. Or that their singing was being choked by the clouds of sand that had turned the sky black above them. Or that around Silverweb, like a shield shaped to her body, there was a clear space where no wind blew and no sand whirled, and all was still; and where all was radiant with a clear golden light that was the same color the evilness had chosen as a strategy to deceive them. Even the stench as the thing lost its control of scent-of-rose and began to pour out the smell that was natural to it could not break the concentration that poured through Troublesome's hands as they gripped her adversary by what might have been its throat.

That adversary did not impress Troublesome, nor could it touch Silverweb; they were the two polarities that served to hold this timespace intact. But the Skerrys were mightily impressed, and they gave a great sigh of relief in Troublesome's mind, all the bells calling out together, as they saw the golden rose crushed and rubbed to a slime in her hands, and they felt the wind fall and saw the desert sky clear once again.

Troublesome bent to rub her arms clean in the sand—she had no least intention of fouling the sacred water with the vile stuff that covered her to the elbows. Scrupulously, she gathered each grain that might have been contaminated by it into a heap before her, and she scrabbled a hole in the sands and shoved those soiled grains into it and laid a flat heavy rock over the spot to mark it. And still she wondered if that would do it . . . might could be there were tiny suckers and cells that would leach out through the sand and make the sacred water a new poison in a Universe already copiously overendowed with poisons. She was hesitating, crouched over the flat rock that seemed a puny barrier against such harm, when she felt Silverweb touch her shoulder, and jumped, startled.

"The Skerrys say," Silverweb told her, "that it is entirely dead, with nothing left that can exist in this world. They say it is not like other deaths, where a substance will recombine as it goes back to its original elements and enter the cycle of life again—it is too alien. You are not to worry, they say; you did what was required, and it is over."

"Well, it wasn't *much*," said Troublesome. "I could do that every day and twice on Sundays."

"They would be pleased if you were denied any such opportunity," said Silverweb dryly. "That's a direct quote."

"Direct as you can make it, I expect. Bells . . . what kind of language might that be?"

"Troublesome?"

"Troublesome looked at her, still shaking the sand off her arms.

"Yes, Silverweb?"

"It worked."

"What?"

"I said—it worked. Look there, behind you."

Troublesome whirled, and had she not been careful she might well have cried, and spoiled her image forevermore. In the silver of the water, Responsible's eyes were open, and she was speaking her sister's name.

9

Over Castle Airy, the giant crystal was beginning to take on the color of the small mallows that grew wild along Oklahomah's seacliffs; a tinge redder than the pale color of peachapple cider well made, but not yet the color of strawberry wine. As the crystal's pulsing grew stronger, its humming more clearly felt somewhere in the marrow of the bones, the point that aimed toward the sky and the point that aimed straight down toward the Castle itself began to look as if they could pierce both targets. They were darker at the points.

The people of Airy had gone inside their houses, and were huddled with their families. If they were to die, they would at least die together, not alone out in a field or a stable, or back of a counter in some store, some workshop. It was better to wait with your children and your kin and whoever you might love close by you. There was no doubt in their minds that they were going to die.

They only wondered how it would be. Would the thing plunge down toward the ground like a missile and explode in rosy flame or rosy poison? A gas, perhaps, spreading out over the Kingdom and taking them all as it coursed the air? And would it be a merciful poison, one that meant no more than a kind of falling asleep? Or would there be convulsions and agonies and desperate clawing at the throat? Or would it stay there in the air and send out its cargo of death in rays, as the lasers did? Or something else, something completely unknown . . . and would it be *merciful* . . . or would it be the stuff of nightmare? They looked at the tadlings, and especially at the babies, and prayed that it would be merciful, and swift.

At the Castle, Charity of Airy and the three Grannys in residence could feel the terror. It took no telepathic powers to sense an emotion like that, coming from every side of you, and they bit their lips and frowned till their heads ached. It wouldn't do to take the contagion of that terror; might could be they would be needed later, and in their right minds.

Castle Airy had no Magician of Rank for the Mules to contact; and given that there were three Grannys there to be put up with that was not surprising. But the word had come in from Brightwater by comset almost at once, Veritas Truebreed Motley passing it along just as calm as he would have announced a blizzard. The women of the Castle blessed the fortune that had made them part of that system, and wondered what it was like for the Kingdoms that were neither part of the Alliance of Democratic Republics nor supplied by a Magician of Rank . . . they would be completely isolated now.

Granny Forthright didn't like it a bit.

"That thing up there," she fussed, waving at the ceiling over her head with one knitting needle, "it scares the bejabbers out of me—and *I* know what it is, not to mention knowing that Airy's not the only Castle so blessed. Now what do you suppose it must be like for the Families that *don't* know those things?"

"Well, it won't *do*," pronounced Granny Flyswift. "And that's all there is to it."

"I agree, it won't," said Charity of Airy, "but talk is cheap—I suggest we give it some careful thought before we go doing anything. Is there truly anywhere that there's neither comset transmission, nor Magician of Rank, nor even a friendly neighbor to pass the word along? Count them off, ladies, and carefully!"

"Brightwater, McDaniels, Clark, and Airy," said Flyswift. "All on the comset, all brought up to date by Veritas Truebreed. That's four."

"Mizzurah's got no comsets," put in Granny Heatherknit, "but there's a Magician of Rank at Castle Motley for the Mules to tell direct, and Granny Scrabble there to see to it they don't kill him in the process. And seeing as Mizzurah's not much bigger all told than our back garden, there'll be somebody on the way to Castle Lewis with a message long since. That's six. And Tinaseeh . . . bad cess to it anyway . . . Tinaseeh's got *four* Magicians of Rank at Castle Traveller, no need to worry about *that* crew. *And* Granny Leeward, which is a shame; I'd of been right pleased to see the four at Traveller get their brains scrambled."

"Granny," chided Charity of Airy. "How you talk!"

"That's seven," said Granny Heatherknit, ignoring her completely. "Seven of twelve."

"Castle Guthrie on Arkansaw has a Magician of Rank, and so's Castle Farson—that's nine . . . oh, law!" Granny Flyswift made a soft and sorrowful noise.

"Aw, law," she said, counting it up on her fingers, "it'll be Purdy and Wommack as think they're all alone in this. No comsets, no Magicians of Rank, no way to know whatever in the world is happening and nobody as would care to make the effort to tell them. I can't say as I'm specially worried about the Wommacks—"

"You should be," Granny Forthright interrupted. "They'll be declaring it's the Wommack Curse again."

"Forthright, that slipped my mind entirely! You're right as right! And wouldn't you know it, wouldn't you just *know* it, it'd be the fool Purdys, as don't know enough to come in out of the rain anyhow, and the Wommacks with their fool *curse*, as are left stranded?" Granny Flyswift raised a finger beside her eyeglasses. "It's near on enough to make a body think they may *have* something with their curses and their poor-mouthing about bad luck following 'em everywhere and everywhen!"

"They make their own luck," Charity of Airy scoffed, "and you know it—don't talk nonsense at a time like this! Anybody wants a curse bad enough can manage to bring one down; you just have to put your back into it. And there's nothing we can do about either Wommacks or Purdys—they might as well be back on Old Earth for all we can do."

"And that makes *eleven*," Granny Heatherknit pointed out. "There's somebody left out."

"That's easy done and easy accounted for," said Granny Heatherknit. "*Nobody* wants to think about the Smiths. The Purdys now, they just need encouragement and they'd be all right. And the Wommacks, a good clout between the eyes'd break them of blaming everything and its little fingernail on their old curse. But the *Smiths,* I declare there's no hope for them! Do you know, they caught one of their Attendants *again*—this'll be what, the ninth time?—trying to tap into the comset transmissions in the dark of the night? I cannot *believe* the—"

"Granny Heatherknit!" Charity of Airy so rarely raised her voice that they all three jumped, and Heatherknit closed her mouth in sheer surprise. "If the whole world came to an end in a thunderclap, you wouldn't have time to get ready, for it would catch you gossiping!"

"Begging your pardon, Charity," said Granny Heatherknit. "I got carried away."

"And I assume," Charity went on in a more normal tone, "that we've no reason to concern ourselves with the Smiths. They've got Lincoln

Parradyne Smith the 39th over there, and whatever else he may be, he's a perfectly good Magician of Rank. It'll be only the Wommacks and the Purdys, poor souls."

"You don't suppose the Mules would call on the Grannys in such a hardscrabble?" hazarded Flyswift. "Castle Purdy has one, and there's two in residence at Castle Wommack."

All four women shuddered at the very idea, and the other two Grannys gave Flyswift a long hard look.

"If they did," said Granny Forthright solemnly, "there's now three less Grannys on Ozark."

"Pshaw! I'm not so sure," said Flyswift. "No, I'm *not* so sure as a Granny's mind is any punier than a Magician of Rank's. Who's to say, excepting always the Magicians of Rank theirselves, and why wouldn't they?"

"You care to try mindspeech with a Mule?" demanded Granny Heatherknit. "*Or* anything else as lives and breathes? Or doesn't, for that matter?"

Granny Flyswift admitted that she wouldn't, particularly.

"Well, then."

Charity of Airy, tucking back a strand of the hair now gone snow white with the long months of hardship and worry, made a sudden hushing sound. That was twice she'd caught them by surprise in one morning —it was not like Charity to be ill mannered—and they thought as they often had lately how she'd gone gaunt and old since pneumonia had taken her daughter Caroline-Ann. She'd doted on Caroline-Ann, had Charity.

"You thought of something, Charity?" asked Granny Heatherknit gently. "*Have* we forgotten somebody? Twelve Families there's always been, and twelve we've counted off—unless a thirteenth's landed, and a fine time they've picked if they have, I must say! We've accounted for all, to my mind."

"It's not that," said Charity. "No, it's something that just struck me. And I may not be right."

"And you may not be wrong, either. Many a long year now you've been solving problems, it stands to reason you'd get good at it," said Granny Heatherknit. "What's struck you, m'dear?"

"Those things. Those crystals."

"Struck us all, I do believe, Charity."

"Yes, but I've been thinking about them. . . . Veritas Truebreed Motley says they're devices to gather up energy, focus it—that they're up there charging, like batteries. And I ask myself, where are they *getting* that energy? It's happening fast, Grannys. You go look and see how much darker they are, and feel how much louder! What are they drawing on for a source?"

"Charity, might could be there's a mothership up there, beaming it down to them; might could be *anything!*"

The Grannys nodded, all in agreement on that; the unknown was, after all, the unknown. But Charity had something on her mind.

"I have an idea," she declared, "and I plan to spread it!" And she was running for Castle Airy's comset speaker, her skirts hitched up in one hand and the cane she'd taken to using lately clutched in the other.

"*If* I can get through!" she called back over her shoulder, and out the door she went, leaving the Grannys staring after her.

"Well," said Granny Heatherknit to the others, "better one of us turn on the set over there or we'll miss it ourselves, and wouldn't *that* be a comedown? Not a one of us as can keep up with Charity, cane or no cane."

Granny Flyswift moved slowly, belying her name, but she was close by the comset stud, and it flickered and came on about three words into Charity of Airy's message.

"—to me," she was saying. "I might could be wrong, but I have a feeling about this. The crystals over the Castles, they're nothing more than enormous batteries, *storage* cells, and till they're charged they can't harm us. And perhaps they charge on sunshine, or wind, or stardust, for all we know. But I'll lay you twelve to three, citizens, seeing as how they come from a planetary alliance that's founded on magic and not science . . . I'll lay you twelve to three they feed and grow fat on the plain scared-sick terror that's coming off this planet like a hurricane. I'll just *bet* you they do!"

The Grannys looked at each other, and back at Charity's confident face on the comset screen. She could be right; she'd always had an uncanny way of knowing things, made up of three parts common sense, three parts intuition, three parts blind luck, and one part they didn't care to put a name to.

"It is just possible," Charity went on, "that if we can't stop them we can at least slow them down some. If we can only be calm, and leave off feeding them fear, while we think what to do. It can't hurt, and it might help. I want you to turn your hand to something else than being scared, you hear me? Times tables, that's always good. Or counting backwards from one hundred by threes, that's even better. You can't keep your mind on being scared if you're doing that. You tadlings as don't have your numbers mastered, or anybody as is so scared they've *lost* their numbers, you do the alphabet backwards. *Backwards,* now! You can't do that and give off terror at the same time."

The people listening agreed that it made sense, and even if it hadn't it would be something to do; and those that had no comsets any longer had neighbors pounding on their doors to tell them.

Charity's voice went on and on, soothing and stroking, going out to four Kingdoms. Even Veritas Truebreed Motley, nursing his aching temples with a cold cloth at Brightwater, was nodding agreement. She had the principle right, however ignorant she might be of its workings.

"Now," said Charity of Airy, "I'll do it with you. We'll all be calm together, calm as pond water. 100. 97. 94. 91. Hmmmm . . . 88 . . . 85 . . ."

In the houses, they said it with her. And the tadlings tried the other thing and were amazed at how hard it was. Glottal stop, that was easy. Z, to go on with. Y, and then X, a person could manage. But from there on it was hard work, and who ever would of thought it? The alphabet, that everybody knew like they knew the look of their thumbs! Backwards it fairly brought the sweat out all over you. X . . . Q?

"Can't be Q!" said a tiny one, crossly, stamping her foot. "It's not time yet for Q!"

"What is it, then?" challenged her brother. "You're so smart . . . oh! I know! W! Before X comes W!"

"Pheeyeew," fussed the little girl. "W . . . now, let's us just see . . ."

Charity of Airy and the Grannys were well satisfied; they could feel the easing in the air almost immediately. It was just as well, under the circumstances, that none of them could see or sense the carnage in Smith Kingdom, where Lincoln Parradyne Smith the 39th was paying the penalty for his phony Granny that *was* no Granny, and the people of the Kingdom along with him. Long before it occurred to any of the other Magicians of Rank to ask a Mule to pass the message along to the Mules of Smith, Lincoln Parradyne had paid his bill in full; he lay dead on the floor of the Throne Room, his brain crisped in his skull like a dead coal. And the only thing spared him was the horror outside and in, where the people of Smith trampled one another in their panic as they tried insanely to flee the menace above them. The crystal over Castle Smith was just a little different; its color matched the color of the blood smeared on the streets and the stairs of the town, almost exactly.

Troublesome of Brightwater lifted her sister out of the spring and held her close, sacred water and all, wondering if she had ever been so happy before. Bring on the giant alien crystals, bring on the slimy alien wickednesses, bring on anything you fancied; nevertheless, her sister was awake again.

Responsible fought herself free of Troublesome's embrace, which was somewhat more enthusiastic than was compatible with breathing.

"Troublesome?"

She tugged at the long black braid, to get Troublesome's attention, and wiped some of the water off her face, and asked plaintively if she could *please* have an explanation. It was not every day a person woke up naked in a creek, with a crowd attending.

She listened, her face growing more and more stern, while she was told. All about the awfulness that had come when she was put in pseudo-coma. The poverty and the sickness and the weather all uncontrolled . . . it sounded like the tales of Old Earth . . . and nobody knowing what might be happening anyplace but the four Kingdoms of the Alliance, except for rumors. All about the Grannys' climb up the mountain, and Troublesome's dreadful ocean voyage. And when the part about Lewis Motley Wommack the 33rd came along, she cried out a broad word in total indignation that startled Silverweb of McDaniels right out of the last scraps of her rapture.

"It would of been when I was asleep, Troublesome!" declared Responsible of Brightwater. "That fool man! *Ignorant*, that's what he is, not to mention no sense at all. Half the night on Brightwater it's day on Kintucky, clear across that ocean on the other side of the world—did he never learn *anything?* I was dreaming . . . I remember the dreams. Oh, I remember them well, and they're not fit for Silverweb's ears. But never, never did I imagine that while I dreamed I was intruding on his mind. . . . The *idiot!* Oh, I'll make him pay, I promise you—oh, how I'll make him pay! He'll curse the day he was born, and long for the day that death releases him before I'm through . . . *stup*id man!"

"He is that," said Troublesome. "He might have asked you—but he wouldn't stoop. That's how he put it."

Responsible struggled from her sister's arms onto the rocks, where she sat hugging her knees and clothed only in her long hair, that was almost dry now in the hot desert sun.

"It was the Timecorner Prophecy," she said sorrowfully, "and no way to escape it. But I must say there's nothing elegant to the way it was fulfilled."

"Nor any excuse," said Silverweb. "For either him *or* you."

Responsible hadn't any interest at that moment in subtle moral questions. "*Now* what?" she said. She was a tad dazed, but she was not so addled that she intended to get into a discussion of how she and young Wommack might have managed to avoid what had been decreed since the beginning of time. What she wanted to know was the status of things.

Before Troublesome or Silverweb could speak, the Skerrys took it up.

RESPONSIBLE OF BRIGHTWATER, THE PLANETS OF THE GARNET RING NOW SEE THIS WORLD AS RIPE FOR THE CONQUERING, AND THEY HAVE COME TO PLUCK IT—IT FALLS NOW WITHIN THEIR LAWS OF COLONIAL RIGHT.

I CAN SEE THAT IT MIGHT, Responsible replied, not caring how much her mindspeaking might startle the other two women. There didn't seem to be much left in the way of secrets anyhow. WHAT HAVE THEY DONE, EXACTLY?

THEY HAVE HEARD THE REPORT OF THE OUT-CABAL, THAT THIS WORLD HAS FALLEN TO ANARCHY AND DISASTERS, AND THEY HAVE SET A . . . YOU HAVE NO SEMANTIC CONSTRUCT FOR IT. NO . . . YOU DO! YOU MUST IMAGINE A STORAGE CELL, DAUGHTER OF BRIGHTWATER, ONE HUNDRED AND TEN FEET FROM POINT TO POINT, POISED OVER EACH AND EVERY OZARK CASTLE AND FEEDING NOW—CHARGING NOW—WHILE WE STAND HERE TALKING. THEY ARE SHAPED LIKE DIAMONDS, AND YOU WOULD CALL THEM . . . CRYSTALS. THEY ARE DEADLY, AND THERE IS VERY LITTLE TIME.

WHAT HAS BEEN DONE? Responsible asked them, and Troublesome realized suddenly that her sister's mindvoice was just that, a voice, and not bells. When she had the leisure, *if* she had the leisure, she would consider the question of why that caused no barrier to the conversation. HAVE

THEY BROUGHT OUT THE LASERS AGAINST THE THINGS? HAVE THEY TRIED A TRANSFORMATION, A DELETION TRANSFORMATION WITH ALL THE NINE MAGICIANS OF RANK—

The Skerry cut her off.

YOU FORGET, it said. THERE HAS BEEN NO MAGIC ON THIS WORLD WHILE YOU SLEPT—YOU HAVE BORNE IT ALL WITHIN YOUR SELF. AS FOR THE LASERS, YOUR PEOPLE HAVE NO WAY OF KNOWING WHAT IT MIGHT DO IF THEY WERE TO PIERCE THE CRYSTALS, OR EVEN IF THEY WERE TO TRY—NOR DO WE, NOR DO THE MULES, NOR DO THE GENTLES. THE GENTLES, DAUGHTER OF BRIGHTWATER, ARE VERY DISTRESSED BY ALL THIS. . . . I DO NOT KNOW IF THEY WILL EVER COME UP TO THE DAYLIGHT AGAIN. NOW, WE ALL ASK THE SAME THING, AND IT SEEMS TO US ONLY JUSTICE, SINCE IT IS YOUR PEOPLE WHO HAVE BROUGHT ALL THIS UPON US. WE ASK THAT YOU DO SOMETHING, FOR THIS WORLD IS IN YOUR CHARGE.

It seemed to Troublesome that that wasn't justice at all, or even likely, and she and Silverweb both protested at once that Responsible was bound to be weak and like a newborn babe for some time, that she would have to get her strength back as anybody does after a long time ill, and that asking her to take on a whole passel of alien planets in her condition was downright ridiculous. It came out garbled, a scrap from Troublesome and a scrap from Silverweb, and some scraps from both, but they were of one mind on the matter.

What they had not taken into account was the strength of the energy that was being lent to Responsible by the Skerrys and the Mules. This was their planet, too, and had been theirs many thousands of years before ever an Ozarker set foot on it, and they had no desire to see it fall to the Garnet Ring, with who knew what consequences to follow. They didn't know a great deal about the peoples of the Garnet Ring, but they knew enough to be sure they weren't anybody you'd want for neighbors, and never mind the details.

Responsible of Brightwater gave her sister and Silverweb one look of considerable irritation, drew on the more than ample reservoir of energy the Mules and the Skerrys were offering her, and before the other two women could so much as draw a breath she had SNAPPED the three of them back to her own bedroom at Castle Brightwater, leaving Sterling to bring the wagon home.

Sitting on the edge of her bed, where she'd lain so long silent and motionless, she clucked her tongue, and glared at Troublesome and Silverweb, both of them more than slightly startled by their unaccustomed mode of transportation.

"This won't do," announced Responsible. "This won't do at all. Let me get something on my bones besides my skin, and I'll see to it."

And she headed for her wardrobe with her hands already busy braiding her hair, pausing only the few seconds it took to advise Troublesome that she'd never *seen* anybody quite so grubby and it would be a good thing if she had a tidy-up before she forgot how the parts of a decent female were supposed to be arranged.

10

"My lady—I am afraid."

The words came from an unusual source; Jessica of Lewis, Teacher Jessica these past seven months, was in the usual run of things a tower of strength. She was a true Three: brilliant, creative, high-spirited, and one for whom everything seemed to come easily. She had slipped into the Teaching Order as a hand slips into a glove made to its measure. None of the usual kicking at the traces for Jessica of Lewis. Not a flicker when her beloved books—"*Real* books!" the others had whispered. "Not micros, *real* books! And three of them!"—had been taken from her and added to the community library in Castle Wommack's north wing. When all the rest were down, it was Teacher Jessica they relied on, to bring their spirits up and to remind them once again that for those that are vowed to poverty the experience of poverty is no hardship.

Now she sat in Faculty Meeting, fifth down from Teacher Jewel of Wommack, so fast had she ascended through the ranks, and said: "My lady, I am afraid."

"We are all afraid," Teacher Jewel responded. "Not to be afraid would show a lack of common sense, or an unhealthy detachment from reality. There is a group consensus; nowhere in that consensus is there space for the crystal suspended above this Castle. How could we *not* be afraid?"

"That bodacious great rock hanging over our heads and ready for to drip down blood, it looks like . . . Law! Teacher Jessica, I should *hope* we're afraid!"

"If it is a rock," said Jewel of Wommack carefully, giving the new Teacher Candidate a measuring look, "what is holding it where it is, Cousin Naomi? Rocks do not float, neither do they fly. And there is no more magic."

Naomi of Wommack met her kinswoman's eyes without flinching; a good sign, thought Jewel. Naomi's speech was rougher than any Candidate's they had accepted yet; one would have thought she was trying for the formspeech used by the Grannys, except that even the Grannys no longer said "for to" before their verbs . . . perhaps in a moment of great excitement one might, but Jewel could not recall an example. Naomi had come out of a pocket on the far side of the Wilderness Lands of Kintucky, from a cluster of six households so isolated they had not had comsets even before Responsible of Brightwater was struck down. The rest of Kintucky had not even known they were there, and given the possibilities of marriage open to them they would not have lasted long—it was good fortune a Teacher, canvassing the Wilderness on her Mule, had stumbled across them.

"There will be again," said Naomi, confident as a child. "As there do be star and sun and tree. Somehow it's got a hitch in it, it's a kind of drought as comes in a bad year for the rains, but no reason for to doubt. *I* don't doubt."

Jewel of Wommack believed her; she was as transparent as thin new ice on a puddle. And—always provided they all lived through whatever this crisis was—Naomi's ways might require more polishing than the other Candidates' had. *Maybe.* Jewel had discussed it when Naomi of Wommack joined them, and there had been disagreement among the senior faculty.

"She will be going back to Teach in the Wilderness Lands and along their borders," Jewel had reminded them. "Might could be that if her speech and her manners are greatly changed they won't trust her there, and trust is the foundation of Teaching. Think of my brother—when he took up the speechmode of the Magicians of Rank, purely to spite them, and then kept it up purely to spite the *rest* of us—think how it changed the way people behaved around him. He has a good deal more difficulty coaxing the young women into the haymows than he had when he spoke like anybody else . . . and a very good thing that is, I might add."

"But how, my lady," the others had protested, letting the matter of Lewis Motley drop, "how can she be respected if she speaks like she does, and drinks her coffee out of her saucer?"

Jewel's eyes, always dark blue, had gone even darker, and she had rebuked them sharply, reminding them for what seemed to her the ten thousandth time that it was *presence* that inspired respect, not fine manners and flowery speech.

"Do you ever look at your Teachers' Manuals?" she had asked them, exasperated. "It's set down there for you clearly enough, if you'd only look!"

It was among the Rules Major:

> The essence of inspiring belief is to achieve *congruence,* so that the channel of the voice and the channel of the body are in every smallest feature in true harmony.

And the codicil:

> And it would be well if the channel of the heart could be harmonious as well, providing always for the protection of the innocent.

That is . . . if you knew too much, keep it to yourself, and never mind the congruence of the heart, which was why it went in a codicil.

Candidate Naomi of Wommack met the congruence requirement to perfection. Her words were rough, her features were rough, her manners were rough, her movements were rough. She strode when she walked, she leaped up when she stood, she collapsed in a heap when she sat. . . .

"It is congruence," Teacher Jewel had said, ending the discussion. "It may be of great value. I know no requirement that Teachers must be like dolls, all matched the way the Grannys are. I may in fact go back to an easier way of speaking my own self; I was more comfortable that way."

A voice in the back of her head had said sadly: *No, you will not.* And she had known it was true. Senior Teacher of the Order, and not yet sixteen—she needed every mark of authority she could get, including the elegant speechmode—not quite his own, but elegant nonetheless—in which Lewis Motley Wommack had drilled her till she wept. He had been quite right.

"My lady?"

Jewel was wrenched from her reverie, and embarrassed that she'd been able to fall into it, considering the circumstances.

"I apologize," she said distractedly. "My mind was somewhere . . . in a pleasanter time."

"We are wondering," said the speaker, a young Teacher whose voice had the granite edge fright gives when held back on tight rein, "if we should go on with the lessons today. We are afraid . . . the children are even more so."

"And what are the children doing at this moment, Teacher Cristabel?" Jewel asked her. "Do you know?"

"Huddled around their parents, sitting in their laps and being rocked if they're little enough, cowering under beds and porches . . . anything to get out of sight of that . . . thing. Whatever it is."

"In that case," said Jewel of Wommack resolutely, "we will of course go on with lessons. And the quicker the better. The most helpful thing we could do would be to present those children with the idea that there is order in their days *despite* that unholy object, and that it hasn't the power to make the grownups set aside the usual daily routine."

One of her faculty had a thought that had been thick on the far side of the world, in Airy Kingdom.

"They are all about to die," she said. "Better they die together than apart."

Jewel felt a rage that would be no help here, and she put it aside to be dealt with another time, and set her questions.

"Teacher Cecilia," she asked, "how is it that you know they, or any of us, are about to die?"

"My lady!"

"Well? If you have information, speak up; and if you have none, hold your peace. Has that crystal done any one of us, or any thing, injury?"

"Not yet, my lady."

"Not yet! But it will, eh? It does not fit the group consensus, will not be poked or shoved into the model we have built and labeled HERE SITS THE REAL WORLD . . . and *therefore,* it has to be a source of death."

"But my lady—"

"Per*haps,*" said Jewel icily, "might could be the time has come for a change in that model. Had you thought of that? It is unknown; one fears the unknown. No doubt the first rainbow ever to be seen in the sky had people running and squalling, too."

Teacher Candidate Naomi was fascinated, Jewel could tell, and before she could call out something disgraceful, the Senior Teacher moved smoothly on into her next sentence.

"Until such time as we have evidence that that thing is a danger, we will behave normally," she instructed them. "That is our duty."

The Teachers and the Candidates nodded, though some did it reluctantly. They could see the rightness of what she said, and hoped those Teachers out riding their circuits or in residence in small towns beyond reach of the Castle would see it as well. The sight of the Teachers at their posts presenting history and grammar and mathematics and ecology and music theory to the children, as they did on any other day, would go a long way toward calming any panic. Business as usual, that was what was needed.

Lewis Motley Wommack the 33rd must have thought so, too. He came into the room in a fury, demanding to know why they weren't already on their way to their classes.

Jewel's voice sliced the air like a whip: "When *I* say that they are to go to their classes, they will go—and not until!"

The other women dropped their eyes and folded their hands; except for Naomi, who would not for anything have missed a single detail of the confrontation between brother and sister.

"Jewel, I do not mean to interfere—" the young man began.

"Then don't. Go on about your business . . . if you have any business . . . and leave us to ours. You have nothing to contribute here, and we have no time to coddle you."

I will never stop paying, thought Lewis Motley; *never. She wanted a home, and a man's body beside hers at night, and babes in her arms, and tadlings playing round her that looked just like that man; that's all she ever wanted. And I gave her this instead.*

It had been necessary, he was still convinced of that. Without the comsets, cut off from the rest of the continents, the people of Kintucky would have been condemned to ignorance and superstition; the Teachers had been absolutely necessary. But she was not going to forgive him.

And there'd been the matter of Responsible of Brightwater . . . that had *not* been necessary.

He gave her a stiff and formal nod, longing for the days when she'd worshiped the ground he walked on and the air he breathed. He wondered sometimes if he would ever love anything or anyone as he loved his little sister. He hoped not.

"I beg your pardon," said the former Guardian of Castle Wommack, and closed the door quietly behind him as he made his exit.

"Now then," said Jewel—and they all understood; the incident had not happened—"the only question is what you are to tell the children. And we must decide quickly, because you should be in your classrooms in ten minutes, and well prepared. Suggestions, please."

Teacher Sharon of Airy, second in rank to Jewel herself, spoke first.

"Do we *know* anything?"

"Nothing," said Jewel. "It was not there; it appeared out of nowhere and it *was* there; it remains there. It grows darker in color, and the Castle throbs with the vibration it is emitting. That is all."

"We cannot tell the children that!"

"Why not? It is the truth."

The protests came from every one of the seventeen who sat around the table, except Naomi of Wommack.

"Dozens," said Naomi. "What point is there making up tales and pretty lies? Reckon any tadling smart enough to do his three-times is going to see we're lying—they do, you know. You can't lie to tadlings. Best they see we know what they know and *howsomever,* pointy rock or no pointy rock, we're there for to teach same as always. *Unless* one of youall has an explanation to offer 'em as will pass for truth."

"Well? Have you?" Jewel asked the silent women.

"It seems harsh," said Teacher Sharon, considering.

"It is quite clear," Jewel of Wommack told her hesitant faculty, "that whatever that is up there, it was not brought to us by the Good Fairies for our delight. What is harsh is letting those children cower and shiver and cry all the day long while we sit here and console one another. You will go to your classes—as usual. If the children ask what that is in the air, you will say you don't know, and you will go on with your lessons— as usual. If they do not bring it up, *you* will not bring it up. As for me, I will get the fastest Mule we have in the stables and ride out to try to reach the Teachers in the country schools, as many as I can, and I will be telling them what I have told you. As usual. Do youall understand?"

"Yes, my lady."

Fifteen grudging yes-my-ladys, and one willing one from Naomi of Wommack; Naomi would of been willing, Jewel suspected, if ordered to lay herself full length in a fire.

"Let's get on with it, then," said Teacher Jewel, and she took up the small bell at her right hand to give the three rings of dismissal.

So it was that Jewel of Wommack was not in Booneville when the emergency alarms shrilled from every comset in the Castle and the town. She was out on Gamaliel, a Mule short in temper but long on endurance, making her way around a thicket of tangled briars toward the thirty-one families of Capertown, six miles beyond the borders of the capital.

There was a delay while the people realized what the sound was, it had been so long. For a few moments they thought it was something new from the horror in the sky, and the Teachers were hard put to it to keep their charges calm as they waited for word to come explaining it to *them*. They kept their voices steady and went on with the measured presentation of principles and concepts, and if their hands trembled they clasped them firmly behind their backs. The astonishing noise went on and on and on. And then, almost everywhere at once, people remembered.

"It's the comset alarm!" It came from a hundred places. People stared at one another, and shouted: "What does it mean?"

The comsets had been silent on Kintucky two years at least; and even when they'd been an ever present part of daily life, the *alarm* had been rare. It was no wonder they were confused. But when they turned to look at the comset screens set in their housewalls they saw that it was true; they were functioning again. The red call light in the upper right-hand corner of each screen was blinking steadily on and off, and the alarm shrilled on. Those that had hung a picture or a weaving over the screen to escape its dead gray eye always staring at them rushed to take away the barrier and get to the ON stud.

"Ah, the Holy One be praised, the Holy One be praised!" cried Granny Copperdell at Castle Wommack. "*Will* you look? It's herself, oh glory be, it's herself! It's Responsible of Brightwater her*self!*"

First a miracle of terror, now a miracle of some other kind . . . life was confusing. But even in the classrooms everything else stopped, while the people of Ozark listened to Responsible's voice.

She began by explaining, for those Castles that might not yet know, what the crystals were and where they came from. She spoke hurriedly and promised them details later, when there was more time.

"But for now," she said, "the details don't matter. For now, youall must listen to me, and pay close attention to what I say, and waste no more time in carry-ons. Listen, now!

"The peoples of the Garnet Ring are not savages—they have laws. By their laws they may move to conquer only planets and systems of planets that are governed, as they are, by magic rather than by science. And of *those* planets they are constrained to conquer only in two situations: first, when the planet they're hankering after has gone to anarchy and has no government of its own to be displaced; second, if the planet they fancy is dying anyway, of natural disasters or of war. Ozark—*this* planet—comes near meeting both those conditions at this very minute, if what I'm told is true; and I've no reason to doubt it. And that is why the Garnet Ring has set those crystals in our skies.

"I do not know what the crystals will do if they aren't stopped," she told them. "I haven't the least idea. I do know, however, that they have power enough to destroy us twelve times over, no matter how it is they go about it. And I know how to *stop* them! If youall will help me, and waste not one second."

Responsible paused and gave them time to take all that in, and beside her, beyond the range of the cameras, Troublesome squeezed her sister's left hand, and Silverweb of McDaniels held tightly to her right hand, and the Grannys sat with their hands pressed to their lips. As for Veritas Truebreed Motley, he paced. There was no way of knowing if the comsets were working on the other continents where they'd been disused all this time. There was no way of knowing if there was anybody left alive on some of those continents to hear the alarm and turn on the comsets if they *did* still work. And there was no way, for sure there was no way, to predict whether, even if everything was working and all the Ozarkers were hanging on Responsible's every word, she would be able to persuade them. The suspense was almost as hard on him as his humiliation. *How* had Responsible of Brightwater been brought out of pseudocoma, without the help of the Magicians of Rank? Nobody would tell him; Responsible had just smiled, a maddening gleeful smile, when he tried to find out.

Veritas Truebreed smacked his fist in his palm, and he paced.

Meanwhile, Responsible went on talking, keeping her voice in the mode that carried the message: THERE IS NO QUESTION BUT THAT I WILL BE OBEYED. "At every Castle," she said, "you will call a Family Meeting, and elect—at once!—a Delegate to the New Confederation of Continents of Ozark. The Magicians of Rank will SNAP the Delegates here to Brightwater as quickly as you choose them . . . if you have no Magician of Rank in residence, be ready; one will be with you within the next half hour, and will not be pleased if you have no Delegate ready to return with him when he arrives, I warn you. Confederation Hall is at this very minute being made ready for the Delegates—"

Troublesome whistled softly, long and low, and Silverweb smiled at the lie, and the two of them—followed by the Grannys at as much speed as the old women could muster—headed out of Castle Brightwater for Confederation Hall, with Troublesome waving the keys above her head to show she still had them.

"Once the Delegates are here," Responsible went on, "they will offer a motion that a New Confederation be formed, second it, and pass it by unanimous vote—they will have ample time and more than ample time to write a new Constitution and work out all the trimmings and doodads they care to, when the crystals have been withdrawn. But that *will not be enough*.

"It will be necessary," she told them solemnly, "to call the roll."

That had never been done within the memory of anyone living, nor the memory of their parents, nor their grandparents. Very early, before the Ozarkers had moved out from Marktwain and their number had been small, it had been done. But now?

"The Garnet Ring wants this planet very badly," said Responsible. "Whatever you have done to it as I slept, and I understand that you have not been idle in your destruction, it is still rich in ores and forests and land and seawater . . . everything that a crowded system like the Garnet Ring needs and does not have. They have set no controls on their population and no controls on their greed—they will not give us up for a gesture. It will be done, one vote at a time, for every citizen over the age of twelve years, Kingdom by Kingdom. Stay at your comsets, and when the Chair says to begin, you will answer one at a time, in an orderly fashion. You will say, for example: 'I, So-and-So of Clark, hereby cast my vote for the New Confederation, and I say *Aye;* let it be so recorded.' It is of course your privilege to vote *against* the New Confederation; if enough of you do so, we will learn what the Garnet Ring proposes to do with us."

And she let them think about *that* a while. As a democratic method of persuasion, it had its shortcomings, and she was conscious of them. On the other hand, death or slavery weren't overly democratic either, and they appeared to be the other alternatives. If the means turned out not to be justified by the ends, she would have some paying to do. She'd worry about that when it happened. Right now, she had a world to convince.

A comcrew tech stuck his head in at the door, then, and raised both fists above his head and shook them at her. That meant the data was back

to the computers; that meant the comsets had been turned on everywhere
—even on Tinaseeh. That meant they were working, and it meant there
were Ozarkers to watch them. Responsible would have jumped up and
down for joy except that it would of introduced an element of confusion
into her presentation.

She nodded at the man and then began again, since there might of
been those coming in just then from the woods or the fields, or only just
finding a house that still had a comset in working order. And she went
through it all one more time. And when she got to the end of that, she
began *again*.

By the time she had reached the third recitation of the manner of
calling the roll of every Ozarker over the age of twelve, the first Delegate
had landed in the yard of Confederation Hall, his arms clasped round the
waist of Shawn Merryweather Lewis the 7th, Magician of Rank in residence at Castle Motley, the two of them seated on a bedraggled and
scrawny Mule without so much as a saddle blanket. Never mind, though;
it had been able and willing—it had in fact been eager—to fly.

They were landing everywhere, and the Grannys of Brightwater
threw open the doors of Confederation Hall and shouted them a welcome, while Troublesome sneaked out the back door and went home,
and Silverweb stood and smiled. Now they would show those cursed
Garnet Ringers, whatsoever they might be! They would show them what
a people united could do, how swift and sure a freedom-loving people
could move to set up a new and a strong government, how quick such
a government could move to take care of such petty matters as weather
and hunger and disease and disaster and war!

The Grannys were as near ecstasy as a Granny could get, and in the
excitement of the moment they had not even noticed that the arthritis
that had been crippling them was gone. They stood on the steps of
Confederation Hall, holding the doors wide, the tears pouring down their
faces, cheering as each new Delegate arrived, and as each Mule and
Magician of Rank SNAPPED out of sight to go after the next one.

They paid no mind to the fact that Silverweb of McDaniels, amuse-
ment in her eyes and cobwebs on her dress, was headed back toward
Castle Brightwater to see what she could do now to help Responsible.
Nor did it occur to them that Troublesome was long gone.

It was a brand-new day.

11

On Tinaseeh there was no need for anybody to ride out into the country-side to search out people beyond the range of the comsets. The Castle stood grim and dark at the central point of the three squares marked off by the logs of ironwood, set upright side by side and lasered to wicked points; this was Roebuck, capital city and only settlement of Tinaseeh, and it had ample room within it for the six hundred and three persons still alive in Traveller Kingdom.

Except for the members of the Family and the Magicians of Rank, except for the College of Deacons and the Tutors—and except of course for Granny Leeward—the people of Tinaseeh were frail and ill. Measles and croup and hunger took the young; pneumonia and cancer and hunger took the old; and at the Castle the Magicians of Rank themselves took turns guarding the secret stores of extra food and the priceless herbs. They could trust nobody else with that duty.

When the comset alarms went off, piercing the stillness that covered Roebuck like a visible miasma, broken only by the exhortations of Jeremiah Thomas Traveller the 26th and his Deacons—no child had laughed on Tinaseeh in many days, and now they were past crying as well—they were like red-hot irons through the ears of the silent people. And Jeremiah Thomas, knowing the high tone at once for what it had to be, cursed in a way that brought the members of his household upright in shock. They had never heard a single broad word cross his lips before, not one; and there he stood shaking his fist at the wall where the red comset light was blink-ing, and shouting fit to turn the air blue for miles around.

Granny Leeward was the first to recover, and the first to realize how little time they had.

"He's right," she said urgently, "though I'll not defend the filth he's used to express himself. . . . I do believe his mind's turned, and no won-der. But we should never of left the comsets in the houses! They ought to have been ripped out, made truly useless, the day we got back here from the accursed Grand Jubilee, aye, if not long before. Leaving them, that was a grave mistake, and Jeremiah Thomas is right thrice over! But listen—it will be a while, might could be quite a while—before the people remember what that sound is. Might could be they won't remember, for that matter; I don't recall they've ever heard it. *If* we hurry! *If* we get out and call them out of their houses before they notice the lights—those, now, they'll remember. All of you, you go fast, you go from house to house and silence the wicked things, cut the wires or whatever it is as makes them go, and we might could get out of this yet! If we hurry, mind!"

"What could it be for?" marveled Feebus Timothy Traveller the 6th, staring around at the others. "What do you suppose?"

"Whatever it is, it comes from the womb of evil," said Leeward viciously, "for only Brightwater has the means to send out that alarm. And whatever it is, we do not care to hear it!"

"Now, Granny Leeward," the young Magician of Rank protested, "it may have to do with the crystal! And if it does, we—"

"No doubt it *does* have to do with the crystal," Granny Leeward threw back at him. "And no doubt you're still not quite over that fever you came near taking, eh, Feebus Timothy? Of *course* it has to do with the crystal; and nevertheless, we do not choose to hear! Where is your *faith?*"

If the people of Tinaseeh had not been so weak and so sickly, the Family might have been able to bring it off. Some would of been in the half dozen stores of Roebuck; some in the schoolrooms of the Tutors; some outside the walls working in the forests or the fields; some would of been walking in the town on their way to or from any of these things. But far too many of the handful of people remaining were housebound by sickness, and from their pallets laid on cold bare floors they had demanded that the comsets be turned on, and they had heard every word spoken by Responsible of Brightwater.

While the rest of the Family and its deputies were racing through the streets to try to prevent that from happening, Granny Leeward and Jeremiah Thomas Traveller sat alone before the comset at Castle Traveller and heard it all—twice through. And when the others returned to report that they had failed, that they had been too late, the Granny was ready for them.

"Call the people together," she said. Her voice made them think of the water that ran deep in the Tinaseeh caves in utter blackness, too cold even for blindfish to survive. "Those as cannot walk are to be carried, and those as try to say you nay are to be offered . . . promised . . . a taste of the Long Whip. Everybody, every last chick and child, is to be brought into the Inner Courtyard to hear Jeremiah Thomas speak against this temptation. Souls are precious things—we'll not see them lost *this* easily!"

It took time, because the messengers were few and already tired from their first hasty dash through the town, but not so long as might have been expected, given the frail health of the people. The College of Deacons met some of them in the streets, already on their way, carrying sick children in their arms. And in not much more than an hour after the alarm had sounded, they were all assembled. The Family, the Magicians of Rank, the College of Deacons—they sat on a platform used in happier times for the feastday services of the church, meant to give space for the Reverends and the choirs. The people that could stand stood, lined up in a squared-off horseshoe with the platform at its open end. Those that couldn't manage that leaned against the rough walls or lay on their pallets on the ground, or were cradled in the arms of relatives and friends.

And Jeremiah Thomas Traveller spoke, while Granny Leeward sat at his right hand with the Long Whip coiled and ready in her lap, and a muscle twitching high in her right cheek just along the ridge of the bone.

"My people," said the Master of Castle Traveller tenderly, raising his arms and spreading them wide in the pastoral embrace, "you know how I love you! More dear to me you are than ever son or daughter was to other man, more tightly bound to me than ever the bonds of blood have been! For you are *the faithful* . . . out of holy suffering you have come pure and filled with precious, nay, with priceless grace; around you the wicked and the weak in spirit have fallen like grass before the scythe, and yet you have stood. *You* have not fallen. You have not shrunk from the blade, not from its very edge; when it was at your throat you have bent to give it the kiss of fearless love. You have never doubted! How I love you—perhaps I love you more even than is fitting, but the Holy One will forgive me that.

"And how do I know all this? How can I be sure? Oh, my beloved people, only think what has been vouchsafed to you this *glorious* day! Those the Almighty loves, those are chastened; those the Almighty trusts, *those* are tested; those the Holy One counts among the elect, those are sent the blessing of ultimate temptation that they may demonstrate their contempt for *all* temptation! And this has come to you, to *you,* to every last and least and weariest one of you . . . for the Almighty knows, knows in confident glory, that there *is no test* your faith is not equal to!

"When I think"—and here Jeremiah Thomas let his hands move in and cross over his heart, and he added a judicious quaver to his voice— "when I think what honor has been done you, my beloved flock, I am struck to the heart. Who am I, that this blessing should pour down on me? Who am I, that I should lead so mighty, so fearless, an army of souls? What an honor has been done *me,* the least of all the servants!

"Fall to your knees," urged Jeremiah Thomas Traveller the 26th, his words honey and oil spreading around him, "fall to your knees! The trollop has spoken again from the citadel of sin, and you have heard her! And unto you, beloved, has come the opportunity to say to the Daughter of Brightwater a *No!* that will echo throughout the farthest corners of this world! *No!* you will say, we are not afraid of the abomination that pulses and grows each moment more gorged with blood above our heads, for it is only one more of the puny tests sent to try our faith, and we *glory* in that trial! *No!* you will say, we are not afraid of your Garnet Ring, of your Out-Cabal, of your bedtime tales invented for the terrifying of little children —for we are not little children, but *warriors* of the faith! There is no Garnet Ring! There is no Out-Cabal! There are no alien peoples prepared to make of us slaves or victims! There is only the just symbol of the wrath of the Holy One Almighty, set in the skies above us as a sign of the anger we have earned . . . and when we cry out *No!* and *No!* and *No!* nine times nine times again to the Whore of Brightwater, that symbol will fade away as do the clouds, that bring the gentle rains, and as the sunlight, that makes way for the healing hours of the night!"

Beside him the Granny sat nodding, her face smooth now with satisfaction, the Long Whip twitching every now and again at a particularly telling phrase from the lips of her son.

The "mighty army" listened in silence, and they heard the man out, as was proper. There were some that had been standing, and as the sentences rolled on, slipped to the ground or leaned more heavily against the walls; but not one left, and not one made a sound.

And then, when the last Amen had been shouted out and Jeremiah Thomas Traveller stood soaked with sweat and glowing with his righteous

exultation, and ordered them back to their homes to take a day's holiday
for prayer, one man stepped forward. Eustace Laddercane Traveller the
4th, him that had had a wife and ten children, and had seen that wife die
in the throes of giving that tenth child birth, and had seen five more of
his tadlings harvested by death since the day he had stood and forced them
to watch the public whipping of Avalon of Wommack. He stepped out
from among the others and walked straight and without so much as a
tremble to his lips right up to the platform. The Granny leaned forward,
uneasy, though her son had dropped to *his* knees and was holding out his
arms to gather in this man he thought overcome with the emotions of the
moment; and the Granny was right in her judgment.

Eustace Laddercane Traveller looked them over where they held
their places. The Master of Traveller, and his Family assembled, not a one
lost to disease or privation. The four Magicians of Rank in their elegant
black. The College of Deacons, all trim, to be sure, but all hearty, all with
color in their cheeks. And when he'd looked them over one by one he
turned his back on them, standing where the Long Whip could wrap him
round without the Granny having to do more than raise her arm, and he
called out in a voice as strong as Jeremiah Thomas's had been.

"The citadel of sin is just behind me," shouted Eustace Laddercane,
"and its whore sits there holding the Long Whip and hovering over her
loathsome son, him that is a *false* Reverend, and a false guardian, and the
liar of all liars! Look at them . . . look well, for I've no skill at preaching,
and I've got no words to sway you with—but I've got eyes, and so have
you. *There* sits evil, and I know it when I see it. And if Granny Leeward
does not strike me down, I will go as Delegate to the New Confederation
at Brightwater, if I have to swim the Ocean of Storms and the Ocean of
Remembrances to get there! And if she *does,* if she does—choose you
another Delegate, and then go back to your homes and cast your votes
for the only hope you have in this life or the next!" And he waited, then,
only the set of his shoulders betraying his awareness of what might fall
upon them in the seconds just ahead.

You would not have thought that dragtail pitiful crowd of people
could manage to cheer or to shout or to clap their scrawny hands together,
but you would of been wrong. Man, woman, and child, they roared their
approval of Eustace Laddercane Traveller's words and of his election as
Delegate, and the Inner Courtyard became a forest of fists, raised high and

waving their defiance, now and forevermore. On the platform, the rats were abandoning ship: the Family was moving back, as far as they could get from the howling mob; the members of the College of Deacons were leaping from the platform into the crowd to join the revolt; and the Magicians of Rank were squabbling among themselves as to which should be the one to SNAP the Delegate to the meeting at Confederation Hall.

Only the Granny held fast, rocking slowly where she sat, letting the Long Whip fall from her nerveless hands in utter disgust. She knew they would not touch her. Not even the father of little Avalon of Wommack. And she knew it was not because they feared her, one old lady deserted now by everything that had made her powerful. It was because they would sooner have touched the most uncanny creature than ever lurked at the bottom of a fouled sea and dragged itself across the swollen bodies of things long dead to feed upon them. She would have many a long and lonely year to rock, and to remember . . . she was the youngest of all the Grannys.

The process of re-forming the central government of Ozark was an orderly one, despite the excitement. The Delegates filled the rows at the front, the Magicians of Rank found a space just behind them, and the Grannys that could get there filled the balcony. Delldon Mallard Smith the 2nd seized the occasion to tear off his purple and ermine robes and his crown and set them afire on the steps of the hall, causing a stink that permeated all the rest of the proceedings before the blaze could be put out; and he had some difficulty explaining the death of *his* Magician of Rank— justified for once, since in fact he did not understand why Lincoln Parradyne had died. But he was there, and though foolish he was willing.

The motion for a New Confederation was put forward, seconded, and carried; and the great roll called by comset, the voices coming in from all over Ozark.

Responsible of Brightwater, up in the balcony where she belonged, could have wept at the pitiful number of votes there were to cast. Ozark had had at least half a million people only two years ago; now, with every Kingdom heard from, and every citizen above twelve years shouting a hearty "Aye!", she could only fight back the tears . . . that number had been reduced to a fraction. It was going to be a long hard pull, rebuilding what had been so wantonly torn down and so casually destroyed, and it would be a very long time indeed before they need concern themselves again with controlling population growth. But she was not going to have any time for tears.

The Teaching Order on Kintucky, that was a good idea; she would be seeing that it spread far and had its branches in every Kingdom that would accept it. Missions of mercy were going to be needed, Magicians and Magicians of Rank, even the Grannys, flying in to feed the hungry and heal the sick and see what must be done to repair the devastation. Other missions, less open, their members very carefully chosen, must go to the Gentles, and to the Skerrys, and to the Mules; debts were owed, and they must be paid. The weather must be brought back under control, and the Magicians sent to hasten the process of regrowth over the wastelands that had been Arkansaw and Mizzurah . . . and if it were true, what she had been told, that the Masters of Castles Lewis and Motley were held hostage at Castle Farson, she would take pleasure in settling *that* score personally. Steps must be taken to work against the prejudice still smothering the Purdys, that the long feuds had only made deeper and more irrational. Something must be done to counter the mythology of the Wommack Curse, that had bloomed and fattened into a monstrous burden on the people that now put their faith in it . . . and that task she might could trust, with a little discreet assistance, to the Teachers of Wommack.

The three monarchies could put away their raggedy trappings now, and if the King of Castle Smith was any example to judge by, they'd be welcoming the opportunity to do so. She would send . . . yes, she would send Silverweb of McDaniels to supervise the long healing process on Tinaseeh, backed by the two Magicians of Rank that were Travellers by birth. High time the Farson brothers spread *their* talents around; with only eight Magicians of Rank left to serve the planet, they'd be needed. And high time Silverweb had something to do that would tie her to this earth a tad.

And there was the delicate problem of placating the Magicians of Rank. For them to know as much as they knew already was chancy and would interfere for a while with their effectiveness; for them to know anything more would destroy them utterly. She hadn't time to be everywhere and do everything herself, nor was that her role. Ways would have to be found, pretty fabrications that skirted the far edge of the truth, face-saving explanations that the eight distinguished gentlemen could grab at and cling to. That line of Veritas Truebreed's, that named her as a cata-lyst, would do for a start.

She leaned over the edge of the balcony, looking down on the back of the Delegation from Castle Wommack; it seemed to her that the shoul-ders of Lewis Motley Wommack the 33rd had lost a good deal of their arrogance. That suited her; and it would suit her to find him something exceptionally burdensome to do for all the rest of his life. Or until her anger was all used up, whichever just happened to come first.

She was still stunned at the lists, that seemed to be endless, of the dead and the injured and the desolate . . . that would be a pain she car-ried to her grave, she rather expected. But she could not afford to indulge it, as she could not afford to indulge herself in any other mercy granted the rest of the living creatures of this planet. Responsible of Brightwater, Meta-Magician of Ozark for this generation and young enough to have scores of long hard years ahead of her, watched only long enough to be certain that the one negative vote to come in on the roll call came from Granny Leeward of Castle Traveller. And then she stood up and stretched a tad, and headed back to her rooms to set to work.

Above the Castles of the Twelve Kingdoms of Ozark, slowly, reluc-tantly, the great crystals were going pale and silent. The thrumming that had filled the whole world for days was no more than a tone just at the limit of the ear's perception, and dying fast. In the stables, the Mules were whuffling their approval.

And Sterling waited, with a message for this Responsible, to be passed on when her death drew near to the next in line, and so on down through time:

THE OUT-CABAL REMINDS YOU THAT THE PLANET OZARK REMAINS UNDER CONSTANT OBSERVATION.

TEACHING STORIES

Why We Are Here
(A Teaching Story)

A very long time ago, and much farther away than you might think, there were Twelve Families, all living on a world called Earth—and they were purely disgusted.

Earth, it's said, had been green and gold and beautiful—a garden-place and a homeplace. But the people that lived there had neglected it and abused it, year after weary year, till it was entirely spoiled, till it was a ruin and a wreck and a pitiful, pitiful sight.

The water was dirty and the air was foul; the creatures all were sorry and warped and twisted. They say the fish that swam the creeks and rivers had become so strange that a person couldn't even look at them, let alone eat them.

And then the people, they say, began to grow twisted, too. Not in their bodies—though living where they did that was no doubt ahead of them—but in their minds and in their hearts. No person could be trusted in those times. Hurting, they say, was done for the *pleasure* of hurting. And the things that were done in those days, we are told, one human hand against another, do not bear repeating.

The Twelve Families, they were a patient people. They had lived a long time on Earth, keeping themselves to themselves, cherishing their homes and their kind, and they waited as long as they could. But the day came, the day came, when First Granny said, "Enough's enough, and this is *too* much!" And everyone looked around at the patheticness of it all, and they agreed with her.

And so, in the year Two Thousand and Twelve—as was fitting—the Twelve Families took The Ship and left Earth together, and went in search of a new homeworld. It had to be a place enough like Earth so that they could fit there; and it had to be hidden away enough so that they could keep themselves to themselves forever and ever more. And they took with them just as little as they possibly could from Earth, with First Granny and the Captain standing right in the door of The Ship, they say, throwing things out as fast as people carried them in.

"The less of that trash goes with us," said First Granny, paying *no* mind to the complaints and the caterwauling, "the less likely we are to have to do this every time we turn around." (By which she meant every two thousand years or so.)

And it would appear that she was right, because a thousand years have gone by, and here we are still, and mightily satisfied with our lot.

And what may have become of Earth we do not know; and the less thought about *that* the better for us all.

How We Came To Lose The Bible
(A Teaching Story)

A very long time ago, and a good deal closer by than you might think, the Twelve Families and the Captain and First Granny turned their attention to bringing The Ship down for landfall nice and easy. Just *nice* and easy!

Made no nevermind that the fuel was almost all gone in The Ship's engines. Made no nevermind that through near nine years under solar sails spread round The Ship like petals of a great lily to gather the solar winds, that fuel somehow had changed. They still had to get down.

"Fool stuff's clabbered," said First Granny with total contempt, tapping the toe of her high-topped high-heeled pointy-toed black patent leather shoes.

"Fuel can't clabber," the Captain told her politely. "It's not even liquid to start with, ma'am—begging your pardon."

"Same thing," said First Granny, sticking out her chin. "Put it into any frame of circumstance that suits you, Captain Aaron Dunn McDaniels, I don't mind! It's *spoilt*—as fuel—and that's the same thing as clabbered."

"Yes, ma'am," said the Captain, as was proper. But they still had to get down.

They had never thought it would take them nine years to find a new homeworld enough like Earth to live on, and lonely enough to make neighbors an unlikely occurrence, and having no other thinking creatures unwilling and unable to let them share the land.

All the food was gone, and all the stuff for making more, and nothing was left but the food seeds packed away dormant in their sterile tubes waiting for new dirt. All of the clothes they'd brought with them were worn out and raggedy and getting too thin even for the needs of modesty.

And the animals, the live ones, they were getting what First Granny somberly referred to as That Look. What might be happening to the stores of embryos sleeping in *their* tubes, no one could say till they were decanted; but it was worrisome.

Going on was out of the question, and had been the last seven days. They had to get down.

First Granny took all the Magicians to the Ship's Chapel, and they did what they could do. And Captain Aaron Dunn McDaniels took all the crew to the bridge and the engine room, and they did what they could do.

And *nobody* stinted.

But the fuel failed them just as they saw a green land rush up beneath them—*just* as they saw it!—and The Ship went crippled into what we now call the Outward Deeps.

Well, what's meant to be will be, they say, and that appears to be true. For even as the water closed over the dying Ship and First Granny told the children to stop their caterwauling and prepare to meet their Maker with their mouths shut and their eyes open, a wonderful thing happened. Just a *wonderful* thing!

Forty of them there were, shaped like the great whales of Earth, but that their tails split *three* ways instead of two. And their color was the royal purple, the purple of majestic sovereignty.

They met The Ship as it fell, rising up in a circle as it sank toward the bottom. And they bore it up on their backs as easy as a man packs a baby, and laid it out in the shallows, where the Captain and the crew could get The Ship's door open, and everybody could wade right out of there to safety.

They were the Wise Ones, so named by First Granny; and it may be that they live there still in the Outward Deeps. Nobody knows, and nobody needs to know.

And it was during that glad wading to shore just before First Granny set her foot on the land and cried, "Well, the Kingdom's come at last, praise be!" that the ancient holy book—its name was BIBLE—was lost to the Twelve Families. First Granny, she thought the Captain had it, it seems. And the Captain, he thought First *Granny* had it. Naturally. And there was a child of three that claimed he'd seen a Wise One swallow it—waterproof, radiationproof, fireproof, crashproof box and all. And for all we know *that* may be true. For sure it's never washed up on any coast of Ozark, all these many hundred years.

"Botheration," First Granny said when they realized it was gone. And the Captain allowed as how he was deeply sorry.

"Well," said First Granny, "I suppose we'll just have to Make Do." And so we have, ever since.

The Flying Dulcimer
(A Teaching Story)

A very long time ago, and much further away than you might think, when the Twelve Families were preparing to leave Earth, there was a young woman named Rozasharn. Now Rozasharn was a Purdy by birth, and it happened that the Purdys had a fine and famous dulcimer. It was of the sweetest fruitwood, and it was cut slim-waisted and curled, and it had inlays of mother-of-pearl in the shapes of hearts and roses and twining vines and little mourning doves. It was purely beautiful, and when they told Rozasharn it had to be left behind, she was outraged. *Just outraged!*

"Rozasharn," said First Granny, "we have on The Ship two guitars, two banjos, two dulcimers, two autoharps, two fiddles—which is one too many, if you ask me—two mouth-harps, two mandolins, and a dobro. Each was chosen because the man or woman that played it was the finest player we knew, and it will serve to while away the time, and to be a model for building more such when we land. But that's *enough*." And then she gave Rozasharn a curled-lip look and said, "You can't even carry a *tune*, Rozasharn, let alone *play* that dulcimer!"

Rozasharn yes-ma'amed, but she went away bitter and she wasn't about to give in. The Purdy dulcimer was the prettiest she'd ever seen, and she intended it to go on The Ship no matter what First Granny said.

So Rozasharn began to plan her magic. There was a Spell of

Invisibility, of course, but that took a lot of work to get going and even more to maintain, and Rozasharn wasn't sure she was up to it. A Spell of Distraction, on the other hand, was a simpler matter, and she decided to set one of those on the dulcimer, to make it appear it was only her shawl. Rozasharn went through her motions and cast the Spell, and found herself a bit embarrassed; she had in her hands a truly splendid shawl, covered with hearts and roses and twining vines and little mourning doves, and *that* was never going to get past First Granny. "Back up a bit, Rozasharn," Rozasharn told herself, "or you'll come out of this blistered."

What she settled on at last was three Spells. The first was to turn the dulcimer itself plain, and that one worked all right. The second was to make the plain dulcimer appear to be a shawl, and that one seemed to be in good shape to the eye, although it was uncomfortable to her shoulders, since she could still feel the pegs and the strings and the edges of the wood; but she considered it her family duty to put up with it. And the third was to take off the other two, and she tried that out, and *it* worked. Nothing was left but to calculate the weight she had to leave behind so no one would suspect, and that meant leaving buried in her back yard two pairs of shoes and a half-slip she'd never liked anyway, and she made it onto The Ship right under First Granny's nose, the dulcimer draped round her shoulders and looking for all the world like a plain old shawl. *Just* like it!

Well, she would of been all right, would Rozasharn—if she'd had a little self-control. But when landing time came she just could not resist letting everyone know the trick she'd played, and as she stepped onto the land of Ozark she cast the third Spell and stood there before everybody, holding the famous Purdy dulcimer and looking like butter wouldn't melt in her mouth.

First Granny looked her up and she looked her down, and then she looked her up once more to be certain her eyes didn't deceive her, but she said nary a word. The Captain looked sorrowful, but he didn't speak either. And as the days passed, and the Purdys settled in and built themselves a homeplace, Rozasharn began to feel comfortable.

And then came the morning when the last stick was in place, and the last curtain hung, and the last dish on the shelf, and Rozasharn looked out her front door and there stood First Granny with Macon Desirard Guthrie the 3rd at her right hand; and young Rozasharn's heart very nearly stopped. Macon Desirard Guthrie was no common person, but a man skilled in Formalisms & Transformations. If there was a more handy Magician on Ozark, Rozasharn didn't know who it might be.

"Stand aside, Rozasharn," said First Granny, "and let us come in."

And Rozasharn did that, most promptly, and there she stood while Macon Desirard Guthrie went through his Structural Descriptions and his Structural Indexes and his Rigorous Specifications of Coreference and his Global Constraints and a lot of other things of that kind and caliber; and when he got through there were just three things that a person could do with the Purdys' fancy dulcimer.

You could hang it on a peg on the back wall of a dark closet.

You could put it in the bottom of a tight and heavy sack long enough to carry it to some similar peg, should you be required to move.

And you could dust it off, from time to time.

If you tried to do anything else with that dulcimer, such as showing it off to the neighbors, or playing a tune, or even moving it off its peg to peek at it your own self, it came flying out at you like a hunting hawk; and starting in the center of the room it would swoop in bigger and bigger circles, faster and faster. . . . Wheeeyeeew! Let me tell you, all you could do then was throw yourself on the floor, roll under whatever you'd fit under, and pray it would miss you.

And *nobody* could put that thing back on its peg but another Magician trained in Formalisms & Transformations.

And that is the tale of the Flying Dulcimer of Castle Purdy, and has something to tell us about being proud of *things*.

The jump-rope rhyme goes like this:

> The Purdys have a dulcimer,
> it cannot make a sound;
> and if you take it off its peg,
> it flies around and round!
> It'll hit you in the back of the neck,
> as it goes flying by!
> It'll hit you in the crook of the back,
> it'll poke you in the eye!
> It'll chase you round the bedroom,
> it'll chase you down the stairs!
> And all 'cause of Rozasharn of Purdy
> as tried to put on airs!

GLOSSARY

ATTENDANT—An Ozark male in domestic service at one of the Twelve Castles. Attendants are reviewed each twelve years for merit of service, and may then be promoted to the rank of Senior Attendant, which carries with it administrative responsibility for lower-ranking staff.

BENISONWEED—A small green herb with white flowers used extensively in magic; it is not a plant brought from Earth by the Ozarkers, but is indigenous to the planet. The strength and efficacy of benisonweed is much enhanced if it is gathered by a virgin.

BESTOWING—One of the three means by which the Kingdoms could grant land on Ozark to individuals. A Bestowing is a grant of land as a mark of special honor, or a reward, and is infrequent. The other two types of land grants are Landholdings (grants of one hundred forty-four acres or more), made only to relatives by birth or marriage; and Farmholdings, grants of forty-eight acres made to friends or close associates—ordinarily for business reasons.

CAPTAIN, THE—Captain Aaron Dunn McDaniels, who brought the Twelve Families from Earth on The Ship originally.

COMSETS—A computerized television network established to provide communication for all of Ozark, with central facilities (including the computers themselves) at Castle Brightwater. The comsets are the individual units, ranging all the way from very simple portable equipment to the most elaborate. Comsets can be used not only for reception but also for the projection of information.

DOZENS!—One of a long list of oaths and exclamations based upon the all-pervasive number twelve. Other examples include: By the Twelve Gates! By the Twelve Towers! Bloody Dozens! Oh, Twelve Times Twelve!

FIRST GRANNY—The very first of the Ozark Grannys, who accompanied the Families on The Ship when they left Old Earth. Only after the Families were established on Ozark and there began to be a number of Grannys did the system for naming them individually become necessary; thus, First Granny had no "granny name."

FORMALISMS & TRANSFORMATIONS—The very highest and most intricate level of magic, restricted to the Magicians of Rank and (without their knowledge) to Responsible. There are four types of Transformations: Insertion, Deletion, Substitution, and Movement. Formalisms are the symbols, gestures, and other symbolic mechanisms for carrying out the Transformations.

FORMSPEECH—A mode of speech, or speech register, used only by the Ozark Grannys. It is marked by archaic vocabulary and grammar, and by a certain ritualistic nagging, but more important than any of these is its unmistakable intonation (the melody of the speech). Unfortunately, no method exists for reproducing this intonation in writing.

GAILHERB—A healing herb, indigenous to Ozark, prized for its property of closing wounds and stopping bleeding almost instantaneously. It takes a practiced eye to distinguish gailherb from ordinary grass; the best method for the beginner is to hold it up to the light, since it is completely transparent and grass is not.

GARNET RING—A group of politically allied planets sharing the same universe as the planet Ozark; their exact number is unknown. All planets of the Garnet Ring base their cultures upon magic rather than upon technology, and their systems of magic are said to be highly advanced. They are aggressive and imperialistic, and are anxious to add new planets to their membership; however, the conditions under which their laws permit this are severely limited. They have had their eye on Ozark for some time.

GENTLES—One of the indigenous races of Ozark, already long established on the planet when the Ozarkers arrived. Because both the Gentles and the Ozarkers share a fanatical respect for privacy, and because the Gentles live entirely beneath the ground, almost nothing is known about them. For the limited data that are available, see Chapter 16 in The Grand Jubilee.

GRANNY—A Granny is an elderly woman skilled in that level of magic known as Granny Magic; it pertains to matters of healing (for simple illnesses), household and garden affairs, and the meting out of elementary punishments such as rashes and warts. The Grannys are also responsible for providing the crucial Proper Names for female infants on Ozark. To become a Granny, a woman must be celibate—by reason of either virginity or widowhood—and must pass rigorous examinations in Granny Magic administered by the already established Grannys.

GRANNY SCHOOL—A system of schooling for all Ozark girlchildren from the age of three to seven, during which a Granny passes on to them a body of oral knowledge necessary to any Ozark woman's welfare. This information is not taught to Ozark males.

HOLY ONE—The Supreme Deity of the Ozark religion; there are no denominations in this religion, although observance may vary slightly from one Family to another.

IMPROPER NAMING—Giving a name to a female infant which is not the one intended for her by destiny. This is a serious matter, and will bring bad luck upon the entire Family in which it happens.

LIZZIES—Twelve-passenger ground vehicles, much like the automobiles of Earth, operating on solar power with backup storage batteries. Lizzies are the most usual method of ground transportation on Ozark, since the Mules can carry no more than two individuals and do well to manage ten miles a day on the ground. (Furthermore, they intensely dislike serving as beasts of burden in this manner, and have no reluctance about making their objections clear in the form of bites, kicks, and unceremonious dumpings of their riders.)

MAGICIAN—Professionals highly skilled in magic, and but one degree below the Magicians of Rank. A woman may become a Magician, but this is extremely rare; ordinarily, boys with a potential talent for the profession are spotted in early childhood and are apprenticed to a Magician for training, a system which does not lend itself to encouraging females for the role.

MAGICIAN OF RANK—The highest level of the profession of magic, and restricted to males without exception. Both the Magicians and the Magicians of Rank are able to make use of Formalisms & Transformations; however, while the Magicians work for the most part with individuals or groups of two or three, the Magicians of Rank exercise their powers for the planet and the population as a whole. Only the Magicians of Rank have the skill of fluent mindspeech, or the ability to SNAP a Mule across any distance almost instantaneously. (The fact that Responsible also shares these abilities is not something that they are fully aware of.)

MULES—One of the indigenous races of Ozark. The original Mules were much smaller and had far less physical strength than the animals of today. Unlike Earth mules, they are not sterile, and the Ozarkers have managed to breed them selectively to their present state—large, strong, handsome animals of great intelligence. A highbred Mule is not only telepathic, but flies at a speed of sixty miles an hour as a result of an arcane mechanism maintained by the Magicians of Rank. The telepathy was there to begin with; the property of flight is entirely the result of Ozark magic. Just why the Mules are willing to cooperate with the Ozarkers to the extent they do, and to serve as domestic animals, is not known, and is a matter about which the Ozarkers feel a certain amount of nervousness; thus, the Mules are much indulged. They are the only form of genuinely rapid transportation available on Ozark.

Although they could communicate in mindspeech with the Magicians of Rank, the Mules will not do so, and the immediate result of any attempt by an Ozarker to force the issue is a blinding three-day headache. They can sometimes be induced to provide ground transportation, or to participate in a race rather than in flight; but this is entirely up to them, always. An Attendant who shows unusual talent for dealing with Mules can be absolutely certain of rapid advancement, large bonuses, and high rank.

OUT-CABAL—The representatives of the planets known as the Garnet Ring who communicate periodically with Responsible. Their physical characteristics are entirely unknown.

PLIOFILM—The usual substance upon which Ozarkers write; it is much stronger, more durable, and less bulky than paper, and is made from an Ozark seaweed. Because it is pressure-sensitive, one writes on it with a stylus rather than a pen or pencil.

PROPER NAMING—The system used by the Grannys of Ozark to ensure that a female infant will have the name intended for her by destiny. The mechanism is simple: a name is chosen, by use of the grid below, so that the sum of its letters will be one of the numbers from one to nine. That is not complicated. (For example: Joan $= 1 + 6 + 1 + 5 = 13 = 1 + 3 = 4$.) What requires skill is knowing which of those numbers is the proper one for a particular girlchild, since each has its own set of distinct characteristics. That knowledge is part of Granny Magic, and is one of the few parts of magic known to them alone. Here is the grid:

1	2	3	4	5	6	7	8	9
A	B	C	D	E	F	G	H	I
J	K	L	M	N	O	P	Q	R
S	T	U	V	W	X	Y	Z	'

(Note: The last symbol beneath the number nine is the glottal stop, which does not appear in the names of Ozarkers and is not part of their language. It was added to the grid by First Granny upon contact with the Gentles, who do have it as part of their language, not only as a neighborly gesture but because it pleased her to be able to bring the grid to an orderly three times nine items.)

Male infants, by the way, are named by their parents, and the name is chosen primarily for the pleasing quality of its sound. A record is kept of the number of times a name is used, and there is no rule restricting that number. Thus, there may be several dozen men at any one time on Ozark bearing identical names differentiated only by the numbers that follow them. Quite a lot of ingenuity is necessary if a family wants the number following a boychild's name to have the significance it had on Earth—that is, to indicate that the child is a "junior." The only real requirement is that a boy receive a first name and a middle name; it has no other significance.

PSEUDOCOMA—A physical state which can be induced in human beings (or other organisms) only by the Magicians of Rank. It is accomplished by reducing all bodily processes to a level just above that absolutely necessary to sustain life.

PSIBILITIES—Psi abilities.

REVEREND—A very ancient term, originating on Earth and still maintained on Ozark. It designates the chief official of an Ozark church, all of whom are male. There have been no attempts by Ozark women to assume this function.

SERVINGMAID—The female equivalent of an Attendant (which see above).

SHAMMYBAGS—Small pouches made of tanned goatskin, used for storing and carrying substances required for the practice of magic.

SKERRYS—The third indigenous race of Ozark. They are very tall and thin, eight feet being an average height, and are extraordinarily beautiful. Their skin is the color of copper, they have long silver hair below their waists—but no body hair whatever—and their eyes are the color of turquoise. They live somewhere in the strange desert on Marktwain, and are almost never seen. They are magnificent, and they are left alone; by tradition, if a Skerry is sighted a day of celebration must be held in honor of the sighting as rapidly as arrangements can be made to do so, and no one is allowed to work on that day. Even less is known about the Skerrys than about the Gentles—no one even knows what their own name for themselves might be, for example. It most assuredly is not "Skerrys."

SQUAWKER—An indigenous domestic fowl of Ozark, much like Earth chickens and used for the same purpose. An extremely stupid bird.

TADLING—Term used for an Ozark child older than two but not yet twelve.

TIMECORNER—A poorly understood sort of "tangle" in time that causes a specific timelocation to be beyond the reach of any of the mechanisms for prophecy or foreseeing used in Ozark magic.

TIMECORNER PROPHECY—The famous prophecy regarding Responsible of Brightwater and Lewis Motley Wommack the 33rd, which goes like this:

> FIRST: For a Destroyer shall come out of the West; and he will know you, and you will know him, and we cannot see how that knowledge passes between you, but it is not of the body.
>
> SECOND: And if you stand against him, there will be great Trouble. And if you cannot stand against him, there will be great Trouble. But the two Troubles will be of different kinds. And we cannot see what either Trouble is, nor which course you should or will take, but only that both will be terrible and perhaps more than you can bear.
>
> THIRD: And if you fail, Responsible of Brightwater, the penalty for your failure falls on the Twelve Families; and if you stand, it is the Twelve Families that you spare.
>
> FOURTH: And no matter what happens, it will be a long, hard time.

This prophecy came to a Granny of Ozark in a dream, and became part of the oral knowledge taught in Granny Schools.

TUTORIALS—The equivalent of Granny School, for boys from age three to seven. The Tutorials are taught by Tutors recruited from among the Magicians, and the curriculum—unlike that of the Granny Schools—is primarily written rather than oral.

WARDS—Any one of a variety of mechanisms from magic, used to shield an area or an individual, or to prevent access or entry.

WILDERNESS LANDS—All territory on a continent outside of the original boundaries of the Kingdom staked out by the settling Family. Such territories are to be maintained as wilderness in perpetuity, and cannot be owned by any individual or group.

WOMMACK CURSE—In every generation, one girlbaby must be named Responsible and must assume the special duties that go with that name. A very long time ago, an inexperienced Granny at Castle Wommack made a mistake and named an infant Responsible in error. The ill fortune resulting from that error, which has persisted over the centuries, is known as the Wommack Curse.